The Spook Tree

MARC LOUIS LEROUX

To my wife Myra, for her steadfast support of my desire to write.
And with gratitude to;
Margaret – my senior class mentor and unwitting major influencing factor in my life,
Claes "The Sailor Man, Nilsson" who criticized me the right way and enough to make a difference,
Dr. William F. O'Brien, ret. U.S. Army (O.S.S.), Ph.D., Founder, Letterman Army Medical Fencing Club Founder, and surrogate father,
and Dave Duarte, for his unflagging encouragement, and friendship.

ACKNOWLEDGEMENTS

A special thank you to the following individuals who supplied various histories, personal or otherwise, or consulted providing information or leads; Don McBride of Antelope, Sacramento County - Scott Graham of the North Highlands Recreation and Parks District, California, for providing access to the North Highlands History documents assembled by Dean and Merrie O'Brien - Ellen Vaughn, of the El Dorado County Chamber of Commerce - Carol Ann Gregory, Ph.D., Associate Planner, Office of Planning and Environmental Review, Sacramento County, California , The Center for Sacramento History, Jeffery Spencer of The Antelope Planning Commission during the revival of Antelope as a town - Dave Duarte, Dirt Diggers North Motorcycle Club founding member, Vice President and former Manager of Penton West and Hi-Point Products — Bruce Young, DDNMC Rt, Mike McGowan, former owner-operator of Mike's Placerville Marine and Cycle, Dan Rasmussen, Dave Buckmaster, and Dan Calhoun, for vital historical information regarding the "Buckmaster Family Settlement Histories," and Don McBride, Chris McKenzie, and Tom Stover for their Antelope memories. Barbara E. Leak, for permission to reprint her articles on the gold recovery history of the Loomis Basin. My special thanks to Herb Garms of the Barton Ranch/Milgate Quarry Coyote Creek Inc., for information regarding the fate of the old roadhouse of "Six-Toed Pete" that was located near the entrance to the present Prairie City State SVRA. James Geddes for his artist rendering of the Haase roadhouse. Torsten Hallman for his vital information regarding Claes Nilsson and motocross' arrival in the U.S.

A tip of the hat to Danny M. Johnson, whose book, "Answering the Call in Time of War — A History of Camp Kohler and the Western Signal Corps School," whose research and material were invaluable for my presentation of Camp Kohler in this book.

TO THE READER;

I grew up in North Highlands, and never learned much about the area. I did not know why Roseville was called Roseville, why Antelope had been established, or when, nor the history of Rancho Del Paso, let alone the rich history of Sacramento County, except in bits and pieces. I spent summer days as a child, wandering around old Del Paso Park on Auburn Boulevard. To me, it was just another park, but with a train ride concession that I never got to ride. It's gone now. I grew up playing in a field with a creek running through it that was only known as "the ditch." I heard names such as Strizek and Kohler and noticed the few remnants of something that had happened, but what? The oldest roads in the area seemed to be Antelope and Walerga. I wondered why they had those names. No one seemed to know or care to know.

As a lifelong student of history, I cannot relate to any event or place without wishing to learn the hows and whys of it. The more I learn about it, the more I see it as a cause in pretty much every issue of the day. It is an idea of mine that better knowledge of the history of where one resides can contribute to a better appreciation of where one lives, especially where one, as a child is growing up and discovering. If I had known more, and perhaps if others had known more, we might have cherished and taken better care in the critical years of North Highlands. Since the story of North Highlands fits many communities, as new people arrive, a new chance comes with them, because people who can learn from history will know better and perhaps act better.

This book is more than a tale of childhood imaginings and experiences. It is a journey through history, sometimes intimate, that is part biography and part historical with bits of fiction for the making of a good tale. The history presented for serious discussion is straight. Notes, sources, a bibliography, and even appendices, are supplied at the end of the book. Outside of some creative embellishments of personal story and that of the 19th-century road agent, Mickey Free, little is fictionalized at all. I should mention, however, that there appears to have been another Mickey Free that operated in the Arizona Territory in the later 19th century. These were two separate people. Where lore around The Spook Tree itself is concerned, I finally divide fact from fiction in the last chapter "Famous Last Words." We hope the reader will understand that the term "Indian" is used in historical usage in its time frame to mean the aboriginal tribes and people of the Western Hemisphere, particularly of North America and especially those inside the borders of the U.S.A., and today most often referred to as "Native Americans." However, anyone born in a place is by definition a native, so this is a misleading nomenclature. "American Indian" is probably the best title. But no offense is meant to be made by the use of the term "Indian." Such walking on eggshell restraints in literature only began after the 1960s, when the Neo-Marxist activists began to successfully label certain words and symbols as oppressive and therefore banned from use, at least by some people. In that and other regards, this book may be viewed as anti-woke literature.

This little story about a dead tree serves here hopefully as a metaphorical demonstration of how a tree branch reaches out and connects the earth and sky, as we are all, through history, personal and beyond, like a tree – and therefore to all consequences. So in telling the tale of the tree, it was unavoidable to delve into local history, which ends up being significant and connected to all the major issues of the day. I realize that this is an old, but tried and true literary device. It always works because it turns out that we are literally connected to everything, right down to the tiniest speck of stardust. Where the report of history is concerned, there are many wrongs to right. So reading this book to the end might be a challenge for some. Independent thinkers will probably like it; polarized minds, perhaps not. I couldn't come up with a better way to tell it than through the eyes of a little boy as he grew up, and the little boy was me. The family and personal history is not meant to be a boast but as a canvas for presenting the historical material and its discussion, which I consider far more important.

Marc Louis LeRoux

CHAPTERS

Other Books by Marc Louis LeRoux

The River Flows – A Tale of the Modern Decline – Trilogy

From Hangtown to Prairie City and Back – The Story of the Prairie City State Vehicular Recreation Area – From a Personal Perspective

History is traped in People & People are traped In History! & I have found two wonderful Books just written by Marc le Preux "The Speaks Tree" & "From Hangtown to Prairie City & Back."

Marc started this journey over five year ago. Marc was able to talk to many persons whom took part in this history experience. I as DDN. MC archivist since 1969, no one has ever collected so much history, Many, Many Details from all Quarters.

Take time to read these books you will be surpised what Marc has found & put on paper. Details of history will amaze you. Lofmember DDN MC

Bruce C. Young

Lifetime Member of the Dirt Diggers North MC and Club Archivist - Bruce C. Young

A VISION OF THE FUTURE BY A PIONEER IN 1913

"The great possibilities of our county are only in their first stage of development. The days of the stock and cattlemen and of the herds that covered the land are gone. The days of wheat raising that followed covered the land are past, and the era of intensive farming has come. The small home of a few acres, where the work that in the days of the wheat farmers was distributed over a quarter or half section is now concentrated on ten or twenty acres, has begun to take the place of the big ranch. Instead of sparsely settled plains where the farmhouse, barns, and corrals were the only signs of habitation, and the rancher depended upon the peddler's wagon to supply him with vegetables and fruit, where perhaps a few struggling fowls were to be seen around the barnyard, and the rancher brought out from the town his butter, eggs, condensed milk, and bacon, are now to be seen the orchard and vineyard, with perhaps a patch of alfalfa, yielding green feed the year around for the cow's and chickens. "The old order changeth, yielding place to the new." The country is daily growing nearer to the city.

The telephone, the parcels post, the rural delivery which brings to the farmer his daily paper and his letters and keeps him in touch with the markets on which depends for the sale of his products – all are making the farm more attractive to the rising generation. The immense holdings of the wheat barons are passing away and in place of the scattered bunkhouses where in winter the men who ran the gang plows and sewed the seed and in the summer harvester gangs passed their nights, are the small farms of settlers with comfortable growing in beauty and attractiveness and the children are to be found who will grow up as the next generation of our citizens.

The schoolhouse, the cornerstone of our nation's greatness, begins to dot the landscape, and the church and post office are soon seen, a nucleus for thriving communities that are springing up and will soon cover the state thickly, as they do in the east. We are coming into our own at last." – William Ladd Willis

"HISTORY OF SACRAMENTO COUNTY, CALIFORNIA,"– 1913

Sacramento K and 3rd Streets – 1953, by permission, City of Sacramento – www.cityofsacramentohistory.org

Where the Antelope Used to Play

I thought a model was something to take out of a box and try to put together and was for older kids. That is, up to that time, my attempts at construction had been miserable failures. I hadn't tried that trick, yet. So when my parents said we were going to look at a model home, I figured we'd be looking at a little house in a display window at a store, or something like that. It seemed strange to me. What was the purpose of making a big deal out of looking at a model home? But then, it was 1955, and I was only three years old. The next thing I knew, I was living inside one. So they made them that big! Okay, what did I know? I'm only three.

No one lived in that house on the corner of Watt and Van Owen Street, the last street of the spanking new suburban development known as Larchmont Village. There was nothing behind it but open prairie as far as my child's vision could discern. Over across the two-lane Watt Avenue was nothing but open field as well, at least, as far as I noticed that day. The sight picture of a three-year-old is limited, but that day it underwent a significant recalibration. I can remember seeing the giant model there with the big sign out front that I wasn't supposed to be able to read because I was three years old. I liked the logo, too.

It was the silhouette of a cowboy with a weed in his mouth, reclined against a corral fence and a slogan, "Larchmont Living."

I already liked the Cowboys. Although I don't remember it, my folks told me that I had a Hopalong Cassidy outfit in those days. It probably fit me for about a month. I think the six-shooter cap gun survived, though, because I always had my one and only until I was about seven, and I always had a hat. It was the classic rope-sewn border type with a cinch for carrying it around on my back; really cool cowboy style. The fact is that from 1950 to 1959, the related industries raked in around 363 million dollars in cap guns, boots, all the accompanying paraphernalia, and cowboy hats and coonskin caps. Early evidence of my indoctrination exists via a photo of yours truly perched on a cute Appaloosa-type pony with a cowboy hat and chaps on that had been taken by a photographer with a good idea, in front of our P Street downtown home. This is likely why I identified with the cowboy silhouette. I think my folks got me a hat to commemorate the occasion.

Once settled on Centinella Drive with nothing but fields to the north and east, I passively understood that I was out on the range where the deer and the antelope were somewhere playing. I was certainly on a kind of new frontier. Because of all of this, I had the idea that I was a cowboy. It was all because of that sign, almost. I also knew what it said because I heard my mother say it out loud. It was a model home. I knew right away; this meant that it wasn't a real house. Nevertheless, I was destined to live in one for a long time.

Not long after that day, we were there again. We left our shady, tree-lined street with its quaint, grassy sidewalk insets, and the shade of the continuous canopy of mature trees in downtown Sacramento and drove out to where that model home was again. I saw it as we drove past. On arrival, I noticed that the field had changed. Suddenly, there were two dirt roads behind that street with the model on the corner. My father drove our Hudson Green Hornet down the second one. There was a lot of lumber lying in neat stacks at intervals along the dirt road that the water truck sprayed continuously to hold the dust down.

The P Street Kid
Photographer – unknown pony photo vendor – LaRue family archive

Those piles disappeared as the homes went up, but more always appeared further up the street, at the last house before the fields began. Before they were done, the dirt road became a black asphalt lane. That day, we stopped in front of one and walked up to a particular pad with its wooden skeleton standing up before us. I remember stepping through the two-by-fours that would soon become the walls of our home.

I had no idea of that at all, but it was warm, the sun was bright, and bugs were everywhere I turned; flitting around in the air, hopping in every direction when I took a step forward when I wandered to the edge of the field, which was just feet away from the pad with the two by four frame jungle. The bugs had no notion of the safest direction to go that was plain to me. All panicked animals flee. Birds flit from tree to tree or bush to bush. I had never noticed a bug before in my life, and now the creatures were everywhere. They were real grasshoppers; the tan-colored ones with wings that showed colors much like a butterfly as they flew away. They made a sound I came to love. I thought of it as "yank, yank, yank," as a happy sound; "yanks," I'd say to myself. And so I thought of them as such, at least until I learned they were called grasshoppers. That sound still evokes the feeling of the warm May sun that was washing over me when I saw the first few of them with their colorful wings, fleeing from my approach. I don't hear that sound very often anymore.

Did I say that I had never taken note of any bug up to that time? Hang a Pinocchio nose on me! One exception, which was a famous one in our family, concerned an event that I was never allowed to live down during those early years. But honestly, it didn't really bother me at all. In our early family years, the entire family, usually during the holidays, would retell all of the funny or significant family stories when after a meal, while we remained at the table, this periodic family folklore time made another round, and these tales were dusted off and recalled.

When my turn came up, my folks would recall what a barbarian I was when it came to dining. Delicate, I was not. Blame it on my Neanderthal DNA. Momma used to keep the floor mopped and waxed because I never ate much of my food while sitting in the high chair at the table. I preferred to dine on the floor. I would fetch it up as soon as I was out of the high chair, according to her, and eat it all up, happy as a clam.

When I was around one year old, and we were living in Oakland on High Street, my older sister came into the house with a bug. It was a caterpillar, the kind with the orange fuzz that used to be so abundant in those days. Martine had found it and made it her pet. That day, Martine had put the cute little critter on the floor too near me. As the story went, I out-crawled her to it, and it was gone. I can't remember doing it, but I do remember her screaming. You'd think I'd recall the taste of it, but I have no special report to offer on that account. So now, here we are, and there is my sister's precious caterpillar wiggling its way across my vision field, triggering the Pavlovian response. I'd hear again about how I grabbed up that orange, fuzzy caterpillar and ate it with one gulp. I retain no memory of the actual incident, so I can't report to you whether it tasted like chicken or not. If I had to hazard a guess, I'd say it probably tasted like a Hostess Twinkie. However, I do retain the memory of my sister crying out, "Mark ate my caterpillar! Mark ate my caterpillar!" The shock of it must have damaged her psychologically. She seemed to have nursed a grudge against me forever after that event, not as a chronic condition, she, after all, was quite a charmer when she turned it on. It only erupted when certain stressors would come to bear, like having me around.

So was it guilt that made me so fond of bugs later on? Was I compensating for that original evil act? I'll leave that question to the hapless psychologists and philosophers who might stumble upon this little tale. But I don't think so. It was just a hungry toddler on the loose and the world was my oyster, so to speak.

I believe that more than one bug flew into the Hudson while we were driving with the windows down in the warmer weather. It was the fashion in those days. It was out of necessity. Few now recall those harsh early times when the pioneers were setting up the first suburbs, and there was no such thing as air conditioning in automobiles, and it was rare enough in homes. Swamp coolers were the status symbol in those days. In hot weather, people had to ride in cars with their windows down, exposed to the vicious bug world. But we took it lightly. When some unfortunate airborne denizen of the insect world would find our car's windshield as its final stopover, the common comment was, "he won't have the guts to do that again!" I only hope that bugs appreciate their capacity for entertaining bipeds with speech centers in their nervous systems like gladiators in the arena, dying for our entertainment. If so, it speaks to their passion for their art, if not the lack of enlightenment of the bipeds who appreciate it as they do, especially when young. But we didn't feel that way then. I mean, no one is making them do that.

The climate in Oakland is refreshing compared to Sacramento and the Valley. I have that early memory and recall standing on a porch in the hazy sun gazing out from a high spot. That would be our home on High Street. I was looking out on the bay as the fog was breaking up in the sun. It was a beautiful sight, and likely still is even today. Those are the sorts of visions, snapshots, you could say, that create those memory engrams. From an early age, I knew that I never wanted to forget beautiful things. Some of those things were inanimate objects like flowers and trees. Others were bugs and even people.

There were unforgettably outstanding events in those early years, such as seeing a mansion being moved from its lot in downtown Sacramento to somewhere further out. We were in the car when the bizarre spectacle appeared to us. Telephone and electrical lines had to be moved so that the imposing giant road hog could be transported out of town to its new location. It was a bizarre sight for a child, at least; a three-story house seeming to float down the road. It so dwarfed the truck that pulled it that it seemed to be moving on its own power, floating on air. I saw at least two being moved this way, I am sure. Some of the old Victorian homes survived this way. I recall seeing a few such homes being jacked up in those days when we made frequent trips into town on some errand or visit. Think of it, that was a time when buying a grand old home, a Victorian, and moving it out to a piece of land was cheaper or at least comparable to building a home. And it saved some historical structures from demolition as modern Sacramento took over the landscape. I think a few of them went to the north, the old Rancho Del Paso Grant land. I believe I attended a party in Rio Linda in 1975 at one such home.

So May I Introduce to You – The Family

My younger sister, Paulette, was born in Oakland, but I don't remember anything of her until we were in Sacramento. Paulette was born with a curious attitude that often came across as humorous without really being intentional. Later, she came to recognize her gift and intentionally embellished what would come to her mind automatically. My first memory of her was an event of what became one of the annual family dinner time stories told around the holidays. It involved her bedtime. Momma told her it was time to go to bed. She was two and learning to walk. Paulette had been lying in her mother's lap and held close. But bedtime had come, and now she had to walk to her crib. "I don't want to be alone." Paulette protested. "You're never alone," Momma told her. "God is with you." "Oh," Paulette challenged, "where is he then?" "He's inside you." My wise mother replied. "No wonder I'm so tired!" Paulette exclaimed. "Why doesn't he get out and walk by himself?" Indeed, who wants to work that hard? Well, not Paulette, at least. Ironically, Paulette became quite religious as an adult, so it turned out that she wanted him in there with her after all. Two personalities in one body; some would call that schizophrenia.

I was much the same. When I was about six, I was doing something in the backyard, which my mother thought I should quit doing and told me so through the kitchen window. I just smiled at her. "Wipe that smile off your face," she scolded. I did just that. I put my hand on one side of my big, toothy smile, and when it crossed to the opposite cheek, the smile was all gone. There was nothing left but an inscrutable poker face. I did it so well, so stone-cold soberly, that Momma almost fell over laughing. I got her that time. Later on, Paulette and I learned to team up to deliver similar stuff impromptu.

Our parents were strict, but we had ways of dealing with them that sometimes succeeded. They were strict, as I note, and there were rules in place that we had to follow, or else. But with four children, all with vivid personalities, interests, and let's call it, "talents," getting all four in sync was not that easy and there were often "fights." If they went too far, they were settled by Daddy, who had a thin leather belt to enforce his authority, and he used it. As we grew physically, we grew in cleverness. It wasn't as if such events were every day or even weekly events, but sometimes we managed to get away with breaking some of the rules because we made it impossible for them to be angry. The best example of this was the code around the dinner table; no singing, no loud talking, and no laughing. All this was no doubt, aimed at preventing choking and getting the nutrition into the location desired, but we were an energetic and active brood. More often than fighting, we were singing, and even more than that, we were laughing, hence the rules for dinnertime. The cause could be any number of things, but most often was the trigger caused by a loaded word that was suddenly forbidden at the table. This did not happen very often, so when it did, it was extreme.

So there we are at the table. The forbidden word has been designated, like a Monty Python skit. Paulette can't look at me. The vibe is contagious; Martine and Gayle pick the energy up and start to giggle. Eating is difficult because our chests are welled up and about ready to explode. Daddy and Momma remain stern and carry on. We just can't. It's a struggle to not laugh. I take the blame. It was always me.

I was the one who would stare at Paulette across the table, as she shaded her face from my gaze and tried to eat. I'd wait for her to weaken, and she always would. Eventually, meaning within 60 seconds, she'd sneak a peek at me and find me ready with my special ambush, which was just a deadpan stare. Paulette would begin to lose control. Martine, sitting next to her would lose control; Gayle was always a reflexive victim as well. By that time, I was losing control. One of them, never me, would jump up from the table and run. One time I recall, we all ended up piled up in the hallway bathroom, laughing hysterically until we had purged the mirth from our souls and could come like reformed sheep, back to the table and finish our meal. The last time this happened, it was summer and we all piled up on the front lawn. We would eventually recover, and return to the table, where both of our parents sat eating as if nothing extraordinary had occurred. I have to wonder about their likely conversation while we were absent. Did they laugh? I think they did.

The killer in this series of events came long after we had matured to the point that laughing like fools at the dinner table had been overcome. At least, a funny face or look could not trigger one. But this one was a classic. Martine was in her phase of supposing herself as the "boss" of the rest of us, being the oldest and having been nominally put in charge of us sans a babysitter for the two hours after school, before our parents would arrive home from work. She relished her power and we resented it, especially me. On this occasion, Martine had a cold. She was sniffling at the table. Momma told her to go blow her nose. She did, but apparently, did not do a very good job. She hadn't sat back down for long when she exploded in a huge sneeze, and a similarly huge, runny gob of expectoration rapidly emerged from her nasal location and oozed over her fingers, which had vainly been placed by her to control that very explosion. The three of us laughed at her comical failure. Martine shouted out, "You think it's funny, but it's not!" (Say that three times fast). Paulette and I saw it instantly and so there was no way to stop the uproar of laughter at that point. And we were at the dinner table. Again, I think our parents were struggling to contain themselves, this time for Martine's sake.

Chronically serious and sober, even Daddy could take a joke. In 1964, I played a prank on him that I was a bit trepidacious about carrying out, but my curiosity and roguishness won out. I had found a little tin of "cigarette loads" at Prang's Variety Store, which was in the strip mall where Safeway was located on the east side of Watt Avenue. Looking back, I'm amazed that such a product would be sold in what was mostly a kid's store. Anyway, they were little bits of wooden matchstick, maybe half an inch in length. You pushed one into the tip of a cigarette so that after a couple puffs it would explode. So one afternoon, while my Dad was sitting in his Lazy Boy chair reading the evening newspaper, I actually picked up his pack of cigarettes, something I never had done before, in fact, no one ever had, not even Momma, and said, "Why don't you have a cigarette?" Maybe he took the one I had pulled up from the pack and sabotaged perhaps because he was curious about what I was up to.

Or maybe he thought I was encouraging him to relax. What do you think? Anyway, he took the thing, and I lit it up as he held it in his lips. I couldn't contain myself. I went to the long drapes on the other side of his chair and hid my face which I knew would have clued him of my plot. In the next moment, there was a bang and I quickly looked out from behind the drape, not knowing what I'd see. Had I harmed my father? Was I about to "get it" like never before? What I saw was the cigarette paper split into four perfect sections, almost symmetrically opened with probably three-quarters of the smoke still perfectly positioned in his mouth. He remained still, but Daddy's wide-open eyes betrayed his complete surprise.

I couldn't bear the tension; I ran out of the house out to the front lawn, simultaneously smirking to myself, and fearing I would be pursued with the belt. When I finally ventured back into the house, he stoically asked me where I got the loads. I told him. He took possession of my remaining supply. I think he was figuring out who he would pull the trick on himself, but wished no further waste of his nicotine supply. Nothing more was ever said or done on the subject. The punishment never came; not even a talk about such pranks.

I've come to think that the reason he didn't punish me was that he immediately recognized that it was the classic prank and that he only wished that he had pulled it on his own father. I wonder did he surprise someone at work. Did they engage in fun like that at McClellan? I wouldn't know. But I have it from his cousin, my senior cousin Olivia, that he was full of mischief as a boy. So where and who did he prank? I missed my chance to acquire more details, as so often happens in families, and so my tale is robbed by my neglect.

We Came From Somewhere Else

It turns out that as the result of another, some have said, tragic accident of nature; I was born in Wisconsin, Oshkosh, Wisconsin, in the Old Northwest, as many of my line had settled before me. (Wait, that's another lie! Our parents were always adamant that they planned each of us. That is, except for the last one, Gayle, who arrived in 1955, and was as they said, unplanned but welcomed). We were old French Quebecois from the south bank of the St. Lawrence River who had settled in the Old Northwest by 1800, first near Detroit. My fifth great-grandfather Jean le Roux dit Vadeboncoeur is recorded as having delivered supplies and picked up furs in the vicinity of Detroit in

1756, during the French and Indian War when he served on the French side. As historians point out, the fur trade was the central issue of that war. Fur trading constituted an early "gold rush" and people like John Jacob Astor, owner of the American Fur Company founded empires of wealth from it.

Jean le Roux dit Vadeboncoeur later established a farm on the south side of the river with his venerable wife, Judith Aymard, who had been a child of one of the original "Filles du Roi," "Daughters of the King" that Louis XIV had recruited as wives for the first men who had established Quebec, so she was a propertied lady. Established on the south shore of the St. Lawrence River, the Raquette (Snowshoe) River settlement became a town later, named after one of Napoleon's marshals by the overwhelmingly Quebecois population. When the U.S. Canadian border was finally settled in 1818, Massena became a town in America as part of New York State, with Cornwall, Ontario as the other LeRoux stronghold and the final resting place of Jean and Judith at St. Joachim Catholic Church with recently upgraded headstones. Members of our line still may be found on both sides of the river in that region.   Through this origin, his son settled in the region of Detroit. Others fanned out in the Old Northwest as it was part of the original New France domain. So at least the location of my birth is less of an accident than first advertised.

When I was born in Wisconsin that year, it was during one of the coldest winters on record in North America, which had seen a record snowpack in the Sierra Nevada Mountains in California. Our trip to California via The Lincoln Highway was undertaken six months later, in June. Thinking back, I believe that trip was closer to what the pioneers dealt with in the 19th century than people do today when coming West; most just fly right over it all. Flat tires, bursting radiators with no help in sight, and no air conditioning, made the trip potentially arduous. There were even a few "highwaymen" still about in the rural regions, as Humphrey Bogart made the public aware of in the films, "High Sierra," and "Petrified Forest." Bank robbers and the like still preferred to "head for the hills," as an evasion strategy in the West.

My father's best friend and fellow grad from National Chiropractic College in Lombard, Illinois, convinced him to come to California, where he grew up in Berkeley. The laws in California regulating the profession were not as restrictive as Wisconsin's. I don't know how he could afford it, but my father bought a 1952 Hudson Green Hornet and drove his little family to California via the Old Lincoln Highway.

Portrait of a young man as a health care pioneer. Dr. James Jonathan LaRue, DC age 21 – 1921 was designated a Chiropractic Pioneer in 1951 by the National Chiropractic Association. His final residence being Folsom, CA, Dr. J. J. LaRue was coincidentally interred at the Pioneer Cemetery there now called "Memorial Lawn" – photo unknown photographer – from the author's family archives

I wish I had asked about that car! Once while reviewing the contents of the family archives which were kept in an old brown suitcase containing the family photos and archives, I read a note my mother made regarding the trip.

In my "baby book," she noted that although I was cutting my teeth, I never cried, so she missed the event entirely. Similarly, the Hudson hummed along through the Great Basin during June of that year. The Hudson was an excellent car in its time. I don't know how he would have been able to buy it since he was just out of school unless the car had been a gift from his father. That is a possibility since he had connections in Michigan as the former doctor of Henry Ford and the fact of his office in Dearborn for years could have afforded him favors such as discounts and favors.

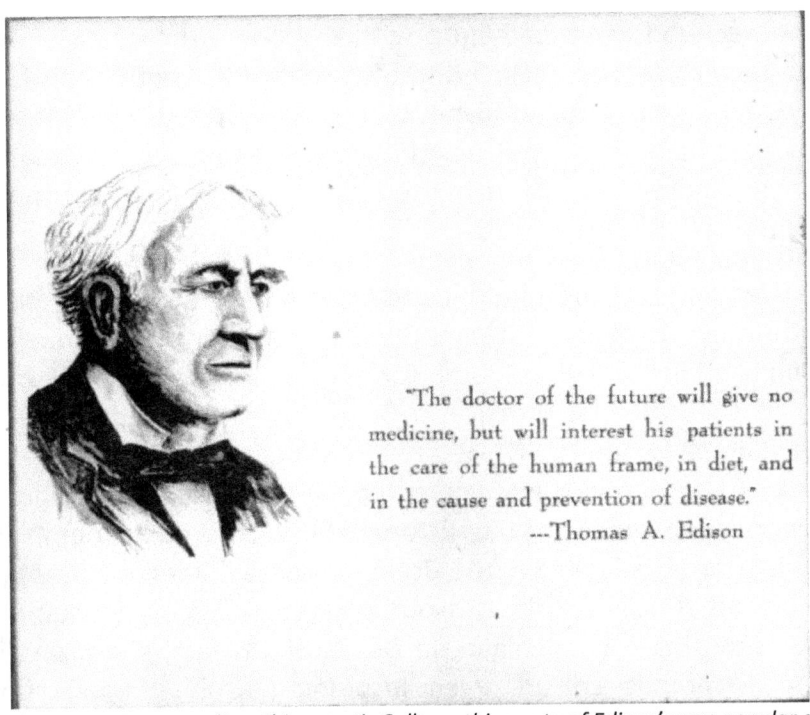

"The doctor of the future will give no medicine, but will interest his patients in the care of the human frame, in diet, and in the cause and prevention of disease."

---Thomas A. Edison

By the time I was attending Chiropractic College, this quote of Edison's was popular and available as a mounted wall hanging that many DCs hung in their waiting rooms. I think I know where he got this notion of the future of health care. The prediction may not have materialized, but Chiropractic was sampled for the principles of "preventative care" and "wellness," concepts of modern healthcare management. Print - Mission Specialties, San Leandro, CA

I have no proof, but something has to explain why we had such a nice car when the family means were so modest. I like to think that it was a gift from my grandfather to his son. He would have been wishing to make up for the terrible times my father and the boys had during the thirties.

With this in mind, we find my father in 1930 as the oldest of four boys at seven years of age. His father was doing double duty at his office in Dearborn and running a second fledgling practice near Jerome, south of Jackson, and more adult expectations were placed on my father's young shoulders. Every day, he was handed a .22 rifle and one bullet. His job was to go find dinner. He hardly ever failed because he would be punished if he missed his shot, not by his father, but by a stepmother who was not gentle with the boys. In fact, she was a sadist. How the abuse occurred so often out of the sight of his father, who would never have stood for it, required some years of research on my part to uncover and understand. But there is no excuse for torturing children, ever, but it used to be institutional, as the film "Hell's House" (1932) illustrates.

I finally learned that grandfather had his practice in Dearborn and had sent the boys with their stepmother to the new place, Bundy Hill, which he had just bought on a tip for none other than Henry Ford. As he established his first practice in Dearborn, he worked at the Ford Motor Company; naturally, Henry Ford became my grandfather's patient. A bright, handsome young man, enthusiastic as the youngest doctor of any discipline in U.S. History, he had entered Palmer in 1918, after his sister, Nellie died in the Great Influenza Epidemic of that year. After a short stint in nearby Missouri where he met my grandmother, he was soon back in Michigan, in Dearborn, in fact, socializing with Ford and Thomas Edison, even inspiring Edison's famous (inside chiropractic, at least) quote about the future of health care. So it came to pass that my grandfather was able to acquire the Bundy Hill property on a tip from Ford. He had decided to move from Dearborn to Bundy Hill, removing his boys permanently from the city's temptations and a more wholesome upbringing. He took this course after his boys began getting into a little bit of trouble in town.

Bundy Hill (no relation to Al) was south of Jackson, near the town of Jerome. It was the highest elevation on the southern peninsula and was a tourist attraction of sorts with an observation tower at the top of Bundy Hill and even a little zoo on the premises. He later sold the land, including Bundy Hill, to a gravel company that used to grade the Chicago-Detroit highway, which sat on the road about halfway between those cities. But there had been an observation tower, a little zoo, a restaurant, and a gas station. He located the boys at Bundy Hill with the stepmother while he worked two practices.

The old lookout on Bundy Hill, Michigan, as my grandfather bought it. After he sold it, the highest point in Southern Michigan became the lowest point as it was mined for gravel to pave the Chicago-Detroit Highway on which it was located. The lumber from it was used to build The Oslo Inn, a smorgasbord restaurant operated by his third wife, Dagmar, during the 1940s into the 50s. – Photo – Michigan Historical Society

I possess a photograph of one of my uncles, "adjusting" another in 1930 au natural in the office downstairs at Bundy Hill. It was on the front cover of the state chiropractic journal that year, but it would likely be considered child pornography today, I suppose, so it is not displayed. It had been on the cover of the Michigan Chiropractic Society's journal in 1930. Perhaps this is an apt illustration of how society has changed since then.

My father ran the gas station as a young teen. They called it "Jimmy's Gas Station." That was his nickname, one of them, anyway. As a boy, I recall my father telling me that he could identify the make of any automobile coming up the two-lane highway where he'd sit waiting for a customer by the shape and pattern of the radiator grill.

"Jimmy" on the left with buddy Bob Ketchum at some bus depot where it snowed in 1940. Photo – LaRue family collection

Jimmy's other nickname was "B.J." He was so named by his father after his teacher at Chiropractic College, the son of the profession's founder, B.J. Palmer.[*1] My grandfather practiced between Detroit and Bundy Hill until he could make a smooth transition financially.

Once he made the proper arrangements, he left Dearborn to live and work at his practice at Bundy Hill. But it was a long time in transition, and in those years, the stepmother, who had been married to grandma's twin brother, had run his front desk. For some reason, Grandma left in 1930 with a man named Johnny, and the sister-in-law became the stepmother. Her twin brother had been married to the eventual stepmother of her boys. She never had any children of her own and didn't want any, it seems. Anyway, in those days, evil stepmothers did not only exist in fairy tales. In fact, they were not uncommon.

Sometime in the late thirties, my grandfather became aware of the abuse. At first, he could not believe it; then, he was appalled. He had to find a replacement for the evil stepmother. It took a couple of years, but he was fortunate to find an angel in a Norwegian immigrant named Dagmar, who not only took my grandfather into her heart but the four boys as well. However, it was a little too late for Jimmy. The need to escape the memory of the abuse drove Jimmy into the Navy in 1939 at seventeen. During the war, he served in signals, mastering Morse Code.

In North Africa, he was the radioman in a Grumman Duck, which was a scout and rescue plane. The "Duck" was ugly, I suppose, but it's beautiful to me. It was the only holdover biplane that was used through World War Two. It was a scout and rescue craft, with a backseat for the radio operator, who could also be a gunner and a bombardier because the versatile aircraft carried two depth charges on its wings. It could also take photos with the camera that could be swung into place in the two-seat rescue compartment beneath his station. While I'm on this topic, I think it is good to think about how vital the Signals Corps are in warfare as communications always have been from the earliest human experiences up to now, when communication is the main event in the world. Imagine a military in World War Two without a well-trained Signal Corps. My father was part of that vast fraternity during the war. If he was alive today, he'd tell you that nothing was more vital to victory. It's obvious.

So in a strange, coincidental way, my father, hence my family's history is linked to Camp Kohler before North Highlands existed. It makes me wonder if my father had ever stopped in there for training as he transferred to serve in the Pacific Theater after his time in North Africa. This is one of the many questions that I wish I had asked him while he was alive. He told me that he dropped the two depth charges on a Nazi sub in the Mediterranean in 1942. He told me they sunk it. I believed him as a boy when he told me about it. I believe it now that I am an old man, and he is gone.* He came from a family that had for generations relied on pioneer skills.

Author's Great Grandfather John Simon LaRue (LeRoux) and son Oril, at his Sturgeon River Farm on the Northern Peninsula of Michigan ca. 1918, with Sailor, the family dog. Oril served in the U.S. Army Cavalry as a horse-mounted soldier - Photo courtesy of Olivia LaRue

My Uncle Reg was on the national pistol team, and his son of the same name became the youngest master-rated pistol competitor in the history of the sport by 1968. When my grandfather gave my father his old Damascus Steele ten-gauge double-barreled shotgun in 1965, my father told me how he had used it to hit 23 of 25 skeets as a thirteen-year-old. So, as many young men of the time, he possessed the skill required to time the drop with the submarine's movement and hit it. I do not necessarily believe the story he told to impress his young son at the time, but it's somewhat plausible.

Gratuitous photo of Oril LaRue of the U.S. Army Cavalry ca 1925 – Courtesy of Hannah (LaRue) Smith Since he was from Michigan, he might have been with the 7th Cavalry.

Like many families, dogs have been memorialized in my family since my great-grandfather's time. His dog's name was Sailor. In those days, everyone but hardcore city dwellers had a dog. The dog of my father's boyhood was named "Major." The youngest brother, my Uncle Johnny, became a police dog trainer after returning from Korea. When he first came to visit in 1959, he was in his uniform, and the German Shepherd he had with him was the same rank as him and named for his rank, "Sargent." Dogs, German Shepherds, in particular, were going to be a key feature in our lives.

My father found a job and worked in Oakland for a year before we came to Sacramento. We first lived at a rental home on Weller Way, across from McClatchy High School. (Named for John B. Weller, California senator in the 1850s). Next, we moved to 17th and P Streets, where my Dad took over Uncle Ross's practice. The house was a split-level affair, with the living quarters over the office. Daddy found it more challenging to get his practice going than he supposed it would be. Later, he told me how naïve he had been. He only charged a dollar for a visit and required no follow-ups. He supposed he'd be overwhelmed with patients. He was skilled and his heart was in the right place, but he wasn't.

I didn't know our car was called a Hornet in those days, or even what a hornet was, until years later when my mother mentioned it. But I do remember that car and how nice it was. I would lie on the generous shelf behind the back seat under the sloping rear window and gaze up at the stars at night as we rolled along. The car rocked me like a cradle. The stars seemed to rotate around magically in the sky as my father maneuvered the car at night.

We were often visiting friends it seems. There were day-long visits to one of our friends in the CCA. It was a close-knit community in those days with many kind individuals among the members. I remember how sad I was when I was suddenly forbidden to lay up there anymore. I must have blocked the rearview mirror because my Dad said no when he hadn't minded earlier. Maybe someone had objected; perhaps someone in a uniform.

The Hudson's seats were of a beautiful brush fabric, tan-colored, which I impacted a bit by forgetting a clam that a man had given to me when we had made a day trip to the mouth of the American River just after we moved into the new house in North Highlands. I recall how the hot, white sand burnt my tender tootsies as I raced to the relief of the wet sand by the water, and I remember the man who gave me the clam after he saw me staring at them in his bait box. This man might have figured to spark my interest in biology this way. I think he did because I was always looking for critters and studying them after that. On that particular count, the poor man failed because I left it in the car, and the unfortunate clam died in the heat. I later found it in the back seat, opened with the clam dried up. It was only then that I realized I had failed in my charge. I confess that failure to you here, now for the first time. It has previously only existed as a secret in my heart. The Hudson was gone by 1956. I am not sure if my poor daddy was involved in two auto collisions in those early years. I only remember one. In that one, he was run off the road by a wrong-way driver just before the railway trestle near the intersection of Roseville Road and Watt Avenue, when it was still a two-lane road, before Gate 1 at about five in the morning.

P Street – 1954 - Momma took the picture

I am not sure whether the Hudson was involved. Later, I remember a CHP bringing him home, but that was when he had been riding a Sears Moped to work at McClellan. So that might have been the second incident. All I can recall is that we suddenly had a Willys sedan. We next made a memorable trip to a wrecking yard to see the Willys, which was the second event, so it had been in the first one.

He was always looking for a better supplemental source of income. Another possibility is that he might have been forced to turn the car in due to our family's initial financial struggles. I will never know the answer to this little mystery. My sister Paulette was born in Oakland a year after me in February. So we came to Weller Way later in the year. The stay in Oakland was brief.

Daddy had two occupations; his office in the daytime and various swing or graveyard shift work. After relocating from Oakland, he focused on practicing his profession exclusively. That lasted until we moved to North Highlands when he began to "moonlight," working a side job to supplement the family. This style of getting a practice going was also a family tradition. But it was one I did not wish to follow when my turn came.

At our first home in Sacramento on Weller Way, across from McClatchy High School, I have two significant memories to recall. One is watching my father make out a check for the paperboy using the porch pillar as a desktop. The other is the day we moved to P Street. I remember being out front and watching some teens standing around a jalopy in front of the venerable-looking, multistoried, school building. (John B. Weller was one of California's first senators and governors).

We remained at Weller Way only long enough for my father to take over Uncle Ross's practice on P Street. Uncle Ross was the friend from college I already introduced. He and his wife, who we called "Auntie Fern," were our "God Parents." I recall my mother telling me this explicitly. Uncle Ross's kids were older. So he had panicked, likely due to the demands of his wife and family. But he didn't do badly.

He had become the fire chief of the Arcade Fire Department by the early 60s. Our families remained close for a long time, and we all learned to swim in Uncle Ross's full-sized built-in swimming pool in 1960, one at a time, taught by Daddy. His kids were kind to us. I naturally regarded them as family. To me, they were cousins. Their daughter served as our babysitter more than once, and the son took us flying U Control planes, which were very popular in those days before radio control arrived a few years later. He built beautiful balsa wood model planes. He was an excellent craftsman. Later as a grown-up, he told me that my father had bought him a sled for Christmas while they were students at the National College of Chiropractic in Chicago in 1950. Maybe that's why he was always so kind to me. Anyway, he mentioned the sled to me during our talks in 2019.

The house on P Street was a split-level affair, with the office on the ground floor. I remember that the lower floor office was off-limits to us kids. I got into it all the same. I recall getting down there all by myself and touring the office unnoticed. Maybe that was before I was told it was off-limits? I can't remember! I do recall that I was a sneaky explorer from that age on, but never a thief. It wasn't about sneaking, either. I was just curious.

The landlords were a sweet old couple that lived next door named Crabtree. I remember seeing them smiling at my sisters and me when we were out front on the sidewalk one day. Many years later, while researching California history, I learned that they were descendants of Lottie Crabtree, a popular entertainer in the region during the 19th century.

My father was struggling at his new practice, so my mom went off to be a typist as she had in Washington, D.C., during the war. I believe she had found the job she remained at until her retirement in 1975, at the General Ledger section of McClellan Air Force Base, and took the bus out to the job. I remember the local bus route from Sacramento out to McClellan and North Highlands. It crossed out of and back into Sacramento by crossing over the old Jibboom Street Bridge over the American River. The name comes from the sight of the jib sails and booms of the old square riggers that used to tie up at the landing in Sacramento. Jibboom Street was the first street a foot would hit once they stepped off a ship. "Jibboom Street," what kid wouldn't like a name like that? Later, when I heard someone on the radio sing, "Shi-boom, shi-boom," I felt I knew what it was all about.

So my two sisters and I had a babysitter from then until we moved out to North Highlands, a German War Bride named Rosie. I have a snapshot instant of her rosy-cheeked face close to mine as my one memory of her. I only realized later in life that Rosie must have just kissed me. That is why I remembered it so vividly, her sparkling blue eyes fixed on mine, and her rosy cheeks so close. Her name made sense to me even though I was illiterate at the time. I remember later thinking, "That is why her name is Rosie." Because of all this, I remember that moment like a snapshot in my mind. We were at Fremont Park, which was just down the street on a spring day, and I believe that Rosie had just kissed me.

That's what I remember; sunny days at John C. Fremont Park, a Christmas when I got a big, funny-looking metal automobile that was about a foot long and bounced on its springs when I pushed it, a birthday party for my older sister Martine, and her friend Linda, at the party. Not long after, at that same table, we sang in anticipation of a noodle-dominated dinner. We mimicked a television jingle about slug bait brand name that rhymed with spaghetti and used a trumpet charge. We changed the brand name to "spaghetti" and sang, "Spaghetti, spaghetti, spaghetti, snails eat spaghetti!" We got an early start at word games, and Paulette and I were most inventive. I was as dangerous as ever, so my mother had to prevent me from eating the pretty oleanders that grew outside the open kitchen window. "Don't eat those, they're poison!" I remember that clearly. But I didn't know what "poison" meant. "Bad," meant, "BAD."

My last memory of P Street is a truck with stuff I didn't recognize at the time as household belongings but with my trike on top of the pile. I didn't realize at the time that this was our last day at this place, or I would have said goodbye to the big trees along the sidewalks, the park, and Rosie. I don't remember her later on at all, except years later, when she came with her husband on a visit, and I realized how small and dainty she was after all.

To a little boy, she was the perfect picture of a fairy princess; "goodbye, Rosie, I will remember you." And I have. Every time I re-watch "The Wizard of Oz" I think of Rosie when Glinda, The Good Witch of the North arrives. Maybe it was because of Rosie that I fell for a certain young woman when I was twenty-four. It was so devastating for me when it turned out that despite her passionate declarations, she didn't love me all that much after all. Not for keeps, anyway. She was no Rosie, that's for sure.

Or maybe she was; both disappeared from my life. But by the time I met that certain young woman; I was no three-year-old boy. I should have known better, bang, bang, you got me, Linda.

Ready for Spaghetti on P Street – 1955 – We liked it because snails liked it. Actually, it's Paulette's second birthday – Daddy took the picture.

Regardless of that, such wiring often travels along the fourth dimension to have its impact later in life in unexpected ways for many people, and literature is full of tales and poems fired by such associations. A favorite old film of mine is "The Life and Death of Colonel Blimp." Deborah Kerr plays a loving female spirit who keeps appearing as the same woman of the same age at remarkable times during the colonel's life. So it can be a good thing. Linda made a huge difference in my life, as it turned out.

I managed to channel the "inspiration" she left me with to get through college and succeed as a competitive fencer. As it is, the experience provided a time divide as big life events often do; so I have a BL and AL as a divide of my age of naiveté; Before Linda and After Linda. Looking back, regardless of the pain, I would not have wanted to have skipped Linda; it was too much love to miss, even if it couldn't last. The Beatles' song, "It's All Too Much" always reminds me of this experience. So I don't listen to it too often.

That day when I was looking out of the window of our upper-story house on P Street, Daddy, and Uncle Ross were filling up that open bed truck with our stuff. It had to be a Saturday because the construction work in North Highlands was so intense that buyers were only allowed to move in on weekends. I saw my tricycle sitting on top of it all, like an afterthought. I thought this was some big cleaning day, and someone had decided that my trike was trash. I said nothing about it. What did I know? Maybe the trike was trash? So to me, so far, anything could be trash, including me.

That was caused by another kind of experience and association at the P Street house. One day, some kids up on an apartment balcony behind our house had called my sisters and me "trash," and other names, I guess, as we stood in our little yard looking up at them. I didn't know what it meant but did after that. Years later, my mother told me about the event when I asked her about it. All I recalled was those kids up there, yelling at us. Momma told me that they were doing worse things than that. She said she went to talk to their mother. When she asked where her children's father was, the woman laughed at her. The state paid her to have children, she said. That was 1955.

If my trike could be trash, I guess I could be, too. I didn't worry too much about it. Luckily for us, this was also goodbye to the kids who called us those names that we didn't understand. Regardless, our mother always forbade us to say any bad words about anyone or any group. She had personal experience with being similarly targeted as a child because she had been raised as a member of a particular religious group and the local kids had learned to hate her from their parents.

It must have been only a brief time from that bright, sunny day when I first saw the skeleton frame of the house we had walked through that our home was finished. That pickup full of junk topped by my trike made a secret trip to our new house because the next thing I knew, we were living there.

I never missed P Street because what had my attention next was the big field behind our home that went on for as far as my eyes could see. It was the opposite of the ancient tree-lined streets of downtown Sacramento. Before me, a vast, expansive, golden field that would wave in the wind, and sparely spotted here and there with a solitary oak tree, or maybe two or three in a cluster. Mostly one lone tree here and there rolled out in every direction as long as I looked north, mostly. The land wasn't exactly flat but described the gentle roll of the land that began just up at the end of our street out of a low hill before it became another street with homes just like ours. A little further east, the land's depressions become deeper and the hills higher until they form mountains out to the east. The Sierra Nevada Mountains that I would come to love dearly and explore as much as I could, on foot, trail bike, and then four wheels, hiking even to its highest peaks later in life. When I was 25, and at the prime of my physical being, I crossed Desolation Valley Wilderness from Fallen Leaf Lake to the top of Pyramid Peak and back in one day. The photograph I made at that time was not yet termed a "selfie," but I took it to log my moment on the peak. Seeing it now, I looked like an absolute wild man. No need to show that one.

I had gazed out to the distance at Pyramid Peak, far off to the east atop El Dorado County, many times throughout my life up to then. The primary school that I attended during my fifth and sixth-grade education was on a hill above the high school. The opposite, eastward view from the school afforded a stupendous view of the land as it folded up into higher and steeper hills. We weren't allowed to hardly stray a foot off the playground in that direction because not far down the hill was the Southern Pacific Railway's track. Trains blasted their wailing horns regularly as they approached the Roseville Switching Yard, which was within sight of the school up the tracks. So I would stand on the edge of the playground and gaze to the east.

Pilot Hill was marked by a large triangulation station and lookout, then ascending up to that outstanding, lone elevation, which was always white except from July until November, when the snow usually began to fall at that elevation.

By standing at the edge of the playground and gazing east, I could see Pyramid Peak, taking note of its contours. It really does have a pyramid-like aspect to it. I loved to spot it way out there and continued long after, often fixing my location in the Valley whenever possible relative to that peak as long as I lived there or traveled in the region when it was clear enough to sight it. This early fascination surely led to my eventual climb up it, more rightly, scrambling up and finally standing on the landmark so often in my vision up to then, and taking in the remarkable panorama of mountain peaks sprawling out in every direction. But then, the more immediate world was the fields about me. They seemed to be living things, full of life and a place of adventure and delight to me in those days. In 1955, the field that began immediately from our house's back door went out to the horizon, north, and east.

Somewhere out there, Cisco and Poncho were on patrol with The Lone Ranger and Tonto, if I could only get out that far in the field to spot them, and the deer and antelope playing. It all blended into me and doubtless many Boomers. The Cisco Kid, Tonto, was the same as Davy Crockett. One memory confirming the universality of these themes in that time, at least in California, occurred one bright day. I have a vivid memory of a song about Davy Crockett. But it was not the usual one. It was in Spanish and the hero's name was Poncho Lopez. The melody was the same; "Poncho, Poncho Lopez," so I could understand what was intended, a version of the popular song for our Mexican neighbors to enjoy. The rest was unintelligible to me, but since I knew one version, I understood this one, too. It did make me wonder who this Poncho Lopez was and what frontier he was blazing.

It Was the Place to Be

In 1920, the Army required an expansion of its aviation, supply, and repair depot in San Diego. Of all the span of the big valley, they chose a spot on the old Rancho Del Paso. It took years for construction to begin as the public was generally pacifist and felt that The War to End All Wars had been fought. That simplistic attitude began to change after Hitler took power in Germany and tensions in the Pacific began to build. In 1936, Congress appropriated four million dollars for the land and construction of Sacramento Air Depot. The depot expanded a little and was renamed McClellan Air Force Base after Hezekiah McClellan, an aviation pioneer who had charted Alaskan air routes. Up to then, the 5,000 acres of pasture and grain fields that had been part of the Rancho Del Paso had been the scene of nature and the occasional pass of a farmer's plow and harvester. Most of it was just open pasture land that had been once grazing land for cattle that had roamed the old rancho in the middle of the 19th century. One of Sutter's early employees at his fort once wrote that the land was so full of game that there was no need to pack provisions when traveling for a few days to get to one work site or another. He described the prairie with wild oats, forage, and flowers so tall only a man sitting on a horse could see the horizon. Commenting after his first journey up the San Joaquin, and Sacramento Valleys in 1845, Kit Carson noted elk, deer, and antelope of hundreds of thousands. Imagine how it must have been! They obviously served as a natural control for the forest floors in the summers when they migrated to high elevations.

But in 1939, things began to change rapidly. By then, there were 600 civilian workers and 100 military personnel at the base. A few families lived across from Gate 1 in the small tract called Plane Haven. This was a triangular plot of land, bounded by Watt Avenue, which at the time ended at Gate 1, A Street, and Poplar Boulevard. I was familiar with that neighborhood from very early in my life because from about five to eight years of age to about nine, I sang in the choir of St. Timothy's Lutheran church that occupied the clubhouse that is now the location of the Lion's Club on Airway Drive. In 1939, and apparently, through the war, there was a small grocery store, and vegetables were sold from a horse-drawn cart two times a week, supplying the civilian worker population in Plane Haven.

After the end of the war and the dismantling of most of Camp Kohler, a developer named Jere Strizek bought 2,000 acres, which included the site of the former "French Village" where soldiers had trained in door-to-door combat. He began the first major construction of homes there in North Highlands in 1950 as North Haven with 364 homes and The Highlands with 189 homes. Fifty Families moved into North Haven in 1951. From these two names, the community of North Highlands found its name.

Excited news articles hailed the new development and planning that saw the modest post office that started in a garage on North Haven Drive in 1951 move four times before arriving at its present location. The space was donated by Mr. Strizek for the first six months. The first postmaster was Ruth M. Hutchins, who became a much-respected member of the North Highlands community. She was paid .72 cents a day, and her office had the only phone in the community for a year. By December 1951, the postal receipts had grown from $120.00 to $2,016.00. All the usual complimentary features of an all-American community were quickly put in place or planned. By 1953, over 5,000 people were receiving mail from the post office. The future was bright and full of possibilities.

The new home my parents moved us into in 1955 was just the beginning. That year, North Highlands was the fastest-growing community in Sacramento County with the latest and most modern homes. For veterans like my father, were a great deal with the help of a G.I. Loan. It was a chance for us and many young families. There was every reason to feel as bright and optimistic as the ever-smiling sun that rained down its glory on the pasturelands of the old Del Paso Rancho. It was considered "the place to be" for aspiring young families.

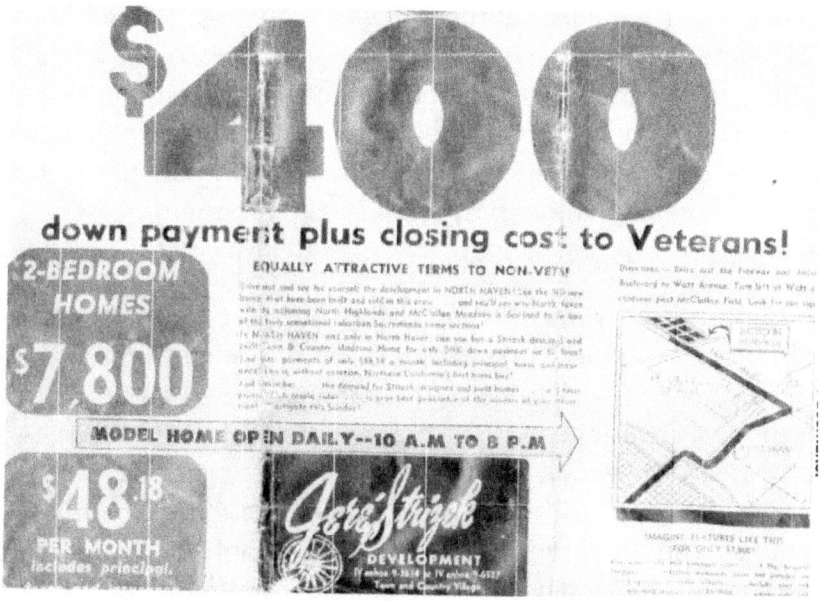

From – North Highlands History 1951-1971 Vol. 1 Full page ad Oct. 12, 1951, in the McClelland AFB Pacemaker Assembled by Dean O'Brien 09/26/2001

By the time I started kindergarten at Village School in 1957, Highlands High School was being built, and Scouting was already established. Martine was in the Brownies before I knew it. In her time, they were very active. She went to day camp in the summer, at Camp Pollack, I believe, and one year stayed a couple weeks. She wrote at least one letter home. I remember its tone, full of confidence and fun. My parents gave her music lessons, and she could play the accordion by ten years of age. The new fire station on M Street came to the school and gave us talks on fire prevention. They left us with plastic fireman's hats, and Fire Department rings that turned our fingers green. In those days, they sponsored an Easter Egg Hunt every Easter. The field they picked was the same one that the Spook Tree occupied, but a distance from it, more toward Watt Avenue, which was also mostly an empty field at the time, with only a few new streets north of M Street. The older kids had the advantage, with wrapped candy eggs tossed randomly through the field not far from the Spook Tree. What a great group these firemen must have been (and they were as records show). At Christmas, the adults and a few older teens from our church choir would go to the homes of congregation members and sing Christmas Carols. Halloween was terrific, with sweet old ladies at the doors very often with homemade treats. Everyone's grandma seemed to be around at that time. The notion that anyone would put a razor blade or poison in anything was never a question. It was a time when people knew they could rely on their neighbors and community.

North Highlands grew as the new civilian support for the base. It had to keep up with a quickly expanding airbase funded to meet the Cold War's challenges as the Military/Industrial Complex grew with it. So the homes were basic structures, made to be affordable even then, for the civilians that would be needed for supporting the Air Force operations there. The houses were simple but reliable, with cement foundations and amenities like heated bathroom floors and installed gas ranges that put today's junk to shame, as well as central heating with thermostats. Cooling during the hot summers was an option. I can't figure that one out. But the developers were from L.A. and the Bay Area, so they probably didn't appreciate how hot the summers in the Sacramento Valley typically became or didn't care. This was, after all, the same period when air conditioning in cars was rare. Swamp cooler technology to the rescue; they worked, to a degree (get it?).

Those gas ranges were commercial-level in quality. It seems that this was the standard universal installation included in the home when sold. The contractors seemed to hold the old adage that the center of a home was the kitchen. A good stove was essential. They sure did not skip on that feature! The idea of cooking with an electric stove was not even on the list of choices, I suspect. I never gave it a second thought until I saw one at an antique shop in Roseville four decades later. It was one of those gas ranges, the stoves installed in the homes in North Highlands, and I don't know where else. They were marvels of reliable construction and function. Seeing one again in the 90s after years of not noticing the decline in the quality of the typical home appliance world was startling; seeing it evoked warm memories in me. I never knew it, but that stove had its own engram of fond recall in my brain, probably low down in the hypothalamus where memories of good meals would reside. But they also did not skip on heating, which was efficient, and also gas. The water heaters had also been plumbed out so the bathroom floors were heated by hot water ducts. So those little cracker boxes were comfortable at least, at least once you got a swamp cooler in for the summer heat. Swimming pools helped, too, and Doughboy Pools became common.

North Highlands continued to grow rapidly. It grew from 150 in 1949 to nearly 40,000 by 1969. The official prediction was that North Highlands would rise from its present population to 80,000 in fifteen years if the growth rate remained the same.

This was how my world seemed to go, changing bit by bit; the fields were retreating, and so was the quality of the simple things. Plastic was the new wonder material. Our stately old wood table was suddenly replaced by some flimsy-looking board with Formica veneer and think tubular, cone-shaped legs. The matching chair's seats came off the frames very quickly. Our generation later became famous for its rebelliousness. But some of that rebellion was justified. One practical feature of that rebellion against cheap, mass-produced junk was hardly political, but it was correct; the planned obsolescence aspect of capitalism seemed not just wasteful, but dangerous to cultural stability. The lack of longevity of that practice has led us to a consumer's hell of lousy quality and slipping standards for decades now as well as dependence on unreliable parties we thought were our "friends." But in those days, the innocence of not knowing made the immediate world a beautiful, bright land of discovery and happiness.

The night sky in our backyard was as starry as it is now in the most remote locations.   One night, our father pointed out the major constellations to my sisters and me as he learned them during his long nights on watch duty out at sea during the war.

I don't know when I first heard the song, but I was four when we moved there, and I already knew the lines, "Where the deer and the antelope play."   This was the place, I figured. It had to be. I was supported in my idea by the same icon used by the developers of our particular set of tract homes, which was called "Larchmont Village," with that silhouette of the cowboy laying way back on an elbow, chewing on a weed. Everything fit together.

I watched "The Cisco Kid" and "The Lone Ranger" on our big, fifteen-inch black and white television.   I liked that genre better than Superman, I think. I imagined they were all out there just beyond my view, in the distant fields, riding about always to right some wrong. It could have been so. In the Roy Rogers shows, there were always cars being chased by horsemen who would always "cut them off at the pass."   When I first heard the name San Fran-Cisco, I felt that I knew who it was named after; "Oh, Cisco!" "Oh, Poncho!" The Cisco Kid, of course! (Was Poncho's surname Lopez)? They were riding out there in the field, too. But my favorite was "Death Valley Days" with "The Old Ranger."   The bugle solo at the opening and closing was compellingly eerie to me, and I suppose the William Tell Overture they used for the Lone Ranger impressed me enough to stimulate a later appreciation of classical music. Every kid knew it, that's for sure. That was probably what sent me on a 1975 road trip to Death Valley with my buddy Jeff; the first of three visits over twenty years. In my estimation, this and the wonderful musical cartoons; Merry Melodies, Looney Tunes, Betty Boop, and such, were later to influence the emergence of Progressive Rock. When you wished upon a star, it really didn't matter who you were. Through the television screen, this promise was made to all children. And at that time, at least, it all seemed possible.

These random but happy and instructive influences were impressed into most Boomers' minds, making them receptive to innovations based on them. Westerns either used classical music or crafted its themes from it up to that time, up to the Spaghetti Western arrival when everything changed. Who doesn't know the theme music from "The Magnificent Seven?" Shame on you; that film further imbued in me the chivalric messages of the earlier "Lone Ranger" and "Zorro" serials, and later "Have Gun Will Travel. "

I suspected I was not the only boy so impressed in my day. I believe these influences came across in the local popular music of the Boomers. The rise of folk music and its fusion with rock, and the pioneering of country rock by The Byrds had counterparts in psychedelia. Quicksilver Messenger Services, "Cavalry" from the "Happy Trails" album, was probably the high watermark of the "Ozone Ranger" subculture of the time; as a kind of Psychedelic Western dream sequence. *[1]

I left out that all Boomers were raised on Little Rascals serials, which seemed to always be on the television set on Saturdays with the usual parade of recycled and new cartoons, quite the alter-ego of Mickey Mouse; Mighty Mouse. I liked the wolf villains, who I only learned later were drawn wearing Zoot Suits. I didn't understand until years later, but this was partial adult entertainment, as were the Rocky and Bullwinkle Cold War-themed cartoons. But we didn't play spy vs. spy, we played cowboy. Or at least we did in our imaginations which were under the influence of local history and Hollywood combined. How delightful it would have been to know that Virgil Earp, Wyatt's nephew, was alive and living in Sacramento in those years. Our pioneer past was still a living thing at the time. Sacramento teamed with it, and I felt it. Fair concessions with robotic gunslingers provided far more comedy than history, as the audio playback after your "shot" hit the target played back.

Oh, ya got me! You miserable polecat!

I was one of those kids who had a cap gun, holster, and hat when I was four or five years old. I remember practicing for a showdown in the front yard against my shadow on the driveway, "reach for it." I think I gave up because I could never seem to outdraw that guy. In those early days, I didn't know the difference between a cowboy and a gunslinger or gun for hire in those days, but "Have Gun Will Travel" arrived to help create that distinction in my mind. (By 16, I had a real Colt revolver and won an impromptu quick draw contest. My father gave it to me for my 13th birthday. I practiced against television gunfighters (with an empty gun, come on)). I no longer believed that I was a cowboy, but the West's romance had been imprinted on me by then, certainly, as it had been on many.

Please note, that I never shot anyone – of course not! Such a notion was absolutely alien to the mind of a Boomer in those years or ever for that matter. We played "army" but the idea that we ought to hurt one another was not remotely part of the play. Today, paintball is a great sport. It doesn't produce "shooters." We might have been cap gun trained using replicas of a more violent time, but we were also taught respect; and first of all, respect for our elders. But I went from cap gun to real gun in a fairly short time. But at that time, this was not so rare. One kid who lived on my block for a short time was on a military-sponsored pistol team when we were both eleven. One day, he showed me his competition piece. He opened its case, showed me without picking it up, and then put it back on the closet shelf in his room where it was kept. I was eager to get going, however.

I wasn't stupid, but I had problems in math because as a left-hander, I stacked digits in a way that sometimes did not line up vertically and my hand blocked the digits, so in moving my hand, again and again, to see what I was doing resulted in me losing my place. (I've realized since that using drafting paper would have solved the problem). So in the summer of 1965, my father made a deal with me. He said that if I attended summer school math class and passed with at least a C, I could take the hunter's safety program sponsored by Sears and get my hunting license. The class was held at Highlands High School. That was my summer project. I regarded the instructions as strict law. Over the years, I've imbued that Colt with deep nostalgia, and consider it a treasured possession.

I wasn't alone in my Western reenactment fantasy. I had a companion, a partner. A kid who lived "around the block" from our house, Mark Miller, was sort of a stray from a then-rare single-parent home who became a close friend and remained so for decades until finally drifted away in the 2000s. His older brother had been student body president in the senior Class of 1968, Martine's class. My mom said many times that she'd adopt him if she could. She knew his mother. She worked with her at McClellan. For a few years, Mark accompanied my father and me on some of our hunting trips and trail bike adventures. Mark and I had all sorts of entanglements in the way brothers would, I suppose. During the winter of 1966-67, we concocted a plan where we'd run away to live in the Sierras. I even had it worked out to the point where we'd spend the summer at higher elevations and where we'd winter lower down.

I realized that food would be a problem. After all, we hadn't had too much luck deer hunting during the season. That's probably why it remained a fantasy. But it was a very active fantasy. Mark soon acquired a Ruger .22 caliber six-gun and holster. My Dad used to drill us at drawing on his verbal signal. We'd stand side by side with empty guns in our holsters. He'd call out "one, two, or three," and we were to find the target to the left, center, or right depending. We also went up into the hills and practiced side by side hitting targets. I also practiced against TV actors when the shows were playing. Daddy joined in on those occasions. We must have been unknowing pioneers of the "Cowboy Action Shooting" sport today.

Later in his twenties, after some college, Mark went up to Alaska for some years. He lived beyond Haines, off-grid as part of the effort of the American Bald Eagle's restoration in Glacier National Park. He later climbed Mt. McKinley, when it was still named Mt. McKinley.

Good for him.   He acted out our mutual Jack London-inspired fantasies. I received regular letters from him in those years.

I had to satisfy my wilderness adventures with extended backpacking trips into the Sierras and Trinity Alps of Northern California. In the 90s, I acquired a great Jockey Club-registered four-year-old thoroughbred named Sands of Time. He was a grandson of Damascus, the horse that made Willie Shoemaker famous in the sixties, but since he was hand-raised, like a pet, as a result, he lacked the orneriness required to be a racehorse, but he was a great show horse. I trained for four years for Eventing, as I considered it closest to what a Pony Express rider would have faced. So I did it differently, but I was still on a branch of the same root as Mark. I came to that divergence in the road, as Robert Frost put it, and took the fork that made all the difference.

Later, when I came to the fork that took me away from Sandy to work and live in Europe, another dream from my youth, I had been training with a saber, hoping to start a trend in mounted saber fencing. It never happened, but it would have been quite a spectacle, I think. Those mounted cowboy photos made back on P Street, not long before we'd moved out to the open prairie range, made an impression on me, at least the photo experience.

Watch the Birdie!

Photographers were everywhere in those days, at parks, at supermarkets, and in their own studios. So one day, I was sitting on a pony on P Street getting my pony photo done and the next thing I knew, I was out of the range, "where the deer and the antelope played.

As far as I was concerned, I was a confirmed member of the fraternity of cowboys. So I was surprised when at a neighborhood birthday party between rounds of "Pin the Tail on the Donkey," when I informed Jan Peterson that I was a cowboy (hat on as evidence), he corrected me. "You ain't no cowboy." He said. "Oh, yes, I am!" I thought to myself. I had no doubt. I only figured out later that it took more than imagination and a cap gun to be a cowboy. But we were always friendly regardless because I never held a grudge over his comment. Up to then, I was a cowboy – I thought. It wasn't a lonely occupation for a little boy in those days, either. After all, Ronnie Howard was one, too! And I received confirmation not long after that confrontation, and from the best source possible, a real Indian!

The P Street Kid Rides Again!
Jockey Club registered as Sands of Time – "Sandy" and author training in Sonoma County –
1996. This isn't anything like riding a motorcycle! – Photo by Dorothy J. Hammack

Going south down Watt Avenue, which is closer to Sacramento's actual city, was a strip mall complex. They were termed "shopping centers" in those days. Country Club Center was one of two on the west side of the county in those days. The Town and Country Village Shopping Center was even closer to Sacramento still, being built by

Jere Strizek in 1945, years before starting the first suburban projects in North Highlands.

This one was rustic style, made up of a log cabin-looking in connected rows as if there could have been a pioneer strip mall, even though Strizek had intended to make it seem more European. The one eatery I remember from it, Brothers Delicatessen, was more European than the one at Country Club Center, which was shorter from home and more modern with an expansive parking lot in the front and rear of the mall.

Another big difference was that the Village had shops, and privately owned and operated businesses in more of what was later called a "boutique" style. It makes sense since it was more European in that sense. Country Club Center was the place for the large chain stores, as they existed then; Rhodes, Penny's, and the then-popular national shoe stores, Buster Brown and Kenny's. There was also a cute little diner called "Harts," although the menu was more pedestrian than Brothers. However, these original "Harts" had been around since the 19th century in downtown Sacramento. The Sacramento Book Collector's Club was responsible for preserving many essential local histories, seeing some published. They regularly met at Harts downtown on J Street beginning in 1939. Over 70 years later, they still meet regularly.

There were many more places, including a toy shop, simply named The Toy Shop. They had sporting goods as well as toys. That is where I first saw a model railroad. I wanted a train set so badly that I could feel the burn of the desire, but I never got one. I was doomed to sit at a friend's house in quiet envy and watch him run his set. The Toy Shop was where I bought my first fishing rod at seven years old by saving my allowance for months. It was not rare to see friends from school sometimes at Country Club Center. Much of the shopping center's business was based around supplying all the Baby Boom households (and childless homes were rare). That meant frequent promotions aimed at kids.

On one day in 1958, that spring, I think, a giant children's event was held there. Kids were already lined across the large parking lot when we arrived. Upon a raised stage, an Indian Chief waited as the kids ascended the hastily built platform's stairs to be in his presence. He was there to induct all the kids into the tribe. I was wearing my cowboy hat and cap gun, so it was no surprise when he dubbed me "Chief Lazy Arrow." His name for Paulette was more charming. She had green eyes and beautiful blonde hair that fell in natural ringlets onto her shoulders. He named her "Princess with Hair Like Springs." That remained in the family lore longer than my less-than-factual salutation.

However, the point is made; I was a bonafide cowboy, and it came with a title as well (so there). However, this did not cover the scope of my childhood fantasies. Inspired first by "Commando Cody, Sky Marshal of the Universe," with his "Lost Planet Airmen," all such entertainment and the fascinations they provided as a nearly daily diet, contributed a great deal to the wonder and innocence of that era. This was true for little boys, at least. I don't know how many girls were influenced by the short run of the "Annie Oakley" series, but I remember the "Bullseye!" intro.

Martine read the girls' adventure books, like "Trixie Belden" and "The Bobbsey Twins." But it was when the Indians, as represented by the cartoon series, "Pow Wow, the Indian Boy," and Tonto (Jay Silverheels), provided feelings of universal friendship with the "Red Man." (They say "White Man" we say "Red Man," Let's call the whole thing off ... it would be nice). A period of good feeling between the Red and White Man had been cultivated by the sixties. It was somewhat ruined by the Marxists who infected our Indigenous friends with their chronic grievance strategy by 1969 and used it for social disruption. Today, they are infected with their version of Critical Race Theory, but happily, not all of them.

I met Kim at Fanny Ann's saloon in Old Sacramento, which was the only time I ever went into that place. She went with me to the last Coloma Gold Rush Days celebration in 1976.

Kalamity Kim?

As a serendipitous intersectional event in real life, in 1976, I dated an art teacher from Auburn High School who had grown up in Los Angeles on the same street as Jay Silverheels (Tonto). She said that it was wonderful to have him as a neighbor as he interacted with all of the kids and was very kind.

Author in Coloma, California, January 24, 1976 – playing harmonica duet with the South Loomis Quickstep Band – Photo by Kim Brown

I used to celebrate my birthday there every year; as it was a grand party that I could privately appropriate for my own since I was born on the day John Marshall picked up that piece of gold in the mill run he was inspecting while building a lumber mill in the Coloma Valley under contract with Captain John A. Sutter, founder of the New Helvetia colony that became Sacramento. Up to then, I had only heard a rumor or two about it, but at her suggestion, we went to the Dicken's Faire in San Francisco, in 1975, and by 1979; I was working at the Dicken's Faire as an extension of my participation at the old Black Point Renaissance Pleasure Faire in Marin County as a fencing instructor. I actually convinced the owner to take on a pirate theme and use the name of a 1976 Roger McGuinn album and song, "The Cardiff Rose," (the song is actually listed as "Jolly Roger").

Fanny Ann's Saloon in Old Sacramento – photo by author

It's all connected in this crazy way, thanks to Kim Brown, I suppose. In 1998, I was corresponding with Roger McGuinn from Europe and told him about the fencing booth. He thought it was great. And this all happened because of Kim Brown.

At William Land Park

The remaining exhibit I have to offer on the cowboy qualifier issue follows thus; my father was active in the Sacramento Chapter of the California Chiropractic Association in those days. In the summer, they held meetings as picnics at William Land Park, which is still a well-known landmark as the Golden Gate Park of Sacramento. Everyone knows about the children's area there, with Captain Hook's pirate ship. It was a children's fantasy land, and thanks to the horse concession, I was christened as a bonafied "horsey rider" early, thanks to my wonderful parents. All I wanted to do and did was talk to the horse as it made its way through the narrow guide ropes to the "end of the trail." (In the 1990s when I owned Sandy, I also talked to him a lot. It turns out that they like it, in fact, most animals do, even wild ones; In my time, I've talked to birds, deer, and foxes. The foxes were especially responsive). One may pick at the fact that I have never roped a cow, let alone met one, but this is a frivolous complication. The matter in my five-year-old head was settled and done. Anyway, I never lost the feeling that I should try to learn to properly ride a horse. I fulfilled that early urge in midlife.

It was a children's fantasy land, and thanks to the horse concession, I was christened as a bonafied "horsey rider" early, thanks to my wonderful parents. All I wanted to do and did was talk to the horse as it made its way through the narrow guide ropes to the "end of the trail." (In the 1990s when I owned Sandy, I also talked to him a lot. It turns out that they like it, in fact, most animals do, even wild ones; in my time, I've talked to birds, deer, and foxes. The foxes were especially responsive). One may pick at the fact that I have never roped a cow, let alone met one, but this is a frivolous complication. The matter in my five-year-old head was settled and done.

Dominant over these experiences continued to be the field that began at my back door in those days. Step outside, and it was there. Even as it began to change, there was something to look at everywhere. The heavy equipment came on like an army of dinosaurs. There were bulldozers, like monsters of another age, which tore the wild oats out by their roots, stripping the land, nearly leveling the land, pushing it into walls of dirt here and there to fill in depressions. The rollers were monsters from another planet that packed down the hardpan into an even denser, man-made material. The big jaws of the shovels looked like tyrannosaurus as they dangled from the end of the steel girders that held them out from the body of the beast. Is this what inspired a B filmmaker to produce "Billy the Kid Meets the Dinosaurs?"*[1]

As these metal monsters prowled the prairie, I expect the Cisco Kid and Poncho were spurring their steeds away to safer havens along with all the wildlife on that prairie, from the bugs to the jackrabbits. The deer and antelope had disappeared long before this. All of their activity would keep the bugs and larger life forms in motion. I would watch ants marching to establish new colonies and then with a magnifying glass as they had their "ant wars," where thousands of ants would hold the other in the death grip of their jaws until one or both died. Then followed the strange aftermath as the survivors carried off the dead ones; to where, I wondered. I always found such phenomena remarkable as a boy, and it still is an odd thing of nature now that I think of it; "No ant left behind" was their instinctive policy. We even had a song in those days; "The Ants Go Marching." It was to the tune of "When Johnny Comes Marching Home Again." What on earth were they fighting over, territory? So it's that much of a basic instinct of evolution? From ants to bipeds, we all need our homes; territory matters.

Then, there were all the other bugs. Being naturally tenacious, many varieties of the less delicate species had made their way back into the completed neighborhoods. I remember quite a variety of spiders, including black widows. My father often took the hose to the outside of our home to wash down their webs in the summer. They liked the exposed underside of the roof that jutted out beyond the outside walls. Daddy showed me a black widow with her strange red hourglass design and warned me about it before killing it. That must have been my first notice of danger in the world. But it didn't make me hate bugs. Beetles were everywhere, including an occasional giant one that would fly straight at you, making an eerie low buzz that was so powerful you could feel the vibrations of the wings as they sought you out. And they did; they saw you. If you moved, they changed course and continued their aerial attack. But not one ever made a landing on me.

I never figured out why they wanted to land on me, owing to my unique backpedaling style, quick retreat technique combined with my ability to turn and flee far enough so that they would run out of momentum and gravity would defeat their attack. But I could see them still looking at me, so I'd leave them frustrated. They only got one try. Sometimes, when they weren't looking, I would step back toward them and marvel at their size. In school, I learned that the Indians around there lived mostly on bugs and acorns. This one had to be equal to a ham sandwich. But I wasn't going to eat it!

My favorite bugs were the grasshoppers, of course, but best of all the praying mantis. They were rarer than the grasshoppers, so it was a special event to find one. My sister and I figured out that we could catch a grasshopper, and hold it just right, delicately with the fingers, so it was belly up and comfortable. That way, we could feed it a blade of grass. They had no problem eating in captivity; they readily accepted the grass blade's end into their proboscis. We would watch their particular chomping style as their mandibles worked. We called the brown juice they produced "tobacco," as if they were bug cowboys taking a "chaw." I don't know why; that's how it seemed to us.

The praying mantis, on the other hand, was on another level altogether. They seemed genuinely smart and even affectionate. My sister became frightened when they would fly from her wrist to her face, but I let mine do it. It just seemed to want to be as close as it could get. I had one once that would drink out of a teaspoon. I would feed it moths. More than once and right into my young adulthood, I'd bring a big female indoors so that it would birth its babies inside my room.

The Dragon Flies arrived in the spring and remained as long as the little water pools in the fields were present. We had butterflies, and when they came around, they made us forget about everything else, not just the other bugs, but anything that was going on. They were a subject of wonder. It was as if a fairy had flown by to visit us. They were friendly, too, and would sit on your arm or in your hand. I remember seeing many that must have just emerged from the cocoon as they were flexing their wings, pumping up their new musculature in preparation for that first flight. Altogether, those early days were wondrous; the land was full of life. Butterflies were once so present in the big valley that in 1804, Gabriel Moraga gave a name to a camp they made in San Quaqin, Mariposa (Butterflies).

Don't ask me why I did not become an entomologist. I don't know. It just never occurred to me that I could make a living from playing with bugs. One of my Class of '70 alumni got the bite; so to speak; Alvin Ludtke did become one, traveled to the Amazon, and named a new species of butterfly that will bear his surname as long as records are kept. I give credit to the fields we grew up in those days.

Sometimes a bluebelly or horned toad lizard appeared. I remember that Mrs. Martini kept a horned toad in a terrarium in my first-grade classroom. But that was the last one I ever saw. They had been banished with the other critters as the streets and homes appeared between home and Village School. Along with the Robins were

Bluejays and Magpies, who came with the valley oaks that dotted the land. But the strangest aviary denizen in the area was the seagulls. They seemed most present in the winter. They seemed to love the pools of water that would form on the blacktop at schools. Village School seemed a favorite for them because it had a large blacktop and grass area. It turned out that these birds were migrating to and from Mono Lake, on the eastern slope of the Sierra in Inyo County, near there was the ghost town of Bodie. I first visited Bodie in 1975, with Rick, who made it with me all the way from first grade and Mrs. Martini's classroom.

One Day We Went a'Wandering

Martine began her school days at the school on Watt Avenue then named Fruitvale. I calculate that was 1955. She went to summer school that year at the only other existing elementary school at that time, Larchmont. She took me with her one day. I don't remember much about the day except the walk home, which was across fields and all the weeds, flowers, bugs, and birds we came across, including a robin's nest with blue eggs in it. It was then that I saw my first pheasant. It exploded out of a bush, which caused us both to jump in surprise.

We entered a construction zone, with ditches and pipes everywhere, traveling inside one deep trench to emerge once again further on in the field, where plenty of corkscrew stickers and wild oats waited, eager to get into our canvas shoes and socks. "Stickers" in the socks and shoes were always the price of a walk in the field during the summer and fall. Pulling them out was tedious, but we had to do it if we wanted to walk very far after getting their points into the fabric. Sometimes you had to stop walking to pull an incredibly clever one out because it had found skin and was actively seeking a way through the skin. Spring was different; the stickers were green and could be imagined as little spears and looked like a shotgun blast of mini-spears when appropriately tossed. I could toss a bunch of them at my sisters if they were around or just into the ground; all good, clean fun.

I had no way of knowing later that the trench we entered and walked through as a "shortcut" was the construction of the next school to arrive in the Larchmont suburb where I would soon be walking to regularly for years. This was the sewer and plumbing work for Village School, where I attended kindergarten through the fourth grade.

So I walked from Larchmont Elementary to Village Elementary and home as a four-year-old. That's quite a loop for a wandering child of four. I thought nothing of it and neither did my parents. Parents didn't worry about harm in those days. No child was likely to get more than a bee sting from such a journey, and I never got even one of those. I got those in the front yard when the honeybees would come for the clover flowers, and we were playing barefoot on the lawn. My parents did have one safety rule; we were forbidden to cross the street in front of our home or even enter it for several years.

I spent my first five years of primary school at Village Elementary through the fourth grade. After that, I was bused up to the school on the hill across from the high school. That hill turns out to be the first official wrinkle of geography that marks the ancient crush of land that stacked up during the primordial ages to form the Sierra mountain range. As such, the school is aptly named Hillsdale Elementary School. I never understood why North Highlands was named as it was. It seemed fairly flat to me. But that must be why; it was north of Sacramento proper and is where the shallow hills represented the higher ground and an escape from the dangers of the flood plain where Sacramento is situated. Sacramento suffered its terrible flood on January 8, 1850, again in 1852, and the next year as well. The Sacramento River levees took years to complete. In the time from those floods to the final complete levy system on the Sacramento River, the city of Sacramento was largely redesigned with a new level built on top of the old. Sacramento has an underground ghost town that is partially accessible for tours today.

The wetlands to the south and west extended for miles. Captain John Sutter erected his fort where he did, a mile from the river precisely to avoid flooding, choosing the first and only high spot available for his establishment. One must marvel at how quickly Sacramento went from a muddy swamp for almost half the year to a town with streets reliably navigable by horse-drawn carriages.

The hamlet of Antelope appeared as soon as the railroad construction began. Workers set up residences at the spot where the junction of the Southern Pacific line and the old Central Pacific line. The Roseville Switching Yard grew from that. On the modest road out to the little burg, travelers must have noticed the land's slight rise. This was the high land to the north of Sacramento. It had long been an unofficial description of the general area of the last stage of the journey to Antelope. When the government wanted to establish airfields in Sacramento County, they chose the higher ground, the prairie to the north and east. It all makes sense. At least I think it inspired Jere Strizek. When a name was required for the residential expansion of McClellan Airfield, Plane Haven appellation made sense. Antelope was there as a lonely dot on the line for some time before Roseville and Rocklin were founded.

It is consequential to our story to consider two types of settlement communities up to the middle of the twentieth century in the American West, meaning everything west of the Appalachian Mountains. The earliest kind of settlement was a fort. Cabins were built, and walls rose around them. A simple castle style was practical for obvious reasons. When it was safe enough for actual civilization to take root, a proper township, with a commercial cause, say a gold strike or a good landing on a river, or maybe simply a landmark of significance. There are many ghost towns west of the Mississippi. Most of them are old mining towns with old train stops created by those mines. But of all causes, perhaps the railway terminal has provided the most permanent settlements.

Antelope was the result of establishing the railroad line, whereas North Highlands is a settlement based on a fort, a military establishment. As Indians did at the various forts in the 19th century, civilians settled around military installations in the 20th century as communities had around Annapolis and West Point in the East in an earlier national development phase. Such causes provide for a different civilian experience. A town might be established by exploiting a local resource, such as furs, timber, gold, or coal, and depending upon that resource's continuation, the viability of that resource. If such a resource played out too soon or was too remote, it became a ghost town. Another sure killer was if the railroad line missed your town. Many a plot of a Western film revolved around the planning or layout of a railroad line and the sometimes violence that accompanied it. "Once Upon a Time in the West" is perhaps the opus of such histories rendered as an old-fashioned melodrama film.

Later, there would be factory towns and mining towns as had been established in the eastern states earlier. Farming communities are where the genuinely free citizen resided by the end of the epoch of Manifest Destiny; which was the idea that the United States of America was naturally destined by geography and political reality to span from the Atlantic to the Pacific. Those visionaries who promoted the idea are responsible for the outcome of the 20th century when old-world ideas about empire and conquest produced the most devastating war in human history (so far)." America saved the world, and then raised the world's standard of living and lifespan everywhere in the Free World. But in the 19th century in California and the West, ranching was still a mobile business that, in most cases, required a lot of open land. Rancho Del Paso was such a place. Antelope was supported by this enterprise as a railroad stop slowly grew into the Roseville Switchyard. Such towns have a center, with a railway station on their main street or near it.

A military installation is the center of the other type of settlement. Where the military is located, security is an issue, so not just anyone can be allowed into the center of that sort of town. A farm town is an industry of its own. It generates its own source of wealth and trade. A military base attracts parasitical populations that depend upon a separated host for wealth that comes from somewhere else. The character difference between the two is essential to recognize. Military service involved the frequent movement of people. A town based on, for example, a farming community usually sees a steady population that may see generations of the same family as residents. This was often the condition up to the nineteen-sixties. There are exceptions and, of course, combinations. Vancouver, Washington, originated from a fur trading post as the most westward terminal for the Hudson Bay Company. During Fort Vancouver's time, some limited farming went on, as with Fort Ross on the Sonoma County Coast of California.

Fort Ross was owned by the Russia/America Fur Company. It is famous for having sold the entire fort to Captain John Sutter, the only interested party when Fort Ross closed down in 1842. You'd think that the Mexican Army would have wanted them, but they were both underfunded and understaffed, and Sutter was their trusted alcade (sheriff/mayor), they left the heavy lifting to him and the Americans that began to arrive soon after.

A town based on a military post is supported by government funding, which is to say, taxpayers. If the base is important enough, it remains permanently. If a supporting industry or agricultural advantage existed and was located on a river, the town would survive as with Fort Vancouver, on the Columbia River in Washington State. Fort Ross had no advantage beyond that of a fur-harvesting endeavor. The Russian River was too far to the south, where lumbering began later as the founding activity. So it decayed into ruin.

With North Highlands, the civilian support of the base constituted a permanent settlement. In those early decades, it was beyond imagination that McClellan AFB would ever be shut down. The town depended on the airbase, but so did many outlying communities and dependent private enterprises of all sorts. In 1971, I had a girlfriend whose family lived beyond Sloughhouse around Wilton at the extreme southeast edge of Sacramento County bordering Amador County, in fact. Her father commuted every day to work at McClellan AFB. The transition after the airbase closed down would be a difficult time.

The differences between the farming community of Antelope and a community based on a military installation were of consequence in determining the character and contrast of the two communities up to the closing of McClellan AFB. One was old and grew with the county, while the other was more hastily created. Antelope had families with ancestors who had settled in the 19th century, whereas everyone in North Highlands had arrived recently. These two communities' history and fate would turn on the military's activities and other government installations and activities. It helped a great deal that Sacramento is the capital of California.

The history of the Spook Tree is very much a railroad story, as we'll see. The railroad brought many changes to the area. One unplanned one was non-native vegetation. The Hillsdale school playground is where I discovered tumbleweeds. They fanned out over the lands from railroad routes. I never understood until long after my school days when I learned that they were not native, but from Asia along with the Chinese workers. Tumbleweeds were most numerous around railway yards and the Roseville switching yard was one of the biggest in the United States. So the railroads spread the tumbleweeds throughout the Southwest and plains. Other reports say the weed came from Ukraine. You decide the most likely route of the plant, from Ukraine through Asia to California or with some Eastern European arriving by ship around Cape Horn or via a wagon train. The weeds followed the rails. We boys found tumbleweeds to be excellent fantasy construction materials. They were stackable due to their prickliness, which provided a convenient interlocking system. We built temporary forts out of them just off the playground's blacktop away from the tracks where the teacher supervisors let us stray out onto the dirt a little. The high winds in the spring and autumn seemed to bring them around. Fired tumbleweed in the wind would be a veritable rolling, flying, fire torch (take note).

When I began kindergarten in 1957, I had to walk through the field about a mile to get there; poor me. But it was no hardship in my view back then. It was always an adventure coming and going. The best part was the little pools of standing water that would appear during the winter and linger into the late spring. They were always host to all sorts of bugs and flowers as the seasonal ecosystems appeared annually.

Fort Ross on the Sonoma Coast – Note the orchards and race track. Fort Vancouver shared similar features – From "Fort Ross – Indians, Russians, Americans." – Fort Ross Interpretive Association, Inc. The author lived on the ridge above Fort Ross for six years – from 1988 to 1994 and was a member of the Fort Ross Interpretive Center.

What was best about the pools was that, like magic, hundreds of little clear eggs would appear. I could see the little embryos as dark life wiggling inside them. Overnight they were gone, and tadpoles were swimming about. Then, their appendages began to sprout out of their bodies. That transition was observable from day to day until they became actual frogs. I would linger around and watch them while most other kids passed by uninterested. I noted the changes every day. I never understood why the other kids did not stop to look. I could see the tadpoles change daily from little guppy-like fish that magically grew until they were completely different animals altogether. Once, I came too close to the water and stepped into the little pond up to the mid-calf. When Miss Wilson saw me, she sent me home to change. That was another two-way trip across the field. I think I got back just as school was ending for the day.

The fields were a distraction. Jackie Cooper was the first kid of significance that I met in Kindergarten. We became instant buddies. Jackie must have noticed I was adventurous. After all, we walked to school by the same route every day as he lived just up Centinella from my home. It was natural that we should pair up. He was an even more precocious child than me. Just as I was, Jackie was led by curiosity. After a while, Jackie began to stop to search the pools with me. We noted such things as the metamorphosis of the tadpoles. Jackie quickly became my best friend in kindergarten and the first grade.

I dug up my father's microscope from his doctor's stuff that had remained in boxes in the garage after our move from P Street. He actually let me have it. Jackie and I put a couple drops of pond water on a slide and saw the little bugs we called "sails." An adult told us that they were amoebas, so we innocently called them "aribas", having no idea what it meant, and that was that for a while. I remember it well because my street had been built up by then, and he was up the road toward the school only by about three houses or so two houses from Cantel Way toward the ponds and Village School, in fact, right across the street from Bobby's house. The practice became a stop by his house to pick him up on the way to school and say goodbye before I continued down the street. I found that Jackie's home had a lawn where ours didn't yet. His was the first backyard I remember ever seeing as a proper backyard.

Jackie moved away before second grade began, and I was sad to lose him. It was the first time I felt the emotion of loss and my first experience of the often temporary nature of so many residents of North Highlands. There were other memorable kids in my class. Some were still around as part of our senior class in 1970. One was a cute English girl named whose surname was a flowering fruit. She had light blonde hair and would smile at me whenever I looked her way. She'd walk by my desk, kiss her finger, and then touch it to my cheek.

On that basis, I think we considered ourselves an item. When I met her again in the seventh grade, she didn't do that anymore, but when she signed my yearbook, she wrote in little parenthesis "First grade." She also included a bad joke; "flunk now and avoid the June rush." This conflicted with my previous memories of her; I didn't exactly take her as having carried a torch for me for five years. In fact, I know she didn't.

Another first-grade acquaintance who was to become a significant part of my life later was Rick. He'd make faces at me whenever the teacher, Mrs. Martini, would throttle some poor kid at their desk as they sat. For all I could see, the act had been triggered by a wrong answer. Rick and his cousin Dave, better known as "Bucky," became my best friends later in high school and young adulthood, and Dave up to when cancer tragically took him in 1997. But Bucky missed out on Mrs. Martini as he sat next door in Mrs. Sanguinetti's classroom. I think it was when Dave made a face at me on the playground and I returned it with my own, that the deal was sealed. Just one look was all it took. Dave remained a close friend until he died too young in 1987 of brain cancer. A favorite photo I took of him in there in 1983, replicates that earlier childhood grimace. It was the same Honda shop that I had worked at earlier where the "She's No Rosie" girl had been on the prowl among the employees and finally found me to play with. Incidentally, Dave had recommended me for the job. The motorcycle community in the area at the time was closely connected, almost literally a family.

Now Mrs. Martini; I never understood why she'd shake a kid up like that. I guess they'd done anything she deemed unacceptable and likely to form into a habit if left unchecked. She'd take their shoulders and shake them so roughly that their heads flew back and forth like a ragdoll. One winter day, I found out how frivolous her standards could be. I was standing on the playground alone, having arrived early. I was facing a low spot on the blacktop against the wall of our cluster of classroom "wings." Rainwater had filled the low spot, which was maybe fifteen feet across, maybe six inches deep, to seem like a little pool. I was attracted to water, I guess. I had become fond of any body of water because of the interesting things I found in them.

So I stood there, almost reverently, staring at this pool of water. As I lingered in my yellow full-body rain suit in the pouring rain, she appeared from around the corner of our classroom wing, seized me by the shoulders, and shook me in the way I'd seen others thus handled. She shouted, "Never stand next to a body of water!" I guess it was worth risking a mild whiplash and medulla insult to provide such a prophylactic lesson in life. She can perhaps be forgiven because hardly anyone in that era understood things like shaken infant syndrome, whiplash, and the mechanics of brain concussion.

My father would have because he was a chiropractor. I never said anything about the incident to him or my mother. I was luckier than her other victims because my father regularly checked and treated my sisters and me. He managed our health, giving us vitamins daily, as a good chiropractic doctor daddy would. He never knew about Mrs. Martini's style of discipline. In any case, other than this ill-recommended practice, Mrs. Martini was not particularly mean. In fact, she was genuinely kind at times. She was old-fashioned was all; a throwback from a rougher, more brutal time, when kids got swept away in floods and drowned in ponds. She likely was merely replicating what she had experienced, herself.

Mrs. Martini even wore her hair in a bun, like an old schoolmarm. I remember noting that she looked a lot like "Mamma" of the Katzenjammer Kids comic strip. Even so, I was intimidated enough to not ask any questions when I got stuck in my workbook. I was afraid of being shaken again. However, these problems did not dominate my world. What dominated my world was the field that filled the space between that classroom and home. In those days, kids were often told to "not bother the grown-ups," adding that "children should be seen and not heard," with the accompanying occasional corporal reinforcement.   So when we were somewhere, at another home or office, we sat quietly and behaved.

The stages of construction in those fields from the vantage point of my backyard as the neighborhood transformed from a vast, open area dotted by oak trees and brush break to more homes like our own, or close to it.   There were three architectural patterns of the houses in the blocks under construction at the time.

Later, the designs would change beyond Thomas Drive, and those lucky bums got fireplaces, solving the severe problem I wrestled with for a few Christmases over how Santa Claus could get into our house. It solved it for them, but not for us. The problem was solved one day when an older kid, full of mischief and glee, informed Jackie and me, and my sister Paulette, who was walking home from kindergarten with us sometimes by then, that there was no such thing as Santa Claus; it was just a story for kids. This was my first crisis of faith. We asked Daddy and Momma that night. Sure enough, they confessed. What other lies were they telling us; "the Easter Bunny, too?" "Yes," they replied. Even the Tooth Fairy was a lie. Paulette and I had the same next question; "What about God and Jesus?" No, they were real, they said. Maybe, but it made me an instant skeptic.   I noticed the same type of belief mechanism was employed for the same kind of unseen beings capable of magical operations.   The difference was the use of the word "faith," which was required to believe in God and Jesus. That made the difference, I was told. But I had faith in Santa Claus, the Easter Bunny, and the Tooth Fairy until I learned they were just cultural myths with no place in reality.   It felt like intentional deception, a trick. I believe that I possessed an inquiring mind from the time I first wondered what a caterpillar tasted like (along with about everything else). This situation served to confirm the skeptic in me.

I couldn't understand why they would teach us such falsehoods. Were the adults also fooling themselves just to feel they were special? And thus, my curiosity, my love of inquiry, and my skeptical nature were stirred at the tender age of six. All while I was singing every Sunday in the choir at St. Timothy's Lutheran Church. I began to wonder what the words actually meant and why everyone was so concerned with death and living forever. The original location in Plane Haven had previously been the first school, but its name is unknown. The experience propelled me forward into inquiry, a student of philosophy, wary of religious fanaticism, but fascinated by its mechanism. Aspiring toward the ideal of the independent individual, "Invictus"*ɸ became my creed, rather than the usual convoluted matrix of beliefs that seems to me to be ultimately aimed at shirking responsibility for anything through creative evasion; just say the magic words and you're free of blame. That was the chief difference; there was no church for Santa Claus or the Easter Bunny. But once, when we were living on P Street, a kind of confirmation had occurred. One spring morning, Martine woke me up while it was dark. She led me to the kitchen table. In the dark, we felt something warm and furry moving around on it. We'd felt it as we grasped at its furry coat. As the light of dawn broke, we discovered that it was a white rabbit, an Easter Bunny. And later, I knew even that had been a trick. Our parents played tricks on us. Authorities like to play tricks on us all. I guess they were getting us ready for real life? But it was years before I ever saw another rabbit.

The next rabbit I spotted, really two of them at once was in a field. Not the area that had started at our back door, though, and they were jackrabbits, not cute white bunnies. This was another field, separate only due to the designs of men. It was a sort of finger of the broader field that remained in a block across the main street that divided the developing suburb from the airfield, mostly. The first business in that field was The Clouds restaurant on Watt Avenue, with the swim club where my sisters and I spent a lot of time during the summers of 1965-66. Our family dined there at least once, as I recall, with Shirley Temple and Roy Rodger as refreshments for the kids. The main road was named after James Watt in the later 1920s when the Inventor Streets were beginning to be laid out. Watt Avenue was one of the two first streets to be named in the North Arcade Creek Area. The other was Howe, with the remainder of the Inventor Streets appearing over time. Of them all, Watt Avenue is the longest. Watt must have existed as a route long before it was named, but there is no known name to report. The road to Antelope is more or less traced over today's Roseville Road. Watt Avenue soon became the two-lane route to the north up to Baseline Road and south all the way to Florin Road.

My first visit to "the field" was when I was about ten. I went out there to try out the boomerang that I had just acquired. The Wammo Toy Company had made their first million (or so) from the hula hoop. They would try the tick again and be most successful from then on. The boomerang marketing might have been coordinated with the sudden popularity of Australian comedy records that joined the Ray Stevens stream of hit after hit with "Ahab the Arab," being the big one. Two from the Australian genre found some popularity in America. Since "payola" was considered racketeering and Alan Freed had famously been convicted for it, justly or not, just a couple of years earlier, we can dismiss the payola idea. So two recordings managed to cross the International Time Zone and get to America on the power of their fun. "Tie Me Kangaroo Down," was a ditty concerning a Wally who had been kicked to death by his kangaroo. As he expires, he asks his fellow mates, in turn, to set his menagerie of Aussie critters free to fend for themselves before asking to have his own hide to be tanned and displayed in remembrance of him. "So we tanned his hide when he died, Clyde. And that's it hanging on the shed!" The second one predicted my lack of skill acquisition with the boomerang. That's right, my boomerang wouldn't come back.

Boo!

Aside from Christmas and all the fun and presents, Halloween was easily my favorite holiday. I loved going from door to door and being greeted by kind adults who laughed as they handed out candy. My favorite was the sweet old ladies here and there who handed out candied apples, popcorn balls, or fudge.

I thought it was wonderful to meet all of these neighbors. It was a real community event. At Village School, there was always an event in the cafeteria, a set of booths with games that even adults enjoyed, as fundraisers for something or other, I never knew. One booth I remember vividly taught the principle of visual deception and its effect on mental assessment via "optical illusions." One teacher had a long mirror propped up on a long table. He was at one end with a hat on his head. When a child entered, they were placed at the other end of the mirror. "Blow," Mr. Mitchell commanded. So when the kid blew, the hat rose up off his head like magic. This delighted us. Once through to the other side, you were allowed to see the trick; the other side of Mr. Mitchell's face was hidden by the mirror, as was the hand that lifted the hat off of his head when we blew at his face. He seemed to love doing this trick. But it was a good trick because it taught the kids something about perceptions of reality. Everything is not necessarily as it seems to be.

But there is a sad part to this little story. Just after I stopped trick or treating, deeming it something teens did not do, I heard that someone somewhere had put a razor blade in a piece of homemade fudge or something. All homemade treats disappeared; who could have done something like that; perhaps the type that condemned Halloween as "satanic" and went off the rails into intolerance?

Halloween was an old European holiday. Originally, it had been New Year's Eve to the Celtic people. They believed that on that night, the spirits of their deceased loved ones were near. They believed they could communicate with them. After Christianity arrived, it absorbed all of the pagan holidays, replacing them with Christian myths that resembled the original myths to make the new faith more palatable. Today, in the more remote places in Europe, such as Slovenia, where I lived in the late 90s for a couple of years, on Halloween, Christians don their best clothes, go to the graveyards, place flowers, and pray. Many widows engage in mourning as their pagan ancestors had, weeping on the graves themselves. The ritual may have been dishonestly borrowed, but its practice is sincere. I am glad to have seen this in actuality during my life's journeys. They still celebrate May Day in the old way there, as well, with the town of Ptuj famous for its parade. They wear the old animist-style costumes, with a version of the hobby horse, and other animals led by the representatives of the "old gods." I visited the museum there in 2000 on a return trip. It was interesting to me that Tito, the communist leader of Yugoslavia did not turn May First into a day for national propaganda, or at least, did not suppress this tradition, as Stalin did in the U.S.S.R.

An Indigenous Indo-European, Celt-Slavic May Day Celebration costume – Ptjui Museum, Slovenia – photo of photo by author by permission of the museum

In North Highlands and the wider neighborhood service region, there were many other delights of the time. I remember many visits to Ken's Red Barn, which was on Fulton Avenue. It was popular and as most were in those years, extremely family-friendly, and therefore always busy. Ken's Red Barn might possibly have invented the tradition of piping "Happy Birthday," and bringing a cupcake with the candle to the happy child who had just heard their name pronounced publically for all to hear and know it was their special day; field training for future narcissists. But it was a great place, actually. Kids learned table manners and other points of etiquette. This doesn't seem to have any place in the national memory today. Whenever we went anywhere we were expected to behave perfectly.

If we didn't, a stinging leather belt awaited our return home. But I can't remember one event where that actually happened; when afield, the discipline was usually limited to the verbal, and it worked.

However, the belt was real enough and was employed over a few other problems, usually initiated by Martine. The worst licking I ever got was over a fight with her. We had struck one another, her first. My father wanted us to apologize. "Are you sorry?" He asked Martine. "Yes," was her immediate reply. I knew she was just lying. She wasn't sorry at all. Then it was my turn. Turning to me he asked; "Are you sorry?" I knew Martine was lying. I noted her insincerity and was amazed that my father did not notice it. I would not be a liar. Even then, I believed that I should say what I really thought and how I really felt. "No," was my answer. And I got whipped; several rounds with the question repeated until finally, I began to feel that I had been wrong, I was sorry after all - Behavior Modification 101 as with the Orwellian program of using pain to change minds. Psychologists have long known that enough pain for enough time changes the mind's perceptions. It can be done as with Pavlov, or as with the Orwellian " Ministry of Love" methods, a la "A Clockwork Orange." At the time, I noticed with some wonder at how my real idea of how I felt had changed. But it's also a biological survival instinct and well understood and it has been employed on more than misbehaving children throughout history. Where my older sister was concerned, this was always the difference of character between us. I noted the cheap dodge by my wily and disingenuous sister and refused to operate in that mode, and it has caused me trouble many times during my life in a world full of deceitfulness.

I had already thought over the consequences of lying at about six years of age and the big problem of having to remember your lies. After I experienced my sister's game, I added a dislike of phony pretension to my little collection of social interaction applications. After hearing quotes such as "honesty is the best policy" and learning of "Honest Abe" and the George Washington myth of the cherry tree early in school, I adapted the virtue as a personal rule of conduct – most of the time. Sometimes myths are useful in the promotion of desirable personal and cultural characteristics. Other times they are used to promote fear and obedience.

The rules of etiquette, especially public etiquette, were reinforced at home without too much need for intervention; no signing at the table, no talking at the table, and no laughing at the table; especially no laughing at the table. Our parents had us, "in hand," at least in the early years. It was part of the experience of Boomer parents to prepare their children for public appearances, for as it might anywhere, so many children out to dinner with their parents at once had to be trained well, or else any public place, especially the restaurants would have been scenes of public chaos. The lack of such training can be seen in the streets of some of our cities today. But they have been prepared, too.

Remnants of that field remain today, forever for sale, it seems. Another bit of the original area of it survived until very late. It was kitty corner to that field, across Watt Avenue. The street nomenclature still demonstrates that North Highlands proper developed from Watt Avenue's east side to the divider created by the railroad line behind Hillsdale Elementary. In contrast, the streets west of Watt Avenue were numbered and lettered as part of an older layout plan for far older and rural Rio Linda, which sprawled out for miles with homes dotting the landscape in family clusters or singly. Rio Linda had been a significant egg and poultry supplier during the war. The economic boom that the war had created took a pause, and the Rio Linda farms suffered.

Most former farmers and new arrivals were attracted to McClellan Air Force Base, which was expanding due to the Cold War's increasing tension. The suburban development ate into the fields to the north and west. Some land to the east, interrupted by the base's runway, remained mostly fields.

I learned later that Dave and Rick's parents had bought large lots on I Street at the intersection of 34th Street and built their own homes before North Highlands and Larchmont Village (named after a former high-end neighborhood in Los Angeles) had developed very far beyond old North Haven's limits. But there was plenty of space behind the homes there; enough for an oval track for brother Jim to run and tune his go-carts, and later for us to use to develop our skills on our Hodaka motorcycles in preparation for the real racing we'd get into later on. I don't think there was ever a question about it. Dave's uncles raced and had friends who raced. Dan Rasmussen and Carl Cranke[*2] were linked in that circle. Not long after, we ran into one another at the Hodaka dealer on Auburn Boulevard in 1967 and realized we both had one.

I began to spend a lot of time at Dave's house. But not so much in his house but in his "backyard" and garage, which was his dad's home machine shop. I always rode across the field on my Hodaka to get there. We'd tune the bikes and discuss the various modifications we'd learn about from Cycle World magazine or the many visitors who would show up to use his dad's machine shop that he had laid out in his garage, including his Uncle Richard and Jim. Dave's father, Joe, was the epitome of a crabby old man, but his brothers were quite affable. Tragic was the death of "Uncle Jim" at Bonneville Salt Flats in 1972, where he entered a Kawasaki-powered motorcycle that was partially custom-built at Joe Buckmaster's garage. According to 1973 ISDT Qualifier Dan Rasmussen and old Buckmaster clan friend, Jim Buckmaster was the two-stroke tuning master that Carl Cranke learned from. Jim Buckmaster learned his stuff from the go-cart racing crowd, which had been using two-strokes for some time before they became popular replacements for the heavy four-strokes previously riders had used. Once Paul Fredricks of East Germany won the 1966

Motocross World Championship on a 360cc CZ, the end of the big four-stroke machines was certain until many years later when the engines could be built to be as light as a two-stroke.

I was at Dave's house when the phone call came and was obliged to leave as Dave went inside the curtains were drawn in mourning. Dave's brother was at the event and many of us, including Dan, heard the story of what had happened from parties actually present with Jim, assisting him. The official explanation of Jim Buckmaster's death is not correct; a vehicle that was not supposed to have been on the track whizzed past Jim and caused him to lose control as he approached the pits on his return from his run, and his shoulder harness failed. (The wrecked Kawasaki sat behind the shop that we both later worked at for several years after).

In about 1963, Dave, Rick, and some other kids had excavated a cave system in the tracks' infield by digging it out as a ditch system and then covering it with plywood and dirt. Some would call that cheating, but I thought it was somewhat clever. I made some visits around that time. Once there was a sort of pow-wow in that cave with the kids; Dave's cousin, and a couple other neighbor boys. Karen was the only girl in the "club." Karen even then possessed striking looks and height. She was taller than any of us boys. She was always around us until later when her Dad forbade her to hang out with the neighbor boys any longer. There was an incident when, as teens, we snuck over to visit her when her parents were out shopping or something. I think she came out to her front yard and stood there, like a siren, silently beckoning.

That was all it took. It was innocent enough; we were standing in her driveway, talking to her about nothing in particular. Just then, her parents pulled up, and "The Daddy" jumped out of the car, yelling at us. We skedaddled off around the fence that formed Karen's backyard safe space. I was last in the order of the escaping criminals. I ran around the back fence beyond, which was also an open field for some ways. At that moment, a pheasant burst out of a bush. I stopped and lifted my right index finger at it as it flew; following it as if were the end of a shotgun, announcing the event to the group. I don't know if even one of them took note because as my finger followed the bird's flight from the ground to the air, it stopped on Daddy, who had popped up from around the fence at the same time. I turned and fled. I was never found in her driveway again. I can't speak for the others. I imagine that Karen's daddy had a good laugh about it.

Karen's home, like those of Dave and Rick, and the few others around there were very different from the lines of standardized designed homes just across the field off Watt Avenue, where I lived because they were made by individuals. Dave's house was very different from Rick's; their house plans came out of their heads, not a contractor's blueprint. Those had to have been some handy grown-ups. They were resourceful too; they used wood grabbed up from McClellan AFB which at the time was under construction. It turned out that pallets of lumber had arrived precut to the wrong specifications. I bet the wives worked on the construction right along with the men. I knew them. Dave's mother worked seasonally at the Del Monte cannery. They were of pioneer caliber; tough but kind. They could keep a garden, make three meals a day, help with barn raising, and serve apple pie after supper, the same way, every day.

I've always loved women like that. One of my favorite Westerns is "Westward the Women." Maybe it's because of what women were willing to go through just to find husbands and a chance at a happy life in a new land. I have read a great deal of pioneer history. People loved fiercely in those days, and friends cared for one another almost as if they were family. The Buckmasters were of this strain, and highly cohesive, even clannish. This bunch was not very demonstrative of their feelings, which was also a common trait, and often presented a harsh front, using cynical, mocking jokes as a façade; especially Dave's father, Joe. I knew it then, I know it now. But at that time, all of the property on the angle of 34th and I Street was Buckmaster property.

Everyone who lived there was a Buckmaster or family of some sort. As the family story was related to me, a sister of the senior members got into some difficulty in Nevada over the legal status of her employees from California. To make up for the error in judgment, she bought her brothers and sisters plots of land. That intersection could have been a settlement named "Buckmaster." It would have been if this had happened before 1914; it has all the elements for the opening of some Louis L'Amour, or better yet, Bret Harte tale. There might even be a saloon there named "Fanny Buckmaster's."

The suburbs represented a divergence of post-war culture in a real way. The kids in the suburbs are associated with their street blocks. You were from this block or that block. The cross streets and fences created a psychological border of sorts. Sometimes it was a little gang-like when we passed down a street that we didn't live on. Some kids would accost us. Martine, Paulette, and I attended summer school at Larchmont Elementary two years in a row. Some kids on La Cienega Drive wouldn't let us pass without a terrible fuss.

The problem was great enough to cause us to elect to take a longer route home to avoid it. It was a bit like half-city, half-country. I never cared much for the city half of it. The kids across the field in the small collections of irregular homes on irregular lots led to a more isolated life. They welcomed every new kid as a playmate. And it had its advantages, as the track and cave illustrate. In that extra field that separated Dave, Karen, and Rick's homes from my tract housing development ran a nameless creek that became a ditch as it passed through North Highlands, which was a natural creek to the west of Watt Avenue. I never heard anyone call it anything but "The Ditch." But it always had a name; Rio Linda Creek, and it eventually runs into the Natomas*₃ Ditch Drainage System to the Sacramento River, as does Dry Creek. Although Rio Linda Creek bisects North Highlands, there has never been a sign to identify it. The little-regarded origin of Rio Linda Creek is on the east side of North Highlands.

It emerges as a little spring beside Walerga Road and travels mostly underground via culverts from near Gothberg Drive to appear as an actual creek near Village Elementary School. There was never a sign that announced its unifying name. The land to the west of the airfield remained distant and unconnected for a long time. It was probably a good thing. After the war, the community of Del Paso Heights and the Grant Union Joint School District's first established high school, Grant Union, became a troubled district.

As it happens, the split between North Highlands and Rio Linda is described by the Fire Districts. They are divided by Watt Avenue, so if you have a fire on 34th Street, or even at the North Highlands Post Office, it used to be a problem to get a response from a fire engine in North Highlands. This issue was resolved in the 1970s after such an incident occurred, just not at the post office. Incidentally, I had a personal demonstration of the time warp between old Rio Linda and new North Highlands in about 1963, when an old man in a Model T Pickup pulled into the new supermarket, The Capri, on the corner of Watt Avenue and I Street. I knew the vehicle was old so was immediately fascinated by it. Little did I imagine that my own grandfather might have had a hand in producing it!

The fields were worlds of wonder to me and as soon as I was deemed old enough to go out there on my own. It was when I was about nine years of age and considered old enough to take myself to Little League games, Odd since I had been taking myself to school since Kindergarten. So I was free to wander the fields at last. That is how I found Dave and Rick on the other side of that field. Up to then, I had no idea where they lived.

In the 1950s, the field around our house was changing very quickly. Those changes did not end until the 1980s when North Highlands finally became a seamless community joined by other developments divided only by the railroad track to the east. This border was made extinct by the 1970s advent of the modern four-lane overpasses. The first was constructed in 1970 and had been renamed after the old Elkhorn Ferry on the Sacramento River far beyond M Street. The new, expanded, and improved route needed a new name, and it was a promotion, too; Elkhorn Boulevard. By the late 70s, the old railroad crossing was gone altogether, replaced by another four-lane overpass that goes into Citrus Heights. That was the final phase of the plan, I suppose. But in the late 1950s, no one was thinking about that.

Larchmont Village was still less than half constructed, and relatively isolated. It was the field across Watt Avenue where The Clouds and the swim club had operated until it shut down after 1966. The Clouds reopened soon after as a nightclub called "The Maverick." The Field remained accessible throughout my life in North Highlands. Today, its huge church occupies the expanded building and its parking lot has an entrance on 34th Street as well as Watt Avenue.

Two I Street Kids – Dave (Bucky) and Karen – circa 1956 - Photo courtesy Karen Rasmussen Note the handmade willow chairs.

Once, when I was 15, for no real reason, I ran away from home. (It was really just a night out without notifying my parents). I slept in that field next to Rio Linda Creek where I crossed on my Hodaka, then Penton, and later, CZ to practice with or without Dave and Rick on the track we had laid out across from Rick's house. That field served as a natural playground as soon as I was allowed to wander to almost the day I moved away from there forever. Now that I look back on it, I am glad that I spent one night sleeping by Rio Linda Creek.

Tar and Cement

I could ignore the cracker-box nature of these homes, but when Pete Seegers' song "Little Boxes" was popular in 1965, I knew what he meant. To put it kindly, these homes merely lacked elaboration. They were distinctly different from those I could recall in the old P Street neighborhood, which I was often reminded of because of our frequent visits to friends and the CCA meetings in the summer at William Land Park. All of the homes there and in downtown Sacramento were older and better built. They seemed old too, and the sidewalks were wide, with spaces for the big trees along the streets inside their concrete design. Because of that, there was always shade in Sacramento. The only trees in the new neighborhood left after construction were saplings; and fruitless mulberries. Every front yard had one.

Someone had decided that the native oak trees were in the way, so as the development grew, little samplings of fruitless mulberry trees replaced them. As a result, the new community lay starkly naked under the blazing sun in the summer. Where downtown Sacramento had the advantage of the shade from its ancient, tall trees, North Highlands had no such advantage. I could see those grand old oaks out there in the fields, where the machine monsters hadn't gotten to yet, but I never met one personally until I was about 12 years old. I actually met The Spook Tree first. But those oaks; I never knew until I played under them what they meant to the wildlife.

Those voluminous branches served as natural shelter, a cool place compared to the fields baking in the sun during the summer. I remember how it felt to lay under one; we had piled up "straw" from some of the wheat shafts left behind by the combines that mowed the harvest under (subsidized farm) and made a "fort" by piling it up under the tree. We made couches of it against the trunk of the tree, and I laid down into it, like a natural armchair, or like sitting on your grandfather's knee.

It seemed to me that I could not sense the tree's real age, so "grandfather" is the only word that comes to mind, although "Methuselah" might be better. These trees were natural oases, and they all served as a respite from hard rain and wind at other times.

When walking among them, it made me feel that I was in a distinctly different place.

And I was. Along with the trains' rumbling and the sound of those big diesel engines, I came to only causally note the constant rumbling and activity of the caterpillars. These man-made mechanical dinosaurs were changing the land. It turns out that they were the brainchild of Benjamin Holt of Stockton. He developed the chain tracks that would allow heavy equipment to work in the region's soggy agricultural land in 1904. His photographer noticed that they moved across the land like caterpillars, hence the name. Later, a visiting British officer took an interest and used the idea to develop the first tanks, which were used with effect during World War One. To me, they seemed more like dinosaurs. They were already there when we arrived, so I accepted them as a natural part of things that came with the territory as a kid does. I witnessed the changes they made to the land. They seemed all-powerful and irresistible. Almost daily during the school year, I saw them prepare the ground for the concrete pads, and then the skeleton frames appeared. I marveled at the fantastic speed of their metamorphosis as they were finished.

The cost was that all of those wonderful, life-filled pools of water disappeared, as Village School, which had briefly stood alone in a field, became surrounded on two sides by 1959. As these changes went on, the wonderful thing for me was that nearly every sight conjured up a melody in my head. It was as if the vibrations of light and sound triggered the activity in my brain. But there was a reason for it; "progress," my father used to say, "progress." Let's hope so.

"**A**ntelope is a village on the Southern Pacific railway. In 1876 a large brick warehouse was built by J.F. Cross, costing $3,000.00. The first store was started in 1877 by the Antelope Business Association and the second by R. Astile in 1879 in the hotel building. The Post Office was established in 1877, with Joel Gardner being the Postmaster. For many years it has been a shipping place for hay and grain into the mountains, and of late, fruit and almond raising is increasing in that section. Arcade is a way station on the Southern Pacific. Within the past three years, the Western Pacific railway and the Northern Electric railway have been built through the township and have established some way stations."*[1]

There must have been some high times in Old Antelope if the Poker Lane appellation is any reflection of fact. It was so named due to the joke regarding the idea that many card games were regularly held by the residents on that street. I bet ya dollars to donuts that they weren't betting with jelly beans, and they didn't drink Tea. But it turns out that the use of the term "poker" was the local joke.*[2]

Whether I was near Antelope or North Highlands, I kept my eyes skinned for antelope, the animals, not the town. I had spotted many jackrabbits by the time I was nine. I had seen them in the field across

Watt Avenue, the same mysterious one I had first seen as a three-year-old when we came to see the model home. I had to cross it to visit Dave and Rick, where they lived. That is how I saw them; they'd pop up from a clump of brush just as I approached it and skedaddle away, panicked. My approach represented a terrible thing to them. I'd learn why later.

Before that, long before I even knew where my friends lived, I had seen a horse in that field in a corral at the far opposite end of M Street. It was big enough to spot from the end of our street, and we saw it up close whenever we passed it in the family car as we drove past its corral on M Street. That's when Watt Avenue was still a two-lane road. I had never seen an antelope, let alone a deer. Up to then, I only had an impression of what a deer or antelope looked like. I had figured them to be big enough to merit being a vital part of the song. Perhaps I instinctively knew what they looked like? Maybe I had the impression from the Challenge Butter wrapper that featured multiple-tined antlers on a buck in a mountain clearing? I always looked at the designs on food packages. For example, in those years (1955), the Hills Brothers coffee cans featured a man in a turban and yellow gown drinking coffee and standing up. (When I called him "The Bubba Man," and Martine heard me, she acted as if I had sworn and threatened to report me to our parental authorities; I have never figured out what was wrong with assigning that gown-garbed, turban-topped fellow "Bubba Man").

I knew they were larger than a jackrabbit and smaller than a horse. I say that because that same year, that summer, our family went on a train trip, "back east," as the pioneers used to say, and as we still said then, as both of my parents were "from back east," a former 19th-century pioneer phrase. We made the journey aboard the then-new and fabulous "California Zephyr." It took us up the Feather River Canyon on the first day of the three-day trip to Chicago. I was up in the famed "vista dome." I spent most of the journey there, anxious to see the new landscapes, when my vision caught a beautiful, four-legged creature with a proud set of antlers, as I would come to know them, crowning his alert eyes, which were looking toward us from the other side of the Feather River. "A deer, "I shouted out! A kindly-looking old gent sitting nearby me in the dome smiled and said, "You've got a sharp eye, son." But really, who is going to make up a song about jackrabbits? "So if you go chasing Jackrabbits..." it just doesn't work. There weren't any white rabbits in any of the Western U.S. fields, either, unless someone freed a pet imported from somewhere like New Zealand. But no one ever did that around there as far as I know.

The old range of Antelope and the original Ranch Del Paso Spanish Grant lands had changed as wheat, and other farming overtook cattlemen politically. The Stockmen had placed the Trespass Act of 1850, which required planters to erect fences to protect their crops from free-ranging cattle. By 1872, the tide had turned, and the farmers passed their "No Fence Law," which was a repeal of the 1850 act that favored cattlemen. As a result, the cattlemen were henceforth required to fence in their cattle. Open-range ranching did see a rebirth via special leases in the National forests once they were established, so the Cowboy lifestyle did not completely die out, but it certainly took a pause.

In 1966, I met a couple of the Sierra cowboys while hunting with my father up near Wentworth Springs. They knew our new acquaintance, the old mineral spring resort's caretaker, an ex-marine war correspondent and veteran of the Great War, as he still called it, Miles Curran. They were staying at Lawyer's Cow Camp, as it was known at the time. They were genuine and even carried six-guns. The occasion of their visit was "to get some of that there Pluto Water," as they put it. "It's good for what ails ya," Miles replied.

That was going on up in the mountains. The course for Antelope and environs had been determined in 1872, and the larger wild animals fled the wheat fields as tractors rolled across the firmament, and the railroad divided the land. There seemed to be a competition between nature and machines going on all around me in my youth. Nature was losing. I had thus far seen nothing larger than a jackrabbit. Even the Sierra cowboys rode in jeeps, Willys Pickups, in fact; but not on horses.

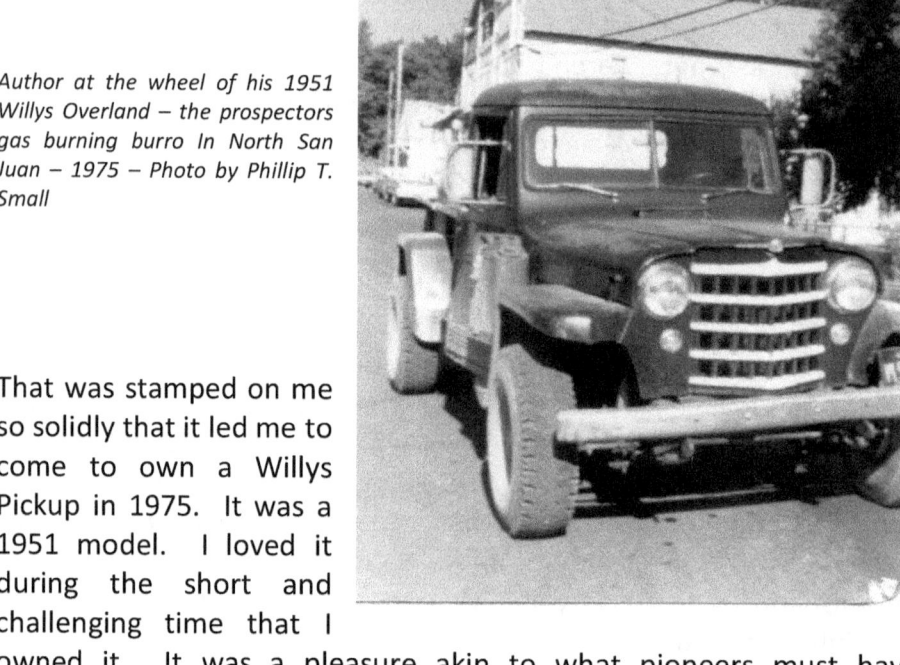

Author at the wheel of his 1951 Willys Overland – the prospectors gas burning burro In North San Juan – 1975 – Photo by Phillip T. Small

That was stamped on me so solidly that it led me to come to own a Willys Pickup in 1975. It was a 1951 model. I loved it during the short and challenging time that I owned it. It was a pleasure akin to what pioneers must have experienced when it broke down miles from inhabited parts outside of Myers near Angora Lakes that summer. The parts search was another adventure that lasted two months and saw me hitchhiking there and back to Sacramento, gathering up various adventures during that time. One of them was being cited at the inspection station by a CHP for thumbing illegally. Another was when I was set upon by two amorous young ladies who picked me up outside of Myers and then took me on a detour to show me some wildflowers.

I recall the first family trip to Lake Tahoe. We went to Stateline, where my parents gambled at the new Harrah's Casino. It was small and wholly constructed of wood. My sisters and I stood outside of a window as my mother played a slot machine and kept an eye on us. Daddy was further within the den of inequity, playing craps, around which he later spent years, perfecting his "system" which never really paid off. We could watch her work the "one-armed bandit" as they were called then, or turn and look to the mountainside and watch skiers plummeting down to the bottom.

That's how small Stateline was then. I recall dinner that evening. We pulled up to a bright little building on a dirt lot in the dusk amid pine trees. My parents spoke of "Talk-Os." (Imagine that, talking food!) We ate some crunchy things stuffed with I don't know what. They did look a little like some sort of creature's former speaking apparatus that had been "harvested" while eating some stuff, but it never said anything to me. I had eaten it before it had a chance, anyway. This was my first taste of Mexican food. I think I liked it. In fact, I know I did, and so did my sisters. Later on, we used to make tacos at home using those kits that used to be available. My wife and I make them now, once in a while.

I apologize for the Talk-O joke. But I was that literal in my early years until schooling began to clear things up. For example, I thought that coffee was for people who coughed because the ones I saw drinking it most often were coughing, at least when I was becoming aware of the term. It just occurred to me one particular day as I watched an old man coughing as he sipped. Hey, it was merely simple logic – rooted in innocent ignorance.

In later years, Stateline developed. Many parents from the nearby California countries made day trips in those days when Harrah's had constructed a Teen Recreation Center, where their patrons could drop off their kids for an hour or all day. It had a penny arcade with a few fun games, including a row of hilarious, quick-draw robots. They'd call you names and challenge you to draw. When you hit them, they'd die with curses like, "You miserable pole-cat, ya got me!" Paulette and I thought it was really funny. There was also a theater, where teen-oriented films were always playing. But most memorable for me was the area with a jukebox and tables and chairs around a dance floor. The last time my parents left us at this teen center, I was thirteen years old.

I met a kid, a really cool guy, friendly, and with a suave manner that was beyond me, a good-looking kid, certainly with a relaxed Elvis style about him. He had to be at least one year, possibly two years older than me, but he accepted me and brought me into his confidence like a real pal. He was a cool dancer. We sat at a table and were soon joined by a couple of cute girls. It became apparent which one was with him. The other one, quite adorable, looked at me and smiled, seeming to be pleased with being stuck with me. At that moment, my name was announced. My folks had come to take us away. My first teen romance was killed in the crib, so to speak.

Martine's Tahoe romance took longer to expire. She was a boy magnet, anyway, having learned how to tilt her head like Brigid Bardot early. At about the same time, she met a guy named Michael Myers. This guy was an early Elvis imitator. They exchanged letters for a while. He wrote one story about playing his guitar on the balcony of their family cabin in Tahoe with all the girls below screaming for him as he strummed his guitar and sang Elvis. Martine thought he was conceited. He even came by one time and visited us in North Highlands, intimating that he had hitchhiked. It didn't work out between them. But years later, don't you know that one day, Martine was telling us about a really popular Elvis impersonator in Las Vegas, Michael Myers. He had his own show.

All this was on the periphery of my interests. The eye-catching feature of downtown Stateline for me in those days was the Pony Express Rider statue just outside of the teen center. It seemed to contrast with everything around it. But it stood out to me as the only genuine thing in the place.

I Learn About Death

The method by which I became familiar with the measure of a horse was tragic. About the time I rode that horse in the park, the horse from the field was killed on Watt Avenue. It occurred almost at the end of my street and Floral Drive, where it was struck by a car. It had escaped its corral in a panic and ran. The poor creature had no idea where it was going. Maybe it saw the expanse of the field out behind our house? I don't know because by then, new homes had been constructed behind our house. But the horse hadn't made for the open field.

It was as if it thought the new suburb would hide it from danger. But there it was, and it was a pitiful sight. Martine and I ran to the scene. The horse was down on one side and not yet dead. Its chest was heaving up and down in pain and fear. I think my dad came and took us home, which was probably the proper action on his part. But I remember the sense of tragedy I felt at the time. I had been there long enough to feel it amplified by the small crowd gathered silently around that unfortunate servant of civilization. It was my first taste of those emotions.

The next wasn't far off. It was a bird, a featherless baby bird that I tried in vain to save. I came home from school one day and found it alone at the front of our house on the rocks that Daddy and Uncle Ross had not long before laid around the shrubs they had planted at the same time. There on the hot stones was the naked little thing with its beak opened, chirping wildly, begging for something to be put in it. I picked it up in my cupped hand. I was alone at home. I had arrived home ahead of everyone else. (I don't remember the house ever being locked, not even in the early 1970s, and I never had a key).

I took the bird into my room and made a nest for it in a shoebox using socks. Then, I went back outside and looked for possible food. It gobbled up a rolling bug that I set into its frantically opened beak. I saw it there, in its little transparent esophagus, stuck where it was, and it suddenly seemed an emergency in itself. So I carefully worked it back up and out of its mouth. I was panicking by then because I just did not know what to do. I desperately wanted to save this starving baby bird. So I took it next store to the parsonage. It turned out that the church my mother decided was for us was Lutheran since that church had established its minister parsonage right next door to us almost as soon as we had moved in ourselves. So I took it to her. I had heard my parents identify her as a nurse. I suppose I knew what a nurse was because of my father and his title. So I took it to the pastor's wife next door. But she was a nurse, not a veterinarian. Her plan of feeding it milk in an eyedropper didn't work. So it died. I buried it out behind the house.

By the time I left North Highlands in 1973, there was hardly a bird to be seen in that neighborhood even though it was lined with trees. Bugs were relatively rare by that time, too. This was not so true by the time one reached the fields that still surrounded Highlands High School on two sides. The airfield's noise and fumes caused while servicing the jets were by then roaring from early in the morning to late evening due to the war in Vietnam. Our neighborhood, being so close to the base, had become the equivalent of an industrial district in an old steel town like Pittsburg, "back east," and the air was filled with the scent of burnt jet fuel. It was possible to ignore the smell, but not the sound. The birds noticed both, as well as the deep rumbling of the giant diesel engines and their blaring whistles as the trains arrived at the Roseville Switching yard, maybe two miles from the McClelland Field airstrip. Two types of tough birds remained in the area; scrub jays and magpies. But all of the delicate little birds were gone, as well as the robins. In the early years during the winter, seagulls were common around Village School. They used to land on the blacktop playgrounds. There were numerous denizens of the two dumps (waste landfills) I knew about in those days; Roseville, of course, but another was on the American River's east side accessed by the old Highway 160 approach to Sacramento. So I assumed in those days that they migrated up the Sacramento River to find food and maybe shelter during the winter. Later, I learned that they nested and hatched at Mono Lake on the eastern side of the Sierras. They aren't just sea birds, or they remember back to when Nevada was an ocean and are just following the old family ways, or instinct, whichever you like.

Even though the early explorers and settlers reported wild oats that grew up over a man's head and droves of antelope and deer plentifully abounding on these prairies, I never saw either a deer or antelope, but I did finally get a clue that there had been antelope around, at least. I put it together the first time we all went to the Roseville Farmer's Market and Auction. From there, I began to map my little world's geography, which was now greatly enhanced.

Let's Go To the Dump (Oh, Baby)

The great thing about my dad was that he always took me along with him on chores, meaning yard work, and related outdoor work. He intended it to be instructive, but the ones that required a trip always had an element of fun. He often took my sisters along, too, but not every time. A trip to the Roseville Dump was never drudgery to us, but an adventure. The old man who was in charge always had a lineup of interesting-looking items in a row along his trailer where he collected the fee. Sometimes, there were old tricycles and bicycles there for sale, along with stuff that I now realize would be coveted antiques, today. I clearly recall a few wringer washing machines, and how many classic motorcycles got tossed into that abyss of human technological waste? I was with my father in 1968, when he finally dumped his long-obsolete cathode ray tube fluoroscope there. No archeologist will ever plumb the depths of such cavities unless they are aliens from another planet in some distant future, trying to figure out what the former denizens of this planet valued.

We never passed through Roseville on a job without a stop at the Roseville Bakery because, in those times, a trip to the dump required driving down the main street, which was Vernon Street, which is where The Roseville Bakery was located. We'd typically stop on the return trip and get a doughnut. Other times, usually in the summer, we'd stop for a soda or Daddy's favorite, an orange freeze, at a hamburger stand. These were called either "drive-ins" or "drive-ups" in those days. Some had "carhops." A&W on A Street had them until at least 1970. They were not to be confused with the "drive-ins," which were where we watched films in the summers in the family cars with a couple of hundred other families, or couples, as the case might have been. There were so many families at the drive-ins on Saturday nights that there were playgrounds for kids while everyone waited for the dusk to become night. The first feature was always a cartoon for the kids. Drive-in theaters were so popular that North Highlands eventually had its own, "The Highlander," which was off U-Street and almost to the opposite of where the Spook Tree had stood across the road.

The first food drive-in North Highlands was Foxie's, but Lou's must have come soon after. It was located on a graveled lot very near Gate 4 on the airfield side of Watt Avenue, across from Brown's Hardware/Rexall Drugs complex that was on A Street. Since the library was behind that building I suppose this could be considered the center of town, if any place might qualify as such in North Highlands. It was never referred to as a "strip mall" back then, just as "Fast Food" was not a term of the era. "Junk Food" wasn't even a term then. These terms were not yet part of the English language. We knew the owners of Foxie's as we attended the same church, Saint Timothy's Lutheran when it was located on Airway Drive in the clubhouse that is still there (St. Timothy's moved to its new location on Don Julio Boulevard by 1963).

When out on an excursion, to the dump, or some other errand, Daddy always pulled in somewhere for a treat. He was a man of the world, having been around it literally during WW2. He also knew wartime Los Angeles and Hollywood. Food concessions were as old as the pyramids, it seems. So if not a drive-in, we'd maybe stop at a delicatessen or butcher shop and get a piece of cured herring or some other handy ready-to-eat meat product. The jumble of odd places that existed before the modern era of fast-food franchises made excursions adventurous. The owners were nearly always there in person waiting on us, and their places of business were always unique in character. At first, North Highlands tried to be a traditional little town, and Watt Avenue Drugs had a soda and lunch counter, just as it would have if it had existed from 1890 through to the fifties. There are a few survivors from that period, Lou's Burgers and Marie's Donuts being the ones I can note with personal knowledge. It's good to see that they are still operating. I'm sorry to see that North Highlands' classic diner, Marasha's, is extinct.

Today, that generation would be considered to have some strange eating habits, but it was mostly due to the war and probably the Great Depression before it. Van De Kamp's beans and Spam had existed since the Civil War, and Sardines were very popular, for example, and made excellent hobo fare, something we kids were very interested in. (Paulette and I once snuck a can of beans out into the backyard and ate right out of the can - what adventure)! The fishing fleets of Monterrey Clippers comprised a vital industry during the war, and sardines were practically a dietary staple back in the day. Without that, maybe half of John Steinbeck's literature would not have existed.

On a particular early trip to Roseville, we stopped at the old Antelope Store, Foote's General Store, properly, which had to be older than Watt Avenue Drugs could have been. It was just a short way up from the railroad crossing we had to take to get into Roseville. That store was a place of wonder to me in those days. I guess because I could tell it was old, like from a cowboy movie. When I looked around and saw how it was arranged, with a post office and a public phone on the wall, it was evident that it predated all the other manmade places on earth; at least to me at that point. That knowledge filled me with awe and a feeling that was almost reverence. Cowboys must have stopped in there for some food for the trail, or maybe to make a phone call. Hey, Roy Rogers used a phone to call the sheriff!

That first foray into beautiful downtown Antelope was a revelation. It wasn't so awful much; downtown consisted of the store and gas pump, and, I suppose, the Grange Hall. But this was enough for me; Ah-ha! This place was the oldest-looking place I had ever seen up to then (Sacramento was a city, and all the old buildings were a blur to me, then). The confirming piece of evidence was that it was named after the very animal in the song! Mystery solved!

I thought I had solved an enigma, and for a little while, I was elated. And after all, it was just common sense. Why else would a town in the middle of a rich prairie be called Antelope? After all, it wasn't named Jackrabbit. Soon my discovery didn't seem to be such a big deal. Only the absence of antelopes and their companion deer puzzled me now.

So as time went on, I began to realize that there were no antelope out there playing, nor were there deer playing with them or anywhere nearby. The feeling grew that these were things of a bygone time. As I learned later in life, my guesses were correct; Antelope was the first town of any sort in what the county planners had established as the Center Township of Sacramento County in the early 1850s. Antelope had been there since the start of the railroad project.

Don McBride is the descendant of one of the first homesteaders. On the 1885 map of Sacramento County, great, great, grandfather's plot can be discerned next to the Finley Homestead as the closest farm to beautiful downtown Antelope. Mr. McBride provided me with his recollections of life in the Antelope community, up to the time of our families' arrival in the area;

"The Antelope store - a post office, was a grocery store (more like a convenience store today), library, gas station. I remember Mr. Ness, the postmaster, could ride a bike backward sitting on the handlebars.

They would put the outgoing mail in a sack hanging from a telephone pole. A guy in the mail car would grab the bag as the train went by and throw out a bag of incoming mail. (This is replicated in the 1944 film, "The Fighting Sullivans," which also featured a motorcycle race organized by The Blackhawk Motorcycle Club).

Ray Gould was president of the Antelope Telephone Company (what they called a farmer line). My Grandfather, Arthur McBride, was the secretary, and my father, Thomas McBride, was the installer and outside plant manager. When they couldn't get wire, he used the barbed wire fence to transmit phone signals.

It was a big party line everyone could hear everyone else's conversation. Each farm had a letter, and it rang with Morse Code, a series of long and short rings to signify who the call was intended for.

The connection to the Roseville Telephone Company was in my Grandfather's house. He had a switch to cut off the rest of the farms when he wanted a private conversation with someone in Roseville. He would occasionally forget to turn it back on, and when someone came by to report the phone wasn't working, he would tell them he'd send my father out to find the problem, wait a while, and flip the switch back on."

The telephone system in North Highlands used the then appellation prefixes. North Highland's was Edgewood or E-D. The remainder of the number was numerical. In the fifties, I remember hearing my mother saying, "Edgewood, 2 – 4777," to someone on the other end. That morphed to "E-D-2," then finally the unromantic - 332. On the other side of Highway 40 (later Interstate 80), the prefix word was "Ivanhoe." It seemed to coincide with the warnings of some popular science fiction stories where people lost their names and became number-named. The television series, "Secret Agent" traded on the idea, as did the sensational British series of the time, "The Prisoner." Dave Buckmaster's older I Street neighborhood was on the party line system until the mid-sixties as a practical part of Rio Linda.

Mr. McBride continues; "My great-great-grandfather Andrew Finley donated land for the Dry Creek School so his grandchildren wouldn't have to go to the Center Joint School on Watt Avenue."

The Center Joint School existed long before 1913, as reported in the Willis history, and long before Watt Avenue was named or reached out across the prairie to find it. The present school at the old location is the McClellan School. That building was constructed in 1960. The original Center Joint School was set where it was so that children from Antelope and the children from the western Center Township farms could have a place for school instruction within a reasonable distance. But the schoolhouse sat in a boundless field with no neighbors for a very long time. That vast area in the center remained Haggin's land as part of his prestigious horse-raising enterprise still called Rancho Del Paso, or else, further north, it was pastureland for cattle to roam. Later, after the land use disputes were settled what had begun as one of Sutter's visionary whims, a fruit orchard, became the origin of the huge citrus fruit farming era in the region and the Roseville Yard became a huge fruit depot gathering up the produce of farms from miles around. The schoolhouse that was built on the land donated by Andrew Finley was on PFE Road, Pacific Fruit Express Road, the western approach to the Roseville Depot. After we had driver's licenses, I passed through Antelope numerous times with Dave, Rick, or both. We liked to mix it up, so sometimes, we'd take Watt Avenue out to PFE Road. We'd always laugh and say, "Don't blink your eyes." Similarly, we called Dry Creek Union Elementary "Dry Creek University" and chuckled irreverently. Such was the arrogance of my ignorant youth. PFE Road was the western approach to the Pacific Fruit Express, an operation that went on from the early days of the area, up to and through WW2, when the Roseville Switching Yard featured the largest ice-producing plant in the world. The fruit from the many family-owned farms, many of them Japanese, sent fresh produce out to the entire world.

Now, I wish I'd stopped and talked to some of the teachers. Today, remnants of Old Antelope are difficult to identify.

Foote's General Store, Antelope, California, 95602
Courtesy of Don McBride

By 1969, the general store was often "manned" by a woman; a blind woman, in fact. Some kids would steal from the shelves right in front of her. A few older kids, the decent ones, would stop them when they were around. This illustrates the transition from a time when a blind cashier was considered quite adequate in the community and doors could be left unlocked, even around a rail yard with "transients" about. However, I'm told that the old woman's senses were so sharp that stealing was a risky venture at the store when she was around.

To my childish mind, it was apparent a very near past was still celebrated, as it was being done in Hollywood by churning out Western films. It was so all-pervasive that I could imagine that I was alive in the Old West.

In fact, some old-timers who had pioneered in California had only died just as I was being born. It took me a while to notice that I was in a different time, looking back but feeling somehow part of it regardless, and the fascination is with me still, although in a more subdued form. World War Two had been the historical divider. Those things had happened between the time when the deer and antelope had been here and the present. I missed them all the same. It would have been a thrill to see at least one Antelope running with the jackrabbits through a field or see a deer slaking its thirst in Dry Creek later on when I discovered it. But alas, it was never to be. Like the song, the time when deer and antelope were plenty, or even if they had been just a few was long gone. Antelope has become a sort of memorial to them, I suppose.

That railroad crossing was the location of many events and memories. It was the only way of crossing the tracks after Watt Avenue, which would require backtracking away from Roseville for too long. So this was the more convenient "back door" alternative in those days. But it was a gamble. You never knew if a freight train would be crossing the road when you got there, and they were very long in those days. Sometimes, we had to wait for a while and watch the other cars and trucks stack up. Inconvenient for the adults, but it was a chance to notice the immediate surroundings; the almond trees, the magpies and blue jays, and the kids that some parents allowed to get out of their cars and try to steal almonds from the trees. Of course, my folks were thinking of safety. So we could only watch those kids put pennies on the rails, pick almonds, and other fun stuff.

To round out this introduction to this neck of Sacramento County and The Spook Tree itself, we must turn back to the vision of what it was like before the first home was built in Aero Haven. What became Aero Haven, North Haven, and finally North Highlands was a signals training camp, an important one that was established at the start of World War Two; Camp Kohler.

Antelope's former general store.

The Original Antelope Store – Courtesy Mike Monahan – The Placer County Historical Soceity

In those days, Antelope and Roseville were the outposts of civilization after Sacramento City. Roseville was consequential to North Highlands and Camp Kohler. The family or just my father and I made many trips to Roseville in those early years. In fact, I lived there in 1974 for a little while. It was almost the same place. But it wasn't, even then.

A Visit to Camp Kohler

Our route to Roseville was always the same, up the block, and left until we came to M Street and then out to Walerga Road, to take a right on Antelope Road, which in those days was designated U Street as a continuation of the earlier county grid naming system. The Walerga Road appellation harkens back to the railroad spur on the line about the time Antelope was established. The name's origin is unknown, but the guess is that someone, possibly Portuguese, had lived there at the time. Vallegra, as the original name, has been suggested. That was not long after the time the Transcontinental Railroad had barely passed through the stop, first known as Junction, and later renamed Roseville, due to the abundance of wild roses in the area. It was called Junction because it was where the Southern Pacific and Central Pacific railroad tracks met. The Roseville switching yard is the largest on the West Coast and had developed there has to be the origin of the army's decision to locate the signal training school there after the transportation of the Japanese population of the San Joaquin and Sacramento area to the camps at Tule Lake in Modoc County. The airfield was already there, having been established in 1936.

The national railroad system was the central infrastructure and the foundation of visual and telegraphic signaling up to then. The rail signal station named Walerga became the name of the Assembly Center in 1942.

Camp Kohler - Camp Kohler 1943 – photo – Army Corps of Engineers

Whatever the wisdom of the time it was that caused President Roosevelt to decide to intern the members of certain ethnic groups for the duration of the war, Japanese in the west, Germans and Italians in the east, it had to be due to the high number of incidents performed by recent immigrants. The sharp national memory of events such as President McKinley's assassination, sabotage during World War One, and other events, including foreign interference in labor struggles, was still alive within the memory of the living. In the thirties, the labor struggles and violence around it were still going on. The advent of the Great Depression led some to think that capitalism had proven to be a failure. The Communist Party USA membership swelled as did its activities. One prominent member, William Z. Foster published a book in 1932, "Toward Soviet America." Many were unsure of the future. Once the European war began, German U-boats were patrolling the Eastern Seaboard and began sinking our merchant ships in sight of land before we had entered the war, and Japanese ships patrolled near our West Coast long before Pearl Harbor.

That worry was increased by the spy network in Hawaii that had been able to embed itself so inconspicuously within the large Japanese population of Hawaii that it had successfully assisted the plans to attack Pearl Harbor. Thanks to their specific reports and photos, the attackers knew where individual battleships were docked on the Seventh of December, as well as hangars and other installations. The worry was that with the Pacific fleet so crippled, the continental coastline was now vulnerable to attack. With so much open space, the remote signal stations were often left inadequately guarded.

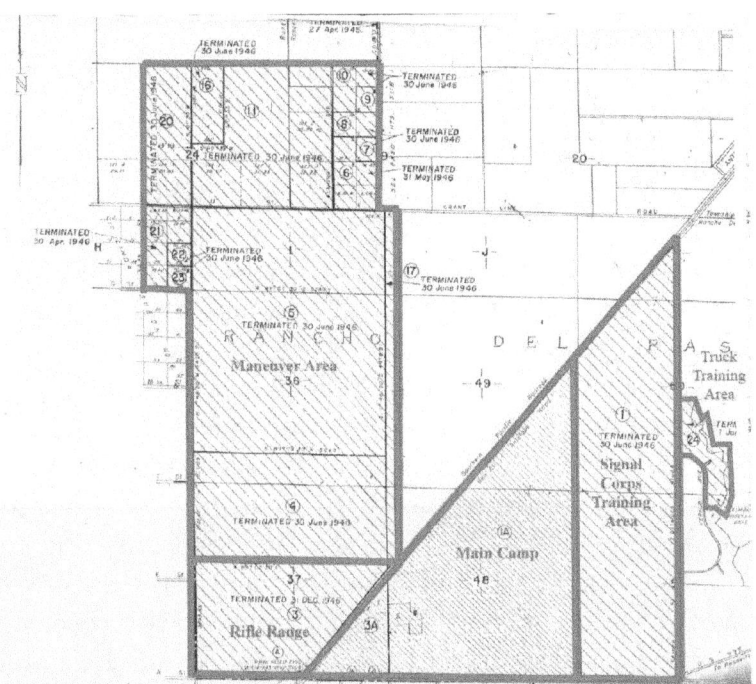

Diagram of Camp Kohler – The Spook Tree would be located in the zone labeled "5." From
http://militarymuseum.org/CpKohler.html

The government and authorities were now dealing with the confusion of the sudden declaration of war. There was a world of new concerns and duties. This meant that intelligence would be that much easier to gather and sabotage that much more likely. As it was, a full third of ethnic Japanese in America were not citizens, nor were they loyal to the U.S., but to Japan, as we shall see.

The decision to intern Germans and Italians was based on known activities and intelligence gained from acquaintances who understood the language. This sort of cultural openness was not as common among the Japanese Americans who tended to be more clannish and closed as a cultural norm. For those who believe the decision to intern Japanese Americans, here is a piece of rarely reported history of an incident that took place on the Hawaiian Islands on December 7th as the attack on Pearl Harbor was underway; Shjenoir Nishikaichi's Zero was hit by a P-39 during the second wave of the attack on Pearl

Harbor. The Japanese Navy had designated the small island of Niihua as the place to ditch if going down. They expected to be able to complete rescue operations. But his crash landed that knocked him out was observed by Howard Kaleohano, who got to the plane and seized the unconscious pilot's pistol and documents. Once he came, Howard helped Nishiskaichi to his home, where his wife tended to him. No one on the island knew of the attack on Pearl Harbor, which was ongoing, but out of sight and sound. Unable to establish communications, Howard went to find his Japanese friends, a husband and wife who lived on the island. They conversed with the pilot but did not disclose the nature of their communication. The next day, when the news of the attack arrived at the island, things became violent. Howard's Japanese friends tried to talk Howard into giving them the documents, but he refused. They and the pilot took two hostages and a shootout ensued. They demanded the documents, but the natives refused. In the fray, the pilot managed to destroy the Zero, but later in the shooting, a native woman fired the shot that brought him down. Nishikaichi finished the job himself. The loss of the captured plane meant that it would be another nine months before another Zero was captured intact enough for U.S. intelligence to learn its secrets and hasten the war. This event directly influenced the decision to intern all Japanese on the mainland. The cause was not based on race.

Camp Kohler was named after one of the earliest combat deaths of the war. He died in China on March 14, 1942, while on the Chinese military mission of Lt. General Joseph W. Stillwell. First Lieutenant Frederick L. Kohler was killed in China when his transport plane, a Douglas DC 2-221-#31, developed mechanical trouble and crashed. There were four survivors, but all thirteen American passengers were killed, including Kohler. He was buried in China. The ceremony was attended by Claire L. Chennault, the American Volunteer Group leader, who was resisting Japanese advances in China with his Flying Tigers air group. His remains were later reinterred at Golden Gate National Cemetery in San Bruno, California, on April 1, 1949. His grave is located in Section K, Site 179. It might be useful to remember that the signals camp was named after Kohler while the relocation center was named Walerga because the details of history matter. Both names are part of the broader historical epoch of World War Two.

Most of Camp Kohler itself was constructed with wood frames and had walls of tarpaper, and corrugated steel roofs. Other wartime temporary housing nationwide was just as flimsy. McClellan had such emergency barracks that lasted throughout the war. The annexation of Splinter City, a quickly assembled set of warehouses, remained a unique tax revenue issue for North Highlands in later years. It had been closer to Sacramento on the southwestern end of the airfield. The transportation to remote camps like Tule Lake in Modoc County was being concluded at the time of the Battle of Midway. This episode of Camp Kohler's use for the Walerga Assembly Center location was a short-term event compared to its larger purpose. The camp was used far more extensively for Signals Training during the war as part of a more massive complex that included U.C. Davis and facilities in the Bay Area. Camp Kohler was a significant part of the war effort, just as those chicken farmers in Rio Linda played their role.

The various branch's signal sections depended on a central system that connected Washington, D.C., and the Pentagon to the worldwide theaters of operations. And just as vital was information, intelligence, and mundane, coming in to be analyzed and acted on. Since the time of primitive man, signals have been critical to survival. Even animals use them. From a shout to drums to fire beacons, and the "Indian Smoke Signals," that delighted the boys' imaginations in the 1950s, to Morse Code, the Boy Scout's signal mirror, and the toy "walkie talkies," many improvements have come since the famous ancient battle of Marathon when a runner saved Athens, with news of victory preventing a planned surrender to the Persian navy that had arrived there. The need to improve military signals has been a significant problem during wartime and emergencies since ancient times. History has often turned on the performance of signals and intelligence.

From Waterloo to World War Two

Before the day of the Battle of Waterloo, which was considered by Creasy*₁ to be one of the fifteen most consequential battles in history, Wellington was served well by his forward intelligence. During the battle, his adroit system of runners kept his commanding officers in place and moving only at his precise signal, avoiding panic and a route when it looked like Napoleon had won. Simultaneously, Napoleon had no such plan but relied on his marshals to carry out missions that required independent decisions in the field. He gave direct orders and relied upon his officers' loyalty and calls for conferences on the field during the actual battle. After the Battle of Marathon, the first one on Creasy's list, a runner took the news of victory to Athens, preventing the surrender of the city-state which was pressed by the Persian navy.

At Waterloo, when Napoleon left the field for a half-hour, Marshall Ney made a fateful decision to charge with his cavalry against the allied infantry without infantry support into British square formations. This, and because Napoleon had no idea where the Marshall Grouchy was when the Prussian General Blucher's black flags appeared on the battlefield because his orders had been given a day before so they were confused by competing interpretations. So Grouchy (pronounced grew-shee) did not march to the sound of the guns when in doubt but pursued the Prussians, from behind, following them, chasing them toward Napoleon rather than putting himself between them. So Napoleon sent in his Old Guard hastily forward and watched it mowed down by Wellington's musketry, and so, Napoleon was defeated. Signals had played a crucial part that day.

Similarly, few today realize that the massacre of George A. Custer and his command at The Battle of the Little Big Horn could have been prevented if General Crook had sent a messenger to inform him that he had been nearly defeated by a huge alliance of Sioux and Cheyenne warriors on the Rosebud; the same that Custer faced later. Crook had retreated twenty miles to the base camp on Goose Creek after his "victory" to await resupply (25,000 rounds of ammunition reportedly spent during the battle), so he could not arrive in time to assist either him or General Terry, with a combined force of 792 was smaller than Crook's total force of 1,325, including 262 Shoshone and Crow allies Crook (as the Sioux and Cheyenne had been raiding them against treaty promises). Gibbon fell ill so Terry took over command of all units. General Terry sent Custer and his command (of 586 soldiers, 33 Indian scouts, and 20 citizen employees) to probe for Indians expecting to meet up with Custer two days before the fatal battle. They had a huge delay and numerous casualties crossing the Tongue River. So General Terry showed up at the Rendez-Vous point a couple miles from the battlefield two days late. Custer expected to Rendezvous with Terry and Gibbon on June 26. They were discovered by the Indians just before they discovered them on the 25th. Custer could not let them escape as his central order was to find and fight hostiles. If they had escaped, the blame would have been laid on him.

Gregory Michno's excellent examination in "The Mystery of E Troop," proved that Custer had set his forces up in a square formation that anticipated the arrival of Major Reno and Captain Benteen's forces to fill in the skirmish lines. Michno noted the earlier success of Custer and other leaders by employing the square formation. At the Battle of Killdeer Mountain in 1864, General Sully had formed a square with mile-long sides and using five companies per side held off and defeated an estimated 1,600 to 6,000 Indian warriors. Custer himself had used the tactic successfully multiple times during his 1873 Yellowstone campaign. Michno and other historians have proved that the Indian's claims that the battle lasted at least a few hours have been borne out by the evidence.

According to the testimony of Indian leaders, the soldiers had succeeded in holding off the Indians until the soldiers were reduced to a few, whereupon they closed in fast. The final fight was fierce with soldiers killed in position. The former guesses at panic and fleeing were shown to be false. For example, a strung-out line of men once thought to describe a scramble to escape, turned out to be one of the "walls of a planned square, and the troop that was accused of galloping away in panic was established by Michno as close as possible as the E Troop, the Gray Horse Troop, which was witnessed by Indians chasing some warriors before disappearing from record. The many interviews of the Indians in subsequent years as well as thoroughly studied battle evidence serve these conclusions. Regardless of the failures of Crook, and the late arrival of Terry and Gibbon, if Reno and Benteen had arrived in time, Custer's smaller-sided square would have had six companies per side. So despite the difficult terrain, Custer likely could have lasted until the Indians either left the field as occurred at Sully's 1864 battle or Terry's arrival, even two days late. The Dakota Column went on, uninformed, even though there was a week between Crook's battle and Custer's demise.*[2]

Custer was not insane, nor did he exceed orders, he had followed orders and responded to the surprise of the size of the Sioux and Cheyenne forces competently. He and much of his command would have survived had Benteen not dawdled and delayed in arriving on the field to find a battle-shocked and indecisive Major Reno. The later hearing (not a court martial) multiple testimonies of Reno, who was known for his alcoholism was drinking on the day of the battle, yet he and Benteen escaped all official blame. But many knew the truth, including Libby Custer, who wrote harshly concerning the court's ruling for years afterward.

The outstanding fact of the main failure of the 1876 Montana Campaign was that the Army got its Indian population reports and locations from the agencies. Because of that Custer had expected to face 1,200 warriors at best. They could not know that four to five thousand warriors had recently arrived from the northwest vector. Moreover, as Libby Custer reported in the last chapter of "Boots and Saddles," news of Crooks retreat arrived at Fort Lincoln too late. They did send out scouts to warn the Dakota Column but there was little hope that they could reach Terry, let alone Custer, who was purposely sent forward in time. So the main cause of the massacre was poor intelligence combined with the failure of communication. The ladies of the 7th cavalry knew of the danger days before the battle and agonized until the final crushing news arrived. They prayed and sang hymns, famously, "Nearer, My God, to Thee."

The controversy among actual historians around The Battle of the Little Bighorn concerns the actions of Benteen and Reno on the day of the battle. Even the many reports of the leaders of the Sioux, Cheyenne, and other Indians such as Kate Bighead (who circumnavigated the battle looking for her nephew who she feared wounded or dead), have been recorded and clearly settled by unbiased historians dedicated to learning the truth of the event. All other "histories" and criticisms are purely political.

Crook learned two hard lessons from the Yellowstone Campaign of 1876. One concerned the need for brass-cased ammunition, as the copper cases had the tendency to turn green while kept in a soldier's ammunition belt which caused it to weld to the breech upon firing. *3 Although archeology and statistics have said that cartridge failure was only 3%, and not the determining factor in the battle, on Reno Hill, a few soldier's duty was to stand by and use their ramrods to clear the breeches so others could fire quicker. The other was the need to improve communication in the field. (Custer fought a battle at the Bighorn River on August 11, 1873, where his 450 cavalrymen faced about 1,000 Sioux warriors. Custer placed 30 of his best marksmen along the Yellowstone River to shoot at the Indians at a 400-yard distance. The best marksman of the group, Private Frank Tuttle used his Springfield 45/70 (although the carbine was actually 45/50) being fired rapidly enough to kill several warriors in rapid succession before any had a chance to fire back. Even so, most agree that at the Little Bighorn, Custer's men would have fared better with their old Spencers).

Note: Despite modern criticisms, Custer was following orders – no debate. One of Reno's officers who kept a record of the event, 1st Lt. Edward Settle Godfrey (commander of Company K), guaranteed that if Custer had not engaged the tribes that day, they would have escaped the campaign entirely without having suffered any significant loss, and Custer would have been blamed (See – The Godfrey Diary). Other sources such as Michno also show that Custer was the forward point and expected to find and attack whatever groups of hostile Indians (off-reservation) he found.

By World War One, carrier pigeons brought messages from the front lines to the rear. By World War Two, the Army Air Force had scout planes with radios on board and men who knew Morse Code.

The Need for Camp Kohler

In the 19th century, the army knew about signals and so the Boy Scouts learned about the use of mirrors, smoke signals, and more sophisticated, immediate signal employment, such as three fires, flashlight signaling S-O-S, or even three shots from a gun as a signal of distress. (Lieutenant Godfrey wrote that a volley of three huge shots had been heard on Reno Hill. Some men commented that "Custer must really be givin' it to the Indians," but Godfrey knew it was likely a distress signal. So did Captain Weir, who tried to mount a rescue but was stopped at "Weir Ridge"). The practice of many early trail bike riders in the Sierra's to carry revolvers was exactly for this reason, (and rattles snakes). We may then consider how vital signals had been during the two world wars. Thousands of men were saved during the First World War because of one pigeon, but it required an entire culture of carrier pigeon keeping and training for that one pigeon to succeed. During World War Two, signal mirrors were included in every naval flier's survival kit. But by WW2, far more sophisticated technology had arrived, which required far more than writing a note and stuffing it into a little tube on the leg of a bird. Radio and huge expanses of geography were involved now. Radio and huge expanses of geography were involved now. Camp Kohler was a vital West Coast Signals training center for far longer than when it served as an assembly center for internees. Camp Kohler was a vital West Coast Signals training center for far longer than when it served as an assembly center for internees. The barracks housed the nearly 5,000 ethnic Japanese detainees used had previously been used by white migrant farmworkers of the "Grapes of Wrath" culture who did not even have permanent facilities on the site. The Army Corps of Engineers and private contractors built the barracks themselves. The same barracks were used by the soldiers training at Camp Kohler after the Japanese had been transferred out after their 52-day stay. Those quarters were never improved and served as excellent fuel when the Fire of 1947 occurred.

As a child, my father was a war hero to me. I had found his war souvenirs in the garage just after we moved into the North Highlands home. So I asked him about the war. As I had already learned, he had flown as the radioman in a Grumman Duck, an amphibian biplane with the capacity to rescue at sea, drop depth charges on submarines, and photograph via the radioman's remote viewer position

A typical migrant labor camp of the late Depression era – U.S. National Archives

.

They were used in the Mediterranean and Atlantic anti-submarine campaigns. So Daddy was in signals on the front line. He knew Morse code. I remember still reciting it as an old man.

As related, Daddy told me how they had dropped depth charges on a Nazi submarine in the Mediterranean "and sunk it." He also told me how he had landed the plane one time after the pilot had fallen asleep due to being out too late partying the night before his patrol assignment. I won't elaborate on the lie he told me about having his seat shot out as he stood up to see if they had hit the sub. And I won't mention how he went AWOL to go home since he hadn't seen his family for five years by 1943 and spent six months in the brig as a result. That's private family business. That tour of the brig resulted in late 1946 mustering out, as he had to make up the six months with actual duty.

Regardless of the incident, my father received an honorable discharge; lucky duck flyer. Later, he was in the Pacific on an aircraft carrier. I found his war memorabilia in a few boxes in the garage of our new home in North Highlands, pretty quickly. That is when I interrogated him and gained the above intelligence. I confiscated his Chinese and Japanese money at that time. I don't know what became of it because it disappeared entirely. Did he steal it back? I don't think so because I never saw it again, ever, and I kept my eyes open if you know what I mean. I still have his copy of the vitamin companies' Navy tribute photo album that I also swiped at the time. But my father never mentioned it to me. I think he knew I had it and thought it was okay, even educational. It was full of sobering photos of war; ships being blown up, Hellcats taking off the flight decks of carriers, Kamikaze attacks, Marines on the beaches of the Pacific islands, and the final ones, burial at sea with a twenty-one gun salute, and the grave of an unknown Marine on Iwo Jima.

It was a war to end tyranny, including the beyond-belief treatment of human beings by the Axis Nations of Germany, Italy, and Japan which saw the starvation, torture, and murder of human beings in prisoner-of-war camps, and concentration camps. But that was not a limit, it happened wherever they went in towns and the countryside. We can look in horror at the Nazi's Russia Campaign, "Barbarossa," and also the "Rape of Nanking," the Bataan Death March," the "Death Railway," work camps in Thailand, Malaysia, and Burma, and the wider spread of civilian camps throughout the Japanese occupied islands from the Philippines to Indonesia, with a complete divergence of history where the treatment of the interned from the U.S. case. Of the now estimated 65 to 75 million deaths during World War Two, the vast majority were civilians killed by the Axis nations, mainly Germany and Japan. No civilians in the U.S. of any race or ethnicity were killed in the U.S. by the government while in detention due to wartime policies. And many loyal Japanese eventually found ways to serve their country, much to their enduring credit and honor.

Camp Kohler Artifact

In the autumn of 1959, I was in the second grade. My best friend Jackie had moved away from North Highlands. Paulette was in the first grade, but there were days that I walked home alone from Village School. The fields where Jackie and I had explored were the scene of new construction. This building was underway during the spring, so we had seen it arrive together. Sometime around October, I was walking home, passing between two skeletal structures of what would soon be more citizens of North Highlands and more classmates.

I always had my eyes on the ground before and around me. I tended to find things; if not an interesting new bug, maybe a small value. Even then, I knew that rings were found lying around in the dirt all the time. What I found that day wasn't a ring, but a tool. As I passed between the two-by-four frames, something caught my eye. It was a brown lump. Whatever it was, I could tell it was not a dirt clod. I picked it up. It was a machinist's hammer but without a handle. I sized it up, and carried it home in my right hand, feeling the heft of it in my little arm all the way. My dad was home, so I showed it to him immediately. He questioned me about how I found it. Satisfied that it was not someone's lost article, he took it. He bought a new wooden handle and kept it in his toolbox. Later, when I was putting my toolbox together for my racing outfit, I swiped that hammer back. Dad never said anything. I still have that hammer today. I believe that it is an artifact of Camp Kohler. Some tank or jeep must have been repaired in the field and the hammer was carelessly dropped and abandoned. So that hammer was a Government Issue item. I believe it is a genuine artifact of Camp Kohler's history.

The link between Camp Kohler, North Highlands, and The Spook Tree becomes obvious; North Highlands right up to U Street was all part of the training area for Camp Kohler. Signs of it could be seen, whether it was Lead Hill, the old rifle range backstop mound at Strizek Park, the remnant of the French Village where St. Timothy's Lutheran Church was first established, that odd shell shot tower at the junction of M. Street and Walerga Road or The Spook Tree.

The Grumman "Duck" – Scout and Rescue plane also carried depth charges on each wing and served during the entire war. The cockpit canopy was often in open-canopy mode. There was a compartment below the backseat with a door to the outside for rescuing downed pilots, reachable through a hatch in the floor of the backseat. A large camera setup was serviced this way as well. Photo – Emigepa on Deviant Art

The Spook Tree

My folks always had a radio playing, at home and in the car. They were music lovers. My father had actually won a jitterbug contest at some bar in Chicago in the late 1940s. He could play "Sugar Blues" on a harmonica, which is how I came to take up the little music maker, myself. One day, he just bought a Marine Band Harmonica, played that tune, and then handed it to me. I think they wanted us to hear a variety of music because they switched stations around a great deal, even though there was only a handful of stations in those days, with KFBK being the earliest of all, going on the air in 1922, while KROY followed in 1937. KXOA arrived as a major pop AM station as was KRAK by the later 50s. KFBK remained a mostly information station. The rest became popular music broadcasters. KRAK became a County Music station by 1964. A radio was always on in our home or car. On P Street, I used to watch the head of the snake wobble over the 78rmp records my mother would play on the Zenith Cobra-Matic record player. The manufacturers had cleverly designed the tone arm to look like a maroon-colored snake complete with eyes on the end where the single tooth of the needle waited to attack a disc of shellack. It turns out that the Cobra-Matic was quite popular in the post-war years until HiFi consoles began to replace them. This was before stereo. Once the stereo arrived, everything changed again.

When a song struck me, I would stop what I was doing or thinking and listen. One day, I heard the song, "There Was a Tall Oak Tree."

That song affected me that way. As I listened to the wistful parable, I thought it had been written about where I lived. In our case, as I soon would notice, they had even burned the tall oak tree.

> "There was a tall oak tree
> That loved a babblin' brook,
> And the babblin' brook
> loved the mountain high,
> And the mountain high
> Loved the sky above.
> The Creator looked down
> And saw everything was love, love, love.
> Then, he took a bone
> And a piece of mud --
> He made a man then a woman
> To be flesh and blood.
> And then along came the devil
> Up out of the ground --
> He tempted the woman,
> And that spread sin all around, all around, all around.
> Now, if she'd left that apple
> On that apple tree,
> There'd be no tears or sorrow,
> We'd live eternally.
> And then along came Man
> To burn the oak tree down
> And now the babblin' brook
> Is solid ground.
> And the mountain high
> Don't stand so high,
> And there's a cloud of smoke
> That covers up the clear blue sky.
>
> There was a tall oak tree. There was a tall oak tree.
>
> There was a tall oak tree."

It wasn't the religious aspect that appealed to me. Even at my age, I understood it as a metaphor. One clue is the implication of "God" using the same dirt to make man and the "Devil." The real state of the world is closer to Melville's narrative from "Moby Dick" as Ahab reviews the ongoing scene beneath the waves where God's Creation "chase and fang one another." And turn's to Starbuck, his first mate, and says, "Who's to damn, man, when even the Great Judge himself is dragged before the bar?"

That's some harsh love. It was The Tall Oak Tree in the song that struck me because we had one, maybe the very one that inspired the song. For years after, I would try to imagine what it must have been like there when elk, deer, antelope, and birds frolicking in the expansive, unbounded river wetlands were the dominating scene in the entire river valley. Historical facts were at the time unknown to me, so those realities could not overcome the wonder of the fields as I found them; they extended forever, it seemed, rolling out over gentle, low hills. Out in the fields, there was room for all sorts of fun. Regardless of that, something bothered me. There was an element missing; the deer and antelope of that cowboy theme.

Moving north up Walerga Road from Camp Kohler on the way to Antelope was one strange landmark that must be logged here as it was known by everyone in North Highlands and could not be missed; the white-painted brick "blockhouse" on the rise at the intersection of M Street and Walerga Road. It wasn't very big at all; maybe fifteen by fifteen feet square with uneven walls that seemed to have never supported any roof. Its floor was dirt but deeper than the ground on the outside. It had a huge hole in the southern wall, which continued through the north wall, and the structure seemed to be slowly crumbling.

According to Kid Lore, which everyone I knew seemed to know, and as I learned very early, this was a target structure left over when the area served as an artillery bombing range for Camp Kohler. No one ever thought to ask an adult, and I certainly never heard a grown-up mention anything about it or many other things; some must have known about Camp Kohler for that matter. The record reports no artillery practice, but since they did have tanks there, I think it is safe to guess that a tank's cannon made that hole. But at the time, the cannon hole was thought to be from artillery. Non-military records only say artillery practice, not specifying. So the hole was made by a tank.

By 1970, someone had painted a green American flag on it as an early statement on the environmental concerns to come into a larger focus in later decades. (I think I know who; Brenda, are you out there)? The issue of the day was the agricultural bug retardant spray DDT.

I grasped the concern. I had seen clear cuts in the Sierras that looked as if a war had torn up the mountains, as well as the ravages of forest fires while on various outdoor excursions from the time of our early family trips up old Highways 40 and 50 to the time of my boyhood explorations in the environs of the property that our family-owned near Placerville and later the hunting and fishing, trail bike rides all over the Sierras. I had even written a short poem, a couplet, I suppose, which I titled "Pollution;" "I settled in the lungs of people, of me, they would not dispose. After a time, deterioration − in my triumph, I saw nature's close."

You can argue about it now if you want to waste time, but I sensed the problem way back then. Just as a free energy machine cannot work because of the laws of thermodynamics, we can't burn stuff and not produce another chemical form that has to go somewhere. It doesn't make sense to pretend that would have no effect, especially after a critical mass of it accumulates. Whatever one might think about the hysteria now, it was a good thing to get DDT out of our food and lead out of our gasoline back then.

The elimination of DDT as a tool of agribusiness was the key factor in the return of the American Bald Eagle from near extinction, as well as a large number of other aviary species. It was later found to affect human male sperm counts. There was concern over the effect of the chemical on humans. This and the elimination of lead from gasoline, among other issues that today, would seem to be common sense by even the staunchest conservative. But it was the concern of "radicals" and "hippies" at the time.

I was neither. I just loved nature and wanted to see it conserved. It was called "conservation" back then, and hunters considered themselves conservationists. "Pollution" was the only "poem" I ever wrote on that theme. The remaining ones I wrote were either about racing motorcycles or borne of pure narcissistic self-pity. I disavow them all, here and now, officially, even though they were never published, except two, and it was a couplet about racing. The other I wrote much later in life. It was published in a Sonoma County community paper. It was about the millions of animals being run over by cars annually titled, "The Silver Fox of Jenner."

By the end of 1970, that little roofless "blockhouse" with that green American flag on it was gone, as was M Street. That structure had no assigned name, but we kids were fascinated by it, and now it was gone forever. It had made way for the new thoroughfare, Elkhorn Boulevard, which now continued east becoming Greenback Lane after crossing over Interstate 80. It then continued after merging with Madison Avenue just short of a mile from what the local youths called "Rainbow Bridge," now its official name. That span over the American River exits the dam in sight of the guard towers of the same appellation as the Johnny Cash melody's prison in the Gold Rush era town of Folsom. In those days, it served as a good central location, far enough from Sacramento's fair city, to serve as a convenient place to congregate the "bad boys" of the era. The road continued on through the glorious woodland climb to Placerville via Green Valley Road. Green Valley Road was part of the Old Gold Rush roadhouse circuit's former loop, although traffic ran in both directions.

Out to the north, there was one sight that commanded my young eye before we even got to U Street on our way to the railroad crossing and Antelope. In the vast open expanse that U Street only briefly interrupted, just a little way up Walerga and across the road from the "blockhouse" to the west, on the North Highlands side, stood what became a local wonder, to the kids, at least. Prior to 1958, Walerga ended at M Street. You had to go up Watt Avenue and turn right, and then onward to Antelope and beyond.

Out there amid the fallow field that always seemed darker than the rest was a tree, not the same as the other oak trees. It could be seen from every direction in those days. No new rows of houses were anywhere near it. Out there in its midst was one, stark, solitary tree, unique and immediate, commanding notice. That tree stood as visual notice of some ghastly past event that had left it as its only reminder. It was an oak alright, but it was dead, obviously dead; dead black in a field of mixed, dried up wild vegetation, brown-yellow and seeming to still be withering unhappily in the hot summer sun. This, my initial view, remained my lasting impression. It remained there until it was finally swallowed up by new suburbs and the landscape many years later. This tree had died in a terrible, unnatural way. It had been blackened from a fire that had consumed most of its branches. Set upon a little rise in the field, it seemed to me that it had once been the monarch of all the trees in the vicinity. It was thicker and taller, even in death than the trunk of any within its visual scope. It seemed frozen there with what few branches that were left charred as black as the trunk, rising and twisting toward the sky as if forever outraged or forever imploring, like the victim of the Inquisition of the Dark Ages, eternally frozen in agony at the stake as a witness to cruelty. The one main forking branch still discernable arched out and away from the tall trunk. The first idea that came into my mind was that it had been a hanging tree. It created a perfect, hoary structure for a natural gallows if ever a dead tree could be; that one surviving branch seemed big enough to have supported a dangling body. And it was high enough off the ground for the hanged to have sat on a horse under it. It was the first real-life symbol of death I had encountered up to then.

There was something both brutal and tragic about that tree. I never heard any adult talk about it, but they must have, as I later learned. I sensed its immediate mystery even at this distance. There was a feeling, a dark secret about it. Standing out there in the sun, it seemed like a mute victim of some old mysterious epic of violence. It stood there neglected as if all consideration had purposely turned from it. It was out of place there in the field, among all of the happy flowers in the spring. Its time was autumn and winter. Only in the worst weather was it in simpatico with its surroundings, and that wasn't what you'd say was a pleasant one. Bolt lightning threatening overhead was its crown, and the following thunder might have been its voice; a voice no one would hear on such a cold, windy, rainy night but in the distance, safe and warm. This is a scene that must be imagined. I imagined it as a six-year-old.

I always turned my head and marked it again, from Walerga Road, and from every other road and vantage that I ever found myself at, even the seat of the school buses that took me up to Hillsdale Elementary school in 1963-4. I think I felt obligated to acknowledge it somehow. But I think I also wanted to make sure it hadn't disappeared. It was a kind of companion, in perhaps an absurd, but strange way, and I was sad when it finally disappeared from the landscape as the suburb development finally arrived in its presence. I wonder if they hesitated. There may be evidence that they did. But from my first notice of it, I was fascinated by the potential of its tale of woe. If only it could speak. If only I could find someone who knew.

I think I was the only one in my family to even ever turn an eye to it, a thoughtful eye, that is. So I never said anything about the tree. For all of its blackness and horror, it looked lonely most of all. How and when it died was a question that always came to my mind whenever I saw it. Why that tree, and no others? This later became the central object and theme of my growing store of Kid Lore. When passing by, it was a sight I never missed. Every time we drove past it on our way to the railroad crossing, I always turned my head to gaze at that stark sight as we passed. My attention could find a new subject immediately, a skill of children and of which I was so adept, but today often termed Attention Deficit Disorder. So once past that strange tree, I was looking ahead up the road. Beyond it was the turn onto U Street and the wonders beyond. Maybe I'd see a real antelope in the field this time?

Past Antelope, a couple of meandering miles was the old, venerable, Denio's Farmer's Market and Auction, which we just called "The Roseville Auction." It still exists today in a modified form. One of our first excursions in my memory was out to the farmer's market. I remember it as a big, dirt parking lot and walk-through rows of sometimes canopied isles of tables filled with vegetable and fruit produce more stacked behind the tables or sides. I still recall the big lug of tomatoes my parents bought on the first trip and how big and tasty those tomatoes were. I discovered my love of lemons in the same way. In 1965, Davy, my best friend, and I walked all the way there and back just to watch the livestock auction, something I'd never seen before. We crossed golden fields with their oak trees, single and grouped, as it was the uniform character of that vast prairie. We stopped at the Antelope store to get a soda on the way back—a real adventure day for a thirteen-year-old. By this time Uncle Johnny was becoming a unifying force in my totality of grasp of geography and humanity.

My Dad's youngest brother Johnny was my favorite uncle, there's no question of that. He was a case, but he was genuinely himself. He personified the Western Man, even more than Uncle Ralph, who reminded me of John Wayne at times. Uncle Johnny was more like Festus from the Gunsmoke television series. Uncle Johnny was an adventurous rascal, who liked women, drink, and ballads; from the frivolous, even bawdy, to the more serious, even religious kind, singing them out loud when we were on outings with my father, who hardly ever joined in. He was all that, but also an army-trained radiography technician after serving in Korea as a medic. Uncle Johnny told me that he was captured at a point. He and his group escaped when an Allied artillery barrage suddenly erupted when they were being marched away by the Red Chinese troops and they got away amid the chaos; a very lucky man, indeed. I believe he was part of the momentous Battle of Chosin Reservoir and Retreat. He was vivid and vivacious, with a hearty laugh, quick to see a joke in every situation, but disciplined when it was time to be so. That's what the Army did for you.

A Genuine Throwback

He was a miner with a heart of gold. Dear Ol' Uncle Johnny ca 1988; Korean War Vet, medic, whiskey-swilling, six-gun toting prospector into his last years, he also taught atomic theory and plane film radiography in the army and set up the first mobile imaging business in Sacramento County and the United States. – photo by Shirley LaRue

As the only member of the family who had been in direct, bloody combat, he had seen some terrible things in Korea and I have no doubt they haunted him. Maybe that is why he possessed a wider spectrum of emotion and expression compared to his brothers; he had seen death's face up close, and personal. He is the only of the four brothers that I ever knew to express true sorrow over anything. But that was probably because he was more intimate with me than even my father.

I have no doubt he suffered from PTSD to some extent. All the boys did from the trauma of their time with Pat. He would drink, cuss, and make lewd jokes, but he worked hard and had the capacity for soulfulness on occasion. I'll never forget the conversation we had about war one day while I was riding with him in his 1952 Chevy pick-up truck, the one my Dad would buy from him, and that we'd take on all the early adventures up to 1968. During the summer of 1965, I spent the weekend with him at his place in Rio Linda. We had heard Barry McGuire's "Eve of Destruction" on his radio console the night before. We were in that truck, and he was at the wheel when he said, "War has shattered many a young man's dreams." It was years later that I learned that my grandfather had intended to open a chiropractic hospital with all of the boys employed there. Uncle Johnny was to be the medical doctor in the group.

He was not only injured in Korea but came away as an alcoholic. I knew he drank too much, my mother complained about it once in a while. But he never let me see him drink anything but a beer. That wasn't shocking, it was common; I saw lots of grown-up men drink beer; it was common. They universally called the opener a "church key;" so much for the faith of our fathers. On the other hand, there was a day I recall, when I sat between my Dad and Uncle Johnny, as he drove the 1953 Chevy pickup we'd later buy from him singing, "Will the Circle be Unbroken." That too was about the faith of our fathers, and my world of contradictions droned on in an odd sort of harmony. Uncle Johnny was an odd variety of "hipster" as well. He frequented bars and loved the ladies there. He played KRAK most of the time, preferring country music, but it was through him that I learned of Wolfman Jack in 1966 when he was playing XERB on the radio when he took me on a fishing trip to Coulterville on Highway 49. We left on a Friday night, so I listened to the wolf howl station ID in a convertible under a full moon. Uncle Johnn could tell a yarn. Oh, could he ever! He had somehow latched or preserved the old-style braggadocio of the Voyageurs that seemed to survive in most Old Northwest French-Quebecois. Uncle Johnny was a personification of that Kris Kristofferson song, "The Pilgrim; "He's a poet, He's a picker, He's a prophet, He's a pusher, He's a pilgrim, a preacher, and a problem when he's stoned. He's a walking contradiction. Partly truth and partly fiction, taking every wrong direction on his lonely way back home."

Even so, he wasn't the type that had to be imbibing at every waking moment. When the work was done, and he arrived at the right place and time, he liked to get a bit wild. I remember one cold morning as we stood on the bank of the Tuolumne River while on a trout fishing trip with him and some of his friends in April of 1967, dressed in an insulated suit of quilted pants and jacket. He said, "After Korea, I swore to myself that I'd never be cold again." He was a sober enough man to succeed. He and a partner began the first mobile X-ray service in the United States. He ended up doing very well with that business. It was through that fledgling venture of his that I met with a profound experience that I've never forgotten.

When he was just starting the business in 1970, Uncle Johnny reckoned that he needed some help, so he called my mom, who then asked me if I'd like to meet Uncle Johnny at a rest home out near Howe Avenue somewhere, and that he'd pay me. Of course, I went. I took requests like that as a call to duty in those days, just as when a classmate at school asked me to take her to a relative's home somewhere near Country Club Center after school, where she had to look after some kids. I did it just because she asked me. I don't know why. It was just how I was brought up, I guess. So I got to the rest home on time. Uncle Johnny was late.

It turned out that there wasn't much for me to do. But I had a memorable experience all the same. That was because of the patient. He was an old man. He told me a bit about his life as a cowboy. That's right, he was a real cowpuncher. He said he was an orphan. He had been picked up by some soldiers after an Indian massacre. He had no surviving family and was too young at the time the soldiers found him to recall his own name. So they named him "Government Standard." That was his name. I only wish I had asked him more questions. I always remembered his name. I thought it was a pity that he was alone in the world in his final moments and that no one it seemed, would know or mourn an old cowboy named Government Standard, let alone know his name. I am so happy now to tell you now, faithful reader, of him and his name. I have Uncle Johnny to thank for that remarkable experience. It all somehow jelled together with The Spook Tree.

By 1970, the auction had grown into a catch-all for just about anything that might be sold; I mean everything, including kitchen sinks. That year, I bought a pot-bellied stove and carried it a half-mile to the Ford van I drove at the time. I used it to add to my bedroom's log cabin theme inside our home on Centinella Drive. I had put in wood-style paneling and mounted the .32 Special, octagon barreled Winchester I bought from a widow at the gun shop in North Highlands over the Ithaca model 37 shotgun my grandfather handed down to me the next year. With the gun shop's help, I looked up the serial number to find it was built in 1913; I had acquired another link to the past. I have also found that the year of the Ithaca was 1942, an interesting year for my grandfather to have acquired the then "high-tech" Ithaca Model 37 Featherlight as it was advertised and marked. All of this was set off by a two-tiered wall-hanging rustic-styled oak bookcase containing the foundation of what is my ever-growing home library today.

Between these and other touches, I was in a different world once I entered the confines of my room. I was buying old books and things like old milk cans at antique shops in Placerville. I found square nails in old buildings and a couple of small gauge spikes at old mines I explored while with my Dad and Uncle Johnny gold prospecting during the summers of '64, '65, and '66. I continue to hold a weakness for collecting old relics of all types and sizes. I guess you could say that I had something on my mind, perhaps influenced by the former five-year-old boy who thought he was a cowboy. But I had plenty of help from my father, uncles, and occasional associates nearer my age. My grandfather got into the act later and contributed a hay knife to my growing collection. My dear Norwegian grandmother, his wife, later passed her Norwegian cast iron cookware on to me after giving me my grandfather's Hamilton railroad watch after he passed in 1974. All of these things are reminders of what has come to be a meditation of respect for those who went before me, working and planning so that I could have a chance at a place in the sun. Respect for ancestors provided support for many societies in ancient times. That is what inheritance is really about. My argument is that the loss of this tradition in the West is one of the main causes of its decline.

Uncle Johnny's last residence was strangely enough, on Gothberg Way in North Highlands. He died a bit too young. But some of his habits had caught up with him and brought his story to a close in 1994. I was at his funeral at the Veterans of Foreign Wars Post on U Street. There was a three-gun, nine-shot salute. His ashes are interned at the Folsom Memorial Lawn, appropriately, just under his father.

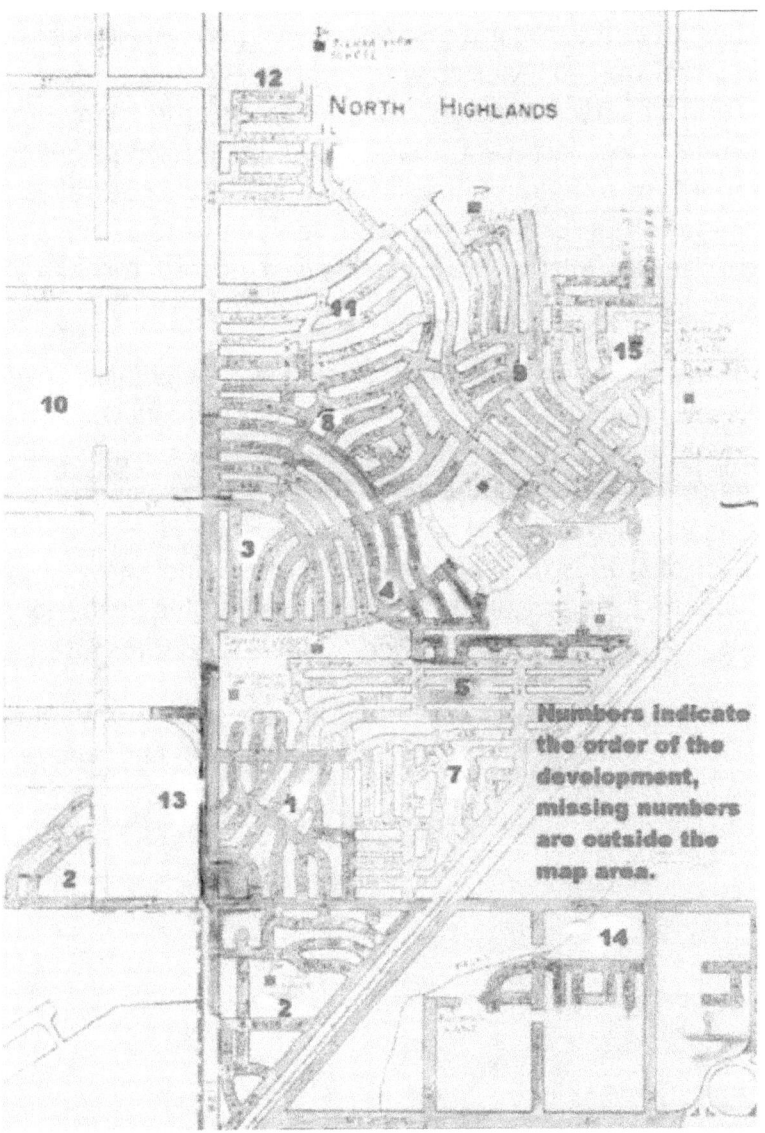

North Highlands – 1958
Village School can be spotted beneath the "Highlands" wording. A short way from the second half of the word stood the Spook Tree. From the Second Annual Chamber of Commerce Directory – from the Dean O'Brien Assembled History of North Highlands – Courtesy of the North Highlands Recreation and Parks District

I still have that old stove as well as a few other items I picked up at the Roseville Auction in those days; a stone corn grinding bowl with a stone pestle, and a small treasure box – both from Mexico. Many a fringed jacket made in Mexico was sold there in those days, and I have one. They all serve as reminders of another time in my life. From that time to the last year that I lived in Sacramento County, an occasional trip to the old Roseville Auction was as natural as stopping at a gas station or local grocery store, only better. Every time I went to the Roseville Auction in those days, I passed through Antelope without thinking about it.

But in 1957, finding that Antelope existed was a significant event in my life because it was obviously old, and that sort of age was attractive to me as something genuine. I guess I sensed the newness and out-of-place nature of North Highlands, at least when you contrasted it with Antelope, which was within a short bicycle ride of it. I knew there had to be a lot of stories to hear about it. Little could I have known of all there was to be discovered beyond it, as my life, experiences, and interests, like an oak tree, branched out into its various forks.

Over all of this, The Spook Tree lurked in the back of my mind, as the unifier of meaning; life, death, and later on, and above all, the inevitability of change.

The Kid Lore Quotient

I n early life, a child focuses attention on what is immediately before them or at their feet. I was a good prospector for treasures that others more hasty or farsighted would miss, even among the other kids. I'd spot a penny in a parking lot first. I'd find an old nail, or as it happened, an old machinist's hammerhead in the dirt in the field just after a bulldozer had made its first scar on the ground of the area, the one full of wild oats, flowers, tadpoles, and bird's nests that I used to explore and observe in those last days of its existence, the highlight of which must have been the time that Martine and I, on a trip back from summer school at Larchmont Elementary School, took the long way home through the construction site of Village School and found a robin's nest in the weeds, with the brilliant, blue eggs in the nest. All such life fled as North Highlands grew to safer locations, but I guess the hibernating frogs were paved over. The bulldozer had turned up a few relics from what age I knew not. But it makes sense now that they were part of the remains or perhaps leavings from the Camp Kohler days. Just as I brought the hammerhead home to my father, it has served usefully again in my father's toolbox and later my own, I once found a horseshoe. I put it on my bedroom wall. To this day, I don't recall what happened to it. Whose horse did it come from? Was it from an old plow horse or a cowboy's mount? I guess we could call what I was doing, "kid archeology," but I have never quite outgrown it. But these were the sorts of attractions that entertained me when my realm was small, and my daily routine consisted of walking trips to and from Village School during kindergarten and first grade. The kindergarten room was separated from the older kids and the rest of the school by a play yard that was hemmed in by a tall white fence. Once we entered the door into the classroom, we were in a world of our own and Miss Wilson was the goddess of the class. I remember her as a very pretty young woman, and she took good care of us all. Some of my favorite kids were in that class and came along with me all the way to our senior year at Highlands High School. Jackie, my first best friend, was there, too. My older sister, Martine, was on the other side and had a different schedule, so I walked alone on those days, but as time went on, I was more often with Jackie.

The next year, I was on the other side of the fence. There was more to see and experience. Mrs. Martini provided some of that as already rehearsed herein. She was the first of the occasional old-school personality that took delight in contradictory and harsh behaviors towards me, and I assume, other children. But for me, such experiences made up my world of impressions. After the departure of Jackie, who had left in the summer between first and second-grade sessions, I found myself alone on the playground. The big attraction there was tetherball, but the older, taller kids dominated it. The girls dominated the four square games or played jacks. I should note that in those years, boys and girls self-segregated because according to the "cootie finders" the girls made out of folded paper, and we boys always had more than one of them on us. (This made the cute English girl who used her index finger to apply a kiss to my cheek a kind of revolutionary). So rather than crowd onto the monkey bars or stand in line to swing on the rings, I'd often go watch the construction of the newest wing of the school. I remember watching the bricklayer work. His white overalls, little cap, and robot-like methodology were neatly artistic as he spread out the mortar on a brick-like butter on a piece of bread, lay it down on the other, tapping it here and there into perfect alignment with the others, and then trimming off the excess mortar. The result was a perfect brick wall.

Here comes Mrs. Martini. Watching the brick masons was wrong, I learned. Did staring kids make them nervous? A good shaking made me sure not to approach or even look their way again. So I resorted to gazing across the fields that began at the playground's blacktop limit out forever to the north and east. By then, the area between the school and home was filling up with a few new rows of houses. It had begun the spring before. Where once Jackie and I had stopped to view tadpoles in pools, new construction was going forward. Instead of searching the pools for fun, we stopped to sample a water station on the way home. It was comprised of a wooden shelter with a big aluminum water cooler raised up off the ground on a shelf. We thought the cone-shaped paper cups were funny. They featured safety messages as cartoons printed on them as reminders for the workmen. Just like the brick masons, these men were like an army dressed in their Union white overalls as they worked like ants, erecting the new houses. There was no danger until they showed up, I thought.

So I would wander around at the edge of the playground blacktop, as we were not allowed to touch the dirt with our shoes as long as the day session was in. Once class was out, well, the route one took home was pretty much of one's choice, so I didn't miss out on anything of interest within my short vision's scope. As the houses went up, I saw the stages. When school had been let out, the labor for the day was done because no men remained in the entire area, whereas they had been everywhere in the morning. The structures were almost as good as a ghost town, and I wandered through it sometimes with that idea in my mind. The wind would blow, and a piece of orange tape on a survey stick would flap listlessly as I passed by. And so the days went by, and the skeletons took shape and final forms as habitations I could recognize as houses. Soon enough, there were people in them. Actually, it often seemed to happen overnight. It was as if they were on a waiting list; they filled up so fast. Maybe they were? After all, we visited our home in 1955, when it was only a wooden skeleton.
The trip to and from school was enjoyable, but the playground had become a sort of surveying station when I wasn't running around with Jackie, who as I, did not fit in on the playground so well.

Jackie and I made things up, and created fantasy worlds based on perhaps TV programs like "Sea Hunt." But then he was gone and I was "alone." So one day early in my second school year, I gazed out beyond the playgrounds' limit and my usual scope and spotted it; the same tree as I had found off Walerga Road not too long before this with its few remaining limbs and black as death. As I stood there and wondered at it once again, a kid, an older one, came up and stood beside me, looking at the tree.

"That's the Spook Tree." He said.
"The Spook Tree," I asked suspiciously.
"The Spook Tree," he repeated.

I said nothing more. My mind was filled with wonder. Not the sort that a Disney film typically inspired, however. This wonder enhanced the feeling of mystery when I had first spotted it a couple of years before, "The Spook Tree," huh? So that was its name! I wasn't the only one that had noticed it. Some kids knew more about it than me, too. Why was it called that? It was obviously haunted. But The Spook Tree was perfect. No other title could top that one; that's precisely what it was; a spooky tree. Were there spirits around it, ghosts? That was my new concern. There was a "don't come near, or else" feeling to it, as well. Even so, the lure of that old, hoary tree beckoned me irresistibly. Out there in the open field, it was too far for a kid to get away with walking out to it. I knew I'd have to be patient and plot a scheme, but I'd get out there one day. At that time, my sisters and I were not allowed to stray off our front lawn when my parents went home. But I would find ways to satisfy my curiosity all the same. In the meantime, my observance from a distance continued.

My toy binoculars; I don't know how I came to possess them. Maybe they had been a Christmas present. It might be that I bought them at the Sprouse-Reitz Five and Dime with the money my grandmother would send from Florida to us every Christmas and birthday. Maybe I traded them for something to another kid. I cannot recall. However it happened, I had at that time a toy binocular set. They were cheap, everything I saw with them had a funny blue aura about it, and the rim was fuzzy. But they did bring distant objects into closer view. No matter, they were better than nothing. So I brought them to school in my lunch pail. At the first opportunity, I took them out to the playground, and as it was not perfectly level, I searched the edge of the blacktop for the best position and put them up to my eyes. They worked well enough to increase the tree's projected hoariness. The imperfect instrument, with its purple aura and fuzz, only enhanced the supernatural look of the Spook Tree. It seemed imbued with a spirit, but not a happy one. My previous feelings were magnified.

How the Spook Tree came to be haunted and so unhappy now fascinated me. It only enhanced my determination to find a way of getting out to it so that I could further inspect it. But this desire did not come without a little fear. If it's haunted, might it be dangerous to get too close to it? I knew immediately that I would not go alone. I needed support. I had to create a Spook Tree Conspiracy. This, I knew, would take time because I had no idea of how to go about forming such a group. I would have to wait for opportunities to create interest among boys I hadn't yet met. That summer, after the last day of school, when some older boys were hanging around trying to flirt with my older sister, I would learn more about The Spook Tree.

My older sister was born with something. Martine had a natural charm and was considered pretty at every stage of her life. She was a born flirt, instinctually effective in "making eyes." She loved to lead the boys on and did right through high school. One was so desperate that he buddied up with me and wrote in my yearbook in junior high to talk to her through me. From what my parents later said of her as a two-year-old, she began her career around then. I sort of ruined things for her by being born, and a quiet sibling rivalry was initiated upon my entrance into the family scene. Later in life, my mother reported an incident to me that concerned Martine in the first year. My sister had distracted her from changing my diaper with an event of her own. Momma was at work, taking care of me, when sister called,

"Momma, look!" Martine felt the need to remind our mother that she could do that, too. That event gave birth to various future issues, where I was always the guilty party by her acclaim. I got over it, eventually. But I wonder if she did. That little caterpillar event I was never quite forgiven of many or any of my faults, failures, and even successes. I seemed inconvenient to Martine.

This is how family politics and complications often begin – innocently. Luckily, at the time, the other two young sisters would arrive and disperse the blame for my existence. With all that, we kids were not solely a study of sibling rivalry. We were a musical family. Boomers were raised on the same diet of media as our parents. The various stations replayed the cartoons and films that our parents had seen at the local movie theaters as kids in the 1930s and beyond. When "The Wizard of Oz" was re-released in the late 1950s, our parents took us to the Starlight Drive-in, near Arcade Creek beside what is now the Hagginwood Golf Course. The lot is there, undeveloped, sitting like a ghost town. With everything that is going on around it, that's curious. My parents were sure to take us to see every Disney film available at the time, along with all the child classics from the thirties, starring Shirley Temple, Judy Garland, and Mickey Rooney. I saw them all; "Snow White and the Seven Dwarves," "Lady and the Tramp," as well as the Biblical Classics. The Starlight was the usual drive-in we used, but my parents favored the old Alhambra Theater. Later, that theatre was the ultimate setting for "Lawrence of Arabia," with its Moorish walls and garden courtyard, which impressed the film deeply enough in me to seek out a book on T.E. Lawrence and read it as a 13-year-old. That theatre was lost in 1973 before the historic building preservation activity got started. Its loss was one of the issues that prompted that movement.

Perhaps the most exciting child film for me at the time was "Darby O'Gill and the Little People." The playful spookiness of that film translated to real spookiness where the Spook Tree was concerned. In Ireland, that tree would have been called a "Fairy Tree." I picked this up when I spent a couple months in the west of Ireland in 1988.

Fairies are mischievous creatures that can appear or disappear from human notice. They have a set of old scores to settle with humans, so it's best to stay out of their way.

In Ireland, and indeed other parts of the British Isles, they are seen to be responsible for strange and tragic events. For example, when I was on Inis Mor in Galway Bay as part of a two-month visit to Ireland I made in 1988, I learned from a delightful little girl named Sophia why a particular old stone house had been demolished. "It's on the fairy path." She told me in a matter-of-fact tone. Something bad had happened to everyone that ever lived in that house, so the people destroyed it. The concept was not unknown in the Gold Country.

Only it was the Tommy Knockers, a particular type that hung around mines that tormented the Welsh that made it over with them, to sabotage a gold mine when the mood took them. The cave-ins, falls, and practically all tragedies, were seen as the work of the dreaded Tommy Knockers. I don't see any reason why they would be limited to the mines. And fairies could go anywhere. They chased the Irish all the way to New Guinea, I've learned. How much easier would it be for them to be hanging around Antelope, with all the railroad activities going on? After all, there were the granite mines in Rocklin, operating in time for the first work on the Transcontinental Railroad.

Beyond the children's films were the Rogers and Hammerstein musicals, every one of which we saw except "Showboat," which I guess they considered too complicated for kids. Martine, Paulette, and I were in the church choir, and we all sang whenever we were on trips, as many families did in those days. These were not church songs but from films such as "The Music Man and "Snow White and the Seven Dwarves." Gale later came up with songs about eating worms, and such (I never heard any about eating caterpillars). My parents also had to put up with the usual silly songs that were circulating in those days. These included "The Bear Ran Over the Mountain," "On Top of Spaghetti," and other such nonsense. Sometimes, we picked up popular songs and sang them. Paulette and I performed a duet of "The Cradle of Love," by Johnny Preston, for example.

There were, of course, the bad songs, "The Bosco Song," which my mother hated; "I hate Bosco! It's rich in vitamin C. My mother put it in my milk to try to poison me. I fooled Mother; I put it in her tea. Now I have no mother to try to poison me!" "Don't sing that horrible song!" Momma commanded. And we didn't. The boys that came to do their best to impress Martine taught us bad songs like that, but we didn't indulge in them, as a rule. I didn't really want to sing about poisoning my mother, anyway. Besides, we didn't even have Bosco in the house. We used "N-E-S-T-L-E-S" because Nestle's made the very best – chocolate... (and the Howdy Doody dog puppet slaps his jaws down – "clop")!

I had wondered, quite innocently, why anyone would want to catch a nickel by the toe. Later, when we found out, my mother issued another command to never, ever, use such a word. It's just not polite. However, I want to remind my readers that in the 19th century, many, many Germans settled in the U.S., especially after 1848, when their populist revolution failed, and many in the South. "Negger" is the German word for "black," just as "negra," is the Spanish equivalent. There is a famous former governor of California whose last name translates to "Black-black." (We mustn't let cultural illiteracy convert to banning or forced speech in a nation whose first founding law is about free speech). When we know that a word is considered impolite, we should refrain from using it. But this should also be a two-way street. Civility in a free country is based on respect, not through enforcement by interest groups. My mother taught my sisters and me not to use racial slurs because they are demeaning. She had personal experience with it as a child, due to her ethnicity, which stood out in the coal-mining Appalachian town of Wilkes-Barre, Pennsylvania. The slippery slope this has created is approaching its apogee, today, as madness is taking the wheel of political culture.

Throughout this period of growth and language learning, Martine was the star. My parents sent her to music lessons, and she learned to play the accordion. Soon after, she had the opportunity to check out an autoharp from the school. Martine first sang folk songs to the family and then taught them to all of us.

She was the star, and that could not be challenged, ever. In some ways, Martine was, and she deserved it. But it was also because she looked astonishingly similar to how Elizabeth Taylor looked at the same age. Along with that, the fact is that Martine was a born flirt. She even charmed the bus driver and used to sit on his lap while he drove all the kids home from school later on when the buses started.

The Bad Boys

Martine was also a star socially, I mean with boys. They had brought the Bosco Song, and then others. She was elected a Little League Princess two years before I began playing when I was nine. And before that, boys would come to our house to visit her. It was the source of some interesting little events. It was also how I picked up the Kid Lore about The Spook Tree.

So the boys would show up. From the very beginning, even when I was four years old our yard had no fence yet. This allowed access from all points for all would-be visitors. The construction of the homes that would block out the backdoor view of the fields was just beginning. The dinosaurs had dug a big hole within the parameters of what would become our fenced-in backyard. The spot would eventually become a manhole as a sewage intersection service point. One day, it came to our attention that these same older boys were out in the yard playing in the hole. This was about when they had taught us the Bosco Song. Martine was telling them to get out of it, but they smirked, and one sat down on a broken piece of red clay piping as if he were doing his business right there in front of us. My sister scolded them again. Those boys were incorrigible.

Soon after, one day, my younger sister, Paulette, almost fell into that hole. I don't remember the incident. Apparently, I was there and pulled her away in time to prevent her from falling in. I do remember my parents telling me about it over dinner at a Chinese restaurant celebrating the event. I was a hero, they told me because I had saved my sister. This was the start of the "buddy" years between us. Actually, I made Paulette into quite a Tom Boy. No worry, she came out just fine in the end and married one of my friends from the racing crowd.

The bad boy's next act was also memorable. Always looking to impress Martine, the boys showed up later that summer with three catfish. They had caught them in a creek. I didn't know it then, but it had to be Dry Creek. So Dry Creek had catfish in it, at least. Later, I would learn from another boy, the son of a woman who worked with my mom at the airbase, that small-fry, striped bass was in it near where he lived in Rio Linda. He had seen them there. From his description, I knew they were striped bass. They must have been spawning there.

The bad boys pulled the fish out of a burlap sack to display them. They looked dead, but the boys claimed they'd wake up if we put them in some water. So they ended up in our bathtub, and soon they were moving around just as lively as you please. The boys, thinking they'd impressed Martine, took off, leaving the fish with us. When our parents came home from work, they were surprised to find three catfish swimming around in the bathtub. My father knew what to do with them. I watched him clean them, driving a nail through their heads into a board and pulling off the skin with pliers. So I tasted catfish for the first time that day.

"Repulsive," you might say. That is the old-fashioned way of cleaning catfish. I don't know of any other method, myself. But then, I haven't been catfishing since the seventies. Skills such as these were more common at that time. It was part of life and considered normal in my family and I daresay, many of the time.

My father had grown up during the Great Depression in rural Michigan. It wasn't that long ago, but culturally, it was closer to the pioneer days by leaps and bounds than to us today. But it is just as easily said now that the fifties were culturally closer to pioneer days than now. Westerns aren't even made any longer. Or if they are, they are mostly a vehicle for anti-American propaganda.

There were some actual pioneers still living in the fifties. Wyatt Earp himself died in 1929 in Hollywood, a good friend of the early Western actor, Tom Mix. John Wayne was given his first job by Tom Mix. Some pioneers persisted in life into the 1950s and beyond, as my report on Government Standard bears some witness. Albert Henry Woolson (February 11, 1850 – August 2, 1956) was the last known surviving member of the Union Army who served in the American Civil War. (There were three claims by Confederates, but one was debunked and the other two were unverified). From this, we may surmise with confidence that the average child's life was far more influenced by the 19th century than since say, 1980, when Country Rock retreated into the "Americana" category along with Bob Dylan and The Grateful Dead. The New Wave and Punk influence combined with dulling heavy metal to further estrange youth from the past. I refrain from any review of the influence of Rap. Suffice it to say that changes in pop culture have further estranged subsequent generations.

The event by which I gained critical intelligence about the Spook Tree involved a German Shepherd, our dog, and the fate of the boy who told me all about it. This boy stood out from the rest in his affectionate persistence toward Martine, which lasted for years, poor boy. His name was Bobby and the surname of the famous Irish poet.*ꙮ Bobby was as passionate as any poet, I believe.

During that summer, he came over often and hung out on the front lawn, talking to her. She didn't like him because she said Bobby bragged a lot. He was a "know-it-all," she told me. Whatever she said to him, Bobby never ceased to carry on his crush on my sister until years later, when he "ended it all," quite dramatically.

Bobby Yates was not one of the Bad Boys, not really. He ran with the two other boys because they lived nearby and they were the only other boys of his age in the neighborhood, which was not very big at the time. On one particular day, we were naturally gathered around, playing with bugs or other games, passing the time until "The Little Rascals" and the afternoon cartoon time arrived on the local television station. "Captain Sacto," the show's announcer said, was stationed "at a mysterious location, somewhere west of Brockville." Brock was the developer of Larchmont Village and much of North Highlands. The mysterious airfield had to be McClellan. But that day, instead of watching TV, I was listening to Bobby telling stories to try to impress Martine. He was talking about an old hermit that lived across the fields by the creek. Bobby was probably a solitary hobo, perhaps serving out a russification sentence for breaking a hobo law. She didn't believe him, what he said about him anyway. But this wasn't what got my attention at the time. What got my attention was when he said, "He lives out on the creek, way beyond The Spook Tree."

This is where I jumped into the conversation. "The Spook Tree," I demanded? What did he know about my Spook Tree?

"Sure, the Spook Tree," Bobby reposted.

"I've seen it," I said. "I've even looked at it through my binoculars."

"You know why it's called The Spook Tree?" Bobby queried me rhetorically.

"No," I admitted.

"Well," he said, "that tree was used to hang an innocent man."

I responded silently with eyes bugged out in surprise. My initial "intuition" was confirmed!

"Yep, in them days, there was a man who killed a ranch owner and stole a herd of cattle. The Sheriff was gone out at the ranch when the news came, and the men at the saloon reckoned that they had to get going if they were to catch the killer. They didn't have the time to go all the way out to the ranch, so they found the deputy who led them out after the man who had taken the cattle. The large cattle trail was easy to follow, so it wasn't long, just by sundown, that they caught up to the man and his herd. They held a kangaroo court and hung him on that tree, the Spook Tree. They only learned that they had hung an innocent man when they got back to town and found the sheriff had returned with the man who had really shot the rancher, and the rancher wasn't even dead. They also learned that the man they had hung had bought the cattle, after all, just as he had insisted all the way up until when they hung him. And that's why the tree is haunted. That man's ghost is in that tree."

"Oh, it is not!" Martine scoffed.

"It is so," Bobby insisted.

"Liar, liar, pants on fire," Martine shot back.

Bobby went home for the day. I guess that showed him.

As I sat there and thought about Bobby's story and my sister's skepticism, I wasn't so sure. She was a know-it-all herself and was always telling me something about this or that. As I found later, she was wrong on most of it. What she liked was to be an authority. So she clashed with Bobby.

But I could not disqualify Bobby's story. After all, I had noticed that brooding tree for a while now. Bobby's story confirmed my childish intuition. But what was most fascinating about it was that the town in the story had to be Antelope. The Sheriff of Antelope had to have been a righteous man, like the one I saw face the outlaws alone in that film when everyone deserted him. That was my impression. I had no idea that there had never been any such office in Antelope.

A day or two later, Bobby returned with another kid. This boy, Bobby declared, could confirm his story. So that was one incident. But the new kid said that was not all of it; he had another one. The tree's history was complicated. Lightning had struck the tree not long after the poor cowboy had been unjustly lynched on it. Later, another man, who deserved what he got, had died on that tree, too, the boy insisted. "A rich kid from Europe was in town, and a man from his country had followed him and his family here, and when he got the chance, he kidnapped the boy and held him for ransom."

"Yeah?"

"Yeah!"

"So what?"

"So the cops chased him, and he got as far as Walerga Road when they were going to corner him. He stopped his car and got out to try to see where the cop cars were coming from so he could pick out his best escape. While he was stopped, the kidnapped boy escaped and ran to the tree. The man chased after him. But the boy got to the tree first and climbed up it, out high onto a branch.

The man had no gun, so he had to climb up the tree, and the cops had driven their cars into the field and were coming for him fast.
So he climbed the tree to get the boy. But the man stepped out onto a branch that broke because he weighed a lot more than the boy, and the tree was dried up, dead, so the man fell. He was caught by the neck by a broken branch sticking up like a spike, and it killed him, just like that."

This was the second event. Martine was speechless this time probably because of the overwhelming detail the strange boy presented. So was I. I would need time to absorb all of this and sort it out. All I could think was that the Spook Tree had to be something special to have, not one, but two horrible things happened with it. The fear I had of its haunting was mitigated by its having next served as a device of divine justice. It was The Spook Tree, but it was also The Justice Tree. But it was dead all the same, and what tree would not rather be alive? It was a haunted tree, that's for sure. Through his recruitment of this boy with his corroborating story and a sequel, Bobby bought himself some time with Martine. Unfortunately for poor Bobby, the next event in his courtship of my sister was not a happy one.

In those days, it was still common for every family to have a dog in town but especially in the suburbs. So in pursuit of the usual family practice of the time, we went through a few until we settled. All the same, not everyone had dogs or liked them. We had neighbors that I don't think cared too much for our dogs.

On P Street, we had a German Shepherd named Brownie. I remember Brownie very well. I recall sneaking out of bed and going to the couch or where Brownie was, putting my arms around him as best I could, and sleeping there with him. My father's brother, our Uncle Ralph, visited during that time and made up a song about Brownie for us. "I know a dog, his name is Brownie, he is a very clever pup. He can stand on his hind legs only, only if you hold his front legs up." Uncle Ralph could also talk like Donald Duck. We liked Uncle Ralph.

Brownie had behavioral problems that were exhibited once we moved out to North Highlands. Two incidents occurred that ended with Brownie's departure from us. The first was caused by the low-flying jets: the second was the undeveloped nature of the neighborhood as far as fences, etc., were concerned.

Things That Went Boom in the Sky

McClellan Field in the early years was a wilder place than it became later as North Highlands expanded. In the fifties, the jets would often fly low. I remember watching an F-80, the one with the straight wings, pass right over our house so close I could see the details of the underside of it. I think I could have hit it with a slingshot. And there were sonic booms, maybe twice a week. The sound made our windows and even the house shake. Perhaps a year later, I remember my mother's comment that they had made sonic booming illegal in populated areas. Up until then, they were considered exciting by all the kids. But for Brownie, one of those booms was his death knell. One day, we left him inside because there was no fence yet. When we got home, the first thing we saw was that Brownie had torn down the new Venetian blinds that covered the patio door. My father was furious and whipped the poor animal. I remember how it hurt to see it done. Not long after, Brownie was gone. I asked why. I was told that he had been knocking over garbage cans in the neighborhood.

Back on P Street, I once left my bed one night, climbed onto the couch, wrapped my arms around Brownie, or tried, and fell asleep that way. Brownie was a good family dog. But poor Brownie, the sonic booms had scared him terribly. Brownie was trying to escape the rattling structure, and the blinds were in the way. I'm sure of this now because we have many stories today of dogs jumping through windows, shattering them on the Fourth of July when the big fireworks displays go off in the neighborhoods. With no fences around and all that delicious garbage to rummage through, it was inevitable that Brownie would get into more trouble. I hope he found a new home and was not put down. It wasn't poor Brownies' fault. No, it wasn't.

My father had to "moonlight" while he was trying to get his practice going. So he was gone until late at night, sometimes even all night in those days. My mother being the paranoid type didn't feel safe without a dog, so now that Brownie was gone, we had to find another one. This effort didn't go that smoothly, either. He next found a dog from the shelter we named Toy. She was a mix of Toy Collie and German Shepherd. But from the very start, she exhibited strange behavior toward my sisters and me when we played outside. She began to snap at us on the first day. We began to call her "The Wolf Dog."

By the next day, she was barking at the TV when a picture and audio of water appeared on the screen. By the time my mother saw her do that, she had been chasing us around, snapping at us. That night, as my father was gone at work, my Uncle Ralph came over. He was working as a guard at Folsom Prison at that time. Uncle Ralph had a revolver shoved into his pocket with the butt exposed as if it were a Western holster. Uncle Ralph had us all get into a bedroom and shut the door as he dealt with Toy. He got her restrained and out of the house without having to shoot her. That is all I know of Toy's fate. This was all we ever knew about it, except Momma said that she had rabies, poor animal.

The next dog was another German Shepherd we named "Bullet" because it seemed that he could run incredibly fast. Bullet loved Martine. He used to jump the fence, go to the school walk into the classroom, and sit down next to her, just like Mary's little lamb, except he was a dog. And it was against the rules. To remedy the problem, my father set up a runner wire where the clothesline had first been located and attached another chain to a collar so that Bullet could not jump the fence. But jump the fence he did, right into the backyard of the parsonage. Bullet did not land on the ground. The old pastor that my mother had dearly loved had moved on, and a new one had arrived. We never knew until much later that our new pastor had stood and watched Bullet strangle to death as he hung on his side of the fence. That pastor's tenure at our church did not last long. I'm not sure why, but maybe this story was responsible. My mom was a talker, that was for certain.

Before long, the houses of a new block behind our house eliminated the fields' expansive panorama. There were homes with lawns and no fence to be seen. We could see the back doors of the other homes. Standing in the space between our backdoors, we could see down the long way to the cross street and beyond. At the time, it seems like a great big playground to me. Just as a few kids were meeting up on that expanse, it was gone. Fences divided up the plots and separated the families and kids in the new homes from the ones on our street, and we'd henceforth play in our back and front yards, and later on, in the roadway. What a difference fences make.

The next dog was the one. My folks had by then learned a couple of lessons about pets and how to select them. No more trips back and forth to the Pound, as it was called then. The family visited a dog show that was held, I think, at William Land Park. In the same park, we enjoyed picnics with the Sacramento Chapter of the California Chiropractic Association. A little while after that, a man coincidently named Masters showed up at our house with a pretty "silver" German Shepherd called "Tinny." She was two years old and already a winner at a few local dog shows. She had impressive AKC lines that went back to Germany with a long list of international champions. And, Mr. Masters told us, she was of the Rin-Tin-Tin family as well. She even looked like Rin-Tin-Tin. Her registered name was "Our own Lady, Cin Tin," or "Tinny" for daily use. She was an instant success in our family. She had something extra that no dog we had known exhibited until that time; she was attentive, and watchful over my sisters and me. An example of her protective instinct was soon demonstrated via the unfortunate Bobby.

It was Tinny who ended this phase of Bobby's tragic attraction to Martine, who could have been a child femme fatale. It was soon after confirming Spook Tree witness when Bobby was visiting during that same summer. Bobby was playful with Martine. They began to wrestle on the lawn. Bobby pinned my sister down on her back. At that moment, Tinny put an abrupt end to the play by taking Bobby by the seat of his pants and pulling him off Martine. Bobby was not hurt.

Tinny had taken the care to seize the cloth that covered his posterior region, not the meat thereof. Poor Bobby was scared to death and ran home crying. The incident came to my parent's attention. It became another dinner-time story for a while, whenever we turned to the exploits of Tinny, our family wonder dog. Poor Bobby never visited us at home again until some years later, when he made his final speech to my cruel, heartless sister, who would not declare her undying love for Bobby at twelve years of age.

From left – Mark Miller, Tinny, King, author at 14 years of age – photo – Wanda Clark

So on another day some years later, Bobby came to visit and took Martine on a short walk in our backyard to the incinerator, which was in active use at the time. He made a speech that, although none of us heard, we observed. Bobby held his open hand over the intense heat of the burning trash, illustrating how angry he was with her neglect of his feelings for her. How anguished his young heart must have been to do that! Exit Bobby Yates; I hope he had a high school romance before he went off to war. I think he deserved it for what he went through over my sister. But thanks to Bobby and my sister's inherited allure; I had acquired the Kid Lore about The Spook Tree.

The last time the Bad Boys stopped by, sans Bobby, they were trying to impress Martine with a cherry bomb, with which they threatened to blow up the hallway toilet bowl. Next was the fish aquarium. Her inherent charm prevented a major event at the house, at least, taking the form of absolute commands to not do any such thing. The bomb went off in the backyard before Martine shooed them off.

It was hot in the summers in Sacramento County, and it still is, but in those early years, we didn't have the benefit of air conditioning. We suffered a few summers with the heat. My parents provided a couple of versions of ring pools – the type where you'd blow up the empty vinyl circles one at a time until you had a pool maybe two feet deep, okay for kids back then, but today, not good without supervision. Back then, we didn't know how to drown in such shallow pools. This helped during the day, but not during the still, hot nights. So the time finally arrived when we acquired the standard cooling device of the time, the swamp cooler.

A swamp cooler was typically set up on the roof of the homes in North Highlands. I don't know who did it, but it was some contracting outfit. They had a big truck with a wide, stable ladder that allowed easy access to the roof.

In that way, I was able to accompany my father up it while it was being installed. So there I was, for the first time, on high ground, for no old oak tree as spotted the fields were ever allowed to remain as the tracts of new homes were installed on the modified firmament. No, when a new home was finished, some guy with a pickup truck and some saplings in the truck's bed would come along and plant a baby tree in the front yard. There were no grown-up trees to climb as there were at every home Uncle Ralph ever lived in out in Citrus Heights and later Orangevale. That was the Larchmont Village Plan, I suppose. Tree climbing around there came a little later when we were old enough to hike out to the distant fields beyond the blockhouse at Walerga Road and M Street and scale some of those old Valley Oaks.

In the early days, there was no shade to speak of in the new developments and the paved roads and homes baked in the summer sun. But up there on the roof, my vision was expanded. I cast my eyes out across the distant landscape. Then, I thought of The Spook Tree. Could I see it from up here? I turned my head in the direction where I knew the dead tree stood. Yep, there it was, further away than when looking from the schoolyard by a mile, but there it was – still brooding, always, all year round, year after lonely year. I kept my eye on it, noting my location relative to it whenever I was in a car on any nearby road; good early practice at reconnoitering by landmarks. In those days, my sisters and I weren't even allowed beyond our front lawn. Stepping onto the blacktop of Centinella Drive would draw a harsh penalty if our parents heard about it, and Tinny was our guard.
Aside from wandering around in the fields on my way to school, and then seeing the "wild" territory disappearing as the homes went up, I could only dream of exploring as far as The Spook Tree in those years.

So out there, standing alone in the dark land around it, The Spook Tree beckoned to me from afar. "Someday, I'll get out there," I promised myself. I'd finally stand in its presence and learn whatever spirit or ghost, evil or good, resided in it. I was sure of that. But for now, I had to sit in the front yard and bide my time.

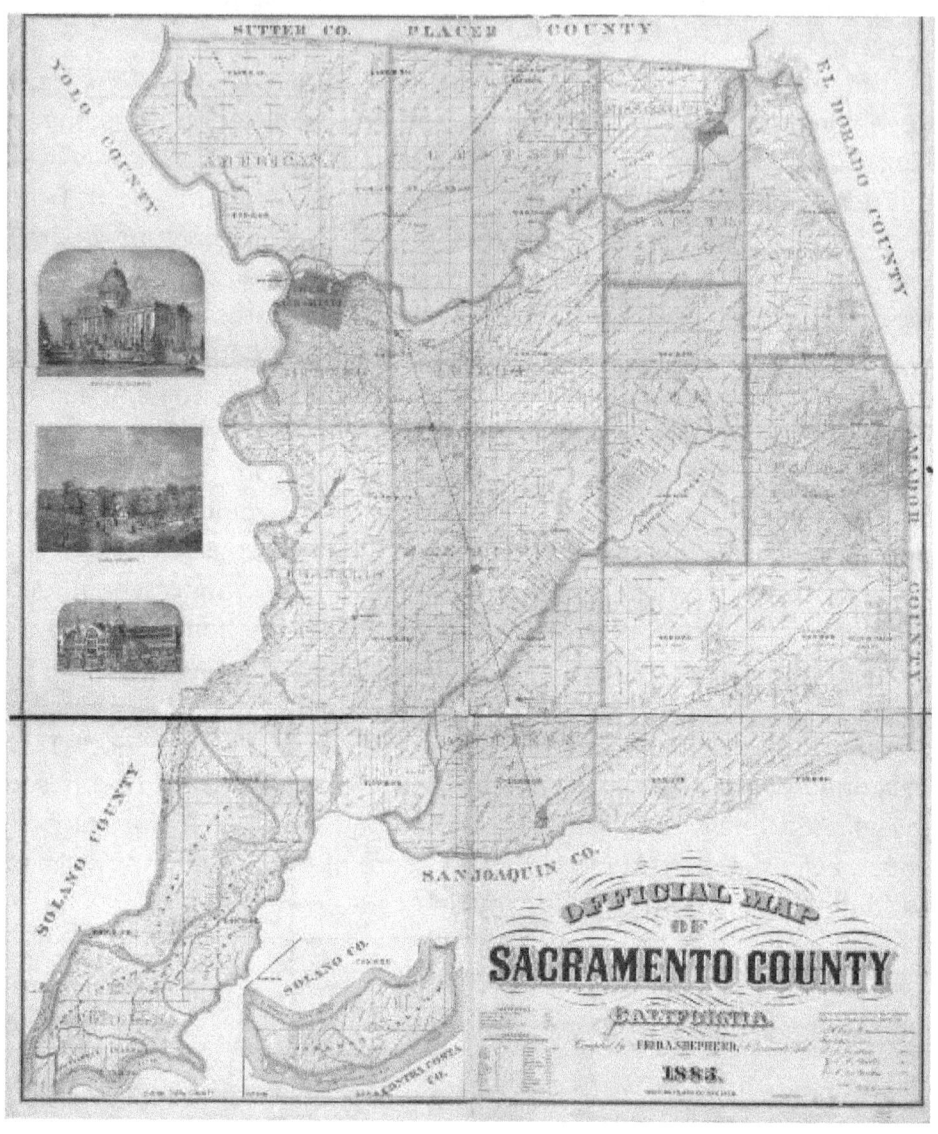

1885 Map of Sacramento County showing the old Mexican Land Grants and townships – From the Free online Smithsonian Museum Collection

A Geographical Round-Up

As the first European into the region, Lieutenant Gabriel Moraga found the confluence of the Sacramento and American Rivers in 1808, the very spot where I burned my tootsies in 1955. The journal kept by a padre on one of the early journeys to the confluence rhapsodized;
"Canopies of oaks and cottonwoods, many festooned with grapevines, overhung both sides of the blue current. Birds chattered in the trees, and big fish darted through the pellucid depths. The air was like champagne, and (the Spaniards) drank deep of it, drank in the beauty around them. 'Es como el sagrado sacramento!'" (It's like the Holy Sacrament)."

This is how the city and the county got their name. Moraga named the American River, Rio de las Llagas, or "River of Sorrow." His official diary notes that the name was chosen as a reference to the sufferings of his Lord, Jesus Christ during "the passion." One later historian claims that it was due to his later lack of success at re-capturing Indians escaping from the missions because once they gained the higher ground near Folsom they could disperse into the hills and elude the Spaniards forever.

I believe the former case because, at the time, all of the rivers and places of importance were given names from Catholic lore. Both the 1806 and 1808 diaries of his expeditions into the valley note friendly receptions from tribes he met. In one case, after initial shyness, an entire tribe marched into the Spanish camp as a regal procession and brought gifts of fish and grain. The priest accompanying him often converted one to over a dozen natives during contacts. Morago named the Sacramento River the Jesus-Maria before the permanent name was settled upon, after a written "benediction" upon reaching the junction of the present Sacramento and American rivers. He had previously named the Feather River, the Sacramento because it ran straight at the confluence while the Sacramento departs to the west for a short while before continuing north. The issues around escaping Indians came later after the mission systems were set up. But they were also pursued for cattle rustling, which became a particular problem the Spanish ranchos faced.

At the confluence of the Sacramento and American rivers was a Nisipoweinan village where Discovery Park is located today but on both banks of the American River. It even featured a cemetery mound. Known as the "Joe Mound," after a Portuguese farmer in the area who was called "Joe," it has been excavated. Findings show that the site had been continuously inhabited from as early as 1,000 BCE. Artifacts that mark their contact with Captain John A. Sutter** and his company dating from 1840 have been recovered also. Some miles to the east, out beyond the banks of the river that the Spanish Lieutenant Moraga had named the Sacramento, The Spook Tree had lived its long life in the north Sacramento County section that was all once part of the much larger Mexican Land Grant titled "Rancho Del Paso."

Captain John Augustus Sutter was not the first to receive a land grant in the Sacramento Valley. Before him in 1833, J. B. Cooper was granted the land known as Rio Ojotska, on the American River, three leagues east beginning at the Sacramento River.*[1] Cooper did not develop his grant and gave it up in 1835. Four years later, Sutter arrived and received the same land as New Helvetia. Sutter first allowed settlement on his grant north of the American River by John Sinclair, with Eliab and Hiram Grimes as absent partners, but then granted them that section as Rancho Del Paso with Mexican government approval. Eliab Grimes applied for the official grant and received it from Governor Manuel Mecheltorena in 1844.   Eliab Grimes had captained a merchant ship to and from Hawaii with Hiram as the firm E&H Grimes. Hiram would later own Rancho San Juan. Sinclair, who had worked for Sutter since 1840, lived on Sutter's land a bit east on the American River (originally called "Rio Ojotska" by the Indians), with his wife Mary in a ranch house beginning in 1843. After Eliab received the grant, they raised cattle and harvested wheat on the land. Eliam Grimes became a consequential man in San Francisco but died in 1848, leaving his share of the grant to his nephew, Hiram. But in 1849, three months after Eliab died, Sinclair sold his interest in the land to Hiram.

As the standard story of the Californios tells, so went the fortune of Rancho Del Paso. The owners spent lavishly and lived high. So in 1852, an immigrant from Denmark named Norris arrived in San Francisco in 1839 and established a profitable business in San Francisco bought the rancho from Hiram Grimes in 1852. Sinclair built the only ranch house two and a half miles east up the American River on the right bank.   For a long time, this was the only and first recognizable settlement to be reached by immigrants coming from the East.

Captain Sutter was known to be kindly and hospitable to new arrivals from the East, and as alcalde (sheriff) of the Sacramento District, he was the one who directly sent aid to the Donner party. (Note that the title "Captain" was often used interchangeably with "sheriff" as with the Texas Rangers etc.). The history of Gibson Ranch goes back to the early 1800s when the area now known as Rio Linda was part of Rancho Del Paso. At that time and in later years, the area began to be homesteaded by a few families and was called Dry Creek. In the 1870s, Sinclair allowed a family named Gibson to settle on the Rancho in the 1870s.*[1] Today, the Gibson Ranch near North Highlands and Antelope is the remnant of a once sprawling ranch and farm. The land passed through several owners until the 1950s when approximately 1,700 acres were owned by the R.H. Gibson family.   The County of

Sacramento purchased a portion of the property in 1962 from the Valley Investment Company and created Gibson Ranch Regional Park.

During the 1850s, Sacramento County became divided into townships, which were districts inside of the original Mexican land grants. In alphabetical order, those townships were Alabama, American, Brighton, Center, Cosumnes, Dry Creek, Franklin, Georgiana, Granite, Lee, Mississippi, Natoma, San Juan, and Sutter.

Some of the place names have remarkable origins. Elk Grove was so named because of many elk horns found in a grove of timber, near which in 1850, James Hall established his hotel and pained on its sign, an elk's head. The name of Florin was given to that locality by the late Judge Crocker in about 1864. The choice of that name was due to the great quantity of wildflowers to be seen in the fields. When the town was started in 1875, it received the same name. Folsom was named for J. L. Folsom, who died there on July 19[th,] 1855.

There was romance connected with the naming of Forest City in Sierra County, and it may not be amiss to mention in this connection the history of the name. The first store at the forks of the Oregon Creek was built by Samuel Hammond and was called Yomana store, from the bluff above the town, which was called by the name meaning "Sacred Hill." In 1853 a meeting was held by the citizens to select a name for the village. There was a vote for Forks of Oregon and Yomana. The matter was compromised by agreeing to call the town after the first woman settler. The first female resident was Mary Davis, wife of a banker. After her death, the town was called indiscriminately Forks of Oregon and Marietta. Davis soon sold out to a man named Captain Mooney, whose wife's name was Forest. Mrs. Mooney was an educated woman and contributed several articles to the Marysville paper. The articles were dated from Forest City. The editor did not know the location of that place but published the correspondence as it was sent in, and thus the name was used for the first time. Afterward, Mrs. Mooney called into consultation several of the leading citizens and succeeded in having the place formally named in Mary Davis' honor.

The name of Galt was suggested for the town when it was laid out. John McFarland, who suggested the name to Judge E. B. Crocker, from Canada, desired to name the place after Galt's town in Upper Canada, where he had served his apprenticeship. The Canadian village had been named in honor of Mr. Galt. The valley of Ione was named before the town was started. It owes its name to Thomas Brown, a lover of literature, who selected the name after one of the characters in The Last Days of Pompeii," by Bulwer Lytton. The town was first named "Bedbug," then "Freezeout," and finally, "Ione."
Natoma is an Indian name meaning "Clear Water." The name was given in 1850 to the Mormon Island post office on the suggestions of the late Judge A. P. Catlin. Afterward, the township was given the same name.

Sutterville was named after Captain John A. Sutter who gained an early land grant from the Mexican governor in California and built a fort by 1844.

Andrus Island was named after George Andrus, who died there in 1852. Rancho del Paso means "Ranch of the Pass." It was so named because it was the first rancho anyone would find after coming over the pass in the Sierras following the course of the Amerian River. It is also often alluded to as the Norris Grant since he had formerly owned the land (before Haggin).

One could say that the American River was named by trappers led by Jedediah Strong Smith, who explored in California and trapped fur between 1826 and 1829, and likely on the American River during the year 1927.   Smith and his party of trappers had arrived from New Mexico by crossing the Mojave Desert. Arrested in Los Angeles, he was instructed to leave immediately upon release. But Smith took an indirect route. It was reasonable. Who would willingly cross a desert again when fertile land with rivers that provided fur for the traps was available to the north? He found the mouth of the river that branched off the Sacramento, and followed its course, camping, and trapping, to eventually follow Indian trails up the Sierras but it is reported that he did not find a way over the pass. He may have spied Lake Tahoe as perhaps the first white man to see it. It is not certain whether he made it to a point that made the big lake visible, but one would think that hearing of such an "ocean" would have urged the ever-curious Smith to try to get a look. I like to imagine that he got on top of Pyramid Peak and saw it from there.

The first official sighting of Tahoe was made by Lieutenant John C. Fremont on February 14, 1844. But the immigrants that later began to arrive at Sutter's Fort have trickled down the trail that Smith had established at least at some higher point in the mountains on the western descent. Smith proceeded up through the coast range of California, which is rough going, to emerge somewhere around Crescent City. He then went north along the Oregon coast to arrive at Fort Vancouver, the western terminus of the Hudson Bay Fur Company, in August of 1828. Because of Smith, the later trickle of American settlers who began to return by the trail he had "blazed" along that river caused the Mexican Authorities to refer to it as "Rio de Americanos."

Hicksville was named after William Hicks (Uncle Billy), an early settler. Somehow, the appellation and only the appellation is all that remains of the town known for the Hicks that lived there. It was a regional slur when I was growing up. The famous local entertainer Dan Hicks took advantage of this during his career from the 1970s until his death in 2016, naming one album "Hicksville," and so on.

The Mokelumne River derives its name from a powerful tribe of Indians, the Mokelhos, who inhabited its lower banks and the adjacent territory. The Spaniards called it Rio de los Moquelmnos. The Cosumnes River was named for the Cosumnes tribe.

Morman Island was named after the Mormons, who settled there after two members passing through camped there and decided on a whim to try to pan for gold using their kitchenware and found pay dirt. Mormon Island became consequential in the history of California.

Routier was named after the Honorable Joseph Routier.

Rancho Del Paso

The "ranch of the pass" was the first rancho one found as they finished the descent from the Sierras. Cattle ranching was the early activity there as it was on many of the Sacramento County grants. The beef supplied the mines of the Sierras. No natives starved because of this fact. The record shows that they came to prefer beef over wild meat and cattle stealing was the initial cause of the Spanish and Mexican issues with them. Beef was highly profitable at the time cattle sold for as much as seventy-five dollars a head. However, due to the Californio's mismanagement of the ranches and a crash in prices due to the large cattle drives over the Sierras that ended up saturating the market, plus the rise of sheepherding Basque immigrants, the ranchos were universally in difficulty by 1856. Its death knell came after the floods of sixty-one and two and the droughts that followed during the next two years. The coup de grace was the "No Fence Law" of 1872.

After California became a state, the grants were "patented," that is, their legal state as private property was made official by the government. It was a slow process. In Norris's case, it took until 1858 to get his patent because the descendants of Eliab Grimes contested his will and, therefore, Norris' ownership of the land. This left Norris deeply in debt to his attorneys, James Ben Ali Haggin and Llyod Tevis, so he sold the rancho to them. So while Haggin might have legally swindled the rancho from Norris, he left a positive and powerful mark on Sacramento County's history. Happily, Norris went on to flourish in his other pursuits in Sacramento and San Francisco. A significant point of consequence for Antelope and North Highlands is that it remained intact as a piece of privately held land until 1910 as the last of the grant landholdings.

Up to then, it had been the home of the best thoroughbred racing horses of the time. James Ben Ali Haggin seems to have been named by a Freemason parent as Ben Ali is a section of the Shriners Temple in the order of degrees. And as I understand it, one only becomes a Shriner after reaching the 32nd degree. Haggin became the operator of a fabulous thoroughbred farm that supplied the best racing horses in America as breeding stock and Kentucky Derby winners. Haggin had the power to see to it that the new railroad would pass through his rancho property. Much of the traffic in later days was the transport of uncounted numbers of horses between Rancho Del Paso and Kentucky, and entire trains for horses only were often employed.

The ranch was divided into two sections, each with different functions. The "Arcade Section" included Haggin's railroad terminal located on what is now the intersection of Marconi Avenue and Auburn Blvd.
He arranged to have Southern Pacific cross his property so that he had a place on his ranch to serve as his shipping center for horses, featuring twenty-four barns, each of which could hold sixty-four stalls. The other section was called "The Bottom," which was close to the American River in the Watt Avenue and Arden Way corridor where Shelby Stables was later located with the horse track that was also used for motorcycle racing before the horse track at the old State Fairgrounds was used and Three Star Raceway in North Highlands came into being in 1958.

Here the most valuable thoroughbreds were kept on approximately 10,000 acres of paddocks. The Rancho also included a regulation mile race track and its own specially designed railroad cars used for moving horses to New York for auction. At its zenith, Rancho del Paso employed over 100 people and had more than 600 thoroughbreds.
In 1891, "The Rancho del Paso Land Company" corporation was formed by Haggin, and he began selling acreage to the Sacramento Valley Colonization Company for subdivision purposes. The deed

transfer took place on December 22, 1910, a year after he died at 91 years of age, and later the sale of 148.34 acres was sold to the Del Paso Country Club in 1916. During the turn of the century, the horse racing industry suffered a decline when the nation slumped into a devastating depression.   In 1905, Haggin discontinued breeding thoroughbreds for a stock farm for cattle.

The glory of the years of 1883 to 1905 ended abruptly when 600 of the finest horses in the world went up for auction as Haggin retired, must be imaged. The majority of the Rancho's land between the American River and what today is Del Paso Heights, where the barns were located, was a huge pasture for his magnificent horses. He sold off a few parcels in the northeast of the rancho to settlers intending to farm during those years.   These parcels may be identified on the 1885 County of Sacramento map. Andrew Finley's and the McBride parcels may be discerned among a collection of others near Antelope. This established Antelope as a farming community.

These earlier sales of land to the grain farmers took his place as the rancho owners found themselves in deep debt due to bad business decisions and extravagant, wasteful lifestyles. One might reflect upon the early days of the rancho, its gaiety, and the lifestyle's generosity. How beautiful the land and happy life must have been in those times! And so now, the farmers were established, and a new era of California history began.   This was the story of Rancho Del Paso, which only started to become subdivided in 1913 as the last of the massive grant holdings in Sacramento County. This was the piece of geography that I wandered on and wondered about as a boy in the 1950s and beyond. This is why the north region of Sacramento County was so vacant by the early 20th century while the south was dotted with towns and burgs, all bearing names such as Sheldon and Franklin, while others such as Hicksville, disappeared. Meanwhile, out in Rancho Del Paso's most neglected part, stood the solitary, ancient oak tree that would be transformed by circumstance, fire, and the imagination of children into The Spook Tree. My child's imagination did not yet plumb such depths of information. However, my main interest as a boy historian after the Civil War was the California Gold Rush. I soon began to gather up information. That was how I was; everything that looked old, or seemed strange, fascinated me. The funny thing is that they still do. These days as many former standing structures have been removed, built over, or those who would recall, less is available to examine and there are no old-timers left to question. That seems like a tragic loss to me. Yet there are records available for those who care to search them out.

One such standing structure was the white, four-walled blockhouse with no roof and a big shell blast hole through it off about fifty yards on a rise on the northeast corner of M Street and Walerga Road. I can find no record that explains the shell hole. Obviously, it was constructed for one-time use, perhaps when some important figure had visited and an artillery demonstration was performed. Camp Kohler did not log such details. The camp had a small arms firing range, and there were reports of the presence of tanks and artillery. Since tanks were there, I am going to surmise that they are responsible for the gaping holes. It was a direct hit. That shattered white blockhouse and Lead Hill were part of Kid Lore in those days and a mystery that I have yet to solve completely. Minor details, you could say. Maybe so, but once assembled, such information often provides the structure of a more significant revelation.

Up Walerga Road, the route to Roseville required a right turn onto U Street. By following the roadway, we would soon come to the option of turning right to the little incline that would take us over the tracks or just remaining on the road and finding Antelope, which we usually drove through with hardly a thought about it.

Before roads, waterways were the most common routes traveled and traded on or by. Dry Creek was a prominent element of the region as the only tributary water in the region. It runs west back toward Rio Linda, meandering across the countryside. At a point, it is cut off by U Street, and then magically picks up again on the other side of the street. It goes on until it gets to Steelhead Creek, which itself meanders south until it empties into the Sacramento River just up from the American River's mouth, similar to Rio Linda Creek. The mighty Sacramento River flows past Old Sacramento and towns of historical significance; Freeport, Clarksburg, Locke, Isleton, and Rio Vista, describing a hundred miles of sloughs and waterways in the delta, not that, unlike the bayou country of Louisiana. The complex even includes the Port of Stockton. The water leads on to Vallejo and finally San Francisco itself. So we could see Antelope connected by Dry Creek, to Steelhead Creek, into the junction of that vital river near the American River's mouth, out to the world beyond the Golden Gate.

Water is Everything

As water courses trace history, this critical natural geography of the little tributary of Dry Creek is perhaps why it came to be a part of Antelope's story as the closest connecting body of water. Was it due to the antelope frolicking on the prairie, or is it that one settler recalled his ship's name? There is no record, except for the vessel of that name that landed in Sacramento in 1850. The most substantial claim for naming the American River itself is Captain John Sutter as the watercourse that brought American pioneers tumbling into the valley up to his fort's gates. Still, it might have come from the Mexican authorities who noted the Smith trapping party some years before as "Rio de Los Americanos."

Fittingly, a rivulet contributing to that greater flow provided the first public school name in Antelope's vicinity. Dry Creek Union Elementary was established by Andrew Finley when he donated the land sometime after 1913. He did this because the farmers didn't want to send their kids all the way to the Center Joint School, which was located near PFE Road, on an essential but lonely dirt road that eventually became Watt Avenue. As it is, Willis notes both Center Joint and Dry Creek Joint schools as existing in 1913 when his history of the county of Sacramento was published. These two schools gave rise to the eventual Grant Joint Union School District. The district spanned the management of public educational facilities from Grant

Union High School in Del Paso Heights, out to most of the old American and Center Townships of old Rancho Del Paso.

Interestingly, the government agreed to pay the donated value back to the family if the building ceased to be a school. I have it on direct authority that in 2018, the government reneged on the promise. (Reader, please note here; that the government has a long history of breaking agreements with everyone, regardless of race, color, or creed, and you can take that to the bank, but not the money. (See what I did there))? This is one of the ironies of democracy; the tyranny of the majority; the thing Socrates hated, now with bureaucracy added.

In those days and before the big changes after 1973, we called that continuation of U Street, U Street. Today, from Watt Avenue to the east, U Street is one of several named Antelope. Antelope North Road and Old Antelope North Road is a no-go road remnant that used to be the only passage through Antelope before 1973. The old San Juan Grant was known as the Mississippi Township in the county plan with the remaining two districts of the old Rancho Del Paso Grant, Center, and American Townships. In the 19th century, until I don't know when, Antelope Road was the only road that exited Sacramento's city and continued directly, near the line of the railroad track, out to Antelope. It seems to have been renamed Roseville Road at some point. Today, Antelope Road is a four-lane overpass over the railroad tracks into Citrus Heights. But for a long time, Antelope Road had been the major thoroughfare along the line. I wonder if there had been any iron horse versus horse races on that road, a la "Dodge City?" Do you think that Higgins or some of his hands on the rancho could have resisted that temptation?

On the roadways near the railroad tracks, there were many sources of entertainment for the roving eye. Aside from spotting a rare bum on a train, there were the almond trees in the orchards by the road with birds flitting around in them. But the sight that always got my attention was the ancient barn standing just before the sharp left turn into Antelope "proper" with the general store off to the right. On that barn was an old advertisement; "Dr. Pleasants' Little Liver Pellets." Yum, I bet they were a treat. I always wondered how long that message had been on the side of that barn because the paint was old and faded, and I never heard my father ever say anything about liver pills one way or the other. He wasn't that kind of doctor, but I bet Dr. Pleasant wasn't, either. Whoever heard of anyone named "Pleasant," anyway? Much later in life, I learned that long before even my father's time, all those sorts of pills were mainly cocaine. That's how old it was! I was innocent of such knowledge then, just like Dr. Pleasants' patients and probably old Dr. Pleasant himself, maybe, if he was a real live doctor at all. I figured that the pills were probably manufactured by someone with a distinctly unpleasant-sounding name like "Dr. Snidely Whiplash" or some such. But I liked the rhyme of the deceptive advertisement, so it stuck with me.

The only other structure in Antelope was the Grange building. With the history of the Grange in Minnesota and Wisconsin, where it began, I have to wonder if there were serious, near-violent negotiations with the railroad, as there were in those states. The Grange had to be secretive to hide its plans for negotiating shipping rates with the railroads. It was serious enough that they imitated the Freemasons' oath and passwords, many of which were likely already members. Was Leland Stanford the robber baron he was accused of being? Did he deal fairly with the grain growers of Antelope? These secrets might have been held in Antelope Grange's archives, but that building was removed in a singular moment in 1973.

Once arrived at the railroad crossing, we'd find out if our fate for the next ten minutes or so would be to sit in a line of gas-burning vehicles and watch the boxcars for bums as the long train went by never in any great hurry. It was slowing down as it entered the switching yard. We knew about bums from very early on. Where this early knowledge was acquired, I have no recollection. I prefer the term "hobo," but apparently, there is a difference between a bum, a tramp, and a hobo. Hobo is an anachronism for "homeless boy."

I gather that "bum" is at the bottom of the hierarchy. The traditions of these perpetual travelers with the Hobo Codes, and the Hobo Code of Ethics, have their origin in the original building of the transcontinental railroad and the Civil War. Veterans were allowed to ride home by hitching on. Some of them didn't find homes to return to and went west, looking for something. Because of vagrancy laws that were originally aimed at clearing out men who didn't want to work, or just could not find work, these denizens of the road took to erecting camps that remained somewhat permanent, except when a gang of railroad "bulls" would set upon it to disrupt the illegal passenger flows on their freight lines. By the event of the Great Depression in the 1930s, what had begun as a benevolent practice following the Civil War became a war of perception between capitalists and communists. However, the story is more complex than that. Not everyone owned a horse or a car. The fact is that public funds bailed out the railroads time and time again in the 19th century. It was planned by the railroad magnates and it was how the West was actually won, with the taxpayer's money.*[1] So it wasn't exactly wrong for one to believe that the rails were a sort of public domain, well established by the time of the Great Depression.

As popular media reminded us a few years back, even the most respectable people might be "hit by a train," while hanging out around the rails, looking for a ride to the next town, state, or nation. Some just wanted to explore. Others were psychological victims of war, likely sufferers of PTSD before it was understood. Some just never stopped looking or never found what they were hoping to find. The term "Hobo" is said to have several origins, but as for "bum" and "tramp," a bum never worked, but a Tramp was originally a migrant worker. Utah Phillips was known to use the terms interchangeably, so maybe this is all too fussy, but Woody Guthrie was a hobo, and Jack Kerouac was a tramp. In our timeframe, the Roseville Switching Yard, riders were not hassled. They carved out caves in Lead Hill for shelter during storms. They never went into the nearby communities or did any harm. All the same, my sisters and I were under strict orders to stay away from the tracks and bums, I mean hobos, and we did, mostly, so the story may have been a lie meant to instill a fear of the iron rails. The truth is that the hobos had a code of ethics that included never harming anyone in the places they frequented and violators inside the "brotherhood" were dealt with via their own sense of justice. This is not to say bad things did not happen on the rails or in the jungles. Of course, they did. The point is that it was more of a haven for those down on their luck. It also became a generator and source of folkways and Americana. Bob Dylan wrote a song that might have been an epitaph to all such men. An excellent version was recorded by Rod Stewart on his Gasoline Alley album;

> "As I was out walking on a corner one day
> I spied an old hobo, in a doorway he lay
> His face was all grounded in the cold sidewalk floor
> And I guess he'd been there for the whole night or more.
> Only a hobo, but one more is gone
> Leaving nobody to sing his sad song
> Leaving nobody to carry him home
> Only a hobo, but one more is gone.
> A blanket of newspaper covered his head
> As the curb was his pillow, the street was his bed
> One look at his face showed the hard road he'd come
> And a fistful of coins showed the money he bummed.
> Only a hobo, but one more is gone
> Leaving nobody to sing his sad song
> Leaving nobody to carry him home
> Only a hobo, but one more is gone.
> Does it take much of a man to see his whole life go down
> To look up on the world from a hole in the ground
> To wait for your future like a horse that's gone lame
> To lie in the gutter and die with no name?
> He was only a hobo, but one more is gone
> Leaving nobody to sing his sad song
> Leaving nobody to carry him home
> Only a hobo, but one more is gone."

Beyond the Shade of the Spook Tree

A growing child has many distractions and interests, and I was no exception. The Space Race was real to us because we knew what the big noise and glow in the night sky meant when Aerojet was testing a rocket engine. I learned about Sputnik because Uncle Ross and my father had held a loud complaining discussion about it as they worked on that landscaping project in front of our home, where I later found that poor baby bird. When Telstar was launched and made its successful orbits, everyone was elated. I watched the launch from Cape Canaveral, which was broadcast live before going to school one morning. The song was playing everywhere. Listening to it now, it recalls such a glorious, hopeful moment. Space was the new frontier, and we were all part of it. Science fiction movies and novels abound. I was reading Ray Bradbury at an early age. Somehow the hit TV series, "The Twilight Zone," fits into it all. Jackie and I watched afternoon matinees on TV such as "Missile to the Moon."

Jackie and I often imitated astronauts shooting for the moon. Sitting on our chairs at our stations in my bedroom/spaceship, we'd imitate the agony of a multiple G Force with screams of pain as we left the earth's atmosphere (leaving Earth has got to hurt). Then, we'd pretend to steer the room toward our goal, a moon filled with rock monsters as we saw in the film. We fought them in the open moonscape, hiding in the shadows of the rock formations to avoid exposure to the sun that could incinerate us in seconds. Between such games, school, and home life, my personal interest in the Spook Tree remained so from the time I last saw Bobby, and he and his friend related their stories until, well, now.

Still strange to me is that nothing of that white blockhouse, Lead Hill, or even notice of that burned oak tree, standing as prominently on the landscape as it was, ever mentioned by my parents or any adult I ever heard. Camp Kohler only very occasionally came up in the early days and virtually never later on even though Kohler Elementary School was one of the two first schools built in North Highlands.

I always think of the old man who sits telling his kids or grandkids about the meaning of landmarks in their region, tall tales, maybe, but occasionally one told with such force and conviction that the listener knows it must be true. The lack of such stories in my time came from new arrivals who knew nothing of their new home. They might have tales of their former regions as mine did, but none of the places I grew up around. I had to do that on my own, and I have all of my life since then. I was always an attentive listener. Later, when I began to meet old men in their element, during fishing trips on the Sacramento River, or even later, when we owned our property near Placerville when I met my first veteran from The Great War. He had been on the German side, and his name was Schmidt. He and his wife were kind people. They lived on a little farm as self-sufficiently as any could imagine. My father remarked on this with admiration that echoed in me as I dreamed of owning such a place someday.

Later during a hunting trip to Wentworth Springs, I met another vet, Miles Curran, who had been with the Marines and, as he told me, met Kaiser Wilhelm because he was a correspondent by the end of the war.

Usually, when it came to adults, the ones I heard in the early days were mostly among our church's congregation at the time. We attended Sunday school after the regular church service. It was the after-service mingling in front of the church where I listened to the adults talk. One memorable one was a cowboy who looked, dressed, and talked just like those on TV. One Sunday, he decided to show my sisters and me how he rolled a cigarette, cowboy style. He got the paper out in one hand and tapped on tobacco so that the crumbles trickled from the white cloth bag he carried in his left shirt pocket onto the little white paper. He deftly rolled it with the fingers of one hand, a skill no doubt acquired from fixing a smoke while chasing bad guys on horseback. The bad part came when he stuck the thing in his mouth and pulled it out all slimy with his saliva. We weren't counting on that show. That was when my father intervened and informed the cowhand that he didn't want him to teach my kids about smoking. He was polite about it. The old boy apologized and went away. Like most adults, especially men of the time, my father smoked cigarettes. The only difference was that he used the store-bought type. It's a dirty habit," they'd say, and take another drag. We used to complain to him about how his smoke filled the car whenever we were traveling together. He finally opened the wing of the window, which sucked out most of it. But the odor remained and lingered at all times. It was part of the reality of my life. Anyway, I didn't know what the term hypocrisy meant, but I understood the event's contradiction at the time. As an adult, I understand why my father didn't want tobacco romanticized by a cowboy as an impression on us. Back then, growing up was full of "do as I say, not as I do" moments. But I never cared about the smoking; it was the man's speech and manner and his type that held an allure for me. There was an air about him that was genuine, while others seemed to be presenting themselves in masks of propriety.

One other major related event of those early church congregation days was when an all-day picnic was held at a member's ranch, maybe this very cowboy's home. It was a way out from North Highlands, somewhere up in the foothills. The adults did whatever it was they usually do that day. Still, one part of it was a hike that I also took with my father, which took us up a path along a ravine amongst many trees, and later, a hayride, and marshmallow roasting on fire pits dug for family groups in an open area. Earlier in the day, they had all of the kids lined up to fish in a pond full of sunfish like crappie and bluegill. A man handed me a pole and set a piece of hotdog on the hook, and told me how to throw it out into the water. It wasn't long before I had what seemed like a big fish in my hands. I took it to show my parents, but I couldn't find them. By that time, I didn't know what to do with it, and a dorsal fin spine had pierced my hand, and it was bleeding. I ran into a kid who had fed his to a barn cat. So I gave it to another unoccupied cat, and we watched them for a while. I don't know why the adults did not take the fish and recycle it. I think that is what they were doing. There weren't fish piled up for the cats, after all, and these were probably not that big even for sunfish. I must have gotten away from them before they could relieve me of the poor fish. But this was just the beginning of fish and fishing in my life. And I don't mean the terrible fish sticks that my mother was trying to feed us every Friday at the time, even though we weren't Catholic. I mean fishing for real fish, big fish, in the Sacramento River.

The Outdoor Sports were a Family Tradition

My father was a sportsman, extracted from the Old Northwest traditions, where he grew up. We came from those French Canadians who settled in that area long before they were states of the Union. "Quebecois," they are called. After the end of the French and Indian War, my fifth great-grandfather began bringing supplies to the Detroit region and picking up furs for the Western Fur Company in 1756. My fourth great-grandfather settled in that vicinity by 1800. Many "Voyageurs" as the fur trapping explorers were called, settled in Michigan and Wisconsin, and often with Indian wives. There were so many of these cases, in fact, that it led to a new tribal designation, the Metis. Life in the Great Lakes region focused on hunting and fishing as a supplement to farming.

This necessity lasted well into the 20th century for many in the Old Northwest. The expectations of hunting for dinner, etcetera, were still common throughout much of America. It was only maybe twenty-five years earlier in his life when he told me about it. Life had changed a great deal, but that experience did not ruin my father's or his brother's love of the outdoors and the sports that had only recently been acts of survival for them. It was part of their identity, and they passed some of that on to me so that when I was deemed old enough to go on hunting trips, I felt as if I was pursuing a tradition, not a deer. It was a matter of family honor to hit the mark "with one shot." I only realized later that I had touched the "holy rock" in 1961 when during our stay with my Uncle Reg and Aunt Becky at Bundy Hill, Cousin Reg had taught me to shoot one day.*[1]   One morning, Uncle Reg disappeared with his car and returned with boxes of .22 ammunition and paper targets. We spent the afternoon learning how to shoot.

I learned how to shoot at the same place my grandfather had practiced and where my father had performed his desperate hunting forays. Myself, I didn't even care about killing a deer, and as it turned out, I never did because I never had the opportunity, except once.

On a trip with a group, Martine's best friend's father, Richard, who was notably, married to a Cherokee woman, shot a deer for me after filling his own tag. Thanks a lot. How did he know that I was coming up that ravine? The fact is that I flushed that deer to him. I remember seeing the flash of the buck I as came up the rocky draw. I think I would have got him, but maybe not. At least he taught me how to field dress a deer. This turned out to be the worst season I had ever experienced, despite his daughter, who was Martine's best friend, naming me "The Great White Hunter," the next Monday as we were going together to school in Martine's first car, a little English Ford. And it was certainly not because Richard killed my deer for me. It was because this had occurred on the opening weekend of the season. After that, there was no more reason for those weekend forays into the high country with the excuse of hunting deer.

I later figured out that I didn't want to shoot a deer at all, just be in the mountains. So I became a high-altitude backpacker where I couldn't drive on old logging roads or pioneer trails in the lower Sierras, even though I still did that, too. But I had been up there on a motorcycle already. I was on the first motorcycle crossing of the Sierras in 1967 when a group of trail riders who worked at McClellan AFB organized a ride from Foresthill to Lake Tahoe cross-country. I was the youngest rider on the trip. By then, I had fairly forgotten about deer hunting. My sights were set on the race track. I found I just did not particularly wish to kill deer. I realized that what I loved about hunting was simply being out there, camping under the stars, and waking up before dawn to tramp out into the forest. Watching dawn break, seeing the sun come up in the Sierras, listening to the first sounds of nature, and the awakening of birds, squirrels, and anything else that might happen, along with exploring new places with historical place names; a more spiritual appreciation of nature, you might say. But the hunting years came later when I was a teen.

First was fishing, fishing for striped bass in the Sacramento River. (Later, I enjoyed trout fishing in the high country). Our fishing adventures on the Sacramento River began long before the time of fish finders, scientifically designed lures, or even Atomic Strike bait oil, the forerunner of the multi-million dollar fish scent industry. There weren't even boats with special seats for the comfort of an old-timer's butt. Similarly, there were no such things as bait wells, fish boxes, or any of that. We didn't even have "sound systems" on the boats. We had to make do with folding chairs and a small transistor radio, which was the new, big sensation in those days. That was how it was in the early times, before the social outbreak of voluntary tinnitus via loud music of which I was a willing victim. On that account, everything my mother warned me about turned out to be true.

The gear was often a Penn Model 60 bait caster and a "boat rod," which was usually a six-and-a-half-foot fiberglass rod with just enough guides to hold the line near the rod and take it to the tip. The job then was to sit there for hours staring at the tip, waiting for a strike. (And we liked it). But in those days, I think even my Dad's gear was inadequate. He passed his rig onto me once I began to fish and he graduated to a better rig; the new high-tech Mitchell spinning reel set it on a nice newly developed spinning rod.

SPACEMAKER 7

Cyclists Complete Trans-Sierra Tour

One flat tire, a broken shifting fork, and some bent brake pedals were encountered during their torturous 200-mile trans-Sierra motorcycle trek, but twenty hardy motor cyclists--most of them from McClellan--came home with hardly a scratch.

The tour, conducted last weekend between Forest Hill and River Ranch, was over terrain that tested the skill of each rider.

Wayne Melvold, a group leader, said that several cyclists--not a part of his group but interested in ac-companying them--decided on turning back after glimpsing the hazardous descent to Eldorado Creek. "It is a rough stretch," he said.

Bob Deston, another group leader, took 8mm moving pictures with a special camera attached to the top of his crash helmet. He operated the camera with controls he designed especially for this purpose.

They did not indicate when their next tour would be. But predictions are that several more cyclists will try to join with them.

The flat tire mentioned was Dad. The author rode many extra miles to procure a tire patch kit from another rider and bring it back to his otherwise, desperately stranded father. – from the author's personal collection of old stuff

My participation began when we started to fish from boats. I was handed down the weird, space-age-looking spinning reel and a flimsy rod that probably would have broken if I had hooked onto anything of size. There has always been sturgeon in the Sacramento River. As a fun note, I recall stopping at Lee's Bait and Tackle on Greenback Lane in Orangevale in those early days. They sold prepared cane rods with a bobber and hook affixed. My father bought one and we took it to Folsom Lake on what must have been our first family trip there. I must make the further notation that in the late sixties, my Uncle Ralph bought Lee's and renamed it "Doc's Tackle Box." After he was diagnosed with multiple sclerosis, he sold it and it became Wild Sports. Spinning reels were a fairly new technology at this point in angling history.

As for the boats, any boat would do once the graduation from bank fishing had been achieved. I made this achievement without ever having fished at all. That was because my father took me along on the first few bank fishing trips on the Sacramento River. I was merely a companion to my father. We were soon joined by an amiable man he called O'Brien. He worked with my father at the airfield.

Daddy had settled into a swing-shift job after a run of moonlighting occupations that ran from taxi driving to a stint at Douglas Aircraft out beyond the new Rancho Cordova development. My life would later intersect with the developer of that suburb and owner of The Cordova Lodge, in a way that is connected to the eventuality of The Prairie City SVRA/Park.

Douglas and Aerojet had been wisely located out there on that prairie land where rows of piled-up rocks seemed to go on forever to my young eye. Hardly a thing grew in that wasteland, so it provided a few thousand acres as an effective firebreak for testing the giant engines for the Mercury Space Program of those years. The rocks were the remaining evidence of the gold dredging that had gone on into the early 1950s by The Capital Dredging Company via a barge-supported dredge. Many years after that, the dredge had remained stranded and derelict on a dry lake, visible just east of Sunrise Avenue. It ran off south beyond The Lincoln Highway into the stony countryside of dredge tailings within view of one of the Aerojet engine test pads.

I knew about it because of the Christmas party held at Douglas while my father was employed there with Uncle Ralph. It was a family event. They had a clown in the parking lot where he was roving as a greeter. Of all the kids around, including her siblings, he strode straight to my giggly little sister, Paulette, and offered her a peanut. As she reached out to seize the treat, the clown quickly stuffed it into his mouth and crunched it up vigorously with his face inches from hers to emphasize his intentional trickery. She burst into laughter, as we all did. Good job, Clarabell. Nearby were the massive cement pads where they tested jet engines destined for the Mercury program space missions. We knew that, even then, which made being there even more special. At night sometimes, we'd go outside when we heard their roar, twenty miles away, and the sky out to the southeast was lit up, glowing with an orange radiance.

Just before the new job at McClellan, a kind of community event occurred that turned my attention, and perhaps the entire community's attention, back to McClellan Air Force Base and, for me, the Spook Tree. My mom had been working at McClellan before we moved to North Highlands. It had become routine; my father ran his practice in the morning but left for his job by the mid-afternoon. He had sectioned part of the living room and den using a curtain to serve as his office. Before McClellan, he had held several evening jobs that ranged from taxi driving to working at Douglas Aircraft, then selling hearing aids at Sears. Various babysitters filled the few-hour gap of parental supervision. Momma got home in the early evening, made dinner, and then waited, dozing on the couch, until Daddy got home not too long after midnight. A major aeronautical catastrophe at McClelland on the landing strip, or instead of its approach, occurred while my uncle and aunt were staying with us after just arriving from Michigan to settle in near us. It was the wreck of a Connie, a Lockheed Constellation. They served as reconnaissance support for the Strategic Air Command. They had been fitted with a high aerodynamic dome over the mid-section like a giant, oblong pillbox with a curved top. An older kid had told me about them and what they were doing. That day, one had not made it to the runway. For some reason, it was broken in two, lying in state, in an open area, almost up to PFE Road. The entire family, plus our uncle and aunt, piled in the car, and we headed out to see the wreck.

It was an event, and many had come to the show. It was spring. I recall the green field as we walked out to the wreck. We drove up Watt Avenue, north past U Street, and past the Spook Tree, which I marked to the east as we passed to the west of it this time.

As it was a clear day, the larger picture might be seen of the formidable presence of the dead monument, the Spook Tree, with a train passing behind it a short distance away, and the snowy Sierras and Pyramid Peak further off in the background. Once there, we found many cars were parked along the narrow two lanes of Watt Avenue, a country road. For some reason, the plane had not made it to the beginning of the landing strip. It was probably a half-mile short, going down in a field. Cars were parked along Watt Avenue out past U Street, where the plane had crashed. The path across the field to the wreck had already been trodden by many feet before us. The way out to the wreck was not unlike ants marching to and from their colony.

We arrived and walked around it, peering into the broken hulk's remains, but we bore back no booty on our return, save the awkward wonder of the disaster. It had the same vacant feeling I got from the Spook Tree. Some tragedy had occurred, but I didn't know how or why it had happened. Once there, the hulk of the plane impressed me with its size. The front was some way ahead of the rear section. I heard someone saying that men had been killed jumping from the plane as it was skidding, but I never learned more about it, ever. And back, across that field and beyond, stood the Spook Tree, the silent observer of another tragedy.

The time came when an opening at McClellan forced my father, with his wife and four children to support, to take what would first be a swing-shift job at McClellan doing sheet metal work on the fighter jets. That eventually led to a managerial daytime job in the air material management department doing a job that a man with a college degree of any kind might secure in those days.   But while he was a sheet metal worker, the strain of doing double time to retain a practice in a shared office further up toward Country Club Center on Watt Avenue led to a heart attack at the young age of thirty-eight. He spent a few days in the hospital, and he recovered within a short time. Not long after that, he told me that he promised himself to enjoy life more.

So he gave up his struggling practice and swing shift work at McClellan as a sheet metal worker for a daytime job after applying for a career in the Air Material Management department. He always said that the other doctor stole his practice while he was out. His wife called all his patients and told them he was no longer available. Life got better for us all after that. He only returned to practice after retiring from "The Base" as a GS14 in 1975. Between his Naval Service during the war and his time at the airfield, he had his twenty years in and could take his retirement pension. What enjoying life meant at the time were more fishing trips and the beginning of my parents' practice of once-a-month weekend trips to Lake Tahoe or Reno. I remember that my Father was always "working on a system" for the dice table. He retained a bit of that 19th-century tendency to believe in practical magic; the idea that ways around the commonly held wisdom could be found. And there were "urban legends" that were centuries old by then, like the work of an alchemist, or the psychic. The psychic craze that began in the 19th century began with people like Madame Blavatsky and perhaps finished with W.T. Stead, who after decades of promoting Spirituality through his popular publication, The Psychical Quarterly, failed to predict his own demise as he went down with the Titanic. It all saw a revival in the sixties, but its influence went in all sorts of directions via the magic show and old-time card shark as circuses with their carny acts continued to roam the land. And some believed it possible to defy the elements.

Daddy's Invention

We all have our faults. Most of us know that even the most brilliant people often have personality and even perception flaws. Tesla displays this with his pigeon, for example, or maybe his ideas about electricity transfer through the atmosphere creating free energy for all forever. Well, my father believed, throughout his entire life as far as I know that he had the secret for the elusive "Perpetual Motion Machine."

At seven years of age, I became aware of his little project when one day, on the way to a colleague's home for a discussion about something important he passed his secret on to me. Taking a dramatic tone he said, "Son, I want you to pay attention to this because if anything happens to me, I want you to understand the principle so that you can complete the project." Quite a charge to lay on a seven-year-old, don't you think? Well, I did my best. As we sat at Dr.

Gaines's kitchen table (all important plans were made around kitchen tables in those days), I listened and did my best to follow the conversation. I don't remember much about what Dr. Gaines said, but I do remember what my father said, up to a point at least. See, the design was this wheel with spokes spaced every so often. At the end of the spokes, a weight on a pivot bar would cause a weight shift forward or back. This weight, my father contended would reach "noon" and then the weight would drop because of gravity and pull the wheel down. Okay, I could see that. But then, the wheel was supposed to keep doing this forever. I saw a problem. As I sought to understand the contraption, I could see that as that weight shifted at "noon" on the wheel, the corresponding weight at the six o'clock spoke did not shift but remained in its position. It further seemed to me that it would remain in that position until it reached noon on the wheel. So the force of gravity, being equally distributed, would not allow the wheel to turn because the "light side" could not rise higher than three o'clock at best. After all, the wheel would be in balance at that point.

What was I missing? Surely, I was missing something, but I could not identify it. Although it seemed that it was all "beyond me," I could not get over the deep conviction that amounted to an intuitive understanding of Newton's Law of Gravity. This caused confusion and doubt in me, but that same intellectual hesitation, made me look at everything more carefully. Anyone would have said that I was a quiet, pensive child. I only relaxed and had fun when with trusted peers, and only intimate with trusted friends.

Over the years and then at high school, I had occasionally taken note of contradicting examples, whenever anything related to science and physics was presented, like Newton's Laws of Gravity and the Laws of Thermodynamics. I also knew by then that my father was capable of error and if I wanted to know the truth, I would have to find it for myself. By 1972, my father had assembled a metal monstrosity he kept on our sheltered patio. I recognized the design that he had explained to me years ago. It didn't move. Once, a man came by in 1972, during the six months that my parents were separated. He was doing an electrical job for my mother. He remarked that he had seen all sorts of attempts at perpetual motion machines. So, this was not a secret!

It certainly wasn't. Over the years, every time I met a physicist, and I met a number of them, two as friends, I would ask their opinion about perpetual motion machines. The last one I asked gave the most illuminating answer of all. He was a former supervisor at Northrop-Grumman who had retired to my town and ran a computer shop. I hired him to teach me how to design web pages. We later went on many motorcycle rides in Marn and Sonoma Counties, which had some great backroads, as well as the magnificent State Highway One. I had already picked his brain regarding String Theory. When I put the perpetual motion machine question to him he repeated some stuff about the law of gravity and thermodynamics and said, "Not in this dimension, at least." There might be a place where everything is backward and gravity is random or can be manipulated, but not in this universe.

Along the way to his statement, I had done my own research. From my first exposure in 1959, I gathered evidence from experience, which went slowly for years. Before my friend's "final" answer, I had come to the same conclusion after taking a course in astronomy and physics as part of requirements for entry to Chiropractic College. Also, along the way, I found the history of perpetual motion machine invention and the big scandals of the 19th century in the U.S. I also found a very amusing insert in a not well-known Shirley Temple film, "Miss Annie Rooney" wherein her struggling but adoring father, explains to her how all will be fine once he perfects his perpetual motion machine!

All of this proved to me that my doubt as a seven-year-old had been a good thing because it had kept me searching. As noted above, anyone can have gaps in their information and understanding. Without information, we are certain to make mistakes in understanding, and the less real information we have, the more often we will make those errors. That is why inquiry is the real perpetual motion of civilization. This is why it was philosophy, not superstitious doctrines, that led to progress and gains, allowing civilization to rise and conquer ignorance and suffering better than any other method in human history. But the same laws that govern physics also govern the biological mass that is the human brain. Consciousness, as Julian Jaynes postulated, must be developed in every new generation. This is why effort is required to maintain civilization, let alone advance it. And it is also why tearing it down is so easy, and deadly.

The Overbalanced Wheel. Perhaps the earliest recorded attempt at perpetual motion was presented by renowned medieval mathematician Bhaskara in the 12th century. The Indian philosopher proposed an "overbalanced" wheel in which weights would swing on one side, applying a greater torque to keep the wheel spinning. A short study of the wheel in motion reveals the cause of failure. One side of the wheel will always have more weight, thus keeping it motionless unless an outside force is applied continuously.

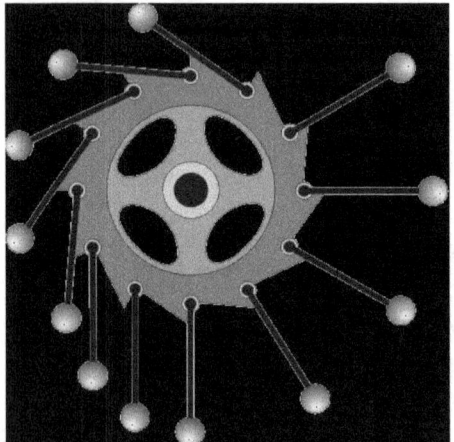

Later, in the 1970s, my father invented something that worked. He designed and patented a device that made adjusting large or difficult low back cases much easier. That time, he used Newton's Law of Gravity correctly and applied it in his field of expertise.

Fishing – Nature's Lesson in Philosophy

All of this made for family stories later on, but the most memorable to me was the fishing trips. They began after my father got the "steady" job at McClellan. O'Brien was his friend from work. He was our first fishing companion starting in 1958. The ritual of a fishing trip saw us up before dawn, then the drive downtown to pick up O'Brien, proceed through town, crossing Broadway down Freeport Boulevard, and finally winding down the levy to Freeport, where there was little more than a little bait and tackle shop. A café operated across the road. Amazingly, they are still there today. They were connected to the marina. For me, just the walk up the funny stairs to the railroad tracks at the top, always making the required look in both directions before the descent down even funnier stairs. That primitive stair in those days consisted of planks of wood with small wood strips nailed across it to provide some traction for a steady ascent. I called them "lubber stairs." I believe I picked up that word from the Robert Newton film version of "Treasure Island," which had repeated showings on afternoon television several times during the summers. Paulette used the name after she began to come with us as my buddy. In those years, Paulette really was my buddy. We even shared the same bedroom until I something changed around her twelfth year and she became simultaneously boy-crazy.

At the bait shop, Dad would buy some foot-long-frozen sardines, which would be wrapped on the counter with newspaper and tied with string. Once at our spot, one of the fish would be taken out of the wrapping, laid on a cutting board, and cut into maybe two-inch square pieces which we passed the hook through two or three times to get it fixed well. Then we wrapped the bait with the thread in hopes of preventing it from separating from the hook during casting or while we would sit for hours, waiting for a wandering "striper" to take a nibble and maybe a good enough bite to hook it.

The rig would be tossed by the fisherman out as far from the bank as possible. Then, he'd sit back and watch the tip, a practice requiring patience and concentration. It was a long time between bites, and I mean years. I learned patience, but eventually, years later, it paid off. Even though fishing on that river was all about sitting for hours, I was never bored. I loved it out there. I noticed everything. I heard everything.

The Sounds Weren't Silence

Quiet really only amplifies the less noticed. The most insignificant things interested me. Besides, the radio was almost always on. So it was while on the river that I heard of Clark Gable's and then Marilyn Monroe's deaths. The sound of the radio as the music wafted out over the water, unimpeded, enhanced sound clarity, and even echo amplification as its sound bounced off the river banks on its way to my ears. I could hear every nuance of a song, despite the low power and tiny speakers. Between Leonard Bernstein, Elvis, The Platters, Surf, and the British Invasion, the fifties, and sixties were a very eclectic and creative time for music. By the fifth grade, I was hooked on classical music as well. After school, I'd switch between Ravel's "Bolero," Rimsky-Korsokoff's "Capriccio Espagnol," and Beethoven's Fourth Symphony.

I suffered from repeated and chronic "earworm" music infections. But I clearly recall that the first earworm I ever experienced was as a two or three-year-old on P-Street. It was Doris Day's "A Guy is a Guy." The first song I remember really liking was "In the Mood." I remember my mother playing it on the Zenith Cobra-Matic AM radio/record player and telling her that I liked it. AM signals were clear in those days because the airways were not as overwhelmed as they are today. I am sure my parents enjoyed the instrumentals such as "Canadian Sunset" and "Blue Tango." But they were impressed onto my mind enough to cause me to catalog them in recent years along with a huge amount of period recordings. Sometimes, like Bob Seeger said he does, I just sit and listen to them by myself. They mean the most to me now because they bring up memories of my parents in those days when they were still young lovely, and alive. Between that and the fact that my father once won a jitterbug contest in Chicago where my parents met, I reckon that my folks were hot stuff, real "hepcats" in their day. I first got grabbed by that particular sound one afternoon while at Uncle Ross and Auntie Fern's house. There was a portable player, probably their daughter's, on the floor in the kitchen. The record on it was a Tommy Dorsey record titled "Boogie-Woogie." I played it over and over. Uncle Ross had one of those player pianos on his enclosed patio that played all sorts of old, rickety tunes as if a ghost was sitting on the bench. Daughter Barbara could play a mean sax.

Out on the boat, I can clearly recall how I felt sitting quietly in our boat, almost suspended in time, as I listened to Fats Domino's

"Walking to New Orleans" for the first time. A man was walking home from a tragedy, it seemed, after learning a profound lesson, and all he wanted to do was get home. It seemed somehow profound to me. I didn't miss out on the rock and roll of those days, either, and Doo-Wop, but when those remarkable guitar instrumentals played, it was magic. When I heard Ray Charles sing "Hit the Road Jack," I could make out the words. Even the car radio was clear. I received a notion of the possible depths of love and devotion when I heard "Mission Bell" and "Tell Laura I Love Her," on the car radio while on a trip to the Roseville dump.

To me, the magic of music was everywhere. When Marty Robbins told his story about "El Paso," it felt genuine to the little boy I was like it just happened last week. Later when I saw the film, "Colorado Territory," I learned how a woman might have the same courage as the cowboy in that song. Afloat on the Sacramento River is also where I first heard Verdel Smith sing, "Tar and Cement." It seemed even then to be a future lament. Perhaps the most stunning of all the music I heard in those days was an acoustic guitar piece titled "Maria Elena." But most memorable of all for me is probably Pat Boone's "Moody River," as it was popular at the time of the big adventure on Dr. McIntosh's Chris Craft.

Now, before I dive any deeper into the cultural aspects of the time, at least the ones I noticed, I want to clarify something; the first dance craze of the sixties was not the Twist, the Mashed Potato, or the Watusi. It was the Cha, Cha, Cha. That's right. It swept the nation. And it was all started by a pop singer named Bobby Rydell. The record industry was looking for something to replace or fill in the gap left by the demise of Rock and Roll after the famous plane crash that killed The Big Bopper, Buddy Holly, and Richie Valens, the arrest of a few bad boys, and the drafting of Elvis. But they had no material. So they foisted up a pretty boy and came up with what must have been the idea of someone like Mitch Miller, who worked for Columbia Records at the time and hosted a Friday night sing-along show. His idea seems to have been a revival of the earlier Big Band Latin craze. Anyway, it was catchy enough with the one, two, cha, cha, cha, rhythm. Out of this came the line that caused the national sensation/habit of finishing every sentence with "cha, cha, cha" when a song finally proclaimed, "Everything is cha, cha, cha!" So it was a national trend for about six months to blurt out "cha, cha, cha!" at the end of any statement, just for effect; "and that's all there was to that; cha, cha, cha!"

It could be meant to be humorous, or in the case of my mother, "brush your teeth, cha, cha, cha," changed to "chop, chop," as we grew into teenagers, and she had acquired a cleaver to back herself up (not really). The effect of that song remained in my family until I graduated from high school. But I'm sure we weren't the only such afflicted household. David Seville's "Chipmunks said "cha, cha, cha," "ruining" another of Seville's songs. In one hilarious case on the radio in 1960, a country song, and I mean a real throwback titled, "The Muleskinner Blues," which was probably the epitome and death blow to the trend, featured the most overdone Hillbilly hyena singing ever put on any recording set against an electric guitar picking out the melody as half-Western, half proto-surf, ended abruptly with a completely out of context - "cha, cha, cha!" I don't know if a funeral was held for the cha, cha, cha, but I sure remembered that song. I was seven years old, so I loved it. Other comedy records came along; "Ahab the Arab,*⊕" "Tie Me Kangaroo Down," and "My Boomerang Won't Come Back," but nothing struck me as quite so outrageously funny until the Trashmen came along in 1964 with "The Surfin' Bird." Martine hated it. I loved it. Dave "Bucky" Buckmaster loved it, too. We used to compete at imitating it for fun. It was the obnoxious quality of both of those songs that appealed to me, I suppose. Anyway, The Trashmen owe "The Muleskinner Blues" for that. That is one type of music we never hear in the 21st century; comedy records. There used to be so many quirky and hilarious artists loose in America. I guess it began with Spike Jones escaping from the Vaudeville stage to the radio and then Wax. Even my seemingly always serious demeanor vanished. He really liked "Alley Oop." Look at that caveman go.

I remember the first time I heard Spike Jones. My folks had a pathetic little phonograph on P Street (but it worked). My folks seemed more interested in the radio and TV after we moved to North Highlands. I found the old 78s one day in the laundry closet and dug them out. They dug out that old Zenith Cobra-Matic from the boxes in the garage, which also contained a stash of Japanese and Chinese money from his later Navy years. I confiscated the money. My Dad didn't care. I had already confiscated his microscope. I had established a pattern by then, and I do believe that my old man was numbed by it, stupefied, even. That was the era when I learned about the Grumman Duck and the submarine. He had a photo album distributed by the vitamin company he used that commemorated the U.S. Navy in the war. I confiscated that, too. In fact, I still have it.

So, I began to play the 78s on my own. My folks didn't care. I found "This Old House," and "Rum and Coca-Cola," (I had no idea what they were singing about), and so on. One day, I found "Beetlebaum," by Spike Jones. This was my first exposure to "novelty" music. It was a comedy cast as a horse race to the music, the "William Tell Overture," somehow presaging the Lone Ranger theme! I think my folks enjoyed seeing their kids go nuts over it. By the late 50s and all the space science fiction movies at the drive-ins and the popular notion of Martians landing anytime to conquer the world, a spate of space records appeared; "The One-Eyed, One-Horned, Flying Purple People Eater," "The Little Space Girl," "The Martian Hop," and others, that all seemed to demonstrate that aliens from space might be friendly, attractive, and even hip. Then, there were the monster records. Everyone knows about "The Monster Mash," but that was just one. "Haunted House," "Dinner with Drac," and then the hilarious, "I'm a Mummy," which featured a cameo by Beat Poet Rod McKuen. There were other even more quirky songs, like, "A Walk on the Moon." But it would be remiss to not mention David Seville's "Witch Doctor." It was wildly popular. After that, he came up with a series of records where his invented singing chipmunks, Simon, Theodore, and Alvin, performed, and always messed up the ending of the song with Seville losing control of the spunky trio, mostly Alvin. Once it was "cha, cha,

cha," joining in on the national trend of the time. That led to a cartoon series to rival the usual fare that children consumed in those days. Such entertainment was almost always musical, funny, clever, but overall cute and charming. It was okay to be that way in those days.

The popularity of "novelty;" weird and funny songs was so great, that by the 70s, a Los Angeles hippy that became known as Doctor Demento, had a syndicated radio show that featured old, and new entries into the genre. Weird Al Yankovich was the last of the purveyors of odd comedy music for public consumption. Then the 21st century arrived and nearly everyone seemed to lose their sense of humor.

Where my memories of my Dad are concerned, it was some of the contemporary jazz pieces like "Cast Your Fate to the Wind" and "Stranger by the Shore" that made a lasting impression. These titles remind me of my father because of his remarks about them. His comments were rare, so when he said that he really liked it, I identified that song with him. When I hear Stranger on the Shore now, I still see him, sitting there alone and silent on the water, lost in his own thoughts. I think he kept a deep-down sorrow hidden from everyone. "Stranger on the Shore," is his song. As it happened, we spent an awful lot of time together, one way or another, in shared silence. Silence was both our bond and our estrangement.

Similarly, I stored my thoughts silently. My father was not an evil man, but he hardly ever spoke to me. He just never knew how to talk to me unless it was to instruct or reprimand. I put it down to his tough upbringing. Whatever the reason, I learned to keep my own counsel at a young age. Despite that, he passed some valuable lessons to me in those early years. When it was verbal, it was short and sweet, sometimes not so sweet, but instructive. Once when trying to reason with me when I was in a stubborn mood, he quipped, "A man convinced against his will is of the same opinion still." I thought about

that a lot; enough to have it memorized sixty years later. He taught me to play chess, and so we spent many long hours over the board.
I could only bring him to a draw or stalemate. He didn't teach me how to close a game, so I had to learn decades later. But I did learn to look at all the angles. However, perhaps the most important of all is how he taught me independence. During the third grade, I was bullied most of the year by a bigger kid. I suffered in silence until it became unbearable. My teacher for some reason did not intervene. Teachers were fairly laissez-faire in those days, letting kids work things out for themselves. I finally told my Dad and Uncle Johnny to find out about it. Uncle Johnny taught me some Judo and gave me encouragement, but my father finally overheard the specific story. He made no effort to intervene but encouraged me to stand up for myself. "Or they will bully you all your life." Finally, one day, the breaking point came, and during the last week of the school year, too; the bully was behind me in the two lines we always formed up after recess, one for boys and the other for girls. He began to taunt me and pinch me where he should not. I exploded. I grabbed him by his shirt, pulled him out of the line, and gave him a perfectly delivered right and left cross with the footwork that gave the blows more force. He tumbled down onto his back. I still can see the shocked look on his face as the bigger kid sprawled out onto the ground under me.

The next year, he wanted to be my friend. I think his parents had a talk with him. But Mrs. Alden, the teacher, never said a thing. On my report card, she noted that I had shown great improvement. But I never tolerated bullies after that. On my fourth-grade report card, Mrs. Roach noted, "Mark plays rough." Sure, if some kid shoved me, he'd get a pop in the jaw. One kid grabbed me from behind one day and found himself flying over my shoulder onto his back.

In 1967, after a risky bit of mob-busting in front of our home, while the folks were gone "up the hill" for the weekend, I had to throttle back, so to speak. I realized my limits without any input from anyone except maybe indirectly, my Cousin Sue who was visiting at the time. She was from Wisconsin and had "run away" to San Francisco. Uncle

Johnny had retrieved her from somewhere on Haight Street. She was lively, engaging, and sweet. We all went on a trip to Reno. When the folks went to gamble, they stuck us in a movie theater. The film was "Bonny and Clyde." Sue went on for a while about the violence of it. For her, it was "peace" at all costs. Impractical, but she had a point and an influence on me.

Another event that I now realize was aimed at giving me some sense of self-reliance concerned the return of a rifle scope that proved defective. For Christmas of 1964, I finally was granted my wish, the wish of many boys of that age in my time; I received a Sears single-shot .22 rifle with a four-power scope. I was very happy. But very soon, the scope proved defective. My parents told me that I could exchange it, saying that they'd take me to Sears, but I'd have to do it myself. So they drove me up to the less utilized back entrance and sent me off with the rifle. I tucked it in under my arm so that the muzzle was pointing at the ground and marched in. I went past some salesman near the door. One of them smiled and said, "The Boss."
I just kept walking with my face forward. I walked to the sports department and did my business. They offered me a better, Ted Williams signature model as a replacement. I accepted. Only now do I realize that they had probably worked it all out with the store ahead of time. But I didn't know that then. I still have the scope. It's held its initial sighting in on several rifles over my lifetime. It's on a Henry .22 lever action now. That's what quality used to mean. One special day, when I was about ten, Dad took Martine and me out on a trip to Rio Linda to run some sort of errand. But the errant turned out to be taking turns sitting on his lap and learning how to steer the car. He thought it was important for us to understand how steering a car felt. This was not uncommon, I think. The wisdom of our elders used to be a cultural understanding. "Time you learned this, son."

It's probably the reason that later in life in 1975, after a couple of years of pondering what to do with my life, having survived the Vietnam War by simply not being called up. Once I had realized that I was not going to make a living racing motorcycles. I wanted to change or at least add to my scope of knowledge and abilities. I realized that the most help I could be to the world was to follow in my father's and grandfather's footsteps and become a D.C. I sincerely believed that helping people by bringing their bodies into better function (harmony) might have a general effect on their lives and choices. In this, I may have been naïve. I even wrote that in my letter requesting admittance into Palmer College in 1978. I was an idealist then. As a student, I joined the Haight-Ashbury Free Medical Clinic, Rock Medicine Section, an all-volunteer operation, and worked at Bill Graham Presents events for fourteen years. I was called from time to time to treat a performer, some with names still recognizable, today. But what I did mostly provided emergency services, everything from holding a bucket for a kid that had too much hooch, talking down a paranoid tripper, holding down a violent tripper so a nurse could administer an injection to counteract the drug effect, and all sorts of orthopedic injuries. People died and a couple babies were born.

A stadium with 50,000 kids in it, going through some sort of initiation into life, is not unlike a MASH unit. The station I served in most after a few years was front-stage triage. Fans would be crushed up against a stage for hours. There was almost always overheating, and sometimes injuries and panic. We'd administer water, and rescue the ones that needed help. I did all of this because I wanted these kids to know that whatever they were going through, they might notice that some strangers cared about what happened to them.

At one of the last shows I worked at, a sixteen-year-old girl had taken LSD and was lost. She didn't even know her name. No one could get anything out of her. Time was running out. The show was over and it was about two in the morning. Soon, her only option would be to take a ride downtown with a police officer and sit in a holding cell for 72 hours. With the help of my girlfriend, who I had brought to the show, we walked the teen around until she could tell me her telephone number. I called her parents. We saved that girl from having a very bad experience in her young life. It might have made a huge difference.

Later, during my time as an intern in the school clinic, I'd spend weekends with him at his office in Foothill Farms, learning the technique he'd learned from his father, and that his father had learned from B.J Palmer. If he were around, I'd thank him better than I did when he was alive. He never learned half of what I did during my career, but he did know that I was selected to work with an orthopedic surgeon in Slovenia, that I had treated rock stars and Olympic-level athletes, and that I had even treated horses.

My father did know that I had been published four times in professional journals, twice in Slovenia, twice in the U.S., and internationally, and once in the CCA Journal through an article about video-fluoroscopy (now, Digital Fluoroscopy), which I was working with after I returned from Slovenia in 1999. He also didn't know that I had assisted the Slovenian State Librarian in producing the first book on Freemasonry allowed in that part of the world where it had been suppressed by the Vatican and then the communists.

These are some of the important things my father did for me. And because of him, I was able to do a lot of good. Aside from always trying to make my services affordable, to the point of taking trades, during my fourteen years with Rock Medicine, I worked with nurses, medical doctors, and other specialists such as psychologists and paramedics. I performed all sorts of emergency medical services, from holding "barf buckets" in the field clinic, field rescues, peacefully stopping fights, talking down bad trips, harmlessly subduing violent trippers as part of an OD (overdose) team, and front-stage triage, to even uniting lost kids with their parents – (important work)). I was occasionally asked to provide chiropractic services to performers, so I was backstage with some classic rock bands. It was a special period of my life that coincided with my competitive fencing career, teaching at the Renaissance Faire, and my professional career, a period of about twenty years.

During the second grade, my class had been displaced for that year from Village Elementary to the new Sierra View School. I'd ride my bike to Village School, lock my bike on the rack, get on a bus with other kids from the lower Cantel Way blocks, and take the short ride to Sierra View. Looking through my classroom window, I could see the Spook Tree, out to the east, perhaps a quarter-mile away. Beyond as a backdrop, on a clear day, loomed the Sierras. One day, after we learned about the Maidu Indians, Miss Imwale took us afield to collect acorns to make the same porridge that the Indians had eaten. I remember she served it out onto index cards, and we used wooden Popsicle sticks to eat it. I was chided a few times by the teacher, Mrs. Imwale, for staring out of the window instead of looking at the chalkboard.

One song that captured my imagination at the time was a folk song titled, "Tom Dooley;" "This time tomorrow, reckon where I'll be. Down in some lonesome valley hangin' from a white oak tree." At the time of its popularity, it was 1960 and I was in the second grade. I'd hear that song every time I looked out to The Spook Tree.

I wondered about what the Indians had used. Almost at the same time, my Cub Scout Den took a field trip to Sutter's Fort and the Indian Museum. My parents were the acting adults on that trip as parents shared duties for the pack by then. But when we went out into that field for those acorns, although passing near, I could not get to the Spook Tree. By that time, I seemed to be the only kid around who found the Spook Tree intriguing. But no one ever brought it up, so I didn't. It was as if the kids had become myopic, while my vision seemed directed out to the broader world.

Rollin' on the River

My distraction from school matters was also caused by all of the fishing trips that began with "O'Brien," one of my father's co-workers at McClellan AFB in the early years there, while he was a sheet metal worker.

When I wasn't out on the river, I was usually thinking about it. Whatever else he might have been, O'Brien was a kindly man. On one trip, he played a game with me where I won a grand total of thirty-six cents from coin-flipping. I thought myself quite a tycoon and gambler. I was quite a sport until I excitedly announced my incredible luck to my sisters. Later after our return home, my father informed me that O'Brien had let me win. Oh, come to think of it, he would shade the coin after he slapped it down on his wrist when he told me I'd won. O'Brien brought fun to fishing on the bank, sitting there talking, and sometimes playing games. Usually, I did not often speak, but my eyes and ears were open. I was silent most of the time when in the company of adults, but especially when I was with my father. It was just the safest way to be. When I was with my sisters, we all spoke more freely, unless we were under orders to the contrary. That was whenever we went anywhere important. Even though I was silent on those fishing trips, it was a good thing to have friends along; because in all the five years I spent fishing with my father from six to eleven years old, I only saw three fish caught, and none of them by poor Dad. But he could catch fish. He almost always outfished me on any trip. Paulette became my buddy because of these trips. And when she was with us, it wasn't a silent day. The truth is that when in one another's company, we were an effective comedy team and kept the remainder of the family entertained, if not annoyed.

Just before things changed and the fishing trips fell off, I finally caught one. It was in 1963 when I caught a big one near the entrance to the locks. To be exact, it was thirty-four and a quarter inches long and weighed eleven and three-quarter pounds, to be precise. I never forgot it. After all, I had waited years for that catch, and I was only eleven when it happened. Five years; that was half of my life at the time, just about.

I was the one who always kept my eye on the tip, as instructed, while the grown-ups seemed more reluctant to take their own advice. But to be honest, I hadn't hooked it like that. He grabbed on and swallowed the bait when I wasn't looking. I only noticed when I went to retrieve the line. The fish reacted immediately, and I quickly struck the boat's gunwale with my knees with the pole bent into a sharp curve to brace myself as I worked for a half-hour fighting the fish close enough for Daddy to net it. It might have been the best moment of my life to that point. In fact, I know it was. But it was really pure luck. That fish might have swallowed my Dad's or even Paulette's bait; now that would have been fun to watch. But Paulette was a Tom Boy and no weakling, either.

The bank fishing days were curtailed after my father lost his fishing buddy, O'Brien. It was an event that, alas, the entire family was witness to. My dad had recruited him to help do some indoor painting, and it soon became apparent that dear old O'Brien was quite drunk. He was taking little breaks to go hit a bottle that he had out in his car. My dad was tolerant enough of drinking. Although I never saw him or heard of him taking a drink in his life beyond an occasional glass of wine at dinner (aside from Paulette's wedding), two of his three brothers had severe drinking problems. I think that my dad didn't want his kids to see any sort of deviant behavior. Looking back, my folks took great pains to keep ugliness from us. They probably overdid it because growing up became a long series of shocks. I think many of the parents of that time did this, but not all. That's what produced so many innocent Boomers who were so easily influenced and seduced by corruptive ideas and practices. They hadn't prepared them for that.

This was partly because they had the idea that since they had survived The Great Depression and won the war, nothing evil was left, except communist subversives, maybe, and they were not in the local area but across the ocean. They were something to talk about, and argue about, but not in the immediate realm. That is where they were in error. I suppose it was the shock of learning of them in our government and society that led to the turmoil of the sixties. It turned out that they were closer than anyone had imagined, except for my father. He had believed McCarthy. I had actively doubted that and everything my father said about it back then. But it turned out that McCarthy was right (if not his methods), and so was my Dad.*₂ Only my Dad often expressed his opinions via tirades of declarations. That caused me to doubt the validity of his claims. It required years and digging through history books to learn what really happened. He was right, but it was more complicated than he knew.

We weren't so naïve in some ways. We grew up knowing about The Cold War. We read the Civil Defense pamphlets in class and practiced "Duck and Cover," drills. I remember seeing Khrushchev's speech on TV as a kind of commercial, where he said he would "bury" us and that we children would be his nation's slaves. I didn't know then that this was contrived propaganda. Khrushchev had actually said, "It doesn't matter if you invite us or not, history is on our side. We will bury you." He had said it in the Polish embassy in Moscow in 1956, during a meeting of Western ambassadors, most of who stood up and walked out; still menacing, yes, but nothing there about enslaving American children. The Soviets were saying things like that all the time during the Cold War. It was no secret that their aim was to take over the world, and not necessarily by force of arms. That was and still remains the aim of Marxism. I clearly remember The Cuban Missile Crisis. I laughed at the dinner table while the news was on, and my mother yelled, "Your country may be at war!" I shut up and paid attention after that.

Indeed, after November 22, 1963, the age of innocence was over for Boomers. By then, I had the presence of mind to appreciate what the assassination of a president might mean. I made a scrapbook of all of the related news stories for a week from the Sacramento Bee, beginning with the colossal front-page headline, "President Slain By Snipers' Bullet." I still have that scrapbook.

I hadn't known anything about O'Brien's politics, whereas I did know about Uncle Ross' because I heard my dad and him talking, actually shouting about Sputnik and the "damn commies." O'Brien seemed more like a nice guy who was fond of the drink, as any Irishman might be as a natural thing, and not losing one bit of his sterling character due to the habit. Both O'Brien and Uncle Ross were early figures in my life, and they are fondly remembered. There would be several more; Miles Curran in Wentworth Springs, Richard Clark, and George Peterson arriving in later years, and at school, Mr. Ramos and Mr. Davidson. But where O'Brien was concerned, my father apparently felt he was a bad influence.

Enter Dr. McIntosh, my father's colleague, and his old Chris Craft cabin cruiser. Dr. McIntosh practiced downtown and, like many in those days, lived next to his office. He kept his boat in a slip at Miller Park, where the land described a natural harbor next to the park itself. At least, I didn't think it was man-made. After our first visit to his office downtown, we went on a series of fishing outings with him. He was a remarkable character to me, then. Dr. McIntosh had a presence. He might have been the California version of Winston Churchill in looks and habits, the ever-present cigar, and the gait of a portly but intelligent man. But the efficiency of that practice must be noted; Dr. McIntosh never wasted anything.

He liked cigars and had the old-time habit of stuffing the stogie into a pipe and smoking it down to the last. Well, he was Scottish, wasn't he? He was of an old, established Sacramentan line. In the history of Sacramento County, we have the arrival of John McIntosh from Kentucky, the in-law of a distinguished Dr. John Cooper. They arrived together in California in 1852 and established stores in Mud Springs (Shingle Springs) and Diamond Springs. They next sent for their families, and the entire clan became families of note in Sacramento.

I remember the Scottish pennant that he flew on the prow of his boat in those days – The Stuart Rampaging Lion. My father, on the other hand, tossed his cigarette butts wherever he might be in those days, much the same as everyone else. These were the days before littering was illegal except in places like New York City, where I saw "No Littering" signs in 1961 when we were there. Neither San Francisco nor Los Angeles had such codes from all I saw, and I cut my foot on broken glass in the sand on our first visit to a Southern California beach. For the most part, regular citizens dropped whatever they had in their hands when they were finished with it, chewing gum, too. To witness, whenever we were at a restaurant, a favorite game of Paulette and I was to look under the tables.

We'd remark on how much chewing gum had been stuck to the underside. They were always numerous. As it is, I can't recall one fishing trip where we came home with a bag of trash leftover from our lunches and so on. I think the trips with Dr. McIntosh were more organized, however. His older Chris Craft at Miller Park was a pretty nice old launch for its size. It had a stove, and a sink with potable water coming out of its faucet. It also featured a john in the cabin with a flushing toilet. It was a comfortable boat with cushy opposing row seats with a removable table inserted between it on a metal post. It also had a recognizable foredeck. This will become important later in the story. The comfort of that cabin was to be the harbinger of a dangerous situation. Of those adventures, the most memorable was the night we all came close to drowning in the river when his boat began to rapidly take on water. We only made it through because I saw it and yelled a warning to him in time for Dr. Mackintosh to turn the boat hard to port and run us ashore on the Yolo side's levy.

I'll never know why my father and Dr. McIntosh spent all of that November afternoon in the boat's cabin, but they did. I only have a theory. As usual, we had started out before dawn, anchored opposite the Freeport marina not far from the bridge, and sat there all day. On this trip, there were four of us; Dr. McIntosh, my Dad, me, and a girl named Penny. She was the daughter of another man; my father worked with who he called "Phil Kill." At least, that's how it sounded to me. Who was ever named "Kill?" Surely, there is an explanation, like a different spelling, but that detail is lost from memory if I ever knew it.

A Memorable Day on the Sacramento River

Dr. McIntosh knew the same people, so maybe the family was his patient of his. They lived just outside of old North Sacramento. I remember picking her up with my father on the way and being there a few times. I think Dr. McIntosh was fond of little girls, we later found. A bit too fond, and my father broke off the friendship after Martine said he had kissed her in a way that was a little "too adult," to put it politely. On this memorable trip was Penny. I'm pretty sure that she was Phil Kill's daughter. She was nice to me from the start. I remember we were standing in the dark on the dock at the office in Miller Harbor, where we were filling up with fuel before heading out that morning. As I stood next to Penny, staring out at the black water, she produced a couple of pennies and gave one to me.

"Let's throw them into the water for good luck." She told me. So we did. The luck might have been that we remained dry and alive that day.

As the day dawned, the sky remained overcast, and it was plain that it would be that way all day. We left the harbor and cruised to Freeport and dropped anchor a little upstream of the drawbridge near the Yolo bank. I took my post with my fishing pole and dutifully sat there all day, waiting for the rare bite.

I don't think Penny had a rod at all. Dr. McIntosh and my Dad hung bells on their rods. It was a chilly day, and the sun never came out, at least on the river. The three of them went into the cabin to get warm and never checked on me once until the time they decided to go home. By the time it came to them to call it a day, it was too late to get home in daylight. It was already dusk. The fog had never cleared and was now thickening. We could barely see the banks of the river. I was too ignorant to know how dangerous this situation had become. To add to it, masses of driftwood in the form of large tree branches were carried by the current down on us as dangerous obstacles to avoid.

It's only my guess, but I think they were playing chess and became engrossed. My father was into chess in those days. He would spend hours playing with Uncle Ross at Uncle Ross and Auntie Fern's whenever we went to his home to swim in their full-sized built-in pool.

Chess is a good game for killing time, and it doesn't waste the mind. He later taught me the pieces and how they moved, and we played a series of games. I recall the nights on the California Zephyr in 1961 on our way east, particularly, when he let me order ginger ale while we played chess for hours. I learned by mimicking what I saw my father do, and from my defeats, so he would always be a step ahead. I could see when it was hopeless, but I'd play on to the bitter end every time.

I have changed that since then. I learned how to turn the tables and win. I recently earned my master's rating, but so far, I have found winning games in that class difficult. It's as if I'm back on the California Zephyr but on another level. So it's back to school for me!

In those days, I finally became frustrated and refused to play any longer. When one never wins, one tends to lose interest and move on to things one might succeed in. I had to try out a lot of activities. But I was always good on a bicycle, building jumps and flying the highest, taking turns fast, and so on. I eventually found sports that I was not just well-suited for but excelled at. They just weren't within the usual scope of a boy's world then. As for my Dad, I think he was using me to practice on. He said it was to teach me how to think, so I guess I can forgive that. My Dad had one of those little fold-up chess boards that could fit in a lunch box. He took it to work. I know because I spied on him. This is where I get my theory about the cause of the situation we found ourselves in that Sunday night on the river. But whatever the reason, they did not emerge from that cabin until it was getting dark, and the fog was settling in. It was a heavy fog. It was apparent that a mistake had been made, and there was some urgency in Dr. McIntosh and my father's demeanor. At the time, I was oblivious to the danger. It's remarkable how a child tends to take everything as an ordinary event. That is the essence of innocence and trust.

Night fell on us quickly. There had recently been heavy rain, and large debris flows, including small trees, were floating down in the current. My father took a flashlight with him up to the bow and was trying to guide Dr. McIntosh by looking out for the many-branched logs coming down on us from upstream. Our progress up the river was slow because of the density of the fog, which only grew thicker. At one point, he signaled an "SOS" to a car passing on the levy. The car stopped, and my dad yelled over to him, giving our telephone number and asking the man on the riverbank to call my mom and tell her we were okay. We continued up the river, but Miller Park was miles away. Suddenly there was a scraping sound under the boat. Regardless of the grown-up's best efforts, Dr. McIntosh just could not avoid that one in time.

Not long after that, maybe five minutes, Penny and I looked down and saw motion on the deck at the transom. It was water. Our boat was sinking. Penny said, "look, Mark, water!" I called out to Dr. McIntosh, "Dr. McIntosh, there's water coming in!" He wheeled about and saw the water immediately. I'll never forget the alarm in his wide-open eyes. He quickly turned the boat hard to port and yelled out to my father on the bow. He increased the speed a little and grounded the boat on the Yolo bank. Everyone remained remarkably calm as we disembarked. Maybe that was because of the relief of making land or some humiliation on our guardians' part? Penny and I took it all in stride as naturally ignorant children do, unaware of the danger.

Now, I think of how it might have been with my father in that cold water, trying to swim with me in tow, and maybe trying to save Penny first? And Dr. McIntosh was sixty-five at the time and not at all in swimming trim unless anything that round would automatically float. In November, the river's water temperature meant that we'd have about three minutes before hypothermia overcame us. We had come that close to disaster. And I thought nothing of it at the time except that it was a great adventure.

I remember taking note of the gallant little cruiser tilted a little as it lay upon the bank with a light still on in the cabin as Dr. McIntosh closed it down. Penny and I were carried to the dry shoreline. Then we all took a walk. I thought we were at some friend's house, but it was an emergency visit to a farmhouse. Still, I recall the folks there being very accommodating. They gave Penny and me some hot chocolate and probably the two adults, coffee, and before too long, a taxi arrived, and we got back to our car at Miller Park and home. My mom said that I had quite an adventure and ordered me into the bathtub to warm up in the hot water. I didn't feel that cold, though. I thought I had had some fun. As always after a day on the water, I could still feel the sensation of the waves. I always loved bouncing on the waves, even big ones out at sea. That's changed a bit in these later years. I take Dramamine now. But it's been a while. I don't know if even that would work now.

It is remarkable to me now that I was too naïve to understand the real danger of the situation. If I had not shouted at Dr. McIntosh so quickly, who knows how it would have turned out? Just another few minutes might have seen a very different outcome. Penny had seemed content to merely point it out to me. But it was Penny's pennies that made the difference if you like; kid lore superstition substantiated.

I never saw Dr. McIntosh again. Did I just say that? Hang another Pinocchio nose on me! I saw him one last time many years later as a young doctor. I saw him at a relicensing seminar in Sacramento. All he said was, "I'm ninety-four years old, ninety-four years old!" It was as if he could not believe it himself. And there he was, renewing his professional license at ninety-four! What a character. But he was such a little man, maybe five foot four! Once, he had seemed to tower over me. How different things look later in life! After the incident on the river, I remember asking about his boat. My father said that he was having the bottom redone. But we never went out with him again. I think I know why.

Ex-Ice Cutter

It wasn't long before we had our own boat. The origin of that boat was curious. My father spotted it sitting with a "For Sale" sign on it at the junction of Roseville Road and Madison Avenue, precisely where Camp Kohler's center had been and a stone's throw over the embankment of the railroad tracks from our little church. It is strange how that railroad and its embankment separated both the land and the mind into particular worlds back then. Everything is more of a blur, now.

I remember years earlier, being at the lumberyard nearby there previously, "Steiner's Lumberyard." I remember the sign, with its image of a hardy-looking blonde man with a tan in a red flannel shirt and a big smile. When the boat was there, all that remained of the army camp were a few old abandoned buildings. That boat was constructed nearby, within sight of The Spook Tree, and maybe, at least partially, with lumber from the old camp, which had been sold off cheap when the camp was being dismantled. It sure looked like it might have been. In my mind, the boat and tree had something in common because of this approximation of geography. But there was something more.

It was a feeling I imagined in those days when I thought I was observing an artifact from a time past. It was all a mystery to me. That tree stood at the center of all mysteries in those days. It provided a common thread in a certain illogical but utterly congruent fashion in my child's mind.

There is a story to how we can to that boat. During that trip "Back East," we visited my mother's old friends in Virginia and then New York. We ascended the Empire State Building and toured the dock. I remember spotting the Queen Mary at the pier and calling it out. Then, we went to stay with a cousin of my mother's in New Jersey. She was one of those types with that heavy "Joisey" accent that used to be common. Nice, but wow, what an audio experience! Anyway, my Dad had made an application to be on a popular game show at the time, which was a daily event filmed live at the Rockefeller Center. I remember seeing the big displays of the Radio City Rockettes. We sat in the live audience and watched a game. It was "Jan Murray's Charge Account." My Dad didn't win, but he won a very nice Japanese-style living room set made of thick bamboo. Not long after we got home from our month-long odyssey on the rails, a truck showed up and there it was in our living room. But we already had a living room set and this one was too nice for a family of four kids. So he traded it for the boat we had seen at the corner of Roseville Road and Madison Avenue.

It was no beauty. In fact, it was definitely an ugly duckling. It was christened in an impromptu manner at one marina, Ed's Brickyard Marina as "Ex-Ice Cutter." This marina is extinct now. I may be wrong with the name. It might have been "Cliff's Brickyard Marina." Those two names seem to compete in a rusty engram in my brain. The "Brickyard" term is due to the establishment of the Callahan and Ryan's Brick Company in 1854, which became Sacramento Brick in 1881.

It was located where Clipper and Brickyard Drive intersect today. Greenhaven Lake was once a clay quarry that supplied the material for the bricks. At its peak, that company produced 50 million bricks a year. Most of them were shipped away for other construction, but the extinct companies' bricks can be found all over Sacramento. The Memorial Auditorium is built of them, for example.

Cliff had named our craft, "Ex-Ice Cutter," owing to its narrow bow and non-existent foredeck. I knew it was a derogatory joke, but I didn't care. A twenty-one-foot cabin cruiser normally has some sort of foredeck, but the one on ours was only large enough for the hatch that served as a station for managing the anchor, which was stowed in the triangular deck space under it. It was a boxy-looking structure with a rectangular structure as the cabin was set on a hull constructed for function alone. I think the cabin was overlong which took up what could have been a larger foredeck but having a roomy cabin meant more to the builder than holding a hoe-down on the deck. It never bothered any of us. My father didn't seem to care, either. I recall my father saying that was a kit boat, with instructions from some do-it-yourself ad from perhaps the Farmer's Almanac, and someone had built it in his barn. I can almost see a couple of handy farm types lifting a flathead engine out of some rusty, abandoned vehicle next to a barn with a tractor. The tractor is clanking over to the barn with that engine dangling from a chain hanging from a homemade crane. Then, with many a "ho, more to the left," they laid it onto the timber stringers in the hull.   As with any farm implement, that boat was built for function first, by someone not that interested in winning beauty contests but in getting the job done. So there, who cares?

Not me. I didn't care about any of that, and neither did my dad. "At last," he said. "I should name it "At Last." The homely craft would provide me with a new dimension of adventure. Its one redeeming feature was the Ford flathead V-8 that powered it. It could move out quickly and set up a big rooster tail as it went. It had a great, low throbbing sound when underway. Since "PT 109" was a popular story of the time because of the 1960 election, I imagined it to be like a PT boat from World War Two, and we were fighting "The Battle of the Striped Bass." It was a new sortie every time we set out on the river, which we did many times over the next several years, even going out on weeknights during the runs. I loved acting in the crew. I'd jump from the boat onto every dock we landed at and had the lines fastened to the cleats properly, overdoing it, with more retention twists than necessary every time.

My father let me pilot it once and taught me how to dead reckon navigate by fixing my sight on a landmark to a point and then picking out another so that the boat's path was smooth and efficient. This and all the exposure offshore and at night would serve me later in life when I was making in at night in a windstorm on the churning Columbia River in my own craft, alone, by myself in the Pacific Northwest. Where others had fallen victim in similar conditions on this river, at the worst point, when my craft was being tossed about, I mastered my fear and focused on the green-lit buoy in the distance that I knew marked the entry to the slough that would take me to the dock and safety. Those early adventures on the Sacramento River prepared me for an event like this, as much as my father teaching me to swim in Uncle Ross's swimming pool saved me in 1970 when I got into trouble while swimming across an inlet at Folsom Lake.

My solitude on these early fishing trips did not last. Soon, I was joined on those trips by my sister, Paulette. At only a year younger than me, we were natural childhood companions, and I had made her into a complete tomboy if there ever was one. So Paulette and I shared almost every fishing trip from then on, and every adventure soon after we acquired that boat.

We were a great comedy team together, so any adult that came near us usually got a show of some sort. My dad once brought along a co-worker named Bill on an evening outing during a weekday. Bill was a Blackman who already liked striped bass fishing. He worked with my father at McClellan. So it came to be that my Dad asked him out for an evening fishing venture one weeknight in the autumn of 1963. Since catching a striper was a rare event, we came up empty on that trip as usual. The day after that outing, my father came to Paulette and me and told us that he was proud of us. He said that Bill had told him that it was the best time he ever had fishing. Bill told Dad that he always went home angry when he didn't catch a fish. Paulette and I had been joking, singing funny songs, like the "Cracker Jacks/Hand Grenade" jingle, as we waited for a fish to bite. Bill had apparently been well entertained. That's a nice thing to remember, now so many decades later with so much anger out there.

Hello, I'm Johnny Cash

In those days, there were only a handful of marinas on the Sacramento River near the city itself. There weren't that many at all. I got a sense of the number the time I cruised the entire river from Vallejo to Sacramento with Uncle Johnny on his commercial fishing boat, but that was a later adventure. To the north, coming south as far as Freeport, there was first, Village Boats, off the Garden Highway. It was a boat repair and sales shop, a bar and café, and docks down on the water. Just a bit downstream was another one we never did tie up at on the Yolo side. The pier for Old Sacramento had not been rebuilt yet, and the old town was a run-down skid row.

We passed through it on the way to Miller Park in those days. Miller Park is at the end of Broadway in the city itself. The next one was "Cliff's Brickyard Marina." That is the marina that we stopped in the most as The Brickyard was a curve in the river with some shallows that we considered a good spot for strippers. I have fond memories of stopping in after the early hours of fishing in the chilling morning for a cup of hot coffee, afternoons for a hot sandwich, and the sight of another customer playing bar dice with the owner to get a free beer and losing. But most of all was the sound of the first outdoor music system I ever heard in any setting. One sunny morning in the autumn, as we approached the marina, Johnny Cash's voice came wafting over the water as "Ring of Fire" was being broadcast outdoors. It was like magic wafting over the river. The owner was certainly ahead of the game; he knew how to bring in customers.

He had speakers set up on the piling tower, once at each end of the marina, so the music could be heard on the other side of the river; the echo effect was random but acoustically pleasing. Even though the music was recorded mono, the effect was almost stereo since the distance between the speakers was so great. The scene at that marina always seemed busy and jovial. Whenever we were there, some were already there playing bar dice with the owner, or someone would stop in and give him a hard time, teasing him about anything that might come into their mischievous minds. To my little boy's mind, Cliff seemed to be a sport with a good sense of humor.

That Marina was convenient as it was near the spot we usually fished; The Brickyard. The other popular spot was across from the Freeport Marina, just before the old draw bridge. A little later, The Captain's Table appeared within walking distance of this spot. But we never visited it. Not far inland was "The Crow's Nest." We went there as a family and had a great time with the Smother's Brothers type folk duo entertaining the diners that night. It was memorable for that reason, but also another. It was the same night as the baby bird incident. I needed cheering up that night, and I got it.

From Freeport proceeding downriver, the next marina was at Locke, which was quite a ways down the river. We only tied up there once that I recall, while on an extended exploration of the Delta waterways one summer day. As an adult, I visited many times and ate at Al the

Wops' restaurant and bar which is right on the levee road in the historic river Chinatown.

Aside from the near-disaster with Dr. McIntosh earlier, we collected several adventures, or more accurately, misadventures on the water in those years aboard the "Ex-Ice Cutter." The first one occurred in 1964 and contains a mystery. I will never figure out how my father managed to get into the water the morning he was setting the anchor in the Brickyard for a day of fishing. One stood in the hatch. On me, it came up to my chest, so for my dad, it would still come to his waist, anyway. But I heard a strange noise and gazed forward to see my father in what is still a snapshot in my mind; arched out over the water, maybe one foot planted on that little foredeck, and both arms out and up with the anchor flying away from him, dramatically. The next moment, a big splash and the sight of Daddy's head bobbing in the water. Paulette and I had to fish him out of the Sacramento River. Luckily we had a ladder that could be placed on the gunwale, so he only had to get a hold of it and climb in. He was soaked, but we didn't go home. Dad could be a tough guy when the event required it.

He was also a righteous man in his own way. Shunning regular church services, he was a Freemason. He also never failed a fellow Mason when hailed. One time, this proved to be a terrible mistake. There were in those days people were called "backsliders." That is someone who takes on the Christian faith but fails to follow the commandments or the preached doctrine of a particular Christian sect. Once "saved," one might live righteously for a time. But that ol' devil comes back to suggest all sorts of forbidden thoughts and fun. So when they'd fail, well, the devil made him do it, you see. That's been a well-used legal defense for centuries. It only recently became invalid as a plea.

In the medieval period, the Inquisition would help you get right again, but almost as often, burn you at the stake so that ol' devil couldn't grab your soul again. That's not much of an issue of concern these days as God has grown far more tolerant, it seems. But the consequences of two backsliding Freemasons did cause our second adventure. It featured a pair of drunks in a boat with the engine off, drifting in the water when we came upon them on our return trip.

This was a big trip out to Rio Vista via the Sacramento Canal. It was a combined trip with Uncle Ralph in his boat with his only son, my cousin.

Our boat, with my sisters along, completed the flotilla. We went through the Yolo Locks across from Miller Park and up the canal to Rio Vista. That cut some miles off the trip, but the channel was pretty dull compared to the river scenery.   It was just flat farmland in all directions. We spent the day watching the tips of our rods, as usual. Paulette and I took verbal shots at any subject that came up, but fishing also featured long periods of silence.

When it was time for lunch, we joked about hooks in our sandwiches; the angels were fishing. My father was not much of a conversationalist. He said what was necessary and that was usually all. He did not tell stories or speak much about anything unless asked. He talked most when I needed a talking to, you understand. When he did that, he usually passed on some ideas about fairness for me to think about. "You can lead a horse to water, but you can't make it drink." I looked around, but I didn't see any horse. I didn't see miss the implication at the time, either. But I had to make the show. It was part of the veil I created to hide my real thoughts. I always knew more than I let on. Happily, fishing turned out to be the binding source between us. Fo ar long after that time, I'd get a call from my mom, telling me that I was expected to go fishing. She had to do the arranging. He was that afraid to talk to me. But even now, with him gone from my life, the good part of him is still with me whenever I am fishing. The silence is the same. This is proof that silence can be comforting. But that day, when we finally headed in, again, with no fish, we had, or I should say, my father had a big adventure.

We came upon a pair of drunken men in their boat, which was dead in the water in the midst of the canal channel. My father stopped as they hailed him. They claimed that they were out of fuel. So Dad transferred my sister and me to Uncle Ralph's boat. He would tow their cabin cruiser with our dear old Ex-Ice Cutter.

It was dark by the time we reached the Miller Boat Park ramp. We didn't see our father until later the next day, which was a Monday. He had run out of fuel, towing them along as they lazed back in their drunken stupors. Those two rats had sobered up, cast free of our boat, and left poor Daddy stranded. Eventually, our father got to the bank of the canal and landed the boat. He had to walk about twenty miles to West Sacramento, return with gas and bring the Ex-Ice cutter in.

By the time he returned with the can of gas, the boat had been burglarized. My fishing rod, the one I had saved up for such a long time and prized so much, was gone, and so were all the other rods and gear. It was my first personal experience with theft, but not my last. I accepted it, but my father felt terrible about it, so he bought Paulette and me new rods. But it never felt the same. Dad never said a word about it. He had fulfilled the duty of any boater, and as a Navy Vet of World War Two, whose job was to rescue others in distress, his response was probably reflexive. It was for those two "Worshipful Brothers" to reconcile themselves to their consciences.

The final story here is a happier, more humorous one. It was one that I missed personally. For some reason, the case was made by someone, I think I know who, that I got to go fishing with my father too much. It wasn't about fishing as much as it was about the fun quotient or the perceived fun quotient. So I was to be left home this time, and Dad would take my three sisters, and Martine would have my rod to use. I remember spending the day doing nothing. If the point was to make me feel bad, they succeeded. I have never agreed with the practice of making some people feel better by making others feel bad. I had early experiences with cruel treatment. This wouldn't be my last. But Paulette alone, of all my family, had some compassion for me. She knew how much I loved the river and being out on the boat, so she made sure I was included by telling me the news of that trip.

They had gone to the Brickyard. She told of how as they pulled anchor and came about to head home, my father had apparently failed to spot two guys in a small twelve-foot rowboat anchored nearby, and his wake rolled over to toss that little craft violently. Well, this guy just stood up in the back of the boat and walked to its prow with both hands up to his nose one ahead of the other, thumbing it at my father's negligent arrogance, and the little boat tipped over, and both of the men flopped into the water. The boat was upside down. They rescued the men and towed their boat into Cliff's Brickyard Marina. Once there, those two guys revealed themselves to be the sweetest two drunks you ever heard of. Still soaking wet, they were so grateful for being rescued. In the bar, they were slapping my dad on the back and calling him "Co-sin," and carrying on in a way that astonished two of my sisters, but not Paulette. In her case, the event provided fodder for some time as she'd call me "Co-sin" and repeated some of the lingo and accent she had picked up on that outing for some time. So through my sweet sister, Paulette, I was there, even though I was not.

Meeting The Spook Tree

W hen I was nine years old in 1961, my mother signed me up for Little League, my mother, not my father. My poor father was working the swing shift at McClellan doing sheet metal fabrication for aircraft maintenance while trying to build a practice at an office on Watt Avenue, up towards Country Club Center with another DC, and driving taxis in between. That ended when he had a heart attack in 1962. But that is how it was for me. My father lost his practice as his partner's wife phoned all of his patients and told them that he was no longer practicing. So my father was obliged to focus on his swing shift job at McClellan until he got a better position at the airbase as an executive in the air material management section, which was the heart of the operation at McClellan AFB. He'd resume practice in 1975 after he retired officially from McClellan as a GS 14 (civilian lieutenant colonel). Lucky for him and us, he was able to transfer over to a desk job, and we fared a little better as a family. The best thing was that he was no longer obliged to drive a taxi or engage in any other moonlighting.

This all took place after we returned from our trip back east and our acquiring "Ex Ice-cutter."

But my Little League days were before that family improvement. There would be no dad at the games for me. Even worse, I didn't know anything about baseball. My mom seemed keener on my playing than my father, who seemed indifferent to the sport. Two of her brothers had been scouted by the minor league for professional baseball and played for a while. That stuck with her, I guess. So Momma would send me off to practice and then to games. Although I played on a team, it was overall a lonely experience. But there were a few highlights.

I recall that first year's Memorial Day Parade vividly as I was picked as one of the boys to ride on a float representing the North Highlands Little League. I got a good tour of North Highlands' main drags, you could say. I also had several items thrown to me by kids while I was on the float. I say "to" because they weren't thrown at me in a vindictive way. One girl threw a piece of candy at me, but I didn't feel like a monkey. A boy with a big smile ran up and tossed a frog to me. It must have come from Rio Linda Creek, commonly known as "The Ditch," as I related earlier. Anyway, I had a pet frog for a little while after that. A very short while, since it was a warm day and there was no water to be had. Even then, I wondered why the kid had made me a present of his frog. In making his friendly gesture, he had condemned it to death.

That first year of Little League in 1961 was pathetic, not for just me but the entire league. Okay, maybe mostly for me, as I was assigned right field and remained there for the whole season as the obviously least-valued player. My team for both years I played was the Rainiers, after the mountain in the Pacific Northwest. That's how I first learned about that mountain and the wider geography of my Western American home. There was only one decent baseball field in the entirety of North Highlands that was open to us. That one place was ironically right around the corner from our house in Larchmont Park, which we called "Thomas Park." We only played there twice and then only because we were playing for the championship at the end of the season. No, we didn't win, but we did win the championship the next year. I had more of a role in the second year. We had diamonds; I mean the cages and fences, backstop, etc. These were made of the same stuff as the storm fences, the galvanized, industrial type used by the airbase.   That was probably where all of this stuff came from as some sort of war surplus.

The playing fields were another story. They were hardpan and strewn with pebbles that could be almost two inches in diameter sometimes. And that wasn't all; there were little rain gutters that seasonal rain had eroded into the hardpan soil from the winter rains that were part of the outfield players' hazards. I can't count how many times I lined up on a ground ball, sure to catch it, just to have it hit a stone and leap over my mitt. Or maybe it would take a dip in the eroded ground and fly by my opened glove as a result. I'd turn and run after the ball. After finally running it down, I would practically break my arm trying to throw it back to prevent a home run as there was no back fence at all – so I could run halfway to The Spook Tree from Warren Allison Elementary. I certainly won no admiration for my efforts; no one likes the kid that just missed a ball even though it hopped over his glove unpredictably. But that wasn't all, no. Our first games were played on a weekend, at midday. So my debut had been a pop fly out to me. I watched it fly up and over me. And just when the time came to begin to tack its descent into my waiting glove, there was the sun, the bright, piercing California Sun – blinding me and defeating me – and the ball would plop down near me while I tried to get my eyesight back. So I was the kid that no one talked to, hardly. There was one, but he was the next one up from me. Even to me, he was a goof.

My one saving grace was that I could hit the ball, usually make it in to score, and I loved stealing bases. I was a pest on base and was always trying to steal a base, which I think I did at least once. Maybe I was trying to make up for my failures in the field. But really, I was just automatically in for the steal, for the sheer fun of it. I do know that I enjoyed being with a lot of other boys. For me, the best time of the game was at the end when we'd all go out and yell, "Two, four, six, eight, who do we appreciate!" I picked up on the idea of sportsmanship quickly, and I disliked cheaters and always have. That has given me a lot to hate in this world. Yet, I engage in this emotion with a more stoic attitude.

That year's season ended. And just as soon as it did, I was whisked off with my family for a trip "back east" to meet all of our cousins, aunts, and uncles that were still located on the other side of the Mississippi River. Coincidentally, my father had been born in St. Louis, Missouri. In Michigan, with Uncle Reg and Aunt Becky, and our cousins Reggie and Diana, we spent a week playing on the old family estate at Bundy Hill. Uncle Reg and Aunt Becky still ran a practice in the home and office complex at Bundy Hill. Uncle Reg ran his practice in the morning and supplemented that with a swing shift job at Jackson State Prison. Competitive pistol shooting was the big sport in that branch of the family. One time, after our aforementioned shooting day, Uncle Reg took my Dad to a range with him. They brought Cousin Reggie and me along but made us wait in the car while they practiced. But Reggie was up for a challenge. He hushed me and snuck out of the car and stole some little green apples from a nearby tree. Back in the car, we ate them. The two authority figures never knew. That part of our family was of some note in the sport of competitive pistol shooting. The remainder of our trip was out to Pennsylvania Coal County in the Appalachians, Wilkes-Barre, where my mother grew up.

We took side trips to Washington, D.C., New York City, and Virginia to visit a friend from Momma's time working in Washington, D.C., during the war. These people were real Virginians. I was already interested in the Civil War. I engaged the daddy of the house in a conversation on the first day we were there out on his patio where he was setting up a barbeque for all of us. I innocently asked him, "Are you a Yankee, or a Rebel? I'm a Yankee." He responded wisely, pointing out that we are all Americans now. Later, he came to me and gave me three large color prints that I still have in my possession today; General Grant, General Lee, and a panorama of the First Battle of Manassas. I had them pinned on the wall in my bedroom for years. Both families went for a day tour of Washington, D.C. together.

I recall their beautiful daughter, Susan, who was my age. We were always paired in the group photos that were made that day. It seems funny to me now. My first "date" was arranged by the grownups. My mother was a first-generation American, so I am sure this was her doing. But I don't mind. I only wish Susan would have remembered and looked me up when I was in high school or even later. My mom showed me a photo of her when I was in my early twenties. It might be best to not elaborate more than to say that she was a contestant for Miss Virginia. But somewhere, there is a photo of her and me in front of the White House, from that 1961 visit to the National Capitol.

The main stops that day were the photo out in front of the Kennedy White House, a visit to the Lincoln Memorial, with a photo taken on the steps, and the Custis-Lee Mansion and Arlington Cemetery to see the Tomb of the Unknown Soldier. At the gift shop, I bought a facsimile of the Declaration of Independence, The U.S. Constitution, The Bill of Rights, The Gettysburg Address, and a book for children titled, "Lee and Grant at Appomattox." This was the first history book in my now huge collection. I actually read it. I still have these items from that trip in my possession; to think that all of that is torn or shut down now. Killing history is surely a crime against humanity at some level comparable to book burning.

With the third grade, the bully, and all entirely behind me, another year with another spring arrived. The question of Little League came up again. I wasn't sure that I wanted to play. My father was still doing double duty, so it was another guaranteed journey through loneliness and shame, it seemed to me. I didn't articulate it to myself as such at the time, but I had very little enthusiasm for going through another season. It was my mother who forced the decision on me. I had shown some interest in science at that point and had expressed the desire for a chemistry set. The choice was either Little League or a chemistry set. As my clever mother put it with ghoulish emphasis to make it seem fun, I would be "hidden away in my lab." The visual I saw was shut in the dark during the summer, concocting some noxious formula for making myself a freak. Or, as she put it, I could be out in the sun, playing with the other boys. The choice was really stressful for me because it was obvious that I had to be a "normal" boy and play baseball. I wasn't all that sure that I wanted to go back to Little League. But I also did not want to be a freak. I didn't have entirely positive memories of the past season, but I made the choice. It turned out not to be as bad as the first season. I had improved. My parents had bought me a bounce-back net, and I became better at catching.

So I found myself on third base and sometimes center field. I could hit most of the time and get in, even in the first year. And in our championship game, I hit one nearly out of the park and drove in two runs, following them in on the next hit. That was a good ending for that saga. So my mother had been right in the end to push me to a positive completion, even though she didn't know how it would end or how it had been for me personally. In the end, I was still no player of any note.

The pitcher was the star, and he got all the love and attention from the baseball coach and his dad, who was always there. I wasn't jealous. The idea that I could ever be in that kid's position never even occurred to me as possible. I had learned to stand apart by then. Besides, I had other things on my mind. I was intelligent enough to sense that there was more in the world than I had found so far. I later found pole vaulting and then motorcycle racing. I found and still see that when I do things by myself, I get more accomplished and even excel. But it wasn't and isn't easy. It is far more rewarding than being carried along by a group of others. The team fencing events were fun, but the medals didn't mean as much to me as the ones I won as an individual. Mastering the horse was the fulfillment of a promise I had made to myself very early in my life.

The Moment Arrives At last

The big change of that season was the big change in the location of the games. That was the first year that Brock Park was opened. Brock Park was named after the primary developer of North Highlands, M.J. Brock & Sons. Their company was located in Los Angeles on Larchmont Drive, so they used that name for the project, Larchmont

Village, and Larchmont Elementary, as well as many L.A. street names, such as Centinella (my street), Melrose, Lankershim, Channing, Clausen, Fairfax, and others. Because of the Brock company donation, we finally had a good field for every game. It was still hardpan, but at least it was graded. There were two diamonds.

Brock Park had been set out on U Street or Old Antelope Road now, far from the then-existing rows of houses. It seemed a long way out at first, and I had to get there on my own. I had a bicycle, so I always rode it out to the park. And guess what was out in that same field, maybe a couple hundred yards away toward Walerga Road? The Spook Tree was there, waiting patiently for me. Up to now, it had been a distant thing, a horror, but not something I had to deal with immediately, emotionally.

Where I had been too young to get away long enough to hike out to it, now all I had to do was diverge just a little from my path to and from home to finally visit it, up close. There was this other kid who would show up early, just after I would. He wasn't on my team, but we'd explore the two diamonds and talk about whatever came up. One time, they had delivered the trailer with dry ice in layers of canvas for cooling the sodas down once the concessionaires arrived and set up. He took a few of the compressed carbon dioxide rocks, and we dropped them into one of the latrines nearby and watched them bubble and smoke up through the blue water in the outhouse's honey pot. So I sorta got a chemistry lesson along with my baseball. (I should have told my mother about it). We occupied ourselves with this sort of activity as we two had one thing in common, a mother that sent us off to the games early. I don't know why that was, either. But that is how it was.

We soon got to the subject because the tree was so near. The kid knew that the tree was called The Spook Tree. I finally formed my conspiracy. One afternoon, we met up while we were both on our way to Brock Park. As we came out into the field, I looked over to the tree as I always did. He noticed, and we talked about it. We agreed to linger after the game and figured we could go over to it and take a closer look. The time had finally come!

By the time the game was over, the sun had set. It was twilight time. The first hundred yards were unremarkable, but the tree seemed to radiate its eerie aura that was increasingly palpable as we came nearer. The sun had already set, but coming closer, the tree's strange feeling seemed to shut out light as if the sky had suddenly gone overcast. My sense was that of deep brooding, of something unknown, dark, and frozen in time, some profound mystery lived on in this big, dark, dead tree. Its one surviving large branch arched up and over us as if it might suddenly snatch us up. As I came nearer, the boy with me seemed to disappear from the scene. Now it was just me and the tree.

There was a certain quality of power about the tree. It was exactly as I had felt when I had just earlier that year stood before a life-sized Calvary Cross at a church where all the local choirs had congregated for an event coordinated among all of the regional Lutheran Churches. A Christian might call me blasphemous, I suppose, but I am not lying; that dead burned tree had presence and power of the same sort; both produced a sense of tragic awe. Certainly, they had both served as execution devices for a long time and after all, a man had died on both the tree and the cross. When the family saw the film "Spartacus" not long after this, I learned to my shock, that untold thousands had been crucified by Romans in "Biblical Times" as many adults tended to put it in those days. Likely enough, that hanged man Bobby had told me about had said his prayers before he died. He might have even wondered why God had forsaken him, as many a Christian victim of lynching must have in the olden times when the law was enforced wherever chaos reigned via vigilante justice. Whether it was factual or not, just as Socrates had been condemned by a mob of clerics, so had the claimed Son of God, and so were the uncounted crucified men of the time.

I wondered how the tallies compare; the number of hanged men versus the number crucified. I later learned that there were more crucifixions than most realize. Once they gained political power in the late fourth century, Christians crucified so-called "heretics," along with pagans, and Jews for some time, like nearly two thousand years, but the initial frenzy that included copious book burnings, crucifixions, and spontaneous executions as with Hypatia of Alexandria in ca 390, lasted about a hundred years.*[1]

Where this tree and lynching were concerned, it seemed like a long time ago to me at the time. I instinctively felt that it was absurd to even think of a lynching now. In my child's mind, things like that were stories; part of a dingy, past. But then, even 1945 and the war seemed like an ancient event to my childish mind. Yet, here before me now, was this ancient tree, standing as a witness. It was one of the first experiences I had of my time separation illusion broken down. Bobby's stories made the leap possible.

It even seemed more tragic to me because it was alone in the middle of a fallow field as a forgotten remnant of something that must have been much larger. But whatever that had been, this tree's burning must have been one of the main events. It was plain that this tree had lived for hundreds of years. It was old enough to have grown a hollow inside of it. It was there to see. It looked to me as if some animal could live there. It could be a coyote or fox den, which it probably had been until the people came and drove them off along with the antelope when the field was green, and the tree was alive and a thing of beauty. That one remaining branch loomed out toward me like a monstrous, dark arm poised to shove me into the hollow to some surprise I had not counted on. That feeling was immediate as I came into its presence. It was both holy and hellish. As that hollow in the tree was frightening because of the unknown that might lurk in its darkness, a burning bush may produce third-degree burns if you get too close.

But there was more to it. There were Bobby's stories, and there was the tree itself. I have never since seen a tree, dead or alive, with so much character expressed on it like this one. The big branch was there, looming threateningly. It certainly could have been used to hang a man.   The few smaller surviving branches seemed to be warding off blows from above, uselessly. They seemed to be pleading to the heavens for salvation, like Joan of Arc at the stake.

Practically etched into the blackened bark was overall an expression of pained outrage. The tree's many prominent, dead roots were knarled and blackened, polished off here and there by the elements. The roots were large, and they seemed to cling tenaciously as they ran out from the base of the tree, seeming to dig furiously into the hardpan earth about it, not ready to let go, not yet. The hollow had opened again a bit further up the trunk and had an almost human aspect, frozen in a scream of agony, and maybe rage. The fire must have gotten inside the hollow so that the mouth had seen fire pouring out from it, creating its final gruesome form. And the ground all around it was bare. It was as if nothing dared grow too near that tree as if there was an invisible "line of death" circled around it like poison, created by the fire that killed it. There was a horror about it as much as there were rage and sorrow. From a distance, it had always seemed a forlorn sight. But now, in its presence, I could not help but feel a little frightened, another thing it had in common with a "life-sized" cross, especially the Catholic type, which always seemed to be horrific in its depiction of the common execution method of the ancient world. But strangely, like the crucifix, the overpowering emotion was the compulsion toward mourning over the tragedy that created it, whatever it might have been.

Certainly, something deeply tragic lingered about it. It was altogether a haunted tree if trees can have ghosts or fairies lingering about it. There was more than enough to account for the unknown kid to first call it "The Spook Tree." Being in the presence of The Spook Tree left me with mixed feelings. It was spooky, it was horrible, and it was tragic. Its death had been a tragedy because trees are not just vital to all life, but a thing of beauty, and the destruction of beauty is always a dark undertaking of all that is good. I could not then articulate them to myself, but I felt it. However, what lingered most from then on was a quiet kind of reverence. It seemed to be some sort of memorial. But I could not know what it might have been. The feeling that the tree had given me for all of the years before was enlarged, magnified by this experience. After a little while, we left and went our separate ways home.

I thought about the tree for days afterward. And I thought of it again, years later, when I read Tolkien and learned of his Ents.   But this tree never had the support of an outraged forest. It was not, after all, a denizen of Middle Earth. From this first meeting onward, whenever I was at the ballpark, I would occasionally look over to the tree as if to assure it that I was here, and I saw it. It almost felt like a duty.

As time went on, I doubled down on my vigilance. It wasn't the foremost thing on my mind. I wouldn't say that I was obsessed with the tree, not at all. It was more like an abiding habit of checking it as a landmark against those rows of streets like my own were slowly marching toward it. They would eventually reach the Spook Tree at some point. Would they leave it up? No, it was dead, and even at my age, I knew that when the men got there, they'd see it as just a dead tree with no aesthetic value or meaning.   After all, they cut down all of the living oak trees they came to as North Highlands expanded. Now I know that this way of doing things, the detached, utilitarian style, had come from Los Angeles, where a teaming city and its suburbs had exploded into being in a short time. The war had even furthered efficiency, and considerations for nature were absent completely during wartime.   Only winning carries any value, and anything and everything will be sacrificed to win at a time of war. That's the reality of wartime, but maybe not the winning policy for constructing a community that is intended to last.

The year went by, and the two final years of my elementary school days were spent at Hillsdale School. I had a constant view of the Spook Tree and out to the almond orchards beyond the wheat fields by the railroad tracks and Antelope. The ever-expanding sea of homes drew nearer to the tree. Finally, one day, I could not spot it. Further attempts from different angles confirmed it; The Spook Tree was gone, just like that.

I imagined it had been paved over or had a house foundation poured over the spot. It seemed like a great sin to me. It seemed to me as if history had been lost; a tree that had observed the years and its seasons for perhaps four hundred years was something that deserved memory. It seemed that it had been unceremoniously discarded, like an old piece of furniture. Or had it? Later discoveries make me wonder.

The Spook Tree was old and attracted no value or sentimentality, it seemed, except secretly, to a few of us. Of course, how could a dead tree mean anything to suburban developers? I knew it was ridiculous for me to think that there could be any consideration for such a thing. At the corner of Watt Avenue and Auburn Boulevard was a gas stop in front of a bar with a sign I always noted when we passed by; "Live Oak." I mean that there were a couple pumps, a little garage, and a larger clapboard structure next to it that wasn't an old-time convenience store.

That bar was next to a prominent living oak tree. It was probably a historic place. This place must have been an old roadhouse because it had a card room. I remember that sign, too. A grown-up could go there and play poker, just like in the old Westerns. From its look, it had probably been there since about the time Rancho Del Paso had opened to development in the early 1900s. It is located on or near the spot where the Oak Gove House, is the site of a famous duel that had taken place there in the 1850s.

The name "Live Oak" likely came from the town of that name, which once existed in Cosumnes Township. We can guess that the Live Oak owner at Watt Avenue and Auburn Boulevard had either come from the original Live Oak settlement or at least memorialized it in a rather bawdy manner. That must have been a lively place in its time. Eventually, that place also disappeared. Progress, as they say. Today, there's an Arco/AM/PM station there, a convenience store.

Palm trees replaced the native valley oak that stood there for who knows how many hundreds of years. Such is the way of urban planning and what some call progress. After they took down The Spook Tree, I could never bring myself to visit the neighborhood where it had stood to see or guess whether its site was covered by a roadway or under some house's foundation. I sure wouldn't want to live in a house built over that spot! It took many years, decades, in fact, before I tried to search for any trace.

Places such as Live Oak existed all along Auburn Boulevard from Sacramento to Auburn as holdovers from the "Days of Gold." All main thoroughfares saw them as necessary and desired. They were not what you'd call "family-friendly," as they served as bars, assiduous gambling houses, and of course, brothels. Many survived very late, as long as the post-war period. In fact, my Uncle Ralph bought "Cliff House" located at the end of the confluence of Greenback Lane and Madison Avenue on Lake Natoma. It was purely an investment as the place had been shuttered for years by then. He sold it and it became a modern restaurant named The Cliff House of Folsom. Just behind it is the Jedediah Smith Memorial Trail, or for the less historical-minded, The American River Bike Trail. It runs from Discovery Park at the mouth of the American River on the Sacramento River, to Beale's Point at Folsom Dam Lake. I have to wonder what these places were like during Prohibition. However, it was, they apparently survived, some of them at least. When I saw these old places, I'd always make the same sort of note I did when I first saw Antelope. Any evidence of older times fascinated me. The mystery of the marks of age left on them by others intimated untold stories of people who had come first, lived, and died. Just like The Spook Tree.

How Antelope Met White Rock

I can't complain that my childhood was hard. It was overall, quite wonderful, despite a few perplexities around the meaning of some of my experiences with my family and the wider world. My personal afflictions were due to my isolation as the only boy in the family and being shorter than usual for my age, which made me an early target of bullies. What got me through it, besides my father's distant, Any Griffith-like managing in a similar crisis, and my Uncle Johnny's better-than-Barney Fife's Judo instruction, was my love of the fields, the rivers, the mountains, and The Spook Tree.

Elementary school and Little League had taught me that mainstream sports were not going to be satisfying experiences. Yet there was something that burned in me, and it needed expression. I had taken a punch in the jaw for objecting to the older kid bullying my sister, Paulette. In hindsight, what he was really doing was trying to get her attention by being obnoxious via splashing water on her by throwing rocks into the puddle we were all standing around at the time. I walked over to him and told him to stop throwing rocks at my sister. When I was bullied for months in the third grade, I found the courage to stand up to my nemesis and knock him down with a right, left cross combination perfectly executed, without any training. What I did get came from my Uncle Johnny, who taught me a few Judo throws, but nothing about fists. What I got from my father was hands-off guidance. He made me work it out for myself. And that wasn't easy. The bully was much taller than I was. As I related, I had finally had enough and acted on the last Monday of the school year. So I didn't see the kid until next fall. Normally, after a fight, kids would come to school the next day and act as if nothing had occurred. I am not sure if that would have been the case. It was good that we had the summer pause.

At the commencement of the fourth grade in September, that kid approached me in a friendly way and invited me over to his house the next day, which was a Saturday. He lived just up Centinella from me beyond Cantel Way. Once there, he tried his best to be friendly and entertain me. We didn't continue any friendship, but we weren't enemies. So the gesture had been made and I accepted it as his apology. I am guessing that there was some parent-teacher discussion behind our backs after the day of my physical outburst. Mrs. Alden was not as negligent as I had supposed.

Mrs. Alden; I remember her well. She had in her own way, and being a shining example of her profession, I now can see how she brought me along, through the trouble caused after we read a story in class about a marble contest. The class would have a marble contest, just like in the book. The ground just off the blacktop of the playground was not yet planted with grass and lent itself well to several marble rings where the class played off with their marbles. Everyone except me, that is. My parents would not let me have marbles. They were worried that my youngest sister, Gayle, might swallow one.

She and I were great mouth stuffers, apparently. I recall the previous panic when my parent feared she had swallowed a piece of glass. My father still had his fluoroscope. I remember standing with him as he scanned her abdomen in real-time. (Those devices later became obsolete due to the freely scattering radiation and the long exposure times to the patient and operator). That had set the policy. So at the marble tournament, I could only stand around and watch in painful envy. I wanted to own some marbles so badly. The boys on my block traded them and I could only gaze at them as they held them up for others to see and judge their value. This made my suffering nearly continual at the time. My abstention from the games marked me. Two boys noticed and separately set upon me, in their own styles, and made me incredibly miserable on the days they acted. Mrs. Alden, after all, couldn't be everywhere and see everything, but she knew something was going on. And there was one boy at least, who befriended me. His name was Ricky. We both had a problem with pronouncing our "Rs" at the time. I was just playing around, imitating Elmer Fudd, but it got Ricky and me into a series of special sessions for language correction. It might have further marked me as an "oddball."

I cannot recall the name of the young woman who coached us, but she was very pretty, and on Valentine's Day she gave us both a very nice candy treat; a chocolate-covered nougat/marshmallow sort of thing shaped like a heart. Things, like, fishing adventures, singing in the Church choir with other boys, and our own family sing-alongs, led by Martine using an autoharp she possessed for a while countered the bad experiences. Apparently, a lover of folk music, Mrs. Alden always took a couple periods a week to spend time singing songs from the American Folk songbook that was issued to us in the primary schools in those days, at least, first through fourth. I don't remember either the books or any singing after that, except as part of the larger annual choral events held by the Grant Union District. Certainly, the curtailing of singing American folk songs in class was a blow to societal continuity and was quite intentional. I've got to say, the folks that ran that district were good people, and Mrs. Alden was a great teacher. And I don't remember singing in any class as much as we did in that third-grade classroom at Village School. Such things and the natural resilience of a child saw me through the bullying episodes. But as the year went on, they increased.

Regarding my final victory of self-assertion over fear; obviously, the bully's parents had a talk with their boy about the bullying episodes that had led to my action. This was how things were handled in those days. The parents talked and were reasonable. It also worked because the boys observed a code of honor, based loosely on the Marquis of Queensbury's rules. For example, kicking during a fistfight was considered a disgusting resort, although wrestling was an acceptable transition. And when a kid said, "I give," the fight stopped. I had been the one who received satisfaction over the bullying I received. Another kid had joined in on the bullying. He had an older brother in Martine's class. She didn't like him at all. They were a difficult set of brothers, it seems. I don't know if their parents were talked to, but they were not living in North Highlands by the new school year that September.

My turn to "give" came early in the fourth grade. There was a kid who had been in my classes since kindergarten. He was a big, burly kid. I mean that he was taller than usual and overweight at a time when kids rarely were. Because of this, he was left alone. Some kids teased him, but I never did that. I don't know how it started but at recess, he was having fights with kids. Every recess, it was one, the next recess, another. A crowd of boys always stood around until he pulled his trick. He'd quickly get the fight down to wrestling and sit on his opponent. "I give," was pronounced inevitably almost as soon as he got his full weight on the hapless boy. I don't know how I came to be in one of those contests, but I was. And I made the same mistake as my predecessors and ended up under him. I couldn't last long. He was so heavy that I couldn't breathe very easily and the gravity of his mass caused a pain that was growing every second. "I give." It was easy to say. But I didn't stop there. As I had been befriended by my previous bully, at least as a gesture of peace, I told this kid that I wanted to be his friend. I remember that day, we walked home together. He had his arm around me all the way. The poor kid only needed a friend. Thus, boys were once cultivated into civility through such experiences. No one got pulled aside and placed on a drug regime.

My fourth-grade teacher Mrs. Roach was fairly conscientious. I think my parents talked with her as I recall the entire family visiting her at her apartment in North Highlands, which was at the McClelland Court

Apartments behind the strip mall across from Fruitvale School (now Joyce School). She had been Martine's teacher before me. I was not doing well in school. It was probably due to having been bullied for so long in the third grade, but I'm not sure about that. I had been out of school for three weeks in the second grade with chickenpox. When I returned I remember how disoriented I felt. I really should have had a tutor. That lack of attention hurt me academically for years. But it wasn't as if I was out to pasture. I had been playing chess with my dad, after all. I think my folks wanted to inform her of my previous history. I improved by the end of the year somewhat. Maybe it had been the most important education that had been achieved; I had found the balance between the extremes of bullying and cowardice perhaps better than most boys did in my time.

My dad had acted much as Andy Griffith did on his show when his son was being bullied at school. He asked me about it and encouraged me to stand up to the bully, but never said exactly what to do. I had to find my way myself. I think that this is the key ingredient to the difference in parent-child rearing by the end of the sixties. By the seventies, the "Little League Father" syndrome had arrived. Parents fought over their kid's issues, and sometimes with fists. It became quite an epidemic, lasting into the eighties.

This problem also arrived in MX by the early seventies. It was the main reason that I did not continue racing at the time partially because of my Uncle Ralph. My cousin had entered the fray and he and my dad wanted to set us against one another as an extension of their own sibling rivalry. I recognized it and refused to take part. I let my cousin, who was six years younger than me, have his time at it, and so he had his day.

This "Little League Father" syndrome grew and created a generation of kids who expected others to sort their problems out for them, and that someone else was to blame. One example concerns the issues around bullying. Up to my time, kids passed on verbal defense methods developed by the previous generations. We all knew how to deal with verbal name-calling; "sticks and stones may break my bones, but names will never harm me!" This was an effective, disarming reply. There were others, "What you say bounces off me and sticks to you!" and "That's what you are, but what am I?" insult banter employed by PeeWee Herman in the 1980s. (It was my sister Paulette who sat me down at her home and made me watch that movie. We almost died laughing at that scene). As a result, not too many ever felt too badly about being called names. When effective bullying happened, it was usually a combination of personal insults and actual physical bullying, which was actually rare. For example, my bully had gotten to me by standing behind me in line after recess and pinching me while making fun of my last name. He had added the physical element and he did it one time too many. It was the ego and laziness of parents that began to affect society as a whole through the neglect to teach kids how to cope on their own. "Helicopter parenting" was a famous term.

First kids, then as they grew up, adults began to feel that there was a larger issue of justice at stake when a child was bullied and so it mushroomed until the backlash and reactions grew into a national phenomenon that affected society. As the traditional father disappeared from the family, along with his particular skill set, particularly where managing bullying was concerned, mothers naturally took over and came up with their own methods. They were assisted by institutional feminism had decided the problem was that the nature of the male animal was the problem. So the solution was to force the boys into passiveness. Exhaustive studies have shown that when boys (like rats) are deprived of their rough and tumble play, they do not develop their frontal lobe functions very well, so they came to be diagnosed with ADHD This was then compensated with drugs including Ritalin. A few concerned feminists like Christine Hoff-Sommers became so alarmed at feminism gone mad, that she wrote volumes one and two of "The War Against Boys."*[1] She warned that the future would be irretrievably harmed if these practices were not ended and boys were helped along more in the way they used to be by wiser parents (fathers). She said that the future would be bleak if it went on. And it was more than that; the schools had changed from the education of American children to the indoctrination of them. In one generation we went from a society of parents who generally understood how to guide their children into learning how to stand on their own two feet, to a society where a significant number, perhaps the majority expect the government to solve their problems for them; too bad for us.

Rough and Tumble Play

Before that societal shift, in my case, I had found my way and I wasn't afraid of risks. I was always the smaller kid, so I was the last to be picked for team games on the block or at school. But I wasn't afraid of a little rough play. Once around that time, the kids on my block used to play tackle football using maybe two adjoining lawns. Since pretty much every home had kids and we were always up and down the block doing one thing or another, adults hardly ever came outside to look much less supervised. One older kid, who was particularly cruel in ways he demonstrated more than once, dragged me after he got the ball and I held onto his foot, kicking me in the face with every stride and laughing as he bloodied my nose. I didn't cry. I plotted my revenge. That revenge wasn't on him, directly, just on my situation.

Later, after someone started dirt clod fights on my block, I responded by forming up a little army to go against the group led by that same older kid. We didn't win the contests. Our contests became so rough that we moved them out to the field closer to M Street by the gas station at Watt and M Street and some kids on Milton Way, including one future long-time friend, Mark Miller joined in the harmless fracas. No one backed down until one day, I hit a kid in the head with a dirt clod that wasn't entirely soft dirt, and that ended it all. It wasn't intentional, I assure you, and I had no idea that the dirt clod contained a harder rock. No matter how much I tried to apologize, the kid wouldn't talk to me and the family moved away not long after, although I don't believe that incident was the reason. The episode of rock battles was over, and I had lost a friend, but I had learned something about limitations. So we found other things to do. Soon we went from merely riding bicycles to setting up ramps on the sidewalk to see how much air we could get. No one dared hit that ramp as fast as I did. I found that I liked flying that way. What stuck with me was the love of controlled risk. As soon as I saw my first motorcycle in an event that I later realized was the Forty-Niner Enduro one day while I was with my dad and Uncle Johnny checking out a mining prospect near Shirttail Canyon in the spring of 1965, I knew I wanted to race. (Shirttail Canyon was named such because of the heavy Chinese presence during the Gold Rush). I had already been primed one year at the state fair when I had an experience that impressed me as a seven-year-old kid. We had just entered the midway of the exposition, where the rides were. There was a tall round structure like a huge wooden barrel standing on one end. But that wasn't so remarkable to me. What was remarkable and caused me to walk to it as if by a hypnotic command was the sound coming out of the top.

It was a loud roar. What was it? I was guessing as I walked up to it. Daddy was walking with me, I noticed. Neither of them forbade me from approaching that roaring tower. There were steps for climbing up to the top. People were already up there looking in. What was I going to see, some unfortunate man being torn to pieces like Ragnar in the film "The Vikings?" I knew about that because Daddy had taken me to see it at the Village Theater on Fulton Avenue in 1958. Jackie had seen it too, and we talked about it at the time.

We finally made the top and I looked in. It was motorcycles. Two motorcycles were riding, defying gravity impossibly on the walls of what now seemed like a huge barrel. They were fast and daring, coming close to the top, almost to the top's edge, where they would fly out and surely die of injuries. But they never flew out. They rode on that edge, up and down, thrilling us all with their daring courage. Now I knew what "daredevil" meant. There is plenty of that in all motor racers. I had seen the old-time "Wall of Death" that along with Barnstorming had been a feature at state and county fairs since the 1920s. The biplanes were gone, but the motorcycles had survived for me to discover. So when the time came to change from the usual neighborhood games to something more, I was ready. (Note; I almost bought a biplane in 1972 to get into crop dusting work, as I saw it as the closest thing to a WW1-style dogfight. But I decided to pass on the idea because of the controversy over the chemicals being used at the time).

It turned out that I found my niche and by the time I was through with that phase, I had "proved myself to myself" as well as a lot of other people. In 1970, my main competition was my best friends, Dave Buckminster, and Billy Grossi; we three swapped victories. Billy topped me at Hangtown where I took fourth behind him and two riders from Southern California, and at a June race at White Rock Motorcycle Park, where I took second. But I got it back on him at a race at the Brisbane track later that summer.

In 1971, one crowd had come up with a nickname for me, "Loco LaRue." The appellation was apparently created after I had pulled off a wild mid-air pass from fourth to first place through a mid-air pass skipping the middle of three jumps on the top of a hill on the Reeder's Mill Shingle Springs tack, a popular District 36 MX site in those days. I launched off the first one, flew over the second one, passed my two competitors, and landed on the third one, which had the effect of popping my CZ up sideways to the track, in a radical "cross-up."

What I remember of it was how after I came down on top of the third jump, my CZ twisted sideways to the track as it flew nearly straight up off the jump. I had enough "hangtime" for a quick decision. My instant idea was to do what I thought World Champion Joel Robert would do in such a situation on his CZ. I opened up the throttle so I was at full power when I hit the ground. The track went left and quickly downhill. After hitting the ground, I rode down the hill standing on the pegs in a full-lock power slide to the bottom, collected myself, opened the throttle again, and took the checkered flag half a mile later. I was a bit angry because these two guys had been cutting a corner in the unobserved section at the back of the course to stay ahead of me up to the time I flew over them into first place. So I backed off a little in time to regain enough momentum to hit those jumps at a higher speed than usual. It worked very well.

There were enough witnesses to relate the event to others, and that was that; I became "Loco LaRue." But that was nothing compared with Danny Chandler, who showed up a little later.

Controlled Chaos was probably the best way to describe his style. But it took him far. But in my little way, I had won some limited admiration, and maybe the respect of enough connected people to be offered a sponsored ride by Penton West when I was working there in 1972. It certainly represents a major fork in the road that I did not take. That was definitely one of the Robert Frost moments when I took a fork in the road that made the difference. But I had also acquired a skill set that included keeping a cool head in a calamity (which saved my life more than once later on).

During 1970 at White Rock, a visiting woman commented to me that in her opinion, those like me, who raced had a "death wish" as she put it. It's not. It is about being on the edge, almost close enough to see over the other side, but avoiding the fall through skill and daring. Sure, it was a rush, an adrenalin rush. I recognized that at a point and used to claim that it was a natural high, believing it to be superior to what most young people were doing in those days. What Jim Morrison and the masses of idiots were doing with drugs, we were doing for real, which made it genuine. The difference is that although there was some blurring in those days, there were some drug-using riders, who tended to burn out quickly or reform. Recreational drug culture was and is about escape and allowing chaos, by default. Racing is about managing chaos, even triumphing over it by mastering the racecourse. In the final analysis, the competition only provided inspiration. As with most of life, the real competition is against one's self. However, as with any such activity, it can become an escape from reality. We should all strive to keep at least one foot on the ground half the time.

As it should be, my future was determined by my father in many ways. Before this, for most men of that era, any kind of motor racing was interesting, and so it was with my dad. Even before I knew it, my folks carried me in a laundry basket to watch the midget's race at Hughes

Stadium or the State Fairgrounds on Saturday nights. My mom told me years later that I used to set up obstacle courses on P Street and ride my tricycle around them. Through the sixties, I went to almost every one of the famous Sacramento Mile National races with my Dad. I had my first bike, a Hodaka "Ace 90" by 1966. I had talked my dad into getting them so that we could use them hunting. I learned how to ride it that autumn during hunting season on the Rubicon Trail out of Wentworth Springs, a place I came to love. We met the old Marine named "Miles" (Curran) there and the only other resident of the defunct mineral spring resort, Baltz Schuler, who Miles called "The Mayor of Wentworth Springs. But Baltz had leukemia. His time came on the second weekend we were there that season. We carried him out to Riverton where a Placerville ambulance took him to the hospital where he expired a few hours later. That event was a turning point for me because it awakened a certain awareness of compassion for those in need that would determine my road ten years later.

Wentworth Springs in its glory days – At one time it was owned by Lon Chaney, Jr. Photo courtesy of Michael Brattland Gerle Wentworth Springs online collection

I would go back to visit that place many times over the years. In September of 1970, after a memorable night MX at the Placerville Fairgrounds, I drove up to Wentworth Springs and spent the night. I walked around the place and took a few drinks from the mineral springs before returning home; the other one, at least. I remember that I was wearing my White Rock MC Park jersey and using my "crash cane," as I had a lingering limp from an odd landing during a race earlier that year in April when I popped up off a jump and my left foot had missed the pedal and my stiff leg found the surface first. That cane had been brought up at a rider's protest over my win the night before. "How can a guy who uses a cane win!?" One man complained.

The Origins of My MX Madness

To begin racing, I had to get permission from my parents. I approached them. To my surprise, they had no objection. My father's approval did not surprise me, but my mother's did. But they had a provision; I must pay for my own bike. So I had to get my driver's license and then get a job. I had all that done by the end of 1968. So I financed by first Penton with the help of my folks and the Bank of America, North Highlands branch.

Gene's Automotive in Loomis was the Husqvarna/Penton dealer and my first sponsor. My first event was in April of 1969, but it was not a moto-cross event. It was the famous Forty-Niner Enduro that the Polka Dot MC had been running since the fifties. It began in Foresthill and ran one hundred miles over logging roads and old miners' trails. My second event was the second attempt at the running of the First Annual Hangtown Motocross Classic.

By 1972, all the paths of my life up to then made a remarkable confluence with Sacramento and El Dorado County history. What began as Antelope in a field beyond my vision opened up into a broader vista of history and meanings. It began in 1964, just after the disappearance of the Spook Tree when my folks bought several acres of land off Green Valley Road just a couple of miles west of Placerville; scrub oak and pine woods with a creek running behind the land named Indian Creek and my life changed in a big way. We had to sell the beloved cabin cruiser to get it, but I never felt too bad about it, even though I was sorry to see her go.

My best friend at the time, Davy Hodges, was the son of my father's patient, whose mother and father owned the land next to the parcel we bought. In fact, that was how my folks learned about the property. Davy and I would have many adventures together up there under the auspice of Davy's grandparents. We had permission to cross through any fence in the region as far as we could walk. So we toted our .22 rifles and took adventures of discovery together. Once in a while, we'd have a wild cookout when we would hunt or fish for some type of meat and gather various edible wild vegetables, including cattail shoots, watercress, blackberries, certain roots similar to potatoes, greens such as miner's Lettuce, and so on. We'd cook it over a campfire. And we had a special drink in those days. From Davy, I learned about Yerba Santa; "Indian Tea." The bushes grew all over the land at that elevation. It was refreshing, and with a little honey, it was very good for a scratchy throat. I was an herbalist by fourteen, at least where one herbal remedy was concerned. Until the time that I left the region entirely, I used to make regular trips to pick some yerba santa and fill my gallon jugs with spring water from my secret spot near Kelseyville.

I became fascinated with Gold Rush history. I dove into it as far as I could at that time. I got my folks to take the whole family on excursions, like picnics at Coloma and other historical places. As the date of the discovery at Sutter's Mill was the same as my birthday, I felt a childish, "meant to be" attitude that I was there as I was at the time. I even read Bret Harte's "The Luck of Roaring Camp" and made an oral book report on it in the seventh grade to a confused class. I didn't do a very good job because I couldn't really talk much about the main character, who was the baby of a prostitute that the miners called "Luck." Yes, I said "a prostitute."

But my geographical curiosity led me to write the El Dorado Chamber of Commerce to ask about a particular mountain that intrigued me. I don't think that they realized that the inquiry was from a thirteen-year-old kid! But I was not deterred. I wanted to stake a claim, but I'd have to put it off for a while since I didn't drive! I explored old mines while I helped my Uncle Johnny on his gold dredge when he and my father would work together in the spring and summers in the mid-sixties. I gathered up Forest Service maps and marked out mines indicated on them for exploration and possible claim jumping in the future. Meanwhile, Davy and I spent a lot of time at our Indian Creek property during the school year during the years 1964 to 1966. During the school year, probably one weekend a month, and a week or two in the summer.

I was always trying to come up with reasons for my folk's drive out to the property so I could come along. The summer days were hot, and turkey buzzards were part of the skyscape as they seemed endlessly on patrol. On the ground were alligator and blue-belly lizards, as well as occasional larger mammals. We saw some snakes but never a rattler. Every so often, we had a wild cookout, as we called it. Once, we had forbidden fish as our main entre. We smoked the remainder in a smoker Davy had set up using a discarded refrigerator.

We were not allowed to enter one place, a property that had an eleven-acre lake on it. It was a vacation property of some party that was never there. It lay beyond the little self-sufficient farm of an old German couple named Schmidt. When we first met them, my parents walked us around to meet the few that lived on Indian Road at that time. I remember listening to old Mr. Schmidt and his reference to WWI. "Those Canadians fought like devils," he said. Later my father said that he reckoned that Mr. Schmidt had indeed been in the Great War, but on the German side! That was very interesting to me. The Schmidt's were very kind people. Their little farm impressed me as it did my father. I remember him talking about how remarkable that small farm was as a self-sufficient operation. I never achieved it for myself, but I have always dreamt of having a similar, off-grid sort of life with chickens, goats, a cow, and a big garden, just like the Schmidts had.

Davy was a year older than me and a bit mischievous, despite his family being "fundamentalist" Pentecostal Christians. Between us, he was the leader. So when he decided we'd sneak onto that property and catch some fish, I naturally came along as it was "his world," so to speak. Besides, he was a year older than me.

There were so many fish in that lake it was amazing. They were bluegill and crappie, and we collected up a good bunch of them quickly. We had already made beef jerky. The next day we were smoking the fish. That's when we got busted. Grandma just came out and told us that Mr. Schmidt had seen us walking in the woods past his place last night at dusk. I said nothing as Davy claimed we had not gone in there but caught them in Indian Creek "down a ways." Fish this size from Indian Creek was hardly likely. I was amazed at his ease with lying but said nothing. All being kindly people, nothing came of it. But Davy's grandparents must have decided that we needed something real and honest.

So they called up their friends, a famous pioneer family of the region, The Veerkamps, whose large landholding included a good-sized pond on it near Rescue, and arranged for us to go fish there. We didn't catch fish because we soon found that the bullfrogs liked the flies dangling off the end of our fishing poles. So we had frog legs that night. Yes, they do jump around in the frying pan, at least, until they're cooked enough. So Green Valley Road and Indian Creek have a special place in my memory. The Veerkamp's are one of the founding pioneer families of El Dorado County, with a historic mine in the region, so it means more to me now than it did even then, as a still ignorant boy.

I last visited Davy on Indian Road in 1995. He had taken residence after his grandparents had passed and left the place to him. He wasn't happy. The reason was obvious. The once open country, the woodsy landscape was now peppered with homes and development in every available location. The pine-speckled, scrub oak, and brushy manzanita acres where we had once roamed about for hours, sometimes on our hands and knees because of the density of the thickets of scrub oaks and manzanita, were hardly recognizable.

El Dorado County CHAMBER of COMMERCE
842 Main Street · Phone 622-3344
PLACERVILLE, CALIFORNIA

December 21, 1965

Mr. Mark LaRue
North Highlands, Calif.

Dear Mr. LaRue:

In answer to your recent inquiry, may we suggest that you
contact the Bureau of Land Management, Federal Bldg., Sacramento on unspoken for land.

Also for information on the different landmarks, may we refer
you to the California Section of the State Library, Sacramento.

Yours truly,

EL DORADO COUNTY CHAMBER OF COMMERCE

Exhibit A – Inquisitive Kid
*I have since come to believe that it was named Iron Mountain because of its iron-red dirt and
that no gold was found there. – Author's collection*

They were occupied by McMansions with sprawling yards. The
rangeland across Green Valley Road was similarly filled with
"ranchettes." In fact, it was all like that. "You can't do anything
around here anymore!" Davy complained. He was talking about
Montana. I assume that is where Davy is now. Carrying his own
personal burden, that only I and one other know of, a Vietnam Vet, he
is resting there now, I expect.*₂ The trip to Indian Creek Road and my
little woodland paradise became sacred to me, so knowing how it all
came to be was important to me. That led to my acquisition of USFS
maps whenever possible. Once my father began to take me on
hunting trips, that became easy as I asked any ranger we ever met for
a map, and I'd steal any my dad came up with. I'd spend hours going
over them, memorizing them, and making notes of interesting place
names to add to the list of locations for future exploration.

The connection to Green Valley Road and beyond all began with Greenback Lane, the old country road from Citrus Heights to Orangeville, back in the day when fruit was grown there and loaded at docks in Newcastle. Greenback was so named as a protest against the taxes used to build it as many felt it unnecessary at the time. Newcastle was the last in the line of towns east of Roseville before Auburn, the Placer County seat; Rocklin, Loomis, Penryn, and Newcastle in that order on the rail line east. Near Newcastle, we can find Antelope Ridge with a westward creek of the same name that meandered toward our little settlement of Antelope.

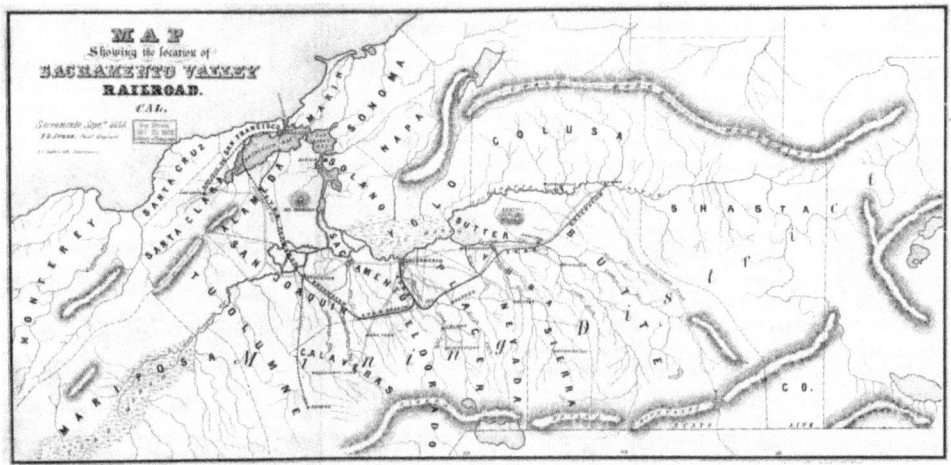

1855 Map of the Sacramento Valley Railroad by Theodore Judah – California State Library – Sacramento – the map has a strange orientation. Can you figure it out?

The development of the Sacramento Valley Railroad was to become the most important event in the life of early California and Sacramento County in particular. The company was formed in 1852, and construction was begun in February of 1855. It reached Folsom in January of 1856. The first railroad to be named Placerville and Sacramento Valley Railroad was incorporated on June 12, 1862, and construction from Folsom to Placerville began in late 1863. The line extended to Latrobe in August 1864. It arrived at Shingle Springs in June 1865, adding 26 miles to the route. Twenty years later, the decision was made to finally extend the line to Placerville. That work was completed on March 29, 1888. On May 15, 1888, it became part of the Southern Pacific, the non-operating Northern Railroad parent company.

Meanwhile, the California Central Railroad was established by Colonel Charles Lincoln Wilson to run from Folsom to Roseville from 1861 to 1864. After it was abandoned, the rail bed became many of the area's surface streets, such as South Cirby Way, which was laid on top of the old rail bed. Folsom Road got its name from being the old rail line and then the road to Folsom Town. The line also followed Linda Creek, and the Roseville shopping Center was built over it as well. Today, Rocklin is but an extension of Roseville. Still, it was once the high-grade granite supplier that supported the trestles and tunnels, allowing the first trains to traverse the High Sierra during the initial Transcontinental Railroad Project.

Owing to its 61 quarry sites, Rocklin was the supplier of some of the world's finest granite. For some time, who knows how long, teens began to use the water-filled quarry pits as natural swimming pools. Today, part of the old quarry is a popular climbing park. The Capitol building in Sacramento and other early government buildings were constructed of Rocklin Granite. "Lin" is a Gaelic word that means "pool" or "quarry." At the time, Roseville was merely a switching junction and a sleepy farm community. Eventually, The Junction became the Roseville Switching Yard and the shipping point for the region's vast citrus production, stealing the attention from Rocklin's granite quarries. Until very late, the Roseville Switching Yard featured the most massive fruit cooler in the United States, which allowed local produce to be shipped all over the United States. But there was another and more common sort of quarrying being done near Rocklin, where two channels of the Tertiary American River provided fine gold at a rate of one dollar per square foot. The Lee Drift Mine was two miles east of Rocklin and was still quietly prospected up to 1970. Antelope and North Highlands are connected by a line of gold to White Rock and beyond. Prospecting in Dry Creek is not necessarily a stupid idea, at least closer to Roseville, where dredging and other types of mining had proceeded in places like Secret Ravine up into the

1930s, leading to the toxifying of Dry Creek in Roseville and civil action after the deer that lived around it was found dead.

In Rocklin, a now long gone landmark, a restaurant and favorite watering hole for the Dirt Diggers North Motorcycle Club in Rocklin was Grouchy's (pronounced Grou-chees). I first noted Grouchy's for the funny face on the sign outside of it that described a less-than-congenial cook. But inside, it featured a fairly elegant dining room. At least it impressed me that way, the maybe two or three times our family visited it. Grouchy's was fine, but our family favored Poor Red's in the town of El Dorado. Once known as Mud Springs, owing to the mess of mud the crowds of draft animals created of the springs there, it finally gained its name from the myth of a golden city that had driven the Conquistador, Francisco Pizarro to rummage through the Andes centuries before in search of it. For their purpose at the time, the literal meaning was "a place of abundance," which was certainly fitting. El Dorado was close to our property near Placerville. It remained a personal favorite of mine up through my early adulthood until I left the region entirely for the coastal counties.

The Genesis of a Motorsports Legend

In 1966, U.S. Husqvarna distributor Edison Dye invited World 250cc MX Champion Torsten Hallman to come to the U.S. to demonstrate the Husqvarna machine at local events across the nation. He was a shocking success. The next year, with Hallman's help, recruited various European riders for a motocross circus that traveled the country as the InterAm event for the next four years until the AMA supplanted it with the Trans AMA events.

Previous page; Joel Robert and Torsten Halllman in 1966. Photo – Courtesy of Torsten Hallman

The Dirt Diggers are known primarily for having founded and run the now-famous Hangtown Motocross Classic, which is now an American Motorcycle Association circuit event that draws thousands of spectators every year. But the event was really the confluence of simultaneous ambitions of three motorcycle shops and one club. This race could be the most significant popular marker/reminder of the 19th century and the Gold Rush left in Sacramento and El Dorado County in 2020. It is linked in a convoluted way to North Highlands and, therefore, the Spook Tree, its history that deserves to be remembered.

The Dirt Diggers North Motorcycle Club could be said to have originated in Rocklin. However, the first meetings were held at the Orangevale Community Center and then at Orangevale Cycle Center, with fifteen members initial membership. Marian, his wife Doris, and Joe Pyle operated there from the early 1960s. According to its surviving members, including Bruce Young and Dave Duarte, Marion Pyle was really the club's grandfather. After the initial meeting, the membership met at the White Front Bar in Rocklin most often, but at Rudy's Hideaway as well. Grouchy's never saw an official meeting, but they saw plenty of Dirt Diggers at what they called "The Great Watering Hole." As a thirteen-year-old, I guess I missed the action at the bar.

Now, dear reader, to dispel any prejudicial thinking on the matter, I would like to refer to the fact that these glorious United States of America, this universally acclaimed Constitutional Republic, was dreamt up by some unsatisfied colonists in bars such as The Green Dragon Tavern in Boston and Fraunces Tavern in New York City. Before, during, and after the Revolutionary War, they were meeting places for the secret society The Sons of Liberty. Fraunces Tavern was the site of Washington's emotional farewell meeting with the officers of the Continental Army. After the war, that same bar became the Confederation Congress, the nation's central government under the "Articles of Confederation and Perpetual Union," and the departments of Foreign Affairs, Finance, and War. Given this and the fact that through World War Two, U.S. troops were fueled by caffeine, nicotine, and alcohol, this dirt-loving motorcycle club was conceived and operated in the loftiest of traditional institutions. Let that suffice.

In those days, European developed and produced motorcycles that dominated the off-road world. The Orangevale Cycle Center had a group of riders in their neighborhood, including Joe Pyle, Bill Dawson, and Carl Cranke.   Carl would later win seven gold and two silver medals at the International Six Day Trials during the seventies and early eighties. (The ISDT (now the ISDE) is considered the Olympics of off-road motorcycling)). The Rocklin group centered around Gene's Automotive, a dealer of the newly developed Penton Six Days Trial 125cc motorcycle that I had focused on as the brand I wished to compete with and the Husqvarna. The majority of Dirt Diggers at the time was a group that orbited Gene's shop, which is where another founding member, Bill Onga, worked. Among the 12 original members were Dave Duarte, Willy Groom (AKA "Lump"), and Marty Devries. These were shops that primarily sold off-road motorcycles, like Husqvarna, CZ, Bultaco, Maico, Sachs, and then the new John Penton-designed model, among others. They were united by their mutual desire to sell motorcycles to customers attracted to off-road activities, showcased by off-road events.

My goal was to race motocross. However, my first event was not a motocross race. It was the famous Forty-Niner Enduro that the Polka Dots, M.C. put on every April at Foresthill in Placer County. As I began riding through trail riding, enduros were not out of the question; they were just a chance to ride longer.   My second event was the Hangtown Motocross race which saw two go-arounds in the winter and spring of 1969.

As the club's story is related to me by founding member Dave Duarte, it was a group of guys who liked to ride, drink, race, drink, ride, and then drink some more that came up with the idea of starting a club. They all knew of the famous Dirt Diggers in Southern California. Many had traveled down as individuals to ride in many Southern California events, such as the Elsinore Grand Prix and Hopetown; why not have a chapter in Northern California? So Bill Dawson traveled down south and met with the Dirt Diggers. He came back, and that was that; the DDNMC would be the sister club of the original Dirt Diggers MC.

By 1968, The Dirt Diggers North MC was operational and inspired by the vision of creating its own GP-sized event in Northern California. They had held a few races in West Sacramento, Lincoln, and Orangevale, but nothing that was very profitable or on the scale they were aiming at. A bigger, better race circuit and room for many spectators were required. In 1968, a group of members including Bill Onga, Carl Cranke, Dave Duarte, Bill Dawson, and perhaps a few others traveled down to the Hopetown GP disguised as riders to spy on the DDMC methods of running their event.

The boys were aiming high. Once home, they began to search for an appropriate track. During September and October of 1968, they were looking for locations for the race. One was the popular track between Shingle Springs and El Dorado, which was known as Reed's Sawmill Track, and land at Latrobe, but no decision was made. The event needed space for enough parking and for a track that would challenge top riders.

Enter the third shop; Mike McGowan owned and operated Mike's Placerville Marine and Cycle. Mike was later a 1974 qualifier for the International Six Days Trial. Mike is the great-grandson of Judge McGowan, who served as a second at a consequential duel in the American Township section of Rancho Del Paso in 1854, somewhere in the area of today's Rio Linda.

During the mid-60s, Mike and his friends had been riding and developing a track on land near Placerville known as The Murray Ranch off Hank's Exchange Road. At the time, Mike's father worked for Bennett Murray and his construction company, running a motor grader. Bennett used to let Mike, Ron, and Gloria Keeping, their families, and other friends ride there. They gradually laid out a track with the dozer. Sometime later, Mike started thinking about holding races on that property as a way to promote his shop, expanding the track with the help of family and friends.

The two aforementioned shops were curiously enough, contemplating the same idea. Races were typically organized and run by clubs recognized by the American Motorcycle Association for points-earning in non-professional sportsman events. The accumulation of points would move a rider up from Novice to Amateur to Expert classifications. Experts could apply for professional licenses and make money racing at professional events. This was the rule, but it was not always followed to a tee; sometimes, the skill classes were divided into "senior" and "junior." Be that as it may, all riders were members of the AMA and naturally wished to compete in events with the possibility of gaining points by placing. So any event hoping to attract many riders had to gain AMA sanctioning.

Meanwhile, a few local members of the Polka Dots Motorcycle Club, Bennett, and some of his friends helped expand the track at the Murray Ranch. This resulted in Mike going to that club, which met just thirty miles down The Lincoln Highway from Placerville, in Rancho Cordova, to see if they wanted to sponsor a motocross race at the ranch. At that time, they were mostly enduro riders and didn't really believe that motocross would become much of a thing in the United States. That Mike wanted to call his races "Hangtown" makes logical sense since he lived in Placerville; his shop was there, and so on. We must take it as a coincidence that the names Hopetown and Hangtown rhyme.

After their earlier history of running enduros around Latrobe, the Polka Dots' use of the Gold Rush era theme "Forty-Niner" for their enduro event could easily have prompted the idea of using "Hangtown." The closest recollections indicate that Mike seems to have first brought his idea for races at the Murray Ranch and his town's traditional nickname to the attention of a few Dirt Diggers at a local race. Mike remembers Bill Onga as the most enthusiastic member initially, as he was likely standing the nearest to him at the time he first mentioned it, but the club took to it instantly.

Within the timespan of a few rounds of beer, several Dirt Diggers North members, including Bill Onga, Joe Pyle, Carl Cranke, Marty Devries, and non-member Dick Mann, were up at the Murray Ranch looking the site over.   They felt that with some improvements, the place would work.   On November 4th, 1968, the club voted to call their event the First Annual Hangtown Motocross.

Author at the third annual Hangtown Classic at Plymouth, in 1971 riding for Cycle Speed, of North Highlands, California – manager, Carl Cranke – photo – B. Greeves

The purse breakdown was adopted at that meeting. And the process started to get the race approved and plan actual logistics. But there was a problem, two actually; the first was problems with the El Dorado County Planning Commission, which was not keen on granting a zone variance for allowing the race to go on at the Murray Ranch. The second was the AMA. The venerable old organization's process wasn't quick enough to get a sanction for the first race. They seemed to scratch their heads and think, "Motocross, what's motocross?

After all, they had scrambles. But the original rough scrambles of the old days that were similar to the English Scrambles of the 1960s had given way to a neat tract circuit where the spectators sat in bleachers as they did and do for the big oval track dirt races that made the AMA famous. And there were hare scrambles and enduros. So they were right in a way. In his book, "The Art of Motocross" (1966), two-time British motocross world champion Jeff Smith explained how the term motocross came to be the term for a then-new sport to the U.S. It was actually the same as the old-style scrambles in Britain. This had also been true of the U.S. from the 1920s until it was somehow lost as the AMA gradually stylized it after their big national flat track races post-war. This change robbed it of its aspect of natural terrain navigation to put it in an arena where the public could spectate from a safe distance in bleachers, not unlike a rodeo or football game, or a Barnum and Bailey circus.

Motocross was a cross-country race, but on a circuit, not a point-to-point race, as with the then very popular "hare scrambles" in Southern California. A motocross race runs regardless of the weather. The short of it is that the British Scramble was termed "motocross" (motorcycle cross country) on the continent. There were many more races in the World Championship Grand Prix season there than in Britain. So that term had become common to the sport by the time it arrived in the U.S. One can almost see the AMA officials in Pickerington, Ohio tilt their heads back and roll their eyes as they learn of an "exciting" new sport from Europe!

Examples of the old scrambling style in the U.S. can be seen in the wartime film, "The Fighting Sullivans." In that film, the members of the Blackhawk MC put one on. Also, "The Wild One" famously opens with an "outlaw" club, that is, a club not registered with the AMA raids a legitimate, sanctioned scrambles race. There is a reference in the film to outlaw scrambles that these outlaw clubs would hold without AMA sanctioning. Where motorcycling was concerned, there was a post-war boom in both Europe and the U.S. In the U.S., many clubs arose for just riding activities as touring clubs and then competition clubs. The AMA sought to organize them. Many went along with it, while others failed to see the need and didn't like regulation. Among them were clubs made up of former wartime fliers, men who had lived the high-adrenaline, high-risk lifestyle and after coming home found they still craved the thrill of combat.

So clubs formed everywhere. Club names were a matter of both expressions of aggression and absurdity of war with ridiculous names like the L.A. Booze Fighters and the Pissed-Off Bastards of Bloomington. A couple chapters from those particular two clubs combined to form The Hell's Angels in 1948. Some members were former Flying Tigers whose squadron had taken the name from the 1929 Howard Hughes film of the same name. Most off-road clubs went along with the AMA, but not always. Also, some clubs mixed things.

As if this wasn't enough, the media got involved to confuse things with the public and affect the public view of motorcycles and enthusiasts. The first in the birth of motorcycle exploitation films was "The Wild One," starring a young, virile Marlon Brando as the ultimate in cool detachment that threatened society because of the obvious detachment his character, "Johnny" portrayed as the archetype of generational rejection of common decency and society for a kind of anarchy on two wheels. That film was based on a real event that had occurred in 1947, in Hollister, California. No one got killed or even hurt seriously. There were a few fights, but no property was damaged. Such rowdy weekends in small towns near cities were common in those years. The nation was still celebrating the end of the war. The San Francisco Chronicle set up some poses during that weekend and ran a story about a biker riot in Hollister. But the fact is that it was no different from when there was a rodeo in town. The cowboys typically raced around on bucking horses, riding them into bars, and so on. The problem was not that the townspeople were unused to some amount of controlled mayhem. The problem was that this was the first big event since the war had ended and four thousand bikes showed up in Hollister that weekend.

The film did a lot of damage. When "The Wild One" premiered in London, England, the kids tore up the theater, resulting in the film being banned in the UK. Nevertheless, clubs arose in the UK that mimicked the gangs portrayed in that film, namely The Beetles. Until Brian Epstein found them and cleaned them up and dressed them up like schoolboys, the Fab Four had been Rockers, leather jackets, and wild behavior in Hamburg, as part of the pervading youth culture of the 1950s in England. So the damage was done to the motorcycling image. It was further enhanced by the motorcycle exploitation films of the sixties that culminated with "Easy Rider" in 1969. In fact, part of the idea for producing "On Any Sunday" was to counter the image of those films.

With this idea for a race, a race called "Hangtown" no less, the Dirt Diggers North MC had found the middle-ground, the twilight zone, if you will. The problem was that the AMA competitions were always divided between sportsman events and professional events, so if you raced for money, you had to have a professional license and the event had to be one or the other. The AMA hadn't yet figured out how to hold combined events. The club wanted to attract the big names in off-road racing, so they raised the purses over any previous at supposed "amateur" events like Hopetown in Southern California. This posed a problem for the AMA. They refused to sanction the race. The club decided to go ahead, anyway. So Hangtown race was a "bandit event."

Organizing the track and event required a considerable amount of planning and logistical organizing. It requires a club full of enthusiastic members to pull off such an event. Carl Cranke designed the race circuit, using some of Mike's existing sections, and adding his own changes. It requires attracting top riders. DDNMC members, Dave Duarte, Bill Dawson, Joe Pyle, Bill Onga, and Willy "Lump" Groom, with the help of Ron Keeping and Mike McGowan, made this considerable gamble possible, along with the general membership of the club. The rules were ironed out by They were encouraged with the advice of the Dirt Diggers MC in the south, particularly Don Kemp and Jack Shook, who at 91, recalls many phone conversations at the time with multiple parties.

The AMA had a problem; there were no rules for motocross racing in their book. So they graciously allowed the DDNMC to write up their own rules. With the race date approaching, the club didn't have the time to wait for the AMA to catch its breath. There were some complications with the AMA, but the club was determined to hold the race as scheduled. So the first race was unofficial or an "outlaw" race. The club wanted to have higher purses than any other such event in California to attract the top riders and decided to go ahead with their gamble, Gold Rush style. And like the days of old, the prospectors came to take a shot at the loot. And they got them, the AMA Pro, Dick Mann, top Southern California riders like Gary Bailey and John DeSoto, Allen Kenyon, and "Desert Fox" Glen Clinton, as well as Northern riders like Brad and Randy Lackey, Bob Grossi, and Mann. The race was on, but would the "outlaw" Hangtown MX cheat the Hangman?

The first Hangtown Motocross was run on January 11th and 12th of 1969. The weekend was so rainy that few spectators showed up. I was there with Dave Buckmaster courtesy of my Dad, who was also interested. In the 250cc race on Saturday, Dick Mann won by almost a literal mile but had a professional date elsewhere on Sunday. A massive storm moved in overnight. Sunday was a disaster with epic mud traps and sloggy going when the open class day when the large displacement machines raced. Gary Bailey won on a 250cc Greeves, an English production famous for mud going in Britain. So many machines got stuck in the mud that the ranch's Caterpillar had to be used to pull them out. Hangtown had gotten attention; the riders loved the mess and the struggle, but the club had lost its... donkey in the bet.

I rode that course as my first MX race in their second go at it on May 25th of 1969. It had one dip that went so abruptly down and up that a rider had to seriously resist the G forces that wanted to force him down from the standing position to the seat. There was a cleverly designed descent. This gradually steepening downhill was a test of nerve at braking skills versus the temptation to pass those more cautious and finally face the rider with an even more vertical final drop-off at its bottom. I got caught. I crashed on each lap because I over-committed, passing other competitors. That caused me to come off the ledge in a cross-up - front wheel down. Slamming into that ditch over and over was getting old. But I kept gaming it on every lap. As a consequence, I came in last. But I had learned a lesson!

I later learned that this section had a nickname, held over from the first event, "The Devil's Stairstep." Chuck Clayton of Cycle News described it thus; "a treacherous downhill that dropped four stories into a muddy ditch with a solid-looking tree on one side and a barbed-wire fence on the other spooked nearly everybody. It would have been bad enough dry, bit with near-zero traction; it was "Geronimo" all the way." It was dry when I raced on it, and I wasn't afraid. I was elated as I passed bikes on the downhill, only to come off the "stair-step" rather sideways and crash. My Penton and I got through it without any real damage. I just felt humiliated and frustrated with myself. This wasn't going to happen at the next Hangtown, and it wasn't.

The second event was an attempt to recover financially from the losses of the first. Everything was set up, so why not? So the daring dirt gang put on another race. It benefitted from a dry, sunny day, but the locals were no better pleased. The additional problem of the county's continued refusal to grant a zone variance put the period on the Murray Ranch location. While the county refrained from any action, the club still needed a site for the 1970 event. It was time for Hangtown MX to git outta Hangtown!

White Rock Motorcycle Park was just establishing itself. Although the DDNMC held two races there during 1970, they either did not know of the park or were more immediately aware of Mike's other land connection in Plymouth in Amador County. It may have been settled when Mike and the DDNMC reps met with the county. A friend owned some acres where a mine and gold stamping mill had previously operated. The Plymouth track would be less hilly, resembling the

Dutch GP, which was famously termed "The Sand Track" of the European Grand Prix events. But this was not natural sand. It was finer sand created by the stamping mill's activity over decades, breaking down gold ore to near dust to extract gold. It was essential to keep a clean air filter on your machine. Mel, the owner, was a customer of Mike's, so the families used to fun ride there. When the Murray Ranch was lost, Mike's other site connection was a natural follow-on. The Plymouth location lasted until 1978. Other sanctioned races were held there during the year. The Hangtown Motocross Classic's permanent home ended up at the Prairie City State Vehicular Recreation Area, just a mile up White Rock Road from its embryo, the old White Rock Motorcycle Park.

They Blazed the Trail

In earlier years local clubs such as The Capital City Motorcycle Club, which came into being after the merger of The Capital City Wheelmen and The Sacramento Motorcycle Club in 1913, The Fort Sutter Motorcycle Club, and The Sacramento Cyclettes, as an exclusive, all-female club in the 1930s, and which must be credited with bringing civilization to the sport, as they put on dances, inviting the boys from the other clubs to attend. But they went further than that, engaging in charity work raising money for the chamber of commerce's fund for underprivileged children and families and for the Sacramento Bee's Christmas Fund. These women must be credited for the eventual participation of outlaw gangs (Hell's Angels) in children's charities decades later. Up until WW2, these were mostly picnic and fun clubs, with maybe a cross-country race or scrambles on the roster with other games, such as balloon swatting, where the passenger had a balloon taped to her back while she sought to swat the balloon on the other passenger's back. While the trick riding has been well eclipsed, but drill team riding they mastered remains a spectacle unmatched to this day. After the war, they became more focused on competitive events, with the Polka Dots MC being the last club of that era to form in the 1950s, stating that they would be a 100% competition club. This set the stage for the growth of competition participants as they opened up the region to more riders who were not club members.

Because of the activities of those pioneers in the sport and likely the great weather, by the early 1960s, California was ground zero for off-road events. So it naturally became the epi-center for the rising popularity of motocross, which arrived to the U.S. by 1967. Lars Larson introduced the two-stroke Husqvarna that year by arriving at just about every shop in the U.S. and launching his bike from the back of a pick-up truck as the beginning of his product demonstration and winning local cross-country events. European professionals like World Champion Torsten Hallman, Lars Larson, and Claus Nielsen of Husqvarna coordinated with Los Angeles importer, Edison Dye, to present motocross circus events. They featured all of the top factory riders from Europe and top Americans chasing them. The Edison Dye "InterAm" events toured California and the nation from 1967 to 1970. White Rock MC Park hosted two such events in 1970. That year was such a pivotal year for motocross and off-road motorcycling that filmmaker Bruce Brown (Endless Summer) was motivated to film "On Any Sunday," that year, a still widely viewed movie. (Fun note: that's the "Giant Mosquito" in the yellow jersey leading Steve McQueen in the Indian Dunes MX sequence; more of him, later). The individual that bridged the old era with the new one has to be Dick Mann, who took to motocross racing immediately.

When the AMA was ready to set up motocross as an official category, they came to the DDNMC for suggestions about the rules. Bruce Young, Bill Onga, and Willy "Lump" Groom set the rules down on Bruce Young's kitchen table. These are the rules for all official AMA motocross races nationwide. By 1971, the AMA had supplanted Edison Dye's InterAm events with their sanctioned TransAm events. But Hangtown was a bandit race until 1974. As founding Dirt Diggers North MC, Dave Duarte put it, "(The) AMA didn't like us and we didn't like them. We said we were going to run outlaw races and we did from the first one in Placerville and the next three in Plymouth. The outlaw way was the most fun."

Finally, (the) AMA came begging and Bill Onga and Bill Dawson got with Mike Dupree and others, assembled at Bruce Young's house and they put together on his kitchen table. So finally, DDNMC races would be sanctioned by them. But they did the AMA a big service, setting up rules for all of their MX events in the future. All of these people were pioneers of the sport in America. The shops and all these individuals of the Hangtown story, the Dirt Diggers North MC, is a tale of a confluence of combined vision whose realization served all and the larger motorsport recreation world. All of these people were pioneers of the sport in America. The shops and all these individuals of the Hangtown story, the Dirt Diggers North MC, is a tale of a confluence of combined vision whose realization served all and the larger motor recreation world. All were pioneers of motocross. There are likely others, but one at least, Mike McGowan, is literally the grandson of a known pioneer in Sacramento County. Mike had been partially raised by a family that owned and operated the Timm Mine off Highway 193, the Georgetown to Placerville highway. The mine was still operating near Spanish Flat in the 1950s. Mike worked there while also attending school at the old schoolhouse in that community, which burned down in the early 60s. Labeled a mystery town by the Placerville Chamber of Commerce in their August 2000 publication of "I Remember," we believe that this photo is of the village at Spanish Flat, near Kelseyville in El Dorado County. He verified it as the one that he remembers on the schoolmarm's mantelpiece in her home. Spanish Flat was named for its first miners who arrived in 1849 from Mexico, South America, and Portugal.

A TYPICAL El Dorado County mining town. All effort to identify the ravine and camp failed in our research effort. If a reader can identify the location, please communicate with the County Chamber of Commerce.   Photo James Gray Family Collection

Photo of a mystery town, identified in the process of researching this book. From the James Gray Family Collection, published in the "I Remember" book, by the El Dorado County Chamber of Commerce – reproduced by permission. The Alhambra Mine was the most profitable of several mines near Spanish Flat, which burned down in 1960, according to Mike McGowan who lived there as a young teen.

There were 81 roadhouses, or inns, if you prefer, along that loop as it is mapped out in Ralph H. Cross's history, the rare 1954 history by Ralph H. Cross titled, "The Early Inns of California." The backstory runs thus;

"To complete the picture of the Overland Road between Sacramento and Placerville, we must now travel over the final location of the western end of the route. The first twenty-two miles of this trip will be by a Sacramento Valley Railroad train to Folsom. In a general way, the railway follows the western half of Sutter's 1847 road from the Fort to his sawmill in Coloma, and for two or three years, this was the most heavily traveled road in California. With the discovery of gold at Old Dry Diggings, Hangtown, or Placerville (placer gold is gold found "in place" not requiring mining or other extraordinary recovery beyond a shovel, pan, and perhaps a sluice box), the local importance of this road began to be shared by the Carson immigrant road, via White Rock, when the freighting outfits, and the later the stages bound for the new diggings, started using the latter route. The Pony Express ran the same route. Sutter's old "sawmill road" continued to carry the traffic between Sacramento and the original placer ground at Coloma for the next eight years, until the completion of the railway to Folsom on February 3, 1856. A new road was then opened to Placerville from Green Valley, on the Coloma road and some Fourteen miles east of Folsom, and with this, the latter place became the stage terminus of the Overland Route. Freight for Coloma was thereafter carried by wagons from Folsom, while many of the freighting outfits bound for Placerville continued to use White Rock Road."

Folsom's importance increased because of its location and the famous New York City newspaper publisher, Horace Greeley, made a trip to that place to make a famous speech in 1859, repeating the advice that he gave first in 1833, "Go west, young man." He would repeat them many times, as his solution to the economic depression that followed the Civil War's close. Folsom was also the designated location for the territorial prison due to its convenient location near the mines but an arm's length from Sacramento where "respectable folks" resided.

The first local railroad line ran from Sacramento to Folsom, as that was the initial jumping-off point for continuing up to Dry Diggings, via the Hangtown and City Road, which is today, Green Valley Road. The first dam was built in 1866 to supply power to the prison that Johnny Cash and Charles Manson would put on the national map once again in the 1960s. Go to jail, young man, and don't collect $200.00.

Greeley's trip led to a mythic tale told as fact by one of the top drivers or "whips" as they were called then, a character named Hank Monk. The story follows Greeley for the rest of his life. Its persistence in the nation's gossip dialogs ruined his bid for a run for the United States presidency in 1872. Hank Monk carried Greeley from Carson City to Placerville for that famous speech in Folsom. To get him there on time, Monk reported that he bounced his distinguished passenger about so violently that at one point; his head had punched clean through the roof of the carriage. The ridiculous image was created by Monk, likely during one of the famous drinking binges that he was famous for; as some reported, he was so scrambled that he served whiskey to his horses and watered himself. The story was a familiar tale on the road for years and survived well up into the 20th century as a factual event. Even Mark Twain involved himself, declaring the story to be wholly fictitious. But Hank Monk lived in the sort of world that many construct for themselves out of single-dimensional considerations. When Monk became aware that his famous passenger was soon likely to be president, he wrote him requesting an appointment to some humbler office in his administration in remembrance of his adventures with him. Greeley responded;

"I would rather see you ten thousand fathoms in hell than give you even a crust of bread. For you are the only man who ever had it in his power to put me in a ridiculous light before the American people, and you villainously exercised that power."

The "Sawmill Road" became the lower end of Green Valley Road, which was established as a lesser, but just as heavily traveled alternative road to the diggings at Hangtown. So my Old West cultural fascination, which was peppered by related traditional outdoor sports carried over from my Quebecois settler culture somehow spliced into replacing a trusty equine mount with a two-wheeled, mechanical horse that snorted smoke. The final ingredient was an inborn need to get into the fray; I was not suited for regular sports, but it wasn't because I didn't have athletic talent, or lacked the desire to be in the arena. So I was now a moto-cross racer and working in the industry.

How did Antelope meet White Rock? First is the deep geographical relationship between water and gold. The ancient ice age gold deposits saw later-day dredging operations that coursed along the American River into Sacramento County. Like a forked tongue, the rivulets that flowed gold went all the way to Perkins Pit (still operating today) nearest to downtown Sacramento, with the other running out north to Loomis and the edge of Roseville on Dry Creek. (Dredging operations went on until the 1930s when a series of problems from the silting up of various creeks, including water quality downstream. The problems for Dry Creek in particular resulted in a lawsuit by Roseville to have the operations cease). Dry Creek was not only a feature of Roseville, but Antelope, and North Highlands. The Gibson Ranch nearby was a recreational park set on Dry Creek. Next, Carl Cranke, DDNMC member, and designer of the Hangtown MX track in 1969 was managing Cycle Speed, R&D by then. Cycle Speed was located in North Highlands. I bought my CZ from Carl there in 1970. Antelope was the geographical union point between the field where Dave, Rick, and I practiced on the track we laid out in a field that was part of the then contiguous fields and The Spook Tree and access to Antelope in a straight line that could be drawn from that track to the tree and Antelope.

Later, in the mid-1970s, a tack appeared off Walerga Road, near the intersection with PFE, west down from the Dry Creek Center Elementary School and Antelope. That practice track was allegedly set up by Danny "Magoo" Chandler. He and Danny Turner were known to ride there.

"Magoo road here." The "Roseville-Antelope-Walerga track was located in the area of the present Dry Creek Community Park. The author believes that it was possible to ride from North Sacramento to Auburn using connected fields that followed the creeks. – Photo provided by Tom Stover – Googlemaps - Maxar

All of this established a quasi-mystical geographical connection in space and time; four dimensions. It turns out that like me and my friends, the DDNMC members constituted a roving threat to open land anywhere in the vicinity, all the way from there to beyond the American River to the south. So White Rock Road, and thereby White Rock Motorcycle Park, McGill's, and finally Prairie City State Vehicular Recreation Area, were joined by these incidental junctions of people and places. Today, the Hangtown MX Classic is on the AMA National Circuit.

Three Gunfights, Two Hangings, and Sutter

I n that neck of the woods, there is no getting away from the history of the California Gold Rush. If it is somewhat overlaid today, it was everywhere and a prominent theme in my time. That was the reason that it had to be obvious that any big race would have to be called "Hangtown" just as sure as an enduro in the mountains in Placer County would be called "The Forty-Niner." All roads start from a point and may diverge into many tracts, but eventually, they all end up in one place. And so the causes of all are the cause of one. The richness and truth of life are to be had through deep, honest examination because it is true that those who do not learn from history are doomed to repeat it, one way or another. And that can cut in endless ways. The proof of the cost of mangling history is on full display today nationally and locally, as the lies of revisionism have come into practice over the past thirty years. Sacramento County's history profoundly affected the entire state, the nation, and even the world. It has everything to do with how The Spook Tree and Antelope came to be. So let's take a look at it, and examine the present criticisms.

It is expected that nearly everyone knows about the one-hanged-per-day reputation of Dry Diggins, Hangtown, later known as Placerville, with its one-a-day hanging reputation. But this is an exaggeration.

What actually earned old Dry Diggins the name was it being the location of the first gold rush-related lynching where mob actions saw a triple hanging in January of 1949 for the crime of robbery. The first big mining town in the mountains eventually acquired the less ominous-sounding name of Placerville. But since this is a Western Folk Tale of sorts, the story of what might be the most colorful character that was ever hanged between Sacramento and Hangtown ought to be noted, along with what might be called "the founding gunfights" that marked the fretful early days of Sacramento City and the eventual county. To tell this story, a long history of Sacramento's origins must be plumbed. As we proceed, note the actuality of the events compared to what occurs today. The differences may seem subtle, but the two issues at least are very different, our gunfights occurred around the struggles to establish civilization, while the present ones involve the decline of civilization. Two of our gunfights occurred as a result of the historical event known as The Squatter's Riot. To gain the proper perspective, we must remember that the calm, even orderly progression of life in New Helvetia to the initial establishment of Sacramento as a city, a port city, was not done by a Mexican government official, or by a priest. It was the result of a Swiss adventurer with a dream of establishing a colony in a paradise called California. While at Fort Vancouver, in British Oregon, he purchased an Indian boy from Kit Carson, and later set him free in California. This illustrates the fact that Sutter did not hold slaves in New Helvetia. He considered the purchase of the boy an act of kindness, rescuing him from an unknown future.

Johann August Sutter, a German-Swiss, had arrived from Hawaii at Yerba Buena in 1839, with the plan to found a colony in the interior. The Mexican authorities welcomed him and his vision for a colony in the interior. They considered such a colony would serve as a buffer against Indian raids, much as they had with the allowance of Americans to settle in Texas around the same time. The origin of those was the responsibility of the Spanish and Mexicans since they had initially enslaved the Indians and hunted them when they escaped. It is unclear to this author whether cattle raiding developed independently, but stock theft was widespread in the 19th century. It was such a problem that punishment was often death, regardless of race. So they allowed him to explore and establish a settlement near the confluence of the American and Sacramento Rivers. He named his realm New Helvetia, paying homage to his native Switzerland. Governor Juan Alvarado then granted him eleven leagues of land in 1841. In return, he would serve as a buffer against Indian raids and develop the region where they had constantly failed up to then. Sutter went to work enthusiastically.

The Mason's Lodges were a major force in frontier charitable work in American history. Every new settlement saw the founding of a new Masonic Lodge, and usually also an Odd Fellows, as many were members of both fraternities. The Freemasons figured prominently in American history from the nation's founding up to at least the Second World War. The great political philosopher, John Locke, who the Founders relied upon for inspiration, was a Freemason, as were most of them. They were active in Sacramento County, as the founders of the first hospital, which was led by the personal effort of the consequential Dr. John F. Morse, with the help of a new chapter of Oddfellows. They set up the first hospital in Sacramento County on Sutter's Fort Hospital's southeast corner, located across Sutter's Fort in December of 1849. Dr. Morse was active in many local efforts to organize the wilderness that was Sacramento into a city and was the California Medical Association founder later on. But before Dr. Morse arrived in New Helvetia, Captain John Sutter converted an old granary outside of his fort's walls into a hospital. This adobe structure served as a recovery home for the pioneers that began to trickle down the American River's course following the Indian trail that Jedidiah Smith had discovered during his earlier trapping and exploring expedition as earlier discussed.

In 1827, Smith and his party made the journey from The Great Salt Lake to Sacramento via the Rio las Lagas, proving that the Great Basin could be safely crossed. This led to the opening of the Oregon Trail and the trail over the Sierras. The Mexican authorities soon renamed the river Rio de Americanos.   The inevitable destination of all immigrants over the Sierras was Sutter's Fort. They were always worn out, sometimes near starvation. It was here that the Donner Party survivors were brought to rest and recover.   In every case, he sent parties to search for struggling groups, paying all of the expenses in most cases with the Donner Party as an exception. That one required more money than Sutter could supply alone. General Vallejo was one of those enthusiastic donors. Sutter welcomed all and gave succor in every case, employing everyone who needed work, regardless of how it affected his books. His worse and later self-admitted error was trusting too much, giving power or attorney to men who later defrauded him. Later Sutter donated the land for the larger hospital. It was the founding facility of the Sutter Hospital network today. All of these personalities were known to each other and associated with such charitable, and civic organizations including later more unlikely ones such as the Fort Sutter Motorcycle Club.*[1]

Recent claims concerning the alleged cruelties of Sutter have no support in the documented history of many witnesses.   On the contrary, we have several historical narratives available that show how the natives were a major part of the early Sacramento communities. In Lee Township, a couple of incidences of horse stealing involved natives as the principal in the meting out of justice to white perpetrators after being adjudicated by white authorities, whipping a man in one case. In most such histories, as with the event of the funeral of the first white woman in California, American Indians appear as; first, willing workers. Sutter described them as "tolerable good workers," who got wages and came to rely on them and community members, perhaps not becoming wealthy, but certainly trusted. Sutter's diary/fort records show they were paid two to three dollars a day. For comparison, my great, great grandfather, born in 1833, worked as a young, recently married man in the 1850s for a dollar a day in Massena, New York. Sutter employed anyone who wanted to work. So when John Bidwell arrived with his wagon train in 1841, he worked for Sutter and remained with him for years.

Race resentments were absent. In a case that took place in Lee Township in 1850, a native administered the whipping. A crooked judge called "Uncle Ben" had attempted to defraud a simple-minded miner of his poke when he set him up as a cattle thief by hiring him to drive them to Sacramento and then reporting a theft. The purse with gold dust, as described by the accused, was found on the judge. A whipping was proscribed. No one was willing, so a native was asked. He administered but three lashes with a lasso. No one was offended because an Indian had whipped a white man. The former judge was run out of town afterward. Later, when several white men were accused of horse theft, the townsmen decided on a lynching because there were not enough present to form a regular jury. The men were left hanged overnight. In the morning, they were buried by Indians, who were the first to feel the need to remove the carcasses from sight.

Play Fair and Tell the Truth

The plethora of fraudulent historical revisionism, complete with forged claims of witness to such bizarre and unsupported claims of genocidal expeditions by Sutter, and even a claim that he kept a harem of tribal women for his pleasure, and fled his wife and children of an unhappy marriage.*2 There is no support for such claims in source documents. Even Berkeley Professor Walton D. Bean's 1968 textbook, "California – An Interpretive History," does not list any such atrocities, let alone genocide. Instead, it reports cattle rustling by Indians, a practice they developed during the years of Spanish rule. Simultaneously, Sutter's diary is corroborated by his ability to win over and attract natives to him for work, protection, and a better life in general. The allegation of the kidnapping of children and sale relates to some activities by others in the Los Angeles region, where they had retained the Spanish/Mexican peonage laws that the Missions had established.   Note that various tribes also kidnapped and traded women and abducted children themselves throughout known history.

In one vignette from Walton's history of the Gold Rush period, the jailer at San Jose, Henry Bee, sought to turn ten of his only prisoners, ten Indians, two charged with murder, to the local Alcade (sheriff), who refused the charge. So Henry took the prisoners with him to help him dig for gold. After he got rich, his prisoners "escaped" and began prospecting for their own benefit. In another example from Professor Beans' book, Sutter made an agreement with the local Indians to lease the land around Coloma for his own mining operations. If Sutter was the slaver and exploiter as our latter-day revisionists insist, no such record would exist.*[6]

The Statue of Captain John Sutter in front of Sutter General Hospital in Sacramento, California, has been removed through Leftist pressures. Sadly, it was relocated to Volcano in El Dorado County and was stolen. Photo – California State Library – Sacramento

Instead, Sutter would have been recorded as having sent in his bullies to murder and otherwise drive off the native occupiers of land he wished to take for his own. The so-called "Kern Massacre" was an event where Sutter had been on a punitive expedition after a specific party of Indian raiders and found himself ambushed. His "army" consisted of eight Kanakas (Hawaiians), a couple local Indians, and a few white men. (The fifteen guards at Sutter's Fort were Digger Indians,** local Nisenan and Miwok). They faced about 200 enemies. After killing about 20 of them, the fighting broke off and was never thereafter renewed. He considered it his mission to care for the women and children and trained many in weaving and other skills at the fort. During the time before the Gold Rush, Fort Sutter was always full of natives, visiting, working, coming and going freely. During 1844, when Sutter led troops to support Governor Micheltorena when Alvarado and Castro rebelled in a power grab as Mexican rule weakened, Sutter had a hundred riflemen, eight, maybe ten cannon and crews, and a hundred native warriors, armed with rifles or bows and arrows. (Micheltoreno's loss opened the door for the Bear Flag Revolt.

Other revisionists interpret descriptions of a visitor of the Indians being fed in troughs and being locked up at night inside rooms inside the fort. It is admitted that some "refused" to come inside the fort.** The observable fact is that under Sutter's Indian guards, which totaled fifteen, some workers wished for protection from hostile Indian attacks, while others were not so concerned. One vividly false criticism fabricated in 1933 from a created account of Sutter represents a German immigrant, Theodor Cordura, held his land further up the Sacramento River, not far from Sutter's Hock Farm. Cordura never wrote that Sutter raided the Indians along the Sacramento River, and the "river ran red with blood." Sutter's charge was to pursue cattle raiders. When he did this, he was fulfilling his duty and protecting the many friendly natives who worked for him and visited often. Chiefs came often to visit and sometimes deliver workers who took wages returned home with supplies. This is closer to the description of the raiding that was performed by Lansford W. Hastings. Hastings was one of a few independent, but highly consequential criminals that made a huge and negative set of historical vectors in motion in those years. If we wish to establish historical truth from fact, a review of these three men is the most useful object for discussion at this point.

The information comes from Dr. Bean's University of Berkeley published, "California – An Interpretive History." Hastings was a lawyer with a reputation for bluster and aggression politically. He was also given to rash and irresponsible advice and actions. I review two here. The first occurred in 1843 when he led a small wagon train into California from Oregon. He and some others decided it would be great sport to shoot Indians they found along the River. This created a cycle of revenge that eventually saw the diminishing of the tribes to a small fraction of their previous numbers. Hastings played a lesser-known role in the well-known tragedy of The Donner Party. Hastings had been active in promoting California from Missouri. His ambition was to foment an immigrant movement with himself as the "Sam Houston" of California. He made speeches and even produced a completely misleading "Emigrant's Guide" that featured a dangerous route to California. His famous "Hastings Cutoff" that rounded the south end of The Great Salt Lake led to the delay time that caused many dangerous delays and landed the Donner Party on the wrong side of the Sierras when a heavy snow suddenly arrived.

Yet another severely consequential and lesser-known, but consequential figure in the history of early California and the American West is one "Dr." John Marsh. Marsh graduated from Harvard in 1823. His arrival to the "West" was caused by his hire as a tutor for the children of officers at Fort Snelling, in Minnesota. While there he "read the medical literature and planned to return to Harvard to study medicine. But he never did. While at the fort he fell in love with a mixed French-Canadian and Sioux woman and married her. They had a child which Marsh reckoned would never be accepted back in Massachusetts. He was appointed subagent to the Sioux. He displayed a bias toward his wife's people against other tribes which led to his dismissal. He had been supplying the Sioux with guns in violation of Federal Law. This furthered the depredations already common between the Sioux and other tribes.

This problem had existed since the very beginning of European presence on the American continental landmass. When the Spanish brought the horse tribal history was hugely impacted. The first Indians to learn the use of horses became the raiders of other tribes, just as the first that gained firearms they used them first on the tribes they had competed with for time unknown. The power balance that European weaponry introduced into the world of the American Indians may have been inevitable, as it has occurred throughout history worldwide, but for our particular story, it is important to point to the case of Marsh's illegal actions because they had a consequence for all of the terrible events that led to the Indian raids and military pacification campaigns that dragged on until 1890 for the Sioux after even the Apache Wars had ended.

Marsh's influence continued after he arrived in Los Angeles, California in 1836. Fleeing a warrant for his arrest, he had fled to California. Marsh secured permission to practice medicine from the authorities thereby presenting his diploma, which was completely Latin, preventing any close scrutiny, so Marsh became the first American doctor to open an office in California. Initially, he accepted hides for his services. He cashed out a cache of hides and was granted permission to purchase a ranch after accepting the Roman Catholic Faith and becoming naturalized and a new phase in his saga began. In 1837, he purchased a huge ranch on the Sacramento-San Joaquin Delta at the foot of Mount Diablo; somehow a fitting location. The original holder of the land had found it too isolated and too available to Indian cattle rustlers. But Marsh made it the first big success in the Central Valley. He managed this by charging fifty head of cattle for his services. But Marsh was to influence more events in early California, as we shall see.

Lieutenant John C. Fremont - The "Pathfinder"

John C. Fremont figures in California history as perhaps the most ambiguous of its heroes. It was he and Kit Carson who forced the first passage over the Sierras in the dead of winter in 1844. Fremont was the son of a French émigré, who had run off with a wealthy, but elderly American's young wife.   Just as with Alexander Hamilton, Fremont grew up in a class-conscious society bearing a soiled pedigree.   But again, like Hamilton, he was precocious and energetic, so sympathetic elders helped him gain security and education.   He was also an impulsive, unstable opportunist all of his life.   In his early years of service, while still in Virginia, he met the daughter of Senator Thomas H. Benton, a beautiful and highly intelligent sixteen-year-old who had been personally tutored by her father in the classics, including civics.   They secretly married after an acquaintance of several months.   After a period of rejection by the senator, he reconciled himself to the fact of the marriage and Fremont gained an influential father-in-law and a beautiful and ambitious wife.

With the prompting of his father-in-law, Fremont was soon appointed to lead a series of five expeditions to the West.   His talented wife wrote exciting travel novelettes that made her husband a household word throughout the country and a national hero.   Kit Carson had coincidently met him while traveling on a steamboat on the Upper Missouri after a rare return trip to Missouri for a visit with friends and relatives.   Fremont had failed to locate a French-Canadian guide he knew of named Captain Drippe, when he met Carson.   Checking up on Carson's previous trapping expeditions and conduct, he took him on as his guide.   Carson would accompany Fremont on all three of his major excursions in the West during the 1840s.   In 1843, Carson married a second wife, Josepha Jaramilla, the fifteen-year-old daughter of Don Francisco Jaramilla.   (Carson had married an Indian maiden in 1838 at Fort Bent.   She died in childbirth, but their daughter, Prairie Flower grew up to marry and live in California).   But in two months, he was off with Fremont to California on his second expedition by a roundabout route to the Columbia River and then south through Oregon territory, purchasing supplies at Fort Vancouver from the Hudson Bay Company.

Fremont had no orders authorizing military actions in California. Regardless, he took on sixty expert marksmen and entered California in December of 1845 and in early 1846 encamped near Monterey.   He claimed that he was merely there to survey the Pacific and to get supplies.   Colonel Castro ordered him out of California.   An angry

Fremont entrenched his outfit on Hawk's Peak (now Fremont Peak) in the Gabilan Mountains overlooking the Salinas Valley and raised the American Flag. Castro raised a volunteer force of approximately two hundred men. Mexican naturalized American named Larkin negotiated and Fremont withdrew to the north without a battle being fought. He moved slowly up the Sacramento Valley. Missing Sutter's Fort for some reason, they found the Sacramento River further north and sought to resupply for the return trip at an outpost run by an American settler named Peter Lawson. While there, American settlers that lived nearby arrived at Lawson's speaking of an imminent attack planned by a large band of Indians, estimated to be one thousand strong. They begged Fremont for his help. Kit Carson's autobiography speaks of the event;

"He and a party and some few Americans that lived near started for the Indian encampment. Found them to be in great force, as was stated. They were attacked. The number killed I cannot say. It was a perfect butchery. Those not killed fled in all directions and we returned to Lawson's. Had accomplished what we went for and given the Indians such a chastisement that (it) would be long before they ever again would feel like attacking the settlements." This is the event that saw the Sacramento River, "run with blood." This is another event that modern Leftists attribute to Sutter (Cordura forgery). The same 1932 forgery claims Cordura's outrage at seeing the natives eating from "troughs." All natives ate with their hands, as did mountain men and trappers. Cordura, in fact, never said anything like this, James Climan, a visitor, did, as well as claiming that Sutter kept between 600-800 natives in virtual slavery. He apparently did not know that Sutter paid his Indian laborers a fair rate and protected them from frauds of whites. To an outsider used to tables, chairs, and crockery, probably fine crockery, the conditions they saw might be expected to shock them. But these were Indians who ate acorns, bugs, and dug roots because it was easiest, with only occasional game hunting. They wove wonderful baskets, but did not use dishes, forks, or even knives as we knew them. Obsidian stone was the source of their tools (i.e., "Stone Age?) Anyone may consult A.L. Kroeber's

"Handbook of the Indians of California" for a factual record of conditions and lifestyles of the tribes, which was as basic as could be imagined.

Fremont and company continued north to reach Klamath Lake and rest there, now being clear of Mexican territory. In a letter to his wife, Fremont lamented angrily is being driven out of California. Carson's comments are that they grew tired of awaiting the attack of the "valiant Castro." Whatever the feelings of the group that Carson numbered at "around forty," and Professor Bean reports as sixty, they were low on supplies and it must be assumed, would eventually be attacked. However, the Mexican government was very weak. Note that it had to ask for volunteers to raise a force they deemed adequate to face Fremont and his party. In fact, it was two Americans, Jared Sheldon, and William Daylor, who built the state house at Monterey for the Mexican government that could not pay in cash for the job. They were paid with a land grant southwest of Sutter's, the Omochumnes Grant.

The Bear Flag Revolt

While Colonel Castro resisted American pressure, his counterpart, Colonel Mariano Guadalupe Vallejo not only liked Americans, he saw the inevitability of them as Mexico's weak and corrupt rule had steadily declined since the Spanish withdrawal. To be complete, it should be noted that there was a great rumor of British interest in California. This combined with other rumors of French and including a ridiculous one about a Prussian plan to borrow ships from Denmark with an order to land and confiscate California from Mexico. The British rumor was the most believed because, of course, the British still administered the Oregon territory, so it was believable that they were angling to expand their dominance. Even the U.S. government feared this, although later records revealed that the Crown had no such ambitions. It would be Vallejo's support of Sutter, and American settlers that would make the difference in the political and military outcomes.

At the Klamath Lake camp, on May 9, 1846, Fremont was intercepted by Lt. Archibald H. Gillespie of the U.S. Marine Corps. With him were letters from his father and law and it is suspected, sealed orders for Fremont. In any case, the two young, impulsive officers decided they would re-enter California, as the war with Mexico was deemed by them to be imminent. They decided to re-enter California and position themselves for the event.

As destiny or a strange confluence of events, Fremont re-entered California and was joined by a gaggle of thirty armed American adventurers, hunter/trappers, and plain land squatters with no hope of ever gaining a title to the land they occupied from the Mexican government, which required citizenship and conversion to Catholicism. They reacted to the rumor of Castro preparing a company for the forcible expulsion of Americans from California and assembled in Sonoma outside of the former barracks and home of Vallejo, who was cheerfully amused at being arrested by them. He inquired concerning what war he was a prisoner of, and invited several of the leaders to come into his home, where he plied with his homemade brandy for several hours. Eventually, Fremont arrived and took him, prisoner, to Fort Sutter, where he remained for about a month as a prisoner. Castro did send a force of fifty who were met at Olompali. Two Americans and six Californios were killed. The Californios, led by Joaquin de la Torre, removed themselves from the north of the bay. Fremont celebrated by needlessly spiking the ancient cannon at the Presidio of San Francisco and naming the entryway of the bay, Chrsysopylae, the Golden Gate. The Bear Flag flew over Sutter's fort and California for about a month when it was then declared a U.S. territory after Commodore Sloat raised the U.S. flag in Monterey on the seventh of July, a few days after Fremont celebrated the Fourth in Sonoma.

The Path of the Pathfinder

The event at Klamath Lake also contributed to the ongoing series of tragedies between Whites and Indians. For an unknown reason the night before their departure, a band of Klamath Indians attacked their camp, killing three men. Why Fremont had failed to post sentries, and Carson missed the error is unknown. We might suppose they believed to be in safe territory, being clear of Mexican territory. They reacted by attacking the nearest Klamath village they could find. They killed all of the men and burned the food supply, in a perfect example of the cycle of revenge by both Indians and Whites, which often victimized innocent parties and spread bitter feelings. It is not clear whether Freemont relented from Indian killing as he followed the Sacramento River back south where many villages lay along its banks it is not known. However, Hasting's initial criminal acts there certainly had precipitated Fremont's slaughter Carson reported during their journey to the lake. Had the rumor of Hasting's slaughter reached the Klamath? It seems so. That the Indians had their own messaging methods and news spread quickly among them is a historical fact.

John C. Fremont, to be fair, was not that much different from many of his American predecessors, in his ambitious and willful actions. His wife, Jesse, the daughter of a senator, was aiming for a stay at the nation's first residence in Washington, D.C. Fremont was following a pattern set by George Washington himself, who as a young officer in the Colonial militia took rash actions on a diplomatic meeting that ended with the killing of the French envoy, sparking the French and Indian War. And other presidents, Tyler and Jackson, among them, had grown their reputations as patriots in the War of 1812 and separate Indian Wars in turn. Although Fremont was instrumental in California's break with the Mexican government in the Bear Flag Revolt and was appointed territorial governor by Commodore Stockton for a short period, it led to trouble. Kearny was ignored by both men. As he was operating under presidential orders, he brought Fremont back to Fort Leavenworth in Kansas where he was court-martialed. Fremont was pardoned but resigned from the army and became one of the two first state senators of California.*₃ Even so, it must be noted that Fremont was of huge historical consequence where the Civil War and the settlement of the American West is concerned. His rash actions in Missouri during the Civil War led to a legacy of crime gangs from the James/Younger Gang down to Dillinger, and the other "Folkish" bandits up to the Great Depression era, including Bonnie and Clyde. His handling of Indian relations, and engaging in the earliest slaughters, was the harbinger of many Indian massacres of settlers to come. (In fact, his atrocities seem to have been heaped onto George Armstrong Custer, who spent a relatively short time in the Indian Wars, arriving after the Civil War, and long after Fremont's five expeditions. Custer learned quickly about captive taking and risks to them in battles. At Washita, he learned that two white captives had been killed. After that, he always negotiated before resorting to force). Fremont never took the time. The Fremonts were hugely consequential in California history. One minor yet notable example is when they purchased the bankrupt Pacific Railroad, and renamed it, Southern Pacific, before failing to make the second installment and losing it, along with several other railroad investments in 1871.

Just as the Depression era Soviet-influenced revisionists worked from a 1933 forgery as a source and willfully inserted the history of Hasting's slaughters along the Sacramento River and elsewhere as Sutter's doing, they similarly spliced in the accusation of Sutter's harem from another figure of the period, a mountain man named James Savage. Savage was an Indian Trader. Such men lived between the two worlds of the Indian and the Whites. Savage is described as a "picturesque character" by Robert Eccleston. He was said to have been short but muscular and possessed boundless energy. His hair was light brown and hung about his tanned shoulders. Savage, it is recorded, had as many as 33 native wives. Five or six of them lived with him, aged ten years of age to twenty-two.*[4] Sutter has been accused of taking children as wives or concubines. Here is the source of that lie. Modern revisionists skip over Savage's and other's records of multiple marriages, but it has always been common for traders, and other free wanders to marry local women throughout world history.

We may consider that Indian women were regarded by their tribes as commodities. They were given as gifts and traded for horses as a common practice. The women accepted their fates dutifully, understanding it to be their father's or the entire tribe's will, done for the good of all of her people. The life that Savage led could be a dangerous dance to maintain as with all Indian Traders. Ironically, Savage was ultimately killed by white men while defending the Indians. James Savage had scouted for Fremont during the Mexican War. He went to work for Sutter soon after and was at the fort when gold was discovered. His wives who lived with him are described as "mostly low in stature, and not unhandsome." Many white men, trappers, (including Cordura), took Indian wives or concubines (girlfriends) temporarily. Later, one of Sutter's former employees, (Lienhard) in furtherance of frauds he (and others) had practiced on him, during later court testimony, painted Sutter as a "Don Juan" with the native women, possessing a harem, that included children. I see no evidence of pedophilia in Sutter. The accusation is ridiculous, and vicious, another modern invention. The record is that Sutter was tender and caring toward children. While it may well be that Sutter kept native women, the fact that Sutter had an army that included as many as two-hundred loyal native soldiers rather stands as testimony that such liaisons were not resented. In fact, one of the attractions of Sutter had always been his kindness and generosity. As tribal culture went, it was a matter of pride that a powerful man should have such liaisons with their women and the women were not unwilling. But this still is conjecture. If Sutter was so unhappy with his wife, he would not have sent for her. She simply had no means to arrive unless she paid.

Savage was very active. He employed a gang of Indians to mine for gold along the Tuolumne River and ran several trading posts along the Merced and Fresno Rivers. All accounts indicate that Savage got along well with Indians and whites. He negotiated a treaty with the Yokut Tribe, which was the most powerful in the Fresno region. The time came when one of his wives told him of hearing the rumor of a raiding plan by the tribes above the Mariposa, where he lived by then, amassing a small fortune as his wives were involved in his business dealings. (No further description of what that meant is found). Savage tried to avert war by taking a prominent chief with him on a trip to San Francisco. He believed that the chief, Jose Juarez, would be impressed enough with white civilization to refrain from war. But instead of impressing the chief, they got into a drunken brawl. Juarez told Savage to not deceive the whites by saying the Indians were peaceful. The chief said their aim was to attack whites as long as they saw them in the country.

When James Savage returned to his home on the Mariposa, after reporting to Governor Burnett, attacks on white settlers had already begun. Burnett had already approved of the Sheriff of El Dorado County's punitive mission against some Miwoks that had attacked wagon trains on both sides of the Sierras. This is what led to Burnett's campaigns against the Indians. The Yosemite Indians were a raider tribe traditionally, as a subtribe of Miwoks. They used the remarkable valley named for that tribe as an unapproachable home, a splendorous "hole in the wall" that not only served them well but was beloved to them. They were the most restive and determined of the tribes for the war on whites. Savage traveled up to Yosemite to parley. He tried to convince them that working the gold from the streams; was something many Indians were doing both under white employment and on their own, and living in peace as they had been doing since the whites arrived. He was rebuffed. Mining gold was hard work, they said, and it was easier to raid and plunder the whites. They said they would ride and kill and take everything from the whites. Savage returned disappointed to his Mariposa home. On his arrival, he discovered an attack had already occurred. Adam Johnson, of Savage's party, investigated. "We reached the camp on the Fresno," he explained to Governor Burnett. "It presented a horrid scene of savage cruelty. The Indians had destroyed everything they could not use or carry with them. The murdered men had been stripped of their clothing and lay before us filled with arrows; one of them had twenty perfect arrows sticking in him." This resulted in the campaign to control the hostile tribes. It resulted in the Yosemite tribe losing their magnificent valley in the mountains and being moved to a reservation.*5

In the present day, after all means have been used to vilify America's pioneers while simultaneously absolving the Indians of having ever hardly done a thing to harm or annoy any whites beyond taking a few captives here and there, which according to recent films and some bogus historians, most whites ended up enjoying, the factual record cries out for reassertion. Beyond the many infamous raids upon the plains of the Midwest and later regions further west, the journey from St. Louis, Missouri to California or the Oregon Country was fraught with dangers. All sorts of injuries, sicknesses, and death occurred along the way. But the greatest of all threats and agents of suffering was the Indian attack. Gregory Michno, likely the most genuine historian of the Old West alive today, has made the observation of the known national trauma experienced at the casualties of World War Two, which amounted to 2% of the serving population, compared to 10-15% of the immigrating whites who traveled and settled in the West during the period of 1830 to 1885, when the Apache War was finally finished. Such a high number of dead and more damaged would have been experienced as a national tragedy with a spectrum of attending emotions. By the time they reached Oregon or California, many would have zero tolerance for Indian depredations.

As tumultuous and violent as the early years of California was, it remains true nonetheless that no one alive today in these regions would be present without that final pacification, and the sacrifice of those pioneering settlers of that period, who often paid dearly for the chance for a new life in a new land. Today, we talk about that as a universal right and literally import immigrants. Their predecessors received no government support, no special allowance, and often, were told a territory was safe when it was not. The numbers of dead, maimed, and psychologically traumatized can easily portray a lingering attitude of intolerance as a result of a cultural post-traumatic stress syndrome, which led to zero tolerance of an outbreak of raids reflected in the response of Governor Burnett, who declared a campaign of pacification in California that had a devastating effect on the native tribes that lasted two decades of back and forth battling until final pacification was achieved.

However, even with these extremes of behavior and policy, the everyday reality of the white and native was far more varied and often illustrated a constant presence of a better nature and possibilities between the races. The fact is that Indians worked for whites at gold claims and on their own during the early Gold Rush. Sutter employed some fifty at Coloma. They were working willingly for him at his fort from the start. The conditions were rough, but life was even rougher out in the bush. Once the Indians tasted beef, they began to prefer it to the roots they subsisted on and hunting game was an arduous activity. Some Indians were rustling cattle from the Spanish long before any American or Swiss citizen appeared on the land. For his time, where labor was concerned, Sutter was no different from the Eastern Industrialists who hired poor whites, entire families, men, women, and children, to work in their factories. These hapless people received wages that were so low that they could never buy their way out of debt for the housing, food, and supplies paid with "script," which is virtually "play money" that the same companies provided them. Today, Sutter's critics complain that Sutter used tin coins as script. Usually, companies used worthless paper stamped with a number and company seal. The Russians at Fort Ross had paid its Russian and Aleut Indian workers with such paper script. The Eastern Industrialists held poor whites in default captivity. Sutter protected his native employees from being cheated out of their wages by only accepting them from the natives in payment for goods.

Facsimile of the Russia-America Company Script used as pay at Fort Ross
From the Fort Ross Interpretive Center

Many could never hope to escape this closed economic system, hence, the coining of the phrase "wage slavery." It was, in truth, a contrived plot, systematic slavery. Later in the century, when freed blacks found themselves subject to it the new sharecropping arrangement, they likened it to the same condition of slavery they had once been harnessed to, except without the guarantee of food, health services, and protection that the antebellum system had provided. In fact, Sutter was merely stern at times, whereas the Eastern Industrial Bosses were outright cruel to their white "wage slaves." These poor whites lived in substandard housing, worked 12 to 16-hour days, with only Sundays off, and labored under harsh and dangerous conditions. When a woman's hair, for example, would become entangled in a machine and partially scalp her, she was not aided in any way by the employer. When a worker was injured severely, he was simply put outside the door to die, if that was "God's way." These methods of labor exploitation provided a perfect opportunity for Marxists later on. Today somehow, when white labor or treatment is historically reviewed, issues are ignored or parsed out as a problem for women, for example. This is due to the rise of identity politics. But it is not based on a balanced view of history. Actual appreciation for the larger picture would inform that as regretful as some chapters of American history may be, such as the first California governor's Indian Policy, the native tribespeople were not the only ones to suffer. In fact, uncounted numbers of whites died. Where miners are concerned, we do have a statistic; one in twelve Forty-Niners died of disease, mishap, or murder, sometimes by Indians. And this would be after the arrival, either as a passenger on an overcrowded disease-ridden ship, or overland, as a survivor of that harrowing journey as gold seekers from all over the globe poured into California, and challenged the new management, posing seeming insurmountable problems. The fact is that the gold rush pressed California into a phase of rapid growth that was nearly impossible to manage. Roving marauders of any race could not be tolerated. Quick decisions had to be made. Governor Burnett's expedient policies were opposed by more humanitarian commissioners, who like Burnett, were from the United States Southeast.

The past can't be changed, but corrective efforts were taken.

The white view of the natives was not entirely malevolent. As with Sutter, peaceful civilizing was the plan. Sutter had brought two native women, wives of two of his Hawaiian Kanakas along for the purpose of educating the local natives (the women were teachers). In 1850, the California government hoped to protect the Indians from white miners and others by negotiating treaties with 139 tribes for a reservation system that made 11,700 square miles or 7.5% of all state lands for reservations to move the tribes out of mining districts where most of the problems were occurring. The treaty included the provision of supplies and cattle. It was a lofty attempt at a solution, but it failed because few Indians moved or stayed on the reservations. Many American citizens objected to the system, stating that even Spain and Mexico had never recognized the land rights of "wild Indians." The resistance was significant enough that the treaties were not ratified in 1852 when they came to the floor at the capital. The next try came from the new Superintendent of Indian Affairs, Edward Beale, who suggested a system of smaller reservations where the Indians would be taught to farm and instructed in other handicrafts along the earlier Spanish Missions lines, but without the harsh "rod" of their Christianity in the hope that they could become self-sustaining communities. The plan was approved. In 1853 five experimental locations of 25,000 acres each were established at Tejon, Nome Lackee, Klamath, and Mendocino on the Pacific coast.

Beale's plan might have worked. He put a great deal of energy into his vision. But in Washington, D.C., The Office of Indian Affairs was particularly vulnerable to the spoils system of political appointments by new administrations. So Beale found himself without a job before he could complete his work. By 1858, a Federal investigator reported that the reservations were dismal failures, having fallen into "alms-houses for a trifling number of Indians." Regardless of this, Beale's system was adopted as the model for the entire West for lack of ability to produce a better model. In 1870, it was decided to recruit Indian agents from various Christian sects. In California, the Methodists were put in charge of the tribes. So maybe this indicts Hastings, Fremont, Governor Burnett, the State of California, the federal government, and most certainly the Spanish who preceded them, the Indians in California, but not Sutter. *5*6

This was the work of the missions. The mission system attempted to civilize the natives by converting them and in effect enslaving them. As the priests considered themselves servants of God, so was everyone else in the community, except under their management. According to Professor Bean, Father Serra, and Zalvidea were harsh, first with themselves, and then on their Indian "flock." Zalvidea is noted as having a lash of metal balls tucked in his belt, which he used several times a day on himself. He treated the Indians with similar strictness. One survivor, known as Victoria, related how a woman who had miscarried was punished by having her head shaved, flogged every day for fifteen days, and kept in irons for three months. But that wasn't all. She was required to stand on the steps before the altar and hold a hideous wooden facsimile of a baby in her arms on Sundays. Victoria reported that they were whipped three times a day, as a routine. On the positive side, we have no record that any pagans, heretics, or witches were tortured and burned at the stake as was practiced in Europe over a period of 1,400 years.

Some of the military leaders criticized the mission's treatment of the natives. Juan Bautista Alvarado wrote that the missionaries "found the Indians in full enjoyment of their five senses, valiant in war... far-sighted in their own way." By the time the padres departed, "they left the Indian population half-stupefied, very much reduced in numbers, and duller than when they found them." The Americans, in comparison, more immediately sought solutions for the problems the Spanish and Mexican rulers had created.

However, by default probably due to the lack of imagination or alternatives, the state assigned the management of the reservations to the Methodists. The Methodists were the hybrid result of New England's colonial period. A major source for almost all eventual sects and social reform movements from abolitionism to temperance, to feminism, the Methodists brought with them perhaps less direct corporal suffering, but the same system of stringent absolutism. For the Indians, it must have been a constant reminder of the Spanish Missionaries among them. This may be the reason for the failure of the system in California.

By 1900 there were less than 16,000 California Indians left. Of the dead, only about ten percent were due to campaigns against them by various military, vigilante, or local white adversaries. During the same period, many whites also died of various infectious diseases, as we shall see. However, before Germ Theory emerged and the advent of Louis Pasteur's new science of inoculation and vaccination emerged; early death was not uncommon among all populations and groups.

It is important to note the drop in native population and activities before Sutter's time. During the Spanish and Mexican period of rule from 1769 to 1846, the native population dropped from more than 270,000 to about 100,000. Most of the deaths were due to disease as they came into contact with the European survivors of Asian diseases that have previously ravaged Europe in an epic of a harsh Darwinian purge of nature there. And there were tensions. Indians found stealing cattle easier than hunting so the entire situation led to increased enmity between the two grew.

There was some eventual recovery in favor of the California Indian tribes. In 1924, after a number of American Indians served in The Great War, Congress gave rights of citizenship to all Amerinds. In 1928, 23,540 living descendants of California American Indians, California Congress authorized California's attorney general to bring a lawsuit against the United States for enumeration for various failures, including the inability to establish the reservation lands they had signed treaties for during 1851. The case was interruptions of the Great depression and World War Two, until 1944. When it was adjudicated, five million dollars was awarded. That came out to $200.00 per person. But also in 1944 was a ruling in a separate case that resulted in the Chowchilla tribe gaining control and income from thirty-thousand acres of rightful tribal land around Palm Springs, resulting in rental collections of $350,000.00, as well as partial income from the land. By 1965, the California Indian population had risen to 75,000, 25,000 short of the population in the 1840s, when the Mexican government had granted Sutter his land.

Since 1965, the same tribes and others all over the United States have been increasingly benefitting from exclusive gambling casino owner/operator rights in many states. Moreover, the combined tribes in the United States own/control more land than any other entity, including the U.S. Government. Today, the American Indian's fate is much like any other American citizen's; a matter of self-determination and self-discipline.

Sutter's Vision

Captain Sutter was not the agent or even cause for these issues of history. Professor Bean reveals some of his bias in comparing Sutter to John Marsh when speaking of Sutter's prehistory in Switzerland. There is no evidence that I know of that his marriage was unhappy. He had failed in his dry goods business, and like many men of even higher station, such as our Revolutionary War Hero, "Light Horse Harry" Lee, fled his country to avoid debtor's prison. And as Lee returned from the Caribbean in due time, so did Sutter send for his family after establishing New Helvetia. John Marsh was a villain through and through. At his estate at the foot of Mount Diablo, he welcomed pioneers and treated them as Sutter for a few days before charging them exorbitant prices for all future food and goods. Marsh was fleeing a Federal warrant. Sutter was looking for a second chance.

Captain Sutter was energetic as much as he was generous to a fault. Aside from the grain and cattle concerns, he planted two thousand fruit trees in 1847, employing as many as six-hundred whites and natives. This was the beginning of the massive fruit production of the future in places like Penryn and Newcastle where many Japanese immigrants benefitted from Sutter's early foresight. The world-record-setting agribusiness of the Sacramento and San Joaquin valleys similarly, has its root in Sutter's early work and example. One pathetic criticism of him that I have read is that he was a drunk. This was predicated on the evidence that he had set up a distillery and produced brandy. This was common on every land grant and estate in California at the time and functioned as currency as it did in the American Colonies and after the Revolutionary War. It's a European tradition. The fact is that every agricultural estate in Europe produced wine and liquor, and today, it's a hobby for many middle-class Europeans with a few fruit trees or honey bees. Sutter was a sober and deliberate man who liked a drink about as much as any man of his time and status, but he was no drunkard. For the close to this account, consider that when Sutter was given his grant part of his expected activities was to pacify the valley and environs as the Mexican government had not been able to succeed through their own efforts. This was because, by the time Sutter arrived, the natives had long come to distrust anyone that spoke Spanish, while Sutter succeeded in making friends of many chiefs and their tribes.

When Sutter and his party were challenged by some Indians on his first journey to the mouth of the American River, they welcomed him after they found they did not speak Spanish. They did, and one Indian accompanied Sutter to interpret for him. But consider the courage of the man, who might have easily imagined himself staked out spread eagle dying in the sun for the sport of the turkey vultures instead of succeeding. Such men as Sutter succeed, because they were not bombastic characters, full of conceit, but were educated, judicious, and had as part of their education, the knowledge of how to spread civilization, not through conquest, but pursuation. And Sutter succeeded far beyond most mortal attempts at personal estate building. He had aimed at a colony, even a state maybe named New Helvetia, not California, but millions of people far into the future benefited from his vision and efforts during that crucial decade of 1840 and 1850. I attribute this not just to Sutter, but to the Swiss civilization in general, which in its development has been one the best modern expressions of Western Civilization, producing an abundance of humanitarians and related projects, such as The Red Cross, which was established by Henry Durant in 1859. For those who love to see him as a villain, they can vainly revel in his downfall. Sutter suffered in turn as his vision of California was crushed by the Gold Rush.

Some were famous; Samuel Clement, Bret Harte, Horace Greeley, etc., spent some time perusing the mines and saloons. Few know that part of the Nightingale family of Florence Nightingale (Crimean War fame) settled in the Gold Country. The Nightingale Family Farm flourished in Latrobe, which is on the Sacramento and El Dorado County lines. James Nightingale and his wife, Jane, and four children from a newborn son to an eight-year-old daughter had crossed the great expanse in an ox-drawn Conestoga wagon in 1853. They had first arrived at Michigan Bluff, in Placer County.

By the time gold was discovered, there were several stores located at Sutter's Fort itself. Captain Sutter's son, John Jr., had arrived from Switzerland with the rest of Sutter's family, and John Senior signed over his majority interest in Sacramento to his son. There was a short economic war between Sutterville and Sacramento. The struggle ended in the latter's favor when after a few frames; construction stores were rapidly set up on the new waterfront streets of I and J. Finally, two large, unique log cabins were built by pioneer businessmen Mr. Gillespie and Dr. Carpenter. But it was the maneuvering and savvy of Samuel Brannan who had a store in that merchant neighborhood, executed a brilliant financial maneuver of speculation, and ended up with five hundred of the choicest lots of the future city. At the close of this deal, the population total for Sacramento was but one hundred and fifty persons.

Brannan, an excommunicated Mormon leader and a young man of 26, had put aside his religious commitments to make strategic gains in California. Brannan, one of the two of that faith who had by chance decided to try a little "sinful" prospecting near their camp while on their way to Sacramento. Carrying no pans or actual mining equipment, they used dishes to dig up the dirt. Brannan quickly filed a preemptive claim to what became known as Mormon Island, one of the first claims ever staked out in the history of California gold mining. Those of his brethren who recovered gold there were obligated to render him one-third of their findings. This condition remained until the non-brethren outnumbered the brethren at his claim. He used that money to put himself into business in Sacramento. When some other of his brethren had come to him for payment of regular tithes, Brannan is reported to have said, "When you can give me a receipt signed by the Lord, I'll give you the money!" He was also the fellow who had rushed to San Francisco and announced by, blowing a horn and parading a banner that read, "Gold! Gold! Gold! To be picked up with little effort from the streambeds of the Sierra foothills." He was the one who had plotted to profit from a big "Gold Rush," not Sutter. Brannan became a real thorn in the side of Sutter. Coming into the possession of one of the two first printing presses in California, he published for his own interests.

Paradise Lost - Again

Captain Sutter had envisioned an American settled colony named New Helvetia with Sutterville, a "city" to the immediate south, three miles from the fort. However, the rebellion of 1846, the arrival of the U.S. Army, and then the gold discovery quickly dashed his dream of a land of splendorous living, of ranchers and farmers; the grandest example of the Californio style of living; gracious and accommodating. John Sutter, Jr. owned Sacramento City outright at this point. Captain John Sutter turned over all of his interests in the City to him after his family arrived on September 14th, 1848. One month later, on the 14th, the transfer was finalized. John Sutter, Jr. immediately retained Judge Burnett (later governor) as his legal actor. Captain Sutter had planned for the town to be called Sutter and had established Sutterville three miles south as the highest ground with a natural serviceable landing.

Sacramento legally wrangled itself into dominance after a brief period of competition with Sutterville. That city was founded in 1844 when Sutter laid out a plan for a landing and trading post there with its first house being constructed by Captain Sutter himself. Next, Mr. Zins finished the third building, the first brick building in California. That initial trading port was located a few miles down the river on the only piece of land that could be relied upon to remain dry all year. It was good enough to have served as the garrison headquarters for a couple of companies of U.S. soldiers under the command of Major Kingsbury during the Mexican-American War. But after the U.S. Army had made its headquarters there during the war, it had struggled along, and Captain Sutter had lost immediate control of it. When George McDougal, Brannan's only other competition, had claimed that he had a lease for four hundred yards of riverbank from Sutter's slough that served his fort directly south, Sutter Jr. challenged it. The court found that Sutter Jr.'s lease superseded that of McDougal. So McDougal relocated to Sutterville to set up in competition with Brannan and John Sutter, Jr. He had an uphill battle before him due to the town site's position amid backwater sludge of brackish water. Merchant maneuvers of one and the other aimed at putting one out of business ensued with all sorts of cornpone shenanigans. But then, McDougal, in a do-or-die strategy, offered the new Sacramento merchants eighty lots in Sutterville if they would move their interests to their city.

Seeing his merchants hesitating at the offer, John Jr. fell took the questionable advice Brannan and Burnett suggested and offered the cost-free transfer of five hundred of the choicest lots in his town. They claimed that this would secure the remnant of the lots to him for future profiting and end competition with his namesake-Ville, forever. Then, Sam Brannan opened a big warehouse by the wharf in Sacramento.   The contest was over, and Sutterville faded into obscurity to the point that today, Sutterville is only known by the road in Sacramento that runs from the old town site on the River towards Brighton. It forms the southern limit of William Land Park to this day. The City's growth was a partial swindle as well. That Sacramento had never been, nor would it ever be flooded, was stated to the newly arrived speculators vigorously.   The few years preceding had been unusually dry years, so the claim was believed. Sacramento was not founded on a lie. It was the perfect location as a junction between the river and the goldfields. The maneuvers involved in its establishment stand as a fantastic tale of courageous pioneering, opportunists, and greedy hypocrites, but overall the triumph of civilization as Sacramento became a gentile city of upright citizens.

Similarly, most who worked in the rivers, streams, and fields searching for the stuff of dreams ended up desperate and broken. Regardless of that, no less than 750,000 pounds of gold were extracted by mines during the Gold Rush years. 1853 was the California Gold Rush's peak year when an estimated 100,000 miners took 80 million in gold in that year's value. Many miners did make a fortune and return home. In one national case, over two million dollars alone was carried to France by Frenchman who had done with prospecting, satisfied with their takings from Mokelumne Hill, where they had discovered a rich vein. Soon, many more miners were there, and fights broke out over claims and claim-jumping. Soon, two armies were camped on either side of the river, ready for war. Luckily, cooler heads prevailed. But those French prospectors had recovered that bounty in two years. Gold grew and sustained Sacramento. The final phase of wealth would be agricultural expansion. In the end, what grew and supported the city, state, and country, was a combination of mineral wealth and food production. In the early days, it was the common morality of the population that held order together.

In 1849, Sacramento saw a steady increase in population. Regardless of that, and there being no law or court in force, the city was peaceful and safe, although the mining towns were decidedly wilder. To be sure, the lure of instant riches was bound to attract types of the least inclined toward civic order and law. Regardless, where Sacramento City was concerned, no thefts, even of gold, were reported in those early days. A miner could lay his poke down next to his hat, come back from his business, and find both untouched.

The first Fourth of July Celebration in Sacramento in 1849 was similarly gentile as well; a ball would be held. The Pavilion, so named, was constructed a few miles east of the city, located near the banks of the American River for the event attended by the first governor of California, Peter H. Burnett.

But there were plans to make. A sufficient number of possible dance partners had to be present for a proper civic function. So a troop of the most appropriate men was persuaded by all the other men to search the countryside, every ranch, house, tent, or wagon, for any and all Caucasian females, regardless of age, education, looks, or manners. Eighteen such females were found, accepted the invitation, and were escorted to the highly attended event.

− Sacramento 1850 −
*Source -Public Domain, **https://commons.wikimedia.org/w/index.php?curid=169428***

The ladies had decorated themselves with any material or means that would add to their presence and sparkle. The women or soon-to-be women faced some two-hundred men burdened with the voracious appetite that the deprivation of such beings always produces, and yet, were not daunted.

The manners of the men were impeccable. They bowed as one to the troupe of gals and displayed every tender rendering of politeness and admiration to every one of them, advancing hat in hand to request a turn on the floor. When one man requested such a tour of a young lady in her teens, perhaps not the most delicate flower among the ladies; the tall, husky girl replied, "You bet!" and commenced to scrub the dance floor with her bewildered partner, as witnesses tell it. Toasts were made and enjoined. One, notably, was refused by a lady as too forward. The civility of the event proves that it wasn't the lack of civilization or the civilized that caused the Squatter's Riot; it was the most basic of all things, the need for home and its security.

In the face of the events of 1849 and 1850, the life's blood allowing Sacramento to survive into 1851 was the gold that flowed from the mines without interruption except for the periods of three catastrophes visited upon the infant city. Only one such event would have been sufficient to bring the life of a lesser-infused town to a permanent end. The first of such catastrophes that interrupted our levee city's forward projection into its glorious future was ironically caused by the gold discovery.

The land that the speculators had laid out for the city was a natural floodplain. In the best spirit of both conscious and unconscious denial, that alarming fact was avoided until the flood of the winter of 1849, 50. Had the new burg's population remained at one-hundred and fifty, there would have been no historical note to make when they scrambled to the heights of the fort or made it out to the higher, drier spots to occupy and camp upon until the waters abated. But the flow of gold seekers had changed the city from a small village of entrepreneur cattlemen and farmers to merchants who may well have abandoned the place for Stockton, or even Sutterville's slight elevation and shorter roadway out to Brighton. However, the dye had been cast by ambitious and energetic men, determined to make Sacramento the monarch of the valley.

Overwhelmed

Men, just men at first, flooded in from all over the world. Most had sold their last possessions or mortgaged their family homes for the fee for the passage to San Francisco. But the majority, the vast majority, had not planned any further than there. As a result, they were marooned in a town too expensive to have been believed before arriving. So even if the prudent planner had a reserve, it was often depleted in a short time. The result of this problem was that humanity piled up. Even though this provided a bottleneck for humanity's regulation out to Sacramento and the goldfields, the numbers were still too large to be managed. The state of most of the men was similarly deplorable. Diaries that survive illustrate the appalling situation that passengers who took the ocean route found themselves in. The ships were so crowded that even the decks were crowded day and night. The food was rotten and water scarce. Many only found succor in the way of food, water, and medical care at some port along the way. Most had contracted sickness and scurvy on the long voyage. The rigors of the journey alone had worn most out, at least long enough to require a recuperation period in Sacramento before the journey out to the mining camps' rough communities.

But it was worse than that. Many that disembarked from the steamers docked at the base of Front Street between I and J Streets could propel themselves no further and collapse on the banks of the river, where many simply expired where they lay. Many were cases of typhus and dysentery. Added to this were the always ragged arrivals from the overland route, which were increasing in numbers daily. Every one of them required assistance, and many of them arrived on the verge of starvation as too many found themselves abandoned by companions, even family, who were afflicted with gold fever beyond human loving. The first of many heroic efforts were made to assuage the pitiful suffering masses that came by that autumn in impossible numbers. John Sutter donated the highest nearby land for a cemetery, ten acres, which went into immediate use and remains the city's oldest cemetery today. The treasury was already exhausted by the time just a small order was established by the erection of a few small hospitals and public buildings.

Just as those losses and the event's grief were becoming manageable, if catastrophe can be ordered, in December of 1849, a downpour of rain of cataclysmic proportions ensued. The Sacramento and American rivers rose to the extent that the city was cut off from all high land beyond the city itself. Sacramento had become isolated. And then, on the eighth day of January, in the dark of night, the rushing water broke into feeble homes and camps of a by then uncounted mass of already desperate human beings.

Hundreds drowned immediately, trapped in beds, tents, and in various inescapable situations where the flood awoke them into a living nightmare, in conditions that the massive inrush of water caused instantly. Only a few boats were present at the dock and were put into immediate service in rescuing women, children, and invalids. They were taken to the few places that had second floors as hospitals.

Capable women became instant nurses. Every able-bodied person was scrambling to save what life could be saved. Merchant supplies, the possessions of all, were stolen away by the flood as it ripped through the streets. To gain an appreciation of the sudden growth of the town and the overwhelmingly poor condition of so many would-be Argonauts, suddenly met with the new catastrophe is best found in the narrative of the venerable Dr. John F. Morse;

"One of them whose blanket enveloped the entire body and head seemed to be rapidly dying, and consequently, he was the first to get the attention of the physicians and nurses. An attempt was made to unroll the blanket, but it was found to be so adherent to the many parts of the body as to make it difficult of removal – so difficult that the effort was delayed after the face was relieved, for the deplorable victim to revive if possible, or if not that death might free him from a sense of his situation. Fortunately for him, death was the speedy alternative. His troubles were ended. A finely developed form a face on which lingered the indices of cultivated intellect, a heart that once beat with manly pride, were enwrapped in a death so dreadful as to beggar description and so appalling as to excite an almost eternal impression of nausea and disgust in the minds of those that beheld it. The blanket was with difficulty detached. When drawn off, the blanket presented a shirtless body already partially devoured by an immense bed of maggots occupying nearly as much space as the emaciated carcass itself. And when one adds to this loathsome mass, the crawling elements of disgust, the accumulated excretions which were alike confined by the agglutinated folds of the blanket, then can a just conception be formed of what was suffered during the sickness of the fall and winter of '49."

Throughout these devastating events, it was the Odd Fellows and Freemasons who raised money for the construction of hospitals, manned them, and after an appalling period of the worst sort of disposal methods for the suffered dead, even the money for coffins so that no one was denied a coffin burial. According to Dr. Morse, these civic-minded organizations were at the center of efforts to succor and guide the city through the worst growing pains that they could never have anticipated. Still unimaginable today, they had to be seen and experienced to be comprehended. Dr. Morse hardly mentions his services but exhorts the highest praise to the doctors who never failed in their oaths to serve, many of whom did not survive the final calamity. This is itself a monument to the good doctor.

Perhaps the most remarkable aspect in the midst of all of this was the frenzy of building, as canvas and wood-framed structures gave way to more permanent edifices. And once they were destroyed by the flood, they were just as quickly rebuilt, only better and more of them. The flow of gold was the only guaranteed condition at the time, so when loans were sought, they were usually granted. And the one man who had been preaching the wisdom of erecting a levy system to protect the city, Hardin Bigelow. He secured the funds necessary to employ a gang of workers who labored around the clock to form the first levy of a system that would end up covering miles of Sacramento Delta waterways. His foresight and forthright, energetic manner of motivating men saw him elected Mayor in an election called in the first week of April 1850. He prevented a second devastating flood by throwing up the levee as its tides were arriving.

The levee had a predecessor, the meager landing where the first theater was erected in October of 1849, The Eagle Theater. It was constructed of canvas on a wood frame. During the summer of 1849, steamer traffic to and from Sacramento commenced in a big way. Among them was one named "Antelope." One may only guess at its influence on the name chosen for our little railroad village of this tale.

The Eagle Theatre was perhaps humble, but it was the first of many entertainments that elevated life in the new city. It wasn't long before the usual gaming of the time, poker, faro, and the wheel became features accompanied by various acts and performances on the stage. George McDougal, who had built Sutterville, was the same man who had managed affairs with Sam Brannan in San Francisco and had once organized a meeting. This meeting included General Vallejo and several international captains of various mariners for the purpose of raising funds and men for the Reed-Donner rescue party of 1846.

McDougal now sat in the upper story of this combination warehouse, gambling hall, and theatre, and drank whiskey with other wharf rats, laughing at his misfortune as his merchandise was carried away by the flood.

Life Goes On

Even amid the losses, Sacramento kept a glimmer of humor and hope as rivals, friends, partners, and legal opponents all, sorted the future out. The city became the heart of the roaring gold camps' life, taking in the gold flow and pumping out food and supplies, and it wished to live. The "Levee City" had its heroes of the day. Of them, many were elected to offices to manage the city and the planning of its future. The first City Council was formed for that purpose.

Meanwhile, the situation that had only begun with a few grumbling squatters in the town had grown into a problem that presented itself as a legal wrangle to be unraveled. Through it, we might study the course of the life of a legal fabrication, filled with admonitions of rights and republicanism in the American tradition when necessity, greed, or both might birth such movements to the point of violence and death.

The early declaration in the autumn of 1849 had been made by a gaggle of illiterate but ambitious men, exhausted from their experiences and feeling the weight of necessity to outweigh property owners' rights. This group, who called themselves "Squatters," voiced the opinion that questioned Captain Sutter's title to the land that the city was laid out upon. Their feeling was of the traditional settler; once one erects a tent on a plot, the plot is rightfully theirs. This grew the opinion until enough men agreeing to question Sutter's ownership of the land seemed legitimate. One of them, John Robinson, settled on a lot and built a house. On December 7th, 1849, it was petitioned by a legal property owner that Robinson's house be removed from the lot, which was adjudicated to be on public property and was removed with grand ceremony attended by all parties. The celebration of those who approved of the assertion of property rights over squatters' rights was sufficient to inflict permanent bitterness among the Squatters.

Much of the resentment toward the Squatters was due to their printing of titles that they claimed were superior to the ones held by those who had purchased lots from Sutter or his subsequent titleholders. For a time after the removal of the Robinson house, the issue was suppressed by the event of the floods. It returned in full force as the crisis passed. The Squatters' declaration implied that their claims would be bolstered by the arrival of new immigrants who they assumed understood the law of settlers and the Republic as they saw it. So the arguments grew into political ideologies of Squatterism and Sutterism.

The Day of Judgment in the court duly arrived. Captain Sutter presented his right to the title first, through the original Mexican Land Grant, and next, through the recognition and guarantee of the transfer of Mexican Land Grants by the United States Government, in addition to his many publically useful improvements of the land. The land had been surveyed and properly delineated by a competent engineer. The land had been handed to his son, John Sutter, Jr., and sold in lots into the hands of thousands of buyers. This was the summary of the titled owner's argument. Opposing was Squatter's rationale that the land's natural boundaries were not in keeping with the imaginary lines and boundaries created by the engineer in his survey. Further, they sought to make the case that the flood had changed the land significantly so that some of the original grant's lines were moved north, which, combined with the initial errors of the engineer, ended up making the entire City of Sacramento public land and therefore opened to settlement.

The first civil suit against the Squatters was filed in November 1849 by John A. Sutter et al. vs. Geo. Chapman. Restitution was granted by Judge Thomas and served by Presley Dunlap. After the flood and its immediate issues subsided, the issue of title to the land in the city rose to the surface once more. This time, it resulted in a gunfight.

As the numbers of Squatter's grew in the succeeding spring and summer of 1850, new, more talented speakers took up the cause. They ridiculed the titled owners as speculators, profiteers, and monopolists, all likely borrowed from the influence of the just-formed Communist Club of New York City and the presentation of Marx's articles that Horace Greeley was printing in his New York Times/Tribune. But they termed it republicanism. As their charges grew in severity, and the number of listeners increased, anxiety among Sutter titleholders grew.

On the tenth of May, 1850, the lawsuit that would spark August's riots was filed. P. Rodgers and Dewitt J. Burnett commenced an action against T. Madden. The judge was B. F. Washington, who being from Virginia, was likely a cousin of the Father of Our Country and first President George Washington. The case concerned a lot located on the southeast corner of 2nd and N Streets. The Defendant pled no jurisdiction and was overruled. Next, the Defendant claimed the land was on public land and, therefore, subject to the title by settlement and improvement, due to his having entered the property in March of 1850 and made improvements.

A demurrer to halt proceedings was entered by the Plaintiffs on the grounds that there was no law to uphold such a claim. The Defendant then filed for a venue change, alleging that the Recorder was biased and that he could not get a fair trial in the city. The application was refused. The trial commenced. The court found against the defendant and fined him $300.00 for costs expended, and ordered the issuing of a writ of restitution. The defendant appealed to the County Court, which was heard on August 8, Judge Willis presiding, which claimed that the City court had no jurisdiction and the verdict be overruled. The case was submitted and considered. Sutter presented his claims, and the Defendant objected. The objection was overridden, and the lower court decision was upheld. The Defendant then asked to appeal to the Superior Court, but no law had yet been created to sustain such an appeal, and the motion was overruled.

The Squatters declared their unified opposition to the judgment of the court. The two opposing sides began to hold nightly meetings, declaring in ever-increasing and threatening tones their dedication to the law as they saw it. But almost as soon as the judge had made his decision known, the Squatters produced a bill titled, "TO THE PEOPLE OF SACRAMENTO CITY," as a declaration of sorts with four points of accusation and argument, followed by a discussion ending with their declaration of intent;

"They will regard the said officers as private citizens, as in the eyes of the constitution they are, and hold them accountable accordingly. And, moreover, if there is no other appeal from Judge Willis, the settlers and others on the first show of violence to their persons or property, either by the sheriff or other person, under the color of any execution or writ of restitution based on any judgment or decree of any court in this county in an action to recover possession of land, have deliberately and resorted to appeal to arms and protect their sacred right, if need be, with their lives. Should such be rendered necessary by the acts of the sheriff or others, the settlers will be governed by martial law. All property and the persons of such as do not engage in the contest will be sacredly regarded and protected by them, whether landholders or otherwise, but the property and lives of those who take the field against them will share the fate of war."

So the day came; August 11, when a Squatter's meeting was held on the Levee. Sutterists soon learned of the meeting and rushed down to engage in a debate with the Squatters. The meeting seemed to be an attempt to supplant the present government and court system via a new declaration of government, of which its first and founding move would be to nullify the findings of the courts they found unlawful. A motion was adopted that the resolutions be taken up separately. At this point, loud calls for various speakers were made; McKune, Kewen, Brannan, McClatchy, Madden, etc. Mr. McKune led off with this diatribe in support of the Squatters. He presented the Sutterists case and then set about criticizing it with the points of issue already argued and denied in court. He then added the claim that Sutter's residence was not in city limits but on the Hock Farm outside of city bounds. This was supposed to somehow cancel Sutter's rights of title by the law of the land supposed as the desertion of a holding. Mr. Brannan, a founding merchant of the city, denounced the claim as an outright lie obvious to anyone. Then, Mr. Brannan asserted his legal agency to have a Squatter removed from his land, adding that his land had been purchased through money he had earned from hard work. The principles of land ownership vs. public dominion were at stake.

After a period of disruptions, marked by pushing and shoving, Colonel K.J. C. Kewen came forward to speak by acclamation. The Colonel proclaimed that many people who were now holding land had been deluded by frauds and forgers, but were at heart honest men of the Anglo-Saxon race. He was shouted down by calls of "Soft Soap" and other less kind epithets aimed at exposing this arbiter as a betrayer of principles involved in this specific set of circumstances. The brave Colonel then modified his tone to support the Squatter's cause by acknowledging Mr. McKewin's arguments denied by Judge Willis. As the chairman of the meeting, the previously aggrieved Dr. Robinson asked permission to address the assembly as Mr. McQueen simultaneously asked for the same privilege. After the court denied his request, Mr. McQueen then turned to the crowd and put the question to them but was refused with roars of laughter. What followed was a war of words with no ear to hear any of the salvos by either friend or enemy in the contest. The meeting was adjourned by Dr. Robinson with his declaration that as for himself, he would defend the property he had settled upon with his life.

Madden's house became the garrison of the Squatters. They gathered up muskets, pistols, sabers, and some very old swords, of likely Spanish origin, as they prepared for an inevitable confrontation of armed parties. Meanwhile, in his office, the Sheriff sought to execute his writs of restitution, discovered some of the resistors to be people he knew, and obtained warrants for their arrest from Judge Sackett; James McClatchy, and John Robinson, among others. Several days passed, marked by outbursts of violence and riots. James McClatchy chose his destiny in the interim, seeing the situation going beyond what he believed was morally and legally supportable, and turned himself in.

On the 14 of August, about forty armed Squatter's sallied forth to the foot of I Street with the intent of reoccupying a lot that had been seized the day before from one of their party. Their aim was to liberate some men who had been arrested during rioting that took place on the morning of August 12th on the specific charge of resisting the process of law. They were being held on a prison ship, which was serving at the city jail at the time. After a little damage was caused, they were repulsed from the lot. The Mayor, in the meantime, issued a request that all good men of the city assemble to prevent a general riot. After being repulsed from the lot, the Squatters retreated in military order back up I Street as far as 3rd, over to J, and from thence to Fourth Street. There, they were met by the Mayor, who ordered them to surrender their arms and disperse. The answer was several fired shots. The Mayor fell from his horse and was carried off to his residence, luckily not mortally wounded. Mr. J.W. Woodland, who carried no weapon, took a shot in the groin and died almost immediately.

Mr. Jesse Morgan, who had only just arrived in Sacramento, had fired the shot at the Mayor. He fell instantly from a ball passing through his neck in retaliation. A supporter of the Mayor, Mr. James Harper, had also been badly wounded. Among the mounted leaders of the Squatters was Mr. Maloney who had his horse shot from under him. He was pursued up an alley and killed with a bullet through the head. Dr. Robinson was wounded in the lower part of his body. Mr. Hale of Crowell, Hale & Company was wounded in the leg. A young boy was also wounded. There were other uncertain casualties of the melee, as well. Acting upon several observers' oaths, Dr. Robinson and an Irishman named Claufield were arrested for murder as seen aiming their guns at the Mayor and Mr. Woodland and firing. It had been a veritable gunfight at the OK Corral decades before that event occurred.

The City Council met immediately and dispatched parties throughout the town to prevent any further violent outbreaks. It was learned that a group of Squatters had occupied Sutter's Fort and was reinforcing it. A mounted group of citizens under the command of the Sheriff rode out to prevent a siege. Soon, quiet fell over the restive scene under the watchful eyes of citizen volunteers, numbering five hundred, having stationed themselves throughout the city that night. Learning of the chaos in Sacramento, Brigadier General Winn, stationed at Sutterville, declared martial law, and Lieutenant Governor McDougal sailed to Benicia to return with a detachment of troops immediately. Thus, calm was restored to Sacramento. With but a few last grumbles, the Squatters seem to have either melded back into the city's population or fled. The City Council held a public meeting to review the events. Among the accolades were those toward Sheriff Joseph McKinney, who was marked as having acted most mindfully and courageously amid the confusion of gunshots, panic, and scrambling for safety or escape. Those known to have been material leaders or participants would have to be located and detained for trial.

Shootout in Brighton

By August 15th, Sheriff McKinney was made aware that some of the violence's principal perpetrators were holed up in Brighton, at the Five Mile House, a few miles outside of Sacramento. He rode out with a party of twenty armed men to affect their arrest.

The big celebration of the Fourth of July that had been held at The Pavilion was near the Five Mile House kept by brothers John and George Berry. The Sheriff and his posse arrived at the Five Mile House to learn that the party he sought was actually located near the Pavilion at a tavern owned by a man named Allen. The horsemen soon discovered the place. The plan was for a trusted man from the Mormon Island community, Mr. McDowell, who was known to the usual patrons, to go inside and report back. But the Sheriff did not wait, perhaps anxious that the men would grow nervous and flee. So the posse rode hastily to the tavern and dismounted. The Sheriff entered the bar alone, and facing eight or ten men, ordered them to lay down their arms. He was mortally wounded by a shotgun blast and died within a few minutes. At the sound of that blast, the posse poured into the saloon, and a general shootout ensued. Two Squatters took shelter behind the bar with Allen. The Sheriff's murderer was instantly killed. Four Squatters were killed, and the bartender, Allen, was wounded but made his escape. Four prisoners were taken, and the rioting was finally over for good.

The effect of the suppression of Squatterism was a slew of bankruptcies and failed enterprises. Still, after September of the year, the people began to go about business in a more regular and sound fashion. This was made possible by the necessities of life and mineral recovery demanded by the mines. The winter of 1849-50 had seen deprivation and starvation at the mines. This impelled them to better planning and supply, which benefitted the quick recovery of Sacramento immensely. The funeral of Mr. Woodland and Sheriff McKinney was attended by the majority of the citizens of Sacramento. Many former Squatters were in attendance, sobered at last, by reality. Eulogies were spoken to the hushed crowd, which afterward broke up soberly to their homes for private contemplation of the previous few days' events.

For Sutter, however, the issues were never concluded. They dogged him until his once expansive holdings had severely declined and his philanthropic largess reduced as a result. Sutter was forced to vacate even his last holdings in California after his Hock Ranch to the north was burned down by a vagrant he had allowed to camp on his land. John Sutter had always been a constant philanthropist and, contrary to some prevalent accusations, never enslaved one human being.

It is only true that some Indians who worked for him under contract to harvest crops had been pursued and returned to duty. It's understandable on several counts. Although they may not have considered their contract binding, they were dealing with a culture that did. Secondly, it concerned the harvest. Due to desertion, the loss was life-threatening to all dependent on that food, some indeed, being other employed Indians. And finally, third, it serves as evidence of the overall goodwill between the natives and Sutter. The Indians that worked for him went willingly at his request as guides for rescuers during the dreadful winter of 1846-7 for rescuing the Donner Party. These and the previous facts should be sufficient answers to such accusations. He never held back but poured out his assistance, wealth, and manpower, for not just the Donner Party but also every one of the stricken early pioneers up to and beyond the discovery of gold. And even when he felt deep apprehension around the presence of John Fremont and his American troops in Mexican California, he gave them succor when they came to him in need.

Sutter had much to fear; firstly, his holdings were vast and had been won through years of sacrifice. He came to California after some years of service as a captain in a Swiss regiment seconded to the French army (this claim is disputed, but we do know that Governor Micheltorlena gave the office to Sutter in 1842*$_8$). Then, at thirty years of age, he left his family in Switzerland for years, looking for success, taking many risks, and finally focusing on California, where they eventually joined him in 1848. Governor Alvarado had given him the right to settle in the Sacramento Valley. He explored the Sacramento, American, and Feather Rivers before locating himself on the site that would become Sacramento in 1839 when the nearest civilization was the northernmost mission. Captain Sutter settled in a wilderness where none but a few trappers had ventured before him. He was granted his acres because the Mexican government had made no progress in the region where the Indians had not yet suffered any white man, Spanish or American, to settle, let alone venture. The initially hostile Indians were soon won over enough to work for him willingly. At first, he was attacked at the fort. In an effort to discourage those attacks, he sallied forth with his little army of eight Kanakas (Hawaiians), six white men, and two vaqueros, which was sufficient to restore peace.*$_6$

Soon, Sutter's peaceful overtures found Indian allies who willingly worked at the fort. In fact, both the Indians and Sutter were guarded by fifteen Indian guards for most of the 1840s. Through working tirelessly to improve the land, his grant had grown into what some have called a kingdom. His fort was the terminus for all overland pioneers and trappers. He even became a contractor with the Hudson Bay Company. By 1848, he owned both the New Helvetia and Sobrante grants, as well as the former Russian possessions at Ross and Bodega. His hospitality and charity were renowned the world over, having not a single enemy but respect from everyone. After the short war, he was a member of the Constitutional Convention in Monterey. He appointed Major General of the California Militia, Indian Agent, and alcade (sheriff) by the appointment of Commodore Stockton.

Lately, much has been made of his alleged misdeeds toward the natives by revisionists, who willfully embellish reports by a few zealots who had personal reasons for criticizing. One example is the claim that Sutter undertook raids into far-flung, primitive regions to capture women and children, which he gave as gifts. But there is no record of this activity. Common sense also contradicts the claim. How could he have been building up his local holdings as he did while on so many such expeditions? It is most likely these are taken from the history of Jim Savage's adventures, embellished by members of today's grievance industry, and applied to Sutter.

Who would be the receivers of these child slave gifts? One of his visitors was a black man who made no report but seemed to approve of Sutter's activities and treatment of the Indians. Sutter did not take slaves nor forced labor except in one instant when a group of Maidu men deserted the fields during a harvest, breaking their contract. Of slavery, the note must be made; there is not one instant of an example of an Amerind tribe that did not take, trade, and hold slaves, and their women were often traded off for goods like chattel. In fact, half of the Cherokee nation sided with the Confederate army during the War of the Southern Rebellion precisely because they wished to keep their Negro slaves and fought the other half bitterly. (Those that sided with the Union merely wished to avoid having to deal with two white governments). For those who appreciate well-documented records, there are hundreds of verified reports of white capture and slavery, beyond the murderous raids on often poorly or unarmed whites during the Westward Expansion.*[9]

Such a series of campaigns by a man with an army of well under twenty such as Sutter possessed would have been financially ruinous if any survived at all. The Modoc War of 1872 further illustrates the phantasm of such accusations. At the very least, that set of tragedies was attributable to Fremont's earlier slaughter and Hastings before him. The more extensive record shows that Sutter treated the Indians better than his Mexican contemporaries and Spanish predecessors. In fact, when Sutter first entered the Sacramento River Delta to explore, the group of Indians they first met began to assault them until they learned they were not Spanish. Once they learned that they were not Spanish speakers Sutter and his party were allowed to pass. In fact, one Indian served as a guide thereafter.

It had been through the Spanish and Mission rule that the California Indians had suffered and seen their population crash. By the time Sutter was granted his rancho lands, the population of the California tribes had been reduced under the Spanish and the mission system from 300,000 to 100,000. Criticism of Mexican or any Hispanic historical wrongdoing is not the order of the day, although it abounded in every land south of the present U.S., Mexico border.

All of Captain Sutter's enterprises became complete losses. All of his vast lands were occupied by squatters, who butchered off his immense herds of cattle, sheep, and pigs, consuming a quantity of it, but ultimately sold off much more to distant buyers in organized rustling, one of which occurred in the middle of the flood of 1851. With the monies gained for seized land and the sale of Sutter's various properties, lawyers were hired, and a legal wrangle began, so Sutter was tied up with expensive lawsuits for ten years. By then, the newly formed United States Court of Land Commissioners had been organized, and his grants were reviewed and found to be without defect and supported by the Treaty of Guadalupe Hildago. The common feeling among Americans was based on the previous practices of the Federal government when granting land to settlers in new territories. Judging them today, given our present situations, might be a bit hypocritical.

The Squatter's lawyers next appealed to the United States District Court for the Northern District of California, but they upheld the Land Commissions' findings. They appealed both cases to the United States Supreme Court in Washington, D.C. That court also found the New

Helvetia grant in Sutter's favor, but the twice-sized grant, the Sobrante, while ruled legal, was decided in favor of the Squatters on "technical grounds." Since most of that grant had been portioned out to legitimate parties already, Sutter had to liquidate the remainder of his New Helvetia lands to satisfy those title losses. It was a calamity for Sutter. But that wasn't the end of it. Sutter had but one piece of land left. He had often stayed on a ranch and had stocked with herds and personnel, the Hock Ranch, which was on the Feather River at the north end of the Sobrante Grant. This Sutter had reserved for his family and himself, as the final redoubt for his last years. And much he deserved that peace and happiness with his family after an epoch of a lifetime!

There is a retort to all the slanders laid on General John A. Sutter by today's revisionist historians. That is an earlier and more thorough history than any done since. In 1934, a genuine, objective, and dedicated historian, Julian Dana, undertook a thorough, in depth effort to produce what still remains as the most complete history on Sutter. He dug into every surviving record, interviewed many parties, including surviving Sutter family members. The history is titled, "Sutter of California." A special edition was produced in 1938 in time for the 1939 Sutter Centennial, a series of events, parades, gatherings, and exhibits that went on for months that year. Ever since then, beginning in the 1950s, with the sardonic comments of Leftist writer, Irving Stone (Men to Match My Mountains), a growing collection of biting criticisms that largely rely on omissions, but also outright fabrications and accusations, building to the latest suggestion by a book sponsored by the Sacramento Public Library, with a founding premise that Sutter's New Helvetia Grant was likely never official. This is a preposterous suggestion, and counts on the ignorance of the reader. Dana' book debunks this and the remaining list of charges of theft of land, cruelty to the natives, drunkenness, and incompetence. His fault was generosity, and trust in his fellow man. He could not imagine that his lawyer would take on his adversaries and conveniently burn down his own office with Sutter's records there, or that his Hock Farm with all of his most important records and documents would be fired by a group of men as part of the ongoing swindles against him. At two in the morning, June 7, 1865, Sutter awoke to cries of "Fire! Fire!," being shouted by innocent deputy who had been sent with a devastating writ to be delivered as Sutter watched his last comfort destroyed. The US Supreme Court had validated his New Helvetia Grant, but there was no order to stop the ongoing swindle of his property. On that same day, far away General William T. Sherman wrote of Sutter as the most important figure in California history.

John Sutter and his wife, Anna, traveled back east to Litiz, in Lancaster County in Pennsylvania, where he fought in vain for reimbursements at the Capitol in Washington, D.C. for losses incurred while having assisted the countless numbers of American citizens settling in California in the 1840s, without success. He died in Washington, D.C., in June of 1880, failing to gain the least monetary consideration for his huge contribution to the nation and world. However, many mourned him in California. Once such was Mrs. S.O. Houghton, nee Eliza P. Donner. In a letter published on the concluding pages of Charles F. McGlashan's "History of the Donner Party," of 1880, her words convey the feelings of the members of the survivors of that disaster, as well as the memories of unaccounted citizens of the time in California;

"I have been sad, oh, so sad, since the tidings flashed across the continent telling the friends of General Sutter to mourn his loss. In tender and loving thought, I have followed the remains to his home, have stood by his bier, touched his icy brow, and brushed back his snowy locks, and still, it is hard for me to realize that he is dead; he who has ever awakened the warmest gratitude of my nature is to be laid away in a distant land! But I must not yield to this mood longer. God has only harvested the ripe and golden grain. Nor has He left us comfortless, for recollections, memory's faithful messenger, will bring from her treasury records of deeds so noble, that the name of General Sutter will be stamped in the hearts of all people, so long as California has a history. Yes, his name will be written in letters of sunlight on Sierra's snowy mountainsides, will be traced on the clasps of gold which rivet the rocks of our State, and will be traced in the transparent characters over the gate which guards our western tide. All who see this land of the sunset will read, and know, and love the name of John A. Sutter, who fed the hungry, clothed the naked, and comforted the sorrowing child of California's pioneering days."

And now, to our shame, we have forgotten, and worse; we have allowed him to be dishonored and intentionally defamed as part of the general political trend to kill all historical memory. End the Leftist, Woke campaign against his name and legacy, which benefited so many up to the present. Stand up his statue inside the fort that bears his name. California should establish and acknowledge him with a "Captain John August Sutter Day."

The Wave of Death that Almost Killed Sacramento

We now come to the final chapter of these the dramatic birthing pains of the City of Sacramento present a further scene of tragedy; the arrival of the Asiatic Cholera ("European Diseases" of usual complaint originated in Asia).

Just as the news of the admission of California reached Sacramento on October 19, the sad news of a most malignant form of cholera landfall in San Francisco accompanied it via the steamer New World at 3:30 am that morning. Stories of the effects of the disease preceded its actual arrival by but a short interval, but in that time, sufficient panic was stirred so as to refresh all memories of the recent suffering. This particular strain was reported to act so quickly that no natural effort at hydration was effective. The general resilience of the population, having been exhausted by the previous winter's stresses and not fully recuperated, provided an even easier opportunity for the plague of death when it hit. Dr. Morse reports that the panic of anticipation seemed worse than the disease itself, but then rued his words as premature. He states that the first case was of a steerage immigrant of a steamer arriving at the dock early on the morning of October 20th when the first victim was found collapsed on the levee. Medical intervention was attempted but to no avail. Germ theory being a few years off, the physician was limited to palliative care, such as it was. The panic canceled many of the typical traits one might see displayed at a fire disaster or after an earthquake because an invisible killer is the most terrifying of all.

The next day, several new cases magnified the panic, which worked to increase the spread of the disease as excited expressions unknowingly spewed forth into the atmosphere from excited mouths into the wide-eyed, shocked, and disbelieving faces of the newly panicking masses. Cleanliness or the lack of it seemed to make no difference in victim selection as it progressed through the city at so rapid a speed that a modern computer model would have been able to show it as a physical wave of death. It surged through the landscape and its inhabitants as if it were a monster invasion for a film that no one could bear to view.

The dead soon became so numerous that little care could be made in handling bodies, which was a terrifying office in itself. Even so, men were continually employed for removing bodies out to mass graves at the cemetery. The death toll soon rose to more than fifty a day, with one hundred and fifty new cases a day. The city's population was reduced to one-fifth of its usual population due to death, as its rapid evacuation exploded in all directions. But even fleeing was no protection, and many died literally in their tracks as they attempted to flee death's final arrest. Families broke apart in panic. Brothers fled brothers, and sisters denied their own. Husbands abandoned wives and wives husbands, fathers abandoned sons, and mothers' daughters as the terror of the disease broke these last civil bonds of humanity. As hope always glimmers through the darkest night, there were heroes in this epic battle against death, principally; the doctors of whom seventeen died before the epidemic subsided, leaving the city with only three living physicians, our Dr. Morse among them.

These doctors, dying in place, had charged as defiantly as any light brigade into the jaws of death to defy it with hardly a weapon in their hand but the love of humanity. Because of the uproar of such a rapid death and panic, no record was made of those terrible twenty days. So the names of the nurses, men and women, and those acting as stewards who conveyed the masses of the dead to the cemetery, or fill some other office, we have no record. Most were members and wives of Odd Fellows and Freemasons; these venerable organizations are to be credited as the stalwarts of the community that gave all when no one else could or would. The future Governor of California, John Bigler, who carried a lump of camphor gum, which he often held to his nostrils, unceasingly toured the hospitals and scenes of the rapidly expiring and suffering masses. Wherever they were located in the city, he lent a hand when he could and admonished the caregivers and patients alike with praise and encouragement against the panic and pain. What gratitude they are owed! What lessons we might take from them today!

By the time the cholera epidemic subsided, Sacramento was nearly wholly depopulated. Those most prone to apocalyptic pronouncements crowed the event as a sign of judgment and determined that the city would never be resurrected. Such voices were soon silenced as Sacramento once again arose from its might-have-been deathbed as survivors caught their collective breath and returned. Once its macabre harvest was complete, the sickness faded away as quickly as it had arrived. The "Levee City" and its dock remained as vital an element as ever.

Once again, thanks to the bounty of the land and the industry of men, the lifeblood of gold resumed its flow from the mines, and demands for supplies continued to quicken the city's failing heart into new, robust life. Never again would the city go to its knees in despair. Never again would its life be in doubt. Regardless of later floods and setbacks, the critical tests had been met. Sacramento City was here to stay.

Out beyond Brighton and the Five Mile House to the south and east flows the Cosumnes River. Michigan Bar was the first gold camp of many that popped up along its course. It was established in 1849 by two men from Michigan. Other camps soon sprouted up in the vicinity. One of them was Cook's Bar, founded by Dennis Cook and had become dominant by 1850. These claims had to be accepted by the Omo-chumnes Mexican Grant owners that William Daylor and

Jared Shelton had received in 1844 as Rancho Omochumnes. The two men quickly became wealthy from mining, trading, ranching, and the hotel business. In 1850, Sheldon built the Slough House on Deer Creek, where Jackson Road crosses the water. It burned down in 1890 but was rebuilt immediately on the original site. It still operates today as a fine restaurant.

Daylor was well established as a trader and hotel keeper along the Cosumnes River about a mile east of Slough House, which became known as the Daylor Ranch and later, the U.S. Post Office. In 1846, Sheldon built a gristmill on the Cosumnes River. He then built a dam, which caused the flooding of the nearby mines. The miners threatened violence. To put them in check, Sheldon placed a cannon in full view of the aggrieved party's prospects. On July 11th, 1851, the miners began to tear down the dam. It is not recorded whether he fired his cannon at the excavators turned dam busters, but after his initial retreat, Sheldon returned after two hours with reinforcements, and a gun battle commenced. In the fight, Jared Sheldon was killed along with two of his men. The dam itself was swept away by raging waters during the winter of 1851-2. The site of the gristmill is about one-mile southeast of Slough House on Meiss Road.

James Pollock came to the state in 1846 with his family and settled on the Cosumnes in 1853. He claims that his daughter, Mary, was the first white to be born in California, but that claim is disputed.

Of particular note is the first death in the Dry Creek Township, next to the Cosumnes Township. On February 4, 1851, Mrs. Jackson died while on a visit with her husband, ironically, at Dr. Russell's house. The only white woman at the funeral was Mrs. McIntyre. Most of the attendees were Indians (Native Americans). They squatted on the ground around the grave and made strange, mourning vocalizations that must be something like the Celtic Keening that until recently was still practiced in the remote West of Ireland.*[8] What is remarkable about this is the grief of the natives at the passing of a white woman. This episode provides a contradiction to the modern accusations of settler cruelty and enmity between natives and the settlers in the Sacramento Valley.

The next hanging tale takes a small leap in time, to 1854.

The Romance of the Highwayman, Mickey Free

Mickey Free was a highwayman, a road agent, as they would say. Everyone has heard of Joaquin Murrieta and Black Bart, and their deeds are well known. For a representative of the region, the choice of Mickey Free and his gang stands as the better of the other less romantic story of Tom Bell and his decidedly far more depraved gang. Mickey Free is the most prominent in the rare histories as the one personality recorded of the unknown masses of claim-jumpers, horse thieves, and robbers hanged from Sacramento to Placerville, Old Hangtown, in these early days. He wasn't a poet-gentleman like Black Bart, nor was he a copy of the dashing, fearsome Joaquin Murrieta, but his story is more or less a classic one. Mickey Free serves well here since the locale of his operations is in our neighborhood of concern. This makes him the best choice among all the wrongdoers who stepped up to take their turn on the gallows in those days.

There can be no doubt of the consequential and massively valuable contribution that so many Celtic peoples have made to America, from the very beginning up until today. The number of stories of our Western settlement and pioneering that don't feature one or two or many Scots-Irish names is few. During the American Revolution, Scots/Irish made up the bulk of the Continental Army. But before I begin to Jones around too much, let me remind all that Jones is a Welsh name, and the Welsh are a member of the Gaelic family. So how did some of them also number so prominently among the rascals, bandits, and terrorists of the 19th century?

When the Great Hunger of The Great Potato Famine struck Ireland in 1845, Mickey Free would have been a teen. "Free" was likely not his real name, but no record exists for any other appellation.

The famine killed a million, and more than a million fled Ireland, mostly to the U.S. and Canada. Absentee landlords had already created a massive class of impoverished Irish, whose labor was near worthless. One must attempt to imagine the scenes of deprivation as penniless, homeless Irish masses were once again told they could go to hell or the rocky, barren land in Western Ireland known as the Connemara. And there, once again, uncounted numbers died of starvation in rocky fields and ditches. Simultaneously, the British PM spoke of natural population reduction that made no requirement for relief unless some might be used as slave labor in workhouses. Who could blame Mickey Free for wishing to be free of such a life?

So when Mickey left Ireland, his mother gave him her Bible. We can only imagine this poor woman's broken heart. No doubt, her husband was absent, likely dead, and her son, maybe the last of her children, left alive, leaving her; and all she had to give him was her Bible and her prayers. What event saw Mickey Free turn to thieving in the new land, where he might have found a better way? We can't know, but stray Irishmen were not in favor in New York City or anywhere at that time. By 1854, he had made it to California, and he was operating mainly around the road's junction from Folsom to Placerville and the Coloma road.

He stayed at the later famous Railroad House in Clarksville, which was owned by Mrs. Margaret Tong. The place was named such in hopes of being on the Sacramento to Placerville Railroad line, but it was missed by three miles to the northeast when the line was finally built five years later. Clarksville itself was named after the ranch owned by Henry Clark and his brother.

The Railroad House was large. Its dining room and bar were seventy feet long, which is probably why of all the places on the road, Mickey Free had the most likely chance of melding into a crowd when he wasn't at work.

Coming by way of Carson Pass, to Silver Lake and Tragedy Springs to get to Mud Springs, Young Gray, and his wife, Mrs. Julia Ann Gray, nee

Porter, who was but eighteen years old when they arrived and took over a hotel. Coming with them was Young's younger sister Polly, who would have been a teenager. It gives one pause to know that she had driven a team of oxen pulling a wagon all the way from Montgomery County, Illinois, to get to El Dorado, which was the last name for Mud Springs (Shingle Springs). When the Grays bought the Lone Tree House in 1854, Free was boarding there. And so Mickey Free saw the beautiful Polly and was fatally smitten. From here, it might be another tale of how beauty killed the beast.

Mickey Free had once bragged that he would commit more robberies and depredations than Joaquin Murrieta. His arrogance and devil-may-care attitude continued up to the moment of his hanging. But a telling moment is recorded by the descendants of the Grays. Before he went to Coloma, to kill a Chinese man, or a man named Howe, or a Chinese man with a name that sounded like Howe, Mickey Free gave Polly his Bible and told her that if he had read it, he might be a better man than he had turned out to be. Not to wax overly analytic, but this report intimates the idea that Mickey Free knew he had no chance with her. What made this even more certain was Young's open resentment of his attentions to his sister. He stole Young's gun, and just as the classic anti-hero does in every story, he rampaged down the road to Coloma where he killed a man over likely nothing at all. The man he killed was Chinese. The highwayman may have thought it less of a crime, but his contemporaries did not despite being of their race and his victim of another. But he must have known he had sealed his fate. Not long after, one of his gang was captured and turned state's evidence, and Mickey Free was easily taken, tried, and sentenced to be hanged. On the day of his hanging, he said he only wished it had been Young instead of the man he had killed. Does this mean that only Young Gray's interference prevented Polly from accepting the attention of Mickey Free?

Hangman's Tree Historic Spot – Placerville, California is said to be haunted Photo – Legends of America by Unlimited License

We can never know. I like to imagine that Polly, as well-loved as she was to her family, might well have seen that young man perhaps as a reform project, deserving of her love. That's a classic element for a romantic plot if ever there was one. Unable to win the love he desired, Mickey Free died as he had lived, careless, on the edge of life. Was his final reckless rampage calculated to end the pain that Polly had awakened? He must have known she was out of his reach. When the day came, he waited his turn to be hanged, joking with the crowd and eating peanuts. When he took his place over the trap door, he danced a jig on it, ere he danced for the last time absent a floor. Mickey Free; what a name for an Irishman who was never free!

Traditional Gunfights

Because it is illustrative of the political culture of early Sacramento, I present the history of a few of the old-school-styled pistol duels that occurred in some of the townships in the 1850s. These were the last of such duels in California, and likely the West as the less formalized gunfight took precedence after that.

Some Background on Dueling

It might be moot to preface these reports with a short history of dueling and the changes in form it went through in the American West. The duel originally began in Northern Europe as part of Nordic, Viking culture, combined with related Germanic cultures. The tradition of the hero tale was widespread in both the Celtic and Gothic tribes from ancient times. In fact, it is such an old tradition that its origin is not known. It may harken back to some of the Indo-European tribes before the "final" expansion into Western Europe after the last Ice Age. The tradition first identified was concerned with the dispensing of justice by using the ordeal of combat to determine a legal outcome. This sprang from the practice of solitary ordeal that we can find in Bible stories, the ordeal of Jesus himself, those trips out to the wilderness, the American Indians' vision quest, and even Odin's ordeal where he had his vision of the world's fate. All engaged in solitary ordeal as a rite of passage or for a vision for personal or tribal determination. That is how old that tradition is; it can be found among primitive people worldwide.

The Indo-European tribes we are concerned with, the Goths, added the refinement of trial by combat. North American indigenous peoples learned this tradition from whites, Quebecois ancestors, in fact. The French were avid duelists by the 16th century. They taught the idea of the practice of "escrime," which we call "fencing" in English, where a cut or "coup" from the French is attained by out-clevering your opponent and scoring without harming. There is even a move in modern fencing called the "coupe'" which is a false attack followed by a quick change of blade direction achieved by "cutting over" the top of your opponent's blade.

Traditionally, a duel arose out of a boast, a hero story that was challenged and defended. Later, it became a way of setting legal quarrels, and even debts. But all that was required was the "giving the lie;" an insult that had to be answered to retain one's honor. Where our tribal practice is concerned, one often finds references to "counting coup" in literature, usually in Western films, dealing with more specific details of historical interactions with tribal peoples in the West. Let's look at some indigenous tribes with French appellations; Sioux, Miniconjou, Sans-arc, Coeur D'Alene, and Nez Perce. Many other less well-known Northwestern tribes were named by French Voyagers. One has to wonder what their names were before then or if they had a name? These and other tribes learned to count "coup" (Fr. cuts) from the Voyageurs directly and other French settlers and explorers, directly or indirectly, long before Lewis and Clark's expedition. Many a French settler or military man had found themselves on the terrible ocean trip to Quebec after an unfortunate result of winning the wrong duel in the motherland. (Note; according to J.W. Vaughn's "With Crook at the Rosebud," counting coup also served as a notice to fellow warriors of his "legal" claim to the scalp and booty located on a downed opponent).

The ordeal evolved among the Germanic and Gothic tribes as trial by combat or the Judgement of Odin —the history of dueling evolved from that. Once Christianity entered the picture, trial by combat took a new interpretation in the form of the knightly contest, where God's Judgement was considered the outcome of trial by combat, but it was really merely a rebranding of an old pagan tradition. This further evolved into personal combat and, from there, became a system for settling disputes.

The French were obsessed with dueling. The English and Italians weren't far behind. In Prussia, it almost displaced Christianity itself as chivalric mercy and virtue eclipsed the earlier penal nature of Christianity during the Dark Age Parabalani and the Medieval

Inquisition.*€   Even though Queen Elizabeth I and Louis XIV made dueling illegal, they could not stop it. During the 17th century, one-quarter of France's male population died in duels.

The chivalric or gentleman's duel became highly ritualized and regulated to ensure cheating was prevented and honor preserved so that the outcome would have consequences. By the 19th century, the tradition was so ingrained in Western Civilization that civil and military conduct can be said to revolve around it. Battles were duels of armies between opposing generals.   They avoided population centers, maneuvering in the countryside in a gigantic chess game until one side had the other in a position that had advantages for the most ingenious general. By the 19th century in America, we still had pistol dueling, which was the equivalent of the high-tech methods of the time for getting to the point, so to speak. Modern fencing is derived from the sword dueling that also continued, mostly in Europe, well into the 20th century. Your author knows of one that took place in the town of Sonoma, in Sonoma County, California, in 1978, on the town square on a Sunday morning at dawn by two collegian fencers who hated the other.

It is perhaps worth mentioning here that the modern Olympics were founded by a duelist and fencer, Baron Pierre de Coubertin. The idea of encouragement of modern sports originally was to preserve the chivalric traditions of sportsmanship and provide motivation for physical fitness among the masses. In America, the situation evolved differently.   The following duels were the last of the old, colonial dueling that more often involved pistols but sometimes, particularly, in New Orleans, a sword duel. Always illegal, it nonetheless was often indulged or ignored.

Everyone knows about the duel in which Raymond Burr killed Alexander Hamilton, for example. After this, the duel devolved into a contest where the one that fired first would be indicted as a murderer. So the game became the well-known quickdraw that sought to beat the time of the initiating party with the intervention of a bullet. "It was self-defense" became the turning phrase for legal determination.

It is a cornerstone of the set of individual rights in the U.S. where the right to defend oneself from harm with qualified legal force is a constitutional right. The principles and assistants in the following duels that took place in the townships of Sacramento County in the early 1850s were almost uniformly originally from Kentucky.

Some will no doubt find the idea of dueling abhorrent. As one who trained in fencing and participated in competitions on the national level in the 1980s, continuing as an instructor until 2007, I can appreciate the history of dueling as a causative cultural aspect that actually created and enforced better conduct. As I observe individual doings and behaviors so common today, I have often wondered if some people would say or do some of the things they do if they knew they were subject to being "called out." With all of its dangers and tragedies, the past was a more genteel time. Today, mobs justify the worst of violence which they often visit upon the most defenseless.

Even so, we could perhaps suggest the notion that delays in personal satisfaction lead to a condition of mass dissatisfaction, individually or collectively. But this is not to justify the trend of the rageaholic" as discipline is diminished in a declining society. And so with that disclaimer, we turn to our duels;

On August 2nd, 1852, there was the famous rifle duel at 30 paces between James W. Denver (then State Senator representing the Trinity and Klamath Counties) and Edward Gilbert (Editor in Chief of the Alta California Newspaper).

The Auburn road ran diagonally through the township, and in the early days, roadhouses were plentiful along its course in short intervals. The most popular of them in 1851-52 was the Oak Grove House, which was about seven miles out of Sacramento. It was kept by D.A.B. Groat. The duel took place near the Oak Grove House, where the two duelers had breakfast on the morning of the tragedy.

This was one of the most famous duels in the early days of the state. Its origin had to do with a newspaper controversy in 1852. Denver was at the time in charge of supplies for overland immigration, and

Gilbert attacked him editorially, charging members of the expedition with dishonesty. He finally sent Denver a challenge, which Denver accepted. Denver, as the challenged party, chose rifles at thirty paces. At sunrise, August 2, 1852, the combatants met on the ground, which was but a few yards from the Oak Grove House. A coin was tossed for position, and Denver won. He placed his back against the rising sun. Mayor Teschemacher was Gilbert's second, and V.E. Gerger was Denver's. Dr. Wake Brady served as surgeon. The first fire resulted in both bullets striking the ground in front of the other.

At the second shot, Gilbert was wounded in the bowels and fell into his friend's arms, dying without a struggle. His body was carried to the Oak Grove House. Gilbert was born in Troy, New York, and worked himself up from the painter's case to a seat in Congress. He came to California with Stevenson's regiment in 1847. Gilbert had previously been an associate editor with the Albany Argus, though he was only thirty years of age at the time of his death. Early in 1849, he combined the California Star and the old Californian, from which sprung the Alta California. He was a delegate to the first constitutional convention. His body was taken to the residence of J. H. Nevett in Sacramento, where impressive funeral services were held by Reverend O. C. Wheeler at the First Baptist church. A procession was headed by a company of cavalry under the command of Captain Fry. The body was taken to San Francisco, and final services were held by Reverent T. Dwight Hunt's church. Every newspaper editor in San Francisco attended the funeral.

Denver went on to become the Secretary of State under John Bigler. He resigned in 1855 and became a member of Congress from 1855 to 1857. He was later appointed by the governor of the territory of Kansas by President James Buchanan. He died in 1894, regretting the duel to his grave. The city of Denver is named after James W. Denver. The Grove House lost its popularity and disappeared a few years after the duel took place.

A duel occurred in the American Township on March 9, 1854. The duel was between Philip W. Thomas, the district attorney of Placer

County, and Dr. Dickson, one of the physicians at the State Marine Hospital in San Francisco. Thomas had made some derogatory comments to the character of J. P. Rutland, one of the clerks at the office of the State Treasurer. McMeans and Rutland sent a challenge, which Thomas declined, saying that he did not regard the challenger as a gentleman. Dr. Dickson appropriated the insult to himself and send the challenge to Thomas in his own name, which was accepted. A hostile meeting was set for the ninth day of March. The parties left the city at 2:30 A.M. but found they were pursued by the sheriff and deputies who had gotten wind of the affair. It was decided to set up a mock duel as a distraction by two of their friends, H.O. Ryerson and Hamilton Bowie (yes, a relative). They took positions and exchanged shots, and Ryerson was immediately arrested and taken to the city where he gave bonds. The principles took their ground about two hundred yards from the estate of H.M. LaRue,*[10] and Bowie acted as the second for Thomas and Judge McGowan*[10] for Dr. Dickson.

The distance was set at ten paces but was increased to fifteen, in the hopes of saving their lives. The weapons were dueling pistols, and both fired promptly at the word Thomas, being slightly quicker, which probably saved his life, as Dickson's bullet struck the ground at Thomas' feet. Dickson fell and was taken to the city, where he died at midnight. James H. Hardy was then the district attorney, and the other participants were indicted, but under the intervention of Colonel P. L. Edwards, their counsel, the indictments were quashed. Thomas was later twice re-elected district attorney of Placer County, and in 1860 was elected to the state senate, but resigned before the expiration of his term. He died in Auburn in 1874 or 75. It is said that Thomas was never the same after this event.

Another duel in 1855 took place between Robert Tevis, a young lawyer and brother of Lloyd Tevis, and Charles Lippincott, a State Senator from Yuba County. In a roast in Downieville, Lippincott roasted Tevis, offending him. They set a date for a duel that caused great excitement because both parties were prominent and distinguished. Ultimately, the contest cost Tevis his life.

Did dueling help civil society, or was it a horrible ritual that replaced reasonable minds in men who should have had the temperance and presence of thought to avoid such calamities? My suggestion is that the lack of law development and practice led to such remedies where a healthy libel lawsuit might have otherwise provided satisfaction and a less tragic outcome. Regardless of that, we saw in the later gun-fighting style of the old west, as we see today in gang wars and political violence that the restraints of law alone are only as effective as the current culture and conditions provide and allow.

The last, tardy entry in violation of the promised three gunfights and one hanging is another lynching, the first hanging in Sacramento City. A gambler named Frederick J. Roe shot a man named Myer, who had intervened in a fight between Roe and another man. Mr. Roe shot Myer dead for his gallant peace-making efforts. Roe was jailed, but a lynch mob of angry citizens broke into the calaboose, seized the gambler, and strung him up on the nearest suitable tree. What became of that tree is not known. However, the famous Hanging Tree in Placerville had a saloon built over it, and it is operating as a lively tourist attraction to this day. The only difference is that instead of the former service to those favoring liquor, it now caters to the over-heated, glucose-dependent as an ice cream parlor.

Indeed, in the West and particularly in California, during the Gold Rush and the rapid expansion that it forced, managing the situation was nearly impossible. It was, in fact, barely managed. The phrase "tiger by the tail" is appropriate, it seems. How these ordinary human beings coped is a matter of wonder. But the history is traceable for those who take the time to unearth it from under the sludge of modern critical revisionism. One element that is prominent enough is that these men all seemed to operate by a code. Due to the prevalence of the Fraternity of Free and Accepted Masons, Odd Fellows, and other fledgling organizations and groups all aimed at the civic good, we can see a code of sorts in operation. It was all based on the well-established principles of chivalry. Inside of it, these men competed and cooperated. They sued the other and settled. When the insult or complexity of issues was too extreme, they resorted to the traditional pistol duel, the lazy man's sword match, but governed by the same ancient rules of honor.   They managed this party because, along with the solemn oaths they took as members of various fraternities claiming ancient and honorable pedigrees, they operated with an unbounded supply of humor.

Related now is one of many to choose from. This one is the prime choice because it features the two most prominent early Sacramento history figures, Sam Brannon and George McDougal. Brannon had just taken part in the meeting at Brown's Hotel that the Alcade Bartlett had called. This momentous convocation commenced when several consequential men convened to raise funds for rescuing the stricken Donner Party. The meeting at Brown's Hotel in San Francisco included General Vallejo, Commander Merine, Leidesdorff, and William D. M. Howard, and succeeded in collecting fifteen hundred dollars to purchase supplies for the party of volunteers that would go up into the treacherous mountains.

 The grand effort completed, Brannon soon found himself the object of the bet of an ounce of gold on his success of negotiating his way around the large hole full of human waste and slop from the hotel out behind the building. He was taken to the other side of the road facing the back of the building, blindfolded, and turned about three times. He completed the bet by losing, walking straight into the pit, and swimming in the filth. George McDougal was on hand, and no doubt had a great laugh with everyone else.   Brannon went on to be a prominent figure in Sacramento and California history.

George McDougal had just completed a prank where he and his fellow pranksters had driven nails into a barrel and fastened firecrackers to it in a way that when lit, they would go off in succession. They took the barrel to the top of Clay Street and then drew straws as to who would take the ride down inside the barrel. The short straw was palmed off on Dr. Jones, who dutifully took his place inside the barrel. The fuse was lit, and McDougal gave it a kick. Dr. Jones was screaming like a banshee all the way down Clay Street. The ride ended when the barrel burst to pieces when it struck the back of Brown's Hotel, somehow missing that gaping cesspool that Brannon would soon make use of. Dr. Jones emerged unharmed except for a few nail pricks and some singed hair. "The harder the work, the harder the play," as is said.

The greatness of McDougal must be pointed out here. After the Donner Party survivors' rescue, the only Donner family survivor, young George Donner, was the benefactor of the gift of two large lots in San Francisco in a trust purchased in his name by McDougal. Brown's Hotel gave the boy room and board until his disposition was settled satisfactorily. These are the men and women who made the future possible for everyone. They were not perfect, but it could be asserted that they were better then than we are now, which is the only conclusion possible because of the present dissolute condition of our society. We could begin to atone by acquiring some respect for them and their memory.

"THE FOUNDATIONS OF THE STATES ARE BUILT UPON THE GRAVES OF THE PIONEERS."

Ghosts of the Glory Trail – Nell Murbarger

Arriving at White Rock

W ithin gunshot of the junction where Mickey Free collected his illegal tolls is Prairie City and White Rock. White Rock was named for the outcropping of white quartz that was hard for passers-by to not notice.

In 1954, Ralph H. Cross published his important, but hardly ever-read history: "The Early Inns of California." On the old map of the roadhouses of the Gold Rush era, there is one just west of the rock, along the White Rock Road section of the road to Hangtown is listed as roadhouse number 19, where "Six-Toed" Pete Haase operated a two-story roadhouse and a dairy beginning in the early 1850s. He did, in fact, have a sixth toe on one of his feet. He ran the roadhouse, and placer mined around his land just off the eastern Sutter Spanish Grant Line. His roadhouse is one of the few that survived long enough to intersect with my life significantly, as it was present on the spot where Prairie House (roadhouse) foundations can still be traced. Six-Toed Pete's land was where White Rock MC Park was located in 1970. His roadhouse was a few hundred yards to the north on Old White Rock Road and its ruins can be located there now. The actual house was moved sometime after Mr. Cross's report to behind the ruins of the Prairie House, which would be the "front yard." That plot is presently bisected by the new White Rock Road.

Peter Haase was one of the more visionary miners of old, who was recorded as reckoning that the gold in the prairie from Folsom to Sacramento was likely to be yielding gold for the next 50 years. They were modest.

From a geological standpoint, this prairie represents the contents of a huge glacial grind down of a large granite cap of the ancient Sierra range. The glacier left its trail across that expanse with a rich blanket of gold injected into the resultant aggregate. By the early 20th century, dredges began to operate in moving lakes that roamed the land from just outside of Folsom down to near Sunrise Boulevard, where an abandoned dredge could be spied just beyond its intersection with White Rock Road up to the early 1970s. The Capitol Dredging Company had used Six-Toed Pete's Roadhouse as a field office. Dredging ceased operations in 1962, and at the time of Mr. Cross's publication in 1954, one was working just above Six-Toed Pete's old diggings. Today, the Perkins Pit still operates as a gravel and sand mine with tertiary gold recovery. You could say it's a deep hole, but it's wide enough for trucks to drive down into it and load up with earth for processing.

I became aware of all of this as a result of my entry into the sport of motocross racing. That off-road racing form was just being introduced in the U.S. Motocross racing was imported from Europe by various promoters, primarily Edison Dye. He arranged for Torsten Hallman to come to the U.S and do some exhibitions at local events in 1966, with the idea of promoting Husqvarna and motocross. The next year, Torsten Hallman arranged for Joel Robert, Roger DeCoster, Dave Bickers, for CZ, and Ake Jonsson, and Staffan Eneqvuist for the Husqvarna team, as a kind of traveling circus for the two teams – the InterAm events. Edison Dye was the U.S. distributor for Husqvarna located in La Mesa, California, who worked with Torsten to arrange logistics. That make was one of the two or three top marks (brands) that dominated the international racing scene at that time (the other being CZ, with Maico, Bultaco, Greeves). Lars Larson was also distributing the newly developed 125cc Penton that the renowned off-road champion, John Penton, had designed and contracted KTM of Austria to produce. So they combined in one effort, under Hallman Racing.

I bought my first Penton at the shop Gene Nunes, had established with his old high school buddy, Bill Onga, who was the shop mechanic. I waited on a Thursday, all day for the two new aluminum barrel Pentons to arrive. I raced one, and Lars Larson rode the other. (My father later bought that one. I raced it a year later at Marysville and took second in a close race with Alan Christensen who was on a Bultaco). I represented their shop at races when I took a trophy at the 1970 Hangtown event the following year.*₁ That year, the forerunner of what was to become Prairie City OHV Park was created on a section of leased land held by the Brighton Sand and Gravel Company.

Earlier that year, Bucky (Dave), Rick, and I had become aware of a new venture that involved "our sport." Dave and I earned money for our bikes. My parents made it a condition. So I worked after school and in the summers from 1969 on. I had worked in the summer of 1967 doing door-to-door sales throughout Sacramento County. (1968 was sort of a summer off). Dave was skeptical about the new White Rock Motorcycle Park from the start. Regardless, Rick and I took a trip out to check out this new place to ride, which featured a mile-and-a-half motocross circuit laid out by a Husqvarna factory rider named Claus Nielsen, who came through Edison Dye's connection. It was located on White Rock Road, next to a large landfill, what we used to call a "dump." This is what had made Dave doubtful, and others hate it. What made some experienced riders hate the track was the way the soil became lumped up. I happen to know that this was due to the Brighton Sand and Gravel's "helpful" application of oil to the track's surface. This was a disaster. Worse still, there was the occasional whiff of nasty biomass deterioration next door. There was also the fact of the searing heat out in those dredge tailings, and an underground fire within the dump was often at large, sending a small spire of smoke up on some days, just like "Indian Smoke Signals."

White Rock Motorcycle Park was the brainchild of a man named Bill Monroe. He formed Red Hawk Enterprises as the endeavor's legal corporation (and I don't know what else). Some said it was as near to hell as anyplace outside of Death Valley in the summer.

It was sort of "no man's land." But motocross racers didn't care about that sort of stuff if a race was on. Bill Monroe banked on that – and eventually lost his bet; not because there were no races there, we had about six races as I recount them, from July to November, when the place was abandoned. It happened because the bread of butter of the place, recreational or even racers who wanted to practice on the course, just did not show up. Very few ever did, I can assert that with some certitude.

With high school behind me in June of that year, I went out to the new park to see if I could find a job. Much to my surprise, I was hired. I later figured out that I was replacing a much older man, a member of the DDNMC, a man who, in fact, merely expected to be paid. I was set to work putting the finishing touches on various aspects of the park, such as shingling the entry booth, painting the tires that lined the track white, driving the water truck preparing the track for races, and generally managing the track during the week, and sometimes on weekends when I wasn't racing, which was rare, but I also raced at events held there, and still have the souvenirs of two of those races. The dump provided the olfactory nodes its odd perfume, and there was almost always a fire burning underground there in the summer heat. The Indian smoke signals would usually be going by late morning and at one point in the summer, I think the underground smolder was going day and night. There were always turkey buzzards around. Sometimes, they circled over me, likely imagining that anything out there in that heat had to be about to drop. Imagine that. Anyone could come out and ride for a modest fee. We even had a handful of MX bikes for rent. I was "in charge" of them. Like me, such parties could come out and take their chances with the buzzards.

There were no usable trees for shade in the front part of the park where the track and my station at the gate were located. I spent many a hot summer day baking among the expansive dredge tailings, sitting in my van with the doors opened, which was the most comfortable place. I was the lone employee who would stand watch over the place all summer for riders who hardly ever showed up. The few that did were gone after an hour, certainly no more than two. It was just too hot to ride, most of the time. Early morning and maybe evening was the time to ride. My only relief was to plunge into the tank of the water truck when I was using it, which was only before races, and there were only four held there that summer; that and the transistor radio that accompanied me. I listened to KZAP all day, every day, so I heard all of the newly released Woodstock music while I was alone, taking day-long saunas sitting in my van, the only shade near the entrance of the park. Only keeping the doors open prevents my roasting inside. As it was, it was a day-long sauna. I spend the weekdays there alone. Others showed up occasionally; Claus just before races, and Bill and his Big Brother boys maybe once or twice a week.

That was okay with me; I never really liked crowds all that much. I meditated and sometimes wrote racing poetry like this; "Two wheels on fire, two wheels they spin. My two wheels are in great hurry, taking me from where I've been." As the summer advanced, my skin burned and darkened while my hair was being bleached by the sun. There have been clinical outcomes over this exposure now that I am older (not too serious, so far).

The park failed due to it being so incredibly hot that no one wanted to hang out there baking in the rocks to inhale the perfume from the old dump. Because of that, and the aforementioned general lack of ambiance in the form of shade or almost anything that would make the place more pleasant, the park did not survive and was defunct by the end of the year. But it did see some significant action, all the same. The Dirt Diggers North MC held two races there, which I not only prepared the track for but raced with Billy Grossi on July 28th, and won on my CZ in the October 18th race. The grand finale was the November InterAm race.

Then, there were the infamous North/South events between the Southern and Northern teams. In researching for this book, I found that the man that I replaced at White Rock was drafted to manage the Northern Team. I had just bought my new 250 CZ at Cycle Speed, so I did not make the cut for the team in the event held as it was the first event I rode it in. That really bothered me at the time. But I was at all the events, including the round in the South, which was held at the

Bay Mare facility. As part of the staff, I went to the events, preparing the track for our event and traveling down to the Bay Mare track in Moorpark later with "The Giant Mosquito" in my van and no giant flyswatter at hand. I brought my new CZ along. One of our team riders damaged his rear wheel, so mine was substituted. So at least my CZ competed, partially!

Billy Grossi of Santa Cruz leads other riders over one of the jumps on the motorcross course at White Rock Motorcycle Park. He and other top riders will compete Sunday in the Dirt Diggers North motorcross at the park on White Rock Road three miles east of Sunrise Boulevard.

Billy leading me on my own track! I beat him next time after Claes Nilsson ported my Penton's Sachs engine at Carl Cranke's shop Cycle Speed, Inc., in North Highlands.
Sacramento Bee Sunday Section

Through Claes Nilsson's connection with Edison Dye and Lars Larson, we held two of the then-famous InterAm races that promoter Edison Dye had developed beginning in 1967 as a promotion for Husqvarna motorcycles.*[1] They were typically held after the Grand Prix season had ended in Europe. This summer event was a special exception promoted as the "Viking Series." That year, even though it was the mid-Grand-Prix season in Europe, somehow, Claus got some of the Husqvarna riders to come over for a summer race held at White Rock

Motorcycle Park on August 7, 1970, right in the middle of the European season. Among my various mementos is the record of a somewhat famous event in motocross history; a photo was taken that day as the first American to spend any real length time in front of pursuing European pros, Brad Lackey (later, first U.S. World Champion – 1983). It was recorded by Larry Montgomery, who made race photos at that time, self-employed as "Fotac." This photo of Lackey leading Thorlief Hansen also features me in the background infield, looking on. This is the only photo record of my time at the park.

The European riders were wilting in the torrid heat and were somewhat saved by Dan Rasmussen, who showed up with a pickup with a pool in the bed. He accomplished this by setting in a huge plastic sheet and filling it with water. I was a native and hardened by constant exposure – if that is really possible. I have yet to learn if it removed one or more years from my lifespan, but my arms are fairly pocked as a reminder of the frying my forearms received that summer. The baseball shirt I am wearing in the photo was purchased in an attempt to protect them. I only came near passing out from the heat once. I was spraying the tires in the photo white in the midday heat.

For some reason, men had forsaken headgear by the late 1950s. No more did we see the stylish fedora in public. Even a cowboy hat was rare. Baseball caps were only used when playing baseball. So I ended up out there with no head cover. The day came while I was painting tires under the blazing sun using the spray rig on a Brighton Sand and Gravel truck, and I suddenly felt faint. I avoided heatstroke, barely, by quickly learning to take off my shirt, soak it in water and wear it, like an Arab headdress. One relief I enjoyed was taking a plunge into the water tank on the truck every time I would finish filling it up. To fill it up, I would make a trip to a remarkable-looking place about a mile up White Rock Road and just across Grant Line Road. There was a large, two-story house out front and a barn behind it. Supplies for race events, such as cases of soft drinks for sale, were located on a platform behind the house. When I first entered the house, it struck me as odd because it wasn't laid out like a home's first story. Remembering now, it was a perfect example of a nice lobby, barroom, and perhaps dining room with a cookhouse outback barely connected to the hotel by a breezeway. The countertop I saw could have easily been a bar as there was nothing behind it but a wall; the open-air or tented kitchen was on the other side of that wall, I believe. I didn't know it then, but I was standing in one of the few still surviving examples of a Gold Rush roadhouse; Six-toed Pete's place.

Eventual world champion (1982) Brad Lackey briefly led Thorlief Hansen at that summer's "Viking Series" White Rock MC Park, the summer held in early July of 1970. It was arranged by Claes Nilsson as a two-event stop in the middle of the regular European GP season as a special favor to Claus and Edison Dye by Husqvarna. Lackey led the race until the last lap when his fuel tank came loose - the author is at the far left with hands on hips and no hat! – Photo by Larry Montgomery

Upon a little hill was a shack. One day, back at the park, a kid, perhaps 13 years old, appeared out of nowhere toting a .22 rifle. He told me some interesting things about the local environs. The kid said that in that shack on the low hill near the "field office" was a collection of old slot machines and penny arcade machines. I felt nosing around up there would be trespassing and off-limits as none of my business. Now, I wish I had gone up and taken a look. At some point, someone bolder must have cleaned the shed out. I even think I saw one bit of the contraband at my brother-in-law's house after he came up with a funny old gambling machine from someone nearby in Rancho Cordova, where he and my youngest sister lived in the 1970s. One building that was not on a hill but right at hand was the barn, tempting me whenever I was filling up the water truck.

One day, I finally became curious enough to venture into the barn. I opened a regular entry door and gazed inside. What greeted me was an extensive collection of antique horse carriages of every sort imaginable. There were fancy coaches, simple buckboards, and everything in between. Some might have been replications, but I doubt it. They were so genuine-looking. There was about one of each type from what I could tell, including a Conestoga wagon. They seemed to represent the spectrum of Western American history's 19th-century epic. Here they were in storage in this dusty old barn, and nobody seemed to know about them or care. I realized that I had to have seen some of these when they were on display in Governor's Hall, at the Old California Fairgrounds at the end of Broadway, when I was about eight years old. That kid was interesting. He lived somewhere out there but I never learned where. When I told him that I was interested in old artifacts, things like milk cans, etc., he made two return trips with a horseshoe and milk can before he disappeared.

I have come to realize that Alan Olson, of Brighton Sand and Gravel, must have been in charge of them. I don't know if he owned them or what became of them.*₃ I never forgot the old fairgrounds. I remember those early state fairs as classic fairs compared to the later cement nightmare Cal-Expo. There were no "Wall of Death" riders at the New "Cal-Expo location, either. I remember also because my father used to take me to the Sacramento Mile every year. The last year I was there in 1970. The event made it into the film, "On Any Sunday." Later that summer, another, older kid from LA showed up at the track riding a loaner Jawa Californian, from Orangevale Cycle Center. Bill Monroe "hired" him to work at the track with me. Now there were two unpaid employees. But it gave me something to do; after he showed up, he would ride the 360cc Husky rental bike, while I chased him on my new CZ 250.

He turned out to be a truant from the Southern California motocross scene. His story was that he had left home because his parents didn't want him to race. So I had instant empathy for him. I talked my folks into allowing him to room at home in my bedroom with me. We set up a cot in my room and made him welcome at the dinner table. He worked with me at the park, more or less officially, for the next month or so until he departed for new "opportunities." The truth is that he skedaddled out of our home because we had figured out that he was using amphetamines. But he was also on the grungy side. He was a "speed freak," as it was termed in those days, as well as a "leech." This is how he came to be known as "The Giant Mosquito" by the end of the year around the local racing community, as he bit probably one out of three, one way or another. Eventually, everyone began to realize that he was on speed and scamming any sympathetic individual or in one case, an older couple. So he went from place to place and initially succeeded in gaining confidence as he had with me at the park and Gene's shop. He was a sort of motocross con man. He eventually disappeared from our midst, after depleting the initial easy confidence of many after enough of his deceitful nature and petty thefts were recognized. But he was fast on any bike, I mean, really fast; zoom, and he's gone.

He had learned how to play on people's sympathy, and thereby got into everyone, weedling whatever he wanted at the time, often using his "fugitive MX racer card" to gain sympathy, and for use in attempts at whatever females were around. But he lacked self-awareness. My entire family figured him out because he lived at our house for a few weeks until it became plain that he was using amphetamines. My sisters, especially the youngest, Gayle, sometimes attended the races. She made friends with some of the other female fans of the sport. One of them shared my fondness for creating rhymes and couplets related to racing. I wrote a ditty about him that set everyone rolling; "His pimply face leers at you; his teeth inside are rotten! His body smells like ten dead fish! My God, I thought I'd forgotten!" That's right; girls don't like smelly, pimply guys, no matter how fast they are on a bike. At least that was how it was back then. When White Rock

MC Park put on a North vs. South competition that summer, The Giant Mosquito was considered a traitor by his Southern buddies. The Giant Mosquito sucked – "blood," but he was fast. Who was he? Except for his nickname, he shall remain nameless. He is the kid I wrote of earlier in the Indian Dunes motocross sequence in "On Any Sunday" as the only rider leading Steve McQueen, the rider with the yellow jersey with black knobby tracks printed on the shirt.

Cycle News – June 1970

I have to admit that I benefited from the race practice we had almost every morning. We didn't coast around; it was an hour-long, high-speed scramble. We'd do it in the morning before it became too hot. Then, we were "off" for the rest of the day, until the cool of the evening, when we'd do it again. During the day, we'd hang out and listen to the radio. During that time, we both drove in the water truck and picked debris off the track when the wind brought new artifacts along, or someone snuck in while no one was around and dumped some trash, vandalized, or some chance event. They would have to have planned well because I was there most weekdays, and someone was there on weekends most of the time, at least, as my boss had a couple of teenage boys in his charge and knew I was off to the races on weekends. But come Monday, I was back on the chain gang.

However, chasing The Giant Mosquito around the track forced me to "find a new gear," as it was said. I was determined to stay on his tail no matter how many rocks that 360cc powered knobby tire kicked up at me. I guess he was only around the track for a month. But he was around the region until the winter. Looking back now, I hope he survived his foolishness and was rehabilitated to a productive and happy life. It might have happened, as there were many such people around the scene then, if not quite so practiced at conning as a lifestyle. So 1970, was coming to a close as White Rock MC Park's time was spent.

It is not at all an exaggeration to say that White Rock Motorcycle Park and Six-Toed Pete's place was pretty much my world that summer. As the summer went on, I began to drive up to Camino to eat lunch at higher and cooler elevations. That led to stops at antique stores where I picked up an old wooden cane I dubbed "The Crash Cane," and used it at times, and then again in 2016 after my left hip finally succumbed to the injury I had taken racing in April of 1970. I discovered most of this history much later in my life when I finally had time to reflect and research these things that had remained curious memories for years.*₂

Up to the end of the dredging era, the old roadhouse had been the Capital Dredging Company's headquarters. There must have been some incorporation, sale, or acquisitions that brought Alan Olson's Brighton Sand and Gravel into control of the place if not ownership, by 1970 when I arrived at White Rock. I even met the company owner, Alan Olson, who I described to my friends then as "Old Man Olson." He must have fancied himself a Marlboro man, with his white cowboy hat and sunglasses in his air-conditioned car. Now that I consider it, he probably had been the very image of a 19th-century rugged individualist in his younger day. After all, I grew up thinking that I was, and he was born closer to the real events. He was a man who had taken part in the county's early history, done something, and came from those who had braved great hardships before him. I wonder if he knew Virgil Earp, Wyatt's nephew. He was living Sacramento in at that time. People ran in wider circles in those days because there were so fewer people and places to publicly meet.

Old Man Olson never paid me any mind as I saw him only a few times. He'd pull up in his air-conditioned Cadillac and roll down the window enough to prevent hot air from getting to him, to have a quick chat with the brainchild, and perpetrator, my boss, Bill Monroe. Whatever he might have been called by others then, I can't write down here.

He presided over the remarkable failure that was White Rock Motorcycle Park. Bill Monroe never paid me a penny beyond my motorcycle payments to the bank with me in person to prevent me from quitting. Once described as an aging lifeguard by a reporter for the Sacramento Bee, he was a good enough confidence-man to have convinced Old Man Olson to slice him off a bit of land as a sublet. The place was a barely adequate piece of real estate that motorcycles could run around on in the expanse of the tailings, next to the old White Rock Dump. Old Man Olson's had his sand and gravel company using the front section of the dump as a gravel processing site at the time. But I didn't really regret it. It was a great if somewhat strange time, compared to what most eighteen-year-olds were doing at the time. Bucky had spent the summer recovering from a broken leg he had suffered in a race in early June that year.

A Gallant Attempt to a Dream

Now to complete the picture of the failure I was involved in that summer, I must make yet another digression. There was a pump house at that spot. Early in the summer, I had been filling the water truck up there. After the first big DDNMC race in July, Bill Monroe and Claes Nilsson must have discussed the heat issue and how to make the park a more attractive place for the public. (How, indeed).... So there was this idea, a plan that was put into action; pumping water up a little hill to a depression that they must have reckoned could be turned into a small lake. Just think of it; happy MX fans cooling off in the lake and watching the race from the little rise on the other side over the track! Nice dream, one could say, with picnic tables and Cinzano umbrellas on AstroTurf. But this was not natural ground. These were dredge tailings that went deep and wide enough in the earth. The unnatural jumble of mammoth dredge tailings was so porous that the water they were pumping in twenty-four-seven was merely seeping back into the ground minus the volume that would have evaporated on contacting the hot outer atmosphere. What dirt surface there was out there collapsed into large sinkholes with small rock caverns where people would have been entrapped and perhaps crushed by massive rocks as the dirt support slipped away to deeper sedimentary locations. It was a potentially hazardous situation—what a disaster. Within a week, they waved me away from the site when they saw me walk out to inspect it one afternoon. I knew it wouldn't work. Bill Monroe didn't seem to grasp that these were dredge tailings or the nature of them. Claes was from Sweden. Sweden is a bit more moist and features lakes that have existed since the last ice age. Claus might be forgiven, but for Bill Monroe, there was just no excuse but wishful thinking.

Watching it all go on was this one lone character that deserves some remembrance. A denizen of the desolate landscape, living alone there for I don't know how long, but a long time, I realized, even then. That old black man, named Oliver lived in a little shack there next to the pump house as caretaker for Allan Olsen. Even at my young age, I sensed the sadness of the old man. He reminded me of that old black man in the Lon Chaney, black and white film "Of Mice and Men," because he was so lonely living out there by himself in that little shack.

One day, the strange wandering kid once came by to say "hi" to me and hang a jackrabbit he had just shot on the outside wall by the door of the old man's shack for his dinner. That implied some kind of relationship but I never asked him about it. I assumed he was acting as a caretaker for Old Man Olson, who set him up there in some ancient time and just forgot about him. I talked to him a couple of times. He spoke of what he saw as he watched the road and environs. "The young people like to park over there on Saturday nights," he told me, gesturing to the gate at the dump entrance. Not me; I brought my girlfriend into the park to hang out with me there, even after it was shut down in 1971. But he said it without a sign of condemnation. He knew life, and I guess he knew his was almost at an end, but I never heard him complain about anything. I hope he died contently; peacefully, at least.

Meanwhile, the disaster of that lake plan had robbed him of his water source. I don't know what he did, but after that, I was driving out to Six-Toed Pete's old place at the new location on the "newer" White Rock Road, to fill the water truck. During the week before the November 8, InterAm race event, it had been pouring rain. I was down with the flu, but Claes called and wanted me to help him prepare the track. So we trudged around, now in the mud with shovels, trying to prevent the course from becoming a series of ponds. As it was, it was really muddy. That race held in the morning served as track conditioning for the professionals later in the day.

I rode in the 250 support class and did well after being pitched off at the start by two bikes closing on me from both sides into the first corner as I dove in with myopic determination to take the lead. I went from last to eighth in a field of over thirty riders in the morning's mud, but no trophy that time! The real thrill that day was a conversation with CZ factory rider, former European and British champion, and future Bond film special effects wizard, Dave Bickers, who was parked next to me in the pits.

The start of the November 8, 1970, InterAm at White Rock MC Park
Photo courtesy of G. Thomas Edwards

By that November, it was plain to everyone that White Rock Motorcycle Park was a bust. After that race, no one ever returned to the track, officially, that is. Bill Monroe's annual trust allowance was spent, and I believe that he was out of investors. One could say he was a more sophisticated version of The Giant Mosquito. The people Monroe had brought along with him, especially Claes Nilsson and his beautiful wife, Lilly, were through with the thing. We had managed one last InterAm event, but when the last van pulled out of the park that day, no one ever came back. White Rock Motorcycle Park was dead. Later, when James Taylor's "Fire and Rain" was popular, I always thought of White Rock Motorcycle Park.

Some consequential racing history that few know about was made, and the future of bigger and more excellent stuff had just survived the embryonic stage. An in-law of Alan Olson, Roy McGill, "Tinker," the one who had used his heavy equipment to cut out the motocross track at White Rock, moved the show up the road. McGill's Motocross Park, on a greener and larger piece of land behind Six-Toed Pete's old roadhouse on former Aerojet, leased land featured the "Moon Room," which was the site of some of Dirt Diggers North MC New Year's Eve Parties, as Tinker was a member. It was struggling along, but the county was petitioned to provide a place for the growing sport of off-road riding by many at the time, including the Trailbike Riders Association (which held its monthly meetings at Eddy's Brau Hof). So the county stepped in and took over. Thus, the financial problem was finally eliminated by the taxpayer and it became first, the Prairie City County OHV Park, later to be promoted to the patronage of the state. The rest, as it is said, is history.

Peter "Six-Toed Pete" Haase and his wife, Gesche, are interned at the Kilgore Cemetery in Rancho Cordova, off Sunrise Boulevard. The tombstone epitaph reads; "Tho lost to sight, a memory dear." I believe that they had a wonderful life. Photo – Myra June LeRoux

Unlike the Foote's Antelope General Store, at least Six-Toed Pete's old roadhouse was moved. Its foundations can be traced. A search of the 1885 map of Sacramento County shows that Peter Haase's land encompassed White Rock MC Park. His roadhouse and dairy were located there originally, and the roadhouse moved up to the site of the old Prairie House sometime between 1954 and 1970. It was updated, too. I recall its interior, which seemed modernized (for the time). "Six-Toed Pete's Inn had been moved about a mile east to the site of the long gone, Prairie House. According to Ralph Cross's 1954 survey, all that was left there was an old charred foundations and an old, dried up fig tree. By 1982, when the house was moved to Folsom, the barn had been torn down years before. Since Alan Olson likely lost his control of the Prairie House plot of Aerojet land around 1973, that control went to an opportunist Teichert employee, Olson had likely been the one who moved the coaches.

The Inn/Home of Peter Haase was moved to its present location in Folsom, California, in 1982. It has served as a private residence to the same party since that time — Pencil rendering by James Geddes.

Although very much unlike the "American Graffiti" version of the graduates' first summer, for me, 1970 was a year for discovery and vivid memories, as one's eighteenth year ought to be, sans the cruises on K Street, buddies, and girls. I had a girlfriend, but I didn't even see her much during that time. That was my fault. She was always ready if I called. But my mind was on motorcycles, not so much on girls and I was off a on with the one I had and did not appreciate as much as she deserved.

Although I spent many long days there without seeing anyone, it wasn't really that bad. I always had the radio on and tuned to KZAP, so I was more or less aware of the music of the time with Woodstock performances airing often. I was racing on most weekends somewhere, and throughout my involvement at the park, I met most of the International Riders of the day and improved my race game as a result of having a near world-class racing course conveniently located at my workplace. On the first night of the September 1970 Friday Night Motocross races at the Placerville Fair Grounds, I took first place in my class over the best junior riders around. It was an exhibition of full-throttle wheelies and power slides. It was the culmination of the previous three months of practicing on the White Rock track. Bruce Young was the announcer for that series. I was later told that as I ripped down the main straightaway in front of the grandstands, he was shouting, "It's up, up, up, for Redhawk Enterprises!" This was the corporation that Bill Monroe formed to operate White Rock MC Park. When I heard about it, I already understood the irony of it. But the next morning back at the park, Bill Monroe showed up with one of his two Big Brothers (of America) boys and gave me the only smile, and positive exclamations I think I ever received from him. When Claus showed up at White Rock Park, I usually went with him in his Porsche to call on various shops with fliers about upcoming races, etc. Claus treated me like a young pal. Then, there was the "archeological" aspect of it. Although as far from "American Graffiti" as imaginable, my five months working at White Rock Motorcycle Park during the last half of 1970 turned out to be a remarkable experience in my life and cherished memory.   I have always considered that motorcycles and racing saved my life. It was a good choice for a male teenager in those days, where I was growing up. It gave me confidence going forward in life.

Cyclists Will Compete At White Rock

More than 200 of Northern California's leading motorcycle riders will attempt to conquer the one-and-one-half-mile European-style moto-cross course Sunday during a number of races at White Rock Motorcycle Park.

Bill Monroe, president of Red Hawk Enterprises stated this will be the first in a series of moto-crosses to prepare riders for a major challange race between Northern and Southern California.

Both juniors and expert riders will compete in all regular 125cc to 500cc classes. Practice is scheduled from 8 to 10:30 a.m. with the first race slated for 11 a.m.

White Rock Motorcycle Park is located on White Rock Road, four miles East of Sunrise Blvd.

Opposite; Bengt Aberg of Husqvarna won the main event of White Rock Motorcycle Park's "grand finale," after crashing at the start and passing back into first place. The author rode in the support class of thirty-plus riders, unloaded in the first turn as well, but only passed up to eighth place by the finish. That's Aberg , minus eight, once removed. The artist who painted those tires is your author. Photo courtesy of G. Thomas Edwards, Right; Article from the Sacramento Bee discussing the Viking Series race at White Rock MC Park mentions Red Hawk Enterprises and Bill Monroe. In a Cycle News story, Alan Olson's son in law takes credit as "owner" and makes the comment that they were still working the "bugs" out, such as dust. I guess he did not know that I was driving the water truck for 72 hours straight up to the race day, with no breaks or food or rest, up to the morning of the race. I only saw him once at the park, pulling out one morning after some illegal deer hunting. Below; Sacramento Bee article announcing the November 8th, and last race ever held at White Rock MC Park, the final InterAm for Edison Dye as the TransAMA took over. Missing from the rider lineup in this article were CZ factory riders Dave Bickers and Rogerde Coster – Bruce Young Collection

World champs race at White Rock

The Sacramento International Moto-cross, one of the most challenging and impressive cycle races on the entire International race circuit, is set for White Rock Park, Nov. 8.

The event will feature some of the foremost motorcycle riders of six countries and the abilities of each promises an exciting contest.

Bengt Aberg, of Sweden was the 1969 and 1970 500cc champion and will be riding a Husqvarna.

Sylvain Geboers of Belgium is the second world champion in the 500cc division and will be riding a Suzuki.

Ake Jonsson, third in the world 500cc championships, is from Sweden and will ride a Maico.

Andy Robertson is from England and will represent AJS.

Wille Bauer is from Germany and will be riding a Maico.

Jacques Yenier is from

France and will be representing CZ.

Rob Taylor is from England and will be riding a Husqvarna.

Along with the European and Scandinavian riders; the cream of the area's riders will also compete in the number of events.

The divisions will be 124cc

Senior, 500cc Junior, 500cc International, 250cc Junior, and 250cc Senior National.

For more information contact the International Moto Cross at 714-466-1261 in La Mesa, California or the White Rock Cycle Park, Highway 50 to White Rock Road, three and a half miles to the signs.

Childhood's End - Growing Up

I n the late sixties, if you were a male, achieving your eighteenth birthday was not necessarily an occasion for celebration. In North Highlands and I assume most of the region, the most common quip from the just over-twenty-crowd was "Now you go to jail," implying that the next time you go too far, no more "slap on the hand" coddling would be administered. For most of us, it was just a tease, devoid of real meaning because we weren't juvenile delinquents, although not necessarily squeaky clean. So it was mostly a joke. But that was not the most sobering aspect of the day. The sobering aspect of a boy's eighteenth fete wasn't a joke but filled that particular day in one's life meant a mandatory visit to the nearest Selective Service Office to register for the draft. We had seen the newsreels of slightly older college students of our sex burning their draft cards in protest of the ever-expanding war in Vietnam. I don't think I am being obtuse if I say that the cause and objectives of that war were not nearly as clear as they had been for World War Two. We Boomers had been raised on its glory. Even so, it wasn't difficult for a young man to ascertain that there was a difference.

Something was wrong. This was a political war with no clear objective. There weren't even battle lines.

I have never liked mobs, even then. I instinctively felt that masses of people most often degenerate into an entity with a cumulative IQ well down into the double digits. This is not a place to get an education in anything. I can't speak for any but myself, but for me, it was a somber duty. I think I can speak for most male teens when I say that it was a confusing time. In 1965 one of the most popular songs on the "Hit Parade" was Barry McGuire's "Eve of Destruction." Some over eighteen former students began to appear in the off-campus, dirt parking lot with upside-down U.S. Flags on display. One of my graduating class had already enlisted in the Marines by 1968, and got to the war; Eddie Pitts, went early and was immediately killed.*[1] He had been recognized all along as possessed of the most courageous of temperament among us all. My future brother-in-law was in Vietnam as a platoon sergeant with the 173rd Airborne Rangers. After a twenty-month tour, he was the last survivor of the original platoon. And even Martine's childhood suitor, poor Bobby Yates lost his life in that war.*[2] I think every male teen was having an internal conversation similar to mine, regardless of all of the distractions of the time.

By my birthday in January of 1970, even my father, a veteran of World War Two, was in Vietnam. As a GS-14 attached to Air Material Management at McClellan, he had accepted a TDY assignment as part of President Nixon's "Vietnamization Program," which aimed to train up the South Vietnamese military as the final phase of American involvement in that war sought to hand over the fight that proxy war to South Vietnam hoping for a better outcome.

History speaks on the efficacy of that program. However, it is important to note that the U.S. military won that war in 1968 by putting down the TET Offensive. It was the success of the Left that made the American people believe that we had lost that critical military event. When North Vietnam saw the American reaction and the protests, they walked out of the Paris Peace Talks and the war went on for six more devastating years and thirty-thousand more American and countless Vietnamese deaths until the peace was announced on January 23rd and the Paris Peace Accord signed on January 27th. I was in Coloma and well aware of the event that weekend at the Gold Discovery celebration, my 21st Birthday.

I had missed the call-up; my lottery number was #337. They had only drafted up to #200.

To add to the drama, when I was nine years old, Daddy had announced to me that if there ever was another war, he expected me to die in it. When I met my eighteenth year that January in 1970, there was no party. It was a rainy day. I drove up into El Dorado County stopping at Greenwood. All that was left of Greenwood was the pioneer cemetery. I spent the afternoon reading epitaphs in the rain. I didn't feel all that depressed; just somber. After all, a week before I had won my first trophy racing in a very muddy event held by the DDNMC at Helvetia Park, on the west side of the Sacramento River just north of West Sacramento. But there was no doubt about it, time had thrust me and my fellows into the world's events and their consequences. One immediate duty that fell on males that turned 18 in those days was signing up for a very active Selective Service System. The quip, "Your number is up," now had serious meaning. Making too many plans seemed useless. Racing was by then, also an escape and a place to work out my thoughts, and angst over some of them. The music I listened to most was Dylan's "It's Alright Ma, I'm Only Bleeding," and the Blind Faith album, especially "Sea of Joy," which has the line, "And I'm feeling close to when the race is run."

By the summer at White Rock, however, I was listening most to Dylan's "Self Portrait" album, whose two songs, "Days of Forty-Nine," and "Little Sadie" seemed to be made to order for my experiences. And whenever I pulled up to Six-Toed Pete's place to fill the water truck, I could hear, "All the Tired Horses," in my head. I had escaped into the old mine tailings around White Rock MC Park, and raced MX, but not completely. I saw the number "come up" for several racers. They all faced it differently. One big name intentionally injured his foot over and over by repeatedly running over it on the track. Another kept reinjuring his finger. It was an uncomfortable time for many young men, to put it mildly. Today, we want to forget about these sort of things, but it was an uncomfortable reality at the time.

North Highlands and I – Forced to Grow Up to All We Can Be?

By 1972, North Highlands had been through some traumas. The growing problems and violence of 1971 had ushered in a period of decay exacerbated by the waning of the Vietnam War and the repeated movements of military residents that saw an increase in rental properties over-owned homes. The scene was not unlike that described retrospectively by Bruce Springsteen in, "Born in the U.S.A,", particularly in the song, "My Home Town." Changes had come, and many old civilian employees of McClellan were retiring in the early 70s. Like my own parents, most of them would sell their homes and move into better homes and neighborhoods outside of North Highlands, and too many formerly owned homes became rental properties.

My father reopened his practice in Foothill Farms on Elkhorn and Diablo and worked there until his final retirement in 1984. By then, I was practicing in Marin County. Sometime during this period, a well-regarded member of our old church congregation from St. Timothy's Lutheran Church was shot to death inside of his home through a window while he sat in a chair watching television, a victim of opportunity. More people began to leave the once-happy community, and a period of decay set in. Real estate speculators began buying up homes and North Highlands was in transitioning into a rental community.

During a visit to Margaret, who was temporarily staying parent's home in North Highlands in 1975, after graduating from Berkeley, her mother declared: "North Highlands is a hotbed of apathy." I always thought that was a little funny, a kind of an oxymoron. Her daughter Margaret was one of the brightest students of the Highlands High School Class of 1970 and a good friend of mine for years, but never my girlfriend. She was a sort of muse, I suppose. She encouraged me to get into public speaking and coached me to two first places in Sacramento Valley Forensic League competitions. She and her boyfriend bought me my first copy of Tolkien's "Lord of the Rings" trilogy, in those days often simply referred to as "The Trilogy," as LOTR was still an underground phenomenon that preachers like Jerry Falwell condemned as "satanic." I read and reread LOTR constantly from then until I returned to college in 1976. As a result, Tolkien had a huge influence on my life choices. Even during the summer of 1970, I'd end my day reading another chapter of LOTR – again. I owe this to Margaret, and her then-boyfriend, who also remained a good friend for many years until his wife died of cancer and he went into seclusion. Margaret, like so many others, would leave as North Highlands increasingly became ironically, the place to leave. Margaret was off to Berkeley by the autumn of 1970. But she had a scholarship to Berkeley. She wrote me a series of letters from there and the Santa Cruz campus that year. I visited her several times in Berkeley between 1972 and 1974. She had made it out to White Rock for the Firecracker InterAm in the summer of 1970. But I don't think that she ever saw me race.

A Tale of Two Suburbs – or – Dr. Jekyll and Mr. Hyde Slept Here

It was as if North Highlands had a split personality. On one hand, its schools up through Highlands High were producing academic achievers, putting in top district athletic performances, and the Highlands High School Marching Band was in the top ten nationally in 1972, and in 1974 flew to Los Angeles to play at a Ram's versus Detroit Lyons game in the L.A. Coliseum. The band later played in Disneyland and made other "professional" appearances. There was a group of citizens who were genuinely working for the benefit of the community. The community was busy, businesses were hopping with activity, and McClelland AFB was still in full swing. After 1969, the Moonwalk Parade was added to the Memorial Day Parade.

Yet, something was wrong and it was beginning to show itself as a chronic issue spelling decline that transformed North Highlands from a vibrant, productive community to probably one of the first to decline to a suburban ghetto.

So What Happened?

The corruption of the later Vietnam War saw McClellan AFB become a secret terminal for drug smuggling. Hell's Angels were frequently seen loitering around in those days. I didn't know why then, but I learned later from some Air Force enlisted men in 1975, ironically at a party at the McCrackin house in Rio Linda where some of it took its toll later that year. Jay McCrackin had inherited Grant School Board Trustee Jim McCrackin's house, which was one of those multi-story Victorians that were moved out from downtown Sacramento in the early 50s. No specific accusations are being made here. Let's just say that the film "Who Will Stop the Rain" was not so much a fiction as it represented the sort of things that were happening at that time.

It wasn't as if North Highlands was an island. One might say that it was a later victim of World War Two when communities were impacted by people's forced movement for war production and support as the Vietnam War became more intense. Wars change societies, perhaps vying with nature's forces that sometimes make significant changes, such as with the collapse of the Bronze Age in the Eastern Mediterranean in 1181, B. C. E. That series of events and invasions became the basis of Biblical myth. The collapse was actually caused by earthquakes followed by massive migrations. The competition between nature and war as the agent of drastic endings and beginnings must be a dead heat by now with humanity as an unnatural force of nature and an added cause. But even before the nuclear age and the overpopulation of the planet by human beings, wars have always created major cultural shifts and power vacuums. Power vacuums are usually filled by the most available, less stable material. This is true for biology as well as in social history and politics. With humans, it's often the most aggressive that moves in. By coincidence, they happen to usually be not the most compassionate members of humanity. North Highlands came to be because of war and it suffered from the subtlest ripples that war creates. But even subtle ripples shape destiny.

The increased activity at McClellan AFB due to the Vietnam War had caused rapid turnovers of military personnel that affected North Highlands' stability and the likelihood of upgrading. Temporary residents are less available to a community, and so cohesion becomes an issue. The activities and movements of military personnel changed the demographics quickly. As trouble began, those who could left for more peaceful communities. And there was trouble. It had been brewing for a while;

Consulting the records of the time, I am reminded and further informed about the problems that faced the community's teens by 1969-70. What strikes me most about these news articles from the archives assembled by Dean and Merrie O'Brien in 2001 for the years 1951 to 1971 are some of the names of the students involved in the community meetings, in this case, the ones held in February of 1970. They were the then-student body president of Highlands High, another officer, and a younger student whose presence there baffles me completely. The Student Body President, Sharon Ratliff, lived behind me, kitty-corner on Milton Way. Student Body Officer Abe Baca lived up the street a little way past the Cantel Way cross-street. I knew them, and I knew the senior president's older brother and younger sister through their affiliation with my older and younger sisters, who were in the same class years, being matched by age. (In fact, her older brother was one of the naughty boys in the earlier part of this story that taught us songs and was one of the boys that showed up with the catfish).

A Strange Array of Teens at the Meeting

Present at the meeting also was a class of '71 member who was quite a case in my opinion. He had followed me around trying to pick a fight ever since his older brother had punched me in the jaw when I was seven years old after I asked him to stop throwing rocks at my sister, Paulette, as we walked home from school together in those days. He sought me out for a fistfight for several years after that as an annual ritual. I guess he wanted to be like his older brother and bash me good. I was always able to prevent that. After years of absence, he showed up at my house in the spring of 1970, wielding a knife. I worked in the evenings after school, so I wasn't there. He told my sister that he had come to kill me. I called him on the telephone and reasoned with him for a while. I made him see or at least agree that we had never had a real issue between us, and anyway, our confrontations after his brother had struck me, not the other way around, and it was years ago when we were children in primary school. I never figured out why he was so mad at me. A look at his high school photo may provide a hint of some actual developmental issues. But there he was, representing some sort of argument or problem that needed fixing to this committee. There is no record of any of his comments at that meeting.

The student leaders put forward an issue concerned with the lack of a facility for the teens to hang out after school and on weekends. Some of these teens had been convening at the county library, where they had repeatedly caused conduct problems.

A few "demonstrations" had occurred there in response to being told to quiet down or leave. The librarians said they didn't want to force the kids to go, but others were earnestly trying to study. They acknowledged the need for a place for the teens to gather and later suggested reserving the library after hours on weekdays or even weekends for the teens' exclusive use.

One member of the class of 1971, reported as A. Murphy, contributed a short report of sorts to the February 4, 1970 article in the community newspaper offering his opinion on the matters, his suggestions, and an accusation of "much prejudice" on the part of the librarians. As the related articles and evidence are recorded, there is no indication of any "prejudice" (then the popular term for "racism") among the librarians or any other authority figure. In fact, over-indulgence and frank appeasement were probably more of a factor in the problems and the events that led up to the 1971 riots.

The truth is that the students of some families that had only arrived in North Highlands once the military build-up around the expanding commitments in Vietnam from about 1965 on came from volatile American regions. They brought aggressiveness and an attitude that was foreign to North Highlands up to then. I can offer an example of this from 1967 as a personal experience involving A. Murphy himself. It has to do with a door-to-door sales business that I had become involved in during the spring of 1967. That business was Emanon Youth. It masqueraded as a youth project when it was really just straight-up candy sales for profit run by a man and wife team, Gene and Fran. We were too young to not see the deception, but it became a news story by August of that summer because we were showing up in neighborhoods all over Sacramento County with our "delicious peanut brittle." We had solicitor's licenses, but it was a subtle misrepresentation. The only activity of this youth group was selling candy for profit. We did hold over after work at the Dairy Queen on Watt Avenue for an hour or so, buying snacks and goofing off.

By that time, we had our first non-white members. In fact, I believe I invited the first one, myself, as I was friends with a couple of new arrivals since, by my home upbringing, I did not judge by the color of anyone's skin, and I was very welcoming of everyone by nature. For example, I was picked by Don Julio Junior High's administration in 1964 to welcome a particular new kid who was very shy. There were, however, disruptions in the classroom by the autumn of 1965 by three of the other newcomers. The disturbances were in the nature of verbal combats between those particular students and involved the use of the then not so dreaded "N" word, which shocked most kids into laughter as they threatened one another with vain insults. Strangely, our famously strict homeroom teacher Miss Douglas made no effort to curtail their demonstrations. This is what I mean by appeasement. But I was raised to appease, too, it seemed.

By the early summer of 1967, there had been a substantial expansion of the number of sales personnel for Emanon Youth. The sales team was about half-white and half-black. Then Gene came up with a horribly bad idea for a competition between the black and white solicitors, which he named "The Steak and Bean Contest." He divided the group by race and tallied the daily sales of each up for a month.

The winners were treated to a steak dinner at the Windjammer Restaurant, while the losers sat across the table and ate beans. The black team won. During the month of the competition, as always, all were subject to various conversations in transit and afterward at the Dairy Queen. Our competitors made no secret of their scorn for their customers who they mocked as they related how easy it was to play on them using inferred race-guilt complexes (again, appeasement at work, ruining these kids). We were also treated to talk concerning a few of the female students at school. They spoke of them as if they had passed them around. I couldn't tell if it was true or not, but it was probably merely a prodrome to planned approaches, as I later observed. It was my first exposure to up and personal racial hatred. I would soon have another.

By the end of the summer, more personnel had been added to the team. All but one white kid, me, had quit, probably due to being humiliated by Gene's contest. A Murphy's older brother was in my graduating class and well-known, had brought in his younger brother. He was with us only about a week before he threatened me personally. It was over a discussion of Jimi Hendrix, the famous psychedelic guitar hero who met an untimely death in 1971.

My mentioning that he had formed his band in London, England and that his two bandmates were white, as an example of integration, and the British influence in Hendrix's style, it seemed, they denied. My point was that Hendrix wasn't Motown. His older brother, my classmate, said something of a threatening nature aimed at me. I replied that he knew he wasn't going to do anything of the sort. This was when "little brother" said, "I will." Nothing ever happened. Gene acted first and separated me from that group. (This is an example of the fundamental element that arrived in North Highlands and brought on the riots of 1971. I was not a participant, but I knew some of those that were; Mark Miller, for one).

All this occurred while Gene was driving us to a location for canvassing. After this, he formed two separate groups, divided by race, in different cars with different neighborhoods for canvassing. I was the last white kid in that group by the end of the summer, anyway. Many quit soon after the infamous "Steak and Bean" contest. Not me. It really didn't bother me, meaning that I didn't let it get to me. I was using the money I earned to fix up my Hodaka motorcycle. Every weekend that summer, I was trail riding with my father and some adult friends up out of Foresthill. That was what had meaning to me that summer. This superseded all other concerns in my life at the time. And I had a great time.

By September, Gene and Fran had expanded their operation, and they had a new group of kids from Foothill Farms now with a driver. I was put into that group of strangers. I quit the job altogether within a few weeks. I was about done with selling candy door to door, anyway. Several intended customers had given me the third degree over the questionable status of Emanon Youth instead of a sale. The whole thing had begun to feel wrong.

I don't know how many of the children and youth in North Highlands were the only child in their homes, but there were some. Others were as good as only children because their other siblings were spread out in years that they were essentially on their own. Our family was one where the children were close in age. Ours was a raucous family, lively and inventive. We played and fought together, as is typical, I suppose, except Paulette and I never fought. We were the middle kids and only one year apart. We had been "buddies" for several years while she played my Tom Boy brother up to about age 13 for me and 12 for her. Once the boys started coming around for her, her Tom Boy time was over. We attracted a lot of kids to our home from the start. First, it was due to Martine's popularity with boys early on, then all of my sisters. I was the one who went out to visit other boys, usually not the other way around. The reason for going over to visit Dave and Rick was obvious; I didn't have a race track in my backyard.

My constant friends Dave and Rick were almost as good as only children because their older siblings were five years older than them, and in Dave's case, were male and serving in the Navy. I suppose I had it better than other boys, including Dave and Rick because I had three sisters who had their girlfriends over all the time. Martine's best friend was so close to our family that she came on a camping trip with us and was often along on family trips to the snow, Tahoe, etc.

In fact, she and Mark Miller were with our family on a particular weekend hunting trip at Wentworth Springs in 1966 that got onto our home movies. But she pops up earlier, and later at MX races in 1971. In this way, my sisters ran an unplanned parade of girls past me. I never made a move, but a few of them did, including Martine's friend who was always at our house. We went on trail bike rides and one hunting trip with her father as part of a larger group that included Paul, who owned the A&W Root Beer business, complete with carhops.

It was located opposite the lot from Marasha's in those days. Between Martine's boyfriend and the crowd, he brought over from Rio Linda, which was considerable since he was the third youngest of thirteen children. One of his constant companions was his nephew, who was older than him. As a result, our house was busy. Something was always going on, and it wasn't always on the up and up, you could say.

The scene at our home became a problem after a while because my parents, like undoubted numbers of others, not only in North Highlands but all over Sacramento County, and likely other nearby counties out to the Bay Area, were attracted to Reno and Lake Tahoe. The Southern California counterpart was (Las Vegas). As far as I know, this situation has not significantly changed.

The parties that happened were the original "home alone" scenarios. The one common feature of these parties in North Highlands in those days was access to alcohol. It found its way into teen hands through older relatives. Martine's boyfriend from Rio Linda had an older sister who had no problem procuring the list of booze he'd bring to her. I got drunk twice in 1966 and found that I didn't like it at all.

I liked cigarettes even less. But there was something else that took me away from this problem; my interest in motorcycles and my desire to race. I guess that I, along with Dave and Rick, were exceptions. We shunned the party scene and focused on the world of motorcycle racing. Dave's uncles were already deeply involved and connected to the local scene, with Dan Rasmussen and Carl Cranke in their circle, so we linked into that quickly. Meanwhile, restlessness in the teen population of North Highlands seemed to be growing. Problems arose and teens had demands, that is, notions of possible solutions.

At the February 1970 meetings, Abe Baca said that there had once been a rumor, a promise of a bowling alley being constructed in North Highlands. Apparently, the contractor that had started the rumor had pulled back as the other contractors had similarly refused to build more expensive homes in North Highlands. The only reason for this that I can think of is that they saw the trouble coming and didn't want the losses. Besides, there was the Country Club Lanes sports facility a couple miles up Watt Avenue. They were savvy businessmen who had built suburb projects in Los Angeles, the Bay Area, and some other valley locations for decades. My feeling is that if such a bowling alley or teen center had been constructed, the trouble that came would not have been avoided. In fact, it would have required adult supervision, something I don't think any of the teens involved wanted. They wanted things that simply could not work at that time. But I don't believe that too many parents wanted much of a role in that sense, either. Where once upon a time, we had a significant Scouting movement in North Highlands in the 50s and very early 60s, it was tiny by 1969. I saw the den mothers pass our Cub Scout pack around until no adults wanted the job, and it just ended. I had only earned my Wolf Badge by the time it was over. The number of adults that wanted to take part was limited.

Abe Baca was near the spot when he complained of the temporary feeling of North Highlands. When an adult reminded everyone that there was already a teen center, he noted that it was a small, temporary building that added to the feeling of North Highlands as an "unstable" community. He had a point in this; the community adults had rejected a measure for raising funds for a teen center three times. Looking at it from their perspective, it can perhaps be understood.

They had grown up during the Great Depression and then faced World War Two's sacrifices and privations. My grandfather had taken his four sons bowling every Friday night, and my father was a pin-setter at the local bowling alley when he was ten. It's remarkable to me how he did that during the Depression while he simultaneously set up and moved his practice from Dearborn to Bundy Hill in Jerome. But the boys still managed to get into trouble. Only moving them out to the country slowed things down. In their view, they were alright. But my uncles, all three of them became alcoholics to one degree or another. How my father emerged as a teetotaler is a mystery I have never solved. I only saw him get tipsy once in my life, and that was at Paulette's marriage reception when she married a good friend of mine from the motocross scene.

If talk I overheard or had leveled at me from time to time growing up is any indication, the so-called Greatest Generation felt that we were all spoiled, that we had it too easy already. So why should they spend more money on something they felt was superfluous? They had a point, too. When Martine was in the seventh grade, there was a teen canteen every Friday night for a while at the junior high. I don't know what happened to it. My guess is that not enough kids participated, or parent chaperons were wanting. I remember her resisting going. She was bored, and Momma was telling her that she could always go there. Not good enough. Not enough excitement? Some problems just don't have easy answers. Martine went on to find trouble on her own. I had a dangerous period myself. It all occurred during my fifteenth year. By the end of it, I had decided that following my desire to race was the way to avoid bad influences and actions. Sue helped, too. She inspired me with her hippy message of love and kindness. Sounds corny, but it worked enough for me to not want to get into fights or other problems, which Martine's boyfriend encouraged in me. Dave, Rick, and I approached racing as athletes, so we were uninterested in drinking or finding drugs to try out.

The kids growing up in North Highlands were not living in a bubble. When I was six, I was going to summer school with Martine. The school district was great, I think. They took us to Iceland to skate on

Thursdays, and on Tuesdays, we went to Grant High School to swim in the large swimming pool complex they had there. I would not be the only kid that saw the old, venerable architecture of that old high school building. I wonder what happened to those summer programs. I went to summer school every year up to the fourth grade. It was a good thing.

Similarly, I had seen McClatchy High School, in Sacramento, on Freeport Boulevard, old 21st Street. We had lived across the street from it on Weller Way, and driven past it many times to go to those early CCA meetings at William Land Park. The youth of North Highlands had a notion of how other schools compared with our comparatively cheaply built, temporary-looking schools and community. The perception was a problem. The grown-ups were not considering how things looked to us, which added to North Highlands' "unstable" nature that Abe identified so clearly. The developer and many adult attitudes were sensed by those growing up there as the first generation of North Highlands while things were changing and the enthusiasm for the new suburb was replaced with turmoil and a reluctance to invest.

Student body president Sharon Ratliff was right; the teens needed something engaging to occupy them. Knowing her as I did, she suggested the activities that interested her, music and poetry writing. I think she threw in arts and crafts and expanded after-school sports programs as obvious, if impractical repetitions of activities already ongoing during the school year, but perhaps she was thinking of summer activities. Well, it had already been done, as summer school programs. The fact is, the teens did not want to do those things.

They were chafing toward scenes leaning more toward adult activities. I shared some of her interests, and we were both on the editorial board of the school literary arts club in my junior year. She wrote a poem about how deep poets must be. I wrote a poem about how shallow most people are. She suggested that parents become involved. And that's the problem; there were already students involved in after-school and other activities. Some of them were the main participants in the problems Sharon sought to address. One of my after-school activities, as with some others I knew, was an actual paying job, which was probably the best solution of all for the restless kids. In 1965, I spent some of August picking tomatoes next to the Braceros out in the Spreckels-owned farmlands and made a little money. I went with Martine's boyfriend from Rio Linda and his friends as the youngest member. This was likely the last generation of White youth involved in farm work during summer vacations. It used to be common.

Some adults were interested in the youth of North Highlands. Mr. Ginotti stands out in my memory, in particular. But there were too few. Most adults worked five days a week and wanted to go home and have dinner when their day was finished. The fact is, on the weekends, many left to go "over the hill" to Reno and Tahoe for adult fun. In this problem of parental neglect, she had a point, and it seems that it was as real in her household as it was in mine. However, she and Abe were projecting and being unrealistically idealistic. There was a touch of hypocrisy involved as well; I know that they both attended various weekend parties that were leading to the problems being discussed. At those 1970 community meetings, she claimed that teen pregnancy was higher in North Highlands than anywhere else (in the region). Because of her orientation, there was no danger of that affecting her.

At the next community meeting a week later, a sheriff's deputy was there and reported that the teen pregnancy rate in North Highlands did not exceed the average in Sacramento County (not that this was a good thing). The meetings ended and nothing was solved.

As for the parties, I never thought I was missing much. I had something that took my attention beyond the mundane, and I wasn't bored. Boredom, now there is the issue. Many kids were acting out of boredom and a sense of being left out of bigger events in a wider world. After all, it was "The Summer of Love" and San Francisco was only 90 miles away. Adults wanted to be controlled by verbal commands from Nevada, but young people wanted action. Despite the usual, common corporal punishment of them as children, rebellion was everywhere and so was an increasing array of temptations, as smart teens noticed the hypocrisy of their parents. We have that history to look back upon, hopefully with wisdom, at some point.*₃

Was the exposition of these dissatisfactions, not a reason to cease incriminations rather than pile them up? It doesn't lead to a solution unless action follows the words. It was the nature of the actions and inactions that determined how things would be in North Highlands and similar communities. The best option for youth was to find a diversion. The nature of those diversions made all of the difference in many cases.

In the autumn of 1967, just as I had quit Emanon Youth, I was with my father picking up our Hodaka motorcycles after a tune-up at the dealer on Madison Avenue. We were preparing to take part in the big McClellan AFB-sponsored trail-bike ride over the Sierras, from Foresthill to North Shore, Lake Tahoe. Ricky Starr, who was attending Mira Loma High School at the time was the only other teen on the ride. We met later on the race track.

I ran into Dave "Bucky" Buckmaster there. I hadn't seen him or Rick while I had been at Don Julio Junior High because he and Rick had attended Campos Verdes Junior High. That's when he invited me to come over with my bike, and the legend of the "Three Musketeers of Motocross" at Highland High began. Okay, we were only that to ourselves. We laughed at the notion as we used it. From then on, it was my interest in motorcycles and racing that deterred me from any involvement in parties and the sorts of problems they brought from then on. The three of us took the idea of racing very seriously. We understood the danger of it and that to excel, we must be sober and dedicated. We trained at home with weights and practiced on the oval track behind Dave and Rick's houses. Later, we laid out a small track in the field between Watt Avenue and 34th Street, right in front of Rick's home along Rio Linda Creek. No one bothered us, and we put in a lot of time out there. Once, in the autumn of 1969, Abe Baca rode his Honda street bike out to the creek to watch us jumping in and out of the creek bed. He said, "You guys are crazy!" Then he rode off. Abe had wheels, but what was he looking for?

The riot that began between the principal's office and Senior Square spilled out into the community and resurfaced sporadically over the next several days to a week. This photo was taken on the first day at the intersection of Don Julio Blvd. and Greylock Lane by Jose Hernandez.

Later, we were joined by Dan Calhoun and a serving officer from McClellan AFB. The last sleepover I ever had at a friend's house was when I spent the night with Rick in the summer of 1969, when we slept outside, next to our MX bikes; more like a camping trip. I worked after school and during summers practicing in the field in my spare time. I had no time for trouble. By the time the community meetings were held in February of 1970, I had already won my first trophy. I had taken our foreign exchange student, Elmar Boje, to that January race. As I began my racing career, my world became further divorced from the problems the other teens were coping with. Dave, Rick, and I had a larger world of excitement to deter us. We were dedicated and uninterested in doing anything that would obstruct our shared goals. In my senior year, Rick and I would often go to Gene's Automotive in Loomis on an open day, spending the afternoon there, picking up on anything we could. Gene and Bill seemed to enjoy having us around. Dan later joined the Highlands High School faculty as an instructor in a program teaching small engine repair and related skills, including machining work.

When my parents would go "up the hill" for the weekend, and my sisters would get a party going, I would lock my room and take my bike over to spend time with Dave and Rick and practice on the track. I'd hear about what happened later; lots of kids and some property damage finally ended the series of parties at our home. Paulette, the hostess was "scared straight." I was glad. I have always said that motorcycles saved my life. They really did.

Did the teens at the meeting, in all honesty, really want what the student leadership proposed at that meeting? I don't think so. The sixties were in full swing with the San Francisco scene just a hundred miles away. And it was everywhere; in London, Paris, and even as it turns out, in the "underground" of Soviet Russia, as The Beatles reminded us (turns out that the KGB failed to suppress the Russian version of Beatlemania, which helped create the generation of Gorbachev and ended the Cold War and the Soviet Union).

Cousin Sue from Wisconsin was four years older than me. She had run away from home to join the "happenings" in "The Haight." Her father called my Dad in a panic; "Cousin, our baby's gone!" Uncle Johnny ended up searching her out and bringing her to stay with us that October. Sue's grandfather had married a Finnish woman, and it really showed in Sue. She had been voted the "Snow Queen" of her hometown of Lake Geneva, and she seemed perfect for that role.

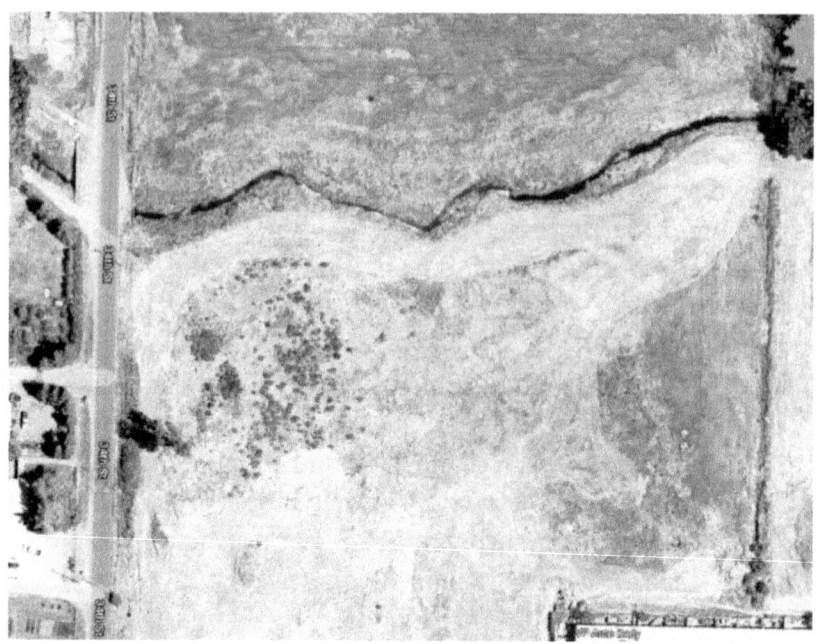

Within the now fenced-off field, the imprint of our old practice track in the field at 34th Street and Rio Linda Creek remains today. Imagery ©2021 Maxar Technologies, Sandborn, U.S. Geological Survey, Map data ©2021 50ft

She was sweet and kind, full of the more positive sixties attitude, and completely a-political (at the time). Her influence helped my decision by the end of 1967 to ignore a certain present influence toward drinking and fighting by turning my ambition to the goal of racing motorcycles, which she seemed to think was great.

There were undeniable, unreasonable pressures on teens at the time. In North Highlands, the teens, especially the boys, were generally suppressed and held to outmoded standards. I believe that many adults felt that if these forms could be successfully enforced, more considerable trouble would be avoided. It was a carry-over of military-style discipline aimed at breaking the spirit of the recruit to reform it. It did seem to be aimed at boys more than girls.

The school dress standards called for a boy's hair to not touch their ears at any point. A boy could be sent home, suspended, if he did not cut his hair. Facial hair was out. Girls were allowed to wear miniskirts, but boys were sent home for hair violations of the dress code. A little liberalization of dress codes for boys at the right time might have avoided a fuller rebellion toward all standards. That was part of the so-called generation gap of the time; the adults wanted to hold on tightly to what they considered superior standards, which had been learned during a very restrictive point in history.

To the kids, it just seemed to be restrictions for the sake of full control. It came across as bullying, at times. Youth wanted to break out and find "freedom." They saw what was happening in Berkeley. What began as some male students not wishing to take the then mandatory officer's training program in place since the war, and being flatly refused, led to the rise of the Free Speech Movement, which opened up opportunities for Marxist-influenced political groups to gain influence and membership. The rest, as they say, is history.

Some thought youth suppression was a question of race, but we all had issues with overpowering adult authority in those days. The race quotient was a product of outside influence and frank mimicry. However, some of it came with the territory that arrived with transplants from traditionally problematic regions of the nation. However that breaks down, the adult reaction seemed to be the same, and their former powers of "remote" control were still in force. The Black kids seemed to have even less parental control. But I could be wrong. They might have been acting out exactly what they heard at home. More supervised activities are not what the kids wanted, in my opinion. They wanted "out" as most Boomers did, out from the cage, out of the cupboard as latch-key kids. Abe Baca wanted out, I am sure. In the spring of 1970, Dave and I overhead Abe on a Monday at school bragging about how drunk he and his friends had been over the weekend. Obviously, Abe wanted "out."

Sharon Ratliff wanted "out," also. In 1974, I met her again as a fellow employee at the ESS stereo factory in Rancho Cordova. She had come out by then and let me know it, unsolicited. I can't say that I was surprised. During the third grade in Mrs. Alden's class at Village School, she presented a series of "Tarzan, Jane, and Girl," modified stories for "show and tell" sessions, and once punched me on my chest for bumping into her accidentally while in line.

At ESS, she approached me, but I never uttered a word to her or, in fact, to any of the Ratliffs. Her little sister and my youngest sister, Gayle were classmates. She was at our house swimming in our pool in 1967. Even though she was very cute and seemed to like me, I kept my distance. Her older brother was one of the "bad boys" with the songs and catfish, you know? I didn't hate Sharon or her family; I was merely stepping around possible landmines on the way to a more compelling horizon.

Both Sharon and Abe had been in my third-grade class at Village School. They were similarly outgoing and seemed to crave the spotlight, as the kids who typically got into student government and activities in an over-abundant way always do (well, someone has to do it). So growing up was going to be hard for the Boomers who survived the Vietnam era because disillusion was epidemic in American youth by 1975. Meanwhile, the teen angst in North Highlands only grew along with racial tensions.

It may have been the inevitability of the times, but by 1971, the racial tensions at Highlands High exploded in the spring as two days of rioting. The initial news reported the cause and actions in a series of fabrications based on the false reports of Principal Mr. R. Ericson. It just so happens that I knew one of the principles of the outbreak of the violence that began on campus on April first, 1971. He was Mark Miller, my good friend, and near-family member.*4 Principal Ericson reported that the cause was the trespass of some underclassmen on the so-called "Senior Square" the sacred ground of the reigning senior class of a given year. (Senior Square was another bad idea of the time. Enforcing the notion of exclusivity is always a bad idea). Ericson reported that after the fight over the trespass, other one-on-one fights broke out. This is not true. Mark was jumped by a crowd of Black students and beaten in front of Mr. Erickson's office. When Mark tried to avoid the beat-down by entering the office, personnel inside locked the door and watched him being beaten up. Mr. Erickson retreated into his office and remained there for some time. This was widely discussed among the students.

Fighting spread out along the approach to the high school on Don Julio Boulevard. This is where the police officers were attacked. Over three days 46 were arrested, 13 on the first day, that's 12 Black and one White, and 32 Whites in later days. Mark was not arrested. After his beating, he was taken to his house on Milton Way. I visited him there. Other concerned classmates were coming in and out of his house during that time. I got the story from them as they and Mark related it. I believed them. I do not believe the timorous Mr. Erickson. The news reported in the Greensheet of the community meetings aimed at discussing and guiding the community out of the crisis reveals the mechanism of Mr. Ericson's conversion of cause, admitting a racial factor after the issue of the causes became an undeniable set of facts.

After the Thursday when the riots, a public meeting was announced and held at Buchanan Hall on the Highlands High School campus a week after the riots. The meeting was reported in the Green Sheet of April 7, 1971. At the meeting, a discussion of the two days of violence on and off the school campus led to the closure not of just Highlands High, but of all the Grant District Schools one day prior to Easter Vacation.

There was also a local news blackout concerning the event throughout Sacramento County. At the meeting, PTA president Jim Smith, Grant School Board trustee John McCrackin, chief deputy sheriff Herb Anderson, and Jess Strandfield, representing area Blacks, joined Principal Ericson in presiding over the meeting of nearly 1,000 community members.

John Banks, a substitute teacher when the April first violence broke out, said, "Many of the frustrations that were being acted out there (at school) are also frustrations of their parents." I can't imagine how he could know that unless he knew some of the parents of his particular community. He said that many of the students he talked to felt the power structure of the Grant School District is not representative (trans; too white). "We're treating the symptoms, not the cause. I'm saddened by the fact that it took violence to bring some of you out here tonight." A two-minute limit per speaker cut Bank's speech short, but it was received enthusiastically. The next speaker was Earnest Cheney, an Equal Opportunities Program employee. He stated that there should be no more "Black Rallies," and that all assemblies should be held for the students by the students alone with no outsiders allowed in.

No doubt under pressure from certain students, who had been making demands since at least the time of the February 1970 meetings that discussed the disturbances at the county library on A Street, Mr. Ericson had allowed "Black Rallies" where the entire student body was made a captive audience. The particular rally that occurred the Thursday that the riot broke out featured the reading of an obscene poem by an adult student from Sacramento State College. Mr. Cheney asked Mr. Ericson why he didn't stop the recitation when heard it and saw the students stirring and talking among themselves. Ericson said, "They assured me that a very minor word here and there was all that was going to be involved in this. We couldn't race out and grab the man, at that time. It would have been inappropriate." Why would that be so? All the talent shows I attended as a student at Highlands High during assemblies were ripe candidates for "The Gong Show." Fear was the motivator or perhaps the non-motivator in this case. Anyone could have predicted what happened because it hadn't begun overnight.

This is what Highlands High School principal Rick Ericson offered as an excuse for allowing a pornographic, racially charged "poem" to be read to minors at a school assembly. It is obvious that the poem was a cuckolding form of racism. That likely went over the student's head and Mr. Erickson pretended to ignore it, but many students felt it. It was a planned, deep insult of one of the most violent types. Arguments broke out after the rally and fighting ensued. The first, or one of the first events was when Mark Miller was jumped in front of the main office as Mr. Ericson and his staff watched from behind a locked glass wall entrance. It was locked when Mark first made a dash toward the door in an attempt to escape the beating. Initially, Mr. Ericson had denied that the rally had anything to do with the fighting, claiming it to be about a trespass on Senior Square.

A teacher reported that initially, the fighting involved about 20 students, but noted that a couple hundred students were "nearby." They witnessed Mark Miller being beaten up in front of the main office, which was directly across from Senior Square, but he was not defending the Square from trespassers. I know what the fight was about. He told me. Regarding the rally, Ericson said that the assembly had been "excellent, and that "the students were entertained." This claim was seriously undermined at the later meeting where the principal could not defend the actual problem of the racially charged "erotic poem." There was also no ongoing issue over underclassmen occupying Senior Square, but there was a demand by the Black Student Union for it to be handed over to them, permanently. On that day, someone not a senior defiantly walked across Senior Square about the time Mark was being attacked. It all exploded from there.

At the core of the cause of the riots were several years of harassment of White female students by many of the Black male students. As I reported earlier, some of these boys spoke as if they passed girls around. It was 1967, and we were 15 years old at the time. At the time I thought it was mostly boasting but as time passed, it seemed to gain factual form.

Later that year when school resumed I witnessed some of it take place in the classroom beginning in my sophomore year when one student went on a verbal assault of a girl with whispered insults using the vilest of language while another recreant instructor, Mr. Vandegriff, pretended to not notice. I couldn't figure out what the situation was between them. Some girls were friendly when they talked to them. Their natural openness was often taken as an invitation when it was a case of just being polite. On the other hand, many of the boys were popular due to sports activities. This was not the case in this instance. This guy was a brooding outlier. My take is that when the demand for more than a polite word and smile was refused, insults and harassment ensued. By 1971, the situation had grown to dangerous proportions. The boys would target a girl. The girls would either comply or give an excuse, the most usual one being that they had a boyfriend already.

Their solution became to find the boyfriend and beat him up. I don't know what the verbal communication, was, but there must have been some. I experienced what could be called a pre-violent form of it personally in June of 1970. One of the school's sports heroes taunted me about a pair of twins in the sophomore class. I met them in the school library in a passive way. They went out of their way to talk to me and signed my yearbook. One of them wrote that she hoped to see me sometime in the summer. Somehow, this senior class sports hero learned of their contact with me. So one afternoon a week or two before graduation, as I was walking to the parking lot after school was done for the day, I found the "hero" walking near me. He asked, "You're talking with "The Twins", aren't you?" I confirmed. "Well, who cares? Everyone's had "The Twins!" He yelled. This was not just a confession to the harassment of minors by a then eighteen-year-old adult, it was also defamation.

I was busy at White Rock MC Park just days after graduation, but a few weeks later, I dropped by the home of the twins. I found them outside, hanging around in their opened garage as many kids did in those days, including me and my sisters. We'd play cards, make jokes, etc., with other kids that came by. I asked them about the hero if they had heard from him, etc. They said that he was making phone calls to them, claiming he was President Nixon, and then hanging up. They weren't scared but seemed mildly apprehensive. The "hero" was a serial stalker.

By 1971, this style of harassment and stalking of white females they were interested in had escalated to physical abuse. If a girl said she had a boyfriend, they'd find him off campus and beat him up. This happened a couple times that I know of. The beatings likely came with verbiage in the form of racial insults and warnings to stay away from so.

I learned of one particular case. It was the trigger event or one of the triggering events that the comments concerning frustrations were about.   These events had been occurring and ignored by the community, the schools, and the district. In my opinion, the Class of '71 was one of the most cohesive classes Highlands High ever saw. They cared about one another in more of a family way than any of the graduating classes I know anything about, including my own.   They stood up for one another. The riots divided them by race, sometimes.

Another notable event at the meeting was Ericson's announcement of the plan to place a security guard on campus. This, Ericson claimed, would be enough to prevent any more such events.   Student Paul Goodwin said that there were many outside agitators on campus and that, "the administers of the Grant Union School District had better get their hands out of their tail ends and get this school operating or shut it down."

John McCrackin said that more and better communication was needed at the administrative level, and left it at that. One woman went into detail about the kind of weapons being used on campus saying that some students "walk around with belts wrapped around their hands with buckles on them." She also spoke of the particular combs, known as "angel food cake cutters" that Black students used as knives, while still others used suspenders as weapons.   Ericson assured her "On Monday when they come back if we can isolate any students with weapons, they will be suspended for the balance of the year if that's what it takes."   There was about a month and a half left of that school year.

One weapon they did not find was a firearm; a revolver. I know because the piece came from my sister's boyfriend. The student who used it later, after this meeting prevented himself from being jumped again. He only needed to let the threatening party hear the clicking as he cocked it from inside his jacket pocket, which resulted in the quick disengagement of that party and his companions.   That probably prevented another round of campus riots. The violence ended after a week of patrols by some Whites who drove around with baseball bats confronting known parties until they no longer came outdoors. This is what put an end to the violence of April 1971, not the feckless communication promise of the Grant Union School District leadership.

As a useful example of the common form of claimed imaginary racism, one man present at the meeting who was Filipino, said, "We find it very easy to very easy to blame our administrators, why can't you parents blame yourselves?" He asserted that there is discrimination in the North Highlands community saying, "When I first came to North Highlands, I was denied a home." This is implausible.

I can guarantee the reader that North Highlands had people of Hispanic, Asian, and Black races from the very beginning and some of the early Air Force families were non-whites. In the second grade, I hung around with a mixed-race kid for a while. Around 1960, My folks hired a Black babysitter for us named Jo. We liked her because she told great scary stories on the first days she watched us. She had three kids and we played together until the oldest boy decided that he didn't like us anymore. She looked after us for two summers after summer school, until her airman husband was transferred out from McClellan. There was an Asian girl in my kindergarten class. She used to swish her black ponytail so it would hit me in the face when I sat behind her on the little bleachers in the classroom where Miss Wilson would assemble us sometimes. She'd smack me with her ponytail and then sneak a peek at my reaction. She lived up the street from me and always smiled when she saw me. She went all the way through with me and many others to senior graduation, smiling all the way.

Other non-White kids were around and had no problems. The trouble kids were later arrivals - implants. People of color in North Highlands might have initially been a small percent of the early population, but none of them had been denied a home. When I was four, a Hispanic kid stole my cap gun, grabbing it out of my hand. I chased him to his house, which was closer to Watt Avenue than ours, so they would have likely moved in at the same time as us. (He chased me back, wielding the toy like a weapon. I had to tell my father. This was the only time I can remember my father ever intervening for me in my life). Tony Valenzuela was from another early family, located around the block on Milton Way. His older brother was the newspaper boy for a long time and was very polite. Tony was my friend all through those twelve years of school. When he and his brother Frank opened a Mexican restaurant in Carmichael in 1975, I visited immediately and met up with a couple of former classmates who were also patronizing the Valenzuela boy's new business. As to that certain man's complaint of insidious racism, and victimization as the routine, there can be other problems with attaining a home.

North Highlands never practiced the sort of exclusion that might be found in some other places at that time. However, if one or more members of a group try hard enough, they can create reactive racism. I am sure that has happened, and not just in North Highlands. Using the excuse of racism as the default for personal failure has become wildly popular, as a tool of the social justice industry gaining millions, even billions of dollars to fix largely fictitious issues, until race hustlers actually created the idea that White dominant communities were a problem in themselves, exclusively. It must be clear, however, that if there had been housing discrimination; neither he nor the parties that had provoked the crisis would have been in North Highlands, to begin with. But the ruse of chalking up any personal problem as proof of racism is an old tactic. It was old even then; and as in the parlance of the sixties, "lame" or "stale." "Thoroughly run into the ground," is another phrase that comes to mind. When words alone no longer intimidate or cease to have the desired effect, the infantilized typically turn to violence.

To the credit of the immediate community, a new "Parent's Grievances Committee," began to hold weekly meetings with the Student's Grievances Committee attempting to sort out the crisis and prevent future problems. The youth group was made up of some of the parties that had been arrested as well as victims. The seventeen-member group was made up of eight Blacks, eight Whites, and one Mexican-American (as he was listed). They were Bob Pugh, chairman of the group, Steve Hubbard, the vice-chairman, Cynthia Burch, Mark Burch, Dave Goodwin, Candy Hefner, Lynn Hill, Randy Hughes, Don

Hurdle, Virginia Krause, Leona Leroy, Kent McBride, Mark Miller, George Sady, Chris Stanfield, Sharon Oliver, and Mike Lopez. How long these weekly meetings lasted is not known. But I gather from Mark's reports that nothing was really solved.

The summer of 1971 was plagued with spontaneous "parties" at parks, one in particular, Larchmont Park was right around the corner from our home. I was unaware of things because I was so involved with racing and working. They were public disturbances where teens were causing damage and disturbing the peace almost every night, tearing up the turf with cars, drinking beer, and using profane language. Others claimed that drugs were being used in the park. In early August, the North Highlands Recreation and Park District Board of Supervisors held a public meeting. Chief Deputy Herb Anderson and Captain Jerry Salter attended. The officers said that they were restricted by the penal code.

They needed citizens to get more involved. Various solutions, including citizen deputy patrols, were discussed. Finally, Slater admitted that he did not consider the parks safe for his own children. This problem was not limited to North Highlands. He said that he would never take his children to Ancil Hoffman Park, which is on the American River in Carmichael, miles away. County Sheriff Duane Lowe later stated during his re-election campaign that he didn't consider any of the parks he works to protect as safe for his own children.

Closing the August meeting, Chief Anderson said, "The biggest problem we have in the world today is overreaction. What we need is cooperation from the citizens, and that's the sum and substance of the situation." I do not know how or if any real action plan emerged. But I do know that later in March of 1972, my youngest sister was brought home by a sheriff's deputy for the possession and igniting of illegal fireworks at Larchmont Park. Later in October of 1971, more unrest led to the suspension of more Black students, which led to parent protests at the school.

In October of 1971, the Greensheet published an article about the suspension of seven Black male students after fighting broke out on campus on September 16th. They had been taken to juvenile hall and held there for more than a week. Four had their charges dropped. A parent of one of the boys had sought a meeting with Superintendent Elwood Keema. He was upset that when he did get to the meeting several other administrators were present. He said that the Grant School District had "failed to face the issues that are plaguing us in this district." According to him, the April groups seemed to have failed at their objectives. This culture of vague dissatisfaction regardless of the excesses of individual and political coddling and awards has only increased that culture to the present.

Bertram A. Graves was upset that the suspension of the boys had been publicly announced. The parents claimed that if White students had committed these infractions, they would not be treated as harshly. Another parent suggested that the severe discipline was pre-planned to quiet down Black students for the remainder of the year. The students were assigned to continuation school.

The parents were concerned with how long their children would have to attend. Assistant Superintendent Lou Jones told them that in most cases, it was to be the current and following semesters, meaning the entire school year. Robert Tyler, chairman of the Human Relations Commission in Sacramento asked what happened to White students exhibiting "aggressive behavior." Jones replied that he was not aware of any such reports. Trustee Dick Lester reminded the audience that both Black and White teachers had witnessed the fighting. Mr. Ericson added that a handful of instructors had witnessed the incidents but only two were required to sign the police report.

Isn't this pattern vaguely familiar? Currently, some organizations responding to the FBI national statistics that show a yearly consistent pattern showing that Blacks perpetrate 51% of all violent crimes say that the cure is to arrest more Whites, as this is supposed to somehow magically make the 51% statistic disappear.*5 The problem is that the Whites aren't committing enough crimes. So new crimes caused by passive "Whiteness" have been invented. First, words were given the power of whips, then, flags, and finally statues, all statues, except those that are held to support the "social justice movement."

One serious event was a murder, or near it, on campus. In 1970, a black student, one I had been friendly with in the 9th grade and I worked with in the candy selling in 1967, struck another student in the head with a baseball bat, turning him into a vegetable. Both disappeared from the scene. I heard that the black perpetrator was accepted into the Marines.

Appeasing the Black community in North Highland was the default management policy. Tolerating the initial disturbances in the library over a year earlier, led to the Black rallies. This appeasement style of crisis management continued when the Miss North Highlands contest, which was usually held in the autumn in the past, was held later in April of 1971 just weeks after the riots. The judges contributed to the appeasing by making Cynthia Burch Miss North Highlands over obviously more talented (dismissing the issue of beauty) White contestants, who danced, and played piano, while Miss Burch merely read a poem by Carl Sandburg.

All of these attempts at coddling and appeasement failed. As history shows abundantly, appeasement never satisfies, but only leads to more of the same activities that drew the initial appeasement. North Highlands spiraled downhill from that time on. By September of 1972, Mr. Ericson left Highlands High after suffering a heart attack that summer. It is never proper to gloat over anyone's health problem, but his management policy of appeasement and denial led to the explosion at the school he managed, and maybe the later series of plagues on North Highlands.

The most egregious betrayal of North Highlands youth has to be laid at the feet of some of the teachers at Highlands High School. I don't know how many were actually involved; I remember noting a few questionable occurrences. Later, I learned that two instructors, one highly regarded, and my homeroom teacher in 1970, were fired from their jobs. One had taken pornographic photographs of a very popular and talented female member of the Class of 1971 while corporally engaged with a non-white gym instructor. What surprised me was that she was well known as being from a very religious family. Today, these two men would have been put on trial, served time, and marked as sex offenders for life.

The photographer, I suspect, went on making adult pornography, at least. In 1973, someone I knew from high school invited me to help set up the new nightclub in Fair Oaks, ironically taking its theme from the innocent works of J.R.R. Tolkien. One of the owners was the photographer, my former homeroom teacher. That was when I learned about the firing and the reason. I believe that he continued to produce pornography. One night, later that year in August, when I was at the club as a patron, I was approached by a porn film recruiter. I was smart enough to refuse (by 1980, many porn actors had HIV). It seems that no one learned any lessons. It seemed that no one gave a damn. Now, giving a damn means everything; the difference between national failure and survival depends on it and clear sight.

I don't know how many of the Class of 1971 knew about this or when, but it might be the epitome of what went wrong in North Highlands as its most harmed children. My sister Paulette was a member of that class. I think many of us went through a few years of disillusionment, at least, but she turned out all right; she married a friend of mine from racing who was as dedicated as we "Three Musketeers."

I avoided the problems most kids were dealing with in North Highlands because I had a passion and I was actively pursuing it. I worked after school to pay for my Penton, and when I wasn't at school or working, I was out practicing on it, usually with my companions in the Highlands High School "motocross conspiracy," Dave and Rick, two of the original "I Street Kids" across the field and Rio Linda Creek. On an August afternoon in 1969, Rick and I rode our bikes through fields, pushing them across M Street, and then Watt Avenue to get out to Walerga Road, near the neighborhood where The Spook Tree had stood until four years earlier. We crossed Walerga Road and rode out into the wheat fields. We were able to ride along the Southern Pacific railroad tracks to get to the Antelope Store where we got a soda. It was a sort of farewell, in a way because although I didn't know it, this was the last time I was in the Antelope Store. Construction of the Elkhorn overpass and the renaming of M Street would begin early next year. The subdividing of that wheat field began soon after. And there was more change to come. But I put in my best year at school in my senior year, making up, perhaps for some earlier spotty performances; I finally made the honor roll thanks largely to Margaret.

There always was and I am told still exists a core of dedicated citizens of North Highlands who work for the betterment of the community. After all of this, some thoughtful people at the Recreation and Parks District decided to take a survey of what the teens really wanted.

Two teen activity and interest surveys were made by teen director Rick Sloan and recreation superintendent Robert Thomas of the park district. The answers were broken down into male and female categories. The age of respondents was also recorded. There were 265 female responses to 248 by males. There were only 15 responses from eighteen-year-olds, while the largest response age was thirteen through fifteen. The resulting plan was to establish teen sports leagues, Friday night swim parties at Highlands High, and dance parties. Three excursions were planned with one being a co-ed campout. The actual participation and history of these plans are not known to this writer, as they are not recorded in any follow-up articles. But I can report some other events of that year.

Along with the ongoing Larchmont Park rendition of People's Park riots in Berkeley, a wave of crime swept North Highlands in March of 1972. "There is probably no time in the history of the United States that law enforcement has been more dire than the one we do now," declared Sergeant Detective Carl Florence to the North Highlands Community Council concerning Citizen's Alert, a crime prevention program that he was directing.

"A certain segment of our society has allowed respect for law and order to slide downhill," Florence contended.   Advice on how to prevent burglary thefts, or otherwise discourage them by engraving valuables, was offered, along with the presentation of a volunteer neighborhood watching one another's property. "There's no time in the history of Sacramento County when we have had more patrol cars than we do now." He praised the dedication of the young patrolmen as "highly trained, and eager to serve the community. But they need your cooperation.

He spoke about the problem of "hot" merchandise being sold by ex-cons at the Roseville Auction. But the situation became even worse.

In December of 1972, North Highlands and Rio Linda were hit by a series of ten burglaries at residents; eight in Rio Linda and two in North Highlands. Three businesses along Watt Avenue were also hit. The Assembly of God Church on Elkhorn Boulevard in North Highlands was also broken into and robbed. Worse yet, at the same time, four white teenage girls, aged thirteen to sixteen, three from North Highlands, and one from Rio Linda were listed as missing in the report. On the fifteenth, a sixty-six-year-old woman from Rio Linda was also listed as missing. No resolution of the missing parties is known to this writer. Many people used to disappear into nowhere in those days before Amber Alerts and the systems that support that program. While the crime rate in Sacramento County dropped, it increased in the afflicted suburb.

As if enough wasn't enough, afflicted North Highlands saw a spate of armed robberies along Watt Avenue that targeted businesses, twelve events in all. Mac's Bottle Shop, Grant City, Albertson's, The Velvet Hammer, The Last Chance, The Roadway Inn, Der Wienerschnitzel, Marash's, and the Mobile Service Station were all hit. Employees were shot at the Food Fair and Stop-n-Go Markets at Kirby and Walerga. The clerk shot at the Stop-n-Go filed a four-million-dollar lawsuit against the unknown assailants and their supplier of guns and ammunition. Detectives believed the crimes to be the work of one gang. Inspector Terrel Dyer reported that after the arrest of a seventeen-year-old Black youth, the incidents ceased. He was thought to be accompanied by two other Black youths, but as of the time of this article in the Green Sheet, which was April 4th, 1974, no further arrests had been made. Dyer said that the perpetrators were definitely "homegrown."

While merchants in North Highlands invested in security systems and security guards, others obtained gun permits. But the worry wasn't over by a long shot due to the incompetence of the armed bandits. In the case of the Velvet Hammer robbery, the perps forgot to announce that they were there to rob the place, and so when they grabbed customer's change from the bar, a dangerous confrontation that might have produced more gunshot casualties ensued until they realized they were being held-up. Armed robbers escaped from Grant City in November with around $40.00 in pennies. They dropped the money bag containing $400.00 in cash. By the end of the year, such businesses began to keep a low cash amount at their businesses along with the addition of cameras, security guards, and their own firearms. After the Food Fair shooting, there was a lull, but the tense feeling at the local businesses remained.

At the November 1973 public hearings held for the North Highlands Central Area Community Plan at Highlands High, Floyd Knapp gave an emotional appeal to the commission for keeping Walerga Road closed to all traffic leading to an isolated development. "Since Walerga has closed," Knapp reported, "it has been like living in a different neighborhood. There are no more fires, no rapes, no crime, and no more garbage dumping."*[6]

Because of so many terrible events, North Highlands seemed to have become a lost cause. But as was proposed, the non-town had a core of enthusiastic citizens who were tirelessly working for the community they continued to believe in. These were adults and teens. They were parents and teachers. While the year of discontent, 1971, was unfolding, other things were going on; the Moonwalk Festival and other community activities continued. The North Highlands Garden Club won the state award for environmental improvement.

Previously, in 1970, it had won a national award for its annual flower show, titled, "North Highlands in Action."

There were other local awards from the Council Award for Child Therapy, along with other community awards, including a certificate for work with mentally challenged children and a Penny Pines Plantation purchase that would reforest one acre of burned forest land. And other great accomplishments reflected positively on some teens in North Highlands, namely the Highlands High School Marching Band. They had always been one of the best in the county. Martine had been "second clarinet" in the band up until she graduated. That year, they competed in the Camellia Festival and received a "superior" rating.

By 1972, their expertise had improved to the point that they took first place in the state at the State Fair competition at Cal Expo. By January of 1973, they were rated one of the top ten bands nationally. This led to an invitation to play at Disneyland, and an L.A. Rams game, all highlighted by an invitation to perform at a festival of marching bands in Brussels, Belgium. Coach Gilbert managed the top tack team in Northern California. Those of that crowd were busy with fundraising. They had no time for hanging around at parks, doing drugs, or otherwise engaging in destructive attitudes and activities.

Except for my personal knowledge of the 1971 riots, the following turmoil in North Highlands was lost on me. I was busy taking twelve units at ARC, working part-time at Carl Miller's Rexall Drug Store, and racing. Sometimes I was delivering prescriptions to customers at home, so I was driving all over the area, but I never saw anything that tipped me on the ugly events afoot, even around the corner at Larchmont Park. I had no idea of the situation until I inadvertently found myself at a house party in North Highlands in the spring of 1975.

I came with a friend of a friend who apparently knew about it. We found a house full of teens and young adults, with no responsible adults present. In a short time, I saw the essence of the problem. We left the party fairly quickly. It was nothing but a vat of young adults victimizing teens. At least one "hero" was there, now surrounded by younger potential victims. By coincidence, this was to be the last time I was in North Highlands.

A Farewell to Antelope

By the end of 1972, the Spook Tree had been long gone for eight years. I graduated from high school in 1970, attended AR for a couple of semesters, raced motocross on weekends, and worked at several jobs. They included a Honda shop and Penton West, which became High Point when KTM began to replace the Penton branded machine. The Austrian factory decided to promote its own brand and not renew the contract with John Penton. I had been injured in August of 1971 at the State Fair Motocross event enough to slow me down for a while. I never got going again, but began to think about my future. The War in Vietnam seemed to be winding down.

My draft number had been 337 and they only called up to 200; lucky for me, but not for others. One friend that did get drafted went to Germany instead of Vietnam while another went to Vietnam and was killed. After a brief attempt at restarting, I quit racing. The knee injury required a couple years to heal. I took up Enduro riding (100-mile cross-country rally) for a time in 1973. Later, when I went back to college in 1976, I was completely done with racing. I would go on now with a clear goal and no distractions, as I had in 1971,2.

By 1972, I had come to a crossroads in my life. My folks had been having difficulties and took some time off from their marriage. At the time, it seemed to be a permanent split. In any case, by that summer, I knew it was time for me to face life in a new way. The adjustment took some time, years, I suppose, but it began with a few sleepless nights where I contemplated the future with some trepidation. Regardless of that "fear of flying," I knew that I had to make my own way from now on. The first exercise in that endeavor was to make a kind of farewell by saying hello. I sold my truck and my CZ race bike. I then traveled east to meet relatives I had never met in Wisconsin and visit those I had met in 1961 in Michigan and Pennsylvania as a nine-year-old boy. Wisconsin was important to me because I had been born in Oshkosh and had never met any of my cousins there except Sue who had come out during the Summer of Love in 1967 after being "rescued" by Uncle Johnny. She was a typical Midwestern "flower child" coming to The Haight to join in the madness of the sixties. I adored her. I'm glad that she seems to have avoided the traumas that many girls suffered on the streets of San Francisco that summer.*[3]

The journey was premised on the plan to eventually make it to Boston, sign on with a merchant ship, and sail to Norway. There my grandmother's family would welcome me as arranged. I'd pass the winter working at their printing shop in Skien. My idea was to join a group that would assemble in Sweden on a specific date the next summer. We'd buy Husqvarna motorcycles at the factory and tour Europe on them. It was a Husqvarna factory program in those days. This idea had its germination in the summer of 1970, at White Rock Motorcycle Park, when Claus Nielsen, the Husqvarna factory rider who had somehow ended up agreeing to help out Bill Monroe with the park. Claus was a typical Swede of the time, he loved using American swear words, "damn" being his favorite one. Claus' wife could have been a model and was more soft-spoken, but almost every time I saw her she would say of Bill Monroe, "I hate that man." I think Bill reneged on his deal with them as he did with me.

However, we had a love of the sport and international races to host. It was up to us to prepare the track and make it work in actuality. Claus also gave me a series of lectures about how I needed to get out and see the world. That is why I planned this trip. After that, I'd return home and re-enter college. None of that happened. I got to Boston, alright, but my passport had been stolen by a middle-aged Blackman in a suit and tie, which I had only passively noticed moving near me when he must have just finished going through my day pack as I dozed on the Greyhound. I was so innocent that I thought nothing of it at the time. I discovered that my day pack was empty later that night.

I can remember the sneer on his face as we both stood up to get off the bus. It puzzled me at the time. I only understood its hateful meaning later when I discovered a cheap camera, and my passport had been taken. The camera's film had recorded the only photo I ever would have had of my maternal grandmother in Pennsylvania. And now it was gone.

I don't blame all Black People for what that one man did. That would be Un-American. It has always been my habit to take people one by one. He puzzled me. He was dressed in a suit and looked respectable. As a result of my experience, I learned to be more careful, and I began to figure some things out for myself. Without my passport, there would be no trip on any ship. It required four months for a replacement, and that put the big kibosh on everything. I came home after a three-month multi-state visit to see relatives, including Cousin Sue's family in Wisconsin, Uncle Reg and Aunt Becky, plus Cousin Reg in Michigan. During that time, my folks had reunited after some negotiations. That didn't seem to change anything much, as far as I could tell.

But it was clear to me that it was time for me to be on my own. After my mishap in Boston, I flew home in a few hours. I was home just in time for Christmas. But the influence of Claus Nielsen remained with me all my life, until after an incident involving a drug gang ransacking my office in Santa Rosa, in Sonoma County, I found myself available for adventures. I contacted my alma mater and found an opportunity in Slovenia. I applied and won the position. I spent two years there and married my American girlfriend in an elaborate civil ceremony as the first American couple to be married in the Republic of Slovenia, at the eleventh-century castle at Lake Bled, Bled Grad, in April 1999. I only wish I could tell Claus about it. I don't know much about what became of Claus and Lilly after the White Rock fiasco. I must guess that Edison Dye, the main Husqvarna dealer and originator/promoter of the InterAm motocross events in La Mesa, California took care of them. The last time I saw them was in 1974 when I traveled south to Carlsbad, California to watch the first official FIM-sanctioned points-earning Motocross GP in the U.S. They were promoting Gatorade. Claus was still talking about building his big catamaran and sailing to Australia. In 2005, Carl Cranke told me that they had divorced. Carl and Claus had run a few long-distance races together and won. He told me of a Barstow to Vegas race where they teamed up. But I think that later on Claus sailed away for good.*₇

1973 arrived quickly. My Dad tried to make up for some things by helping me out a little in re-establishing myself. I spend a couple of months sporadically looking for work while visiting with friends and extended family friends. It was a busy social life in those days, and everyone loved to gather up and party at someone's house or another. At one of those parties, which happened to be at a house in Arden Park, I met a young lady who had attended Rio Americano High School, who I will call, Janey after the character in the Bob Seeger song. She was on that level that we often term "Super Model" today. I had met Janey and dated her until work took me out of Sacramento County for the summer. Almost simultaneous to meeting Janey, I found a job in Rancho Cordova one of the new industrial parks making stereo speakers for a still existing, high-end brand, ESS now located in Los Angeles. The factory was right across the street from where Penton West was located, which seems remarkable to me now. I dropped in to visit my old employer one day and reunited with Carl Cranke. He was in the market for speakers so I arranged a demo for him at his home in Placerville. That led to some years of occasional visits there until he moved to Washington State. I did not know then that I would follow him twenty years later, but I looked him up and we rekindled the friendship there. I made regular visits to Carl's place, which was an active "meeting place" for his many friends. I won't call it a "party house," because Carl was busy working at Penton West, and off, either riding at an event, or on one of his "Half Day Trials" out on the trails of El Dorado County, getting ready for one, testing a product for some company, or doing the occasional interview. But somehow, Carl had time to "have fun," and I was along for some of that "fun." It could be said that in those days, right up to the end, Carl possessed abundant energy for engagement.

A significant requirement for growing up is gaining a developed understanding of the world and one's relationship with it. I had to move on in order to grow up. I knew that. And I also knew that I had a lot to work out. These are some of the things I learned "growing up" so onward, as that is a constant, dynamic process we hopefully never complete.

Old and in the Way

I am an old man now. When you're old, you think about the past more often. When I was eighteen in 1970, and near graduation, I was at the top as far as my educational experience so far in life. I discovered forensics and public speaking due to the influence of a couple of my egg-head friends and found that I excelled in public speaking. It drove me to a new vision of my possible self as something beyond a motorcycle racer, eventually. I was on a casual visit to the then-popular Tower of Books,*[8] which was next to Tower of Records on Watt Ave, south of North Highlands, a few miles in the same strip mall as the famous Country Club Lanes bowling alley and final location of Sam's Hof Brau today.

Carl Lee Cranke – September 24, 1948 – November 14, 2020 – racing at the Third Annual Hangtown Motocross Event at Plymouth, Amador County, California, 1971
Photo – B. Greeves

That is where I found a little booklet by a philosopher titled "As a Man Thinketh," by a 19th-century philosopher named James Allen. This affecting short essay provides inspiration through simple, eloquent language without the complications and authoritarianism of religion. It encourages the idea that what we nurture in our thoughts is the cause of our experiences and that we have power over our thoughts if we only assert ourselves by will.

Cranke Bags 2 Placerville MX's

By Bruce Young

PLACERVILLE, CAL., July 4, 1971 — Heat reduced the effort by some, but Carl Cranke wasn't one of them today as he bagged two motocross overalls sponsored by the Placerville M.C.

His first overall came in the 250 combined Am-Ex. class with a runaway effort on his CZ in all three motos. Amateurs Mark LaRue (CZ) and Lonnie Forman (Hus) made valiant pursuit, but the nimble Expert was untouchable.

Not a major event, but a great personal memory – Cycle News – July 1971

One other simple point it made was that one can always change oneself; when my friend Davy wrote in my seventh-grade yearbook, "Past is past, but the future can be controlled," he was on to something. His words then probably caused me to pick up James Allen's little classic five years later. All that is required is the decision to change and the will to mean it. At the time, I understood it clearly because of my experience of racing motocross. It requires a particular type of self-control, clarity, and determination to rev up a two-wheeled machine, ready to charge "full bore" toward a narrowing lane that you know many others are making for and with a similar amount of commitment.

The rider is completely exposed and vulnerable. I was quick off the line, and by the autumn of 1970, I was enjoying many successes on the track and was often one of the first group of the pack to arrive first at the first turn if not first of all. But I never beat Carl to the first turn. By the summer of 1971, as an Amateur/Intermediate, I was on the starting line next to the remarkable Carl Cranke,*9 and right behind him on the track, learning quickly from the master by watching him choose lines.

I learned how to manage my racing by reading, listening, and experimenting. I managed the psychological aspect of competition thanks perhaps to my father who forced me to think for myself via chess so many years before, and Margaret, who showed me that I could memorize a famous speech, and analyze and repeat it dramatically. She proved to me that I had scope and possibilities. Eventually, this would take me beyond the race track, and North Highlands. But I had also learned early to avoid ideas and people who were set to manipulate or control my mind. "Bench Racing," was a realm my friends and I recognized and avoided.

It's not as if I did not make bad decisions at times or make mistakes,*[10] but I do feel that as I faced my forks in the road, with the occasional exception, I made the best choice I could, given my options, which were never ideal. But I never forgot the little book and its message. I still have it; it is displayed prominently on a bookcase in my home today. And it continued to prove correct; I put years of work into my studies and years of effort to learn the art and skill of fencing, all as part of the effort toward self-improvement, as imperfect as the result might be. That effort removed me far from my earlier self, and the limitations that were sure to hold me back and retain me as a low-income blue-collar employee of some better achieving blue-collar boss as just another cog on the wheel, another brick in the wall. However, in those early years, I carried just enough wisdom to survive the inevitable foolishness of young adulthood, so I never took a side trip into any corrective institution. The worst public disobedience I scored was a hitchhiking citation issued by an irate CHP in South Lake Tahoe because I failed to bow as he first drove past me as I stood by the old inspection station. I guess I had mistaken what I thought was a safe place for a car to pull over. I was in violation of something. I never have figured out what.

As it is, I reckon that I only really finished growing up after I finally was married in 1999 at forty-seven years of age. In my defense, I had been very careful about who I got involved with after a few bad experiences. I was determined to not end up divorced with children I could not visit, a common situation at the time. I was wise enough to avoid that unhappy situation, at least.

In 1973, I was still in the preliminaries. I knew I had a lot to work out and I was searching for the way, but I was also distracted by the times and ideas that I required fuller engagement knowing this was the only way to find out what a thing was all about. I like to think that I was "gathering intelligence." By April, the truck driving and religious plunge I took afterward lay ahead in the year. I was in the field with Janey, learning those "night moves." I'd go to her home, pick her up and drive all the way from American River Drive north up Watt Avenue to North Highlands, and the spot between the old Spook Tree and the railroad yard.

The year before, 1972, I had taken a job at Penton West when the Oregon and Southern California warehouses were centralized in Rancho Cordova. They needed a local guy to help set up and asked Gene in Loomis for a recommendation. And that's how I ended up there. Dave Duarte was already there as the road man, traveling to shops all throughout Penton West's huge territory. However, after the warehouse was set up and things began to settle down, there just wasn't enough work for me. Fred, the manager would lay me off on a Friday, and then call me Sunday night and rehire me. This went on for a few weeks. I told Bucky about the problem. He was assembling bikes at Vicker's Honda, which was on Fulton Avenue near Eddy's (restaurant), and Fulton was the region's exclusive "auto row," in those years. So I joined Dave at Vickers. The family was in crisis that year, and I grew restless. I left Vickers and sold my truck and bike, and went traveling. By the start of 1973, I was back and looking for work. That's when I simultaneously met Janey and started at ESS. Before 1973 and ESS, I had taken my ill-fated, interrupted year-long road trip that terminated early in Boston. The best part of that journey had been meeting my relatives in Wisconsin and Upper Michigan and seeing Cousin Sue again.

I was able to visit the farmhouse where my grandfather had been born, the little house in Oshkosh where my parents had lived with my father's Cousin Floyd and his wife, and where I shared a baby crib with my cousin Deedee until we made the trek to California. Near old Bundy Hill, just south of Jackson, I stayed with my Uncle Reg and Aunt Becky for a couple weeks. While there, I was "taken" on a date by my Cousin Reg's friend, Lisa. I accompanied her one day at her job as a substitute teacher, where I met her friend, Eric. Eric was very friendly, and soon we were off together as a couple of tomcats running up and down a straight stretch of highway outside of Jackson locals termed "The Zip Strip."

As an odd disruption of my mundane travel style, Eric suggested that I try the rails to get to my next destination which was Harrisburg, Pennsylvania, from where I planned to take a bus up into the northeastern Appalachian coal-mining region of that state where my mother had grown up to visit my grandmother and other family members there. Eric showed me where to get on and even dropped me off near the "jump point" on the day of my departure. It was a lonely, cold, and wet trip. Even the bums knew better than to ride that time of year. I passed a miserable twenty-four hours pretending it was romantic despite the reality of it. I got lost trying to find my way out of the yard in Harrisburg. I went back to riding the Greyhound after that. Strangely, the first song I heard in the bus station in Harrisburg was a new one, "City of New Orleans." It became my favorite right into 1973. "Good morning America, how are you" became a national slogan. It even provided the title for a morning news show that is still being broadcast as of this time. In Pennsylvania, I was passed around until I finally realized that the only way for me was to go back home. It was my hair length that did it. So the song with the haunting theme matched my mood at the time. I began to wonder if I was a stranger in my own country.

The Exploding Railroad Blues

The dramatic end of a humble 19th-century farm town on a modern railroad line. One of the explosions at the Roseville Railroad Yard on April 28, 1973 – Center for Sacramento History – Sacramento Bee Collection

Suddenly, on Saturday, April 28, 1973, reality changed. I had come to work overtime due to the orders pouring into ESS at the time, interestingly, mostly from Japan. Even though we had our saws and nail guns actively engaged, we heard distant booms. The strange noise caused us to stop working and go outside to determine the nature of what we were hearing. We were hearing railcars exploding in the Roseville Switching Yard. In moments, the Old Antelope Store was gone along with several other structures. Windows blew out of homes up to a mile away. People were knocked off of their feet. A general alarm went out, and all the nearby districts, Citrus Heights, Foothill Farms, and North Highlands, were ordered evacuated.

A call came into the office, and the message was brought to me. Martine had called to say for me to go to her house in Arden Park rather than go back to North Highlands when I finished my day at work as it was evacuated under an emergency order. Going home that night was a strange feeling, but since our home had not been damaged, it was not traumatic beyond the knowledge and view that we saw on the news reports and saw in person when we went out to the site itself. The feeling of loss at seeing the vacancy where the Antelope Store had been felt similar to the way I felt when I had looked out to locate the Spook Tree and found it missing years before. It was a feeling of the loss of an irretrievable past. I have that feeling every day now.

The first thought for many must have been that some radical group had bombed the railroad switching yard. However, it was hard to imagine that actually happening as it was not easy to get into that switching yard undetected. That would have required quite a plot. We eventually learned that the cause was that the brakes of the cars had heated up so much on the downhill grade coming off the Sierras as a load of ordinance bound for Vietnam in one car had been ignited when the wooden floor of the car caught fire in a freak accident or twist of fate. A taste of that war had come to the oldest settlement of the former Rancho Del Paso and left its mark.

There were 7,000 two hundred and fifty-pound bombs in those boxcars. Not all of them exploded. During the rebuilding of the railyard, hundreds of pieces of the ordinance were hauled away. But some were not found until years later. When that later find was announced, it caused an understandable bit of local panic.

There are a plethora of personal stories available about how the event affected people in the area. The blast effect reached ten miles in some cases. People were knocked over, and thrown across rooms. Windows were shattered. Antelope itself was reduced to rubble. Amazingly, no one was killed, but three hundred and fifty people showed up at the Roseville and Mercy San Juan Hospitals, the Kaiser Permanente Center in North Sacramento, and the Twin Lakes Hospital in Folsom. If those boxcars had gone off just a day before when work crews were active, there would undoubtedly have been multitudes of dead and injured in addition to the costly destruction and the loss of the oldest township outside of Sacramento City.

Governor Reagan declared a state of emergency in Sacramento and Placer Counties, but by Monday following the Saturday event the State Office of Emergency was asking for a federal disaster area designation because Southern Pacific Company was paying for damages in the area. Southern Pacific established a special claims office in Roseville to pay displacement and repair costs to affected property owners. The most affected neighborhoods were the southwest corner of Roseville, the northern part of Citrus Heights, Hillsdale, and Antelope. I believe most of North Highlands got off with mere evacuation and window-rattling because the rise of land that Hillsdale Elementary School sits on protected it which ran out to U Street to the spot I had parked with Janey. I was able to come home by Saturday evening. Many others were not that lucky.

The National Guard was deployed and heavy forces of Sheriff Deputies were patrolling for possible looting. Some arrests were made as plate windows had been blown out of many businesses along Auburn Boulevard. Many returning home faced loss and difficulties; 400 homes had glass blown out of them and damaged door frames. Altogether, around 5,500 structures were damaged. Many homes had been tagged by building inspectors urging residents to not turn on their electricity until they had been inspected. All the homes in the area were serviced by gas lines. The stores along Auburn Boulevard from the county line to the Arlington Heights shopping center suffered cracked plate glass and had to operate with them boarded up for some time because of the backlog that was created. Fires flared up in the neighborhood closest to the railyard, the Grand Oaks neighborhood, as falling debris from the explosions landed on homes and property. In the yard, Earl Grundy and Steve Rodgers at the Antelope station of the Citrus Heights Fire District had just left their trailer quarters on the first dispatch of the fire when their trailer was flattened by an explosion. In a nearby trailer was Grundy's wife, Kathy, who was six months pregnant. She fell through the new hole in the floor when an explosion demolished her trailer moments later, cutting her foot badly. She was treated at Kaiser and released. In all, eight fire and rescue units were deployed while Sacramento and

Roseville police directed the evacuation from unsafe "off-limits" areas, and medical units from McClelland AFB and the Sacramento Army Depot's radio network assisted with dispatching.

The disaster created problems for over 250 people who had no relatives to go to. Several public schools including San Juan High School were opened up. Food donations immediately arrived along with bedding, clothing, and other necessary items mostly with the help of the Red Cross. Citizen Ban "Ham" radio operators coordinated and aided families searching for missing members. The command center was set up on the land owned by Fred Rusch was 92, but able to go visit friends in Auburn so that authorities could use his 1914 constructed home. The land next to his home became Rusch Park.

The cause of the brake heat that had started the fire was located. To prevent another such fire, metal shields and non-sparking brake shoes were installed on all boxcars. Paying for the damage would require decades. A school chum worked at that Southern Pacific Switching Yard until retirement. "Sufferin' Pacific" was the popular term for the company, according to him. It must have been quite an extended recovery for SP, financially speaking. The rebuilding of the railyard alone was astronomical. A railroad employee said that a set of wheels from a boxcar weighing more than a ton was hurled 100 feet in the air and fell near where he was working. After a helicopter inspection of the destroyed railyard, Sacramento County sheriff Duane Lowe said that it was "a mass of craters and twisted debris" which "looks like a hydrogen bomb might have been dropped in the middle of it."

During May after the explosion, Janey and I had passed a late night hardly a stone's throw from the railyard, working on our "night moves" while listening to Fleetwood Mac's "Then Play On" on my tape deck. I remember that I commented to Janey how much Peter Green's acoustic in "Oh, Well," sounded like the lament after a nuclear war.

Aftermath
Copyright – California Governor's Office of Emergency Services. Creative Commons
- Attribution 3.0 Unported (CC BY 3.0)

I didn't know why I felt so compelled to play that song while we were there; the impact of the event affected me less at the time than later as I listened to the tragic music that might have been composed for this very event's aftermath. At the same time, I had come to realize that it was time for me to get out on my own and learn to be a man. My initiation was soon to come.

My last date with Janey was with a couple of friends to the now legendary June 2nd, 1973, Led Zeppelin concert at Kezar Stadium in San Francisco's Golden Gate Park that led to the city banning all rock concerts in the park for twenty years. I worked at the next concert allowed in the park as a volunteer with Rock Medicine in 1987. Ironically, it was the 20th anniversary of the Summer of Love event in the Polo Field. After the 1973 event, I immediately joined my brother-in-law, his younger uncle, and an old buddy, all Vietnam Vets, on a venture hatched by his much older brother. It was more a scheme for making money trucking produce from the San Joaquin Valley fields to the canneries in Oakland and San Jose that summer.

I didn't call Janey until about six months later after making some life adjustments recovering from the truck driving episode and an interlude with what I will call intense Bible study. Her mother told me that she met and married a Hollywood film director. Good for her. I am sure she was up to the challenge. Anyway, I hope she has survived and is doing well now. Why she was interested in me, I'll never know for sure, but it must have been my racing reputation. She had been to a couple of races, and I did have a name locally, at least, among some of that crowd. It was in her company that I spent my last days living in North Highlands, parked in the field that I used to stare across as a ten-year-old from Hillsdale School, in a version of what Bob Seger reminisced about in "Night Moves." That field had just been started in development. The roadways had been plotted and bulldozed but were still of dirt. I drove us up one of them to the highest point in that field, within sight of the railyard and a long stone's throw from old Antelope. We had visited that spot before and after the big event. It was always night time or we would have seen the mess. The site of the Old Spook Tree was off in the opposite direction. We were parked between them. All I would say to her now, wherever she might be, is "thanks for the memories."

I left my home, my job at the stereo factory, and a beautiful girl to make "big money" driving an eighteen-wheeler pulling doubles. The whole thing turned out to be a fiasco. We were scammed coming and going, and I almost got killed several times, driving the junky truck that my dear brother-in-law's older brother had assigned to me as the "least valuable" member of the bunch, I suppose. It was marginally hip, to be a truck driver, I suppose, as a couple local bands, such as The New Riders of the Purple Sage, and Commander Cody and His Lost Planet Airmen had taken up doing covers and original truck driving songs. Country Rock was cool, including remakes and new songs about truck driving.

Even my brother-in-law's surname was the same as the title of one of the then-popular songs. But I can testify that it was anything but cool. In fact, it was hot, damned hot, and damned dangerous. If it was 90 degrees outside, it was ten degrees higher in my rig, which had no firewall between me and the engine. In fact, it was so bad that the rivets on the engine cover were mostly gone, allowing a view of the engine as the sheet metal vibrated and flexed, and of course, the heat and fumes came straight up as we all know how heat rises. The zenith of the entire experience was when my dear brother-in-law offered me to drive his sleeper cab-over tractor after his nephew blew up my truck on a short run a couple days earlier after he heard the sandwich truck girl tell me to give her a call as she'd like to go on a run with me and hand me her phone number.

I'm glad I didn't call her. It seemed wrong to have done it anyway. But if she had been there, who knows what would have happened. This was because my brother-in-law had not told me that he had adjusted his brakes higher than the trailer, something we had been told not to do. So when I was coming down the two-lane Pacheco Pass grade, which twisted and turned steeply around midnight in the fog, I found my brakes fading fast. I looked in the rearview mirror and saw smoke billowing behind the tractor like the smoke from an old steam locomotive. My racing experience probably saved me by allowing me to keep calm and think of what to do. I was considering rubbing the truck against the sheer earth wall on the passenger side of the canyon to slow me down when the fog cleared enough on the only spot where there was a pullout on that mountainside. I stood on the double foot brake pad and whipped the heavy truck around and onto the dirt lot, just under rollover speed. That was the end of my day. I grabbed a couple tomatoes out of the giant bin on the nearest double trailer and ate my dinner. I then settled into the sleeper and forgot about it - what fun!

That was not the only risky event, but I somehow survived, and by August, had my old job back at the stereo factory, and a Class A license that I would never use again. That is when Rick and I decided to move out of home and become roommates in a tiny old farmhouse that a friend of his family-owned out just off Edison Avenue near Mira Loma High School, but out of North Highlands for good. I think it had been built in the 1930s at the latest. But it was quaint and had enough land for us to have four chickens. It seemed appropriate since there was a little farm next to us and a horse stable up the road around the corner in those days. There I was, playing out some of that P Street Kid stuff, but Rick was fine with it. In fact, he played along, coming up with the connection for the hens via his mother's friends in Rio Linda. I also took him to Coloma in January for the Gold Rush Celebration in 1974. We camped there for the whole weekend.

The War Against North Highlands Goes On

As I made this move, I knew it was the end of some things and the beginning of my journey into an unknown future without the training wheels I admit that I had relied upon up to 1972. By then, sadly, North Highlands had changed from a quiet little suburb of church-going working families to a district that had been wracked by riots and the kind of crime that evolves in the wake of such unrest.

Those perpetrating the "war on North Highlands" were not finished. Area schools were targeted by arsonists. On October 13th, a Sunday morning fire broke out at the Woodridge School in the Hillsdale area on Brett Drive. Seventy-five firemen fought to save the school. They came from the North Highlands, Citrus Heights, and Rio Linda districts. The damage there was around one million dollars and displaced 400 students. Next, Village Elementary, where I had attended kindergarten through the fourth grade had its library destroyed in an arson fire on December 14th, the same year.

The total damage there would cost $172,000.00 to repair. Then, Sierra View Elementary saw $3,500.00 in damage, and the Allison Elementary school fire total was likely around that figure. Finally, the arsonists set fire to the Highlands High School Band Room, causing $183,000.00 in damage. From what I've gathered the marching band never quite recovered. Whatever party or parties perpetrated these horrible acts, I'm sure they weren't thinking about their futures, too much, or the kind of world they want to live in. The 1973 Railyard Explosions seemed somehow part of it all.

The trouble at the parks remained an issue throughout the seventies. Memorial Park, which was established in 1965, the same year as The Spook Tree was removed from the grounds of the new elementary school being built next to the new Memorial Park, saw the same problems as Larchmont Park by 1972. In August of 1978, alcohol was banned from the local parks. But by October, a new wave of complaints grew out of ongoing activities at Memorial Park. Noise, drug use, drinking, foul language, and lewd behavior were the major complaints. A uniform park curfew was suggested and a petition was circulated. It was said that 95% of residents favored the idea. The move was resisted by Mary Morgan, who served as chairwoman of the NHRPD board said that a 9:00 PM curfew would be hard to enforce. There is no evidence found that any curfew ever was established or that parties ever refrained from drinking at the parks. "Neighbors become so sick and tired of the conditions but they are forced to ignore them," a sheriff's deputy said at the meeting "This leads to passive acceptance of the unacceptable." Sheriff's Deputy and Highway Patrol presence was increased at the problematic parks. Also in that year, forty citizens of North Highlands picketed the complex of porn shops at the intersection of Roseville Road and Watt Avenue where Cycle Speed had been relocated before it closed. It had become known as "Porno Corner."

Today, they'd be laughed off as "church ladies." But sometimes, the Church Ladies are right. The movement spoke on radio KBFK. But the county superior court ruled in favor of the owner of the businesses on First Amendment principles put forward so cleverly by a lawyer representing the ACLU. , Jim Tucker. "Nobody's forcing anyone to pick up an adult book or go into the movie." He added, "What they are trying to do is force their views on what is proper and improper on everyone else." Today, we're swimming in the same stuff, up to our necks.

The North Highlands committee claimed that the porn complex had hurt property values and the community image. Other businesses at that location had been forced to move at a loss because patrons were embarrassed to be seen in the area. They suffered a double whammy when Don Green, a lobbyist for the California Attorneys for Criminal Justice implied that there was no concern because "pornography was being well controlled at the state level." As far as the records this author reviewed go, there was no challenge to this ridiculous statement. This was the era of topless bars, and "Deepthroat." Many adults, including my parents, snuck to San Francisco to see it. Many of the then adult population patronized topless bars beginning with North Beach in San Francisco, (where Carol Doda made it famous at The Condor Club) so the trend grew and was filled in with the other former "port of call" vices that North Highlands was forced to suffer as a military town became an every town commonality. And the women who danced in those places were their "neighbor's children." These were the same people who went to those churches; "Harper Valley PTA," indeed.

The Other Side of the Tracks

These events, conditions, and decisions resulted in owners of businesses in North Highlands and higher-income people, including some members of the community's governing bodies, such as community administrators, teachers, and park district leaders, moving out of North Highlands. One member of the Recreation and Parks District had never lived there at all. This was compounded by developers' refusal to build better housing, so as some people's income increased, they would move into better homes and out of North Highlands. Moreover, more of the homes in North Highlands became rental properties. Renters usually do not take as much pride in their homes, and landlords often, especially in those days, were less responsive to the complaints and needs for repairs than getting the rental payments from their tenants on time. The reason North Highlands became one of the first examples of a suburban ghetto conversion was that over half of the homes became rentals fairly quickly. So today, North Highlands is still struggling with a four times higher crime rate than the average in Sacramento County. It is a place where many residents tend to live temporarily until they can afford to buy a home somewhere else. This harms community cohesion, obviously. But there is more to it than this, as any community has more than one issue.

The efforts of the best-intentioned citizens of North Highlands were simply steamrolled by the times. After the burning of the band room at Highlands High, the band never seemed to recover. On December 17, 1980, the community newspaper, The Green Sheet, ceased production. North Highlands was left to wander in the dark. Still, the valiant of the community soldiered on. In 1981, Highlands High School principal George Porter reported to Community Quipa that he has been successful in getting students, "out of the halls, cars, and convenience stores, and back into the classrooms where they belong." That's a generation of lost youth that grew up and had children in their turn. By the end of the 20th century, North Highlands had undergone a facelift, with the Town Center Mall renovated, and a new coat of paint on the community center. They were looking at reviving the Moonwalk Festival. By then, the cyber universe was opening up and no community would be able to resist its lure and pitfalls. Today, the problems that faced North Highlands then have over time become the common denominator nationally on a scale no one except, perhaps, Aldous Huxley and Isaac Asimov could have predicted.

The phony angst at Highlands High School may have had its root in "The Blackboard Jungle" and "Rebel Without a Cause," which goes back to those "huddled masses" on Ellis Island and the Gangs of New York lore revision by Hollywood. But it took the Bolsheviks and Neo-Marxists exploiting the power of race and sex for destroying American, Western society. The tragedy of North Highlands was the success of this overarching strategy. By July of 1973, my solution was to get away. Rick and I moved in together at a little old farmhouse near Mira Loma High School, that a friend of Rick's mother owned. The world was calling, and I was off. I left behind a North Highlands in decline. But the worst was still ahead for the beleaguered suburb. And it seems the problems have remained right up to the present.

By 1970, Martine was working for a senator at the State Capital.

Knowing that I was already a collector of information, she offered me a copy of the Senate Fact-Finding Subcommittee on Un-American Activities, 15th Report. I have found it useful as a historical document since becoming more interested in the roots of our present-day issues. In their conclusion of the Students for a Democratic Society, the last paragraph stands out as a sadly prophetic query of college and high school administration; "With all of the available knowledge about the true character and activities of SDS and the two factions (Weathermen, Socialist Workers Party), it seems utterly incomprehensible to us that university administrations and the heads of high schools, junior colleges, and State colleges should continue to afford official recognition and status to this organization, provide State-owned facilities at taxpayers expense, while SDS goes about its business of revolution and its activities in disrupting the campus, blowing up its buildings, terrorizing students who presume to disagree with its principles and propaganda and arrogantly defying all authority."

Even if some in North Highlands were merely aping the outright violence occurring on high school campuses in Southern California in 1969, the destruction found its way to Highlands High School and the community. The effect of it remains today, not just in North Highlands, but everywhere.

Lately, in keeping with the national trend for self-loathing and Leftist annihilation of history, there have been discussions about Camp Kohler, for example. An expression of it appeared in the local online bulletin board where one resident spoke of how Kohler Elementary School should be renamed. I saw another online post by a young woman living in Foothill Farms who was shocked to find there had been a "concentration camp" right "over the fence" from where she lived. All of the misinformation and misrepresentation of history must not go unanswered. For that reason, and for the sake of historical accuracy, clarity, and continuity with the line of this story, we return to Camp Kohler.

Camp Kohler Revisited

T he symptoms of infantilization*₁ have seen a plethora of manifestations over the past forty years or so on their way to the present building crescendo. One of the minor issues that entangle this history would be the idealizing of fond childhood reminiscences and local history, so it must be addressed within the actual local historical experience. We can think of it as the guileless observations that fell under the view of our Spook Tree as a sentinel on the scene, finally given a voice.

It is merely the march of history that found the old railroad signal station of Walerga becoming a U.S. Army Signals Corps Training Station as part of the greater Western Signal Corps School and intelligence operations on the West Coast during the War. That old signal station along the first line of tracks of the Transcontinental Railroad had served a growing nation since the railroad's very start. The training programs at Camp Kohler were of utmost importance during the war.

It was not exactly comfortable, either. Soldiers in training lived in pup tents regardless of weather conditions or time of year.

Whether they were Japanese, German, or Italian, the internment of any citizen, the decision was made by a Democrat president whose wife was an active advocate for civil rights during all of her life. Was it a lack of imagination or the influence of ideas from the then very active Communist Party USA? The fact is that Franklin and Eleanor Roosevelt's son James was an open supporter of communism.*[2] But FDR understood that war was coming and he was still a patriot with a long list of problems to address from 1933 on. Today, we have homeless camps and a kind of tyranny caused by neglect that is reminiscent of the Dust Bowl Refugees of the Great Depression. I'd argue that the Japanese Internment was more humane than the conditions tolerated and even approved of in many cities headed by Democrats that typically abuse history to accuse others.

The popular mode is to claim the internment of Japanese citizens is a replication of Nazi-like behavior. The use of internment camps by Stalin, Mao, and other communist regimes far outstrips the activities of the Nazis, even if we only examine the Soviets during the same thirteen years that the Third Reich existed and limit it to that. Contrary to belief, the persecution of Jews in the U.S.S.R. was vigorous if not to the extremes of Nazi Germany. They shared an undertow of the inherent intolerance of Christianity in common that had relied on Anti-Semitism since the New Testament's formalization in 325 CE. During the 1930s, Stalin had twenty million Soviet citizens put to death and an even larger number interned in Siberia. Therefore, it is not a stretch to see the tendency toward incarceration based on race and ethnicity in America as influenced by communism, especially since the Soviets and communism had so many collaborators in the U.S. government, even among a couple of presidential family circles during the critical years of 1922 to 1970.*[3]

My preference would have required all concerned groups to take the same test or interview they took once they were interned before they were taken away from their homes. But one must consider the time and personnel required while the nation was ramping up for world war and 40,000 Japanese agents loose in America would still be a potential problem and could have done an enormous amount of damage while evading the examiners. That same 40,000 could have evaded the test and gone into "hiding." The government must have had some cause to believe that a fairly large number of dangerous persons were hidden among the 120,000, and they turned out to be right. In the end, taking the situation out of its historical context is hypocritical.

The war years were a period of discomfort for just about everyone. According to historians like Carroll Quigley (Tragedy and Hope), the vast majority of the over fifty million people who died during World War Two were civilians and suffered horrible deaths. Current estimates are sixty to seventy million total deaths in World War Two, most of them civilians. The vast majority of those deaths were not in North America or North or South Americans. They were, in fact, mostly Russians or citizens of the Soviet Union.*₄ In WW2, one of every three dead was Russian. That number has increased since the collapse of the Soviet Union when more archives became available to Western researchers. The number of Jewish exterminated during the Holocaust went up by one to two million, as well.

Aside from these deaths, many times more lives were interrupted, and many a young man was drafted into service and thereby obliged to put off his life plans and sometimes forfeit his life altogether. Families were permanently impacted, and society changed abruptly, and not always for the better. The Zoot Suit Riots in Los Angeles and San Diego resulted from direct harassment and violence toward civilians and sailors by gangs that included draft dodgers and Pachucos.*₅ All over the U.S., populations were moved to industrial cities for war production. It was a national emergency. Any history that reviews the internment of Japanese citizens and omits this information is not history. It is propaganda intended to stir resentment and guilt to cause harm. That is the plan of the enemies of freedom.

During my time in North Highlands, it was rare to hear anything about Camp Kohler. When it was discussed, it was in a practical sense among adults. The camp's sewage treatment facility had treated all of the wastewater from McClellan AFB and North Highlands, including Larchmont Village and Foothill Farms. In 1959, the federal government released all interest in it. The initial $128,770.00 the federal government had spent to build the treatment plant required another $500,000.00 investment from developers over time as it was expanded to serve the expanding community. The county got a free lease for processing McClellan's wastewater at no charge. It was demolished in 1972.

To us as kids, it was a place of mystery and fascination, but not much information. This was probably because people either did not know or were just too busy. But I believe that it was also because no one involved had made an issue, including the former Japanese interned. (My mother's supervisors at McClellan AFB were a Japanese American man named Yozo, a German man named Heinrich, and a Mormon man named Jensen). Camp Kohler was there, and the laundry, at least, was still being used by McClelland AFB. One of the first elementary schools was Kohler Elementary. We kids knew about it, and so we had the rumors of Lead Hill and the firing range, the strange white structure at the T intersection of M Street and Walerga, and so on. In those days, the war felt near, like it was just finished. And that was true; I had been born only seven years after that war had ended, during the Korean War.

It required the emergence of a social justice industry that recreated a version of a new traveling inquisition. That social justice system was aimed at reviewing the sins they now alleged, confident in applying a remedy by setting a big, "Scarlet R" on the body of the white race, forever, or at least, or at least long enough to subvert society and make way for a new "order." The propaganda lately claims that many Japanese internees died due to the conditions. If this is true, no records and not even Reeves discussed it.

It is useful to note here that where German internees were concerned, of the 16,440 that were interned, one hundred were given jail sentences for convictions in court that totaled 1,880 years. By 1943, six more had been executed by court decision. The reason that this occurred might be because of the old history of Germans in America and therefore comparatively open entry for patriots of German background as witnesses willing to not just fight against Germany (in two wars), but give evidence against German U.S. citizens engaged in subterfuge of various sorts, compared to the far more brief period for Japanese assimilation combined with the closed nature of the Japanese culture inside of the U.S., as a general cultural characteristic. It required the interment for the splintering of the Japanese community into loyalties that could be identified.

The camp's use as an assembly center for carrying out a federal mandate is not a cause for shame for Camp Kohler, the Western Signal Corps School, Lieutenant Fredrick Kohler for whom the camp was named, or North Highlands and Foothill Farms. Both names should be held up in honor wherever it is applied today unless we plan to label the U.S. efforts in WW2 racist and a series of war crimes. Such terms could only be possible after all memory has been erased. No serious person could claim this, and certainly, no true historian would.

To examine the issue, I selected perhaps the most accusatory publication on the subject published at the height of the renewal of grievances already processed during the sixties and seventies. This and now other already addressed historical issues are being revived for the sake of their usefulness to the social justice industry during the years from 2008 to the present, where they have finally provoked a national existential crisis. This might be one of the earlier entries in what is now known as "Cancel Culture," where new political and racial capital is created through historical revisionism. Revisionism has operated as a political mechanism wherein gains, often realized as actual monetary payouts and even government grants and boons, etc., are obtained through branding one group as exclusively guilty for events whose social memory has faded just enough to allow the "plausible deniability" of history for recycling as new grievances. That book is the work of Richard Reeves, ironically titled "Infamy."

Note that as a result of the activism of the 1970s and 80s, reparations were made in the form of cash payouts to all Japanese Americans that had been interred during the war. Regardless of whether they had owned any property or business, this was done uniformly were adults or children. So what would be the motivation for reviving the issue in the 2000s?

Yes, the words of President Roosevelt are usurped as the title. They mock while they cancel all the suffering of American soldiers and citizens at Pearl Harbor, with an assertion that nothing between December 7, 1941, and August 15, 1945, could rise to compare with the abuses heaped upon the 120,000 ethnic Japanese interned in relocation camps during the war. Please note that very few of the additional 120,000 Japanese living in Hawaii were ever interned, but joined in support of the United States actively. They were so angry with the Japanese attack on Hawaii that they changed the signage on their businesses and homes to English with no trace of Japanese almost the next day. They were vigorous in their contributions to the war effort on many levels.

As I dug through Reeve's book, I found it straining to establish this picture. It succeeds, but only by isolating it so vigorously as to present it in a historical vacuum. I found the story's main thread to be not of cruelty but a witness to the overarching kindness of both the Internees and the Interred, one toward another. Yes, many were inconvenienced. We note that all wars and this one significantly interrupted many lives, some permanently. No one in those camps was tortured or executed. They were left alone to govern themselves from the moment they were assembled, and that is how it was at Camp Kohler for the approximately 5,000 that were gathered up there.

There was no abuse of the Japanese detainees by military personnel during the internment. Every effort was made to see to it they had recreation and entertainment, cinemas and canteens, and even libraries and schools for not just the children, but adults. And not one Japanese person was forced to work for the government or private industry as the Axis powers did universally and with massive, genocidal extremes during WW2.

Prisoners of War, on the other hand, were made to work. There were a few German prisoners of war working at Camp Kohler. On July 13, 1945, Georg Gerst, 25 years old, and POW, was temporarily at camp Kohler as a work detail summoned from the Stockton, California Prisoner of War Camp. On July 17, he was spotted by some boys aged seven to ten, who pretended to be playing within view of the escapee. They went straight to the police station in Roseville. Captain Joseph Zanolio contacted Camp Kohler and the FBI. The Army Air Force at McClellan sent a detail of thirty-five soldiers to find him. He did not resist arrest, as he was corralled while he was shaving at the bottom of Dry Creek.

Much has been made in various books about the camps' poor construction, food shortages, and the lack of various materials. But as one might review the worst claims of atrocities, they might have missed a literal world of mitigating information. Food shortages were universal during World War Two. Many in the wider world died of starvation, tens of millions, in fact. The Japanese government and military violated many Geneva Convention mandates and starved prisoners of war to death. The ethnic Japanese in the camps were never forced to do any work beyond taking care of themselves. In the U.S., everyone was issued food and fuel rationing cards. Anyone who committed fraud was prosecuted. Kids were involved in rubber and metal drives, and many valuable possessions and keepsakes were sacrificed for the war effort. If your whatchamacallit broke, you would probably have to do without it and wait until the war was over for a replacement. Many citizens remained at home or near home for the duration of the war. Most people worked long hours. The omissions regarding Camp Kohler are around the fact that even Camp Kohler's buildings, which the military used for work and rest everywhere, were built the same way. They were constructed of wood frames with tarpaper walls and metal roofs. After the Internees were moved out for the permanent Tule Lake camp in Modoc County, the buildings were inhabited by U.S. Army personnel as they trained there through the war's remainder.

Shortages of food and other articles were occurring all over the country. Whites suffered shortages and deprivations along with everyone else. New dormitories for recently arrived workers from the South and other places in industrial zones were built the same way as Camp Kohler's buildings. They were substandard uniformly because the nation was in an emergency, so they were hastily approved for use as the basic shelter for all temporary structures. One claim I read with disbelief concerned the obligation of detainees to use outhouses as if it were an outrage of inhumanity. My mother had used an outhouse as a child right up until she left to work in Washington, D.C., during the war. She was from Wilkes-Barre, Pennsylvania, and that had been the norm throughout less developed towns and rural locations since White settlements had existed in North America. Whites who had to live in the same sort of quickly-built habitations just did it. Nonwhites, such as the blacks in Detroit who had been shipped there for war production work, rioted several times during the war. The modern claim is that it was due to the terrible buildings they were forced to live in. Other reports say that the first riot erupted when Whites retaliated for vulgar advances toward local white women and an actual incident of sexual violence.

Once again, context defuses the claim. During the Great Depression, almost up to the outbreak of World War Two, there were camps for whites. Far more than 120,000 were "interned" in them. That is an exaggeration; they were free to go – if they wanted to starve. These were the CCC; Civilian Conservation Corps camps. Tens of thousands of young men labored ten to twelve hours a day on public projects, many in the national forests and dangerous, and lives were lost. Just as with building the Golden Gate Bridge in that same period, the work open to whites by the government was risky, and men were killed and maimed. They lived in huts and used outhouses. Most will not recall the "Hooverville's" of whites camped out because they had lost their homes and livelihoods while Japanese farmers prospered. Still fewer will remember the 1932 bonus army of white World War One veterans and their families. They were charged by saber-wielding cavalry of the U.S. Army and shot during the summer of 1932 when they gathered in

Washington, DC, to demand the remuneration of certificates they were issued in lieu of cash in 1924, as war vets. They were over 40,000 people there, 17,000 vets, and their families; they were out of work, and they were starving. Meanwhile, other whites were migrating from the Dust Bowl to work in conditions in California far worse than those slaves experienced in the Antebellum South.*₆ But there is a more significant, far more compelling piece of factual record that even the most critical publications could not ignore, and it is in Reeves' book. This issue is that of the 120,000 total Japanese detained during the war, one-third of them, or 40,000, were loyal to Japan. Reeves attempts to infer that the written tests given to determine loyalty were somehow rigged, but no explanation of how that was tricky or unfair to do is provided. Those loyal to Japan made no secret of it. And they fought against, that is to say, attacked the loyal American Japanese at the camps where they were located.

It was not a sport; the Japanese loyalists viciously attacked the Japanese loyal to America, sometimes, in the dead of night. Loyalty had been determined by questionnaires, which, contrary to the complaint Reeves attempts to lodge, were a series of simple questions that anyone could have lied about by checking the box or writing the best lie. 40,000 did not want to do that as they considered it dishonorable to deny Japan. They formed into a gang with names like Black Dragons and Kibei groups, who were young adults who had as children been sent by their parents to Japan to be "educated." So, 40,000 admitted their loyalty to Japan, and just about that amount were not U.S. citizens. The worst ones were shipped to Fort Sill in Oklahoma. There were a couple of deaths by guards there, but it is not as if they were guards' victims, but looking to escape or otherwise cause chaos. Some expressions of anger and hate were initially by some of the public and guards later at the camps, but no outright murder or atrocities. Those 40,000 were distributed among camps.

Yet Reeves revels in using the term, "Concentration Camps" because that term had been used sometimes as interchangeable with "Relocation Centers," etc., knowing the weight the word would carry with the post-war, post-sixties generations of increasingly indoctrinated youth, including the children and grandchildren of the detainees.   They, with the American public, were reminded continuously of German atrocities during the war, but not Japanese ones. In his introduction, Reeves admits that the post-sixties civil rights movement influenced the detainees' children and grandchildren. The latter were encouraged to replicate their version of the Marxist-influenced Civil Rights Movement,*W unaware of the disunity and Machiavellian exercise they had been enlisted to perform, masquerading as social justice. Eventually, all are exposed as "useful idiots," puppets of the Marxist masters, and as such removed and eliminated.*₇ In the meantime, they are used to create division in America, becoming what their parents strove so diligently to disprove.

At Tule Lake, those loyal to Japan were a large enough group that when they rioted, meaning they attacked loyal Americans of Japanese ethnicity, only U.S. Army tanks and tear gas could stop the fighting.

Think about it.

If there had been no internment, one-third of the 120,000 Japanese detained at camps, 40,000 people, would have been free agents inside the U.S. They would have been free to spy, sabotage, and otherwise undermine the U.S. war effort. What if they had learned of the Navajo Code Talkers and informed the Japanese military?

Many now forget, if they ever knew, how fanatical the Japanese Empire was up to and through the Second World War. Today, many today know nothing or little about it but are fed, from time to time, a new version of the Internment. By design, whites fret about any appearance of prejudice and racism, while even today, many Japanese view marriage with a non-Japanese as a betrayal and an anti-Japanese deed. In Japan today, most neighborhoods do not welcome non-Japanese or mixed residents. The much-celebrated 442nd Regimental Combat Team fought whites in Europe. The 6,000 translators used in the Pacific did not have to face one person of Japanese ethnicity as a foe.

White Privilege – Christmas Dinner during the Great Depression
photo – Dorothea Lange

At the same time, those of European ancestry were obligated to fight, often knowing the city or town they were blowing to bits was the one their grandparents had lived in before coming to America.   The true test of loyalty would have been to land them on an island like Iwo Jima or Tarawa and see if they were as loyal as the white Americans who were killing hundreds of thousands of white Europeans at the time. Such present guilt mongers should remember that Japan had deemed itself racially superior to all peoples and arrogated the idea that Japan should control all of the Eastern Pacific and Asia, including Hawaii. It was they who believed the destiny of their race was to rule inferiors. They allied with Nazi Germany, which had the same view. Thankfully, we never got to see how they would sort out the final question of whether the Germans or the Japanese should rule the world entirely.

Japanese American Couple at the Walerga Barracks – Center for Sacramento History –
Sacramento Bee Collection

There are complaints that the Japanese family was being broken up because the children and teens would sit together at meal times in the cafeteria. The women gathered up in various interest groups. The unhappy were apparently of two categories: older men who felt they had lost their position in their families because of the camps' communal nature and the 40,000 loyal to Japan who became engaged in various violence, raiding, and rioting incidents. Reeves could not deny or fail to report on the jitterbug parties, the sports, the cinema, the choirs, women's circles, and on and on; the many activities, and the many experiences of whites' kindness toward them while they were in the camp. In fact, Reeves's book would have been much shorter had he failed to report all of this contradictory history and neglected to say, for example, how sorry many Japanese were to see how lonely the white guards were, especially during the holidays.

In one case, the Japanese interns came out to the guards, sitting in their desolate towers in the cold, and sang Christmas Carols to them. To my mind, these Japanese were examples of humanity at its best.

As it is, 25,000 Japanese internees were released in the three years up to 1945 to go to work, to college, or to serve in the military. This provides witness to some degree of whites' beneficence and the American culture of forgiveness and the value put on merit, regardless of identity or skin color.

Many photos are presented and try as he did; Reeves just could not find enough interpretative adjectives to hide the fact that you can't force that many smiles on people; he claims to have been so unhappy and outraged. One photo was of Eleanor Roosevelt, the First Lady while visiting the Gila River Relocation Center in 1943. She is surrounded by detainees, adults, teens, and children, all dressed smartly, obviously well-fed, and full of smiles. The caption also pretends that FDR didn't know about the 442nd Regiment existing, hinting that the military hid that fact because he must have been such a racist. FDR had to know because he awarded eight Presidential Unit Citations and 21 Medals of Honor to members of that regiment. Are we so infantilized that we cannot see through such a shallow set of lies? If so much racism existed, and so infused our society, wouldn't such awards be withheld or minimized?

At Camp Kohler, the detainees were allowed to govern themselves and did so through democratically elected committees without outside interference or input. At the remote camps, they continued the same way. There was no interference from the outside. Even the stills that produced Saki and hard liquor were not dismantled or even noted by the guards or army officials. The attitude was likely sympathetic; a man needs a good shot during such times, and saki was a cultural comfort. Ironically, the laws against stills continued to be enforced in the broader U.S., against U.S. citizens in general.

When the war was over, these Japanese detainees were given priority even over returning military personnel for relocating home and finding them housing. The trains that took the soldiers and sailors home carried these internees home before them. This caused a great deal of anger among the non-Japanese populations. Yet, after the war, no more violence against Japanese Americans is recorded. Quite the opposite; after the war, San Francisco's Japan Town was expanded. The "Peace Pagoda" was erected in the 1960s.

There were some incidents of violence, particularly in the Pacific Northwest, which had experienced civilian deaths by a Japanese balloon bomb in 1945, just before the end of the war. The government suppressed the story nationally, but locally, it was known. The Smithsonian article about it uses the following introduction;

"Elsye Mitchell almost didn't go on the picnic that sunny day in Bly, Oregon. She had baked a chocolate cake the night before in anticipation of their outing, her sister would later recall, but the 26-year-old was pregnant with her first child and had been feeling unwell. On the morning of May 5, 1945, she decided she felt decent enough to join her husband, Rev. Archie Mitchell, and a group of Sunday school children from their tight-knit community as they set out for nearby Gearhart Mountain in southern Oregon. Against a scenic backdrop far removed from the war raging across the Pacific, Mitchell and five other children would become the first—and only—civilians to die by enemy weapons on the United States mainland during World War II.

While Archie parked their car, Elsye and the children stumbled upon a strange-looking object in the forest and shouted back to him. The reverend would later describe that tragic moment to local newspapers: "I...hurriedly called a warning to them, but it was too late. Just then, there was a big explosion. I ran up – and they were all lying there dead." Lost in an instant were his wife and unborn child, alongside Eddie Engen, 13, Jay Gifford, 13, Sherman Shoemaker, 11, Dick Patzke, 14, and Joan "Sis" Patzke, 13."

This article makes the distinction between American civilians killed on the mainland during WW2. During the Pearl Harbor attack in 1941, forty-nine civilians were killed, and thirty-five were wounded during the Japanese attack on Oahu on December 7, 1941. Many of them were of Japanese ancestry.

There had to be a certain amount of fear among the West Coast populations because of general knowledge about the balloon bombs. The Smithsonian article provides us with some idea of what the level of tension on the West Coast might have been like as these bombs approached the West Coast of the U.S.;

"Though relatively simple as a concept, these balloons—which aviation expert Robert C. Mikesh describes in Japan's World War II Balloon Bomb Attacks on North America as the first successful intercontinental weapons, long before that concept was a mainstay in the Cold War vernacular—required more than two years of concerted effort and cutting-edge technology engineering to bring into reality. Japanese scientists carefully studied what would become commonly known as the jet stream, realizing these currents of wind could enable balloons to reach United States shores in just a couple of days. The balloons remained afloat through an elaborate mechanism that triggered a fuse when the balloon dropped in altitude, releasing a sandbag and lightening the weight enough for it to rise back up. This process would repeat until all that remained was the bomb itself. By then, the balloons would be expected to reach the mainland; an estimated 1,000 out of 9,000 launched made the journey. Between the fall of 1944 and the summer of 1945, several hundred incidents connected to the balloons had been cataloged." (Japanese work on atomic bomb*[8])

If we consider this and add the knowledge of it with the resentment and fear that the sneak attack on Pearl Harbor created on the West Coast and combine it with the revealed fanaticism of the Japanese during the war, the massacre on Wake Island, the Bataan Death March, the genocide in China, and the systematic abuse of young women as sex slaves, the starvation of prisoners of war as well as civilians. All told, during the war, the Japanese Armed forces held 300,000 people, mostly civilians in camps like the one that Agnes Newton Keith describes in her 1946 story of her family's internment, and separation in Borneo. The men were kept separate and worked to exhaustion, with many dying of abuse and neglect, while the women were worked, abused, and bullied. Failure to bow to any Japanese soldier was punishable by a severe caning. Any sign of arrogance met similar treatment. They all starved, including the children. And although she cleaned it up in her book, it is clear that rapes occurred. Keith was nearly raped (or perhaps actually raped). Complaining about it led to a series of interrogations and beatings. Moreover, on August 1, 1945, the Tokyo War Ministry announced the plan for the complete extermination of prisoners of war. Some of this was completed with others rescued just in time (see – The Great Raid, book, film, Ghost Soldiers). Lately, information about the medical camps in China and Singapore, run by a sadistic officer named Ishi, tortured and murdered 10,000 to 12,000, men, women, and children, including some POWs. Compare this to the 1,000 victims of the Nazis in their hospitals. May I suggest that the contemporary methods of the Americans were far more humane, in fact, not even comparable?

But it's a more stark contrast than that. Mark Felton is a well-known historian, his specialty being WW2. He has published "The Real Tenko" (list), which is the record of the mistreatment of women and their use as sex slaves during the war. Thousands of women were forced into sex services as "Comfort Women." In one case, Felton presents for the first time, the treatment of the three hundred Dutch women who were captured in the Netherlands West Indies. Although older women "volunteered" to protect them, the Japanese officers soon focused on the sixty or so virgin teenage girls. They were inspected like cattle and loaded into an open truck and delivered to a brothel where they were initially raped by dozens of men, officers first, then sergeants, then the enlisted men, all night long. The prettiest of them was treated exceptionally cruelly. Their lives were ruined. The fact is that the Japanese treated the whites far harsher than any other racial or national group short of murder. In Japan, Americans were portrayed as lumbering, hairy, grotesque semi-humans on their propaganda posters. The government convinced the civilian population that the American soldiers would torture and kill them. That propaganda was spread so widely, that Japanese civilians on Okinawa jumped from cliffs to avoid capture. I think Mr. Reeves should read Mark Felton's book. The Japanese government still has not apologized, let alone acknowledged these atrocities. Maybe some of our Japanese citizens today should as well.

The ones that did surrender were clothed and fed, giving the lie to complete the propaganda of victory that was believed until at least 1944. On top of it all, we have the loss of actual family members during the war; one might begin to comprehend the extent of removal from the context of circumstances that "Infamy" and similar media produced for public consumption in the 1980s. This book represents a renewed salvo in the cultural wars, published during Barak Obama's time as president, and the Cancel Culture strategy was becoming the new tool for the grievance industry. It might be pertinent to ask why it was deemed necessary to stir up a new wave of resentment and shaming in the 21st century.

The jet stream from Japan to the U.S. arrives over the states of Washington and Oregon. Most of the violence against Japanese Americans after the war occurred in those states. California was a far milder case. There was some resentment and difficulties, but in Northern California, the only incident that Reeves found was where three boys burnt down the barn of an absent Japanese family. There are vague claims of prejudice and a burned-down house, but fires happen during wartime, and often they are more frequent and devastating, as I will soon illustrate regarding the core of my story. My living witness reports a different reality from the one Reeves portrays regarding Loomis and the region. Reeves seems to relish that the son of the farm owner was serving in the 442nd. But how could those boys have known that? (A new claim is that the boys were white soldiers that had gone AWOL, but the record and even Reeves's book report them as being teenage boys. They have been aged for propaganda use).

My direct source tells me that the Japanese farms were not violated and returned with rents paid and profits handed over by the local whites who had taken them over by agreement. Reeves appears to feel that any resentment at all is disallowed because whites are required to be superhuman towers of virtue or be damned. This, while their counterparts in Japan engaged even more egregiously in racist propaganda against whites to the point that the average civilian believed that the white monsters would kill them on contact and eat their children.

For his part, Reeves doesn't fail to emphasize the words of the defense of the boys who burned that barn, and who were put on trial for it, as he accuses the defense of angling via his concluding remarks for a race-based adjustment; "Remember, this is a white man's country." The claim is that this led to the young men's acquittal. My sense of it is that they were not the only barn-burning cases that occurred in the U.S. The fact is that there were riots and many instances of civil unrest during the war. The judge may have thought it wise not to antagonize feelings any more than they were by sending three teens to prison for burning a barn down. We don't know if any of them had a brother who had just been killed in the Pacific. If Reeves had cared to research that far, it might have compromised that narrative's intended power.

This obsession and upset with whites only where accusations of "racism" might be leveled is an implanted system for planned societal dysfunction, and Reeves performs as trained for that purpose. According to the Marxist-steered narrative, it's a sin for such a thing as a "white country" to exist. This idea is not even being slightly concealed today. The Kalergi Plan that the EU is based on is a plan to replace the Indigenous and historical European Caucasian population with non-Europeans via discouragement of family and encouragement toward pairing with non-Europeans. Meanwhile, on this side of the Atlantic, Reeves and his ilk work hard to ensure that this nation will not long endure. Their aim is to present such material to be understood as a product of justice and virtue. The more numerous, ninety percent world majority of non-white nations, such as Japan China, and Africa, and their racially homogenous and relatively uniform populations believe in their right to racial dominance. It is only a crime when it is a "white nation." The solution is now proclaimed often and openly; clear those nations of Caucasians, by force, if necessary. In France, President Sarkozy proposed a policy that would force white French to marry non-whites. He saw this as completely reasonable. He lost the following election, but this is broad evidence of the Kalergi Plan's influence in European politics. This, paired with the Barcelona Agreement of 1995.*ق

It is as if Whites are the new Jews for a new kind of Nazi extermination campaign. Why is this so? Because Europeans and their Western Civilization are the oldest cultures of democracy, they have expectations rooted in traditions. So those traditions must be destroyed and then the people themselves, whether it is through displacement and limiting of opportunities through acclaimed justice for past alleged atrocities against peoples of color, or direct, forced extinction through miscegenation. The resultant populations will have no past to cling to and therefore, no identity beyond what the state provides. Other groups are considered easier to corrupt and manage by the future ruling cabal (CCP).

As the return narrative in Infamy reports it, poor treatment was usually defanged by the new intelligence of, for example, the death of that Japanese families' soldier in service of America. Some, but not all, resisted when they attempted to return or had their former homes or businesses denied to them, one way or another. No one was killed or even beaten up. Even Reeves concludes that particular chapter about the evils of the white people in the Loomis area with the tears of a white man as he confesses to a returned Japanese neighbor, who was egregiously wounded in the war.

He confesses that he had misbehaved by displaying signs at his gas station that read, "No Jap Trade Wanted." I have to wonder, how many Japanese people were around for him to sell gas to during the war? Answer; not many, if any. Nasty sign, but how many were there to be offended? It was more of a demonstration to his contemporaries in a time when "Jap" was a common word as "Gringo" still is in the Hispanic community, and "Cracker" or the trend of the

"Broke Becky" in the Black professional sports community, or "Haole" is in Hawaii. While unflattering appellations for non-Whites are taboo, crimes punishable by complete and total cancellation, the derogatory nouns used by non-Whites for people of European heritage and genetics has no penalty attached and are used regularly. Whites accept them and even act as if they enjoy the abuse as if Aldous Huxley's formula had worked through racist social justice efforts to produce Whites that enjoy social servility. No red flags going up in those communities, however. Now the practice has been extrapolated into the creation of a two-tiered justice system based on political allegiance. No more un-American practice could ever be short of actual concentration camps for political prisoners (Gulags).

Uncle Johnny served as a medic in the Korean War, which was primarily an action to defend Japan against a Sino-Soviet invasion. He similarly was wounded as the man in the above Loomis story. He had to suffer through repeated surgeries through the late fifties and live in a body cast for months after each surgery. I have never resented this, nor did my uncle ever say anything bitter about it beyond a sincere conversation I had with him on the subject of war when I was thirteen in 1965, when he said, "War has shattered many a young man's dreams." But his experience in the war doubtlessly contributed to his early death at sixty-six years of age, and I lost my favorite uncle early.

The plan was that he was to medical school and serve as the medical input in the chiropractic hospital that my grandfather, the classmate of Leo Spears, DC, who ran a successful one in Denver, Colorado for a decade, intended to replicate in Michigan. These plans were foiled by the Korean War, and our family fortunes were dispersed as my grandfather sold off the land he had reserved for the hospital, and my father moved his family out to California in 1952. Should I blame the Japanese people for this? No, I blame the fortunes of war and the course of history, against which to complain is not only useless but also an exercise in solipsism.

I have never thought of making this an issue. It has only occurred to me now because during the past few I have continually heard it said that such losses only matter if you are not white. The impression of the non-white world is that nothing bad ever happens to white people. It's as if whites were never enslaved. They have always been enslaved directly during Roman times, in the Arab world before, by design after the advent of Islam, and then in Europe, as serfs, bound to their lords' land in permanent servitude for centuries. Serfdom only ended in Russia in the later 19th century, and by then, it was too late. As for the infamous 400 years that we are always being lectured about, white slavery was concurrent with the Africans in the Americas in the 17th and 18th centuries, at approximately a million. Then, we may look to the history of the over one million taken by the Barbary Pirates of North Africa up to the early 19th century.*6 This is not to mention the millions of Slavs held in serfdom until 1917 in Russia. How my mother's parents got out of there in 1913 is still amazing to me. But no, it is my privilege, I'm told, to have had our family plans and their potential legacy ruined by a war fought to defend a people who seven years before had been our mortal enemy. Maybe the eradication of distant relatives in Western and Eastern Europe during World War Two is also a privilege? This is just my family history. There are no genealogical records on that side of the family beyond my great-grandparents. I am only one of how many others?

By the time Imperial Japan surrendered, there were just over 40,000 evacuees left in all of the camps and about 15,000 at Tule Lake. Even Reeves reports that these were Japanese who had been somehow convinced while interned, that Japan was winning the war and that the emperor would reward them for their loyalty. The rumor was that Japan would give each family $10,000.00 each, plus $7,000.00 for each child as payment as compensation for their time in the camps. The end of this delusion came on March 20, 1946, when Tule Lake was closed permanently. These last internees were given $25.00 and a train ticket to wherever they had been first picked up.

This means that the U.S. government sent 40,000 anti-American Japanese back into society without any follow-up. Some understandably failed after they got home. A few of them, old men, attempted suicide. Reeves lists only one case where a suicide attempt succeeded. Yet, even this is held up as an example of white American atrocity in Reeve's estimation. But, imagine the surprise among these people when they found that everything they thought was true turned out to be lies.

We should focus on these facts rather than obsess over the occasional failures. America revealed its true character when it nurtured its conquered enemies and rebuilt their war-torn nations to recover soundly and prosper. We might also reflect on how this might have influenced Japan in bringing about its transition into a loyal ally. As for the home front, nowhere in the history of detained groups of any sort has there been an effort by private, white citizens as voluntary caretakers of their property. In fact, in most cases, some I know of personally in Europe, homes were ransacked and looted by other locals. That this wasn't one hundred percent can hardly remain a complaint. The ones that gave their word and even turned over profits that the Japanese American businesses made combined with the previous facts overturn any comparison with the Germans and Japanese atrocities during the same war.

The one big, outstanding, and reified "sin" that Reeves ends with as a fully intact complaint despite so many exceptions and even admittances of innumerable acts of sympathy and kindness is that it was racist to have interned the Japanese and that somehow, Americans, the White ones, exclusively suffer from "racism." The term has become so common and applied so often that its meaning has become a weak, subjective complaint. But again, to such assertions in his book, I merely repeat the long set of contradictions, and hypocritical omissions as mentioned above that charge, repeating, Germans and Italians were detained, too. And if we eliminate that and turn toward "nationalism" as a sin, dragging patriotism with it, then we must indict the entire human race because no nation can long stand without a foundation based on patriotism. Without it, there can be no cohesion. Those who deny this, pretending that a global community of borderless occupation is realistic or supported by history, are either simpletons or intentionally deceptive. Given recent events and revelations, including frank confessions of purpose, we can settle on the latter case.

Up to and during World War Two, the Japanese were far more a nationalist nation, and today, they invent robots to deliver health care to the elderly rather than import non-Japanese for the task. And for a bottom-line indication of current racial attitudes, one American blogger who lives in Japan has noted that in Tokyo's large red-light district, only Japanese men are served. Is that racist? At least they can recognize Japan as a Japanese nation with a clear culture based on Japanese traditions and beliefs. I'm all for that, but for all people. A truly multicultural nation is desirable if there can be mutual respect. That is where the problems lie as there is a natural tendency for one or the other to dominate. Nothing is or remains equal. This is a major lesson in history. The supposed alternative is a grayed-out humanity that has no identity or meaning. The Marxist plan is to create this final class of humanity and supply meaning through a global elitist dictatorship.

The Ruse of "Racism" - Part 2

In examining the universe of abuse this term has come to represent in politics and modern culture, it is important to know the origin of the term. "Racism," the term was invented by none other than the Bolshevik Leon Trotsky, who recognized its potential power and use in dismantling multi-ethnic, especially, multi-racial, and especially, therefore, American society. The Bolsheviks understood history. By that, I don't mean dates and events. They understood the meaning and the philosophy of history. They knew that every multi-cultural, multi-ethnic empire had fallen because it became impossible to manage due to the plethora of cultures and people inside of it. But they also observed that empires manage the problem by setting one group against another. This is what the Romans did with Christianity versus the Jews in the first century, and it worked so well that it lasted two thousand years, so far.*k Those familiar with Edward Gibbon's classic tome on the decline and fall of the Roman Empire will understand how this occurred. Whatever empire one might examine,

British, French, Portuguese, Russian, Hapsburg, the same mechanism holds true. When the U.S. political system began to assign benefits or penance due to racial or ethnic (or sexual) identification, it became tantamount to an empire in this sense and destined to collapse.

It could be argued that the emotion that political actors have come to term "racism" is due to an instinct shared by all living things, even vegetation. Differences are recognized and a natural cause of caution and in the world of botany, the development of characteristics that resist the particular plant from being wiped out.   Single-celled amoebae have cilia, little sensors that sense the outside world and give feedback the creature uses to discriminate against that which will harm it and that which will nourish it. The failure to resist nature results in the extinction of a species, or subspecies, which often possess different but rare and naturally developed characteristics. The religious would say "God" created, while a scientist would say "evolved," but both are normally held as sacred in their own way and worth preserving, it could be argued. How against nature and God, then, might it be to actively seek to destroy groups of people because of their racial or tribal identity?

Writers like Reeves wish for us to bow our heads in shame and redeem ourselves through demonstrations of virtue as penance. Those that also harm us seem to be the most desired by them. They wish to make these changes that affect our culture, society, and nation by the publication of interpretations of history set in sensational language and out of the context of the times and ignoring piles of mitigating well-established and documented historical facts. In fact, every return narrative is countered in Reeve's own book with a mitigating counteraction of kindness and apology on the part of the whites involved. This is exactly the use of "racism" Trotsky had in mind. Meanwhile, Japan never did apologize for its war crimes in China, the Philippines, or Indochina during their long war of conquest that began in 1937.

I can offer a personal witness to this narrative. Later in my teen years, when I began racing, I had an older acquaintance who had been interred at the Tule Lake facility as a boy, Bill Onga. He was a great guy who bore no resentment toward anyone and a founding member of the Dirt Diggers North Motorcycle Club. One of his closest friends who grew up with him in Penryn, Dave Duarte, was where Japan Town was located before the war, told me that there were many Japanese families there and many in school with him. The site of Japan Town was on Penryn Road just before the intersection with English Colony Road. The old church back down the road from the intersection among the tall, ancient palm trees was the Buddhist "Church" in that time and the center of the Japan Town community. The Japanese there were universally engaged in farming citrus, and fruit production was Penryn's big business. When the Japanese were sent off to the internment, white friends ran their farms, collected and banked their profits, and turned the farms and money back over to them when they returned. The Reeves "Infamy" claimed that this was rare, but I think it was more common than the impression given by that biased review of the event. It certainly did not report the experience of the Japan Town citizens.

Bill was universally liked and respected by all because of his character and his skills as a racer. As earlier reviewed, he worked in Loomis with Gene Nunes at Gene's Automotive repair shop that sold off-road dirt bikes, Husqvarna's, and then the new Pentons, the brands used by world champions at the time. As previously reviewed, Bill was one of the Dirt Diggers North Motorcycle Club founders. He was a tough competitor and won the famous Elsinore Grand Prix in 1969 by virtue of his superior skills in dealing with muddy conditions. Bill never spoke or behaved in any way that reflected any bitterness about anything, let alone his time as a boy at that camp.

Fellow surviving co-founder Dave Duarte talked to me regarding Bill's attitude and memories as told to him by Bill. Bill would have been at the Tule Lake facility. Bill said that he and the other kids had a great time overall. The long list of deprivations that the various social justice advocates have utilized for their political and fundraising interests did not traumatize Bill to any significant degree. Bill was quiet but friendly and engaged in the clubs' many activities, including a vigorous party ethic. In the impromptu photos of boys at the Walerga Assembly Center, they are chumming about smiling.

I can't believe the adults' smiles in the pictures I've seen were ordered under the muzzle of a gun. Any such suggestion is ridiculous in the extreme, yet Reeves makes that suggestion. In fact, for those boys, it was probably a great adventure, as the Blitz in London was for the many children there. The difference is that the British kids were sometimes killed.

Reeve's also missed, along with just about everyone else, a very interesting wartime film produced by United Artists titled, "Jack London." It was a film biography of the California, San Francisco Bay Area author's life. It went through his life from childhood as an orphan and struggles from a lonely childhood to the harsh conditions of working for less than a dollar day, twelve hours a day at a cannery in Oakland, to his time as an "oyster pirate," and on to join the Alaska Gold Rush in the Klondike. His early stories land him a job as a rookie reporter just in time for the Japanese-Russo War of 1905. This section covers that last one third of the film. He goes with some veteran reporters on assignment to Japan to get the story as the war unfolds. But the authoritarian government won't let them out of Tokyo. Relying on the savvy acquired from his rough past, he smuggles himself to Korea where the Japanese are staging for battles. He gets caught and imprisoned in terrible conditions along with Russian prisoners of war with no food and hardly any water. His colleagues back in Tokyo learn of his plight and the story is communicated to President Theodore Roosevelt, who springs London through his then famous "Big Stick" diplomacy methods.

The film was obviously a piece of wartime propaganda made to illustrate the cruelty of the Japanese as a chronic condition. In the film, it is given out by the actors that Japan already has a plan to dominate the Pacific and rule Asia, understanding that the U.S. will stand in the way and must be dealt with. A nasty sneak attack on Russian forces is described. None of this happening in a film made in 1943 is surprising. What is perhaps surprising and notable is that the actors playing the numerous role of Japanese soldiers, officials and officers, were Japanese Americans who not only obviously agreed to play the roles, but did it with obvious zeal. From this and other information revealed here, it is obvious that the Japanese Americans of the time were largely loyal to the U.S. to the point these facts of history illustrate. Even though it was a less than happy chapter in American history, they bore it, and even seemed to understand the necessity of it. This has changed today. The Neo-Marxist agitators have also penetrated the old Japanese American communities. At least one or two noted spokespeople have chosen to bask in the "shame on America," and the whites who "perpetrated this injustice."

While in that geographic neighborhood, it might be moot to mention the year that the Japanese captured and occupied several islands in the Aleutian Chain, including Sitka Island after the Battle of Midway. A U.S. and Canadian combined force of 100,000 was required to dislodge them. There were thousands of causalities. Why was it so important to drive the Japanese form a few small islands; because from there, the airfield on Sitka could be used to bomb the U.S. and Canada.

Isn't it time to admit that at that time, President Roosevelt's difficult course was the only way to avoid a worse set of events on the U.S. mainland and perhaps even have prevented U.S. success at crucial moments? The fact is that President Lincoln had used the same executive powers to suspend Habeas Corpus during the Civil War and imprisoned individuals and groups such as the peaceniks known as "Copperheads" and journalists deemed to be a threat to national security at the time. He had journalists that criticized his efforts too much and put them, along with Copperheads, into prisoner of war camps. President Wilson similarly suspended Habeas Corpus for security reasons, as did FDR. These were national emergencies. World War Two was a national emergency such as this nation had never seen.

It is a matter of fact that by the time the transfers were completed, the Battle of Midway had been won. This great sea battle turned the tide of the war and relieved, to a degree, the fear of a Japanese strike on the West Coast. The battle occurred during the last month of the transfers. Even though some historians have said that a Japanese attack on the mainland after that battle was nearly impossible, this is not a sensible criterion for making the argument that release should have been affected during the war. There would have been 40,000 fanatical agents of Japan running free in America. They would have been free to set off bombs at factories, and schools, even haunting Los Alamos, and so on. Japan, like Germany, had been pursuing the development of the Bomb. I read interviews of former Japanese commanders who told interviewers that if they had developed The Bomb before the war was over there was no question that they would have used it.

Our Own Worst Enemy – Or?

America has been self-flagellating over this and other drawn-out social justice industry issues since the 1960s. Addiction to virtue has been manipulated and used to further Marxist objectives. This must be recognized. Everyone has done everyone wrong at some point. So if we are to be a society based on reasonability and justice, we must keep the balance of history and meaning in perspective. Isolating events for political and social exploitation is sure to result in imbalance. That is intended. Today, ideological enemies are jumping in freely with their whips. Are we a land of social masochists or the land of the free? Thankfully, some signs of correction are beginning to manifest.

The way to excise the demon of trained self-hatred is knowledge. It is always knowledge that clears the fog, regardless of its composition. The enemies of civilization and reason always seek to blind their victims. There are many ways that this can be done. Nietzsche argued that dividing analysis of the human condition into a contest of good and evil insured a future of suffering without the correcting details of causality, those shades of gray that the details of history provide us for learning how to act and not act.*9 The danger of the assumption of the absolute supernatural as a parental force leads to the abandonment of self-reliance and responsibility. The psychologist Carl

Jung observed, that synchronicity is separate from supernatural causes but is a psychological phenomenon that aids in the individuals' development of spirituality. I posit that it must be free of conditions to create useful meaning and not as a yoke to harness the soul. Joseph Campbell further developed the Jungian ideas of positive independent spiritual development and heroism and others today, people such as Jordan Peterson, follow on but have limited audiences. During the past 20 years or so, the road has been made muddy, and extremes have taken the place of reason. True adulthood means thinking for oneself in the knowledge of real cause and consequence.

Down the Corridors of the Ages

Oswald Spengler was a famous philosopher of history who wrote, "The Decline of the West" at the beginning of the 20th century. He showed how civilizations rise and fall according to a predictable formula. He showed that like the four seasons, and as with life, there are four phases; spring, summer, autumn, and winter.

The historic philosophers recognize the period termed the "saeculum." This is the period of an average human life or about eighty years. Some ancient civilizations had founding myths that contained a termination myth. We can look to the East, and even the Americas, but for lineal dialectic's sake, I focus on the Western Civilizations. The Etruscans believed that their civilization would last for eleven saeculums, and it turned out that they were conquered and absorbed by the Roman civilization after eleven saeculums. Rome had its founding myth which also included a similar terminal myth that turned out to be true. The civilization that replaced the Romans was not civilization as much as it was a termination myth. Christianity and early Christianity especially were based on the expectation of the End of Time and the changing of the cosmic order. We are currently wrestling with the residue of the history of that belief and the forces that naturally form to oppose such ideas. This happens because saeculums expand from the human generations which overlap, to historical epochs, which also overlap. However, the complete cycle of a civilization comes with huge cataclysms, as we can see from the end of the Bronze Age, onward. They are usually events that share both social and natural destabilization and social collapse.

It amounts to this; the human saeculum is divided into its four seasons and sees four generations, with a new one emerging about every twenty years. Marxists have long understood that only one generation's brainwashing is required for bringing about the demoralization of society; that is, just fifteen to twenty years is required to demoralize society. To escape the cycle of repeating the decline and fall of civilizations there must be a breakthrough in the host society's habits of historical anticipation. This requires a change in the perception of an absolute cosmos.

The Founders of the American Republic realized this. They provided a system of government wherein an enlightened populace might be provided the tools for perpetuating the opportunity for liberation from constraining conditions that absolutism always places on human existence. It provided for the checks and balances against the assertion of any tyranny against the free mind. That means our consciousness must be free of anticipation of command and free to operate unrestrained as has occurred for most of human history through monarchal and religious rule, which historically phased into dictatorial governments. Unless we abandon these habits, we doom ourselves to the cycle that Spengler warned the world about, just as he predicted the devastation of the Second World War while the first one was finishing.

From the perspective of historical philosophy, the Second World War was the end of Western Civilization. Europe was exhausted and has never recovered. Socialism and bureaucracy have replaced the notion of human initiative and independence. The vacuum has been created and those forces that would once again assert tyrannical rule over human life seem to only be opposed by other forms of the same goal. At present, they seem to be feeding on the other. But the future of humanity does not look happy unless the individuals inside of it "grow up" and become responsible in their time.

"The most effective way to destroy people is to deny and obliterate their own understanding of their history."

— George Orwell

Those who intend to rule over others always seek to murder memory. History represents any people's collective memory. Destroying a society or civilization requires a set of acts executed sequentially. There are many cases of this being done in the West for the last 2,000 years.*[10] The first phase involves the destruction of collective memory. This is done by falsifying history just enough to make the big lie seem plausible to the masses. This goes under the heading of propaganda. But it doesn't stop there. The last 60 years of American and even Western social history illustrate that process at work. In countries without a First Amendment, it is possible to be jailed for what is guessed about your thoughts. You can be jailed for your speech. We are very near that in the U.S. This process has finally been identified as "cancel culture." But this is not a new phenomenon. Religious persecution and shunning producing isolation and destruction of the individual have been a part of Western Culture since the Fall of Rome and the rise of Christianity. What we are seeing today is just a prelude to worse scenarios. We are at last arrived at a historical precipice that all can recognize if they have thus far retained their senses intact. Some have begun to recognize these things and discuss it more openly than ever before.

It was the monarchs in Europe that gained and retained their rule by divine right. Our Founders were deists but not theocrats. On that much, we must be clear. No divine power will save us. The only apocalypse there will be is the one we create through our neglect and ignorance. If we are to be saved, we must act on our own behalf. We must not be dulled by calls to limit our understanding to the faith of a child. We are not sheep to be led. So we must prepare ourselves truly and correct our vision so that we might survive into the next epoch of history.

Then we must unite in that clarity. The U.S. Constitution is the most sublime governing document to have ever been written. The next twenty years will determine the future not of only America, but the world. If we fail, we face a future dark age-matched by no other in history from which there may never be a return. There is no time left for squabbling or self-degradation. Respect yourself! Hear Aldous Huxley's final plea; drop the dope and take up hope!

Vote in leaders who know what is at stake and do not serve internationalists and their organizations. Whatever illusion you suffer under, free yourself of it enough at least to act in the moment we find ourselves in now and fight for our collective freedom. It begins first with the assertion of the right to think and express oneself in real-time, with the understanding of what it truly means. Ban the banning of words! There is the easy way; pick a side and join in "the struggle." Escaping into "End Times" fanaticism is actually cynicism of the worst type and neutralizing in many ways. It may seem comforting, but it is dishonest and contributes to the collapse. But it isn't easy to walk alone. I find it akin to a tightrope walk before a jeering crowd.

I reflect that some may hope to bask in the one comfort that if such a national emergency should ever arise again, our country is now so diverse that no such camps would be practical or even possible. I agree such places would be quite useless. But it is more likely they'd be used for the now popularly designated supposed domestic terrorists described most often today. That most likely would include the adult version of the child in this tale, your author, for merely writing this book.

The End of Camp Kohler
and the Birth of The Spook Tree

A fter the end of the war, the process of shutting down Camp Kohler began. By May 4, 1946, almost all service personnel had been discharged, and by the summer of 1947, activities at Camp Kohler were finalizing. Previously, in 1944, the camp had been turned over to the Army Air Force and became the embarkation point for airmen for mustering during the last phases of the Pacific war. However, the transition was slow, and Signals Corps personnel remained up to the end of the war. In March of 1945, 600 high school cadets spent a week training there under the California State Guard's auspice. After that time, the camp remained an official "Embarkation," and the army returned to its management role as Kohler was made into the fourth embarkation location as a branch of Camp Stoneman, under the overall command of the San Francisco Port of Embarkation at Fort Mason. By 1946, the 3,453 acres of Camp Kohler were designated surplus land and put under the Army Core of Engineers' management to see to its disposition. 72,173 square feet of building space was given to the AAF, McClellan Field. Land that had been assumed from owners was returned while other parcels were sold. At the time, a residual contingent of Army personnel remained; ten officers and fifty enlisted men.

In October of 1945, Japanese internees began to arrive at the Camp for resettlement in society. This was delayed due to a shortage of housing. So the U.S. Army Liaison Officer working with the Federal Public Housing Administration and WRA made the barracks at Camp Kohler a legal temporary residence for those who did not have homes or farms to return to. Out of the 5,000 internees shipped out in 1942, 234 were obliged to remain at Camp Kohler until good homes could be found for them. Many personnel and families living at the Camp through the VFW (Veterans of Foreign Wars) complained to the Sacramento Chamber of Commerce on November 10th, as almost criminal as veterans of the Pacific War were obliged to remain in holding areas themselves while the internees were seen to. Regardless, the Japanese were allowed to stay at the camp until they had been appropriately resettled. No former internee was put out on the road to fend for themselves. Meanwhile, in Europe, millions of refugees starved while sometimes walking thousands of miles to get home to poverty, and sometimes the total destruction of their communities where persecution often met them as a plethora is possibilities, including local civil wars.

The main activity in 1947 was a railroad spur that supplied a post lumberyard as McClellan Field was building out. The settlement of Plane Haven and Aero Haven was being expanded. I remember the remnants of this in 1955 as a commercial operation on Roseville Road at that spur, "Steiner's Lumber," which I visited with my father that year. This was also the location where we'd find our agriculturally developed cabin cruiser for sale years later.

How the huge Camp Kohler Fire broke out on June 20, 1947, has never been determined. Chief of the Hagginwood Fire Department said that it began as a grass fire at Camp Kohler, while another theory says that it was caused by sparks from the brakes of a railroad car, an ironic pre-cognition of the 1973 railyard explosions. One witness report puts the fire's origins just north of the Camp itself. The tar paper walls of hundreds of buildings exploded into flames, and the high winds spread them wide very quickly. Many smaller fires coalesced into one major conflagration with a mile-wide front, driven mostly eastward by the winds. I can imagine flaming tumbleweeds swirling around in the chaos. As the bulk of fire crews worked to stop the eastward advance, the fire in an open field just to the west of the fire's origin and just a good stone's throw from the center of Antelope must have been considered a mop-up or secondary consideration.

The fire destroyed fifty buildings in the camp and twenty nearby homes. The losses would have been even more devastating had there been a higher population. Still, as it was, the wind gusts of up to forty-seven miles an hour drove the fire to the outskirts of Carmichael, threatening that community, with a fire line a mile wide.

Ten civilian fire departments, the State Forestry, and hundreds of volunteers, men, and women, joined the battle. Fifty people were treated for burns, and one Arcade Fire Department volunteer, Charles Gay, died of third-degree burns. This event must have been one of the last ones that took on the old, pioneer scenario of total community involvement. Women provided water, food, and nursing, while the men fought the flames. No doubt, some of the women took up a hose during the events during those four hours that must have seemed like a year to the communities involved as there were so many flare-ups that melded into the lingering aftermath of the event. One reminder lasted until 1964.

When it was over, a field just off Walerga had been burned black. A tree, a very old oak tree that had stood alone as the monarch of its realm in the midst of that field for hundreds of years, had been burned almost entirely, leaving an eerie, desolate sight for the next sixteen or so years, where kids who saw it recognized its haunting presence inspiring their lore around it, naming it, The Spook Tree. I have come to see that tree as the object that became a catalyst for wonder and meaning in my early life and again, in the present, as I have rediscovered it through the writing of this book.

The early stage of the 1947 Camp Kohler Fire – It would expand to present an eight-mile front fanned by winds up to 47 mph – Center for Sacramento History – Sacramento Bee Collection

Fighting the Fire at Camp Kohler – Center for Sacramento History – Sacramento Bee Collection

A partial view of the distribution of hot spots as the fire fanned out. – Center for Sacramento History – Sacramento Bee Collection

The Last Round-Up

Although it is obvious that few could have foreseen what the twentieth century would bring, one cannot help but wonder what old Bill Willis would say if he could see how his vision of the future from 1913 turned out; profoundly sad, perhaps?

Is the species Homo sapiens finding its limits in the 21st century? It would seem so. Long before the Left seized upon Global Warming as a political tool for societal and global control, MIT researchers in 1972 produced a study called World3 that used all available empirical data to predict that without a major change in human activity and population growth, society would collapse worldwide by the mid 21st century. In 1980, the great physicist and writer of the landmark science fiction, "Foundation" series, Isaac Asimov,*[1] predicted that same scenario at the 1980 convocation of The Futurists, a group of scientists and writers that used to gather every ten years to discuss and explore future scenarios as civilization progressed into the unknown future. And there is hardly even a voice in the wilderness pointing to a way forward.

No Sane Man's Land

On one side are the Leftists. For them, the solution is worldwide human enslavement led by a government, not unlike the present Communist Party of China, that uses the same population control methods that

Mao Tse Dong learned from Stalin. Communism's Marxist policy is a struggle that never ends, even when the world has been made communist; for individuals, just as with religions, are corrupt, because "absolute power corrupts absolutely" (Lord Acton, quoting by George Orwell in "1984"). Orwellian manipulation of language is used to form thought patterns in the general population. Just as with the most fear-mongering religions of the world, they promote themselves through the use of fear and the fire that panic can provide. They are currently working at buying off those who suppose themselves free to choose their destiny. But once they chose the Left, there will be no future for them. As history shows, the only ones safe are the elite, and then, not really even them. Ironically, communist nations, including and especially the former Soviet Union, had horrible records where the environment is concerned, which makes Western nations and capitalists look absolutely hermetic; at least since around 1970.

Then, on the Right, we have the Deniers. Bolstered by religious convictions and lulled by the promise of their faith that ultimately, God will intervene at the exact right moment, much damage is allowed. "Neglect" is the operative word here. Ironically, they simultaneously demonstrate the belief that there is no contradiction in the unrestrained acquisition of possessions and earthly wealth. This challenges the Christian doctrine of poverty as a virtue and even the requirement for entry into the "Kingdom of God." Thanks to the two-thousand-year tradition of Christian Apology, it turns out that God is fine with high profit-taking, regardless of how that might be done, at least, until Armageddon and Judgement Day arrives.

The problem is that Magical thinking doesn't solve problems; it only confuses the issues, making workable solutions more unlikely. Worse, the 2,000-year expectation of THE END hangs over every thought process in the West. This generates a subculture of absence where future planning and emphasis of purpose are concerned.

At the center of this social and political maelstrom is the United States of America and its unique Constitution, as the sole beacon of freedom in a world beset by the symptoms of the MIT predicted collapse. Whatever lies ahead, no reasonable American would agree that we can only save our planet by surrendering the basic freedoms that are natural to all humankind.*₂ In another odd contradiction, it is the Right that supports the preservation of the Constitution and the rights of mankind as the light of the world. If they could only parse out their tendency toward theocratic assertion! However, for the present, the hope lies with the Right because the vision of the Left is both financially and strategically impossible.

The current crisis doesn't seem to be aware of the roots, the foundation of the completely unhinged declarations we see coming daily from the Left. Most have forgotten if they ever knew, that the modern Left was created by The Frankfurt School, and its Critical Theory of revolution. Its members, Herbert Marcuse, and Eric Fromm, among others of this neo-Marxist think tank, escaped from Germany in the late 1930s. They landed in New York to find haven at the already Left-leaning campus of Columbia University. politicians, and their "New Left" of the sixties, who view the One World Government model as desirable- the ultimate goal.*₃ Marcuse and other members worked particularly on usurping the American Democratic idea of civil disobedience to "The Great Refusal," against what they first labeled "consumer society," or capitalism, in favor of eventual world socialism. His writings, "Eros and Civilization," "One Dimensional Man," "Counter-Revolution and Revolt," An Essay on Liberation," (which is an update of his earlier books in 1969,) and his unbelievable tenures by indulgent universities, combined with other members publications, such as Eric Fromm's "On Disobedience – Why Freedom Means Saying "NO" to power," and related themes, including feminism, racial justice, any issue that would disturb the status quo and create instability was fair game for essays on alternative, utopian ideals based on first dismantling the present order.

Unable to learn the lessons to recognize the foundational flaw of communism; that it is a closed economic system that always bankrupts itself, even after exploiting the workers often worse than the previous capitalist bosses that provided the cause for their movement, the neo-Marxists came back with a new, improved version. Herbert Marcuse was born in 1898, and his ideas, like Marx's, were borne of 19th-century conditioned analysis, which was rooted in the French Revolution, but now cured in a marinade of various, and extreme socialist utopian experiments, such as The Mormons, The Oneida Community, The Shaker Movement, The New Harmony Community, and Brooks Farm. Some had a religious foundation while others, such as the Oneida Community were free-love communes, along with extreme forms of New England Christianity such as The Millerites (later, The Seventh Day Adventists), who fostered not one, but two famines after farmers failed to plant crops due to twice believing William Miller's prediction of the Return of Christ (which ended up supplying factories with entire families for their capitalist "communes"). These various communities had many imitators or branches throughout the U.S. Other events, such as traveling tent revivals, and medicine shows, crisscrossed the region for decades, sewing such excited and fanatical thought seeds that by the mid-19th century was termed "The Burned-Over District" owing to the endless religious and social experiments that erupted there, again and again, creating both poverty and extremist thinking. Other radical movements, including, feminism, a preacher named Lyman Beecher, and scion, John Brown, who was backed by Boston Industrial bosses. One of them, Gerrit Smith, checked himself into an insane asylum after Brown's attack on Harper's Ferry failed, while others took vacations in Canada. These happy social and financial manipulators were joined by thousands of socialist Germans who arrived after the failed revolution of 1848. By 1850, some had created The Communist Club in New York City. The leaders ended up in Lincoln's government and the officer class of the Union Army, while many other German immigrant volunteers filled the ranks in 1861.

After the end of the war, the neo-Marxists reckoned a new way, less directly violent, perhaps, but more insidious, using social movements grew in America, as discussed above, but also with counterparts in Europe, but with a new, more subtle method; rather than work on the peasants, they'd impose themselves into the institutions of higher learning. So by the early 20th century, The Frankfurt School*₪ came up with a new idea that coincided with the plans of the Bolsheviks where undermining capitalist societies for the Revolution was concerned. Their Neo-Marxism viewed Marxism as expressed through the repression of sex in the poor. So their most prolific exponent, Herbert Marcuse's "Eros and Civilization," published in 1954, was particularly devoured by the "Beats." Coincidentally, Betty Friedan wrote "The Feminine Mystique" soon after just as The Pill, also coincidently, became widely available.

The Frankfurt School members were the creators of the so-called New Left in the United States. These collections of political theorists were members of what amounted to what was a Neo-Marxist think-tank. Herbert Marcuse, Theodore Adorno, Walter Benjamin, and Eric Fromm were the most prominent members, with the most published being Marcuse and Fromm. Their core principle for social influence and change was their theory of how economics relates to the economic and social superstructures of a society. They proposed that the latter gains a certain amount of autonomy from the material base. This means that if one understands this and dissects it, opportunities for influence present themselves ripe for exploitation for a desired social consequence. Just as with Sun Tzu's "Art of War," once the vulnerable points of your target are identified, classic strategies, such as the Machiavellian, may be employed. But the powers that be in the U.S. were not so circumspect in any notion that they might in their arrogance and error, provide opportunities for their own demise and the victory of the darkest side of humanity possible.

Blame Enough to Go Around

War changes history. The process varies, but some things are constant; populations change, and purges occur as new opportunities present themselves to survivors of active movements as societies and cultures change as the result of the violent upheaval of war. Complications arise when the strangest of alliances form. One such would be when the U.S., France, and Great Britain found themselves allied with The Soviet Union in World War Two. In Europe, the main issue was Hitler; how to stop and defeat him. As a Jew and a Marxist, Herbert Marcuse and his colleagues in Frankfurt naturally fled to America. Marcuse was welcomed into Columbia University, which was a Jack Kerouac noted in 1943, an institution, "that only wanted to teach communism." Kerouac may have been a lot of things, but he was not a Leftist by any stretch of the imagination. It turns out that during the war, the OSS found Marcuse useful. They rewarded him with control over the nation's universities where he taught, lectured, and practiced his Critical Theory, produced radicals, and encouraged every departure from capitalist consumerism, and middle-class lifestyle; all this while practicing his theory of "eros and civilization on the daughters of the bourgeoisie. The debauching of America's youth began at universities, but by the end of the sixties, as can be noted in our example at Highlands High School in North Highlands, the practice had trickled down to the high school level. Is it any surprise that it has lately trickled down into elementary schools as Critical Race Theory? But it is fully intentional as the "coup de grace" of American society.

Post-conflict, the OSS became the Central Intelligence Agency. One branch had been investigating Lysergic acid dimethylamine for possible use as a truth serum. They quickly determined that LSD was not useful for such applications and some called for all investigations of it to cease. However, there were a few who saw "useful" possibilities for it. One of them was a frank enthusiast, Captain Hubbard, who became the original "Captain Trips." He was the agent who figured in the CIA purchase of the then-existing Sandoz Lab cache of LSD in Switzerland. Captain Trips had a vision; he believed in the hallucinations he experienced on the drug. He envisioned a future of

LSD-enlightened world leaders marching forth into a glorious world of peace, harmony, and brotherhood. So like a psychedelic Johnny Appleseed, he went from high place to high place, pushing his idea and the acid. He was also referred to as "The Candy Man." Many then world leaders whose names would shock the public then and now "turned on." Clinics in London, New York, and Hollywood sprung up to serve the elites in politics and the arts. He even dosed the Bishop in Vancouver, BC, who then made LSD an official Holy Sacrament in his parish. But he felt this stuff was too powerful and well, elite, to be wasted on the common folk. But Hubbard did not have a monopoly on the stuff or its distribution. The CIA had meanwhile established its MK-ULTRA department for LSD and other similar "research" projects. So the army had its own program of experimentation. This is how Ken Kesey, the all-American athlete, and writer from Oregon who was studying at Stanford University in California came to it. He signed up for the program at the VA hospital where he worked as a janitor while studying writing at the university after watching patients dosed with it.

Kesey became the second "Captain Trips." He called his program, "The Revolt of the Guinea Pigs," in an unofficial sort of way that an anti-establishment writer might do. At the same approximate time, a pair of Harvard professors of psychology, Timothy Leary and Richard Alpert became interested in LSD and Psilocybin. They established a program that lasted from 1960 to 1962, ending because of the concerns of other professors around the requirement of students to imbibe the drug under the two protagonists' observation and control. During this time, an old girlfriend of then-President John F. Kennedy, Mary Pinchot-Myer, was taking LSD classes at Leary and Alpert's retreat at the Millbrook estate, owned by the "enlightened" heir of the old, and fabulously wealthy Mellon family (Mellon Bank). Mary Meyer's former husband was Cord Meyer, an officer at the CIA who hated JFK with a passion. Mary warned Timothy Leary that he was being watched at Harvard, but it did not seem to deter him until he was finally dismissed. He and Alpert went on to fame as a sort of "independent contractor," Alpert taking on the title of "Ram Dass."

These men fancied themselves as some order of Indian Gurus with drugs. This book is not a treatise on the assassination of JFK but only reviewed as an illustration of the close connection between LSD, the CIA, and the top echelons of government at the time. The reader must decide how much importance to place on the fact that one year after the assassination of JFK, Mary Pinchot-Myers was assassinated mafia style, with one bullet to the abdomen, and a second into the skull. Her diary went missing.

And so, the exploiters of the Baby Boomer generation sallied forth to "enlighten" and otherwise raise havoc in a loose alliance with Marxists, Feminists, Civil Rights Movements of all brands, and of course, the Vietnam War, where the boys were providing both theatre and jobs for their elders. These influences flowed out and down into communities nationwide, especially ones near military establishments. So North Highlands was one of the first such suburbs to be inundated. It was both innocent and open. And the wolves rushed in.

The methods for demoralizing society were illustrated by Yuri Bezmenov*[14] in filmed interviews in the early 1980s. Its methods include infantilizing and have echoed on through society to the point that when combined with religious denial, conservatives think their refusal to accept long-proven protection, scientifically proven during and after the Great Influenza Epidemic of 1918, over one hundred years ago. The delusion of the mechanism is clever; both sides believe that they are standing up to tyranny. They are merely the mirror image of their Marxist brethren, driven not by a rational set of values, but by values of superstition and emotion, all made possible by the infantilization of society in general as Christianity made "sheep" and "children" of us. "Rendering to Caesar" means obeying the rules, especially, for example, when you take an oath when joining the military and accept the Military Code of Justice. The insertion of the infantile expectation to always have one's way has come into dominance in general, due to both Christianity and Marxism, both of which declare themselves the parent, the caretaker, or the shepherd of the proletariats, otherwise known as peasants, or Biblically, sheep.

Right Thinking Depends on Critical Thinking, not Theory

What stands in our way is the unreasonableness of the unreasonable. They are everywhere on all sides. One cardinal mark of modern democracy is the existence of a substantial middle class. The rise of the merchant and craft guilds was what pulled Europe out of the Middle Ages and into the Renaissance. The death or even suppression of the middle class is a sure sign of a collapsing democracy.

The enemies of reason and freedom have always understood that demoralizing a people is the first step to conquering them, and the work begins early in life. The first realm of freedom is the mind. Disinformation parading as truth is not new, but it was never as thoroughly weaponized in a free society as it has been now for years since the Dark Ages when the slightest departure from Church doctrine and proscribed behavior resulted in torture and death. The new Inquisition is the New Left. The New Left invented Critical Theory, which had focused on race from the start in the 1850s after The New York Communist Club was established in 1850.*[4] It is only logical that Critical Race Theory would evolve from that.

Misinformation is the vehicle of choice for those movements that wish to erase knowledge. To change a civilization, the history and memory of the preceding one must be eradicated. We may observe three historical examples of this process. Each one was followed by decades, even in the first case, a millennium of death and destruction. Each one of them radically changed civilization through the use of fear, the forbidding of free thought, the burning of books and public symbols of the past, including and especially statues and buildings, and most importantly, the rewriting of history. They all tore down statues, executed the rulers or representatives of those civilizations, and replaced them with tyranny. These events began with the rise of Christianity (Christian revolution if we go by its political form) that brought down the Roman Empire*[5] was repeated during The French Revolution which terrorized Europe and created modern communism, and revolutions, to the Russian Revolution, and later Chinese. The Chinese event is but an extension that survives to this day, becoming the main existential threat to not just the United States, but all freedom-loving countries in the world. This is no secret intimation, I realize. They all shared a single goal: the people's subjection to control by controlling thoughts and lives.

As Mark Twain observed, "A lie can travel halfway around the world before the truth has put its shoes on." Half-truths are even more dangerous because the truthful part of it gives the lie-staying power. But a half-lie is a total lie because the truth has been deconstructed by the half-lie. Imagine how quickly that lie can travel in a pair of Air Jordans with a cyber connection.

For decades, our children have been simultaneously traumatized mentally through being infantalized while they have been simultaneously sexualized. Starting sometime in the 70s, with the rise in single motherhood and more working mothers in general, the childcare industry arose. Although there has been much support thrown behind it, including taxpayer support in some cases, its regulation has not been that uniform, and the emotional neglect of the children under care produced the first mass-produced generation. That generation is completely known as Gen X. They have now had children that their Boomer parents have often been obliged to raise as each new generation became more dysfunctional. The compensation for the neglect has been coddling, often by strangers, through the adoption of ridiculous new "rites of passage" such as kindergarten graduation ceremonies. That coddling led to the practice of interrupting the normal course of childhood experience as this style became the rule rather than the exception. It combined with "Summerhill" ideals converted into a mania around positive reinforcement which only magnified the coddling, expanding the same coddling that "benign slave owners" used in antebellum times, and that the Marxists continue up to today to keep our Black community inside its cycle of misery. The idea since the end of World War Two has been to "make everyone Black," at least those not of the expected political ruling elite. But the real point has been to produce a two-tiered society of the haves and have-nots because the resistance to the Leftist rule has always come from the middle class. So every issue is used to diminish the middle class.

Our educational system has been the battleground since the start. In a perversion of the idea of equality, to prevent "hurt feelings," everyone had to win. To create a better future, children were "given confidence" as the cue was taken from Feminist representatives like the singer Helen Reddy who claimed, "If I have to, I can do anything!" (Just don't expect me to actually do it). That became, "I can do everything," which became, "Get out of my way." That mutated into the notion that any suggestion of limitations constituted vicious oppression. Suddenly, college campuses reverted to pre-schools in function.   But also, a real war on boys ensued.*6   The initiates into Critical Race Theory are taught that they are both the victims and the virtuous avengers by the enemies of freedom, similar to the original Frankfurt School Critical Theory, which was erroneously aimed at everyone, including white people (according to CRT).

The symptoms of this infantilization are observable in various personal and social dysfunction syndromes, rage addiction, and chronic non-cooperation, from the anarchist movements to the outright hypocrisy of our leaders and of laws currently accumulating on the books. Throughout history, such operatives have required scapegoats. Christianity has theirs, their "Lord" and his "Chosen People," and the Left has theirs, Whites, in particular, White Males. The lengths of fabrication and irrational pronouncements made verbally and on paper are only possible due to the fruition of the previously inserted condition of infantilization.

Now the Time has Come and There Are Things to Realize

"Time" was a relevant song in 1968 and remains so today. Two related but opposing, authoritarian systems are fighting for control over the world's minds and bodies. In between them, our Constitutional Republic seems to dwindle and wane. The dystopia that invaded North Highlands by the late sixties and wreaked catastrophe on the community was not a sudden event or caused by the declaration of war in Southeast Asia, or even by the then often-quoted "four hundred years of slavery." One reason that this complaint is bogus is that for half of the time, whites were slaves, too. Later, during the first two decades of the existence of the U.S., whites were being captured and enslaved in North Africa by Islamic Barbary Pirates; untold numbers of white children were kidnapped, captured, or sold in Britain to toil in the American Colonies. Only one in four lived to adulthood.

Indentured white slaves were treated worse than African slaves because they were chartered, obtained at no cost. Their terms of service could be extended for the smallest infraction or error, and children were often made responsible for the accumulated debt assigned to their parents. They were used for more risky work like swamp clearing, logging, and mining. As earlier reviewed, in the 17th century, Cromwell sent over 50,000 Irish into perpetual slavery in Barbados where they were cruelly treated by black taskmasters, and have never been relieved to this day in Barbados where the remnant lives on in degradation. From 1790 to and during the Civil War, black masters owned black slaves, most of who were not their relatives, and profited from their labor just as white owners did. *℗

Moreover, when President Monroe established the African colony of Liberia for the purpose of repatriating slaves bought out of bondage in the U.S. for that purpose, they immediately set up plantations there and enslaved black Africans to labor to enrich them just as their former masters had. And when we review the plethora of material on the issues, we find that black slaves in the South fared far better than their white wage slave counterparts in the North who were only technically free, but lived in far worse conditions and for longer than black slaves who were released from their bondage officially in 1863, and in fact in 1865. For the poor whites, the struggle would extend into the 20th century right up to and including the Great Depression.*⊕ From this, we can dispense with the effective but magnificently overused false complaint that blacks were enslaved exclusively and repressed exclusively.

Roots

To plumb the question of how North Highlands became a victim of social history, we must look to the birth and rise of modern communism. Just as the United States was finalizing its Constitution and setting itself to the work of establishing the Republic, France, whose king had exhausted the nation's wealth in supporting the Americans in their war for independence, was entering into its own effort toward a more just future. It requires a philosopher of history such as Oswald Spengler or Simon Schama to better parse out the extraordinary circumstances such as a thousand years of absolute Church and Monarchal rule that saw a crusade against itself in the Languedoc in the 13th century, and religious civil wars ravaging the land up to and during the 17th century. The absolute rule of Louis IXV was the true catalyst for the slow fuse that finally went off on his hapless grandson and his naïve, pretty wife, Marie Antoinette. (She never said, "Let them eat cake. That was a later fabrication implied by a novel written by Jean-Jacques Rousseau in 1767, about King Louis XIV's wife. (Anyway, the phrase was "Qu'ils mangent de la brioche." Brioche was a very nutritious bread made of eggs and whole wheat). However, she was the victim of a false press story about some expensive jewelry. However, once the Paris Commune established itself, it quickly formed its own Inquisition for revenge for over a thousand years of outrages and abuses by the Church and Monarchy.

A ruined people become worse than their former oppressors and the mass that peopled and supported the Commune had been ruined by their history. Their revenge was insatiable, and when it was over, the former leaders became their last victims. Out of the ruin arose Napoleon who frightened Europe and wasted a generation of French males. While he organized France into an efficient, modern state, the monarchies feared his example would prove catchy; so a twelve-year war-ravaged Europe again pitting the old church-supported monarchies against Napoleon's new secular empire. Out of the confusion it left behind was a new revolutionary concept, state communism (as opposed to the clerical brand).*k

Napoleon gave rise to the concept of the modern dictator, but the Revolution gave rise to modern communism. After his era, various plots arose around Europe. In 1848, a revolution exploded in the German Confederation of States, Austria, and other places in Europe. Called the March Revolution in the German states, three factions were involved, the aristocracy, the middle class, and the working class. The aristocrats were able to suppress the uprisings because the two other classes would not unite. The middle class was idealist, influenced by Christian Socialist ideas, while the workers were more radical. After their defeat, members of both classes were persecuted in Germany. Known as the "Forty-Eighters," many fled to America to settle in the western frontier from Wisconsin to Texas. But the elite, the activists came to New York. By 1850 they had established The Communist Club in New York City. Because of the failure of the Revolution of 1848 in Germany, Lincoln found himself rich in cannon fodder as these recent arrivals volunteered for service, and rounded out both his officer corps and Cabinet.*₇

Meanwhile, during the 1850s, Karl Marx was living in London and publishing articles in the London Tribune. Soon, Horace Greeley was reprinting the articles in his New York Tribune. Greeley had previously been an advocate of Fourierism, a radical form of communism that led to the Revolution of 1848 and later, to the Paris Commune in 1871. (In "Eros and Civilization," Herbert Marcuse wrote "Fourier comes closer than any other utopian socialist to elucidating the dependence of freedom on non-repressive sublimation"). Charles Fourier's social philosophy included "free love" communes, and many think it was he who coined the word, "feminism." Earlier, Mary Wollstonecraft had merely copied the Jefferson/Lafayette produced "The Declaration of the Rights of Man" naming it "The Declaration of the Rights of Woman," and advocated for the improved education of women so that they might become better wives and mothers. Her daughter, Mary, had married the poet Percy Shelley, who was a genuine communist of French Revolution influence. Ironically, his influence seems to have inspired her to write "Frankenstein" perhaps as a warning of the tragedy of men seeking to imitate God (divine rule over secular rule) in subtle contradiction of her husband's absolutism.

Then, through political evolution, Marxist/Anarchists arose such as Emma Goldman, who inspired the assassination of President McKinley in 1901. And some of our most consequential members of society were part of that evolution. But the spectrum of communist-inspired idealist and religious communes was wide. As such, they presented a plethora of choices from the Free Love Oneida Commune of John H. Noyes, Mormonism, whose founding principle was multiple-partner marriage, and Christian Socialism. All were in one form or another Christian apparition. Fourierism a product of the French intellectual Charles Fourier was another one of them.

Greeley broke his association with Fourierism after 1848, because he was also a pacifist, but he began to publish Karl Marx's articles in the Tribune in 1851 after Marx was officially made the Tribune's official correspondent in London. Marx used his paper to promote the idea of a slave uprising in the South as a perfect starting place for his plan for a worldwide worker's revolution. His New York Tribune had the greatest distribution in America, even after it was banned by the Southern States just before the war he had at first opposed, broke out (he advocated peaceful secession).*¥ But Greeley's influence was enough to continue the attraction of the wildly experimental region of central New York State known as "The Burnt Over District" as the hotbed of radical religious and utopian experiments, including, the Millerites, Mormonism, the free-love commune at Oneida, and the first encampments for feminist conferences at Seneca Falls.

Even the new European phenomena of Spiritualism, which Charles Dickens, the great friend of W. T Stead (Borderland publications), was known as an adherent, made it into Boston society and beyond. Few now realize the reality plethora of "utopian communes" that blossomed and quickly failed in many locations during the 19th and early 20th centuries in the U.S. (however, the Millerites morphed into The Seventh Day Adventist Church) and the Mormons found a permanent home as well.   Spiritualism continues today as The Theosophical Society.

These influences also produced new radicals in the form of the fire-brand circuit preacher Lyman Beecher and his children, including Henry Ward Beecher and Harriet Beecher-Stowe. It was Henry who purchased rifles and exhorted young men in New England to "go to Kansas and kill Southerners." Meanwhile, Harriet met a runaway slave and from that claimed "visions" that informed her of the reality of slavery in the South and wrote her famous, although completely fictitious melodrama, "Uncle Tom's Cabin." Once again, the methods of Christianity utilized violence; Henry's rifles, termed "Beecher's Bibles" were so-called because he had reckoned that they would be more effective than Bibles in bringing about the abolition of slavery, while Harriet's book was galvanizing social idealists at home and abroad.

It may be that Greeley's eccentricity, his early acquired, anti-coffee, tea, anti-tobacco, and vegetarianism was due to his likely affliction of Asperger's Syndrome, as the utopian commune named after him in Colorado, as some of his biographers have suggested.   Whatever his affliction might have been, it produced a great deal of inspiration and support for radical ideas and practices because he owned the nation's most influential newspaper.

This likely also caused him to flit from position to position during the long decades of his influence via his New York Tribune. Through him, although not always intentionally, the most dangerous ideas of the 19th century, having their birth in the bloody French Revolution, were able to find a home in the American heartland as well as the coasts, as deeply influenced immigrants from Germany and Scandinavia settled the regions in high numbers. With the addition of Christian virtue as a motivator, the extremes of traditional Christian socialism became institutionally established as formal Christian Socialism.   From this strange but steady evolution of history, the nineteenth century became the century of revolution in Europe, and it had its influence on

America. The line from the 17th-century English Civil War to the American one is straight; the factions that battled in England then, faced off anew in 1861. "God" driven Oliver Cromwell led the self-righteous Puritans in an echo of the Continental Thirty Years War by beheading England's Catholic monarch and warring with the "loyalist" troops to finish Oliver Cromwell's reign as Britain's only dictator in its history. This is the same Cromwell who committed genocide in Ireland in the name of his religion and God, even sending over 50,000 Irish men, women, and children into perpetual slavery in Barbados. Whatever anyone says today, the color-blind nature of the slavers is abundantly evident in history. It required socialist/anarchist radicals to make it see only one color as part of its Machiavellian design.

This time, however, the religious fervor of it was only part of the cause, although an underlying political tow that found active expression and influence in the Lyman clan. Protective tariffs were favored by the Whigs and other parties up to the passing of Stephan Douglas' Kansas-Nebraska Act. That law caused the Whig Party to fracture. Greeley had left it just before and had begun to organize a new party. That party became the Republican Party in 1854. Tariffs were at its center of concern, along with anti-slavery, both inherited from the Whigs. Greeley did not always agree with it, and at first, opposed Lincoln's candidacy and then endorsed him later on after the Confederate Army attacked Fort Sumter, and his paper actually criticized the President for not having attacked sooner. Perhaps Greeley did not know that Lincoln had forced the South's hand by sending a flotilla of supplies into Charleston Harbor, which was in effect the territory of the new nation. Even though that nation saw a vigorous debate preceding the decision, the same decision that had been made in 1776, was made in 1861, and for the same reasons. The South had realized that they would never have a voice in Congress, and combined with the higher Morrill Tariffs set to begin in 1861, it amounted to much more than simple "taxation without representation."

The issue actually rested on the question of the protective tariffs and their effect on the South. For decades, the Northern Industrialists had insisted on a protective tariff in order to compete and grow in the face of the Industrial Revolution in Britain. The Whigs and then-Republican Party supported it. But the North became dependent upon them. A class of men was growing rich and wanted more. The cotton produced through forced labor in the South was enriching the shippers in the North. As the taxes collected from the tariff were used to build up infrastructure in the North, especially railroads, the South was completely neglected. The Northern rails were intentionally of a different gauge, so the cotton had to be shipped up the coast. This ensured that the merchant ships from Northern ports could collect the tariff on that end as well as the delivery end and the South was isolated and helpless. So by the time the Morrill Tariff bill passed Congress in 1860, the Southern States were the economic captive of the Northern Industrialized States. You could say that they were enslaved by the North.

But the Southern States had been brilliant; in their own constitutions, they had made tariffs illegal, so the goods into the North were expensive, while goods coming into the South were cheaper. When the South seceded, they removed most of the North's revenue. The new Confederate States negotiated a more reasonable 6-7% tariff on British goods, and so the merchant ships of New England moved to Confederate ports. This left the remainder of the Union in dire financial trouble. Invasion of the South became their only option.*ⁿ During the same time, Lincoln was discussing a colonizing plan for emancipated slaves to be sent to the Central American region that became Panama. His policy was for no blacks in the Western or Northern States. The states that joined the Union during that time included Oregon which became a state in 1851. This was to halt the spread of slavery, but also to contain the black population for planned evacuation from the U.S., and North American Continent. When Lincoln made his January 1863 Emancipation Proclamation, he did not liberate the nearly one million slaves that were either in Union states or under the Union's control in conquered regions such as Louisiana and Tennessee. Toward the end of the war, Lincoln's postwar plans grew fuzzy. His assassination removed all possibilities from the table.

The Radical Republicans had their own plan, however. This entailed a new invasion of the defeated and largely destroyed South as Carpetbaggers, and corrupt politicians exploited the chaos for self-enrichment.   Whatever arguments one cares to make about his period, by 1868, every publication, newspaper, weekly, and periodical pronounced Reconstruction a failure.

The failure was largely due to the brutality of the war in the South and then the rampant exploitation of it. Martial Law was applied sparingly by unsympathetic officers who also saw many opportunities for self-enrichment.   This led to the rise of vigilantism. The KKK was not the only civil protection group that arose at that time. After the war in Texas, the Union Army left the state to fend for itself against Indian raids, favoring the pro-Union territories across the northern border.*W The Wild West truly got its start in the American South as the lawlessness exploded into the territories, and ex-Confederates from families that had been abused during the pre-Civil War conflict in Kansas Missouri led to the new age of the outlaw gangs that so romanticized, especially during the twentieth century.

This period also saw the first major depression over-speculation in railroads led to the Depression of 1873. It lasted until the late 1880s and was termed The Great Depression until the stock market crash of 1929 produced its successor.

But there were positive events; after leaving the increasingly unreasonable and violent Klu Klux Klan, Nathan Bedford Forrest, a successful businessman before the war, became a successful railroad builder, using free black labor the Yankee way. The Illinois Central, based in New York, clawed its way out of desperation in the 1870s by gambling everything on one railroad line along the Mississippi to New Orleans. It was a great success. In three years Illinois Central traffic rose 500%. The road's president Stuyvesant Fish said that the line was the company's salvation.   In contrast, New York Central's owner Chauncy Depew complained that the Illinois Central was "stealing" business from New York for New Orleans. Fish replied that he was only trying to take back some of what had been stolen during and immediately after the war. But there was even more progress; U.S.

Senator Leroy Percy, who was a friend and hunting partner of Teddy Roosevelt's, began investing, buying up huge tracts of land in the Mississippi Delta. At the same time, Percy was writing tax legislation to tie railroad development to the lands around the Delta. Soon he owned half of the land in the Mississippi Delta.

By 1881, he finished his future empire by buying and lawfully marrying up two more tracts purchased from Illinois to a railroad that never laid a track or owned a locomotive. Eventually, it became the Yazoo and Mississippi Valley Railroad, the Y&MV, coming to be known as "The Yellow Dog," in the Mississippi Blues musical culture of the region.

The purpose of Percy's investment was simple; cotton production. Cotton was in high demand and Percy set up what became the model for the sharecropping arrangement that lasted until the Great Depression. The lingering problem in the South was the black labor force. For reasons other books explore in detail, the black labor situation in the South had been in crisis since the end of the war, and it only grew worse over time. Whatever the meaning of freedom might be for some of the emancipated in addition to travel, freedom from the drudgery of labor was among them. Reality soon eclipsed that notion and many cases of proto-sharecropping arose between former masters and slaves. But in many other cases, labor was unreliable; the hired man would show up late and leave early, or perhaps not show up at all. The low wages and dead-end nature of it was the likely reason. Vagrancy laws arrived and men once again found themselves slaves (poor whites, too) as convict laborers (see – "I am a Fugitive From a Chain Gang").

Percy made the freeman a better deal; he would not only pay better, but the possibility of buying the land you worked on was part of the arrangement. Black labor flocked to the Mississippi Delta and Percy and his family made huge profits while the region flourished. A kind of golden age ensued. However, the rowdiness of the freemen didn't disappear. Most of the blues songs about fights, breakups, murders, and traveling, came out of this period, as bars, gambling, and prostitution thrived in this huge span of private land that was lightly policed, if ever at all. Murder was so common that often the newly dead could lay on the floor in a public bar for hours before anyone took notice, let alone showed up to claim the body. Yet overall, everyone was making money and carrying on. This was the other "Wild West" we had never heard about, even as we listen to popular songs from the region as Delta Blues and a few that popped up in the 50s, such as "Staggerlee" and "Franky and Johnny."

It all came to a sudden end when the Great Mississippi Delta Flood of 1927 brought the era to a close. Desperate times brought out desperate actions. The City of New Orleans deemed that the only way to save itself was to dynamite the lower end of the river, which would flood out the near indigenous Cajuns living there. Further upriver, at the town of Greenville, masses of blacks arrived on the levee as refugees. Expecting to ride the ferry to safety, they watched the last boat sail away with only a few white officials and their families aboard. They had to stay. They were needed for their labor. And since no one volunteered, the work was unpaid. This meant that the agitators had found an inroad. Soon, it was realized that no supplies could be had without getting them from a white man. When they grew unruly, soldiers of the U.S. Army showed up. So they did their work to save their homes and jobs under the guns of white authority. They felt betrayed, and some violence followed.

Percy, who had always taken the administration of justice into his own hands in the huge corporate cotton land, had only seen three hangings in all the time of his management of the large population, and no vigilantism. Of the three that happened, one was a white man who was hanged for killing a black man. Now, his son and family were losing control of their empire and could only watch sadly as brutality broke out. Because Hoover had ordered in the troops, blacks began an exodus from the Republican Party.*⻊

The events of the Great Mississippi Delta Flood of 1927 have often been cited as an example of the depth of racism in America, then, and allegedly now. But it is really about a legacy of an old national tragedy, and a fight over labor and taxes.

If we look a few years later we can see President Hoover's even greater rashness in his response to the 1932 Bonus Army incident. Twenty-thousand overwhelming white protestors, mostly veterans of World War One and their families, who had become homeless due to the Great Depression, converged in Washington D.D. to demand that the promised pension be issued then because of their desperate situation. The Democrats voted to move up the date of the pension from 1945 to the present date, 1932, but the Republicans blocked it from passing. The next act was the one that guaranteed that Franklin Roosevelt would win the next year's election. He ordered in troops which were led by Douglas MacArthur, who with cavalry brandishing sabers and a bayonet-wielding infantry, used tear gas and violence to drive the mass of protestors out of Washington, D.C. This and the Scottsboro Trials were a great boon to the Communist Party USA. We saw it again with the abuses of the CIA regarding LSD experimentation after World War Two, which led to a major social upheaval and advantage for the New Left, led by Herbert Marcuse. No one ever seems to learn. The Marxists have always been skillful in taking advantage of conservative overreach. This is a lesson conservatives should take to heart. But also, this event is an answer to the cries of racism as the central issue around the events of 1927 during the Great Mississippi Delta Flood. It should also be remembered that the City of New Orleans dynamited the lower levees and flooded out the Cajuns living there, who were considered to be of unimportance as subsistence farmers.

Baby Boomers will be familiar with the most familiar song about this event from the British band, Led Zeppelin, who produced an apocalyptic version of the Memphis Minnie song, "When the Levee Breaks." One of its last lines, "I'm going up to Chicago," as the guitars simulate a raging flood and Robert Plant screams/sings, "Goin' down, goin' down now" serves as a prelude to the mass migration out of the Delta to Northern cities and the tensions that came with them as a result. The legacy that rolls on daily on the streets of Chicago has truly become a self-devouring Frankenstein Monster.

In 1909, the NAACP was established. George Washington Carver opposed it, believing that the road to equality would be necessarily generational. DuBois and the NAACP believe in the absolute, immediate reality of equality by direct demand, in the tradition of the 19th-century European revolutionary movements. He received the 1900s equivalent of "canceling" treatment. The founders of the NAACP were all white socialists, except for one, WEB DuBois. DuBois was of mixed racial background. He was from a Massachusetts family of European and African heritage. His mixed father left his mixed mother when he was two years old. Although it is reported that he was treated well by white kids and in general in Great Barrington, Massachusetts, he would later write about the racism he felt there as a child, starting with his father's desertion. If you try, you can find racism in everything, and WEB DuBois did. When he attended the all-black college, Fisk University in Tennessee, he found the strife he saw and its harsh laws up close. He was given a seat at Harvard, which somehow was not too racist to let him in and from there received a scholarship from a white philanthropist who spent the fortune he had amassed via capitalism to send DuBois to Germany from which he returned as a fully committed Marxist. Even the NAACP found DuBois to radical at times, so he had an on and off again membership with that organization.

In 1920, DuBois in his wisdom published a book of poetry titled "Dark Water." In it was a poem that called for the total extermination of the white race, worldwide. He called on God to do it, "Christ, I hate them, I hate them well, If I were God I'd sound their death knell, this very day." WEB DuBois repeated himself at the 1949 World Peace Conference in a speech wherein he warned the white world that "They may arm themselves against Armageddon, but the Brown Tide is Rising and will engulf them." DuBois wrote and talked himself into suspicion. When Stalin died in 1953, Dubois eulogized him, praising him for his ability to bring members of various ethnic groups together peacefully, even though he had visited the Soviet Union, which had attempted a tragic, but predictably unsuccessful black colony. It is interesting to note that the CPUSA had injected itself into the

Scottsboro trial fiasco, which DuBois himself used to his benefit. It will never be known whether Ruby Bates, who was eighteen years old at the time of the alleged crimes had been bribed or threatened into recanting and claiming they were merely prostitutes; prostitutes at eighteen years of age. The pressure on the two young women was national and intense.*ᗷ The issue remains a hot topic today. But that the rape of white females by black males is a political fantasy is countered by decades of FBI and other records.*ᗤ

In 1919, the Russian Revolution had devolved into a genocidal pissing game, as civil war broke out there. The Bolsheviks were already emigrating abroad to spread the revolution, and so, transported through newspapers, wires, and Ellis Island, the ideas of Bolshevism spread. The KKK had a revival that was no longer about state's rights or slavery, but about America, and against the various races and ethnic groups it considered to be in on the overthrow of the nation. It had memberships in all of the states of the union. It was the paranoid reaction to the threat of a new civil war, this time with clear, international influences. So every prejudice, every xenophobic button was pushed, and so with the post-war recession and lack of jobs helping, the Red Summer of 1919 exploded and race riots erupted in various cities across America. DuBois ended his illustrious career by joining the communist party officially and then moving to Ghana, where he died in 1961. From his early childhood on, DuBois had been the subject of the racial experimentation of white people.

Ironically, though he wrote and spoke viciously of his hatred of white people, both of his wives had been white. By the time of the Scottsboro tragedy, which is all it can be called, the Communist Party USA had published "Toward Soviet America," by William Z. Foster (Foster was a member of the Garland Fund, which financed the CP USA until at least 1934). At the same time, international communism - Comintern, empowered by the Scottsboro trials, was identified by the FBI as a form of warfare managed by the Soviet Union through the then-powerful Communist Party USA. Combining with four domestic communist movements, Comintern had already published a declaration of purpose in creating a separate Negro state, to be carved out of a few existing states in the South. Ironically, this was fielded in the full face of the arguments of the time and now that segregation was unjust, and equal rights were the goal of black folks universally. The Soviet goal was to foment an uprising within the South that would in turn attract black workers and white sympathizers from the North. The plan was when the opportunity came as was expected, the two groups would unite and reconstitute America into a Soviet sister state. The Soviet Union may not exist today, but these ideas are being fielded today. Part of the strategy is to subvert suburban life. North Highlands was merely one of the early victims of the revival of this process. Socialists/Marxists use people. They were there at the beginning. They agitated for war in the 1850s, playing every angle, and they used emancipated slaves to divide and conquer America.

While the highly flawed character, Martin Luther King, Jr. preached peaceful protest in the tradition of India's Gandhi,*⊕ the effect of DuBois on African Americans was not only real, but reportable historically. DuBois was a frank communist, while MLK was a Christian Socialist. Our black population has been manipulated by the Socialists since even before the Civil War, as Marx called for a war of liberation in the South as a useful flashpoint for a worldwide worker's revolution. Much has been made of the debt owed for America's era of slavery and many organizations have benefited from keeping that complaint alive. In fact, it became an industry and has made many people extraordinarily wealthy. You may be sure that they have no intention of killing the "racist" white goose that lays the golden eggs.

This has to remain a myopic consideration through the suppression of the history of slavery, which that illustrates whites suffered alongside blacks in the colonies and then internationally, and that slavery was the major source of labor in the world until the 19th century when Western Civilization, that means whites, began to eradicate it worldwide.*⊕⊕ Whites stand in the way of world authoritarianism because they have such a long history and culture of democracy, they are the most stubborn about giving it up. The solution is to use race to first vilify and then destroy them systematically. And every method has been employed short of out and out violence, although that is becoming more often spoken of in some corners by some people on the public stage.

While slave-taking and its abuses continued, including the taking of whites by American Indians in the western territories, where they were only sometimes ransomed and later only sometimes released as part of treaties that were often violated, black slavery ended in the U.S. at the close of the American Civil War. It has been the Leftist manipulators that have led blacks and whites alike into the historical amnesia that allows for outrageous demands and actions, that have now risen to the level of existential concern nationally. Be that as it may, the national focus on Black slavery as the sole historical example of slavery in the U.S., colonial history, and the plethora of non-black examples of the same period, constitutes racial solipsism.

The Union's prosecution of the Civil War as the first modern war was uncivil, violating the later adopted Geneva Conventions by attacking cities and civilians, intentionally burning homes, and destroying crops to cause mass starvation.*Ŧ Sherman intentionally burned an irreplaceable historical archive of early American history during his sweep across the South. Grant and Sherman led a total war against the South in a way that did not appear to be aimed at an eventual reunification, regardless of President Lincoln's sanguinary tone after Lee's Surrender. The Uncivil War led to uncivilized activities in the conquered South. It is far too simple to chalk up all the atrocities to the Southern reaction. And of course, it was being guided by Lincoln's Marxists.*₇

Today, they appear have nearly achieved their final end. The one-two punch involved the exploitations of racial tensions while working to see more sympathetic populations grow in the U.S. through immigration from countries on the verge of revolution. In Brooklyn, a young man named Emanuel Celler ran for Congress and won a seat in the House of Representatives. He remained there for nearly fifty years, from 1923 to 1973 (the son of Jewish immigrants from Germany, he attended Columbia University, from which Beat Poet Jack Kerouac would drop out in 1942, saying, "All they want to do is teach communism"). Like the Roman Catholic Church as the Vatican, the Marxists understand the value of playing the long game, so they inserted themselves into politics the moment they were able. Even the seemingly innocent poem on the statue of liberty was written by Emma Lazarus, a fourth-generation American, but a socialist, feminist who wrote the poem as she saw the increase of fellow Jews and Socialists as a good thing, and after all, they were refugees from Christian political persecution. Truly, it is the grand errors of Christianity and authority that have opened the door to the Socialist opportunists every time, and right up to the present via the age-old alliance of Church and Monarchy in Europe that led to the French Revolution and the rise of modern communism, and the alliance of Church and State in the United States*† that led to the prejudices that even the social idealists from Germany perpetrated in the Midwestern states after their arrival in the 19th century.

Celler sat on the board of the Garland Fund, which financed the Communist Party USA in its early decades. Celler was obsessed with immigration law because of his desire to see more fellow Eastern and Southern Europeans admitted to the U.S. after the Johnson-Reed Immigration Act of 1924 became law and brought the immigration moratorium that has been credited by some historians for allowing just enough time for assimilation to allow for a united U.S. military to win World War Two. As even a broken clock is right two times a day, Celler acted when "his people" required it. To his credit, he worked hard to find destinations for Jews fleeing Nazi Europe during World War Two. However, his overall legacy is the Ted Kennedy sponsored, "Immigration and Naturalization Act of 1965, the provided the turning point for American demographics, and oddly enough, politics, even though Ted Kennedy insisted that it would have no noticeable effect on American demographics. The result is a new post-constitutional America. One piece of evidence of this is the declaration of the Washington State Supreme Court regarding crime and punishment. They had announced that whites will be punished more severely than non-whites for the same crime, establishing the national trend of recent years.

The game if nearly completed. The whole thing was a plot to ensure a Democratic/Socialist majority forever. The Clower-Piven Social Welfare Strategy*$_{12}$ was devised at the same time to produce another one-two punch for creating a future government-dependent population of diverse ethnic and cultural groups that could be counted on to never successfully unite, especially if identity politics were developed and exploited, and so they were.

The rest is, as they say, history, and we have arrived just in time to see its crescendo. Today, the drive toward white genocide in Western nations, once dismissed as the claim of a fringe of ultra-right-wing white racists is not even being slightly disguised.*℗ Today, the specter of mass population control via legalized drugs to stupefy them, a supplemented or guaranteed income, an array of computer distractions, the tolerance of violence, and a handy pill for use when the dissipation finally becomes too much to bear, complete the once considered dangerous vision of Aldous Huxley.*

During the sixties, radicals used race and claims for liberation campaigns of every sort. The Frankfurt School, a collection of Neo-Marxists led by Herbert Marcuse and Eric Fromm, immigrated from Germany to the U.S. before World War Two and brought their radical political Neo-Marxism with them and developed the political action tactics known as Critical Theory with them.*$_8$ Quickly put, Critical Theory is the active application of Machiavellian principles into Marxist aims by dividing people by race and sex and playing on the vanity of one to set it against the other by exploiting and enlarging the sense of historical grievances. Marcuse was an old hand at subversive activities by the time the war was over. He had been born in 1898. Virtually none of the main movers and shakers of the sixties were Boomers, but they converged in the 1960s to exploit the first post-World War Two generation. As it turned out, it was a perfect storm of Left and Right atrocities perpetrated on children.

The Baby Boomer generation was not the cause of the present crisis; they were merely the first guinea pigs. Ken Kesey had early on declared the LSD explosion as "The Revolt of the Guinea Pigs." And their parents and the government created prime conditions for their exploitation as they served as both actual guinea pigs for the CIA's MK-ULTRA program which once it "got out of hand" because a new project for both private and government social scientists, as well as cannon fodder for a war that drove the Military/Industrial Complex through the sixties.*9   This author heard the argument for the economic benefits of that war directly from parents and community members in North Highlands at the time. The military kids had always been "more worldly" than we local kids. When I was fifteen, someone took me to a party for the military teens that was held on McClellan AFB. I was amazed at the crowd, the live band that the base had recruited for the kids, the lack of any adult chaperone, and the goings-on. These kids were running wild, and they had an influence on the less worldly kids in North Highlands. A hike across the field on the north side of U Street, north of the former Spook Tree, to Capehart in the summer of 1968 with a friend enlarged that impression. Later, my Air Force family girlfriend was two years younger than me but far more forward than me. I just didn't think it was right to get started that young.

As with the Jack Kerouac example*Щ, history illustrates that Marxism was creeping into the profession of educators earlier than most think. In California, after Proposition 13 defunded many school programs and left the teachers relatively impoverished, many moved on to make a better living. The ones that took their places were Marxists that didn't mind taking less money because they were doing what they considered important work. This allowed for a major tide shift in American education.

Howard Zinn was a Marxist who became highly consequential to the present national crisis of America's meaning and future direction by capturing the historical narrative in public school curriculums.*10 Educated in history, he led the efforts to revise history textbooks used in public schools. Zinn had inserted himself into the mechanism of school textbook editing beginning in the 1950s. By 1980, he was in charge of it. In that year, his revisionist campaign in elementary schools on upward began in earnest. His efforts to produce generations of youth that would hate America are thoroughly exposed via the historian, Mary Grabar's latest work, "Debunking Howard Zinn."*[11]

Gandhi wrote his "Seven Blunders of the World" as his view of the bad habits that he considered the primary causes of suffering in the world.*[12]   His grandson Arun added an eighth, "Rights without responsibilities." The mechanism is on full display today, I believe. A mousetrap works because the mouse thinks the cheese is free. The Cloward-Piven Social Welfare Strategy implemented beginning in the 1960s is the historical root of the current central issue.*[13] When we focus only on our rights to exclude the notion of responsibilities, we end up with "infantilization," forever raging at the consequences of that free cheese. Like a baby in a high chair, we only scream for more.

As a consequence of my understanding of this deeper set of historical events and the highly developed strategies that were played on the American public for over one-hundred-and-fifty years, I lay no blame on any group, except the puppet masters and those who would take power for themselves over the naturally free populations of the world. The Bolsheviks had the most cynical word for the people they manipulated "useful Idiots," who would be eliminated as soon as their usefulness was exhausted.

The creation of grievances for social disruption was a large part of that effort. It often requires the distortion or complete rewriting of history or the trick of simply leaving it out while suggesting an alternate focus. They systematically and intentionally promoted victimhood. One of the products of these efforts, which attacked almost every facet of life, has been the infantilization of future generations. Through radical feminism, the family unit and masculinity were attacked. Converting women from marriage to a man to marriage to the state or a corporation was the goal as part of the strategy to eventually, cause all to be dependent on the state. Antagonism of all sorts was encouraged so that emotions have become more important than the weight of facts. This created a social justice industry that has long been dependent upon the continuation of the notion of an overwhelming, permanent oppressor.   Once a critical mass of infantilized population is achieved, we have a potential army of zombies. In fact, studies and people like Andy Ngo, who has infiltrated and widely reported on ANTIFA found that most members of ANTIFA are aged 18-29 and live at home with their parents. This is a symptom of a larger failure and dysfunction that was planned seventy years before, arguably earlier. This has become the norm, not for just one side, but for almost everyone as the bleed over into even conservative culture has occurred in its own way. Both sides mythologize history, for example. The critical mass for societal implosion was reached sometime in the late eighties and early nineties.

The culture of drug use and social rage has been learned by everyone, even if they do not use drugs, a la "Brave New World," to produce an Orwellian dystopia via a combination of drugs and the internet. Since then, the increase in infantile thinking has been encouraged through social media, as Allan Bloom warned in "The Closing of the American Mind, in 1988. Now, the age of the cyber world arrived and became dominant in influence and danger. Entropy is the dominating force in the universe. It requires a great deal of determination to roll the rock uphill. But everything depends on doing that every day, especially in our minds.

The strategy of any totalitarian regime, or the individual who wishes dictatorial rule, is to erase the memory of the people they plan to rule so that they cannot muster up an alternative to the reality supplied to them by that regime or dictator. This is what Stalin did. This is what Mao did. This is what Hitler tried to do.

This is what historical revisionism does. The final move is on to destroy the last remnants of cultural and historical memory. When this is done, society will be like a victim of advanced Alzheimer's disease. The West will be an empty shell where new occupants may be transferred in, like Dr. Frankenstein planting the wrong brain into the monster he already created out of pieces of several once identifiable human beings. I may not be a Christian or believer in a supernatural cause, but I could agree with anyone who says that everyone needs to take a step back, forgive one another, after acknowledging the facts of history, not the myths, and then stop doing this stuff right now! We're out of time;... we're crushed by the tumbling tide of time.

Lines of History, Lines of Thought - Connections

So what has this to do with my tale of the Spook Tree and the lore around it? Nothing happens in a vacuum, and one thing leads to another, connecting all as one. This is obvious to me.

The Spook Tree was created by the same causes that changed the land from wild pastureland to what we call a civilized state. The civilized state has finally arrived at its existential crisis. It becomes increasingly difficult in such a maelstrom to find meaning, and even purpose, unless it is packaged for us. Yuri Bezmenov lectured on the use of distractions and misinformation, which is also the point of Critical Theory; bend meanings and inject them with modified meanings, create a system for policing language using the ruse of social justice to destroy the capitalist state and open it to the new socialist ordering. This Mr. Bezmenov explained, is how the KGB operated. It was a passive exercise; appealing to the emotions by exploiting every possibility for ethnic and racial division, encouraging any and all decadence, music, film, feminism, and so on as long as it leads to the goal of destroying the pillars of civilized society and creates so much confusion that the average person cannot determine what is true. As Bezmenov noted, "to the point that it does not matter how much proof you pile up in front of the person; it will not prove anything to them. This increasingly became the condition of America and the West during the sixties, and increasingly after.

The true believer operates the same way. For them, "faith" trumps facts every time. We end up faceless souls under the rule of a seemingly indifferent god, or else our "god" strangely takes on an identity closer to our own. This is demonstrated by the fact that today there are approximately 42,000 sects of Christianity.*†† I don't think any Christian alive today, including the Pope could pass the

Inquisitions inspection. The point being, as Carl Sagan noted, "Christianity has become a social lubricant, allowing people to feign to tolerate people they really don't tolerate." But Christianity holds the title of the world's first intolerant religion. Up to then, all religions accepted others, and Rome was tolerant of all religions, including Judaism, with which they had worked out special arrangements so that for example, Jews did not have to participate in required public religious festivals, like the winter solstice festival of Saturnalia, which the Christians converted into Christmas while exterminating the pagans that had tolerated them for four hundred years, even sheltered them from the infrequent Roman persecutions of the third century, which was dangerous.

The early Christian "Taliban" known as the "Parabalani" expanded to be the Inquisition, which was only more formalized by the most ironically named Pope, Innocent III, organized to aid the Albigensian Crusade against a "heretical" Christian sect in southern France called "Catharism," in the 13th century. Stalin trained for the priesthood before becoming a Bolshevik. He used the form of show trials and mass murder based on politics as the Inquisition had.

The only difference is Stalin was living in the industrial age and so could be more efficient in his purges. Stalin accomplished what took the Inquisition centuries, thanks to industrialization. But there is no doubt that if such means had been available they would not have been utilized. The intent and proclivity are abundantly evident in the records of history. The French Revolution was the product of those centuries of oppression, and human beings, flawed as they are, only created another oppressive system out of it. The pendulum is still swinging and the power gaps instability creates are created opportunities for the most aggressive. Such people converged in America in the sixties and projected their ideas into the present to great consequence.

Sixties radicals of the Weather Underground wrote that once "the revolution" took control they reckoned 25 million Americans would need to be purged.*15 We are hearing strangely familiar comments today.   That 25 million by the projection of population increase becomes something like 60 or 70 million. It's as if Stalinists are setting the stage for the future of America, beginning with a big purging of political undesirables, the big, big basket, you might say, not imagining, as Yuri Bezmenov illustrated, that they will, in turn, be purged themselves.

As it is, the proponents of Critical Race Theory have pronounced their findings that melanin-spare skin is the cause of racism, contradicting the American philosophy of individual determination and everything Martin Luther King, Jr. ever said about being judged by character, not skin color. It seems that the reactive hatred of WEB DuBois has won out in the end.   Today, we are seeing the calls for a separate black state in the American South again from certain quarters. They are of the same ideological and historical line as the Marxist Radical Republicans of Reconstruction, and the various communist organizations in the thirties. The wedge that drove the parties apart was 19th-century Capitalism and Socialism.

This is why knowing genuine history is essential, especially the details, where true meaning is revealed. Erasing historical memory is the main activity of the Marxist/Socialists. The encouragement to be distracted, indulge one's senses, and use substances, is part of the strategy. They do this to create a population that will accept their enslavement, as Aldous Huxley warned a society that was too self-indulgent could easily become.*[16] But this has lately been combined with outright annihilation as the Fentanyl epidemic has moved in as an apparent plan to kill as many U.S. citizens are possible. The circumstances that have allowed matters to get to this point are important to understand. An examination of details is dangerous without an appreciation of the full historical period, concurrent events, and similar accounts throughout the ages. While history does not exactly repeat itself, it often imitates the past as a new version of the same old human issues. The question now is, how many times can we flaunt its lessons? This question has to be a concern of all thinking people. Rule by guilt and fear must be rejected entirely.

On top of all of this is the fact of climate change due to human activity. But once again, the Left only finds it useful as a tool for asserting universal control of socialist bureaucracies and a two-tier social system, with a self-selected elite in charge and the dependent masses under them. Currently, there is a move to remove the middle class by attacking the suburbs and making them equivalent to inner cities by buying up land and mass immigration, legal or not. Accommodation is the new boom as constructing apartment flats while eliminating the typical suburban three-bedroom two-bath and backyard culture goes forward. The idea of personal property will be eliminated and large corporations like Blackwater Global, and other international companies owned by landlords connected to the CCP. This deception is only possible because of the exploitation of the real problem by the Socialists. The idea that any real-world solution would be possible without making China responsible for its huge and growing output of polluting agents is simply ridiculous and a clue to the fact that this is not about solving the global warming problem, but suppressing the West, especially the U.S., to make way for the "Chinese Century." It would actually be the beginning of a new Dark Age which the world might never recover from.

It's impossible to imagine how anyone could be ignorant of the CCP's record on human rights, its treatment of its minorities, even to the point of its monstrous human organ harvesting program that victimizes their Uighur and Falun Gong populations in crimes against humanity that eclipse the activities of the Nazis during World War Two. It's this country that wants to be exempt from any environmental responsibility while they profit from the solar panels and windmills that will likely break down in a relatively short time. To any serious, investigator the fact of human-caused climate change is indisputable. While the politicians politic, the world literally burns. The Great Barrier Reef is producing 87% less new coral as the old coral dies off. The polar caps are melting. The Greenland Ice Sheet has collapsed. Now evidence has emerged that the Atlantic Meridional Overturning Circulation is failing due to the warming of the ocean and the dilution of salt in the seas. The AMOC has been operating since the last ice age and human life and activity have become dependent upon it, as it controls climate and resultant food production. Salty water cools quicker. As it is diluted, the current slows down. Scientists fear that it will stop completely in a few decades. But the build-up will be noticed. I'd argue we're witnessing it now.

The predictions of the 1872 MIT report, Limit To Growth, and its thirty-year update show the predictions to be accurate and on schedule according to the projections made in 1972. That update is now nineteen years old. However, its projections are being exceeded by reality. We don't have a lot of time to mess around.

Is There Any Hope?

There is always hope. And by that, I mean tangible hope. But it is not windmills birds. Nor are solar panels that might be nice for homes in the suburbs, but not the answer for the national power grid. Manufacturing and disposing of them is a source of highly toxic pollution. We are close to the development of hydrogen fuel cells for homes which will render solar panels obsolete. I accept that the internal combustion engine must give way to cleaner technology. I have no problem with electric cars, trucks, ships, etc., except, where will the electricity come from? Here is the real answer; we are only a few years away from the realization of the fusion reactor. Since 2007, thirty-five countries have worked together, aiming to generate a significant amount of energy from hydrogen fusion for the first time. The first experiments are scheduled for 2025, and full nuclear operations in 2035, although the senior management knows that further delays are unavoidable. "The complexity of the project is built-in," as they used to say. So, between 2035 and 2040, the reactor will heat up minute amounts of hydrogen isotopes (only 2 grams) at 150 million degrees (plasma), which will trigger their nuclei to fuse, like in the sun and the stars. This should generate a tremendous thermal power of 500 MW.

Molten Salt Reactors (MSRs) differ hugely from the light water uranium types by virtue of these features; the molten salt is both the energy producer and coolant. If it overheats, a plug in the jacket melts and the liquid flows into a tank under the plant. But this is not likely because molten salt is both the fuel carrier and coolant due to the nature of the salts used. This means that they can be built anywhere because they don't require cooling towers. This is because the melting point of salt is 1,500 degrees centigrade, while water is 100c. In order to facilitate fission, the water must be heated far beyond the boiling point. That means that it has to be pressurized. This is why light-water reactors are dangerous. All three major nuclear accidents occurred because the cooling systems broke down or as with Fukushima, the generators were flooded and knocked offline. The reactor was automatically shut down because of the earthquake, so when the generators were flooded the cooling only lasted while the batteries remained charged. After they expired, the core overheated. Molten Salt Reactors operate between 600-700 degrees, well under the boiling point of salt. Not only does it take the major risk out of nuclear energy production, but it also eliminates the high cost and maintenance of the Light Water Uranium Reactor.

They can be of almost any size. They have no measurable radioactive waste product, they cannot be used to create fissile material for nuclear weapons development, and they produce more energy more cheaply as they are far more efficient than light water uranium reactors. As a spectacular bonus, they will be able to produce so much excess energy that oceanic and atmospheric carbon capture will be possible and go in tandem with desalinization as a stopgap for drought-ridden areas like California until the natural balance of nature returns. They will be able to produce so much energy that they will represent a new age for humanity. Thorium Liquid Fluoride Salt Reactors technology will produce refinements that will improve nuclear medicine by providing specific radioisotopes that can be bound to specific antibodies and target specific cancer while not harming local tissues as the less precise types of the past and present, by making it possible to kill cancer cells individually. They can produce abundant hydrogen cheaply for the fuel cells that will fuel cars, trains, jets, and ships, and provide homes with cheap electricity. Kirk

Sorensen of Flibe Energy has shown that carbon-free diesel fuels can be produced. Last year, Cummings announced the production of a hydrogen engine for commercial use. MSRs can produce huge amounts of free hydrogen. His design is for a Thorium rather than a Uranium type. Thorium has 200 times the energy potential than Uranium, and it is as common as lead, so it is literally dirt cheap. Modular Reactors now seem the to represent the way forward due to their flexibility.

After Water, Energy is Everything

In the U.S., two were being set up in Wyoming and Texas as of 2012, but funding and construction have been stalled up to now by adversarial laws and red tape that favor big oil and/or plans for billions of windmills and solar panels that will have to be built in China, which is no guarantee of realization or stability. There will always be a need for oil as all plastics are made from it, but we have to make changes where energy production is concerned. We can't even guarantee that these limited mechanisms' supply is guaranteed. There is no time to waste. The hope is that politics can be bridged by politicians for supporting this ultimate alternative to smacking birds out of the sky with inefficient windmill blades and poisoning our environment through the solar panel industry of China.*₪

China is currently producing 27% of the world's carbon emissions, while the U.S. is at 11% and falling. They are installing more, not less coal plants to make solar panels and windmills for the U.S. Moreover, these forms require huge pieces of land or sea for occupying which displaces all sorts of life as it imposes on the natural landscape. And once the energy is captured, it will require hugely expensive, giant bands of cables that must also be routed for miles, sometimes hundreds of miles, creating more environmental harm. Is this the way to save the planet and ourselves?

The good news is that recently, legislation has been introduced in the Senate by a Republican for a secure and legal pathway for Thorium as a fuel source for molten salt reactor development projects underway by numerous U.S. companies. So the possibility of bipartisan support has possibilities. Molten Salt Reactors can be erected on old coal plant sites, and present nuclear power sites can be refitted to MSRs. Thorium as fuel seems to bring the best overall results and it is abundantly available worldwide. Four times more than uranium, which is almost as abundant. Thorium is 200 times more energy dense than uranium. It is 2,000 times more energy dense than carbon-based fuels. Thorium is so abundant that it is considered a waste product of rare earth mining. Thus, it represents an incredibly cheap fuel source. They are much cheaper to build than light water uranium reactors, and far less problematic than them and the so-called "renewable" energy solutions so widely discussed by many nations today. They can be built anywhere because they don't require water to cool the fuel and they don't produce fissile material, which is why they were unselected in 1969 when President Nixon had the Oakridge National Laboratory Thorium program shut down. This was because Light Water Uranium Reactors produced nuclear fissile material necessary for national defense. The other reason is believed to have been as a favor to the oil, gas, and coal industries, which feared being put out of business. But now it is 2022, and we see the need to move beyond the dependence, politics, and toxicity of carbon-based fossil fuels. Thankfully, all sides are recognizing this and at the same time, the danger posed if China, which has had 700 scientists working on their LFTR development for several years, using the plans that were developed by the U.S. Oakridge National Lab in 1957. They had an operating model there for several years until Nixon shut down the program over budgeting concerns and the fact that MSRs are not very useful for producing nuclear weapons. Other reasons, such as competition with the fossil fuel industry were a possibility that has been discussed lately. However, now, the enthusiasm is bipartisan.

Kirk Sorensen, a NASA astrophysicist with a foundation in nuclear physics was searching for ways to produce usable water for future Mars colonization when he discovered the old archives from the Oakridge National Lab project in 2000 and put them online. If they could work on Mars, they can work on Earth. He turned his concern from Mars to Earth. This is how the Chinese got the plans as well as other countries. The plans were stored in a closet at the children's library at Oakridge. They were almost destroyed. Since then, he has been building momentum. He established Flibe Energy in 2011. Sorensen is altruistic in that he sees all efforts domestically and internationally as a necessity for mankind's survival. If we can create an atmosphere on Mars out of nothing we can reverse the unhealthy trends on this planet. So Kirk Sorensen switched from his work in NASA to a private venture based on a most earnest vision of future chaos if the work done at the Oakridge National Labs in the 1960s was lost to future generations. It had to be rescued and revived. Currently, Flibe Energy is working in conjunction with the Pacific Northwest National Laboratory. Terrapower, also located in the PNW, has been granted a construction permit for the long-delayed Wyoming project. Modular Reactors can be set up as MSRs, or in several other configurations. Three are now planned for Washington State.

The movement was very small at first, but now it is about to be realized. But the U.S. Department of Energy is moving too slowly, while China accelerates. They seem to have a problem permitting the construction of an MSR yet still permit LWURs. Molten Salt Reactors, and the emerging Hydrogen Fuel Cell technology, will effectively end the age of oil use in transportation. Of course, oil is used for many other purposes. One would think they might be satisfied with survival, if not dominance since it means the survival of all. The good news is that Republican support for Molten Salt Thorium Reactor development has developed. The effort is bipartisan. The current development is driven by private companies such as Terrapower, which has three related projects in progress in the Pacific Northwest. Other private companies internationally involved are Terrestrial Energy, Flibe Energy, Moltex Energy, Copenhagen Atomic, Thorcon Power, and Sea Bors, as well as other now emerging entities such as Elysium, which is designing a reactor that will burn the waste from light water reactors exclusively. ThorCon, with a model ready for production but lacking the DOE permit, is constructing a shipborne MSR for Indonesia, which has no such red tape to defeat. India and

China have government-sponsored programs. In 2016, Thorcon announced that they can build Liquid Salt Thorium Reactors within a two-year window. Most of these companies are waiting on the DOE and NRC to issue licenses for construction, a process that drags on for five years for purely bureaucratic reasons. It's time to get going!

Discipline and Flexibility are Required

We must become realistic and pragmatic. Isaac Asimov wished for a type of "One World Government." This he always said, was the only way that we could solve the huge problems that lay before humanity and that space exploration would only be possible if the Earth was united, which means, they will have made war obsolete and peace a constant. He was naïve in this statement and demonstrably incorrect. He said that it didn't matter what you called it, The United World, or even Anarchy. Since he lectured at universities and college campuses for decades, he was one of the driving forces behind the violence of the young Left that we see today. If he were alive today, I wonder if he would say that his influence had produced the outcomes he was hoping for. But his purist requirements are wrong; we made it to the moon as a national goal. In Arthur C. Clarke's "2001, a Space Odyssey," there is an international space station where frenemies" carried on their socializing while working for opposing governments in a sort of Cold War-style Detente. The International Space Station has been a reality for some time. Today, all the theoretical physicists and Futurists are saying that the only way for the human race to survive will be as a multi-planetary species. With the invasion of Ukraine by Russia, the emergencies we face are complicated by the possibility of wider war, even world war. Clearly, the human race has arrived at its historical crisis point. Indulging in "Doomsday" apocalyptic beliefs only guarantees that a portion of people is taking the religious form of the Huxlian model and escaping from reality.

Far from international cooperation, China is space planning strategically, and the U.S. has established its "Space Force." "Satellite Wars" may become the real-time version of "Star Wars," but as a thematic collision with "Mad Max" as the resultant earthly landscape devolves. But none of this will be survivable without enough energy. One certain thing is it will be fairly useless to shoot for Mars if the earth is staggering under expanding population and its present set of future goals, fighting Climate Change with windmills and solar panels made by the greatest polluter and tyrannical government in the world. In his final two short stories, "Nightfall," and "The Last Question," Asimov presented two possible scenarios in a world where humanity faced immediate annihilation due to the same issues of overpopulation and factual biological limitations that we face today. In the former, the population goes mad and is lost. In the latter, they quickly learn to cooperate and survive. Oswald Spengler demonstrated that as civilizations decline, the general population becomes more superstitious and religiously fanatical. The decline and fall of the Roman Empire was only the most well-known and spectacular model because of Edward Gibbon's six-volume tome, but this principle of human nature is all too real throughout history. As then, the Christian tendency to withdraw from worldly considerations increases as world stresses accumulate. This produces neglect, which is what Gibbon said was the root cause of the Roman collapse. Today, we are in danger of repeating history again, but in a far worse way. Today, the former Soviet Union has reverted to the old Church and State alliance. They say that defeat is not possible for them in any scenario because they have nuclear weapons. Armed with their Abrahamic faiths, they claim a nuclear holocaust is tolerable because Heaven will be their reward. They know it. They have declared that they will regain their former imperial glory through war or submission to their enemies. And this time, God is with them. Soviet Russia knew this was not an option.

Is this Really the 21st Century?

In his epic history of the twentieth century, "Tragedy and Hope," historian Carrol Quigley explained how the twentieth century up to and through the Second World War was not actually the 20th century. He claimed that the 20th century did not begin, historically until the event of the atom bombs being detonated at Hiroshima and Nagasaki, beginning the Atomic Age, and a new historical epoch. This was because World War Two was caused by the cultures, prejudices, policies, and events of the 19th century. Even though the technology was 19th century, even though it had been extrapolated into some very highly technical engineering, it was based on 19th-century ideas. Few realize how dependent the German army still was on horses in 1940. Most of the supply and support were horse-drawn, and tanks maneuvered and fought like the horse units of Napoleon and Wellington had at Waterloo. Quigley saw the great divide in history as The Bomb influenced it. One might now argue that we are actually still in the 20th century for similar reasons. The 21st century will begin when we finally can cooperate enough to calm the current anti-nuclear prejudices, based on an obsolete form of atomic energy, and embrace the new. If and when we do, it will be possible to open a new era of humanity, one wise enough to manage itself intelligently, rather than engage in population wars previously driven by religious competition; The Second Atomic Age. If we can do that, and retain or even reestablish true morality and ethics, we might even avoid the end that Isaac Asimov laid presented in its stark certainty in 1980.

Looking to the future, we must recognize that discipline and flexibility will be required of us individually and as a society. Western Civilization now stands opposed to a new, rising Eastern Bloc that menaces freedom on every level. They are counting on our weakness, our infantilism, and they encourage it on every level. They love to see us squabble and fail. Their activity facilitates it at every opportunity. We must rise to the challenge. To do that, we must set our own house in order. I will not comment over much on that as it has become obvious. I trust Christians who at least are largely evolved from the barbarism of the Middle Ages, more than the chaotic promises and practices of Leftists who seem to not even understand themselves beyond the immediate idea of getting things for nothing out of a system they think has an endless supply of "stuff" to reward them with if they will behave.

Diversity is Not Our Strength Unless the Merit System for Success is Followed.

The Founders of the United States were aware of this and tried to avoid it, but the divisions that caused its civil war had a strong religious compulsion as well. This is why I argue for the natural religions of philosophy over the dogma and intolerance of "revealed religions." Is it possible to retain the ethics and morals that are natural to the enlightened mind and reject the superstition, exclusivity, and intolerance of the true believer? Moving beyond this and Marxism, the stepchild of Christianity, we might find a space for the sort of cooperation that allows for real progress. Once the Molten Salt Reactors are in place, the present environmental and energy-driven clashes evaporate. In the meantime, natural gas is clean and cheap. If we suppress that source and sour the economy as is the present plan, we will not have the financial resources to afford the final development and distribution of these new reactors and the infrastructure that a switch to mostly electricity will require.

The British, the French, the Spanish, the Portuguese, and famously, the Ottoman, Russian, and Hapsburg Empires all collapsed due to the problem of increasing ethnic diversity and the inability to manage them justly. In fact, they did just the opposite; they used different groups to control other groups by setting them against one another. Tito did it, too, and the Marxists in America have been doing it throughout most of U.S. history.

The empire model always ends up using one ethnic group to suppress another. The weakening Hapsburg Empire combined with their former enemy of over three centuries to suppress the Serbs in Bosnia in 1878, led to the revenge of the Black Hand when Gavrilo Princip shot Archduke Ferdinand and his wife, Sophia in Sarajevo in 1914, leading to the cataclysm of World War One, and its sequel, World War Two. After 1945, Tito used the historically clashing religious ethnic groups to check each other in Yugoslavia.

But the chess master was mortal. And while he was dying, an event that required ten years to realize, his government was corrupted. Civil war broke out and the old religious and ethnic divisions rose and produced the specter that most people alive today can recall in living memory. The author was nearby in Slovenia for that war's sequel in 1999. The United States has been traveling the same path since the sixties.

China is winning because it is Chinese-centric. The overwhelming majority literally walks in lockstep. One of the most critical historical issues that needs to be examined is the effect of multiculturalism on civilization. In every case, this condition was the result of empire-building. When we examine the history of empires, we find that what collapsed them was the inability to manage the diverse cultures inside of them. We can go from Ancient Greece to Rome, to the early empires in Europe for whom just a split as Christian sects was enough for division and endless purges and civil wars. But as we reach the extremes of both systems' worst weaknesses, it becomes a contest of which will collapse first, China or The United States? The United States of America became equivalent to an empire when it opted out of the system of personal merit for the system of awarding boons to certain groups over others to control them or the other groups. This began in the late sixties. The result has always been division, not unity. All studies show that as diversity increases, trust, even among people of the same racial/ethnic groups diminishes. Today, the calls or guarantees of unity are tangibly fraudulent. In short, America has become Balkanized as well as stratified by race far more than previously seen. They only mean unity within a certain set of politically motivated racial and ethnic groups against our basic American philosophy of personal merit and individual freedom. The confusion that results prepares the way for the CCP, which is already ensconced in our university system, and many of our institutions, including science and technology. They are even buying up farmland and food production plants on the U.S. mainland.

Are You Spooked Yet?

Marxism/Socialism/communism is a historically proven failure. We must face reality and stop using race as a determiner of merit. Philosophy with its children, science, and technology are the basis of Western Civilization, not religion. We must cease to suppress and mythologize history; for the human race, time's about up. So short of a visit from Klatu we cannot rely on belief in alien intervention any more than we can count on Armageddon solving our problems. Science fiction and religious delusion are equally the stuff of the human need to escape reality and feel comforted. They do not help solve the crisis of civilization we now face.

"Who controls the past controls the future. Who controls the present controls the past." – George Orwell

A great American named Patrick Henry once made a speech in the House of Burgesses. He was concerned about the future where the intention of the British Crown was concerned. He said, "I know of no better way of judging the future but by the past." History matters; its accurate report or distortion is the cause of everything.

Civilization depends upon its accurate report. A democracy depends upon people who know their history and can be identified by an over-arching culture of law and justice. Our Constitutional Republic is a form of representative democracy. This is why American and even Western history has been so assailed. All civilizations and people have their dark side, but how many have brought the unending list of benefits to more people than ever before in human history than Western Civilization and the United States of America in particular? When history is preserved and consulted objectively, it informs of the answer. That is why it is attacked and mythologized so constantly, principally but the two struggling polarities have more in common than they realize. Will we be able to overcome ourselves enough to save ourselves?

The effect of these conditions provided for the dysfunctions that led to the current critical impasse we find ourselves in. While Herbert

Marcuse was constructing The New Left at our colleges and universities, conservatives were saying "America, Love it or Leave it." Politicians either wrapped themselves in the "Cross and Flag" or unleased dialectics of deconstruction and the erection of a socialist state through the ideas that the Civil Rights Movement had brought to the fore a few years before. Every minority that could be identified created a similar set of grievances for joining in on the social justice graft system forming. In many ways, Feminism led the way. It was The National Organization for Women that first proposed white genocide through their pronouncement in the 1980s that "no conscientious white woman should bear the children of a white man." So while Marcuse encouraged all of this, elements supported by the Soviets through the CPUSA worked at encouraging every corruptive practice and socialist construction. So while the Right dithered away at supporting big corporations and cheap labor, the Far Left was moving the chess pieces into place.

As Howard Zinn was rewriting school books, The Moral Majority was focused on abortion denial legislation, rights to school prayer in public schools, and the teaching of Creationism as a First Amendment Right, missing the authoritarian aspect of it all. The result has become polarization into mutual camps of infantized political philosophies, neither of which recognizes the meaning of the U.S. Constitution or is now even in favor of it at all as the actual destruction of America is being manifested as ecological, environmental concern, a new wave of justice for imagined or regurgitated claims of historical crimes. As this preceded the habit of ethnomorphism, the fallacy of judging the culture, behavior, and morals of a past time with a selected model of modern assumptions became normal, as encouraged by media, academics, and Hollywood. The damage is not only to history and our sense of it and ourselves, but now it threatens science and even the function of reason and logic in society. In one of his last interviews, Carl Sagan worried about the rise in ignorance of science. He said that in the present situation where schools were graduating fewer and fewer scientists, while personal power and political power were growing to unprecedented levels, the combination of power and ignorance did not bode well for the future. And it seems the future has arrived. Only a few years after Carl Sagan's death, philosophers and psychologists found themselves grappling with a new social phenomenon of enough concern to warrant the recognition of a new field of study, agnotology, which is literally, the study of ignorance, with the problem of the Dunning-Kruger Effect as its central mechanism. It applies to the condition where the less educated consider themselves more knowledgeable than those trained in a field of knowledge. They don't know what they don't know and no one can tell them that they don't know it.

Reclaiming Culture is the Key

Some scholars are writing that the end of history is upon us in this postmodern, post-postmodern civilization where our minds may actually be fading back into the pre-conscious state of functional schizophrenia. It is manifesting, at least in many of the political postural functions of active denial of reality as Julian Jaynes demonstrated as the birth of consciousness, but in reverse. Such extreme political and personal abandonment of reality presents a host of looming dooms – a perfect storm of doom, in fact. It has been proven that as times grow more dangerous the religious become more fanatical. The End Times never end, but nearly every generation has had its fling with The Apocalypse. Its final expression seems to be the re-emergence of a religious medieval empire, with nuclear weapons, engaged in war with the world, armed with that threat and the assurance that their mission is holy and heaven will be their reward for making the ultimate sacrifice universal as a fulfillment of Scripture.

J.R.R Tolkien wrote his Trilogy for several reasons; one was simply to try his hand at the telling of a very large tale. But as Norman Cantor points out in "Inventing the Middle Ages," Tolkien was trying to encapsulate all that was dear to him and what he thought to be representative of the deep values of Western Civilization. He did this through the use of British and Germanic myth idioms for producing what Joseph Campbell later identified as the "Heroic Journey." This journey is about the conquering of darkness with light. It has hereto only seemed to be embraced in the realms of religion and mythology, but science has revealed the dichotomy of the universe. All things come in a binary construction; negative and positive, dark and light, etc., and yet we see all of the heroic and meaningful acts occurring in the ground between. As we walk one road or another in a forest, life exists off the roadway, not on it. Getting off the road, outside of the box, in modern parlance, is where we find the future. The search for knowledge is the true quest.

The Trap of Dichotomy

When Robert Frost wrote "The Path Not Taken," we must wonder if he realized the totality of his metaphor. We can certainly see the mechanism working in our personal lives. I chose to be a D.C. rather than pursue a degree in history and literature. This makes me an amateur writer. I quit racing because I believed I saw the limits and a narrow avenue of opportunities, rejecting some viable opportunities at that moment. One chooses their destiny daily, whether one knows it or not. This is the literal interpretation of a dichotomy. The metaphorical view of it is as expansive as the universe. Between the dark and light is a realm once popularly called "The Twilight Zone." This is where most events occur. The dichotomy can be found in extremes and polarity. Zoroastrianism is the earliest known dualistic religion that posited a struggle between good and evil. Judaism adopted Zoroastrian dualism along with the Babylonian Creation myth "Enuma Elish" when it was created. The view of a struggle between good and evil has become imprinted on the social/cultural Western mind. The meld of government and religion in the ancient world was the political reality. The Abrahamic religions are each an expression of a ruling system based on a dualist cosmic view that requires an overlord that battles with the "evil," and since it was already a cultural habit to project human characteristics and needs onto gods and the elements. Since evil is personified in the form of Satan, Beelzebub, Lucifer, etc., the need to pick sides becomes obvious. This is the root of polarity. We might notice that as the earth has polar opposites as a magnet, life evolved and flourished the furthest from those extremes. In the end, our problem is that dichotomy does not allow for alternatives. In this condition we are told, you are either with us or against us.

This expression is ironically seen first in the Christian Gospels. As a result, Christianity became the world's first intolerant religion. Modern communism (as opposed to Christian forms), arose during the French Revolution. Karl Marx formalized it as a secular religion with the State as the god that must be obeyed. That two of our own Founders, Benjamin Franklin and Thomas Jefferson were present in France before and during the French Revolution, and Jefferson himself (with the Marquis de Lafayette), wrote the "The Declaration of Rights of Man and Citizen," and think of the catastrophe that followed in France and Europe, the importance of alternatives to dichotomous polarity, might be best appreciated. Both the religious and secular polarities declare that you are either with them or against them. They both function to root out individualism and replace it with sameness. They use a myriad of tools and they are very clever. Both act as cults because they seek to indoctrinate from birth or early age. Emotions, biases, especially confirmation bias, **ethnomorphism**, and the dichotomous traps, create a "doomster" culture that cannot appreciate and develop possible alternatives. The frightening part is that this is just one little issue in an enormous stack that must be solved. From the best solution for energy production to whether we continue to burn our forests and police our cities, it all depends upon a citizenry of informed and truly open-minded participants.

An Example of an Alternative Method for Western Forest Management Using Informed Reason

One of the keys to the future is the most intelligent use of lessons to be gained from knowing the past but knowing it well enough to make the correct decisions going forward. One simple example of how this might work in a practical sense is regarding the increase of wildfires in the West, particularly in California. While continuing drought and lighter precipitation due to climate change is part of it, one of the main issues around prevention has been controlled burning. The politicians quote experts who happen to also be pro-timber harvesting, that proscribed burning is the answer. Your author thought so too until some of the research I did from this book created a "Eureka" moment. Going back to the first reports of Kit Carson in the 1830s, he noted "herds of deer, antelope, and elk by the hundreds of thousands everywhere." Some of Sutter's early employees noted that they need not take any food provisions while on a journey to the mill in Coloma or anywhere else, as the game was that plentiful, that all one needed was a rifle. Those wild herds would have been migrating up to the higher elevations in the summer. It is not difficult to connect the dots; these vast herds kept the undergrowth under control.

It is true that as civilization moved in, the herds were reduced in size by huge a huge amount. They were somewhat replaced by cattle herding in the Sierras, the type that we touched on in previous chapters. This began during the Gold Rush in the 1860s and continues today but on a much-reduced program. So we are left with proscribed burning programs that destroy nearly all of the feed for the radically reduced endangered species to the point that no animal life can live in it, wild or domestic. Regardless of good intentions, it is the extremes of management style that are destroying the forests and environment. The problem is also that those who favor controlled burning often deny the issue of human-caused climate change, claiming that the extremes of weather are but a short phase in the story of natural history. But the extinction that is taking place today is unparalleled and possibly final. The current mass extinction rate is 10,000 times higher than any past natural extinction. The result is that there is not enough time for various life forms to adapt. It is not possible to bring back endangered species to the numbers needed to keep undergrowth down naturally. So commercial, domestic grazing of some type must be restored.

Despair is not an option. Neither is escapism, in any form, as superstitious recipes called faith, material obsessions, or chemical. We might examine the idea of life for its own sake, knowledge, and its acquisition as a good in itself. The right to inquire is what authoritarians hate the most and it is exactly what all human freedom and progress require.

As Albert Camus illustrated using the Myth of Sisyphus, we find meaning in the moment we live in. If the work seems hard, the recognition Is in the joy of accomplishment, regardless of the task. For, as Sisyphus was doomed for eternity to push the boulder up the mountain, he also could experience joy in the burden-free journey back down the mountain. The claim of relativism is false. It is instinctual to recognize limits and the emotions of empathy, love, and self-sacrifice need not be insisted upon as an institutionalized formula. We know how to self-regulate using the words of philosophers. Life is happening now. But we got here because of the intellects that were willing to risk straying off the path to find a new way. They understood where they had come from and where they hoped to arrive. Apocalyptic dreams are now nuclear nightmares. As we "wind on down the road" this question is whether we pass this ultimate Darwinian cut where we are our own extinction machine? With the addition of some old-fashioned stoicism, otherwise in modern parlance "keeping your cool," we might collectively find the way forward in the "Twilight Zone" of alternatives. We have attempted to present a viable one here as the paths to true progress are blazed, not followed. The twilight zone of the unknown may seem risky, but it is also where creativity and opportunity exist. It's where you have the only real opportunity to own your own mind.

Famous Last Words

T hanks to the North Highlands Recreation and Parks District, I have been able to study 800 pages of newspaper and other documents that illuminate the History of North Highlands, most of which Dean and Merrie O'Brien assembled in 2001. The maladies that struck North Highlands were to become common in the seventies in nearly every suburban neighborhood in the nation to the point that eventually, no community was unaffected, regardless of income or average educational level. But North Highlands might be one of the first once foremost communities that held out a promise to the future to become what could be termed, a suburban ghetto. Because of increasing community leadership failures at Highlands High School, some too dark to describe here, and in the community up to 1971, cynicism and apathy set in by 1975. The document trail illustrates how a little community goes from blossoming promise to something far less contained in North Highlands' full history if it is studied and contrasted to the wider developments in America during the last fifty years.

Possibly the most damaging trend for North Highlands was its transition from a homeowner-dominated community to an approximately fifty percent renter-based one. Toward the late sixties, the transition began. This change had many causes. Aside from real estate hucksters pushing get-rich-quick schemes through Amway and real estate hustles, a real problem existed because developers refused to build more expensive homes in North Highlands.

This had the effect of driving more successful people to other communities. The situation grew to one where nearly all civic, educational, professional, and business owners were no longer residents of North Highlands, a condition dominant in inner-city ghettos at the time.

The years 1970 -1979 were pivotal years for determining the future of North Highlands. There has been a small ongoing struggle to see a better North Highlands. Those stalwart, energetic souls that have worked to hold up the civic banner deserve great credit. But there are too few of them and the tide is not on their side. This, however, is something that can be changed if enough people join with understanding. The effort must be more than nostalgic reminiscing and living in the past. However, the general voting public must embrace the values that create a stable society. The tragedies of places like North Highlands were only possible as such values were eroded.

It doesn't have to be that way. The Squatter's Riot in Sacramento ended abruptly when events forced their way into the conscience of all involved, regardless of which side of the issue they stood on. That happened because they shared a common set of values as Americans. So the question becomes, "are we of one common set of values with common goals, or are we not? It's not as if we haven't had riots around lately, or all sorts of afflicted suburbs. North Highlands happens to be one I know about enough to talk about because I grew up there into young adulthood from the time of its birth to the time of its pivot. Today, when one searches online, the information they will find on North Highlands is its crime rate and the accomplishments of having a rap artist and an award-winning porn actress as its products. North Highlands is capable of more than this. It has to be. From the hard-pan firmament of North Highlands, many citizens of great character have emerged. I can bear some witness to a few here.

My older sister, Martine was in Highlands High School band and it was great then, in 1968, but it achieved even more afterward, playing at an L.A. Rams game, Disneyland, and even by invitation in Belgium. This went on until the fire that destroyed the band room put an end to the glory era of the Highlands High School Marching Band. They could not replace the bagpipes for example and so Highlands High School and North Highlands lost one of their distinguishing cultural marks. The Highlands High Track Team led by Coach Gilbert set many records statewide. And others of us made academic achievements; the lists of the ten Toppers, and my little contribution in public speaking at Sacramento Valley Forensic League Tournaments, thanks to the tutelage of Margaret Godwyn. And North Highlands produced good, reliable young people. I think the greatest number of employees of the now legendary Tower Records of Sacramento, which became an international phenomenon, is greater locally than in any other community in Sacramento County, at the Sacramento Stores. My youngest sister worked at Tower Records on Watt Avenue, I used to visit several friends at the store on Broadway in 1975, and I even worked one summer at Tower Water Beds, myself, in 1977. (Tower Records is defunct, but the Japanese branches were bought by a Japanese investor and they are still going strong in Japan, at this time).

During 1969, from spring to just before the new school year, I worked at Eddy's Brau Hof. It's how I paid for my first Penton. Many older locals will remember that popular rival to Sam's Hof Brau on Auburn Boulevard, just off the Fulton exit on I-80. It turned out that most of the employees there were boys from North Highlands. Eddy's was a bustling place due to the multitudes of gambling and ski buses chartered in the Bay Area that regularly stopped in beginning on Fridays through to Sunday evenings. It had three two large and one smaller dining room and a full bar with its own seating at the bar and a row of tables against a low wall that separated the bar from the main dining room. The owner was a travel agent and had worked it all out. He even had a special parking lot for the convenience of the buses behind the restaurant. During the weekends, the bus line that led from the buses to the restaurant's cafeteria-style counter lasted for hours.

Once popular spot – long gone
– postcard image – Commercial Printers, PO Box 875, Stockton, California
– color by I.E. Lundholm – cardcow.com

The ladies served whatever was selected from the menu behind them on the wall and in front of them in the steam trays and set it on the customer's tray while a skillful carver whipped his sharpener up and around his long knife in quick, clean sweeps before making his precise cuts to lay them on a plate or open faced bun. The scene created a kind of controlled chaos that lasted for hours. These conditions kept us boys hopping from the moment we clocked in up to the moment the place shut its doors at the end of the day, which was 2:00AM on weekends. During the summer of 1969, I often worked 60-hour weeks, with split shifts on Saturdays.

The manager of Eddy's was Chuck Berry. (Not the musician doing a gig on the side but a white dude with the same name). He happened to have friends on Centinella Drive just up the street from where I lived. In fact, the kids of his friends were good friends of mine. So one evening, my boss came strolling down the street with our neighbors and knocked on our door. He came to meet my parents. He talked about what a hard worker I was and commented that for some reason, the hardest-working kids they have had at Eddy's consistently came from North Highlands. We may have had issues here and there, but overall, we were all generally good kids with little exception, until things began to change.

One of the best of all the citizens and youth to have lived or been produced by North Highlands has to be Roy Edward Pitts. Eddie was a member of my class of 1970, although his Marine record shows him as born in 1950. Eddie Pitts received the Navy Cross and Purple Heart posthumously due to his amazing heroic conduct in Vietnam in 1969. He was one of the only two recipients from Sacramento County to ever receive the Navy Cross, which is only second to the Medal of Honor. I encourage all readers to consult the Honor States site and read the page and citation that describes how Eddie gave his life to save a fellow Marine during a firefight, dragging the wounded Marine across a wide clearing under heavy fire while also verbally directing return fire.*ሕሕ

I knew Eddie; he was a member of our Church. I once came across Eddie in the passway for school kids coming and going to Village School on Stoneman Drive, the very location of the former fields where I had once stopped at the little ponds to spot tadpoles and watch dragonflies. In that alley, Eddie was managing a fight between two younger kids who seemed to really have it in for the other. He made them fight fairly. By the time his instruction was finished, Eddie had them shaking hands grudge-free and better for the experience because they had learned honorability. That was Eddie. I have never known a more fiercely and truly righteous guy personally in my life.

I like to think that Old Man Willis would nod with approval and pride. I also have to wonder whether Eddie Pitts was inspired by the kid lore around the Spook Tree? I know that he knew about the tree. They were mystical hero stories, after all. One time, while I was standing on the playground at Village School, he noticed me staring out and came to see what it was I looking at. He already knew it was called The Spook Tree. Certainly, some sort of thin thread of common knowledge passed through a few of us back then. Many of the boys in North Highlands, at least, shared a common faith in the value of heroism.

From the Highlands High School Class of 1969 Yearbook – I think Eddie's girlfriend wrote this memorial in every yearbook she could get her hands on at the time, including mine.

Then there is this; in 1993, a few of us of the Highlands High School Class of 1970, with the help of one of a dedicated and honorable former instructor from our old high school, Mr. Davidson, organized the first California International Marathon, as the active coordinators for the Sacramento Running Association. (It was Mr. Davidson who had introduced me to the works of J.R.R. Tolkien as I was in his English class in my senior year).

I was one of the two medical coordinators; the other was Robert Klass, R.N. Gary Green (Mr. Scot, 1970) was another fellow alumni organizer. This marathon was an Olympic points-rated marathon and had a big turnout. We reprised the effort in 1984. By 1985, more powerful people sought our positions and moved in.

Author greets KCRA TV News with Bob Klass at 1984 event at the finish line in front of the state capital on Capital Mall – photo by Deborah S. Lortz

This event exists due to the efforts of some people from North Highlands, graduates, and one truly dedicated teacher of Highlands High School. This is something to be proud of! Every year when this event is run, North Highlands should take pride and proof that great things from North Highlands are possible. The past can't be changed, but one can control your future, and one should at least try.

Carl Cranke did not grow up in North Highlands. He was from Orangevale, but he has a significant history in North Highlands. He began his illustrious racing career at Three Star Raceway, which was located near Splinter City and where the later Orange Grove industrial park emerged years later. Three Star was a flat track race track next to old Splinter City," an industrial area on the south side of Roseville

Road and west of Watt Avenue, famously in and out as an official part of North Highlands. I remember going there with my whole family a couple times. Carl managed a popular dirt bike shop in North Highlands for a few years. Cycle Speed, R&D, was located on Orange Grove Avenue, and then on Watt at the strip mall that intersected Roseville Road, which the top riders in Northern California frequented (and I raced for in 1971). Carl spent long hours at the shop, working on a project often late into the night. His favorite restaurant in the area was Marasha's, where he knew he could get a T-bone steak at any time of the day.

Today, I look back on this time and am proud that I was part of that scene and one of Carl's lifelong friends. By the way, Marasha's was owned by a pair of Lebanese immigrants. I don't see why a couple of Russian immigrants might not make that spot a success today. My experience is that Russians are great cooks.

Similarly, noted flat track racer, Mike Ellis was of the Class of '69. Tony Septinelli was a '70 classmate. His father belonged to the veritable Polka Dots MC, which put on two major events in the AMA District 36 (Sacramento) region; the Wilseyville Hare Scramble (Amador County), and the Forty-Niner Enduro (Foresthill, Placer County). Tony's Dad was killed in 1968 while laying out the course for the enduro when a cable brace of a tower caught him as he descended a hill. Starting in 1971 the club held the Septinelli Memorial MX. I rode the event at Cal Expo that year and am proud to have taken home a trophy from that event. All of this came once again, out of North Highlands. Off-road motorsports continue to be a positive arena for building character in and around Sacramento County.

Finally, we have Mike Burton, of the 1972 U.S. Olympic Swim Team, who was from North Highlands originally. He lived near us and had an early crush on Martine during those early years. He won the gold medal for the long-distance event as the only men's category that wasn't taken by Mark Spitz that year.

When I think of it, just up our own street's length was Mike Burton, Abe Baca, Tony Thorton, and next door to him, Eddie Pitts. I could report other outstanding personalities from just that short block in North Highlands, but these were long-time residents who had arrived on Centinella Drive, like my family, in the mid-1950s. I don't doubt that there are other great achievers from my hometown that I don't know about. We should be proud of them all. North Highlands should realize that it has produced more than its share of outstanding persons. There's no reason that this should not continue as a renaissance of sorts.

Antelope was established as a railroad village when antelopes were still plentiful on the surrounding prairies. North Highlands came into being because of the anticipation of war. North Highlands should be proud of its military origins. It was my idea that a forgotten geographical anomaly that transferred into a street layout blip could have a story behind it. And it does. Antelope has its founding tales, the great railroad story, the stalwart homesteader/farmers, and even Poker Lane, which was actually about one big bridge game during a long storm where everyone was stuck at one house. Now North Highlands has a little story if it wants it.

North Highlands should be proud of its rise as a significant part of the effort that resulted in the defeat of tyranny and philosophies of world conquest in World War Two. Camp Kohler was a major part of that effort as a major signals training facility and should be remembered for that, not denigrated by modern propagandists who are driven by forces and ideologies that seek to divide and destroy America, Western Civilization, and ultimately enslave the world. History is about the past, but it is made daily and it has consequences. Some have said that history repeats itself. It doesn't repeat; it echoes. As time goes on, good ears are required to perceive that echo. North Highlands needs more than ever, a well-tuned ear for providing meaning and projection into any possible future.

As Oswald Spengler*[13] famously noted in "The Decline of the West," all great civilizations are based on a founding myth. The caveat is that such myths usually also contain the elements that cause civilizations to decline and fall. In fact, they always do.

New civilizations sometimes arise from a reconfiguring of old ones, using more constructive aspects. Europe rediscovered the Greek and Roman civilizations and their gifts after a thousand years of relative darkness and struggle due to the advent of Apocalyptic Christianity. The Renaissance revived ancient art, architecture, and philosophies but rejected the coliseum and crucifixion for the rise of the philosophical pursuit of Reason. It is that thread of history that led to the establishment of the United States of America, or more precisely, the Constitution of the United States of America as a secular republic.*Ŧ North Highlands is certainly not a great civilization, but great civilizations are echoes of smaller communities and vice versa; one reflects upon the other.

Spengler showed that great civilizations came out of rural experiences. Inspiration comes from individuals who spent time alone in "wildernesses." And so there are some relevant aspects of a great civilization required for any community inside of a civilization that hopes to survive; much as a brick affects the structure, it helps to form; every brick must be of good quality. Little things can influence the larger results. I offer a kind of folk tale, to North Highlands to add to its complexity. A little mystery can do a lot for image enhancement. In the 1920s, Spengler recognized the 19th and early 20th century's advances in freedom of thought and concurrent advances in science and technology and contrasted them to the effects of the centuries of religious suppression and the new Marxist/Fascist governing models. He wrote;

"Formerly, no one was allowed to think freely. Now it is permitted, but one is capable of it anymore. Now they think what they are supposed to think, and this they call freedom." This is the pervading condition of the present.

That is as it is said, a mouthful. Spengler is famous for predicting much of the catastrophes' of the twentieth century and laid out its historic anatomy and physiology. We must recapture truth before we can hope to survive the birth pangs of the present. If we succeed, we will go on as a free people and the "Fourth Turning" will succeed. If we don't the scene will be that of an earthly stillbirth.

In a Democracy, the People Have the Government They Deserve – Alexis De Tocqueville

North Highlands, like many communities, nationwide suffered through a decline marked by increasing violence. One question is if this is the "new normal;" have the masses accepted this as normal. Perhaps one more significant event besides the Spook Tree is the tale of another tree. The venerable old oak on the grounds of Highlands High School was cut down by some errant youths from Foothill Farms High in the mid-seventies. A reexamination of how and where we place values, especially artificial ones; Interschool rivalries, the petty campus competitions' the jocks against the nerds, the "mean girls" the later trends of cyberbullying. How was it possible that some of such formerly innocuous traditions as a Senior Square would be seized upon in order to create controversy. Those who wish to destroy work this way; whether it's a word, a symbol, or even a flag, it is imbued with false meaning, which is repeated until it changes, and brainwashes the public. This mechanism was used to foment racial tensions leading to the riots and destruction that plagued North Highlands and damaged its schools for a decade after? In the sixties, the Left claimed free speech as its cause. Today, the "Yuri Bezmenov Effect"*⊤ finds fragility everywhere, ready to cancel ideas and speech. Things can't go on long as they are. It's a question of whether a town or people can learn from their own history or do they retreat into various shelters for comfort?

When I lived on the Marin County coast from 1984 to 1987, the local politics used to get me down. One exercise I found marvelously effective was to ride my motorcycle up onto Bolinas Ridge and look down on the lagoon and the two beach towns. The issues always took a new proportion in my mind, less prominent and more in perspective. It all felt less threatening, which allowed me to cope with it better.

Taking the "Olympian View" is to rise above; to be circumspect, even stoic. Remaining "in the hole" has the psychological effect of keeping one "in the hole."

That is also what the study of history does. The deeper one digs into history, the more the simple, pandering accusations and answers become exposed as not so much about factual truth, but preferred political thinking of one type or another, gained by a dishonest focus on one event while ignoring the mitigating history. Politics aren't about truth, they are about power. What we need are statesmen and leaders of the Socratic tradition. Politicians always mangle truth, regardless of party or position. They can't help it because their greed for power overcomes them, in most cases. We cannot allow ourselves to be herded like sheep or treated like children; there are things to do, trees to plant, and land to save.*Ш We must throw off the ideas and false philosophies and belief systems that infantize us. But we must police ourselves as individuals. That is one way to find personal pride and even dignity. When you own your own mind, which is real power. Then, you can go on to do constructive things because you're not being turned against yourself. And North Highlands should be for itself; all for one and one for all. There are ways to end the dissipation of youth in North Highlands and for that matter, the entire nation.

As I wrote it, this book started out to be a simple story about a dead tree that had fascinated me as a child. As a student of history, I soon realized that I could not isolate the tree from the region's history. After all, The Spook Tree wouldn't exist without it. History really is a logue; the memory of many matched to the evidence their activities produce and leave behind as their time comes and goes. North Highlands began as one of the new suburbs. It was a new idea about how America would henceforth establish its way of civic management offering an alternative lifestyle somewhere between the city and the farm. As new potentials are created, a vacuum is also created. So elements from the city and farm found its way into North Highlands. But its story is not all that different from many others. It was perhaps one of the earliest to see a quick rise and fall. The violence and violations of the 1970s drove many away, but others arrived to take their place from regions of the world further afar than as with the founding years of our subject suburb. Compared to many cities today, North Highlands is not such a bad place. In fact, it has more power to be whatever it wants now than perhaps it ever had. McClellan AFB closed down as everyone feared. Today it is a business park and the airfield is still active and the home of one of the main US Forest Service Firefighting fleets. That is something to be proud of. Someday, I hope they will have a Liquid Fluoride Thorium Reactor charging up the drones that will speed out to the forests killing baby fires with sound waves. As a famous Grateful Dead song goes, "you can't go back and you can't stand still. If the thunder don't get you then the lightning will." If we are to survive, we must plunge boldly into the future intelligently. Again, the future remains a matter of choice.

The Mystery of The Spook Tree

This is the "true confessions" section of the story. The first one ought to be my own. I was never a cowboy. When I trained for eventing, I used German Steuben saddle and trained "English Hunt Seat." Except for a couple times up at a friend's ranch when I helped castrate and brand some calves, I never wrangled cattle. I don't know of any LaRue, LeRoux, etc., who was ever a cowboy. When we were in the rural regions, we were fur traders. I have some indication that some of my Quebec ancestors were Voyageurs. There's a chance that one or two even made it to Fort Vancouver, in the Oregon Territory which is in Washington State on the Columbia River, today. I have a record of Antoine Leroux, who was a scout with Kit Carson on the tragic failure of the Ann and Virginia White abduction rescue attempt of 1849.*ↄ If as a child, I had known my family history and understood the difference, I would have claimed that I was more of a Davy Crockett type, a frontiersman. But this is a superfluous consideration.

More germane our theme is fire that created The Spook Tree led to the Kid Lore around it. During my research, I found the truth of that lore. As for the hanging tale; it was based on two films. One film was the excellent 1942 film, "The Oxbow Incident," which I recommended to all. It is loosely based on events in Johnson County, Wyoming, in 1890, namely, the lynching of Ella Watson, "Cattle Kate" and James Averill. The Lincoln County War in Arizona is perhaps the most famous because of Billy the Kid's character caught between two "cattle barons fighting it out for control of the territory. Billy was caught between the wealthy cattle barons. The other is an old Zane Grey Theater production titled "The Justice Tree." In this tale, a criminal on the lamb takes a mother and her son hostage at their rural home. He is killed by a dying tree while chasing the boy who flees up into it and slips from a cracking branch to be skewed on the remaining spike of another broken branch.

The story of the kidnapping is true. It just didn't involve The Spook Tree. In 1942, Marc de Tristan, a three-year-old boy and the son of Count and Countess Marc de Tristan, was kidnapped on the street in Hillsborough, San Mateo County, while his nurse had taken him out for a walk. A ransom of $100,000.00 was demanded for his return. His kidnappers were driving a two-door Ford Sedan. A day after, a deer hunter reported his car stolen at gunpoint on the Ice House Road above Riverton in El Dorado County. From there, he fled with the boy to Amador County, where two local residents, Cecil Wetzel and Ellis Woods, saw a strange man on a logging road near the Omo Ranch, near the old sawmill. The crime was in the news and on the radio. They saw the boy, and he fit the description. Cecil and Carl began to question the man. When he pulled out a gun, it was clear to them that he was the kidnapper. Cecil was close enough to the man, so he grabbed the kidnapper's head, held it like a football, and flipped him to the ground. Cecil dropped on top of the man and took the gun out of his hand. Ellis was right there, and between them, they tied him up, hand and foot, and took him to the River Pines Grocery Store, where they waited for officers from San Francisco to pick him up.

The kidnapper was Wilhelm Jakob Muhelmbroith, a German alien who spoke four languages and was a barber by trade. Cicel Wetzel weighed two hundred pounds and had been a football star known for his flying tackles at Washington State College. There was a big reward for capturing Muhelmbroith, but the two men refused it.

So the Kid Lore around The Spook Tree was made up by kids. I always thought that Martine was probably right to some degree, at least as I grew older. The stories were too grand. In truth, the fire that destroyed Camp Kohler might not have burned the tree. It might have occurred due to a fire caused by artillery practice that we know went on in that area. I can easily envision the scene; it's 1944, maybe a month after D-Day. A tank crew of young soldiers, beginning to feel that all the fun and glory will be over soon crawl about the landscape on a hot summer day. Spotting a prominent tree out in the near distance, they aim and fire; "Bulls-eye!" The observer yells, and the tank turns back toward the base and a cold beer. It could have easily been that way. I remember the dugout nature of the cavity over which The Spook Tree sat. Rather than an ancient animal borough, it could easily have been a shell crater that lit the natural internal cavity on fire and killed the tree. These young men were typical young men, often thoughtless and rash. To them, a tree out of many was just another of many trees. And besides, it was on their designated firing range and it was a time of war, total justification in all cases. They probably never marked the mournful looking remains of a formerly beautiful work of nature. Wars are made by men like me, but you know who only can make a tree. Surely, war is a major crime against nature, beyond what human beings do to themselves. The Creation of The Spook Tree was a minuscule aspect of the larger tragedy of World War Two, and the tree was one of the likely billions that were destroyed. But that tree, standing there in that field like that, was a statement. And after all, no one can know the factual story behind The Spook Tree. However, I think my guess and the alternative are good and likely.

An enigma remains around the Spook Tree. When the developers drew up the plan for the latest North Highlands expansion in 1958, they had to decide what to do about a big, dead, fire-blackened tree in the middle of their planned neighborhood. Typically, these developers tore down the old oaks. Interestingly, when David D. Bohannon and company laid out their plans for the Spook Tree field, they did something extraordinary; they drew up a street and named it

Blackfield, and behind it, another one called Bainbridge Drive. They drew up Bainbridge not in a straight line but around the site of The Spook Tree. An elementary school was planned and built, with a park behind it on Blackfield Drive. They chose to leave the site of the tree uncovered and preserved. It's a bulge on the northwest end of the playground/parking lot of the school. Why did they do this? Why did they give it such a wide berth? Did they know something? Were they superstitious about the tree, too? Did they have some understanding about that tree? Were some of the workers on the Bohannon project former volunteers during the Camp Kohler Fire? Imagine the hundreds of personal memories of that fire that must have remained in the memories of those people. Such records as there is can be found on the Citrus Heights Fire District website.

I could not find out why the site of the Spook Tree was given such a wide berth and not simply filled in and built over. Most, if not all, of those who might know why are gone, and no notes have been found. So I can only speculate. Could it be that some form of superstition or reverence was responsible for the strange bulge of Bainbridge Drive - The Spook Tree Bulge – (TSTB) if you'll indulge me)). Today, the site of The Spook Tree is located on a school campus. The former public school on Arutas Drive is now a charter school.

At the moment of the completion of this book, Memorial Park, on Blackfield Drive, remains in limbo. Vandalized and degraded in the past, its new theme remains unresolved. This author's humble suggestion would be that it be made into a memorial of the 1947 Fire and the sacrifice of volunteer Charles Gay, who gave his life to save the communities threatened by that fire.

After eighteen years of extinction with Antelope assigned a Sacramento zip code, 95841, the township of Antelope was restored because of the work of Jerry Montjoy and Jeffrey Spencer. They were members of the Antelope Community Planning and Advisory Council formed by County Supervisor Grantland Johnson in 1991 with the zip code 95843. So Antelope arose, like a phoenix from the ashes, literally, to a place name on the map as a community. Why stop there?

Imagery ©2020 Maxar Technologies, U.S. Geological Survey, USDA Farm Service Agency, Map data ©2020   100 ft

Can you spot the site of The Spook Tree?

The Spook Tree? I have done my best to point to its significance. Something is certainly responsible for the Bainbridge Drive "bulge." Maybe this set of wishful thinking is unlikely, given current attitudes and sentiments. People must decide that they want to build up on its older legacy, not ridicule and tear it down. And rather than investing in shame over Camp Kohler, why not an exhibition for displaying the full historical situation rather than continuing with the same sort of divisive rhetoric that is so dividing our nation today?

Yet it remains a wonder to me, to look back and know that once, and for a very long time, the place that is North Highlands and Antelope had wild oats that reached up over a grown man's head for as far as one could see, and deer and antelope roamed and played. The beautiful land must have literally hummed with nature, while the Maidu people roamed and played in the bounty, gathering acorns from the many grand Valley Oaks. Then, it was a cattle range, then farms, and finally, a training area serving during the largest and most cataclysmic war in the history of mankind – so far. Finally, it became

North Highlands, and a part of the world's drama played out there and plays on yet.

It is strangely ironic that an oak tree should be the sacred object of a Christian-themed song since oak trees had always been held as holy by most pre-Christian European cultures. As the first of the two world's most intolerant faiths,*† it caused the advent of modern intolerant communism as any unbiased review of history must inform. Today, they are at last locked in a death struggle like ants at war. And we, who glimpse the narrow path of survival, must wait them out because we're outnumbered. But nature will eventually sort it all out, with or without us. In the end, whether they come along is not up to us – personally and collectively. It might be that we've run the clock out. Coping in a time of great change and upset is challenging for all. I think that if we strive to recall our humanity and honesty, and refuse to let ourselves be fooled, but anyone, including ourselves, there is a chance. One inspiration we might take can come from knowing the past of the region and the struggles that required it to survive and grow, we might survive our current existential crisis, if we can make ourselves truly worthy, in the real sense.

As for me, I know that I am but one in a sea of causality. So I continue to search, gather, ponder, and hope. When my thoughts go to my old hometown, The Spook Tree immediately comes to mind as the memories flood in. Suddenly, I am once again that curious boy, standing on the edge of the school playground, staring out to a dead tree, wondering why it should be there, innocent of the future. And its song plays on the radio in my head;

"There was a tall oak tree.

There was a tall oak tree.

There was a tall oak tree."

The End

Notes and Sources

Where the Antelope Used to Play

*German Warships of World War ll, page 113 lists U.74 attacked by British ships, and allied airplanes, sunk off Cartagena by two destroyers and aircraft on February 5, 1942.

A Visit to Camp Kohler

*[1] The Fifteen Decisive Battles of the World – From Marathon to Waterloo, by E.S. Creasy, M.A. - 1851

*[2] The Godfrey Diary – Battle of the Little Bighorn, The Montana Column – March to the Little Bighorn – The Journal of Lieutenant James H. Bradley, 1876, With Crook at the Rosebud, J.W. Vaughn

*[3] The third might be to ban known alcoholics (Reno) from command positions, at least. According to the Gordon Diary, which quoted Chief Gall, who led the attack against Reno, they were in confusion, and Crazy Horse was finishing the evacuation of the villages when Reno fled the field. It was only then that the order to evacuate the village was reversed and all the Indian forces were focused on Custer. Custer had initially been correct, and his following pursuit would have driven the Cheyenne and Sioux into the Montana Column of Terry and Gibbon, as planned. (See also – The Reno Court of Inquiry – 1879)

It Was the Place to Be

*[1] No such film exists, but you know what I mean.

*[2] Carl Lee Cranke – American Motorcycle Association Hall of Fame Member – winner of seven gold and two silver medals at the rigorous International Six Day's Trials – famous for tuning and development of Penton and KTM Motorcycles – from Orangevale, California – manager of Cycle Speed R&D in North Highlands, 1969-72.

*[3] The Natomas Company is very interesting with a history that spans 133 years. It began in 1851 when A.P. Catlin and others organized early mining and water companies as loose associations to divert water from the South Fork of the American River. A few of the historical moves by the Natomas Company; In **1853, the Natomas Water& Mining Company had been formed and a 16-mile ditch system to Prairie City had been completed by November of 1853.** See Appendix B for a complete timeline of the remarkable history of the Natomas Company.

*ϕ Invictus – "Out of the night that covers me, black as the Pit from pole to pole, I thank whatever gods may be for my unconquerable soul.   In the fell clutch of circumstance, I have not winced nor cried aloud. Under the bludgeonings of chance, My head is bloody but unbowed. Beyond this place of wrath and tears looms but the Horror of the shade, And yet the menace of the years finds and shall find, me unafraid. It matters not how strait the gate, how charged with punishments the scroll, I am the master of my fate: I am the captain of my soul." - William Earnest Henley

Old Antelope

*₁ William Ladd Willis, "History of Sacramento, California," 1913

*₂ They really were only playing pinochle.

*₃ Historic Spots in California, Douglas E. Kyle, Fifth Edition, Page 304

A Geographical Roundup

** Historic Spots in California – "Sutter's Fort, as it soon came to be known, was not merely a fort; it was a trading post and a place of refuge as well. Robert Glass Cleland writes;

"In addition to Sutter's military activities, he displayed a vast amount of energy in more peaceful endeavors. To care for the ever-growing needs of his colony, and especially to meet the pressing demands of his Russian debt, he branched out into a great variety of pursuits and tried all sorts of experiments, most of which impoverished rather than enriched him. He planted large areas of wheat; built a flour mill; diverted water from the American River for irrigation purposes; grazed large herds of cattle and horses; sent hunters into the mountains and along the rivers for furs and elks skins; set up a distillery; began the weaving of coarse woolen blankets; ran a launch regularly between his settlement and San Francisco Bay; employed nearly all foreigners who came to him for work, whether he needed them or not; trained the Indians in useful occupations; at times chastised the thieving war-inclined tribes which the Spanish Californians could not subdue; administered justice as an official of the provincial government; and, in short, made his colony the nucleus of all activity, whether political or economic, in what was then the only settled portion of the interior of California.

In addition to these varied activities, with their decided local and personal interest, Sutter contributed in much larger ways to the making of California history through his aid to American immigration. Few people today realize how large a part of this hospitable, visionary, improvident land baron of the Sacramento played in the American advance to California. His fort occupied the most strategic position in all of northern California, so far as the overland trails were concerned, and became the natural objective for parties crossing the Sierras, by the central and northern routes, or coming into the province by way of Oregon.

At Sutter's these immigrants, exhausted and half-starved as many of them were, found shelter, food, and clothing, and an opportunity to learn something of the new land and people to which they had come. More than one company (the most famous of which was the Donner Party) caught in the mountain snows, was saved from destruction by a rescue party sent from Sutter's Fort. The situation of the latter also made it impossible for the California authorities, had they been inclined, to check or turn aside the stream of overland migration. The passes and trails of the northern Sierras lay open to American frontiersman so long as Sutter maintained his position on the Sacramento."

*[1] The first settler from the East was "Dr." John Marsh of Massachusetts. He graduated from Harvard University in 1823 and came west to tutor the children of an army officer at what later become Fort Snelling, Minnesota. He studied medicine under a surgeon there. However, the surgeon died before his studies were completed. He took a French-Canadian/Sioux wife and was appointed sub-agent to the Sioux. He became a fugitive from the army and the U.S. government after selling guns to the tribe against federal law. Somewhere after that exile, his wife died. He lived in Independence, Missouri for a short period, but then made his way to Los Angeles via Santa Fe, where he gained permission to practice medicine by showing his Latin-inscribed bachelor of arts diploma to the lesser-educated authorities there. He traded hides for his services and finally sold them to buy a ranch near the foot of Mount Diablo near the Sacramento-San Joaquin Delta. His predecessor, Jose Noriega, had found it too isolated and too exposed to Indian cattle thieves. However, Marsh made the place a great success by charging 50 head of cattle for his medical services as a general rule. Marsh is not memorialized for any grant of largess. Two years later, Sutter arrived in the Sacramento Valley. Source; California – An Interpretive History; Walton E. Bean, Professor of History, University of California, Berkeley, 1968

The Kid Quotient

*[1] It may not have turned out to be the standard, but it has contributed to the practice of medicine and other health care delivery modes as preventative care and more interest in the cause of health problems has become more prevalent in recent decades.

These are the basics of Chiropractic Principles and Philosophy as taught by D.D. and his son B.J. Palmer since the inception of Chiropractic by D. D. Palmer in 1895.

A Geographical Round-Up

*[1] Railroaded – The Transcontinentals and the Making of Modern America, Richard White

Beyond The Shadow of The Spook Tree

*⊕ Ray Stevens did the "Ahab, and other satirical comedies survived to make another online hit in 2020 concerning the "pandemic."

*[2] Blacklisted By History, E. Stanton Evans

Meeting The Spook Tree

*[1] Constantine's Bishops – The Politics of Intolerance, H. A. Drake

How Antelope Met White Rock

*[1] See – Christine Hoff-Somer's "War Against Boys" Vol 1&2

*[2] David C. Hodges – 1950 – 2016 - Dave was a very talented craftsman, in taxidermy and woodcarving – he was one of the first to do chainsaw art – carving out a bear in the early 70s.

Three Gunfights, Two Hangings, and Sutter;

*[1] Today, the Fort Sutter Motorcycle Club (Est. 1932) makes an annual donation to the Shriner's Hospital, in keeping with their namesake affiliation with the Freemasons and Sutter's early acts of establishing New Helvetia's first hospital and providing great humanitarian services in keeping with his Swiss heritage.

*₂ No indication of a troubled marriage; Sutter had left his wife and five children in Switzerland but sent for them after his success. His wife and children arrived in New Helvetia on September 14, 1848. His wife stayed with him in a faithful marriage for the next 30 years up to Sutter's sad, penniless death on June 16, 1880. His wife Anna died the following January. Both were buried in Lititz, Pennsylvania, adjacent to the Moravian graveyard called "God's Acre."

Similarly, many 49ers were men with diplomas and learning who had failed for a myriad of reasons and had left families behind to get a new start by succeeding in the goldfields. Source; The life and work of Gen. John A. Sutter / by Jacob B. Landis. - 1913

https://www.lancasterhistory.org/images/stories/JournalArticles/vol17no10pp279 300_573778.pdf

** "The Deadliest Indian War in the West," G. Michno – page 346, explains that the term "Digger" was used by whites to describe tribes that dug roots and otherwise lived on bugs and small reptiles. First applied to the Paiutes in the Great Basin Desert and then to the various valley tribes in California. But it should not be taken as a racist term, as it was also common usage among other Indian tribes who considered Indians who did not ride horses and "rooted" for subsistence as the lowest caste among the tribes. The Shoshonis called them "Shoshokos" or "walking people," who could not hunt big game and were also termed "earth eaters." It is obvious that a horse would not be practical in deserts because of a lack of forage. In California, however, there is no explanation found for why the California tribes did not ride. One possible explanation is that the Spanish controlled their herds better than their counterparts in Texas and New Mexico in the early years, preventing a native horse culture from developing. However, this did not stop the California tribes from raiding the Mexican settlements on the coasts. Part of the expectations placed on Sutter in exchange for his grant was that he would pacify those inland tribes and serve as a safety buffer for the established Californios.

Troughs may have well been an improvement over what the Indians were used to when taking their nourishment. Natives made baskets and ground acorns into meals and cooked, but they ate off hollow slabs of wood. No record that any Indian was forced to sleep inside the fort at night. It seems they were free to choose. But since in the early days, there were raids, some choose to sleep under guards, Indian guards, who kept a lookout over them, as well as Sutter himself.

*₃ False narrative of Sutter's Indian Wars; "When Sutter established himself in 1839 in the Sacramento Valley, new misfortune came upon these peaceful natives of the country. Their services were demanded immediately. Those who did not want to work were considered as enemies. With other tribes, the field was taken against the hostile Indian. A declaration of war was not made. The villages were attacked usually before daybreak when everybody was still asleep. Neither old nor young was spared by the enemy, and often the Sacramento River was colored red by the blood of the innocent Indians, for these villages usually were situated at the banks of the rivers. During a campaign, one section of the attackers fell upon the village by way of land. All the Indians of the attacked village naturally fled to find protection on the other bank of the river. But there they were awaited by the other half of the enemy, and thus, the unhappy people were shot and killed with rifles from both sides of the river. Seldom an Indian escaped such an attack, and those who were not murdered were captured. All children from six to fifteen years of age were usually taken by the greedy white people. The village was burned down, and the few Indians who had escaped with their lives were left to their fate." (Cordua – 1933)

"The Age of Gold"® – Pages 33,34, describes the attacks on the Indian villages along the Sacramento River precisely as above, except that it is part of the larger narrative of Captain Fremont's erratic and semi-official campaign in California during 1846. He joined the Bear Flag Revolt in Sonoma, taking the friendly ally, General Vallejo, prisoner. Fremont next took Sutter's Fort by domination if not by force and imprisoned Vallejo there for two months under the protest of Sutter. Fremont berated Sutter for seeking to make Vallejo more comfortable in his bare cell. From there, he sallied north after hearing that the governor had issued a proclamation to Californians to attack Fremont and his forces wherever they might be found. Hearing that Castro had also encouraged local Indians to attack American settlers, Fremont attacked an Indian Village and killed as many as 175 Indians. He then removed to Oregon to await orders in the vicinity of Klamath Lake. In May of 1846, Gillespie, a secret agent from Washington arrived with a message whose contents have been lost to history because the agent destroyed the orders before crossing into Mexican territory. This history is easily found in any serious historical account of California history. Walton Bean's university textbook, "California – An Interpretive History, page 98, reports that after Captain Fremont's camp was attacked at night by some Klamath Indians and three men were killed, he attacked the nearest Indian village and wiped out every adult male and destroyed the villages food supply. Professor Bean comments that it was common practice in the West for both whites and Indians to attack innocent parties in the absence of the guilty parties.

It should be noted that Captain Fremont's ambitious wife, Jesse, made it no secret of her ambition for her husband's eventual ascent to the highest office in the land. Fremont would rise by following the examples of George Washington and, more lately, Andrew Jackson, gaining national acclaim through military exploits in California and elsewhere with her at his side on a throne of her own. It is not a matter of court findings that Fremont persecuted the Indians in California, but it is a matter of record that he exceeded his orders. He faced a court-martial proceeding and was almost dismissed from the U.S. Army. However, although, Fremont survived and went on to serve as a colonel, in this, his wife may have been his Lady Macbeth. After his court-martial, she complained that if only he had been a little more ambitious, he might have made it to the White House. But the Fremonts continued to have great successes and failures throughout their lives.

A further example of Fremont's excessive zeal comes from his activity in Missouri in 1861. In 1861 Missouri was the testing ground. It had been caught up in the violence between slave owners and abolitionists before the war and had become brutalized by guerrilla conflict and banditry. By then, Colonel John C. Frémont, the Union Army's commander in the West, placed the state under martial law. Confederate guerrillas were executed, their supporter's property seized, and their slaves freed. The brutality of the actions caused the rise of bitter resistance that produced "bad men" for decades, even up to the Great Depression. They included Quantrill's Raiders, which of course, included the Younger brothers, Jesse, and Frank James, and the infamous "Bloody" Bill Anderson.

Lincoln, looking to avoid reprisals, relieved Frémont of his command but a precedent had been set. Later in 1863, General Ewing, a German immigrant General, one of many in Lincoln's Army, (See – "Lincoln's Marxists," Benson and Kennedy) issued the infamous Order Number Eleven in Kansas City. The Thomas Building there was owned by one of the guerilla's wives, Elizabeth Cockerel. The army took the first floor as their headquarters. Arrested prostitutes were kept in the basement. They imprisoned eight wives, cousins, and sisters of Quantrill's Raiders on the third floor, none of them over twenty or under seventeen years of age. The soldiers had made three large openings in the wall in order to have easy access to the prostitutes. One day, the wall collapsed and killed all the women on the third floor. Most died more or less immediately, except for Martha Anderson who the troops had shackled because of her complaints. She survived with two broken legs and a broken back; her face was disfigured by lacerations. Everyone in the town was enraged, but for the men of Quantrill's Raiders, it was far more personal than merely a war over a tariff or slavery. It was proof of the tyranny of the Federal Government.

General George Armstrong Custer, is a national figure who has been similarly maligned by modern "historians." Freemont's early morning attack on the Klamath Indians in 1846, and his wholesale slaughter of the natives along the Sacramento River just before seem to have been transferred to Custer. From all factual accounts, after the Battle of Washita, where women and children fought against his command, and killed two white captives whose presence in the camp he had been unaware of, he always negotiated with the Indians before attacking as captives might be present. This practice lasted until 1876 when the Montana Campaign and superior command gave him orders to find and chastise any and all Indians he encountered.

®"Age of Gold - the California Gold Rush and The New American Dream," 2002, - H.W. Brands, Professor of and holder of the Melbern G. Glassock Chair in American History at Texas A&M University, New York Times Best Selling Author "The First American," an acclaimed biography of Benjamin Franklin, which was a finalist in the Lost Angeles Times Book Award for Biography, as well as "T.R." a celebrated biography of Theodore Roosevelt.

*₄ One prominent online article titled "The Lesser-Known History of John Sutter" –

https://www.davisvanguard.org/2017/01/the-lesser-known-history-of-john-a-sutter/

The article contains a litany of lies as described in the text and disproven by historians such as H.W. Brands in "Age of Gold," and the University of Berkeley, California Professor Walton Bean - "California – An Interpretive History" (1968). The Indian Trader recorded as named Savage, in fact, had 33 wives with 5 or 6 said to live with him constantly. They were said to be between the ages of ten and twenty-two. " This appears to be the source of the "harem" and child molester slander against Sutter. "Age of Gold," pages 307-8. The nearest source that could be found of Captain Sutter and the alleged relationships with native women is Walton Bean's guess that Sutter may have had a native lover at his Sawmill Gold Claim.

Since Professor Bean made the simultaneous error and omission regarding the arrival on September 14, 1848, of Sutter's entire family, including his wife, and his story that Sutter turned his interests in Sacramento over to his son August (he turned it over to John Sutter, Jr, his eldest on October 14, 1848, BEFORE he had a mining operation in Coloma), the error of report seems to lie with the good Professor. Professor Bean's speculation has no doubt served to assist an expanded story of rape and sex slavery on Sutter's part.

The details of Sutter's family's arrival are in the First History of Sacramento City – by Dr. John F. Morse, 1853.

*₅ Governor Burnett had made his oft-abused comment that "A war of extermination will continue to be waged between the races until the Indian race becomes extinct." But it was all bluster. The historical narrative proves that there was no general war against the Indians. The level of violence against Indians was at the same level as anywhere else. It was disease from the Spanish that reduced their numbers most. – Walton Bean, "California – An Interpretive History."

Historians of the American West, including Gregory Michno, have shown government policy was to civilize the tribes, not exterminate them. There were many successes, while the failures are the most famous. The so-called "Indian Wars" occurred, most often, because they were raider tribes. Raiding, regardless of race, is a criminal activity. The plan's flaw might be that; "The institution of slavery among Indian tribes is not as well-known as its white counterpart, but it perhaps partially explains the Indian affinity for captive taking. According to Russell Managhi, in "The Indian Slave Trade," Indian slaveholding was a pre-Columbian practice that was given fresh impetus when they learned they could raid other tribes and sell captives to Europeans. In the West, early Spanish and French traders gave the tribes an outlet for their captives and the number of captives incorporated into tribes lessened as Europeans stimulated the profit motives. In about 1694, Navajos captured some Pawnees and brought them to Santa Fe, demanding money for their lives. When the Spanish did not pay, the Navajos killed their Pawnee captives, causing the Spanish to issue decrees authorizing the use of royal funds to ransom captives. It had long-range repercussions. Indians fully realized that captives could be used as bargaining chips or sold for a profit. It started a vicious cycle." – (A Fate Worse than Death – Michno – page 469).

As early as the 1820s, the U.S. Government had determined that it cost much more to kill Indians than to feed them. Therefore, efforts were made to make treaties that would bring tribes to agencies where they could be served and eventually civilized.

This was done through treaties, and some tribes converted easily. Continued raids by treaty tribes led to penalties (costs of losses deducted from annuities). This would typically be resented, setting up the pretext for the next series of raids (see – Spirit Lake Massacre to the Lakota Uprising of 1862 as perfect examples). Some tribes made treaties to cease captive-taking for annuities and went on taking captives (ex, - Cochise). This added to the earlier influence in captive taking and bargaining, ransoming captives, etc., formed many tribes into dependents who gained through violence. The last phase of the Indian Wars began when the official U.S. Government edict against ransoming captives was ordered and had the opposite effect regarding depredations. Sutter was operating in a world where Indian slavery was common, and captives were sold. But there are no indications that Sutter either captured slaves or bought them (the one noted case where he bought an Indian boy and left him with Indians at Fort Vancouver). His workers, regardless of race, were paid.

One modern journalist has noted that Sacramento County's tribal population is a mere three percent today. But Sacramento County holds little attraction for anyone who loves the outdoors. It is a modern metropolis with the problems of a modern metropolis. The Indians fled Sacrament due to the Asian Cholera outbreak of 1850. The presence or lack of presence of Amerinds in Sacramento County today is no measure of an outcome to be lodged by any social justice warrior today except as a deception. It has to be admitted that the Gold Rush forced situations into being that may have not ever been if the compression of events and human tides in such a short time had not been so intense. However, we may rest assured that the sufferings of humanity ran across all racial and ethnic lines.

*6 "New Helvetia Diary – A Record of Events Kept by John. A. Sutter and His Clerks at New Helvetia, California, from September 9, 1845, o May 25, 1848." San Francisco The Grabhorn Press in Arrangement with The Society of California Pioneers – Sutter's early education came from his mother, who was the daughter of a clergyman. Later, Sutter learned French and Latin in a public school at Kandern from a local clergyman.

Sutter's failure in his printing business in Switzerland is attributed to his generosity, over-trustfulness of partners, and lack of worry about the bottom line. His migration to America to redeem himself was a common solution for many during the 19th century. The same qualities that garnered him praise and endorsement in California's efforts were the same that caused his demise in Switzerland. But that Sutter could have been a miserly slave taker and trader, and a lecherous rapist of native females of any age has no direct evidence and is highly unlikely given his early Christian influence. His personality contained a large portion of the Swiss national tendency toward humanity, enterprise, and home defense. Sutter's contemporary countrymen organized the International Red Cross in 1866.

Reports of capturing children for gifting as slaves are another current slander. Sutter was noted as purchasing an Indian boy at the Wind River Rendezvous in 1838. He appears to have left him with the Indians at Fort Vancouver. Sutter's "raids" for capturing children were instead a dragnet for collecting orphans created by "raids by others, principally Captain John Fremont, for adopting civilized Indians and interested whites. Sutter hoped to create a colony and did not care about the origins of his subjects. He had eight Hawaiians, the Kanaka of which two had wives Sutter employed to teach the Indian women and the children.

Description of the battles James Savage took part in – "Encyclopedia of Indian Wars – Western Battles and Skirmishes, 1850-1890," Gregory F. Michno, pages 9,10

*₆ A passage in I Remember – Stories and Pictures of El Dorado County Pioneer Families – supplies some insight into the state of Indians of the time as Mrs. Lyons recalls the Washoe Indians around Tahoe; "There were Indians in the area, a lot of them. They couldn't stand being closed up all the time." One named Ida went to live with a Stockton family but soon presented with diabetes and died. (Likely spoiled her on rock candy). "It was Ida who had solicitously "cumb'd Mrs. Lyon's very fine hair and who made a papoose dress complete with doll one Christmas. My mother would've trusted Ida before anyone else,"

Mrs. Lyons says.

"Then there was one (Washoe) named Susie, who washed for Mrs. Lyons grandmother, and who, she recalled: "loved to tell tales." Susie delighted the guests with her stories. One of her favorite expressions was "I so scare," (leaving the "d" off). She was "so scare" when the white men came in covered wagons. The Indians would go back of the rocks and hide."

*₆ (from page 165) - Outrageous, some will complain. But consider this; the Yosemite tribe was a raider tribe. They had raided the local tribes around them and holed up in the magnificent Yosemite Valley against all comers from time unknown. The Americans arrived, and things changed. When the Yosemites began to raid the white settlers, there was a large enough power to bring the age-old pirate tribe's reign to an end. Some call for recompense, "returning land." Should one small group of people be able to prevent the world and even science from accessing one of the wonders of the world for a return to what some imagine a return to blissful primitive living? All evidence shows that such living was not all that free from trouble, and life was usually violent and short, long before the white man arrived (see Lawrence H. Keeley's "War Before Civilization").

*₆ From Sutter's Diary - http://www.sfmuseum.net/hist2/sutdiary2.html

Note -["f" and "v" with Sutter were interchangeable-- save becomes safe

"It took me eight days before I could find the entrance of the Sacramento, as it is very deceiving and very easy to pass by, how it happened to several Officers of the Navy afterwards which refused to take a pilot. About 10 miles below Sacramento City I fell in with the first Indians which was all armed & painted & looked very hostile; they was about 200 Men, as some of them understood a little Spanish I could make a Kind of treaty with them, and the two which understood Spanish came with me, and made me a little better acquainted with the Country. All other Indians on the up River hided themselves in the Bushes, and on the Mouth of Feather River they runned all away so soon they discovered us. I was examining the Country a little further up with a Boat, while the larger Crafts let go their Ankers.

On my return all the white Men came to me and asked me how much longer I intended to travel with them in such a Wilderness. I saw plain that it was a Mutiny. I answered them that I would give them an answer the next Morning and left them and went in the Cabin.

The following Morning I gave Orders to return, and entered in the American River, landed at the former Tannery on the 12th Augt. 1839. Gave Orders to get every thing on Shore, pitch the tents and mount the 3 Cannons, called the white Men, and told them that all those which are not contented could leave on board the Isabella next Morning and that I would settle with them imediately and remain alone with the Canacas, of 6 Men 3 remained, and 3 of them I gave passage to Yerbabuena.

The Indians was first troublesome, and came frequently, and would it not have been for the Cannons they would have Killed us for sake of my property, which they liked very much, and this intention they had very often, how they have confessed to me afterwards, when on good terms. I had a large Bull Dog which saved my life 3 times, when they came slyly near the house in the Night: he got hold of and marked them most severely. In a short time removed my Camps on the very spot where now the Ruins of Sutters fort stands, made acquaintance with a few Indians which came to work for a short time making Adobes, and the Canacas was building 3 grass houses, like it is customary on the Sandwich Islands. Before I came up here, I purchassed Cattle & Horses on the Rancho of Senor Martinez, and had great difficulties & trouble getting them up, and had to wait for them long time, and received them at least on the 22nd October 1839. Not less then 8 Men wanted to be in the party, as they were afraid of the Indians and had good reasons to be so.

"Before I got the Cattle we was hunting Deer & Elk etc and so afterwards to safe the Cattle as I had then only about 500 head, 50 horses & a manada of 25 mares. One Year, that is in the fall 1840, I bought 1000 head of Cattle of Don Antonio Sunol and a many horses more of Don Joaquin Gomez and others. In the fall 1839 I have built an Adobe house, covered with Tule and two other small buildings in the middle of the fort; they was afterwards destroyed by fire. At the same time we cut a Road through the Woods where the City of Sacramento stand, then we made the New Embarcadero, where the old Zinkhouse stands now. After this it was time to make a Garden, and to sow some Wheat &c. We broke up the soil with poor Californian ploughs, I had a few Californians employed as Baqueros, and 2 of them making Cal. Carts & stocking the ploughs etc. [manada : the Spanish for drove or herd.]

In the Spring 1840. the Indians began to be troublesome all around me, Killing and Wounding Cattle, stealing horses, and threatening to attack us en Mass I was obliged to make Campaigns against them and punish them severely, a little later about 2 or 300 was aproching and got United on Cosumne River, but I was not waiting for them. Left a small Garrison at home, Canons & other Arms loaded, and left with 6 brave men & 2 Baquero's in the night, and took them by surprise at Day light. The fighting was a little hard, but after having lost about 30 men, they was willing to make a treaty with me, and after this lecon they behaved very well, and became my best friends and Soldiers, with which I has been assisted to conquer the whole Sacramento and a part of the San Joaquin Valley. [The French lecon for lesson: Sutter's polylingual accomplishments creep in here and there.]

They became likewise tolerable good laborers and the boys had to learn mechanical trades; teamster's, Vaquero's, etc. At the time the Communication with the Bay was very long and dangerous, particularly in open Boats; it is a great Wonder that we got not swamped a many times, all time with an Indian Crew and a Canaca at the helm. Once it took me (in December 1839.) 16 days to go down to Yerbabuena and to return. I went down again on the 22d Xber 39. to Yerbabuena and on account of the inclemency of the Weather and the strong current in the River I need a whole month (17 days coming up) and nearly all the provisions spoiled.

March the 18th [1840]

Dispatched a party of White men and Indians in serch for pine timber and went not further up on the Amer. River as about 25 miles, found and cut some but not of a good quality and rafted it down the River. On the end of the month of March there was another conspiracy of some Indians, but was soon quelled when I succeeded to disarm them." – End of Quote from Diary

Kanakas were Hawaiian natives. Sutter arrived from New Mexico to the Columbia River in the Pacific Northwest by 1838. At a rendezvous near Wind River, he bought a native boy, apparently for the purpose of setting him free/getting out of the slave market. At Fort Vancouver, he made many friends but found that California's travel was too hazardous by land. So Sutter was obliged to take a ship to the Sandwich Islands (Hawaii) and hope to find a ship to California as they were fairly regular. He again made many friends due to his affable manner, honesty, and the treatment of all he met. He finally found a passage to California via Sitka, Alaska. Once again, he made many allies there. So when he finally arrived in Monterrey and asked for permission to settle, he had thirteen persons with him, three white men, and ten Kanaka, two wives of two of them. They would teach the Indian women in California. He paid them ten dollars a month and carried letters of introduction and recommendation that gave glowing reports of Sutter's character and reliability. At the expiration of their contracts, they all chose to remain with Sutter. – Introduction – "New Helvetia Diary – A Record of Events Kept by John. A. Sutter and His Clerks at New Helvetia, California, from September 9, 1845, to May 25, 1848," – Published 1939, San Francisco The Grabhorn Press in Arrangement with The Society of California Pioneers.

*€ The parabalani had neither orders nor vows but were enumerated among the clergy and enjoyed clerical privileges and immunities. In addition to performing works of mercy, they constituted a bodyguard for the bishop. Their presence at public gatherings or at the theaters was forbidden by law. At times they took a very active part in ecclesiastical controversies, such as at the Second Council of Ephesus. They received their name from the fact that they were hospital attendants, although the alternative name parabalani also became current because they risked their lives (παραβάλλεσθαι τὴν ζωήν) in exposing themselves to contagious diseases. It has been asserted, though without sufficient proof, that the brotherhood was first organized during the great plague in Alexandria in the episcopate of Pope Dionysius of Alexandria (second half of the 3rd century). Though they were chosen by the bishop and always remained under his control, the Codex Theodosianus placed them

under the supervision of the praefectus Augustalis, the imperial governor of Roman Egypt. The parabalani were believed to have helped murder the Alexandrian philosopher-scientist Hypatia in 415. Because their fanaticism resulted in riots, successive laws limited their numbers: thus a law issued in 416 restricted the enrollment in Alexandria to 500, a number increased two years later to 600. In Constantinople, the number was reduced from 1100 to 950. The parabalani are not mentioned after Justinian I's time. They could be seen as a stylistic forerunner of the Crusader order of St. John, and the Knights Templar.

*[7] The distortions of American history, its representation, and especially meaning, is a planned event. The Cordua quote arrives in 1933, long after the man's death, and the same year that "Toward Soviet America" was published by the CPUSA and William Z. Foster. This attack on American history was created by Herbert Marcuse of the Neo-Marxist Frankfurt School, as part of its Critical Theory for social revolution that began operation in the U.S. after WW2. Starting at Columbia University in New York City, and then nearly all Ivy League and state universities by Marcuse and other members such as Fromm and Adorno. In short, Critical Theory is the active application of Machiavellian principles in Marxist activism. The aim is to divide society by appealing to social injustices inflicted by one group on another with no cure until the issues are historically blurred and confused and primed for the final ascension of the socialist order for administering social justice and managing diverse populations as the manager of social grievance and discourse. But utopia is never attained, nor is utopia the aim; the power of control by a political elite is the aim.

Marcuse himself ended his long career of sewing social dysfunction at San Diego State University from 1965 to 1970. The Critical Theory dialectic taught by Marcuse became a method of inciting racial hatred through omission, the falsification of witnessed and documented history and establishing outright falsehoods with the aim of creating resentment in groups that hold the most insistent racial and tribal identity as their core human value. This has culminated in un-American political movements such as the current Critical Race Theory crisis, whose only aim was to destroy the establishment and capitalism, and the ideas of democratic republicanism. The fruits of his efforts are the current Globalism and Leftist rise in America with the mushrooming curtailing of Constitutional Rights.

Howard Zinn was another open member of the CPUSA who gained a history degree after WW2 and subsequent teaching positions. He could be said to be the father of historical revisionism. He wrote the history book used in public schools nationwide since 1980, "A People's History of the United States." (See Mary Grabar's

"Debunking Howard Zinn – Exposing the Fake History that Turned a Generation Against America."

Marcuse believed he was promoting a liberated society as one that has broken free of Industrial servitude and the rule-laden society it creates. His cure was worse than the disease, which had been corrected by the time he wrote "Eros and Civilization" and "One Dimensional Man." His ideas were reactions from the 19th century as Marcuse was born in 1899. When it came to the means of implementing this brave new world, his Neo-Marxism was essentially based on Machiavellian principles of divide and conquer, conquer and divide. He did this by actively setting races and ethnicities against one another in the U.S., continuing Marx's own theory of inciting a civil war of liberation in the American South in the 1850s. His articles were published in both the London and Horace Greeley's New York Times. Greeley was an avowed Socialist and Abolitionist. He with Lincoln were co-founders of the Republican Party. The Frankfurt School continued with these by now Far Left, revolutionary tactics, which melded well with the Civil Rights Movement and other activism of the 1960s. That these ivory-tower political philosopher megalomaniacs gave themselves license for thoughtless social experimentation without pausing to make new assessments of the current era is remarkably fantastic. Hopefully, this dark time of deception and engineered hatred will pass, and factual truth and reason will return to our greater society for the benefit of all.

On the other hand, Freemasonry was well-founded in the ideas of democracy and rule by consent. Freemasonry was a common feature shared by nearly every male member of most religious sects in the Anglo-American world, except for Catholicism.

The Roman Church had been the original cause of its formation. In 1307, the French King ordered all of the Knight's Templars arrested via a conspiratorial plot at dawn on Friday, October the 13th, 1307. Later in 1314, after years of imprisonment and torture at the hands of the Dominican Inquisition, the Grand Master, Jacque de Molay, and the Templar Preceptor of Normandy, Geoffroi de Charney, were roasted to death in front of Notre Dame Cathedral, in Paris, after recanting their forced confessions on the scaffold. The secret oaths and such resulted from a long period of persecution in Europe and England, not some modern plot for asserting world power with other mythical conspirators. Until after World War Two, the RCC forbade its members from joining FM but had organized The Knights of Columbus as an alternative public fraternity. The venerable order dedicated to universal brotherhood arose from these violent persecutions. It carried the embryo of reason and democracy through arduous periods of history through deeds such as influencing Charles II to establish the Royal Society in the 17th century, and later, the emerging light that the United States of America was intended to bring forth to the world. So it supplied the foundation and binding glue of American cultural and civic function until the 1970s when criticisms based on false historical interpretations and a loss of continuity in the fundamentalist Christian community began to result in the gradual diminishing of FM in American society.   However, there is enough membership left for Shriner's Children's Hospitals to continue to function. And they were an important influence in Sacramento's early history as they were throughout America.

*8 Regarding the controversy of Sutter's military experience, Sutter served in a Swiss regiment, so he was not listed in French records.

His grandson would not be able to find them because he was searching the wrong records. Here is the recorded dialog of that issue as it explains itself;

- Here is a letter received from a descendant of the Captain. It has to do with this much-disputed point in Sutter's eventful career.

"Reverend Schoonover who wrote Life and Times of General Sutter [T. J. Schoonover, Sacramento, 1895] claims that he (Sutter) served as Captain in the French Army under Charles X, and you state that he did not...Which is right? You or Reverend Schoonover? I say you are right. John A. Sutter never served in the French Army. I know this to be perfectly true because I had investigated it, and nothing could be found in this regard in the French Records ...."

The above, quoted only in part, addressed to the writer of this foreword, is signed; "Reginald Sutter, grandson of General Sutter."

The error of assuming that Sutter served in the French army when it was actually a Swiss regiment seconded to the French army. His name would not have been recorded in French rolls. Captain Sutter's grandson would have been thoroughly Americanized, and as one of his time, unaware, as many younger journalists of today, that since the time of William Tell, every Swiss male is automatically in the national militia as an obligation of birth citizenship. He was raised in a village that was occupied by German troops during the Napoleonic Wars. As we witness Sutter's diplomatic and organizing abilities, it is not a stretch to conclude that his claim of officership in the Swiss army or even the French army was not deceitful. The grandson worked from the information that led him to assume his grandfather had served in the French military in a French unit. John A. Sutter was not a liar or charlatan in any of his known dealings. So that he would create a false claim is not supported by any but those wishing to discredit Sutter. There is a record that John A. Sutter was commissioned as a Lieutenant in the U.S. Army during the Mexican-American War. Previous to that, Sutter had been made a Captian by California Governor Micheltorena in 1842. Later in life, many came to title him "General," by acclaim as even his grandson does in the same paragraph where he claims to have debunked his grandfather's French captainship.

Moreover, fleeing debt was common, as was the debtor's prison. Some famous Americans had gone bankrupt or fled debts, including U.S. Grant and the father of Robert E. Lee, Revolutionary War hero Harry "Lighthorse" Lee, Thomas Jefferson, and Abraham Lincoln. Many famous artists have fled debts or lived in perpetual bankruptcy, including Beethoven, Mozart, Richard Wagner, and countless other famous artists. Many of those who came to the California gold fields had fled debt and were looking for a way to either pay them off or find a new start. Ergo – overwhelming debt is no proof of character one way or the other. From Sutter's dairy, the actual book's 27-page introduction, Sutter was born in Kandern in 1803, a tiny town near Balse, where he grew up. Sutter grew up during the Napoleonic Wars and was ten years old when the Battle of Leipzig was fought, and Napoleon was forced to cross the Rhine into France. The Allies, Germany, Russia, Austria, and Prussia made their headquarters in Balse. Balse was an armed camp. Sutter grew up wishing to be a soldier, and again, as a male born in Switzerland, he was automatically considered militia.

*[9] The recent historical publications of Gregory and Susan Michno ("A Fate Worse than Death," "Dakota Dawn," "Circle the Wagons," "Encyclopedia of the Indian Wars," etc.), and the historical records of people such as Herman Lehmann ("Nine Years Among the Indians," and Lieutenant Charles Gatewood – "Apache Memoirs," G.A. Custer's, "My Life on the Plains," etc.

*[9] (Willis pg 326)

*[10] Fun Facts; H.M LaRue, is not a relative of the author who was born with that surname spelling variant until he changed it in 2010. Hugh LaRue was a Protestant descended from the American colonial settlement of French Huguenots, whereas the authors' roots are Quebecois and Catholic. #2 Judge McGowan was the great-grandfather of Mike McGowan, of Placerville (Placerville Marine and Cycle) who

partially grew up in Spanish Flat which served the Timm Mine on Kelsey Ridge nearby and was a key figure in creating the Hangtown Motocross Classic.

Quote; "The Foundations of the States are laid upon the bones of the pioneers," from the preface of "Ghosts of the Glory Trail," by Nell Murbarger – 1956

Arriving at White Rock

*₁ The InterAm was a big show as it traveled across America from coast to coast, and beyond, to Hawaii. It began as a sport that today is considered a major motorsport and the cause of a substantial off-road recreation industry.

*₂ The acquisition of "The Early Inns of California," by Ralph H. Cross, published as a limited edition of 500 copies, provided the story of "Six-Toed Pete" and other points of history presented in this book that exist nowhere else that I have found.

His old roadhouse survived until the early 1970s, when the entire compound apparently razed to the ground, likely intentionally. The foundations can be located near the entry of the present Prairie City SRVA just off White Rock Road near the junction of Grant Line Road, south of Folsom and present-day Highway 50.

*₃ A staff member at the Sacramento Historical Society told me that they likely were sold off to private parties.   But they have no knowledge or records of any actual sales.

Childhood's End – Growing Up

*₁ Eddie Pitts – See page 573

*₂ https://www.vvmf.org/Wall-of-Faces/57712/ROBERT-A-YATES/

*₃ Recommended reading; "Acid Dreams – The Complete Social History of LD, The CIA, The Sixties, and Beyond," Lee and Shlain

*₄ Mark Miller – Class of 1971, Class of 1968 Steve Miller's younger brother – Mark was a good friend and spent a great deal of time at our home for many years during high school. He came on hunting and later trail bike rides and campouts with my father and me. Mark lived near Haines, Alaska for some years in the 1980s. We went on many day hikes near Wentworth Springs, until the late 90s. Mark and I kept in touch until the late 2000s, after I returned from Slovenia when he seemed to drop out of circulation, with no phone responses, etc.

*5 Heather MacDonald — The Manhattan Institute - https://www.manhattan-institute.org/html/reality-black-crime-1845.html

*6 Rape was a constant complaint in North Highlands during that time, but rape had been an epidemic in California since the so-called "Summer of Love" in 1967 (Acid Dreams," page 186), and has remained a national problem since. Coerced rape is an unexplored issue, but real.

*7 July 2021, founding member of the Dirt Diggers North MC, Penton West, Hi-Point general manager, contributor, and friend, Dave Duarte, contacted Lars Larson (my MX workshop instructor in April of 1970 and Husqvarna factory rider), to ask him of the whereabouts of Claus Nilsen. Lars emailed back that Claus "The Sailor Man" was out around the Philippines, forever sailing, and gave an email address. I have emailed Claus, but it might be a while before I hear back.

*8 Tower Records began in Sacramento and grew into a worldwide phenomenon. A number of Highlands High alumni have worked at Tower Records, including, Barry Akin, Tony Thorton, my youngest sister, and others that I cannot recall. See the film, DVD – "All Things Must Pass," with Bob Akin '70, a contributing photo/videographer.

*9 Carl Lee Cranke, off-road, ISTD legend with seven gold, and two silver medals won eight years straight, mostly for Penton Motorcycles. Carl Cranke managed Cycle Speed in North Highlands from 1969 to 1972 and was an active member of the Dirt Diggers North Motorcycle Club, as well as active moto-cross, speedway, flat track, and hare and hound cross country races such as the Baja 10000, Barstow to Vegas. See – It Was The Place to Be *2

*10 British two-time World Champion Jeff Smith, in his book, "The Art of Moto-Cross" writes that in order to improve, one must ride a little beyond one's current skill level. Because of this, he explains, crashes are inevitable, but the smart rider learns from his errors and his skill level rises as a result. The author told his English professor at American River College in 1971 that a race was like a lifetime; every move and decision had a bearing on the race's outcome, just as in life. Because of this understanding, errors in life are inevitable. The determiner is the vision and discipline of the traveler.

Camp Kohler Revisited

*1 In psychology - The act or process of infantilizing, or treating a non-infant as an infant. In politics/social engineering, repressing through the manipulation of

education, and laws, to make and retain dependency on government agencies - the removal of consequences for actions that would normally draw penalties such as jail time.

*[2] James Roosevelt supported communist party member Hugh DeLacy (D-Wash) in 1946. When the Red Chinese took over mainland China in 1949, Roosevelt was delighted and worked actively for its admission to the U.N. He served as an executive officer of the communist-dominated Independent Citizens Committee of the Arts, Sciences, and Professions. From 1955 to 1965, he was in the House of Representatives. Most of his activities were aimed at the abolition of the House Committee on Un-American Activities. In 1962, he edited "The Liberal Papers," which is a manifesto of the Far Left. He supported Khrushchev's demands that the U.S. remove all missile bases from Europe in 1962. A son like this does not arise from a loyal American conservative family founded on Constitutional principles but from socialist elitists. – Biographical Dictionary of the Left, Volume 1, Francis X. Gannon, pgs 506-7 – "Blacklisted by History – The Untold Story of Senator Joe McCarthy," M Stanton Evans

*[2] As revealed after the collapse of the Soviet Union when records long ignored were released and available to historians' world community.

*[3] This is well illustrated by historians such as Nobel Prize winner Robert W. Fogel and Stanley L. Engermann), "Time on the Cross – The Economics of American Negro Slavery."

*[4] World War II was the deadliest military conflict in history. An estimated total of 70–85 million people perished, or about 3% of the 1940 world population (est. 2.3 billion). Deaths directly caused by the war (including military and civilian fatalities) are estimated at 50–56 million, with an additional estimated 19–28 million deaths from war-related disease and famine. Civilian deaths totaled 50–55 million. Military deaths from all causes totaled 21–25 million, including deaths in captivity of about 5 million prisoners of war. More than half of the total number of casualties are accounted for by the dead of the Republic of China and the Soviet Union. – From Wikipedia

*[ق] The Barcelona Agreement of 1995 – discussion link article by Israel Today – **https://blogs.timesofisrael.com/barcelona-agreement-treaty-on-growth-of-islamism/** Four main points of action;

1. The Barcelona Agreement is based on four basic principles and requirements, which practically include:

2. Europe opens its doors to Islamic immigrants. Preventing laws that violate the rules and bureaucracy of countries that hinder the interests of Muslims and their religious practices in accordance with the teachings of the Qur'an.

3. Facilitate the spread of Islam in Europe.

4. Presenting and promoting attitudes that present a positive image of Arab and Islamic culture.

The educational materials of schools in this field should focus on the sins of European culture against Islam and pay attention to positive propaganda.

*5 The word "pachuco" is uncertain, but one theory connects it to the city of El Paso, Texas, which was sometimes referred to as "Chuco Town" or "El Chuco." People migrating to El Paso from Ciudad Juarez would say, in Spanish, that they were going "pa' El Chuco." Some say "pa El Chuco" comes from the words Shoe Co., a shoe company that was located in El Paso in the 1940s during the war. The majority of Mexican migrants would cross the border in order to work for this famous shoe company in El Paso. Throughout the years the term "pa El Chuco" was used when Mexican immigrants were heading to El Paso looking for a job. To cross the American border with success, the migrants would have to dress nice and look nice otherwise they would get rejected at the border. These migrants became known as pachucos. "Pachuco" could also have derived from the name of the city of Pachuca, Hidalgo, Mexico,[7] as the majority of Mexican migration to the United States came from the Central Plateau region, of which Hidalgo is a part. Another theory says that the "word" derives from pocho, a derogatory term for a Mexican born in the United States who has lost touch with Mexican culture. The word is also said to mean "punk" or "troublemaker." Yet another theory is put forth by author Laura L. Cummings who postulates a possible indigenous origin of the term. Connections have also been found between "Pachucos" and mixed civilians who lived near the Mexican–American border during the turn of the century, and between "Pachucos" and the poor soldiers who fought in the Mexican Revolution in the armies of Pancho Villa. Pachucos called their slang Caló (sometimes called "pachuquismo"), a unique argot that drew on the original Spanish Gypsy Caló, Mexican Spanish, the New Mexican dialect of Spanish, and American English, employing words and phrases creatively applied. To a large extent, Caló went mainstream and is one of the last surviving vestiges of the Pachuco, often used in the lexicon of some urban Latin

Americans in the United States to this day. The influence of Valdés is responsible for the assimilation of several Caló terms into Mexican slang. - from Wikipedia

*₆ See – "Time on the Cross – The Economics of Negro Slavery," Robert W. Fogel, Nobel Laureate in Economic Sciences and Stanley L. Engerman - "White Cargo" – Don Jordan, Michael Walsh, "White Gold –

The Extraordinary Story of Thomas Pellow and Islam's One Million White Slaves," Giles & Milton, "To Hell or Barbados" – Sean O'Callaghan

*W Martin Luther King, Jr. is listed as a Christian Socialist in a Wikipedia article online. As reported by evidence in *₇ below – served the purpose of disruption the Soviets, CPUSA, and various anarchist revolutionary groups as planned since the late 19th century – see Thomas Sowell's articles regarding the CRM and Black Social History.

*₇ (see – David Garrow's "Bearing the Cross" for Stanley Lewison, Highland Folk School, Robert Kennedy, FBI, CIA, – "Blacklisted by History," E. Stanton Evans), "Acid Dreams – The Complete Social History of LSD, The CIA, The Sixties, and Beyond," Lee & Shlain, not long after this, 1970 Soviet KGB defector Yuri Bezmenov gave a series of lectures on how all of these movements and undertakings, and foolishness were either directed by the KGB or at least encouraged as it would demoralize society (mainly intellectually, but ethically and spiritually as well) and cause the fall of capitalism and the West. (see – Love Letter to America," Thomas Schuman (Yuri Bezmenov) quotes; "As I mentioned before, exposure to true information does not matter anymore. A person who is demoralized is unable to assess true information. The facts tell him nothing, even if I shower him with information, with authentic proof, with documents, and pictures. ...he will refuse to believe it... That's the tragedy of the situation of demoralization." –Yuri Bezmenov [1984] "Deception Was My Job" - A collection of lectures by defected KGB Agent Yuri Bezmenov

*₈ https://www.atomicheritage.org/history/japanese-atomic-bomb-project

*₉ Fredrick Nietzsche broke with his sister over her Christian beliefs writing to her, "Hence the ways of men part; if you wish to strive for peace of mind and comfort, then believe. If you wish to be a devotee of truth, then inquire..." Nietzsche abhorred anti-semitism and broke with Wagner over it, as well as his sister. After his death, she reworked some of his writings to support the political philosophy of a

rising new leader, Adolf Hitler. (see — "The Holy Reich — Nazi Conceptions of Christianity, 1919-1945," Richard Steigmann-Gall)

Note; Wagner was not a Hitlerian precursor but held common attitudes of his time, once quipping, "Service in the army would do Jews good, it would Germanize them." (Many had arrived from Russia, fleeing from the Tsar's Pogroms. Germany officially welcomed them in). Many Jews served in the German Army in WW1. Jewish scientist Fritz Haber developed chlorine gas and directed its first use at the Battle of Ypres, in 1915. (Haber had previously won a Nobel Prize for his invention of synthetic fertilizer which saved the expanding German population from starving and allowed the entire world to enjoy a great expansion of farm production. Ironically, Cyclon Z, which was used to gas millions of Jews and others during the Nazi era was developed from chlorine gas fundamentals (but not by Haber who had fled Germany to Switzerland)).

*₁₀ "The Decline and Fall of the Roman Empire," is a six-volume study by 18th-century historian/philosopher Edward Gibbon, who developed the "Historical Method," for historical research equivalent to the forensic examination of criminal acts based on the scientific method of collection of corroborating evidence and correlation to provable or evidentiary facts. Gibbon showed that early Christians falsified history (see - Eusebius — 4th century) as a method for asserting themselves into it as a main cause or champion where it had in fact suppressed and controlled information as with the 4-5th century suppression of the teaching and use of rational logic, math, and any application of reason as "Satanic," resulting in the intolerance explored in that period by Drake in "Constantine's Bishops — The Politics of Intolerance." The practice continues to this day as righteous opposition to communism. The contest between those who would rule our minds and lives goes on. Yuri Bezmenov goes deeply into the Soviet/KGB deep understanding and implementation of these processes in overthrowing capitalism and democracy.

*k Caesar's Messiah — The Roman Conspiracy to Invent Jesus," Joseph Atwill

The Last Round-Up

*₁ The premise of the Foundation stories is that, in the waning days of a future Galactic Empire, the mathematician Hari Seldon spends his life developing a theory of psychohistory, a new and effective mathematical sociology. Using statistical laws of mass action can predict the future of large populations. Seldon foresees the imminent fall of the Empire, which encompasses the entire Milky Way, and a dark

age lasting 30,000 years before a second Empire arises. Although the inertia of the Empire's fall is too great to stop, Seldon devises a plan by which "the onrushing mass of events must be deflected just a little" to eventually limit this interregnum to just one thousand years. To implement his plan, Seldon created the Foundations—two groups of scientists and engineers settled at opposite ends of the galaxy—to preserve the spirit of science and civilization, and thus become the cornerstones of the new galactic empire.

One key feature of Seldon's theory, which has proved influential in real-world social science, is the uncertainty principle of sociology: if a population gains knowledge of its predicted behavior, its self-aware collective actions become unpredictable. (Is infantilization a social certainty)?

Issac Asimov spoke on the limits of growth at the 1980 Futurists Convention. He noted the mathematical certainty of closed biological systems and noted the earth's position as life/death graph used in the typical high school science lab to show that life on earth had reached its endpoint of stabilization and would soon see higher life forms plunge to zero or near zero as all the toxic accumulations. He said that the death drop would occur almost immediately and we'd see it begin in the 21st century. "It may be through pandemics, war, natural disasters, or a combination of them, but it is a mathematical certainty that it will happen."

*$_2$ The Founders were uniformly influenced by two things; Freemasonry with its tolerance of all faiths and promotion of science, and the ideas of the English political philosopher John Locke. John Locke observed that man's rights to his freedoms were natural, not "God Given" as many of the Right assert almost daily on various media platforms. Moreover, the Founders were very clear in their writings about the need to keep religion and the state in a separate relationship, not cooperative on any level. This was due to the lessons learned regarding the history of Church and State in Europe since the fall of the Roman Empire. Here is a statement by Madison that is echoed in the commentary of Jefferson, and Paine, among others; "Religious bondage shackles and debilitates the mind and unfits it for every noble enterprise... During almost fifteen centuries has the legal establishment of Christianity has been on trial. What have been its fruits? More or less, in all places, pride and indolence in the clergy; ignorance and servility in laity; in both, superstition, bigotry, and persecution." Just before he left office George Washington wrote the 1797 Treaty of Peace and Friendship Between the Unities States of America and the Bey of Tripoli. This treaty was passed by Congress and signed by President Adams. It emphatically

states the U.S. was not founded "in any sense" - on Christianity in Article 11 of that treaty.

*₃ Refer to this link for useful research material on One World Government - https://www.brexit-watch.org/the-danger-of-political-delusion-part-one-world-government

*₄ See *₂ – Beyond the Shadow of The Spook Tree – Lincoln's Marxists," Benson and Kennedy - The French Revolution generated the modern communist movement which became Marxism. It was focused on Machiavellian tactics using race from the start. In the 1850s, New York Tribune publisher Horace Greeley was publishing Karl Marx's articles that advocated for a war of liberation in the Southern States as a righteous, Christian endeavor, adding the religious fanatics of the time as his "useful idiots," of whom Horace Greeley could be counted. Misinformation was employed then, as with radical preacher Lyman Beecher's daughter Harriet Beecher Stowe's entirely fictitious novel "Uncle Tom's Cabin," and her brother's exhortation for young men to "Go to Kansas and kill Southerners," disregarding the basic tenants of Christianity including the Ten Commandments, and the directive to "leave it to God," which to the secular mind could mean, "let it resolve itself naturally." It arguably would have if the Southern Plantation system had been left alone to find its limits. As it is, many owners were beginning to shrink from the practice as the pressure of the larger world anti-slavery movement was in motion, largely led by Britain. Queen Victoria was vehemently anti-slavery and sponsored many wars throughout the British Empire aimed at eliminating slavery and slave trading worldwide.

(The U.S. joined the international ban on the Transatlantic Slave Trade that had been initiated by Britain in 1807, in 1808. Both led other European nations in patrolling the Atlantic for violators (see 1930s film, "Souls at Sea")). However, because of the vastness of the ocean and the rural nature of much of the U.S. east coast, lucrative smuggling operations continued and even led to the development of faster ships aiming to outrun the patrolling nation's efforts.

Increasingly, many owners, including George Washington's son, Parke Custis, left a directive to free the slaves at Arlington, upon his death. The executor of his will was son-in-law, Robert E. Lee, who endeavored to comply but found certain interference from unknown agents agitating the slaves on the estate. That and the prerequisite of certain endowments to survivors be completed first, delayed the emancipation order since repairs on various properties included in the estate had to be made before such could be sold in order to raise the endowment funds. Horace Greeley made a public scandal of it, even spreading the rumor that Lee had whipped a female slave who had escaped. No slave was ever whipped at Arlington. Lee was against slavery and was such a devout Christian and gentleman that the idea of his ever laying a hand on any woman, slave or free was ridiculous to anyone who knew him. Moreover, the claim was not supported by the victim herself. (In "Time on the Cross – The Economics of American Negro Slavery," Nobel Laureate in the economic sciences, Robert Fogel and Stanley Engermann showed that any and all harsh or unjust treatment universally resulted in the shirking of work, claims of illness, and other dodges that cost the planter. Keeping the slaves content and healthy was a question of economics, which was reinforced by the general Anglican morality of the Christian South. This is supported by Professor, Eugene Genovese in his historical tome, "Roll Jordan, Roll – The World the Slaves Created." Ill-treatment costs money. And the cost of keeping slaves would only increase over time.   This stands as another argument for the natural mortality of slavery in one or two generations).

The Republican Party was originally formed for the purpose of supporting the interests of the Northern Industrialists and never had a constituency in the South. They had become dependent upon the harsh tariffs on Southern-produced goods, which largely meant cotton and tobacco that was shipped to Britain and Europe. In 1860, a major plank of the Republican Party was a high protective tariff as a solution for a mild recession that had hit Northern Manufacturers.* The high tariffs forced the Southern States to sell to the Northern Industrialists at their prices. The loss of a seat in Congress meant the loss of support for the tariff. The 1828 tariff almost caused Southern secession but was avoided by Henry Clay and his "Great Compromise."   By 1860, the new Morrill Tariff would raise the tariff to 50% and even higher on some goods. Lincoln supported the Morrill Tariff.   After Lincoln won the general election, Southern states began to secede and form the Confederate States of America, with a constitution that was almost exactly the same as the one ratified in 1789, except that it dealt with slavery. An interesting note is that the way the laws were written, slavery would have gone extinct within a short time because importation, exportation, and interstate transportation, of chattel slaves by anyone but citizen owners was prohibited. With the sole right to import, the financial burden of slave international slave trading, being illegal internationally since 1807, anyway, would have meant that the trend toward owner-willed emancipation was the likely eventuality, as carrying it on would have become cost-prohibitive soon, largely due to the rise of the medical profession and concurrent costs associated with it (slaves required a lot of medical attention, while emancipation mean personal responsibility). Sharecropping was a natural result of the ending of the slave, and it carried on until The Great Depression when corporate farming became its replacement. (*See- "When in the Course of Human Events – Arguing the Case for Southern Secession," Charles Adams – Pg 94).

The question becomes, did the CSA realize the slavery amortization process that they had set up in their constitution? The copy used by the author is a typical booklet form, the same as the type we often see for handy versions of the U.S. Constitution. On its back cover is a comment about the nature of the document inside. "The constitution contained many of the phrases and clauses which had led to disagreement among the states in the original Union, including the Supremacy Clause and a Necessary and Proper Clause. The Confederate Congress had powers almost identical to the U.S. Congress, however, all the minor differences added together amounted to a much more constrained federal government than the U.S. government of the times and of today. The Confederate Constitution contained clauses which increased the powers of the Executive Branch, such as the line-item veto power given to the president. However, they also granted essentially a line-item veto to the Senate and Congress by limiting each bill to one issue written in the name. By making both the executive and legislative branches of government more powerful they did more to tie the hands of the Federal government overall – enhancing the planned ineffectiveness of the central government, one of the founding premises of the U.S. Constitution. The framers of the Confederate Constitution, having studied the various constitutional crises which had arisen in the United States between 1787 and 1860, tried to revise the constitution to eliminate the grievances which had been raised in that period."

*[5] Edward Gibbon – "The Decline and Fall of the Roman Empire"

*[6] See – Christine Hoff-Sommers "The War Against Boys," volumes 1&2 Early negation of the male has likely led to the gender wars of the present, the drugging of boys to "normalize them" has converted to gender modifications via hormone therapy – as well as a myriad of consequential social dysfunction

*℗ See – "White Gold," Giles Milton – "Barbarian Cruelty – An Eye-Witness Account of White Slavery Under the Moors," Francis Brooks, "White Cargo – The Forgotten History of Britain's White Slaves in America," Jordan and Walsh, "They Were White and They Were Slaves – The Untold History of the Enslavement of Whites in Early America," Michael A. Hoffman II – "To Hell Or Barbados – The Ethnic Cleansing of Ireland," Sean O'Callaghan, "Black Slave-owners – Free Black Slave Masters in South

Carolina, 1790 – 1860," Larry Koger (includes a brief history of Black masters in other states in the Introduction).

*⊕ "Roll Jordan, Roll – The World the Slaves Made," Eugene D. Genovese, "Time on the Cross – The Economics of American Negro Slavery," Robert W. Fogel – Nobel Laureate in Economic Sciences and Stanley L. Engerman – (Actual conditions for the vast majority of slaves were not just humane, but of far better quality than for poor whites in America. The slave diet in the antebellum South was more nutritious than the average American diet in 1964).

*ⴽ Simultaneously was the rise of Christian Socialism, which is based on the Beatitudes and the traditions of early Christians (Acts 2, Vs 44-45) using collectivism and condemnation of wealth and materialism practiced by various Catholic orders and early Protestant sects from the 13th to 18th century.

*¥   Horace Greeley on peaceful secession; "If the Cotton States shall become satisfied that they can do better out of the Union than in it, we insist on letting them go in peace. The right to secede may be a revolutionary one, but it exists nevertheless ... And whenever a considerable section of our Union shall deliberately resolve to go out, we shall resist all coercive measures designed to keep it in. We hope never to live in a republic whereof one section is pinned to the residue by bayonets."

*₇ "Lincoln's Marxists" – Benson and Kennedy

*ᚾᚺ "Slavery Was Not the Cause of the War Between the States – The Irrefutable Argument," Gene Kizer, Jr.

As the panic of the Morrill Tariff's effect on the Union bereft of revenue from the South, and the higher cost of goods resulted in its spread into the North, Lincoln began the plan for an invasion of the South. The CSA offered a peaceful withdrawal from Fort Sumter as Lincoln dealt in duplicitous negotiations with representatives from Virginia, which had not yet seceded. Despite overtures of peaceful withdrawal, Lincoln sent a three-ship flotilla to Fort Sumter and landed troops at Fort Pickens, Florida on April 12, 1861, the same day that the bombardment of Fort Sumter began, as an invasion force. The remaining six states of the South seceded during May, with Kentucky taking a neutral resolution and refusing to send troops to the Union call-up.

*₩ See – "The Settler's War," Gregory Michno

*⚵ See – "Rising Tide – The Great Mississippi Flood of 1927 and How it Changed America," John M. Barry

*⊕ Or was he? Even sympathetic chronicler, David Garrow, and partner in the Southern Black Leadership Conference, Ralph Abernathy reveal in their books MLK's hypocrisy and contradictions; his rejection of basic Christian doctrine, plagiarism, extreme sexual deviancy, etc. (King, in fact, is listed as a Christian Socialist). One of King's less popular quotes was his demand for a monthly stipend for all Black Americans in perpetuity. This he claimed was required for justice and as long as these demands or not met "the Black community will represent a knife leveled at the throat of America."

*♭ The International Legal Defense, sponsored by the Communist Party USA, competed with the NAACP for defense priority applying mass pressure on the Alabama political and judicial system, individual liberals and radicals, as well as their organizations, bombarded officials, including the governor, with telegrams, postcards, and letters demanding justice, including a retrial of all the defendants. Ruby Bates, in a move that blew up the case, then changed her testimony. Her motives for the dramatic change were apparently mixed. She was annoyed because the other witness, Victoria Price, had pushed her out of the limelight. But the element of conscience was also present, for as she wrote in a letter to a boyfriend, "I wish those negroes are not burnt on account of me." Whatever her reasons, it took considerable courage for her to change her testimony in a racially charged case in the Deep South of the 1930s. Bates found herself vilified, being accused by many of the local elites that she had been bribed by the defense team, which as far as they were concerned was comprised mostly of Jewish Communists who had no right to be in the South. After her testimony, Ruby was taken from the courtroom and hidden by several National Guardsmen.

Recognizing Bates' publicity value, the Leftist defenders of the Scottsboro boys took her on a tour of New York and Washington, D.C. At New York's St. Nicholas Arena, she spoke as a poor white woman before a crowd of over 5,000, saying that her initial false story of rape had been the result of having been "excited and frightened by the ruling class of white people."

Back in Alabama, hostility toward Bates increased. The Huntsville Times noted with sarcasm that she had become "Harlem's darling" and called on the state attorney general to institute perjury proceedings against the "former Huntsville guttersnipe." The teen girls were examined by an M.D. retained by the defense, long after the events, and declared that they had not been raped. How that could be a found fact is unclear. Yet then and today, we are to believe that nine black teens had thrown a group of white boys off the train over some issue that we are to suppose had nothing to do with the girls, and then the girls remained on the train, voluntarily, we are to accept, and not one of the nine blacks, ages ranging from thirteen to twenty years of age did any harm to the girls. Even when during the first trial, one of the accused had confessed and another pointed out the members of their group that had raped the girls. Yet a myth was constructed and a book based on fiction was published and held up as representative of the event, to this day.

*∞ Annual average Violent Victimizations, 2012-2013 – sample – stats have expanded along the same lines since – especially during the 2020 riots.

Table 10. Race of victim   Number of victimizations/Race of offender, %

Race of victim	Number of victimizations	White	Black	Hispanic	Other	Unknown
White	4,091,971	56	13.7	11.9	10.6	7.8
Black	955,800	10.4	62.2	4.7	15	7.7
Hispanic	995,996	21.7	21.1	38.6	11.6	6.9
Other	440,741	40.3	19.3	10.6	20.3	9.5
Total	6,484,507	42.9	22.4	14.8	12.1	7.8

Data Source: BJS, National Crime Victimization Survey, 2012–2013, Special Tabulation

Some observers argue that the overwhelming preponderance of black-on-white over white-on-black violence suggests that blacks deliberately target whites for violence. Others argue that since there are 4.7 times as many whites as blacks in the population, it is to be expected that black criminals are more likely to encounter white victims than vice versa.

Both positions must be evaluated in light of several considerations. First, blacks who commit assault, robbery, and rape are likely to be members of the underclass, who live in largely black neighborhoods.

If they chose victims without regard to race they should be more likely to encounter other blacks rather than whites. Second, black/Hispanic interracial crime fits the same lopsided pattern: Of the 256,074 violent crimes involving those two groups, blacks were perpetrators 82.5 percent of the time. Unlike the nearly five-fold difference in numbers between blacks and whites, there are only about 30 percent more Hispanics than blacks. The high black-aggressor figure suggests that blacks may also deliberately target Hispanics — perhaps even more than they target whites.

The imbalance can be expressed differently: When whites commit violence they target other whites 82.4 percent of the time, blacks 3.6 percent of the time, and Hispanics 7.8 percent of the time.

In other words, white violence is directed overwhelmingly at other whites. When blacks commit violence only a minority — 40.9 percent — of their victims are black. Whites are 38.6 percent and Hispanics are 14.5 percent. Hispanic assailants also attack their own group less often than they attack others. Their victims are Hispanics — 40.1 percent, whites — 50.7 percent, and blacks — 4.7 percent.

Finally, interracial crime can be expressed in terms of the greater or lesser likelihood of a person of one race committing violence against a member of the other. In 2012/2013, the actual likelihood of an attack was extremely low in all cases, but statistically, any given black person was 27 times more likely to attack a white and six times more likely to attack a Hispanic than vice versa. A Hispanic was eight times more likely to attack a white than the reverse.

*⊕⊕   In 1807, Britain banned the international slave trade and convinced other European nations to join in the ban, except Portugal. The U.S. followed in 1808. The Atlantic was patrolled by British and U.S. ships. Slave smuggling continued and actually led to the development of faster ships as outrunning the sea-policing was considered possible and rural coasts were plenty on the U.S. Eastern seaboard, but even more so in the Caribbean islands, and South American shores. Britain extended this crusade to its colonies, fighting wars in India, China, and Africa, famously in Sudan, in that effort, spilling considerable blood and treasure "By Order of the Great White Queen," Victoria. Today, Queen Victoria is vilified by the Left for having ruled over her empire as white rule over non-whites without any other consideration.

*⊤ The Geneva Conventions, which were adopted before 1949. were concerned with combatants only, not with civilians. The events of World War II showed the disastrous consequences of the absence of a convention for the protection of

civilians in wartime. The Convention adopted in 1949 takes account of the experiences of World War II. It is composed of 159 articles. It contains a short section concerning the general protection of populations against certain consequences of war, without addressing the conduct of hostilities, as such, which was later examined in the Additional Protocols of 1977. The bulk of the Convention deals with the status and treatment of protected persons, distinguishing between the situation of foreigners on the territory of one of the parties to the conflict and that of civilians in occupied territory. It spells out the obligations of the Occupying Power vis-à-vis the civilian population and contains detailed provisions on humanitarian relief for populations in occupied territory. It also contains a specific regime for the treatment of civilian internees. It has three annexes that contain a model agreement on hospital and safety zones, model regulations on humanitarian relief, and model cards.

*† See – The 1797 Treaty of Peace and Friendship Between the United States and the Bey of Tripoli"- Article 11 - **As the government of the United States of America is not in any sense founded on the Christian Religion,** — as it has in itself no character of enmity against the laws, religion or tranquility of Musselmen, — and as the said States never have entered into any war or act of hostility against any Mehomitan nation, it is declared by the parties that no pretext arising from religious opinions shall ever produce an interruption of the harmony existing between the two countries. - https://usconstitution.net/tripoli.html   The treaty was written by President George Washington, ratified by Congress, and signed by President Adams.

*℗ 1948 Convention - 29-03-2004 – Statement of the International Committee of the Red Cross;

"Genocide is a serious crime under international law. It is currently defined in the Convention on the Prevention and Punishment of the Crime of Genocide, adopted on 9 December 1948 by the United Nations General Assembly. Alain Aeschlimann, jurist, and head of protection activities at the ICRC explains:

Genocide is described as a specific act (killing, serious bodily or mental harm, etc.) "Committed with intent to destroy, in whole or in part, a national, ethnical, religious or racial group, as such". The parties to the Convention (at present almost 120 States) undertake to enact the necessary legislation to ensure its application, and in particular to provide effective penalties for persons guilty of genocide.

Persons charged with genocide are to be tried by a competent tribunal of the State in the territory of which the act was committed, or by a specially constituted international tribunal. Genocide is never to be considered a political crime for the purpose of extradition.

Lastly, the Convention provides that the States party may call upon the competent organs of the United Nations to take such action under the United Nations Charter as they consider appropriate for the prevention and suppression of acts of genocide (for the text of the Convention see Schindler/Toman, The Laws of Armed Conflicts, 1988, pp. 231-249).

Scope of the law "compromised"

Following protracted negotiations in 1948, the States decided not to include political and cultural genocide in the Convention.

In addition, the scope of the Convention was seriously compromised by the reservations made by the Soviet Union and its allies concerning the provisions relating to the implementation of international obligations.

The word "genocide" is very often used in error and exaggeratedly. In the eyes of the public, it has an incriminatory connotation.

The term "genocide" is not used in the Geneva Conventions or in their Additional Protocols. It is nevertheless obvious that all the acts that constitute genocide are grave breaches of the Geneva Conventions and represent war crimes if they are committed in the course of an international armed conflict (Articles 50/51/130/147 of the Geneva Conventions; Article 85 of Protocol I). **By the same token, any act that constitutes genocide and is committed in the course of a non-international armed conflict is a violation of common Article 3 and of Protocol II."**

*8 *₪ Critical Race Theory is hardly different from Herbert Marcuse's and the Frankfurt School's Critical Theory. In Norman F Cantor's Inventing the Middle Ages, the chapter "The French Jews" presents one of the clearest definitions of the Frankfurt School's theory and how it was implemented in universities by Cantor's example of how it influenced the interpretation of Medieval History in the departments of the top universities and the United States. Early 60s radicals learned at Marcuse's knee. Among them is Angela Davis, who was famously involved in the murder of a Marin County Superior Court Judge in 1969 as part of the Black Panther's activities of the time. Saul Alinsky's "Rules for Radicals," published in

1971, was a kind of "Revolution for Dummies" version of Critical Theory. Combined with the KGB's simultaneous work in influencing American culture from Hollywood to the local school boards, it was intended to demoralize society to the point of dysfunction and collapse. They spawned the Weather Underground, The Black Panthers, and many other movements, including the Women's Liberation Movement. They understood that destroying capitalism and its civilization would require ruining a generation and the next from then on. Any destructive trend or fad was exploited as the best means available.*² Concurrently, the KGB encouraged demoralization in the West as a favored passive method for defeating the West. Yuri Bezmenov's lectures in the early 1980s came too late. The dye was set.

*₉ See – "Acid Dreams – The Complete History of LSD, The CIA, The Sixties, and Beyond," Lee and Schlain

*₁₀ Born in 1922 in Brooklyn, NY, Howard Zinn began at New York University and emerged from Columbia University in 1958 with a Ph.D. in history. Zinn began teaching at Upsala College, Brooklyn College, and then Spelman College in Atlanta. He became chairman of Harvard University's Center for Far Eastern Studies and was director of the Non-Western Studies Program at the Atlanta University Center. From 1964 on, he was an associate professor at Boston University. Zinn invented modern historical revisionism. Among his books are "La Guardia in Congress," SNCC, The New Abolitionists," "The Southern Mystique," and "Vietnam: The Logic of Withdrawal." Note that the Student Non-Violent Coordinating Committee was anything but non-violent. His contribution to the United States' destruction was his book, "The People's History of the United States." It ignores all mitigating historical facts to present America as a brutal mechanism of race hatred and exploitation for the benefit of a few. This book became the standard history textbook for use in public high schools nationwide since 1980. Happily, a thorough rebuttal has finally been published by Mary Gabar, "Debunking Howard Zinn: Exposing the Fake History That Turned a Generation against America." – Zinn is also listed in "The Biographical Dictionary of the Left," Francis X. Gannon, Vol 1.

*₁₁ "A People's History of the United States." (See Mary Grabar's "Debunking Howard Zinn – Exposing the Fake History that Turned a Generation Against America." – Mary Grabar - is a resident fellow at the Alexander Hamilton Institute for the Study of Western Civilization and the founder of the Dissident Prof Education Project. She taught at the college level for twenty years, most recently at Emory University. Her work has been published by The Federalist, City Journal, Townhall,

American Greatness, and Academic Questions. Mary Grabar was born in Slovenia and immigrated with her family to the U.S.A.

*[12] Gandhi's Seven Blunders of the World – Wealth without work, Pleasure without consciousness, Knowledge without character, Commerce without morality, Science without humanity, Worship without sacrifice, Politics without principle.

*[13] Cloward-Piven Strategy – review online – plan for creating the welfare state Intended to cause the collapse of the system and establish a permanent welfare state – also below;
https://www.discoverthenetworks.org/organizations/clowardpiven-strategy-cps

https://en.wikipedia.org/wiki/Cloward%E2%80%93Piven_strategy

Cloward-Piven Social Welfare Strategy

History

Cloward and Piven were both professors at the Columbia University School of Social Work. The strategy was outlined in a May 1966 article in the liberal magazine The Nation titled "The Weight of the Poor: A Strategy to End Poverty".

The two stated that many Americans who were eligible for welfare were not receiving benefits and that a welfare enrollment drive would strain local budgets, precipitating a crisis at the state and local levels that would be a wake-up call for the federal government, particularly the Democratic Party. There would also be other consequences of this strategy, according to Cloward and Piven. These would include: easing the plight of the poor in the short-term (through their participation in the welfare system); shoring up support for the national Democratic Party-then splintered by pluralistic interests (through its cultivation of poor and minority constituencies by implementing a national "solution" to poverty), and relieving local governments of the financially and politically onerous burdens of public welfare (through a national "solution" to poverty).

Strategy

Cloward and Piven's article is focused on forcing the Democratic Party, which in 1966 controlled the presidency and both houses of the United States Congress, to take federal action to help the poor. They stated that full enrollment of those eligible for welfare "would produce bureaucratic disruption in welfare agencies and fiscal disruption in local and state governments" that would: "...deepen existing divisions among elements in the big-city Democratic coalition: the remaining white middle class, the working-class ethnic groups and the growing minority poor. To avoid a further weakening of that historic coalition, a national Democratic administration would be constrained to advance a federal solution to poverty that would override local welfare failures, local class, racial conflicts, and local revenue dilemmas."

They further wrote:

The ultimate objective of this strategy—to wipe out poverty by establishing a guaranteed annual income—will be questioned by some. Because the ideal of individual social and economic mobility has deep roots, even activists seem reluctant to call for national programs to eliminate poverty by the outright redistribution of income.

Michael Reisch and Janice Andrews wrote that Cloward and Piven "proposed to create a crisis in the current welfare system – by exploiting the gap between welfare law and practice – that would ultimately bring about its collapse and replace it with a system of guaranteed annual income. They hoped to accomplish this end by informing the poor of their rights to welfare assistance, encouraging them to apply for benefits, and, in effect, overloading an already overburdened bureaucracy."

Focus on Democrats

The authors pinned their hopes on creating disruption within the Democratic Party:

"Conservative Republicans are always ready to declaim the evils of public welfare, and they would probably be the first to raise a hue and cry. But deeper and politically more telling conflicts would take place within the Democratic coalition...Whites – both working-class ethnic groups and many in the middle class – would be aroused against the ghetto poor, while liberal groups, which until recently have been comforted by the notion that the poor are few... would probably support the movement. Group conflict, spelling political crisis for the local party apparatus, would thus become acute as welfare rolls mounted and the strains on local budgets became more severe."

Reception and criticism

Michael Tomasky, writing about the strategy in the 1990s and again in 2011, called it "wrongheaded and self-defeating", writing: "It apparently didn't occur to [Cloward and Piven] that the system would just regard rabble-rousing black people as a phenomenon to be ignored or quashed."

Impact of the Strategy

In papers published in 1971 and 1977,[6] Cloward and Piven argued that mass unrest in the United States, especially between 1964 and 1969, did lead to a massive expansion of welfare rolls, though not to the guaranteed income program that they had hoped for.[7] Political scientist Robert Albritton disagreed, writing in 1979 that the data did not support this thesis; he offered an alternative explanation for the rise in welfare caseloads.

In his 2006 book Winning the Race, (Losing the Race – 2000) political commentator John McWhorter attributed the rise in the welfare state after the 1960s to the Cloward–Piven strategy, but wrote about it negatively, stating that the strategy "created generations of black people for whom working for a living is an abstraction". Thomas Sowell has also criticized the Clower-Piven model as a major cause for the decline of the black community.

$*_{14}$ "Deception Was My Job" – Yuri Bezmenov DVD – videos of lectures online at various sites

*†† See – "50 Simple Questions for Every Christian," Guy P. Harrison – 2010 - New Testament makes salvation a critical and highly refined. How can all 42,000 or uncounted individual interpretations be right or qualified?

$*_{15}$ The Sixties Papers – Albert/Albert, Rules for Radicals; prediction/plan for political/racial genocide of a quarter to one-third of the population of the U.S.A. – Saul Alinsky; codification of Critical Theory. Yuri Bezmenov; Interviews – "My Job Was Deception." Yuri Bezmenov stressed the KGB/Marxist strategy of promoting all and any trend that would result in the "demoralization" of capitalist society to the point that no one can recognize the truth regardless of how much proof might be presented or how well it might be argued.

$*_{16}$ "Within the next generation I believe that the world's leaders will discover that infant conditioning and narco-hypnosis are more efficient, as instruments of government than prisons, and that lust for power can be just as completely satisfied by suggesting people loving their servitude as by flogging and kicking them into obedience." – Aldous Huxley, in a letter to George Orwell

*Щ Many believe that Jack Kerouac died of alcoholism, but this is not true. He died as a result of a bar fight in St. Petersburg, Florida. He and a friend had gone out drinking and were beaten up badly by several angry Blacks. Kerouac died within a couple weeks of the incident; ironic for a man who had written about his "wishing to be a negro." Self and situational awareness matter. The first "Beat" was a victim of the delusion that he could be someone else and it would be accepted because he was "hip."

*Ѧln its January 2012 report to the United States Secretary of Energy, the Blue Ribbon Commission on America's Future notes that a "molten-salt reactor using thorium [has] also been proposed." That same month it was reported that the US Department of Energy is "quietly collaborating with China" on thorium-based nuclear power designs using an MSR.

Some experts and politicians want thorium to be "the pillar of the U.S. nuclear future." Senators Harry Reid and Orrin Hatch have supported using $250 million in federal research funds to revive ORNL research. In 2009, Congressman Joe Sestak unsuccessfully attempted to secure funding for the research and development of a destroyer-sized reactor [reactor of a size to power a destroyer] using thorium-based liquid fuel.

Alvin Radkowsky, chief designer of the world's second full-scale atomic electric power plant in Shippingport, Pennsylvania, founded a joint US and Russian project in 1997 to create a thorium-based reactor, considered a "creative breakthrough." In 1992, while a resident professor in Tel Aviv, Israel, he founded the US company, Thorium Power Ltd., near Washington, D.C., to build thorium reactors.nm

The primary fuel of the proposed HT3R research project near Odessa, Texas, United States, will be ceramic-coated thorium beads. The reactor construction has not yet begun. Estimates to complete a reactor were originally set at ten years in 2006 (with a proposed operational date of 2015).

On the research potential of thorium-based nuclear power, Richard L. Garwin, winner of the Presidential Medal of Freedom, and Georges Charpak advise further study of the Energy amplifier in their book Megawatts and Megatons (2001), pp. 153–63.

About a dozen companies have incorporated in the United States, to join the many worldwide ventures aimed at developing the optimum form of the Liquid Flouride

Thorium Reactor and related models, Terrapower, Thorcon, Elysium, Moltex, Flibe, Terrestrial, and others while the governments of India and China are racing ahead with government supplemented programs. Chinese students in America discovered the original documents and notes of the original Oakridge Nuclear Facility project that operated there from 1957 to 1969. Today, Chinese is reported to have 700 scientists working on developing these reactors for domestic use and sales abroad, no doubt via "Belt and Road" style programs. If the U.S. and Europe do not step up their programs Western influence will not just fade, it will disappear. Happily, the amazing potential of LFTR and related nuclear technology has become a bipartisan concern. In early June of 2022, Senator Tommy Tuberville introduced S.4242 – Thorium Energy Security Act of 2022 onto the U.S. Senate floor. It makes the first step in creating the conservation of Thorium as a valuable material (which is so plentiful it is considered waste tailings at mines and many other places for smelting to extract the Thorium and other rare earth elements that are gained by processing Thorium ending the rare earth issues for the U.S. and setting the stage for access for the companies who want to develop reactors. Interestingly, Elysium is focused solely on a reactor that will burn nuclear waste from the light water uranium reactors that have been built in the past.

Famous Last Words

*[13] Spengler used the nomenclature of historical philosophers as saeculums, eras, and epochs in the discussion of the course of the life of a civilization. A saeculum is the approximate number of years of the average human lifetime or eighty years. These periods are divided into natural seasons as a biological echo that transfers to the historic measure; Spring, Summer, Autumn, and Winter. Life sees a birth, growth, stable period of "harvest" and decline and death, or winter. Every generation born is influenced by the season of history in which they are born.

*Ш On his website The Lookout, Zeke Lunder talks about a future where forest management and wildfire prevention becomes an industry in a near enlightened future. Ideas such as making sure replanted forests are not the same age, and ensuring biodiversity thereby are but one of his advocated projections. **https://the-lookout.org/** However, a new technology for extinguishing forest fires is being developed using sound waves. In the likely future, drones will be the firefighters and deployable to the most remote locations.

*Т Statements of Founders and first five presidents of the United States of America on religion/Christianity and government;

"Believing with you that religion is a matter which lies solely between man & his god,... that the legitimate powers of a government reach action only and not opinions,...legislature should make no law respecting the establishment of religion, or prohibiting the free exercise thereof, thus building a wall of separation between church and state." – Thomas Jefferson – Deist – Third U.S. President.

"Of all the animosities which have existed among mankind, those which are caused by a difference of sentiment in religion appear to be the most inveterate and distressing, and ought most to be deprecated." – George Washington – Diest – First U.S. President

"The priesthood have, in all ancient nations, nearly monopolized learning. And ever since the Reformation, when or where has existed a Protestant or dissenting sect that would tolerate A FREE INQUIRY? The blackest billingsgate, the most ungentlemanly insolence, the most yahooist brutality, is patiently endured, countenanced, propagated, and applauded. But touch a solemn truth in collision with the dogma of a sect, though capable of the clearest proof, and you will find you have disturbed a nest, and the hornets will swarm about your eyes and hand and fly into your face and eyes." – John Adams – Unitarian – Second President of the U.S.

"...Experience witnesseth that ecclesiastical establishments, instead of maintaining the purity and efficiency of Religion, have had a contrary operation. During almost fifteen centuries has the legal establishment of Christianity been on trial. What have been its fruits? More or less in all places, pride and indolence in the Clergy, ignorance and servility in the laity, in both, superstition, bigotry, and persecution." – James Madison – Deist – Fourth U.S. President

*⊤ The "Bezmenov Effect" refers to the idea Bezmenov espoused regarding the aim of the Soviets to create and encourage social and political confusion in order to demoralize society within one generation to the point that facts and evidence can no longer be agreed upon, producing an increasingly polarized and dysfunctional society.

*† A fully informed statement would view the Abrahamic faiths as intolerant by their exclusiveness, and then resort to coercion on the part of the last two although there is a case of coercion in the Old Testament as well. See – Bibliography "Constantine and the Bishops: The Politics of Intolerance," by H.A. Drake.

*⋔ On October 24, 1849, Ann Dune White and her daughter Virginia White were abducted by Jicarilla Apaches led by Lobo Blanco after their small wagon convoy was attacked on the Santa Fe Trail near Point of Rocks, New Mexico during the nighttime. All were killed except for the mother and daughter, and a black servant girl. In November, a search party was formed after James S. Calhoun, the Indian Agent, wrote to Washington and received permission to search into Indian Territory. Captain William Grier, of the 1st Dragoons, led a rescue expedition. They were joined by Kit Carson as they passed through Rayado. Once they caught up to the raiding party Antoine Leroux advised Grier not to attack because the Indians might want to parlay. Kit Carson advocated that they charge immediately. Once the Apaches saw the troop hesitate, they quickly packed up and began to leave in haste. Grier realized that he had made an error and ordered an immediate charge. Virginia White was spotted being forced onto a mule. When Virginia White saw the troops, she leaped to her feet and tried to run to them. The squaw that had been trying to get her mounted onto a horse quickly set an arrow into her bow and shot Virginia dead within feet of her would-be rescuers. When Carson reached her he described that he found her, "still perfectly warm." She had been starved and obviously cruelly treated. Her bare feet were bloody and her body showed the marks of many whippings and beatings. Her face portrayed the lines of a lifetime of sorrow.

After the failed rescue the troops searched the abandoned camp for signs of the two other presumed captives. Near where Virginia fell, one trooper found a little book, a sensational dime novel of the Ned Buntline style. This one featured Kit Carson executing a daring rescue of a similar captive damsel in distress. The trooper showed it to Carson, who at the time, had no idea of this type of literature and his glorification in them. As he was illiterate at the time, he had the trooper read it to him. Virginia White had held onto life in the desperate hope that Carson would come to her rescue. Now Carson had to see how he had failed her. It was said that Carson was tormented by the incident for the remainder of his life. It is reliable to say that Antoine Leroux and the entire command were impacted similarly by the terrible event. It is believed that the servant girl and Virginia were killed soon after their abduction because their bodies were never found. – A Fate Worse than Death – Gregory and Susan Michno, page 99

It is important to note that the later 20th century to present notion of the American West has been plundered by the Marxists and their social grievance industry. They began with film and then the classroom where Howard Zinn would have influence in this and all American historical representation for the generations following the

Baby Boomers. The view of the peace-loving but unfairly treated red man is the product of film and dishonest parties that willfully distorted history. In his book, "Circle the Wagons," Gregory and Susan Michno present the mechanism of this distortion in the book's preface. Former Secretary of the Interior Stuart L. Udall led the opinion-forming at the Western History Association conference in 199. It had an agenda. According to Robert R. Dykstra, the Columbine High School Shooting in Colorado left "historians" with a political task, that of de-emphasizing violence in the present by deemphasizing it in history. Frontier violence, according to Dykstra, was a hoax. They then changed the narrative up to the claim that all the violence there came from the white population and the military against the American Indians.

To prove the new history studies were required. One study, in particular, was done by an itinerant historian in 1962 regarding wagon train raids. George R. Stewart didn't research beyond his own locale and since he did not find an appreciable number of Indian raids, he assumed that this was the common history, besides, he reasoned that it made no sense that Indians should make targets of themselves by attacking wagon trains. Later parties produced "studies" that covered limited years on selected routes and generalized them to the entire period and geography of the West. So his study left them out. All subsequent historians who wished to represent a tranquil West where only the white man was the villain, used him as a source. And then the next one used Stewart and the former, and so on, building a cadre of "valid" studies for arguing against the earlier plethora of evidence and documentation. The fact is that the Western Expansion was accomplished at the cost of many lives lost and many more ruined. Indian attacks alone took 50,000 lives, while many times more survived with injuries both physical and psychological remaining from their captivity that often sorely afflicted them and often shortened the survivor's lives substantially.   This is what the factual, documented records prove. Further, the actual history of Western Expansion from 1830 to 1885 was a period of repeated attempts by the government to appease the various tribes with treaties for compensating tribes that allowed settlement to occur peacefully. In Kansas, Dodge City, Sante Fe Trail, and Texas the trade in white captive-taking and ransom had begun in 1800 when a priest bought the freedom of a white captive from the Comanche tribe. By 1868, the government would no longer allow ransoming of captives. The policy became pacification to end these and other depredations for which there is an overwhelming trove of factual and documented evidence for the sincere seeker of truth. If historians do not tell the truth, they are not historians. So we must ask what is their purpose?

Appendix A

Bibliography

Books consulted for the history presented in The Spook Tree

History of Sacramento County – William Ladd Willis, 1913 – Scholar Select

First History of Sacramento City by Dr. John F. Morse, 1853 – California Book Collectors Club 2018

Jedediah Smith – No Ordinary Mountain Man – Barton H. Barbour

Answering the Call in Time of War – A History of Camp Kohler and the Western Signal Corps School, Danny M. Johnson – I Street Press 2018

The Early Inns of California 1844-1869, Ralph Herbert Cross, 1954 – Cross and Brandy

New Helvetia Diary – A Record of Events Kept by John A. Sutter and His Clerks at New Helvetia, California From September 9, 1845, to May 25, 1848 – San Francisco: The Grabhorn Press in Arrangement with the Society of California Pioneers – 1939

The Gabriel Moraga Expedition of 1806 – The Diary of Fray Pedro Munoz – Kessinger Publishing – **www.kessinger.net**

Diary of Ensign Gabriel's Expedition of Discover in the Sacramento Valley 1808 – Translated and Edited by Donald C. Cutter – Published by Glen Dawson 1957 (300 copies)
California – An Interpretive History, Walton Bean, Professor of History, University of California, Berkeley, 1968 – McGraw and Hill, Inc.

Gold Districts of California – State of California – Scholar Select
Encyclopedia of Indian Wars – Western Battles and Skirmishes, 1850-1890, Gregory F. Michno

H.W. Brands – The Age of Gold – The California Gold Rush and The New American Dream, 2002 – Double Day – Random House"

I Remember – Stories and Pictures of El Dorado County Pioneer Families, El Dorado County Chamber of Commerce – 2000

Charles F. McGlashan – The Donner Party – A Tragedy of the Sierras, 1879 – Dover Publications

Historic Spots in California – Revised by Douglas E. Kyle, Fifth Edition, 2002 – Stanford University Press

Railroaded – The Transcontinental's and the Making of Modern America, Richard White – 2011 – WW Norton and Company, Inc.

Sacramento Street Whys – The Wise Guy's Guide to Sacramento Street Names, Carlos Alcala – 2007 – Big Tomato Press

The Art of Motocross - with Jeff Smith and Bob Currie – 1966 – Cassel & Company LTD

Sacramento Motorcycling – A Capital City Tradition – Kimberly Reed Edwards

Handbook of the Indians of California – with 419 Illustrations and 40 Maps, A.L. Kroeber

Circle the Wagons – Attacks on Wagons Trains in History and Hollywood Films, Gregory F. Michno and Susan J. Michno

A Fate Worse than Death – Indian Captivities in the West – 1830 – 1885, Gregory and Susan Michno – Caxton Press
North Highlands History documents assembled by Dean and Merrie O'Brien

Biographical Dictionary of the Left – Volume 1 – Francis X. Gannon

Infamy – The Shocking Story of the Japanese American Internment in World War II – Richard Reeves

Lincoln's Marxists, Benson and Kennedy

The Decline of the West – Volume I: Form and Actuality, Oswald Spengler – Alfred A. Knopf – Publisher, New York

Losing the Race, John H. McWhorter, Winning the Race, John M. McWhorter

Acid Dreams – The Complete Social History of LSD, The CIA, The Sixties, and Beyond, Lee and Schlain

The Communist – Frank Marshall Davis: The Untold Story of Barak Obama's Mentor, Paul Kengor, Ph.D.
The Real Tenko – Extraordinary True Stories of Women Prisoners of the Japanese – Mark Felton

Blacklisted by History – The Untold Story of Senator Joe McCarthy and his Fight against America's Enemies," E. Stanton Evans

Toward Soviet America, William E. Foster
The Sixties Papers, Albert/Albert

Biographical Dictionary of the Left – Francis X. Gannon

Fifteenth Report Un-American Activities in California `970 – Report of the Senate Fact-Finding Subcommittee on Un-American Activities to the 1970 Regular Session of the California Legislature Sacramento, California

Time on the Cross, - The Economics of American Negro Slavery, Fogel and Engerman
White Cargo – The Forgotten History of Britain's White Slaves in America, Jordan and Walsh

They Were White and They Were Slaves – The Untold Story of the Enslavement of Whites in Early America

White Gold – The Extraordinary Story of Thomas Pellow and Islam's One Million White Slaves, Giles, Milton

Barbarian Cruelty – An Eye Witness Account of White Slavery Under the Moors, Francis Brooks

To Hell or Barbados – The Ethnic Cleansing of Ireland, S. O'Callaghan

Black Slaveowners – Free Black Slave Masters in South Carolina, 1790-1860

Roll Jordan, Roll – The World the Slaves Made, Eugene D. Genovese, Ph.D.

The Dying Citizen – Victor Davis Hansen

Jack Kerouac and the Decline of the West – an essay by Semmelweis

Constantine and the Bishops: The Politics of Intolerance, H.A. Drake

Not Stolen – The Truth About European Colonialism in the New World, Jeff Flynn-Paul

The Fourth Turning – an American Prophecy – What the Cycles of History Tell Us About America's Next Rendezvous with Destiny, Willam Strauss and Neil Howe

Appendix B

TimeLine – Natomas Company History 1851-1984

1851 – 1852   A.P. Catlin and others organized early mining and water companies as loose associations to divert water from the South Fork of the American River.

1853 – Natoma Water & Mining Company was incorporated as a public corporation on June 25, 1853. Construction of Natoma's 16-mile canal/ditch system completed to Prairie City, November 1853. Water sales began.

1854 – Natoma Water and Mining Company recapitalized, from $200,000 to $300,000, on October 13, 1854.

1854 – A.P. Catlin and other principals of Natoma Water & Mining Company organized a second company, the American River Water & Mining Company, on December 9, 1854. It was capitalized at $150,000, to divert water from the North Fork of the American River.

1857 – Natoma Water & Mining Company purchase 9,654 acres of land, i.e., the eastern portion of the Rancho de Los Americanos from Charles Nystrom, for $36,000. The tract became known as the Natoma Purchase.

1864 – Horatio Gates Livermore and his sons, particularly Horatio Putnam Livermore, obtain controlling interest in the Natoma Water & Mining Company. Begin plans to build an industrial center in Folsom.

1864 – After seven years of court battles, the Natoma Water & Mining Company receives the patent to the Natoma Purchase.

1866 – Construction started on the first Folsom dam by Natoma Water & Mining Company.

1868 – First convict labor contract made between Natoma Water & Mining Company and the State of California, June 10, 1868. The state was to receive 350 acres for Folsom Prison in exchange for 30,000 days of convict labor. (That's 82.19178082 years!)

1881-1886 – Natoma Water & Mining Company completes planting its 2,000-acre vineyard. It was the largest vineyard in the world until surpassed by Leland Stanford's "Vina" in Tehama County.

1883 – Natoma Water & Mining Company recapitalized at $600,000, on March 27, 1883, to complete vineyard expansion.

1885-1886 – Natoma Water & Mining Company builds a large winery complex for producing its own wine.

1888 – Natoma Vineyard Company, incorporated by Charles Webb Howard, Herman Bendel, and others, on September 6, 1888. Livermore is no longer in control of the Company.

1891-1892 – First Folsom Dam completed late 1891, Folsom Prison Powerhouse completed in February 1892.

1895 – Folsom Powerhouse was partially completed & single dynamo operated in June-July, 1895. All four dynamos working by the time of the "Electric Carnival" in September. The powerhouse completed by November 1895.

1898 – First commercially successful gold dredge in California was completed & placed in operation in March 1898.

1898-1899 – First gold dredge at Folsom on Mississippi Bar. Prospecting begun in September 1898, construction started in January 1899, the boat launched in February, and digging commenced in April 1899.

1903 – Natoma Water & Mining Company's 49 year-year charter expires.

1903 – Folsom Development Company, backed by R.G. Hanford & a Colorado mining syndicate, was incorporated in San Francisco County on March 4, 1903.

1906 – Natoma Development Company, backed by W.P. Hammon, was incorporated in San Francisco on September 25, 1906.

1908-1909 – Natomas Consolidated of California was formed by a merger of all but one dredging company in the Folsom area. Natomas Consolidated incorporation was officially dated January 1, 1909.

1911-1912 – Natomas Consolidated of California completes a series of dredges, Natoma #8, Natoma #9, and Natoma #10. #8 was the largest in the world when completed in March 1911. #10 was the first all-steel dredge operated in California.

1914 – Natomas Company of California was incorporated on December 24, 1914, when Natomas Consolidated of California was reorganized after defaulting on bond interest payments.

1915 – Main river and drainage levee system for Reclamation Districts 1000 & 1001 completed. The total enclosed area is approximately 86,000 acres.

1917-1918 – First Bulldozer Blade was designed and constructed by Natomas Company of California. Installed first on a Hold, then Best tractor, and used to level tailings of reclamation dredges Natoma #1 and Natoma #4.

1918-1940 – Mather Air Field started on 780 acres of land leased to the United States Government by Natomas Company of California for $1 per year. Offer of sale for $100/acre for undredged land. In 1940, Natomas Company sold 4,500 acres to Mather for a bombing range.

1928 – Natomas Company is formed by reorganization of Natomas Company of California, November 10, 1928.

1934-1935 – The price of gold was raised by FDR from $20.67, beginning in late 1934, and fixed at $35.00 in January 1935.

1946 – Sacramento War Industries, including Natomas Company, is awarded the Army-Navy "Big E" for wartime production efficiency, 1942-46.

1948-1956 – United States Army Corp of Engineers finished construction on Folsom Dam. Work had begun in 1948.

1950 – Natomas Company sells out the last of land holdings in Reclamation Districts 1000 & 1001 in 1950. Price was always below book value.

1952 – Folsom Powerhouse shut down after over fifty years of successful operation.

1956 – Natomas Company merger with APL Associates, Inc. Other mergers also had been examined, including Gallo Wine and Continental Uranium.

1961 – American River Parkway was first proposed by Natomas Company to the Sacramento County Department of Parks and Recreation. About 1,000 acres of land in the flood zone of the American River were converted to equestrian and bicycle, and other recreational uses.

1961 – Constructed the International Building in San Francisco, sold in 1983.

1962 – Western Geothermal, Inc. organized to engage in geothermal exploration and development.

1962 – Natomas Company shuts down the last dredge at Folsom, Natomas #6, on February 12, 1962.

1962-1972 – Natomas' only foreign venture was in Peru, where Poto No. 1 (a rebuilt dredge from Snelling, CA) began digging in November 1962. The operation had many problems. Dredge sank in 1964 and again in 1972 when operations were abandoned.

1966 – Oil refinery completed on the Caribbean Island of Antigua. Sold in 1976.

1966 – The state of California acquired through condemnation 1,800 acres of Natomas lands in Butte County, California, in connection with the construction of the Oroville Dam.

1968 – Independent Indonesian American Petroleum Company stock acquired. IIAPCO held oil concessions off-shore Java; both became highly profitable.

1974 – Thermal Power Company, the holder of 25% of the interest in the Geysers geothermal areas of Sonoma County, California, is acquired.

1976 – Apexco, a company with extensive oil and gas holdings in the United States, is acquired.

1978 – Kentucky coal properties of Brown Badgett, Incorporated are acquired.

1979 – Acquired the minority interest in American President Lines, Ltd., from the Signal Companies, making the shipping company a wholly-owned subsidiary.

1980-1982 – Planning for development of Natomas Company lands as residential communities are completed. Construction of "Gold River," begins in 1982, and planning for "Natoma Station" gets underway.

1983 – Magma Power Company, the holder of 25% interest in the Geysers steam field in Sonoma County, California, is acquired by Natomas.

1983-1984 – Natomas Company was acquired by Diamond Shamrock Corporation, through an exchange of stock, accompanied by a "spin-off" of the shipping and real estate interests to a new company, American President Companies, Ltd. Natomas ceases to exist as an independent company, ending a corporate history spanning 133 years.

Appendix C

LOOMIS BASIN HISTORICAL SOCIETY'S THROWBACK THURSDAY:

Gold Dredge Legacy

In the late 1930s, numerous dredging projects were in operation around the Loomis Basin. The sharp devaluation of orchard property during the Depression led to the opening of land for mining purposes.

E.B. Skeels started a dry land dredge near Rocklin in 1935. He soon started another dredge on Secret Ravine near Loomis. Also near Rocklin, the Walton Gold Dredging Company was working on the Burt Moulton ranch, with a water supply from Secret Ravine.

In addition to the gigantic dredge named Loomis No. 1, operating near Barton and Rocklin roads, the Gold Hill Dredging Company launched a second dredge, Loomis No. 2, on Antelope Ravine. Closer to Penryn, the Antelope Creek Dredging Company worked the same ravine near Humphrey Road. And the Rohn Brothers completed negotiations for a dragline dredge on a large pear orchard near Penryn known as the Kayo property.

East of Loomis, the Panob Dredging Company's doodlebug worked near Horseshoe Bar and Val Verde roads, and E.L Hill, of Roseville, began gravel washing operations in an old hydraulic tailings deposit that had lain idle for almost a half century. Hill adopted a simple method of operation, consisting of running the gravel through a fifty-foot sluice, fed by an elevated hopper. The hopper was fed by a dragline power shovel.

In the Allen's District (now Granite Bay), the Oro Bell Dredging Company began operating in 1934 on Miner's Ravine. Its large dredge was following an old river channel starting near the Allen's dance hall. The company had rights to dredge about 900 acres.

On July 30, 1938, the City of Roseville filed suit against the Gold Hill and Oro Bell companies seeking to restrain them from discharging mud and debris into the tributaries of Dry Creek. The complaint stated that the muddy waters constituted a nuisance to Roseville's Royer Park. Before dredgers began operating, Dry Creek was naturally clear and clean, but now quantities of soil, gravel, grit, filth, and mud had been discharged into the stream, ultimately being deposited along the banks in the park. The mud not only affected the beauty of the park, it was detrimental to the deer and elk that drank the water and often became mired in the mud. The channel was being filled with debris, causing the stream to overflow its banks.

Edward Von Geldern, engineer and witness for the City of Roseville, testified before the court that water samples from Dry Creek showed impurities running as high as 20 percent. Dr. Seth Law, Loomis veterinarian, testified that the intestines of five deer that had died in Royer Park were coated to such an extent they could not function properly. The deer were anemic and much yellow water, similar to that in Dry Creek, was found in the stomachs of the animals.

In October 1939, Placer County Superior Court Judge Landis ruled in the City's favor, granting an injunction against the Oro Bell Dredging Company. In his opinion, the judge found that the bed of Dry Creek was naturally clean, composed of rock, sand, and gravel, free from filth, sediment, and debris. The dredge mining operations caused large quantities of debris to be carried downstream, polluting the water so that it caused deer, elk, and other animals kept in the park zoo to become unhealthy. The banks of the creek were made unsightly and offensive to the senses of the people of Roseville and the acts of the defendants constituted a public nuisance.

The injunction against the Gold Hill Dredging Company was denied on the ground that the company had ceased all operations in Placer County on May 14. At the time of the trial in June, it was removing its gigantic dredge to the Mokelumne River. Royer Park, one of Roseville's chief beauty and recreation spots, could now return to its original charm and usefulness.

On June 22, 1940, 19-year-old Jack Dacey, of Folsom, drowned in an abandoned dredge pool on Secret Ravine about two miles southeast of Penryn. An investigation showed that the dredge hole sloped out gradually for several feet, then dropped off suddenly into deep water. It was surmised that Dacey stepped off into the hole and was unable to swim out.

Appendix D

Timeline of the California Gold Rush

1775-80 – The first known discovery of gold in California was made in the Potholes district, Imperial County. Mining extended into the Cargo Muchacho and Picacho districts.

1828 – A small placer gold deposit was found at San Ysidro, San Diego County

1835 – The placer gold deposits in San Francisquitto Canyon, Los Angeles County, were discovered

1842 – Gold was discovered in Placerita Canyon, Los Angeles County. Some sources give the date of this discovery at 1841.

1848 – Gold was discovered at Sutter's Mill at Coloma on the American River by James Marshall. Although the exact date has been the subject of some discussion, it is officially designated as January 24. The first printed notice of the discovery was in the March 15th issue of "The Californian" in San Francisco. Shortly after Marshall's discovery, General John Bidwell discovered gold in the Feather River and Major Pearson B Reading found gold in the Trinity River. The gold rush was soon in full sway as thousands of gold seekers poured into California.

1849 – Quartz mining began at the Mariposa mine, Mariposa County. A stamp mill, probably the first in the state, was installed.

1850 – Gold-bearing quartz was found at Gold Hill at Grass Valley. This led to the development of the great underground mines in that district and a major industry that continued for more than 100 years.

1851 – Gold was discovered in Greenhorn Creek, Kern County. This discovery led to the rush to the upper Kern River region.

1852 – California's annual gold production reached an all-time high of $81 million.

1852 – Hydraulic mining began at American Hill and Yankee Jim's, Placer County.

1853 – The placers at Columbia, Tuolumne County, began to yield vast amounts of gold. This continued until the early 1860s. At that time, Columbia was one of the largest cities in the state.

1853 – The Fraser River in British Columbia caused a partial exodus of miners from the state.

1854 – A 195-pound mass of gold, the largest known to have been discovered in California, was found at Carson Hill, Calaveras County.

1855- The rich surface placers were largely exhausted by this date, and the river mining accounted for much of the state's output until the early 1860s. All of the river gold regions were mined.

1859 – The famous 54-pound Willard nugget was found at Magalia, Butte County.

1859 – The Comstock silver rush began in Nevada. This development caused a large exodus of gold miners from California. However, it stimulated gold and silver prospecting in eastern and southern California.

1864 – By this time California's gold rush had ended. The rich surface and river placers were largely exhausted, hydraulic mines were the chief sources of gold for the next 20 years.

1868 – The first drills were introduced. However, the widespread use of air drills did not come for another 30 years.

1876 – The stampede to the Bodie district in Mono County began. The rush lasted until about 1888.

1880 – Hydraulic mining reached its peak in the state. Vast systems of tunnels, reservoirs, ditches, flumes, and pipelines supplied water to these operations.

1883 – Gold production figures began to be collected for the calendar year instead of the fiscal year.

1884 – Sawyer Decision, in the case of Woodruff vs. North Bloomfield Gravel Mining Company, Judge Lorenzo Sawyer issued a decree prohibiting the dumping of debris into the Sacramento and San Joaquin rivers and their tributaries. Action against other hydraulic mines soon followed. A few mines constructed tailings storage dams and continued to operate, but hydraulic mining has not been important in the Sierra Nevada ever since. For a few years, drift mines partially made up the loss of output of the surface placer mines.

1890 – Beginning about this time and continuing for several decades, great improvements were made in mining and milling methods. These changes enabled many more lode deposits, especially large, low-grade accumulations, to be profitably worked. The improvement of air drills, explosives, and pumps, and the introduction of electric power lowered mining costs greatly. The introduction of rock crushers, an increase in size of stamp mills, and new concentrating devices, such as vanners, lowered milling costs. Cyanidation was introduced in 1896 and soon replaced the chlorination process.

1893 – The Caminetti Act was passed creating the California Debris Commission. This commission licenses hydraulic mining operations in the Sierra Nevada. It is empowered to assess such mines to build debris dams.

1893 – Gold was discovered in Goler Gulch in the El Paso Mountains in Kern County. This led to other discoveries in the area and the influx into the Rand district, which began in 1895.

1898 – The first successful bucket line dredge was started on the lower Feather River near Oroville. Gold dredging soon became a major industry that continued for more than 65 years.

1904 – The lost, high-grade Tightner vein was rediscovered at Alleghany in Sierra County. Large amounts of rich ore were taken from this vein, and mining activity, reviving in this district continued until 1965. This was the last district in the state where gold mining was the chief industry.

1916 – The general prosperity that began during WW1 and continued until 1929, with accompanying high costs, caused a decrease in gold output.

1922- Argonaut disaster; A fire on the 3,350ft level of the Argonaut Mine in the Jackson district, Amador County, caused the loss of 47 lives.

1929 – Peak of the post-WW1 boom. The lowest point in gold production since 1849.

1930 – Gold production started to rise because of the Great Depression and resulting in lower operating costs.

1933-35 – The price of gold increased from $20.67 to $35 per fine once. This rise ultimately resulted in a large increase in gold output and in much greater exploration activities.

1940 – Gold output nearly $51 million. This was the most valuable annual output since 1856. Thousands of miners were employed in the quartz mines at Grass Valley, Allegheny, Nevada City, Jackson, Sutter Creek, Jamestown, Mojave, and French Gulch. There were many active bucket-line dredges, and dredgeline dredges became important producers of placer gold.

1942 – World War II caused a precipitous stop in gold output. War Production Board Limitation Order L-208, issued on October 8, caused the gold mines to be shut down.

1944 – Gold production touched the lowest point since 1848.

1945 – Order L-208 was lifted effective July 1. Some of the bucket-line dredges resumed operations, but only a few important lode mines in Grass Valley, Allegheny, and Sutter Creek were reopened. Production increased slightly for 4 years.

1950 – Gold output resumed its decline because of rising costs and depletion of dredging ground. This trend was accelerated by the Korean War.

1953 – The Central Eureka Mine at Sutter Creek, the last major operating lode mine in the Mother Lode Belt, was shut down.

1956 – The mines of Empire-Star Mines Ltd., and Idaho-Maryland Mines, Inc., at Grass Valley were shut down. The industry of gold mining completed nearly 106 years of operation in this locality.

1960 – Gold output fell below $5 million as the dredges continued to curtail operation.

1962 – The last dredge of the Folsom field held in Sacramento County was shut down, ending more than 60 years of operation. One of the last active lode-gold mines in California, the Sixteen-To-One in the Allegheny district, curtailed operations.

1963 – The large dredges of the Yuba Mining Division, Yuba Consolidated Industries – in the Hammonton district, Yuba County - - were the only major sources of gold in the state. The small output from the substantial number of part-time prospectors, pocket miners, snipers, and skin divers did not offset the decrease in output from larger commercial operations. Several mines in the Allegheny district obtained U.S. Government exploration loans.

1964 – The Brush Creek Mine, a substantial source of gold in the Allegheny district, Sierra County, ceased operations.

1965 – Governor Edmund G. Brown signed Senate Bill 265 designating gold as California's official state mineral. The Sixteen-To-One Mine at Allegheny, Sierra County, was shut down at the end of the year. This was the last lode mine in the state that had been operated on a sustained basis.

1967 – Two of the three remaining dredges at Hammonton were shut down.

1968 – The last gold dredge at Hammonton was shut down on October 1. This was the last sustained commercial gold mining operation in California.

1968 – The U.S. Treasury suspended purchases of newly-mined gold. The free market price rose to $44 an ounce in early 1969, falling by November to $38.50, because of greater stability in international currencies.

IN MEMORANDUM

The honored dead of the Vietnam War of North Highlands and Highlands High School

Michael Archie Blakey
Randolf "Randy" Brown, Jr.
Ned Davis, Jr.
Richard Deffner
Gene Howard Ellis, Jr.
Garfield Evans
Kenneth Vern Jensen
Daniel Wilburn "Danny" Lawson
Russell Edward Metzger
Curtis Lee Nelson
David Leslie Palmer
Roy Edward "Eddie" Pitts
Michael Christopher Smartt
Stephen "Steve" Renier Tubre
David George Williams
Robert Alan "Bobby" Yates

The Author's grandfather, Dr. James Jonathan LaRue, D.C., final resting place in the Folsom Pioneer Cemetery, now The Folsom Memorial Lawn, Folsom, California
Photo by Author

His fourth son, John, was the only son who did not attend chiropractic college just beneath.
Photo by author